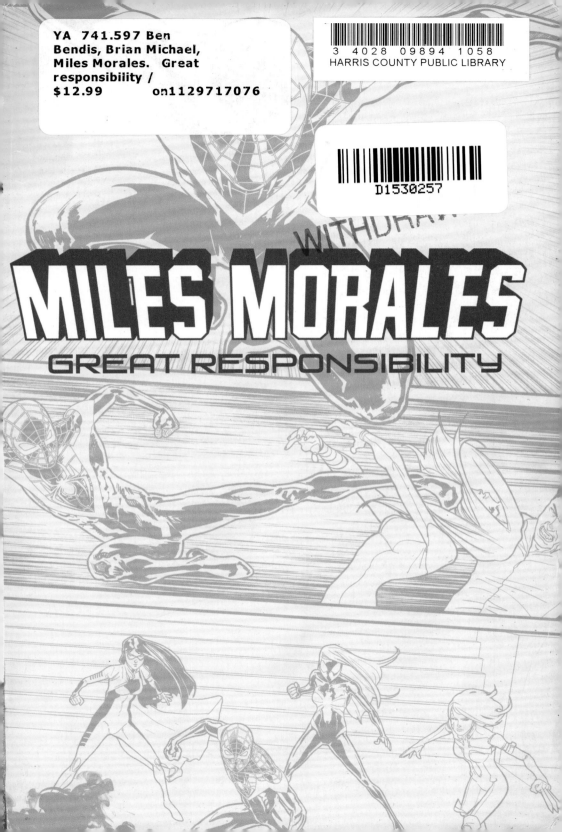

MILES MORALES
GREAT RESPONSIBILITY

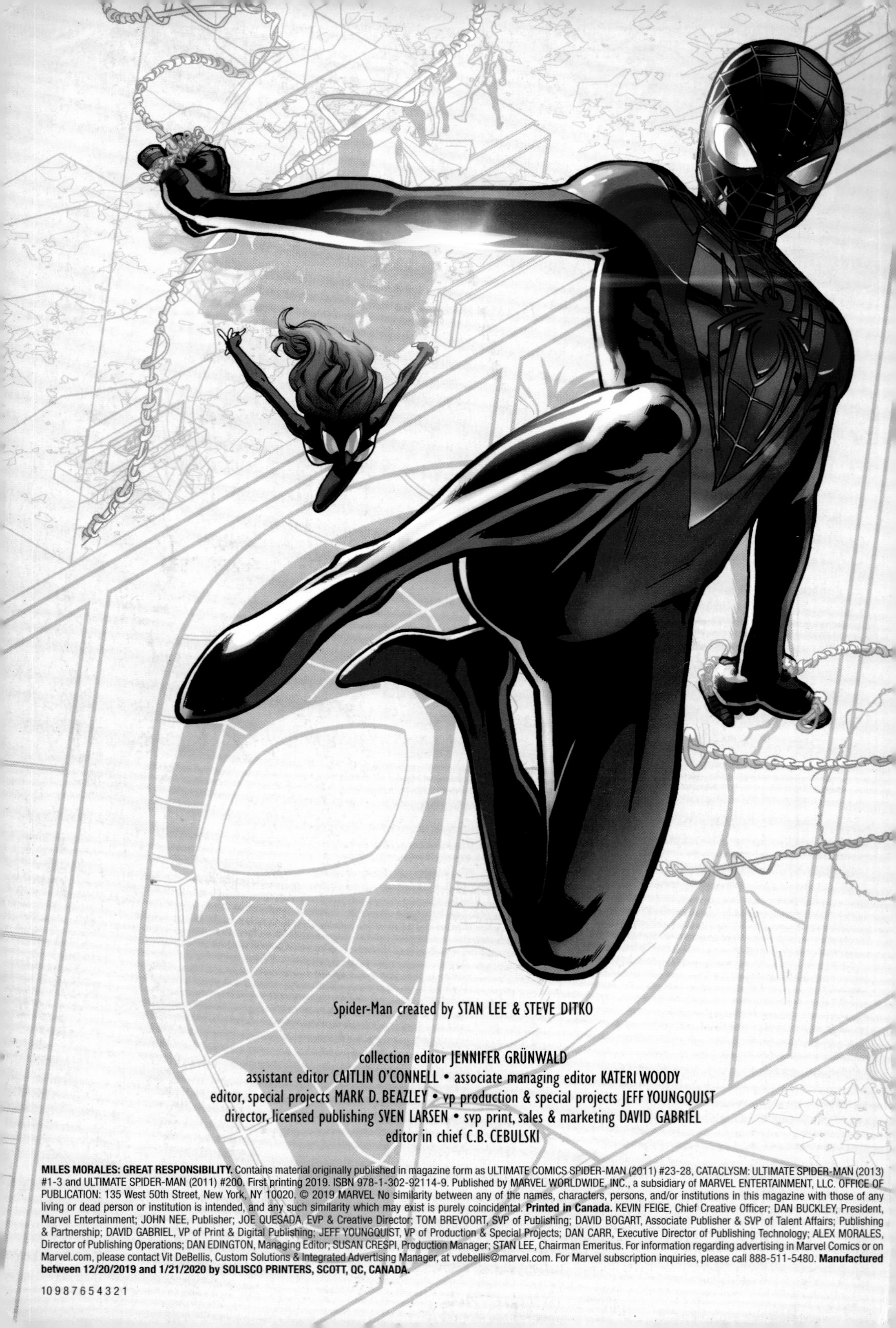

Spider-Man created by STAN LEE & STEVE DITKO

collection editor JENNIFER GRÜNWALD
assistant editor CAITLIN O'CONNELL • associate managing editor KATERI WOODY
editor, special projects MARK D. BEAZLEY • vp production & special projects JEFF YOUNGQUIST
director, licensed publishing SVEN LARSEN • svp print, sales & marketing DAVID GABRIEL
editor in chief C.B. CEBULSKI

MILES MORALES: GREAT RESPONSIBILITY. Contains material originally published in magazine form as ULTIMATE COMICS SPIDER-MAN (2011) #23-28, CATACLYSM: ULTIMATE SPIDER-MAN (2013) #1-3 and ULTIMATE SPIDER-MAN (2011) #200. First printing 2019. ISBN 978-1-302-92114-9. Published by MARVEL WORLDWIDE, INC., a subsidiary of MARVEL ENTERTAINMENT, LLC. OFFICE OF PUBLICATION: 135 West 50th Street, New York, NY 10020. © 2019 MARVEL No similarity between any of the names, characters, persons, and/or institutions in this magazine with those of any living or dead person or institution is intended, and any such similarity which may exist is purely coincidental. **Printed in Canada.** KEVIN FEIGE, Chief Creative Officer; DAN BUCKLEY, President, Marvel Entertainment; JOHN NEE, Publisher; JOE QUESADA, EVP & Creative Director; TOM BREVOORT, SVP of Publishing; DAVID BOGART, Associate Publisher & SVP of Talent Affairs; Publishing & Partnership; DAVID GABRIEL, VP of Print & Digital Publishing; JEFF YOUNGQUIST, VP of Production & Special Projects; DAN CARR, Executive Director of Publishing Technology; ALEX MORALES, Director of Publishing Operations; DAN EDINGTON, Managing Editor; SUSAN CRESPI, Production Manager; STAN LEE, Chairman Emeritus. For information regarding advertising in Marvel Comics or on Marvel.com, please contact Vit DeBellis, Custom Solutions & Integrated Advertising Manager, at vdebellis@marvel.com. For Marvel subscription inquiries, please call 888-511-5480. **Manufactured between 12/20/2019 and 1/21/2020 by SOLISCO PRINTERS, SCOTT, QC, CANADA.**

10 9 8 7 6 5 4 3 2 1

MILES MORALES
GREAT RESPONSIBILITY

WRITER
BRIAN MICHAEL BENDIS

ULTIMATE COMICS SPIDER-MAN #23-28
ARTIST
DAVID MARQUEZ
COLOR ARTISTS
JUSTIN PONSOR
WITH **PAUL MOUNTS** (#28)
COVER ART
DAVID MARQUEZ
WITH **RAIN BEREDO** (#24-25 & #28)
& **JUSTIN PONSOR** (#23 & #26-27)

CATACLYSM: ULTIMATE SPIDER-MAN #1-3
ARTIST
DAVID MARQUEZ
COLOR ARTISTS
JUSTIN PONSOR
WITH **PAUL MOUNTS** (#28)
COVER ART
DAVID MARQUEZ &
RAIN BEREDO

ULTIMATE SPIDER-MAN #200
ARTIST
DAVID MARQUEZ
ARTISTS, MJ AND MAY PARKER SEQUENCES
MARK BAGLEY & ANDREW HENNESSY
ARTIST, GWEN STACY SEQUENCE
MARK BROOKS
ARTIST, MILES MORALES SEQUENCE
SARA PICHELLI
ARTIST, KITTY PRYDE SEQUENCE
DAVID LAFUENTE
COLOR ARTISTS
JUSTIN PONSOR
COVER ART
MARK BAGLEY, ANDREW HENNESSY
& JUSTIN PONSOR

LETTERER
VC's CORY PETIT
ASSISTANT EDITORS
EMILY SHAW & JON MOISAN
ASSOCIATE EDITOR
SANA AMANAT
SENIOR EDITOR
MARK PANICCIA

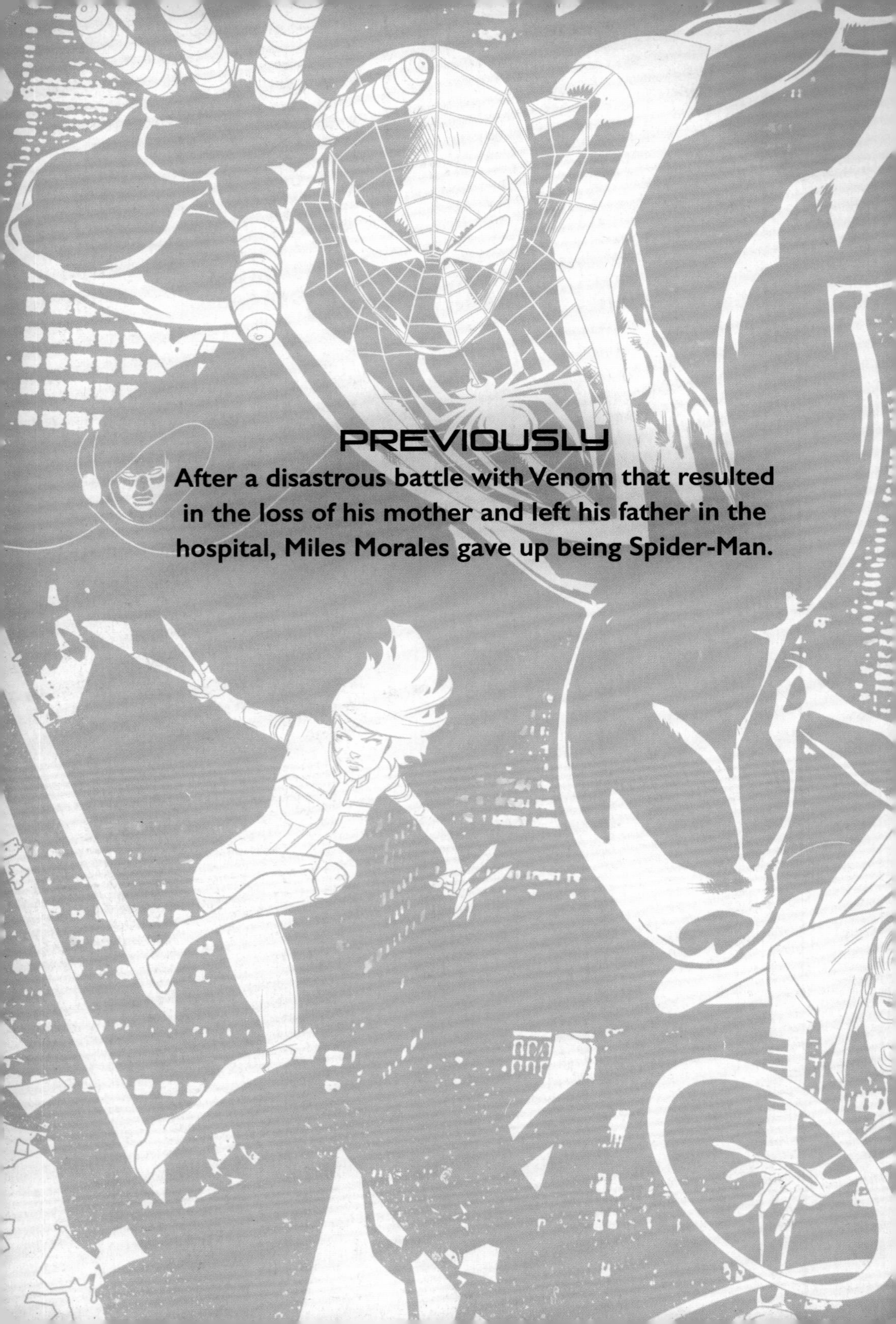

PREVIOUSLY

After a disastrous battle with Venom that resulted in the loss of his mother and left his father in the hospital, Miles Morales gave up being Spider-Man.

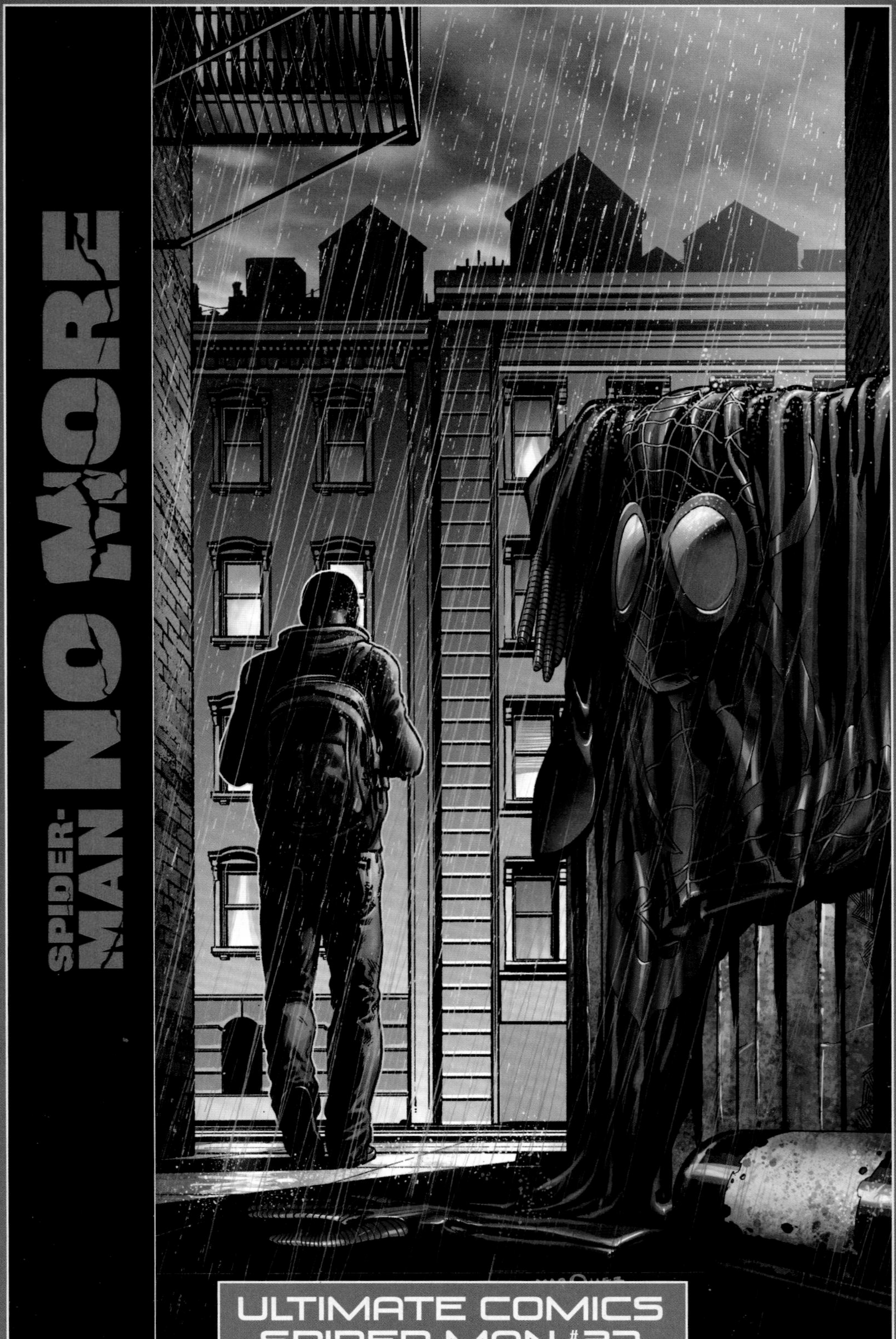
SPIDER-MAN NO MORE
ULTIMATE COMICS
SPIDER-MAN #23

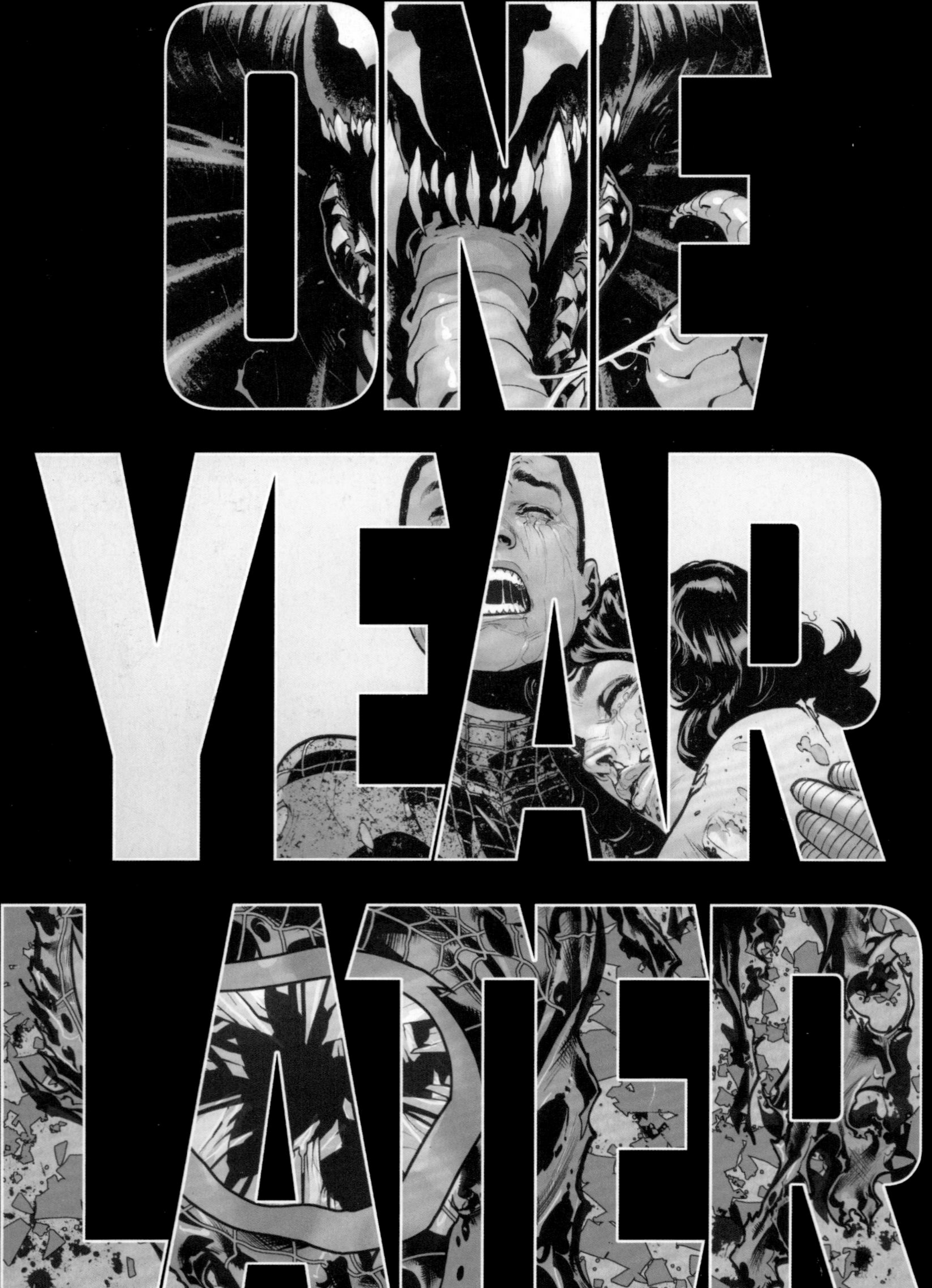
ONE
YEAR
LATER

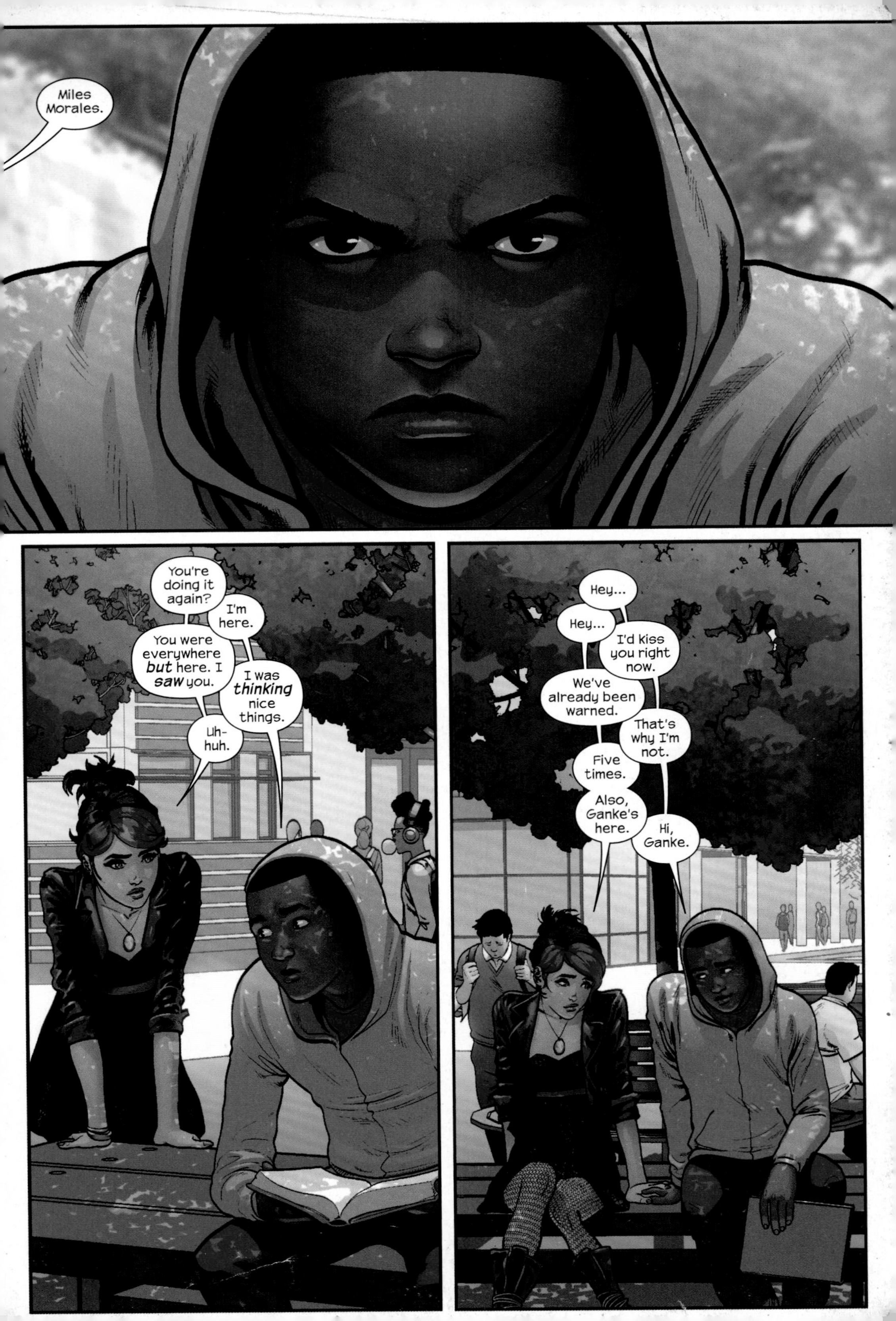
Miles Morales.
You're doing it again?
I'm here.
You were everywhere *but* here. I *saw* you.
I was *thinking* nice things.
Uh-huh.
Hey...
Hey...
I'd kiss you right now.
We've already been warned.
That's why I'm not.
Five times.
Also, Ganke's here.
Hi, Ganke.

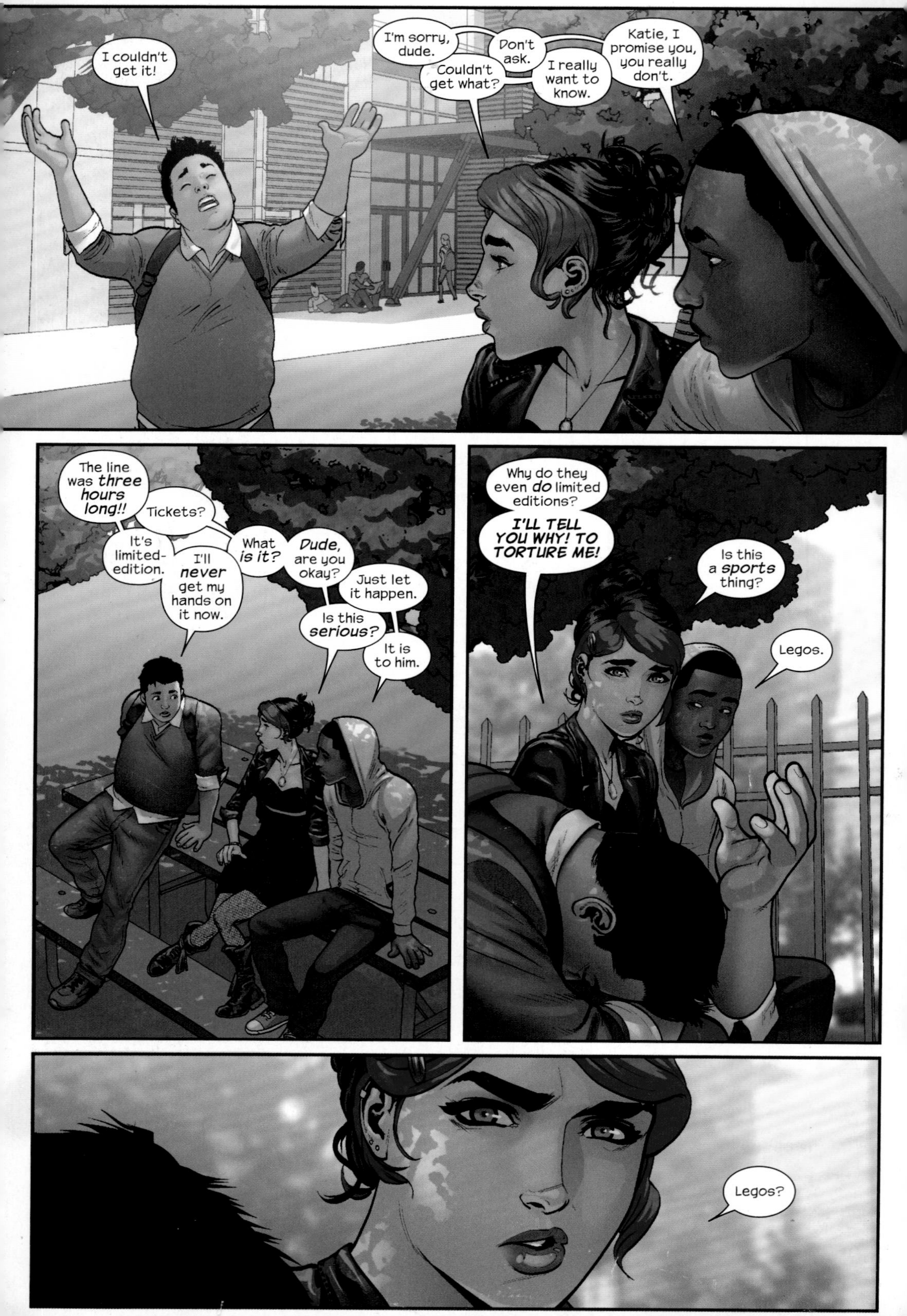
I couldn't get it!
I'm sorry, dude.
Couldn't get what?
Don't ask.
I really want to know.
Katie, I promise you, you really don't.
The line was *three hours long!!*
Tickets?
It's limited-edition.
I'll *never* get my hands on it now.
What *is it?*
Dude, are you okay?
Just let it happen.
Is this *serious?*
It is to him.
Why do they even *do* limited editions?
I'LL TELL YOU WHY! TO TORTURE ME!
Is this a *sports* thing?
Legos.
Legos?

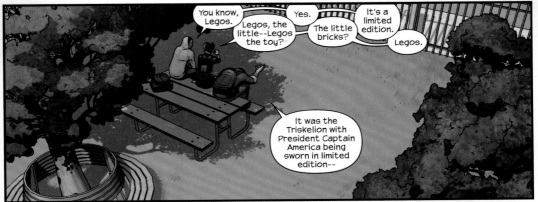

You know, Legos.

Legos, the little--Legos the toy?

Yes.

The little bricks?

It's a limited edition.

Legos.

It was the Triskelion with President Captain America being sworn in limited edition--

Edition. Yeah.

YES!!

I'm sorry.

Thank you!

So, uh, I'm going to go to my room and, let's say, e-mail my parents.

Yeah, okay.

See you after dinner.

Sure.

I ask for so little.

I think I'm going to tell her.

Tell her you love her?

What? No.

You haven't told Katie Bishop you love her yet?

No.

Girls like when you tell them.

Oh yeah?

She would.

You know what girls like to hear all of a sudden?

Sure.

This from the man who just chased another girl from our table crying over Legos.

That's not why she left. She had to e-mail--

Dude.

She had to go--

I promise you I don't know what girls want from us but I know they don't want to hear about you and the Legos.

The right girl will.

Wait, what were you going to tell her?

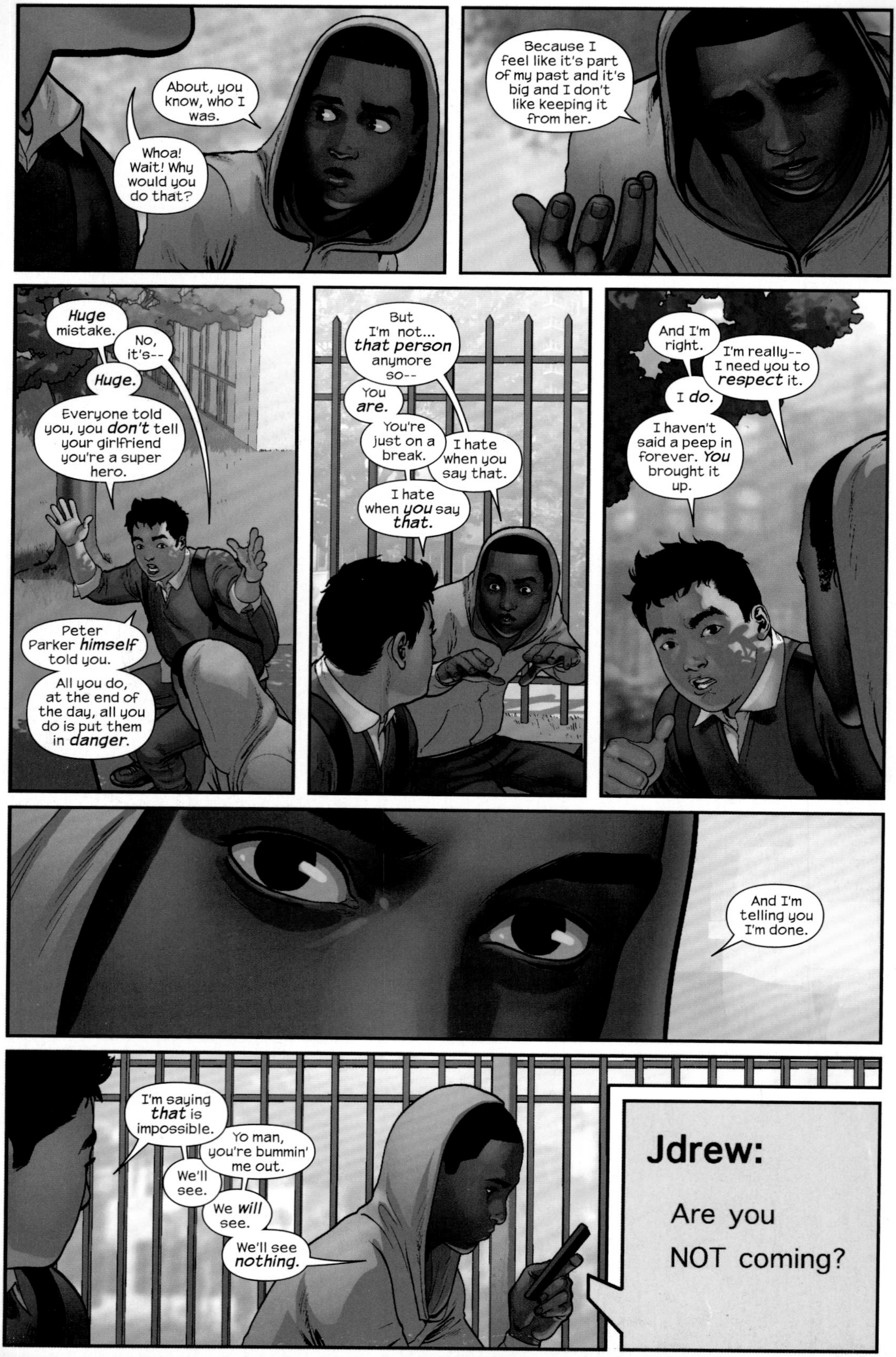

About, you know, who I was.
Whoa! Wait! Why would you do that?
Because I feel like it's part of my past and it's big and I don't like keeping it from her.
Huge mistake.
No, it's--
Huge.
Everyone told you, you *don't* tell your girlfriend you're a super hero.
Peter Parker *himself* told you.
All you do, at the end of the day, all you do is put them in *danger*.
But I'm not... *that person* anymore so--
You *are.*
You're just on a break.
I hate when you say that.
I hate when *you* say *that.*
And I'm right.
I'm really-- I need you to *respect* it.
I *do.*
I haven't said a peep in forever. *You* brought it up.
And I'm telling you I'm done.
I'm saying *that* is impossible.
Yo man, you're bummin' me out.
We'll see.
We *will* see.
We'll see *nothing.*
Jdrew:
Are you NOT coming?

Uh-oh.

Who is it?

It's, ugh!! It's Jessica Drew.

Who is *that*?

Spider-Woman.

She just texted you?? Right now while we were just talking about--??

I was supposed to meet her.

Now?

Yeah.

Why?

She probably wants to have the same damn conversation *we* just did.

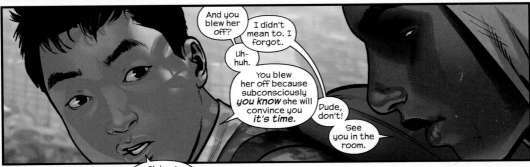

And you blew her off?

I didn't mean to. I forgot.

Uh-huh.

You blew her off because subconsciously *you know* she will convince you *it's time*.

Dude, don't!

See you in the room.

Oh hey! See if she can get me the limited edi--

Not going to happen.

MILES:

I'm so sorry.

Jdrew:

Don't make me come down there.

MILES:

Where r u now?

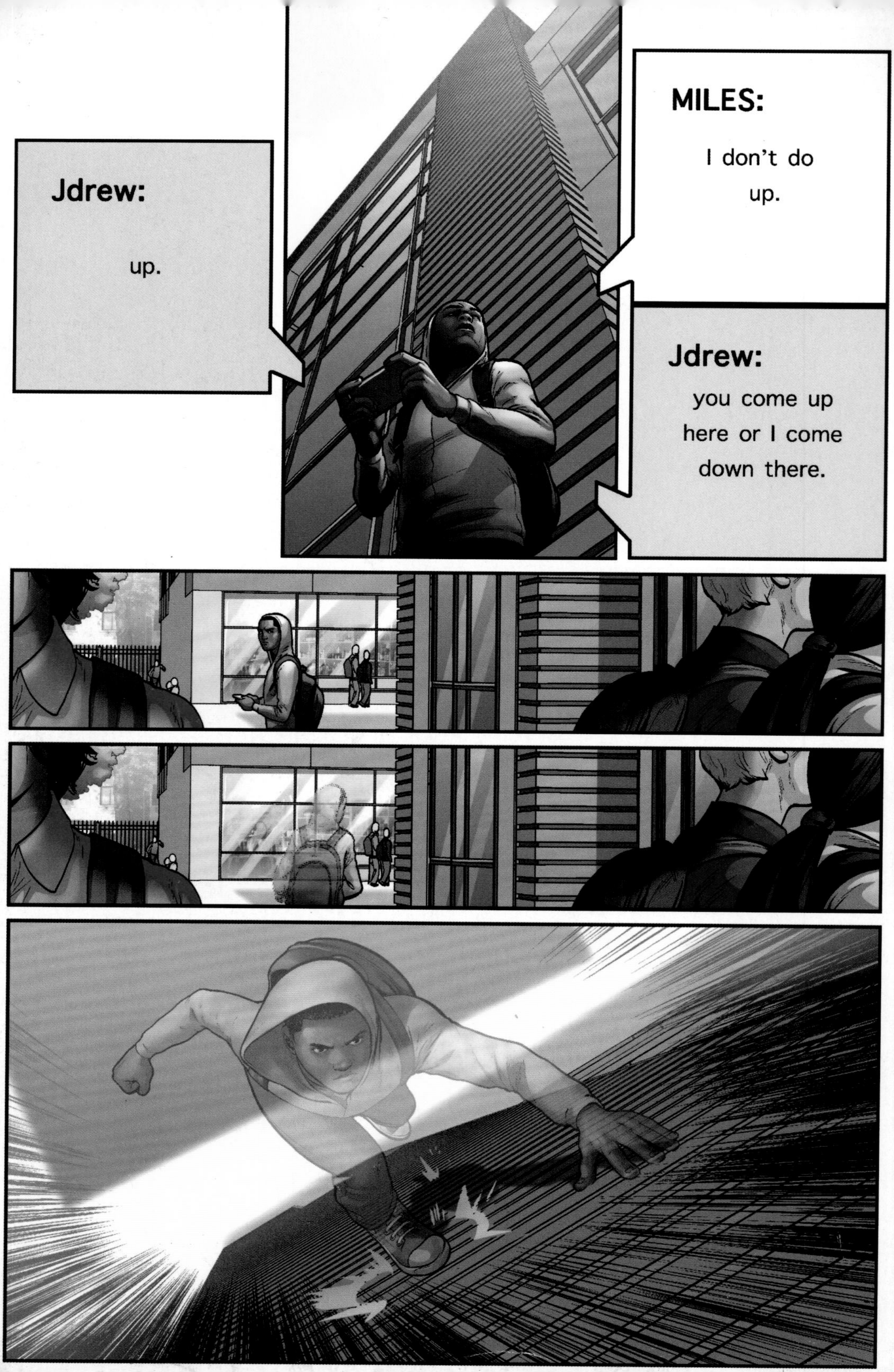
Jdrew:
up.
MILES:
I don't do up.
Jdrew:
you come up here or I come down there.

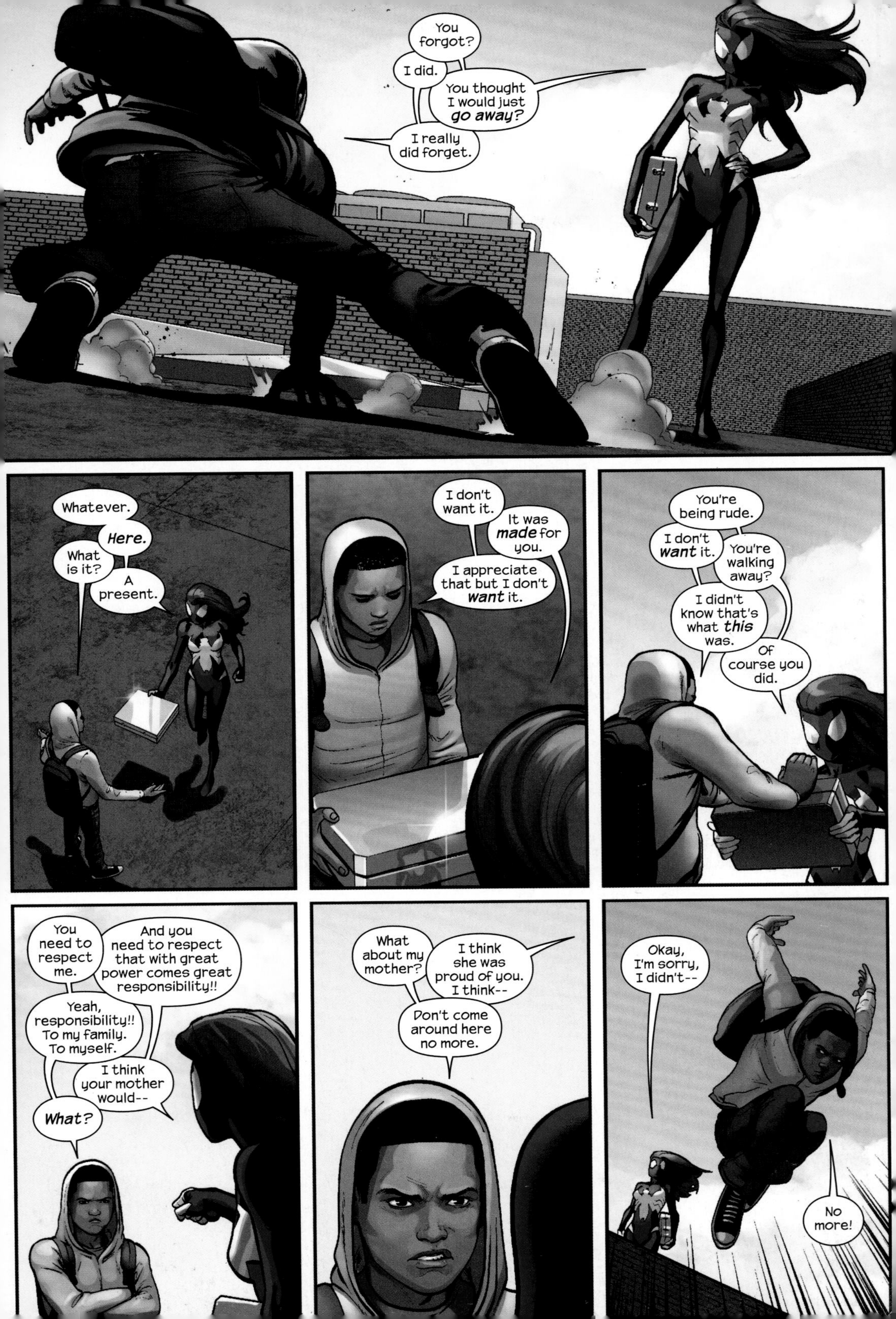

You forgot?
I did.
You thought I would just *go away?*
I really did forget.
Whatever.
Here.
What is it?
A present.
I don't want it.
It was *made* for you.
I appreciate that but I don't *want* it.
You're being rude.
I don't *want* it.
You're walking away?
I didn't know that's what *this* was.
Of course you did.
You need to respect me.
And you need to respect that with great power comes great responsibility!!
Yeah, responsibility!! To my family. To myself.
I think your mother would--
What?
What about my mother?
I think she was proud of you. I think--
Don't come around here no more.
Okay, I'm sorry, I didn't--
No more!

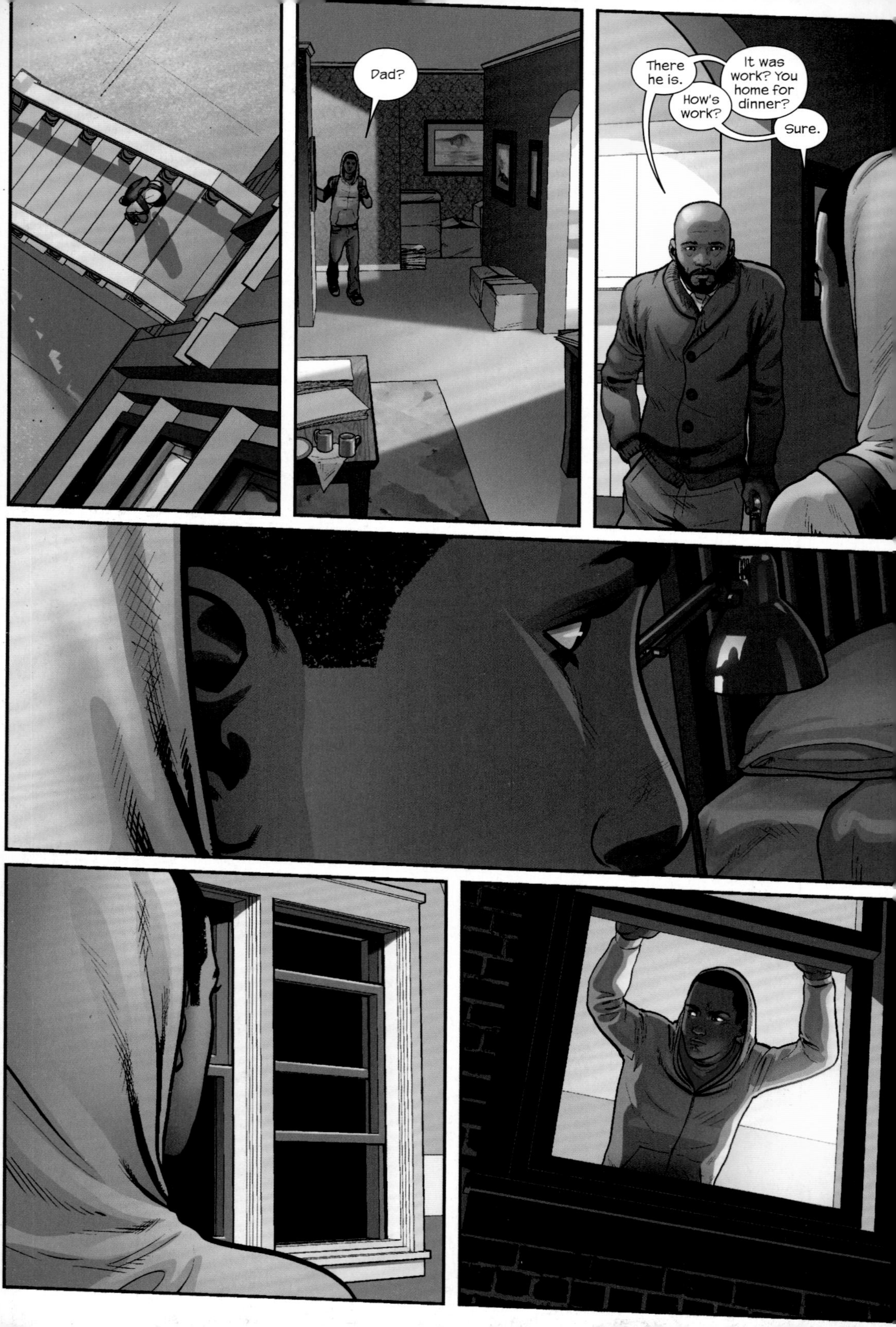
Dad?
There he is.
How's work?
It was work? You home for dinner?
Sure.

Does the school know where you are?

Yeah, sure.

Go wash up. We'll order in Chinese.

Let's, uh, let's go out.

We can go out. Give me a few minutes.

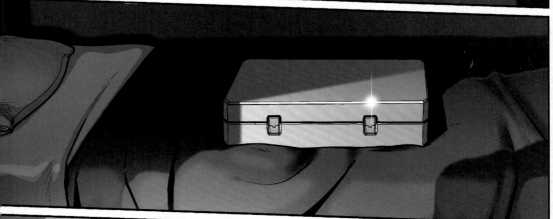

A year is a long time. How many people could you have saved?

You fall off a horse, you get back on.

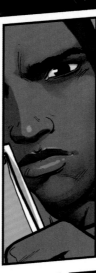

You ready?

Almost.

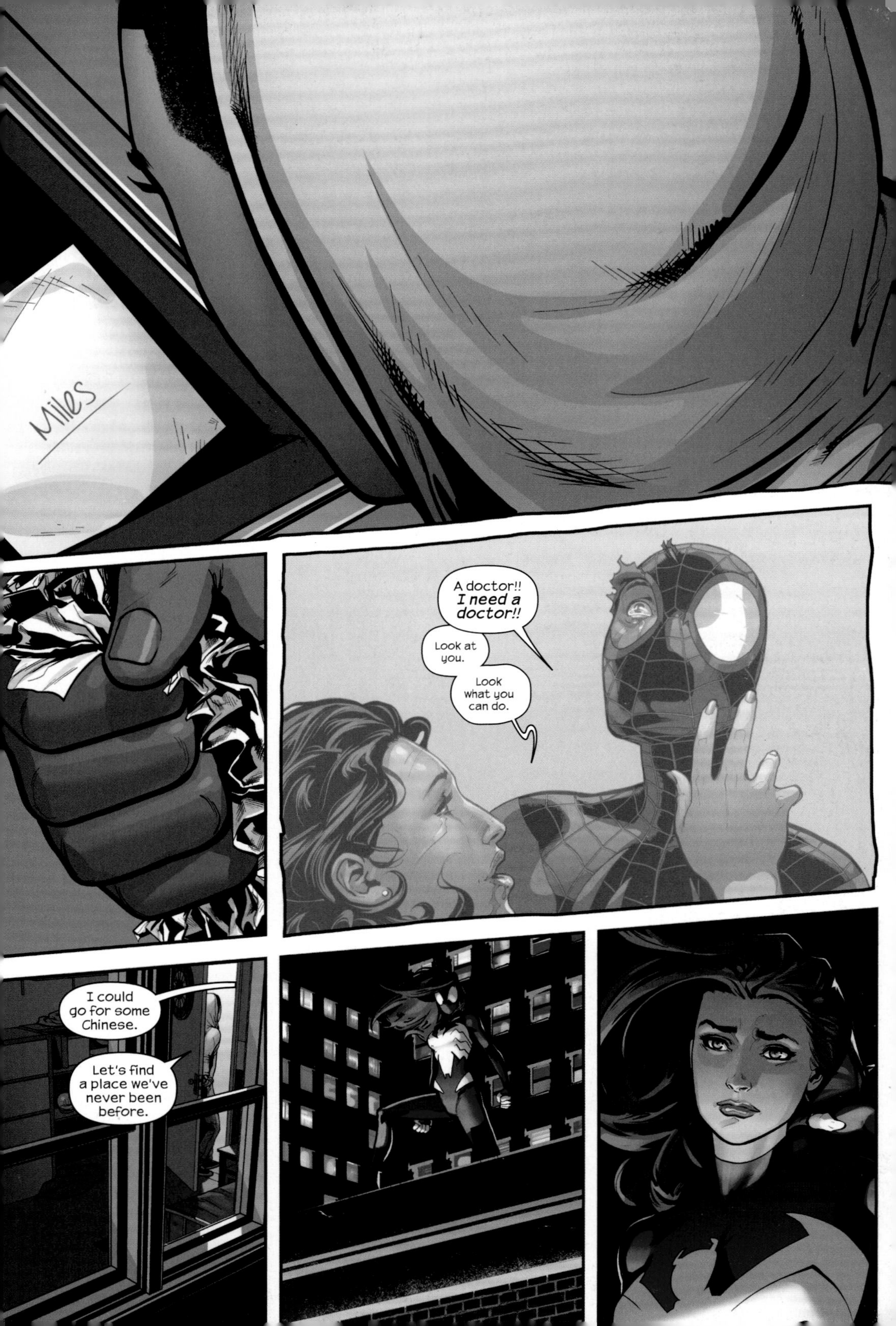
Miles
A doctor!! *I need a doctor!!*
Look at you.
Look what you can do.
I could go for some Chinese.
Let's find a place we've never been before.

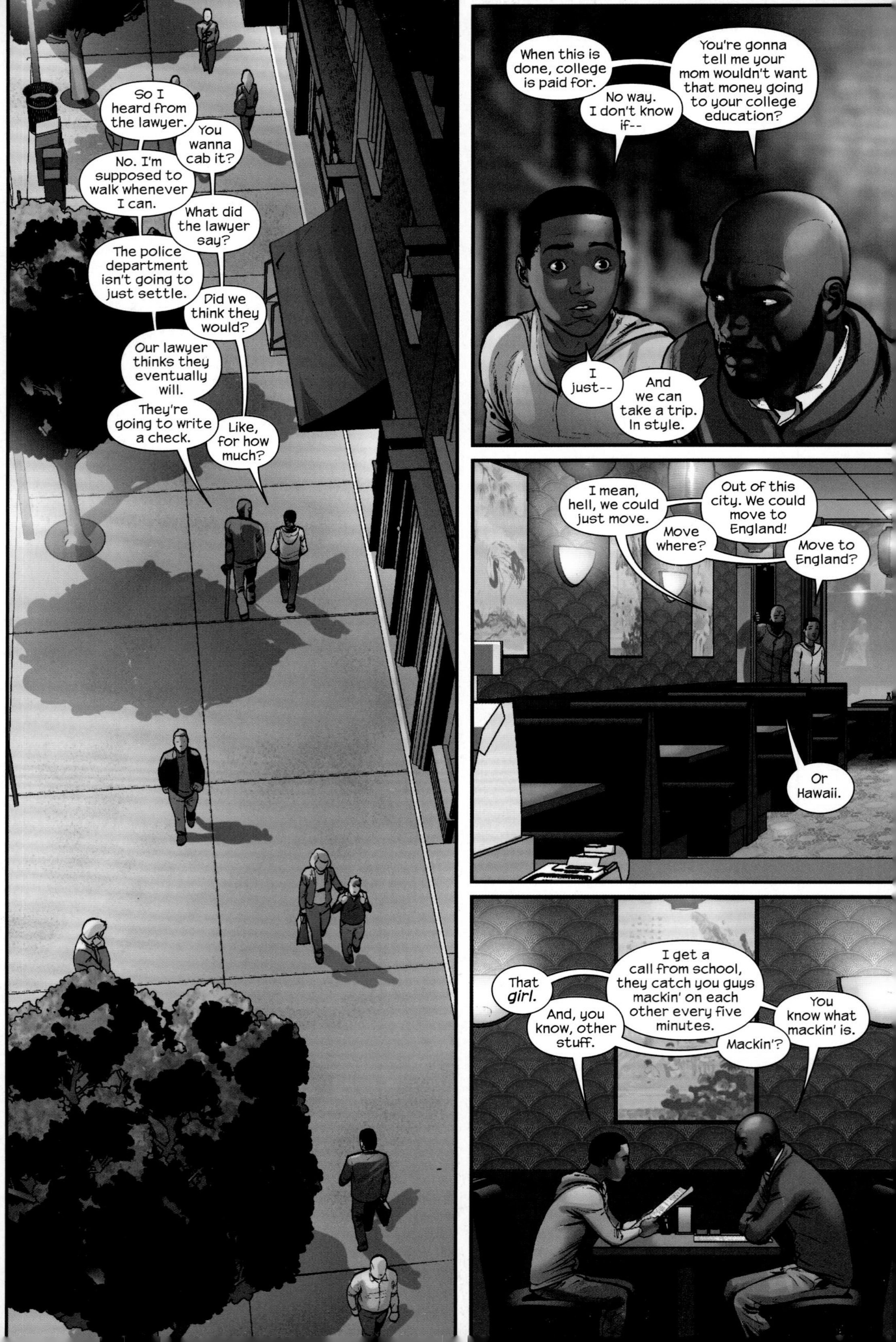
So I heard from the lawyer.
You wanna cab it?
No. I'm supposed to walk whenever I can.
What did the lawyer say?
The police department isn't going to just settle.
Did we think they would?
Our lawyer thinks they eventually will.
They're going to write a check.
Like, for how much?
When this is done, college is paid for.
No way. I don't know if--
You're gonna tell me your mom wouldn't want that money going to your college education?
I just--
And we can take a trip. In style.
I mean, hell, we could just move.
Out of this city. We could move to England!
Move where?
Move to England?
Or Hawaii.
That *girl.*
I get a call from school, they catch you guys mackin' on each other every five minutes.
And, you know, other stuff.
Mackin'?
You know what mackin' is.

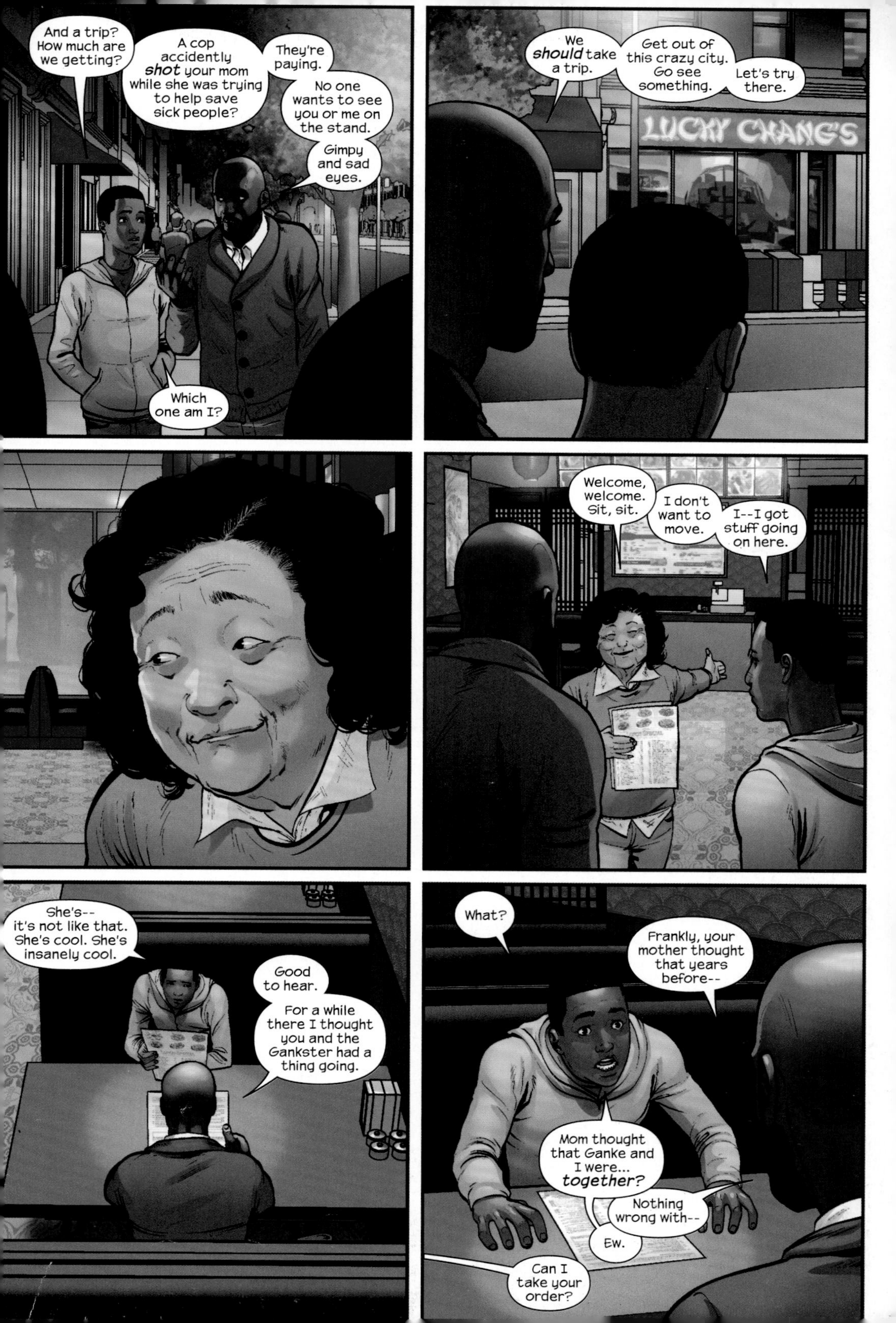
And a trip? How much are we getting?
A cop accidently *shot* your mom while she was trying to help save sick people?
They're paying.
No one wants to see you or me on the stand.
Gimpy and sad eyes.
Which one am I?
We *should* take a trip.
Get out of this crazy city. Go see something.
Let's try there.
LUCKY CHANG'S
Welcome, welcome. Sit, sit.
I don't want to move.
I--I got stuff going on here.
She's-- it's not like that. She's cool. She's insanely cool.
Good to hear.
For a while there I thought you and the Gankster had a thing going.
What?
Frankly, your mother thought that years before--
Mom thought that Ganke and I were... *together?*
Nothing wrong with--
Ew.
Can I take your order?

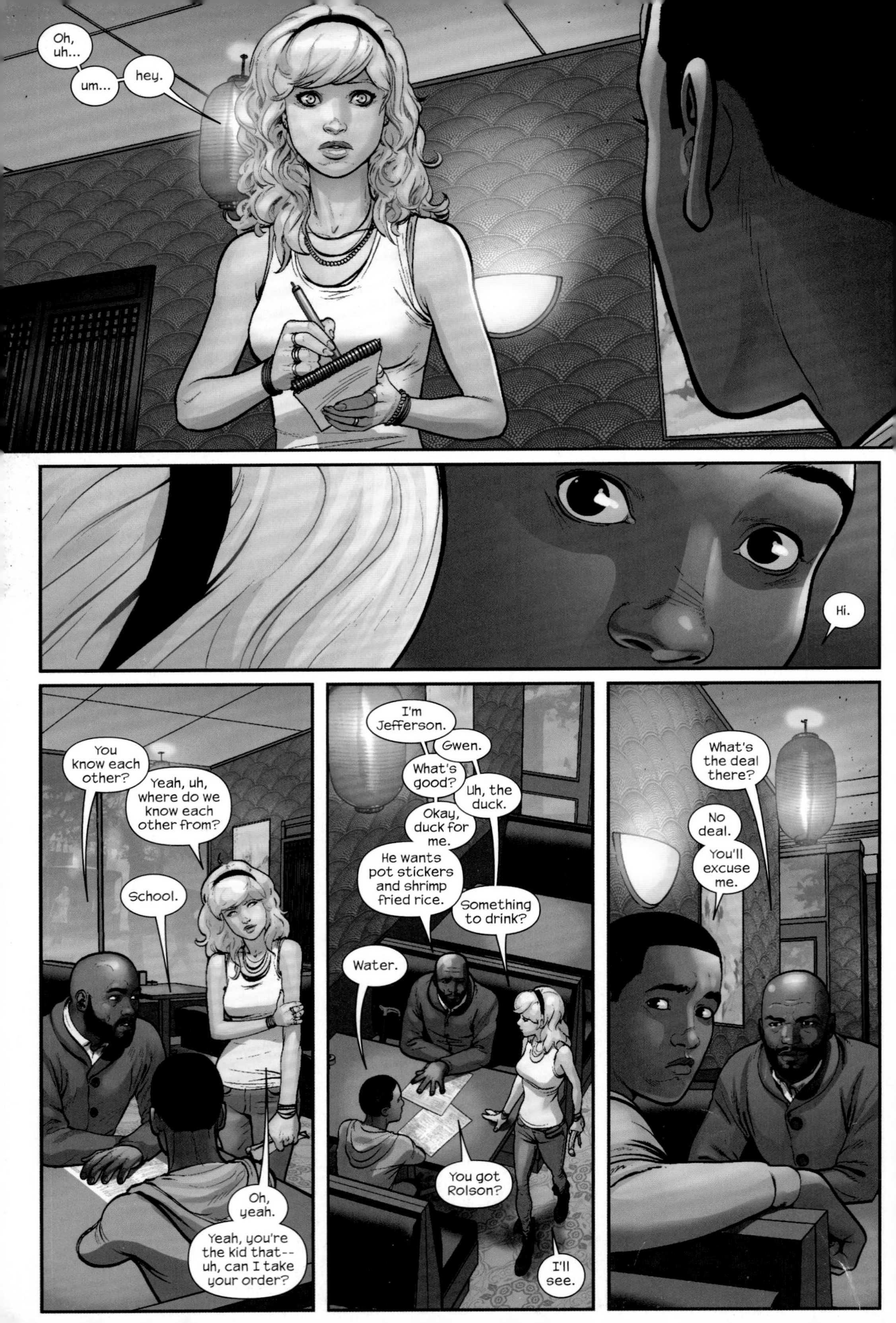
Oh, uh...
um...
hey.
Hi.
You know each other?
Yeah, uh, where do we know each other from?
School.
Oh, yeah.
Yeah, you're the kid that-- uh, can I take your order?
I'm Jefferson.
Gwen.
What's good?
Uh, the duck.
Okay, duck for me.
He wants pot stickers and shrimp fried rice.
Something to drink?
Water.
You got Rolson?
I'll see.
What's the deal there?
No deal.
You'll excuse me.

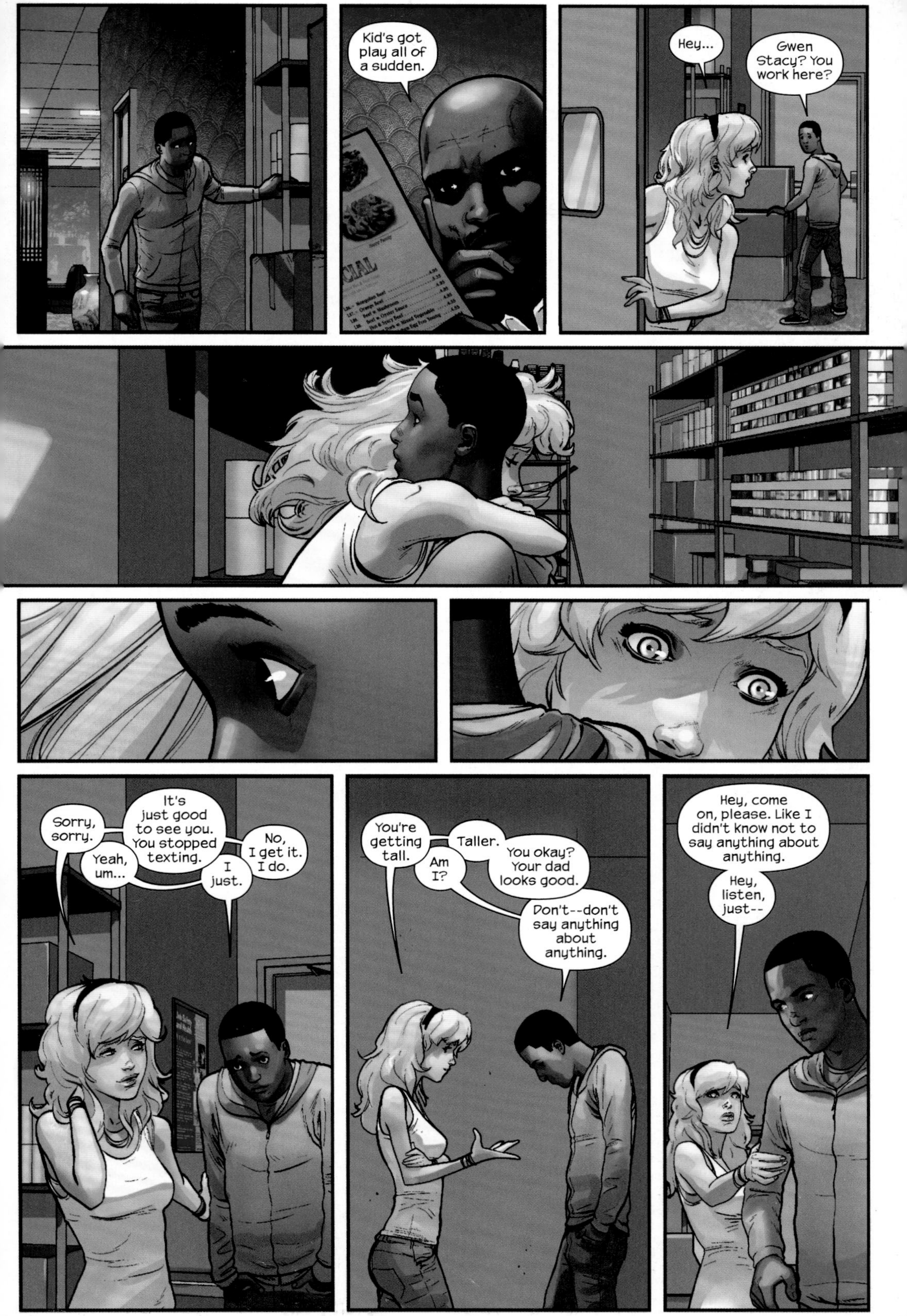
Kid's got play all of a sudden.
Hey...
Gwen Stacy? You work here?
Sorry, sorry.
It's just good to see you. You stopped texting.
Yeah, um...
I just.
No, I get it. I do.
You're getting tall.
Taller.
Am I?
You okay? Your dad looks good.
Don't--don't say anything about anything.
Hey, come on, please. Like I didn't know not to say anything about anything.
Hey, listen, just--

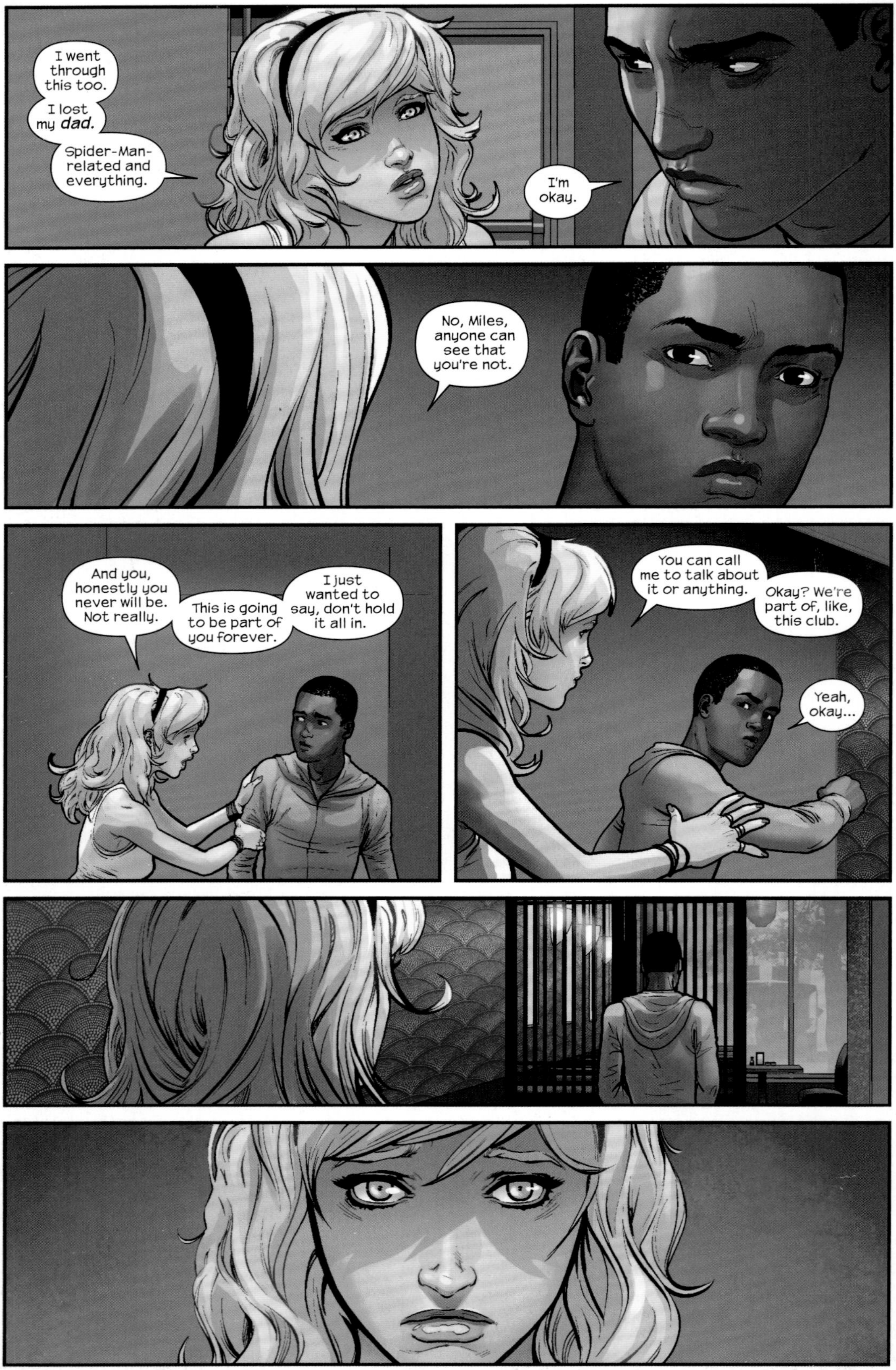
I went through this too.
I lost my *dad.*
Spider-Man-related and everything.
I'm okay.
No, Miles, anyone can see that you're not.
And you, honestly you never will be. Not really.
This is going to be part of you forever.
I just wanted to say, don't hold it all in.
You can call me to talk about it or anything.
Okay? We're part of, like, this club.
Yeah, okay...

Everything okay?

Yeah. She's just--

You want to go?

Kinda, yeah.

Okay.

Okay?

Sure.

You "sure" sure?

We'll go.

Hey, miss, we have to go, actually.

You know what? I didn't see the time.

We'll have to cancel the order.

Really?

We cook for you.

We have to go.

What did you do?

She didn't do anything. It's the time.

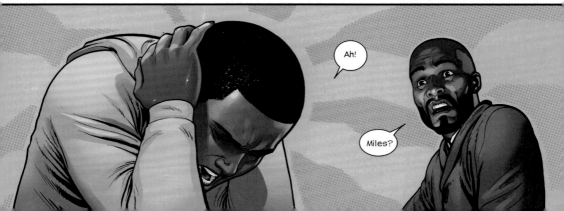

Ah!

Miles?

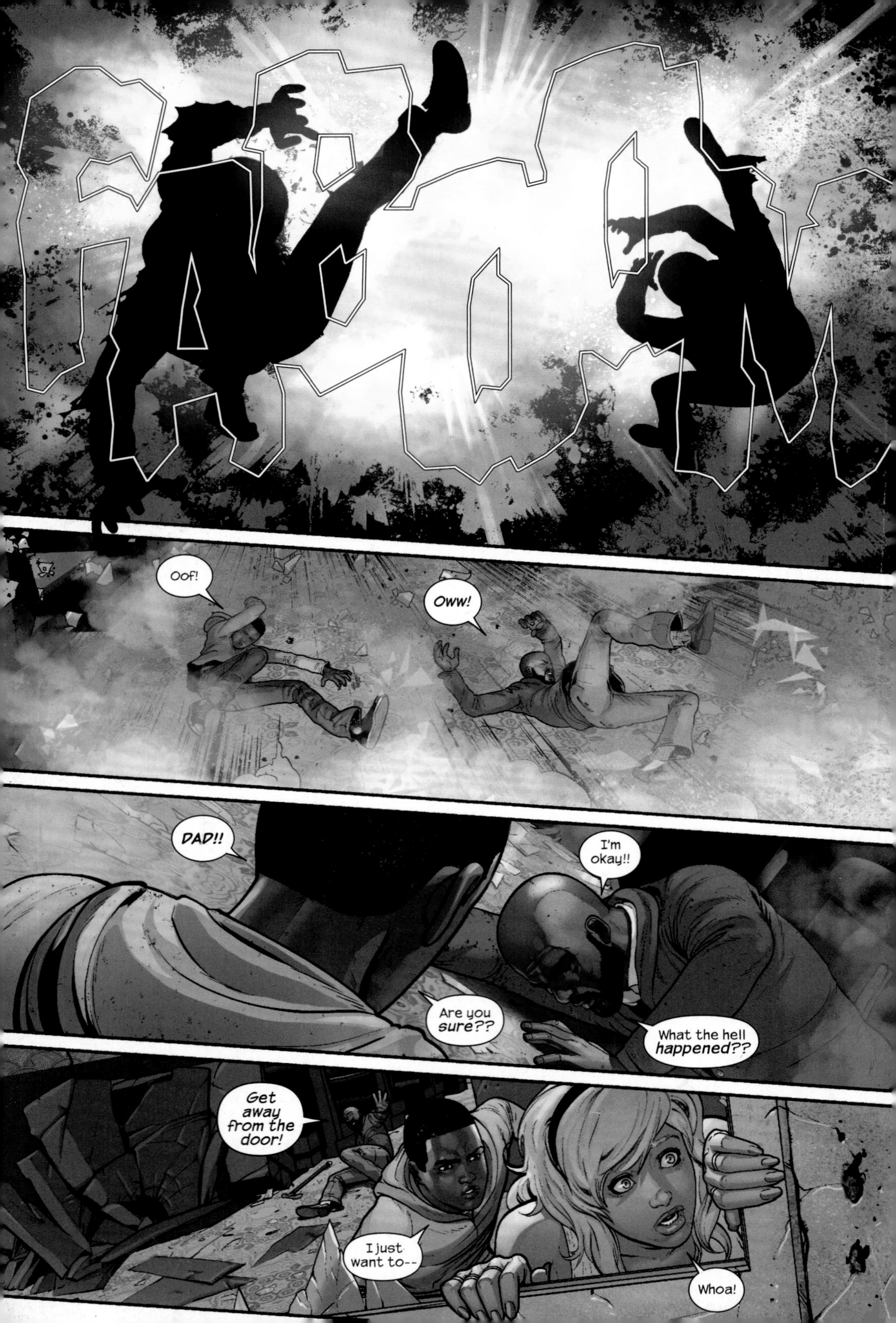
Oof!
OWW!
DAD!!
I'm okay!!
Are you sure??
What the hell happened??
Get away from the door!
I just want to--
Whoa!

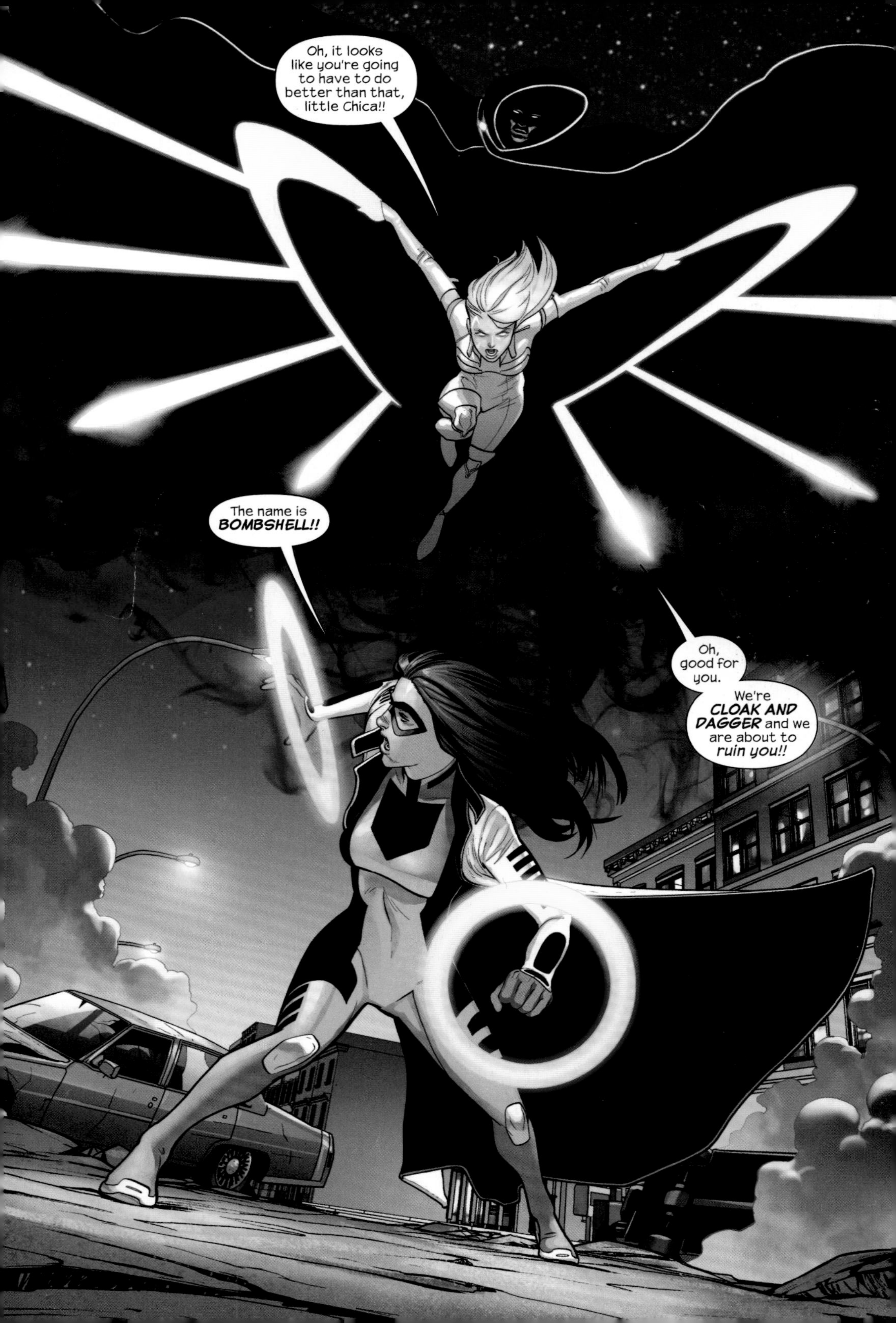
Oh, it looks like you're going to have to do better than that, little Chica!!
The name is BOMBSHELL!!
Oh, good for you.
We're CLOAK AND DAGGER and we are about to ruin you!!

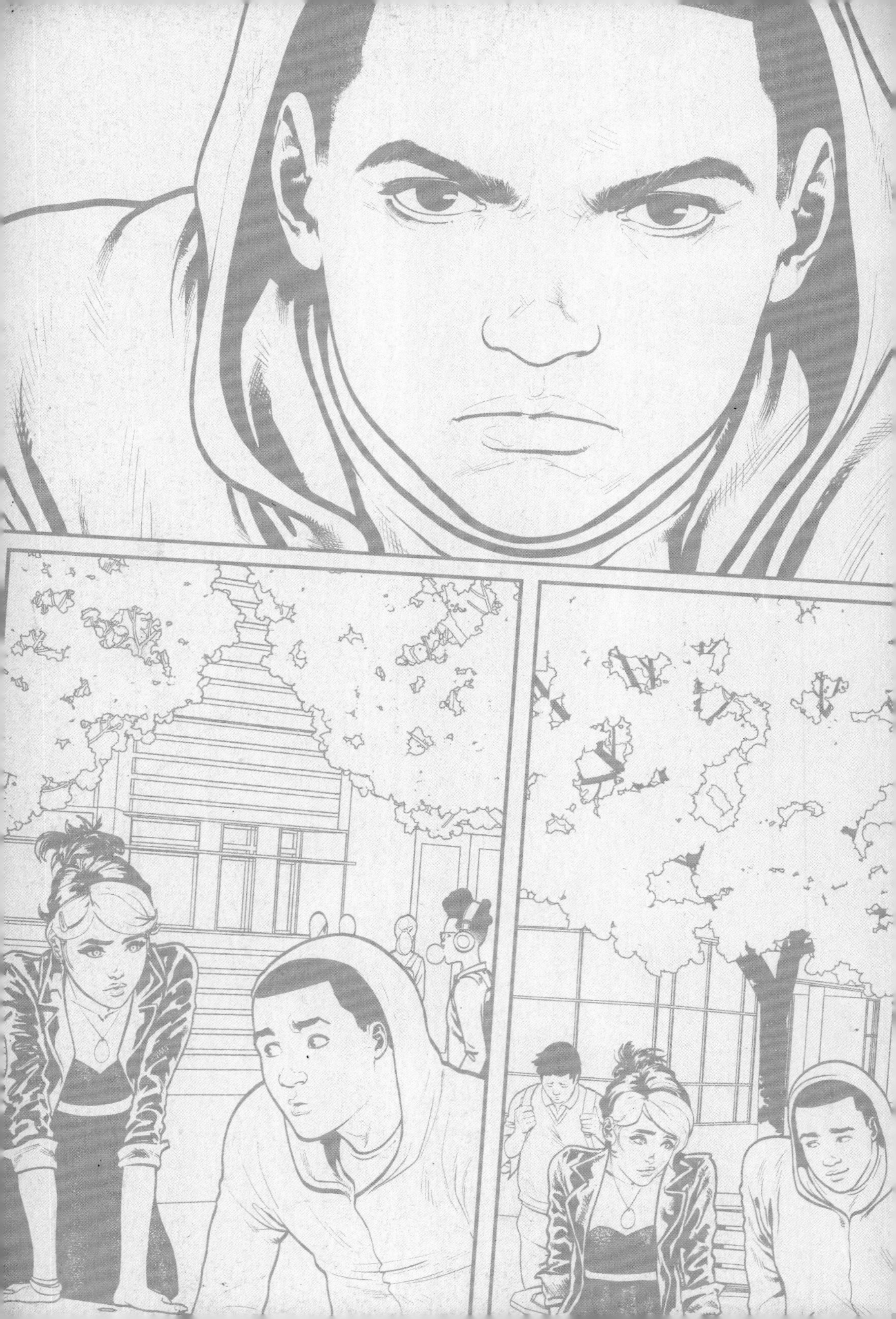

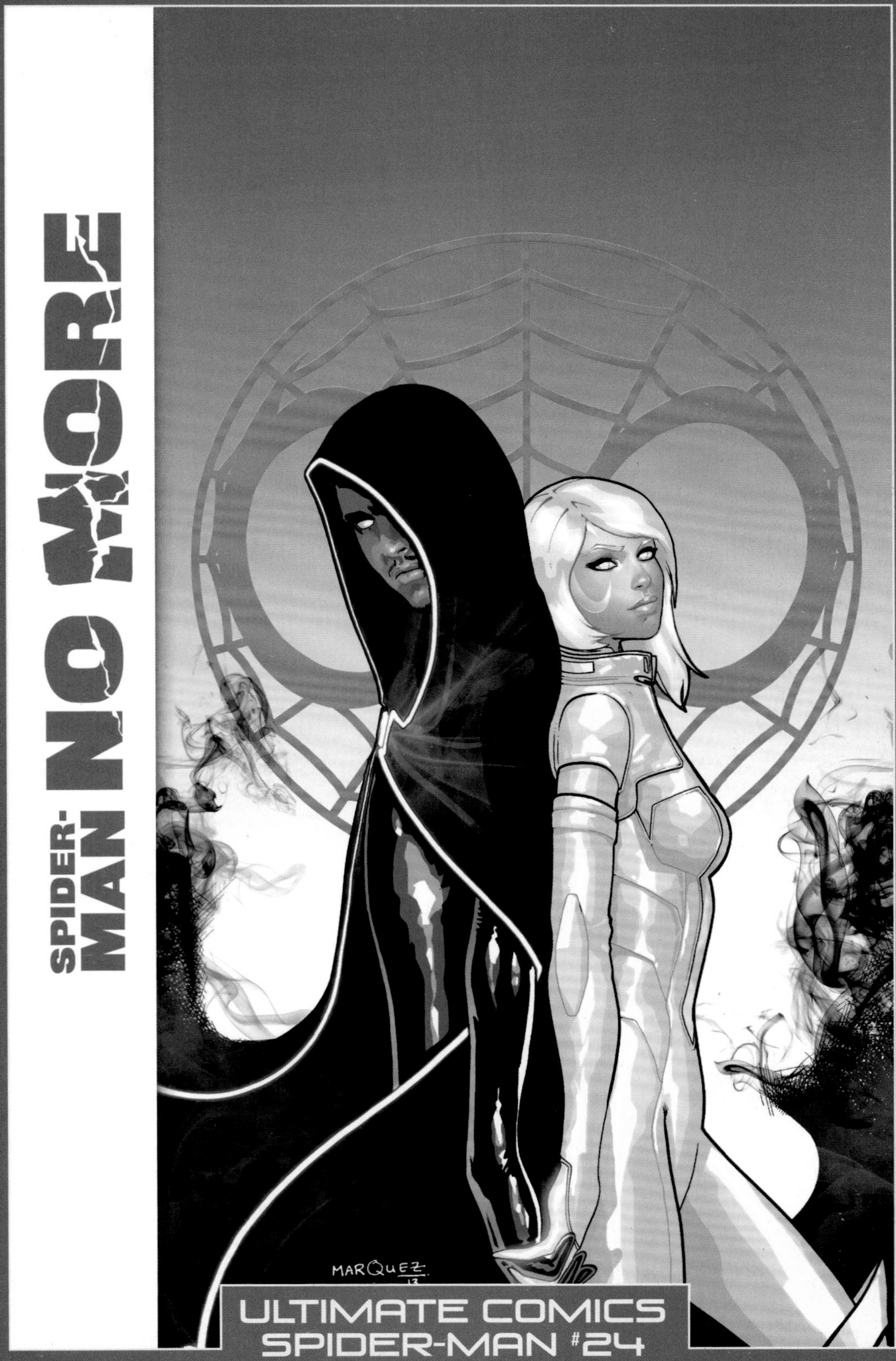
SPIDER-MAN NO MORE
MARQUEZ 13
ULTIMATE COMICS
SPIDER-MAN #24

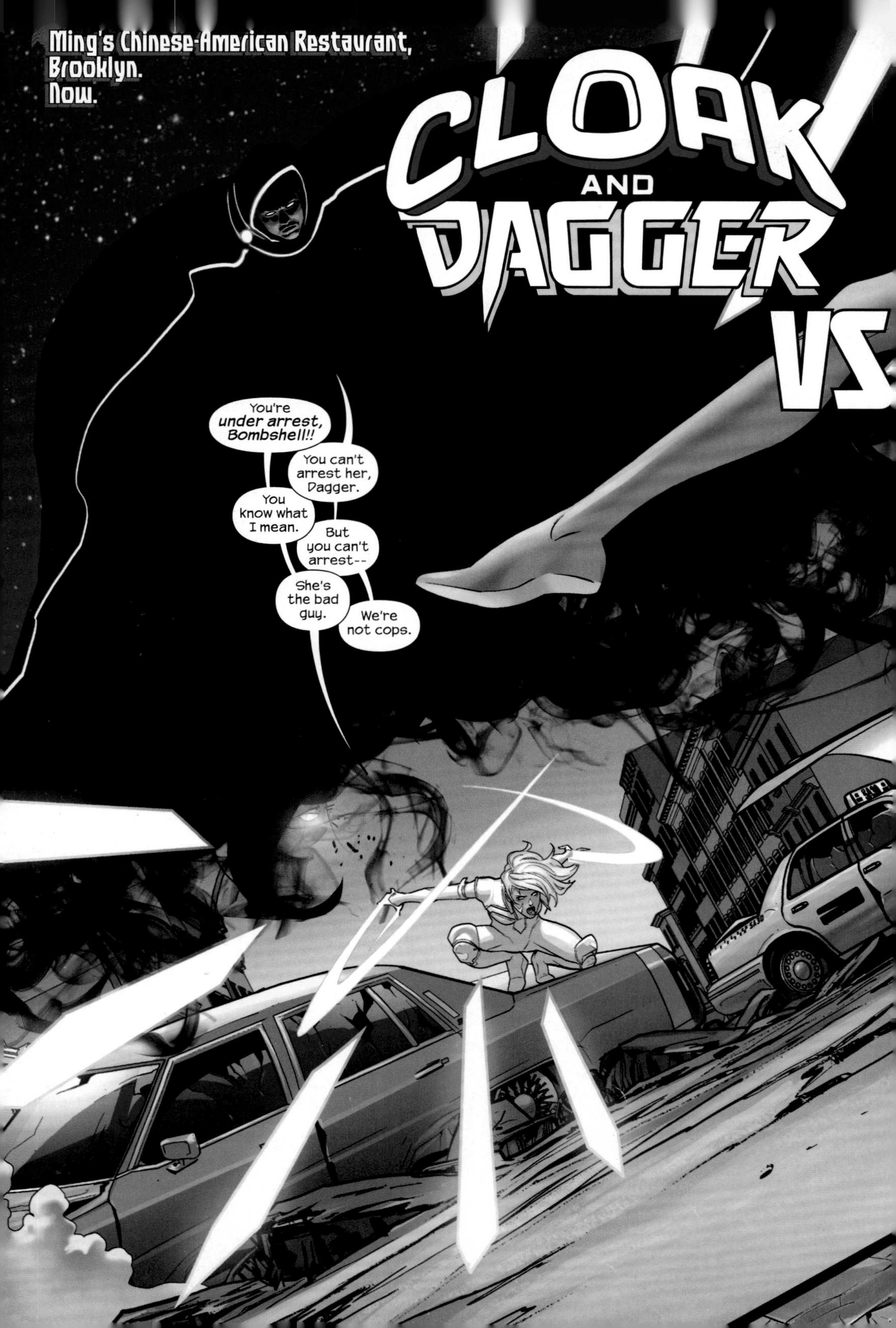

Ming's Chinese-American Restaurant,
Brooklyn.
Now.
CLOAK AND DAGGER VS
You're under arrest, Bombshell!!
You can't arrest her, Dagger.
You know what I mean.
But you can't arrest--
She's the bad guy.
We're not cops.

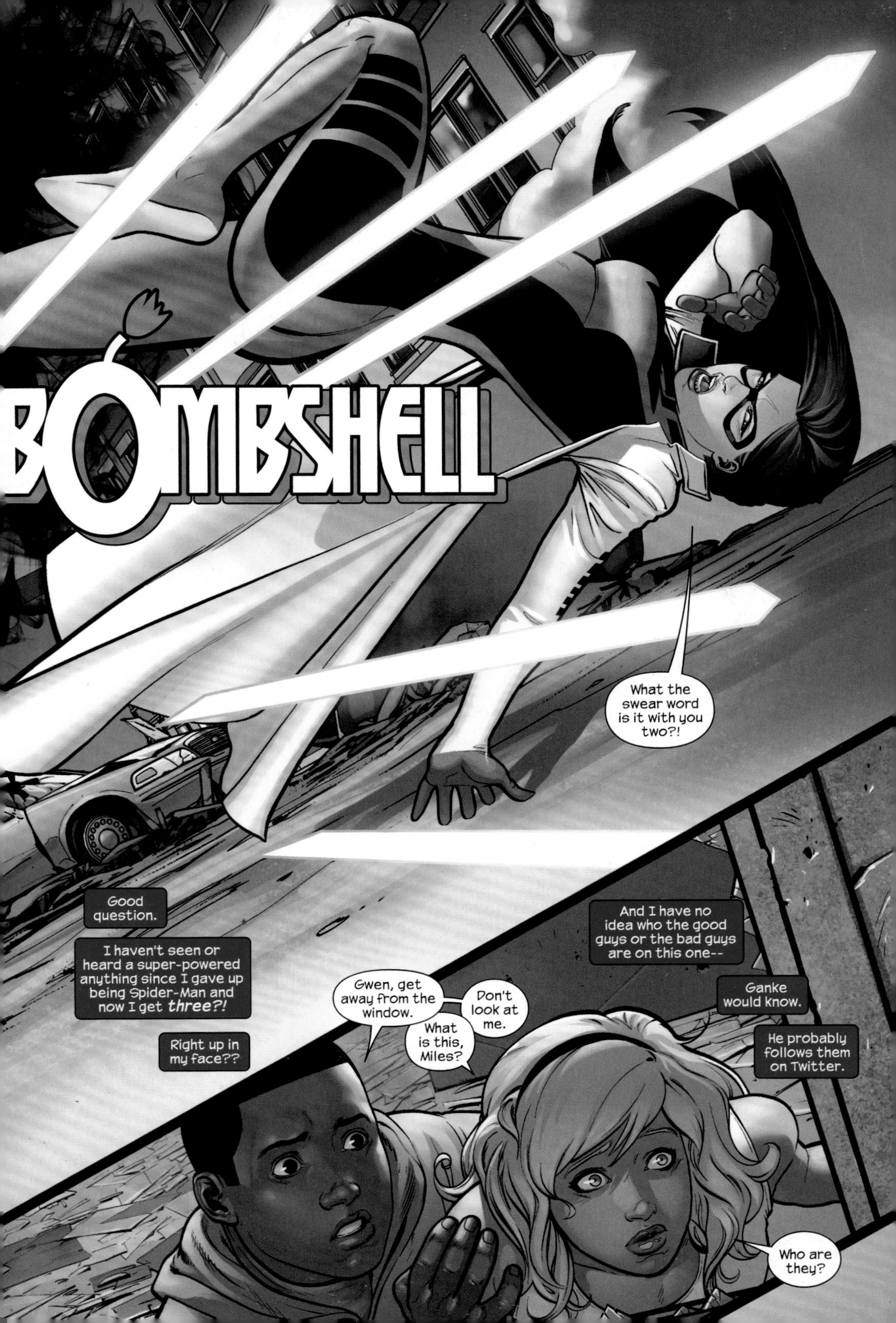
BOMBSHELL
What the swear word is it with you two?!
Good question.
I haven't seen or heard a super-powered anything since I gave up being Spider-Man and now I get *three?!*
Right up in my face??
And I have no idea who the good guys or the bad guys are on this one--
Ganke would know.
He probably follows them on Twitter.
Gwen, get away from the window.
Don't look at me.
What is this, Miles?
Who are they?

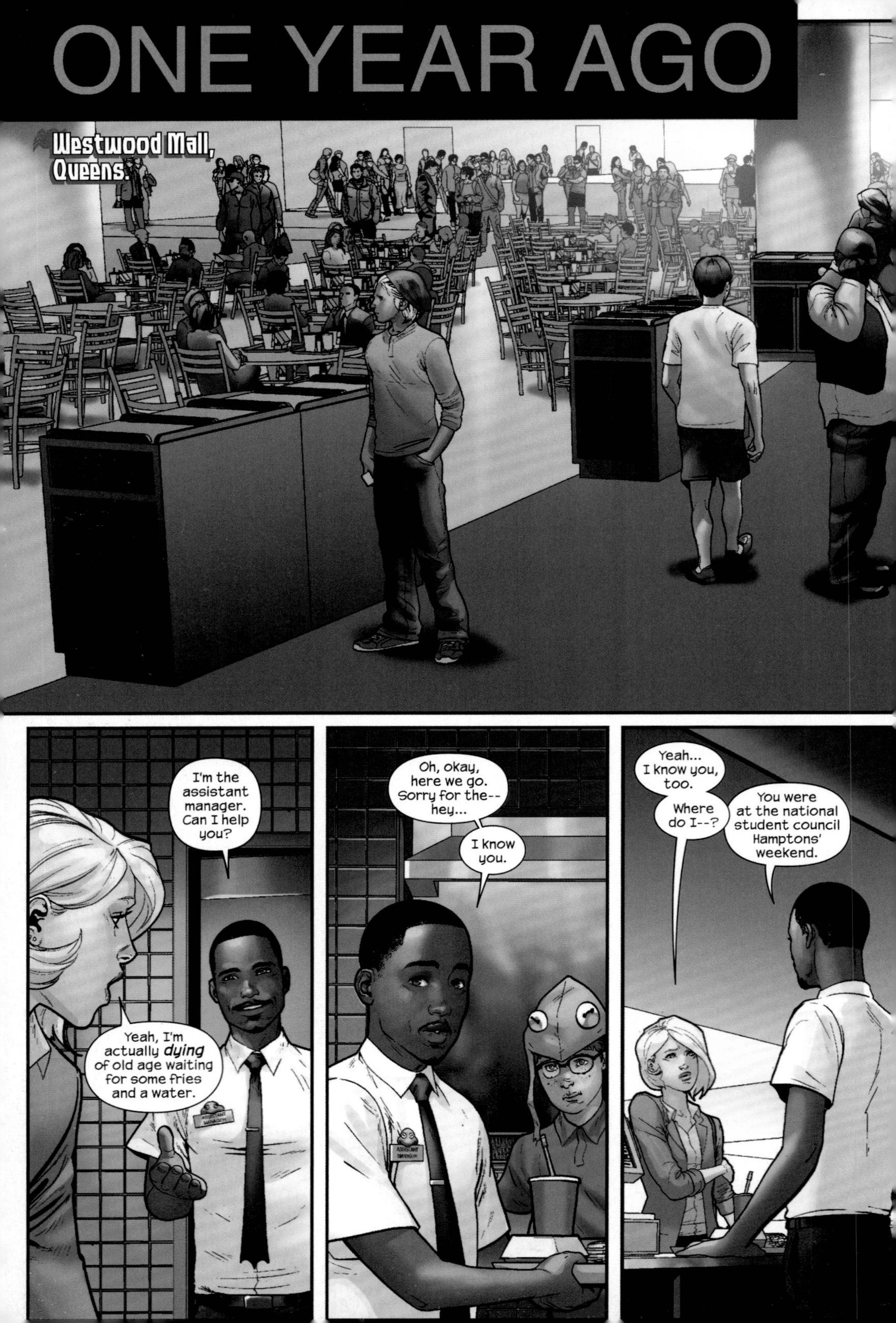
ONE YEAR AGO
Westwood Mall, Queens.
I'm the assistant manager. Can I help you?
Yeah, I'm actually *dying* of old age waiting for some fries and a water.
Oh, okay, here we go. Sorry for the-- hey...
I know you.
Yeah... I know you, too.
Where do I--?
You were at the national student council Hamptons' weekend.

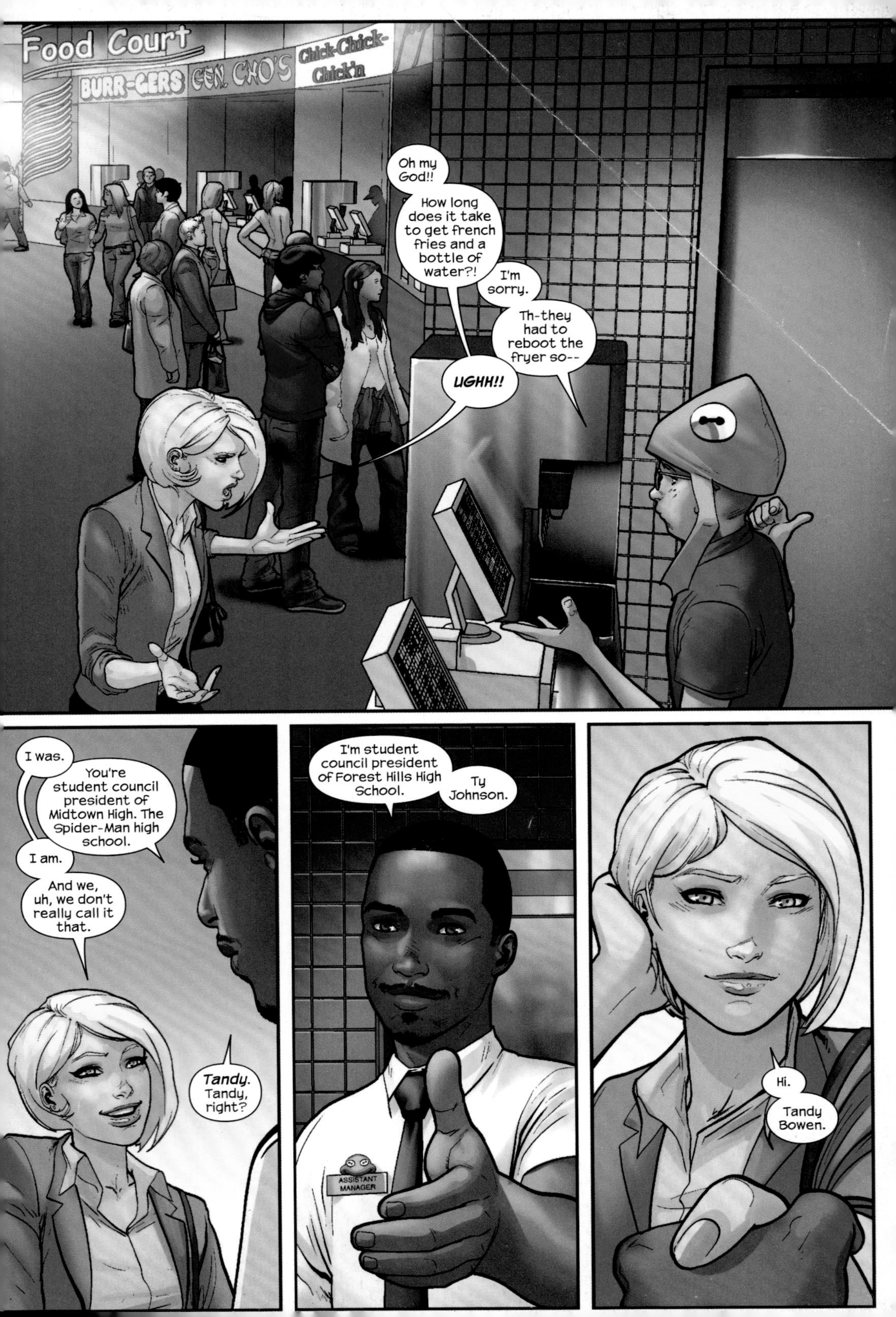
Food Court
BURR-GERS
GEN. CHO'S
Chick-Chick-Chick'n
Oh my God!!
How long does it take to get french fries and a bottle of water?!
I'm sorry.
Th-they had to reboot the fryer so--
UGHH!!
I was.
You're student council president of Midtown High. The Spider-Man high school.
I am.
And we, uh, we don't really call it that.
Tandy. Tandy, right?
I'm student council president of Forest Hills High School.
Ty Johnson.
ASSISTANT MANAGER
Hi.
Tandy Bowen.

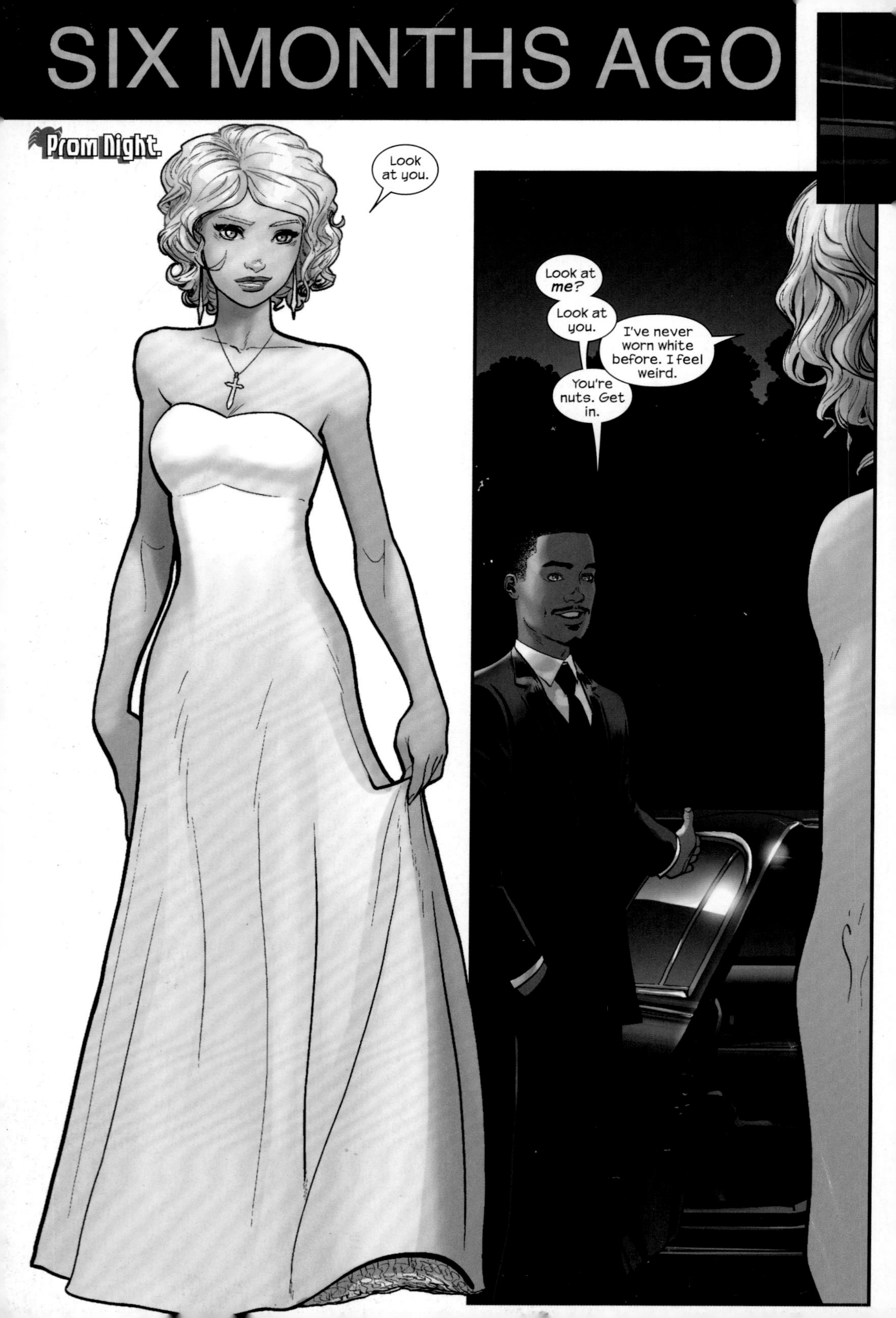
SIX MONTHS AGO
Prom Night.
Look at you.
Look at *me*?
Look at you.
I've never worn white before. I feel weird.
You're nuts. Get in.

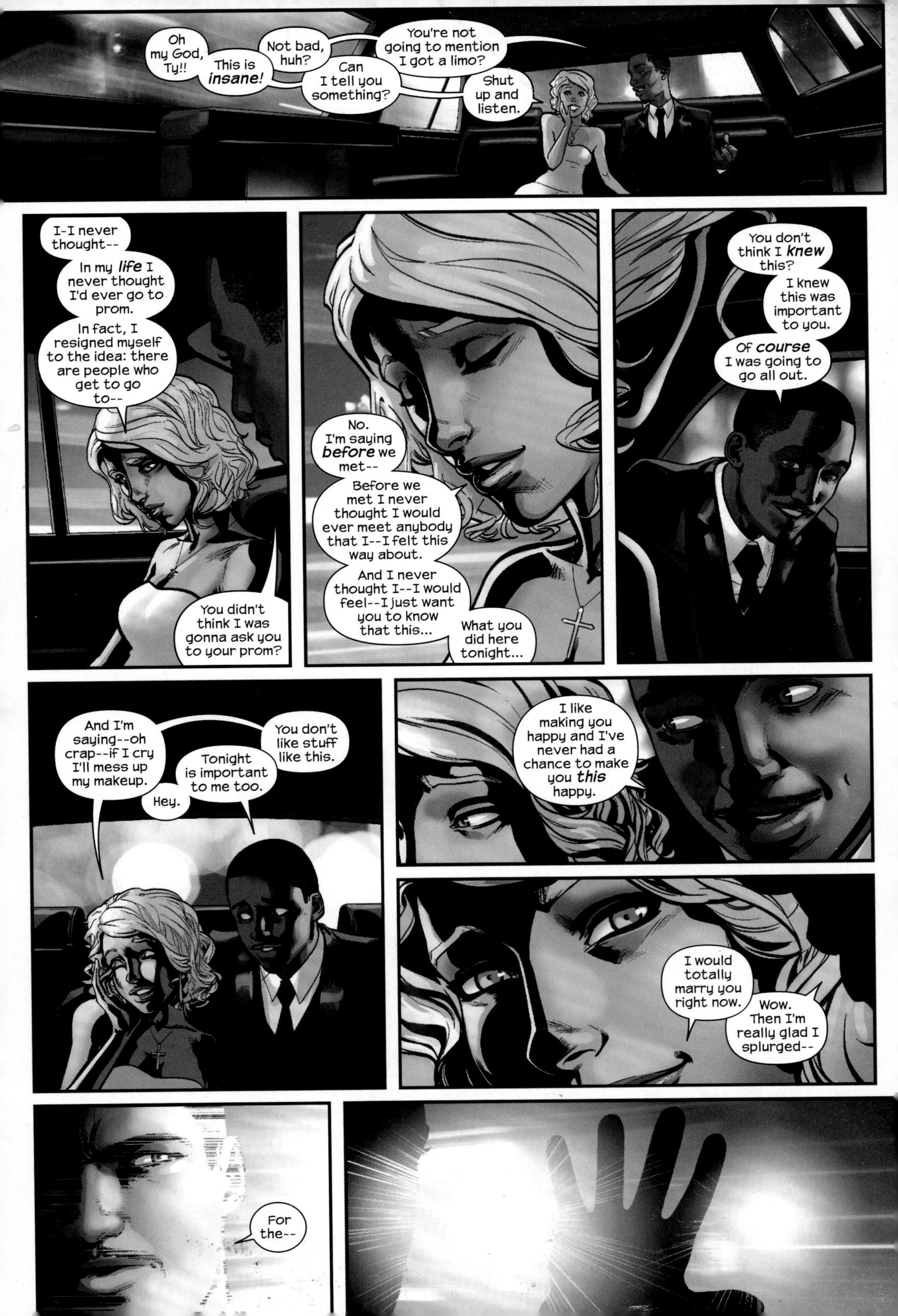

Oh my God, Ty!!
This is *insane!*
Not bad, huh?
You're not going to mention I got a limo?
Can I tell you something?
Shut up and listen.
I-I never thought--
In my *life* I never thought I'd ever go to prom.
In fact, I resigned myself to the idea: there are people who get to go to--
You didn't think I was gonna ask you to your prom?
No. I'm saying *before* we met--
Before we met I never thought I would ever meet anybody that I--I felt this way about.
And I never thought I--I would feel--I just want you to know that this...
What you did here tonight...
You don't think I *knew* this?
I knew this was important to you.
Of *course* I was going to go all out.
And I'm saying--oh crap--if I cry I'll mess up my makeup.
You don't like stuff like this.
Hey.
Tonight is important to me too.
I like making you happy and I've never had a chance to make you *this* happy.
I would totally marry you right now.
Wow. Then I'm really glad I splurged--
For the--

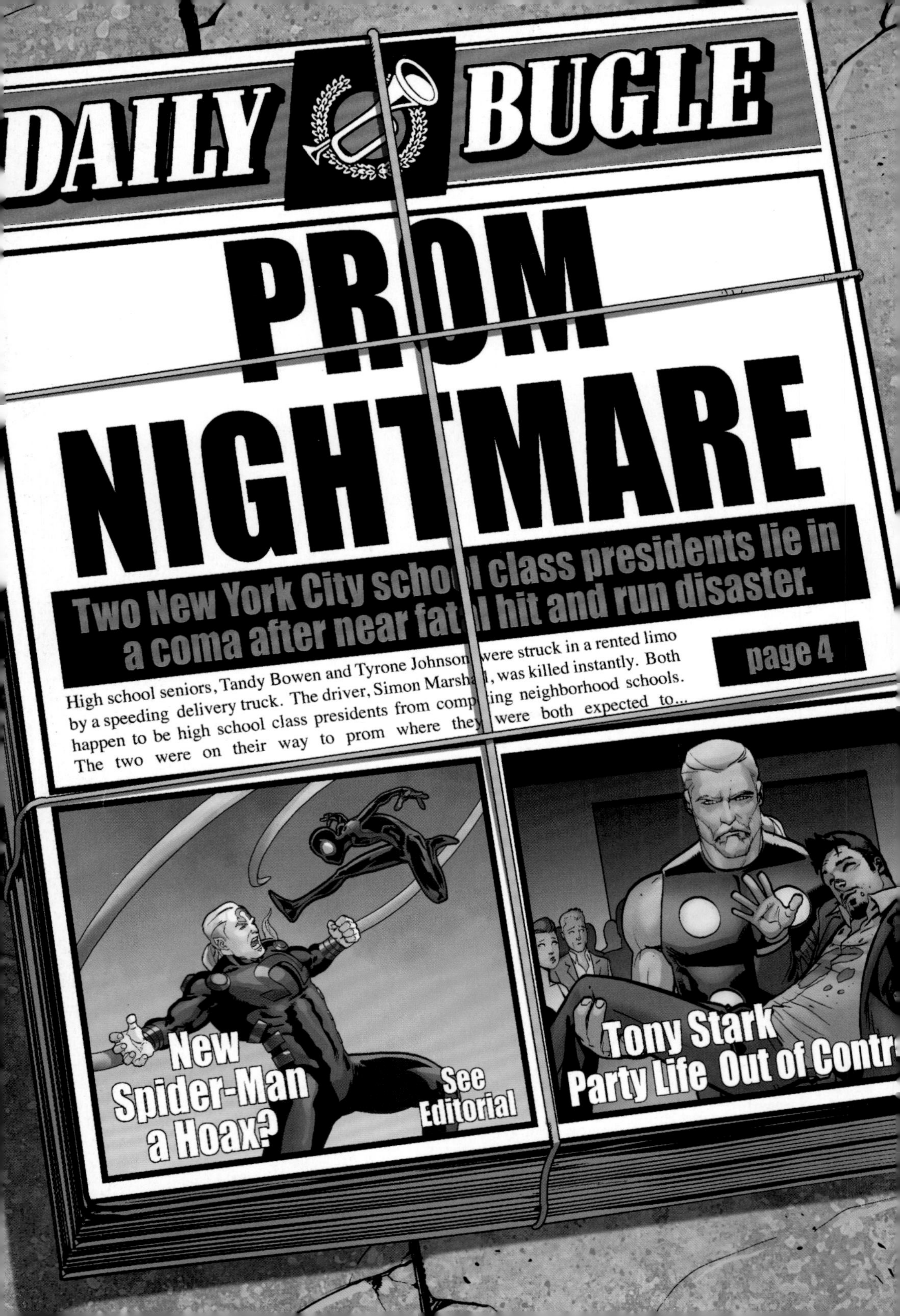

DAILY BUGLE
PROM NIGHTMARE
Two New York City school class presidents lie in a coma after near fatal hit and run disaster.
page 4
High school seniors, Tandy Bowen and Tyrone Johnson were struck in a rented limo by a speeding delivery truck. The driver, Simon Marshall, was killed instantly. Both happen to be high school class presidents from competing neighborhood schools. The two were on their way to prom where they were both expected to...
New Spider-Man a Hoax?
See Editorial
Tony Stark Party Life Out of Contr

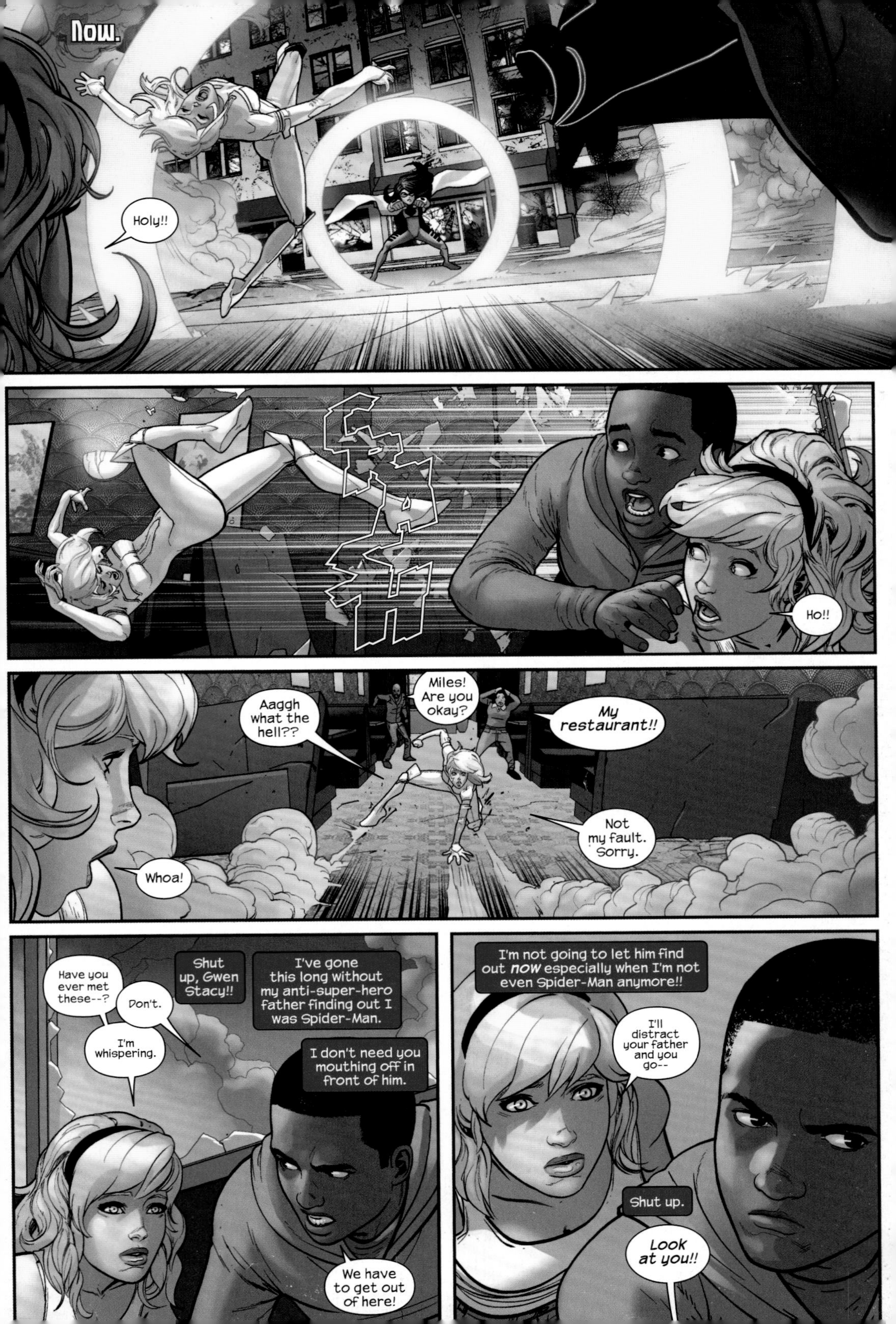

Now.
Holy!!
Ho!!
Aaggh what the hell??
Miles! Are you okay?
My restaurant!!
Not my fault. Sorry.
Whoa!
Have you ever met these--?
Don't.
I'm whispering.
Shut up, Gwen Stacy!!
I've gone this long without my anti-super-hero father finding out I was Spider-Man.
I don't need you mouthing off in front of him.
We have to get out of here!
I'm not going to let him find out NOW especially when I'm not even Spider-Man anymore!!
I'll distract your father and you go--
Shut up.
Look at you!!

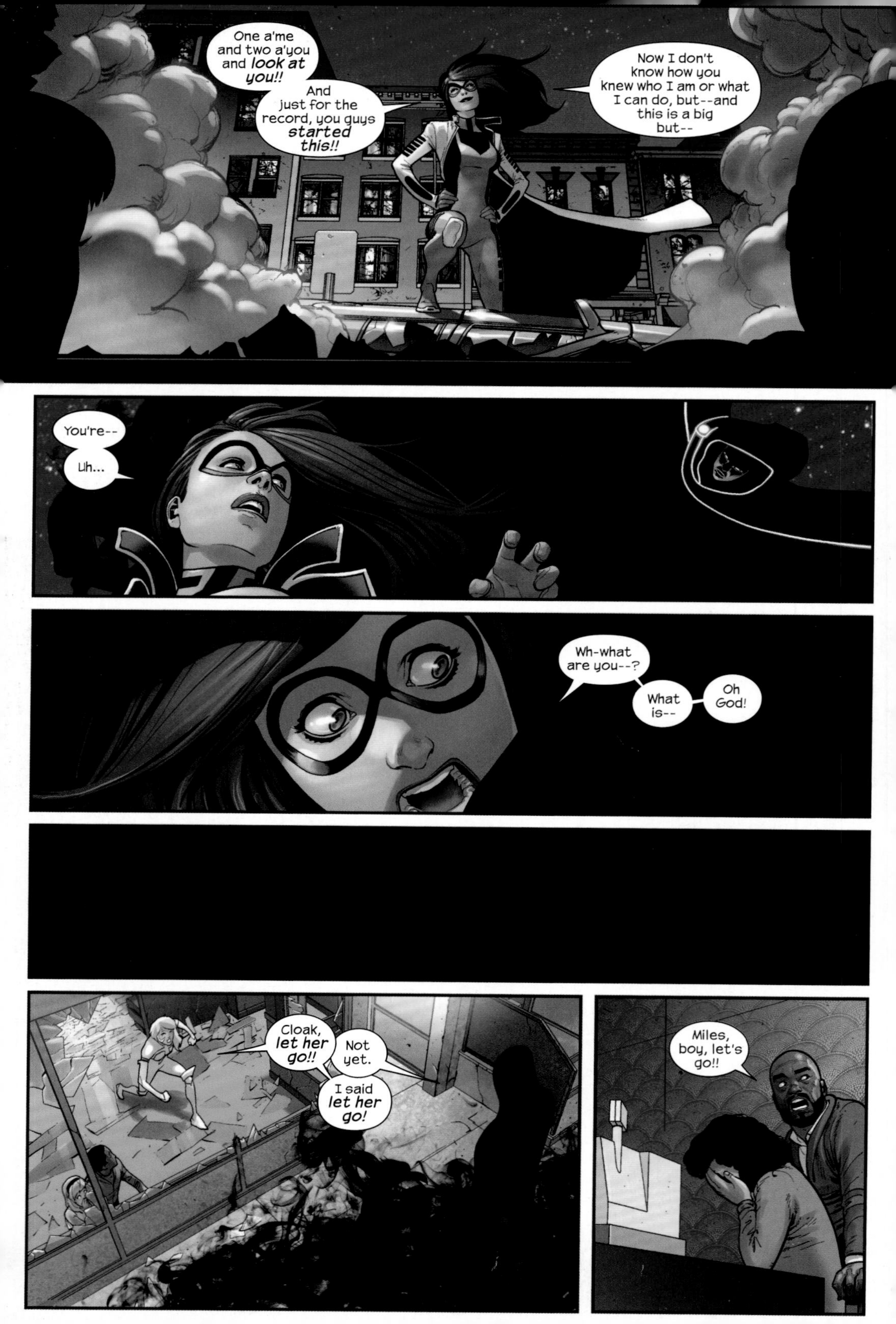

One a'me and two a'you and *look at you!!*
And just for the record, you guys *started this!!*
Now I don't know how you knew who I am or what I can do, but--and this is a big but--
You're--
Uh...
Wh-what are you--?
What is--
Oh God!
Cloak, *let her go!!*
Not yet.
I said *let her go!*
Miles, boy, let's go!!

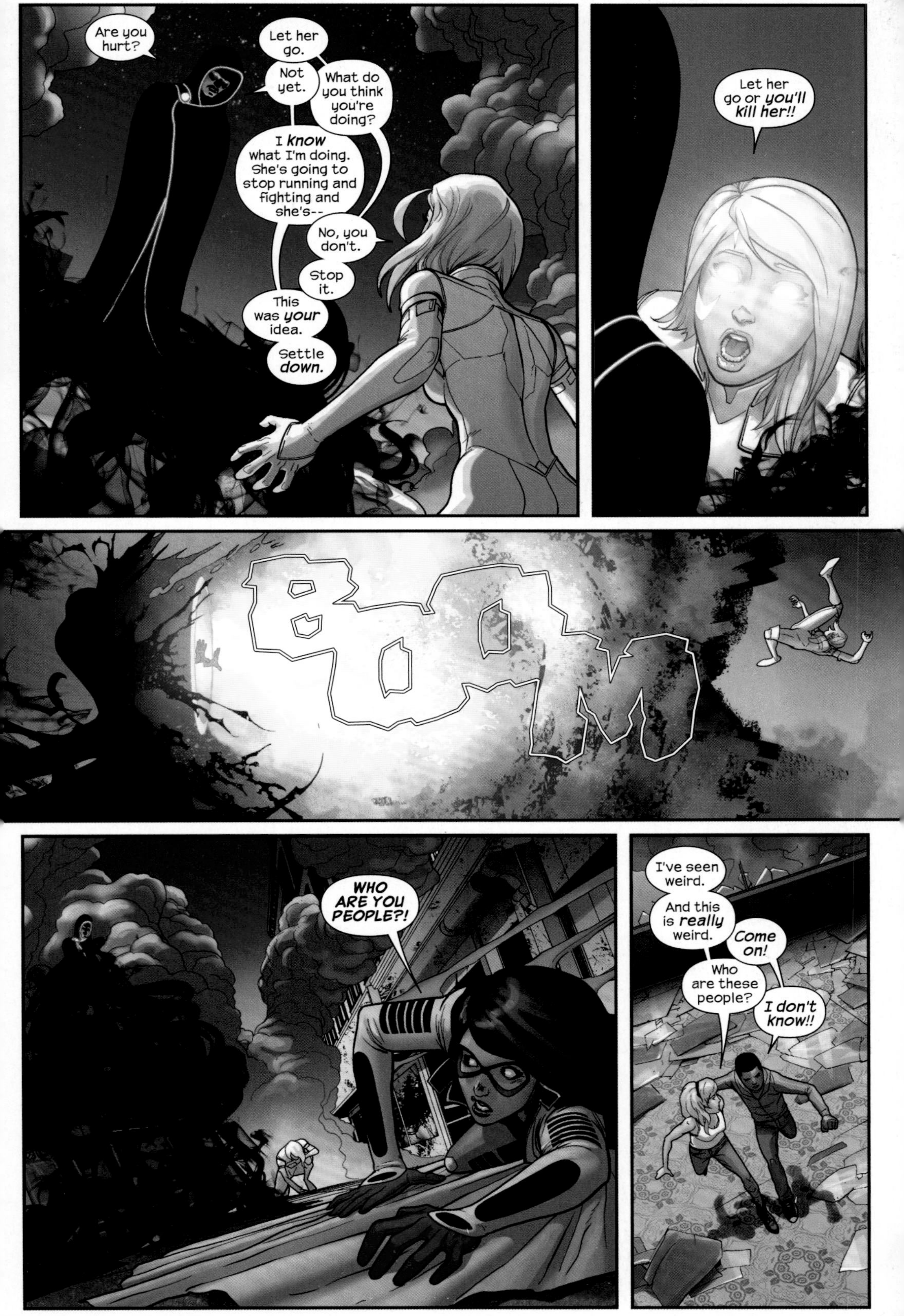
Are you hurt?
Let her go.
Not yet.
What do you think you're doing?
I *know* what I'm doing. She's going to stop running and fighting and she's--
No, you don't.
Stop it.
This was *your* idea.
Settle *down.*
Let her go or *you'll kill her!!*
BOOM
WHO ARE YOU PEOPLE?!
I've seen weird.
And this is *really* weird.
Come on!
Who are these people?
I don't know!!

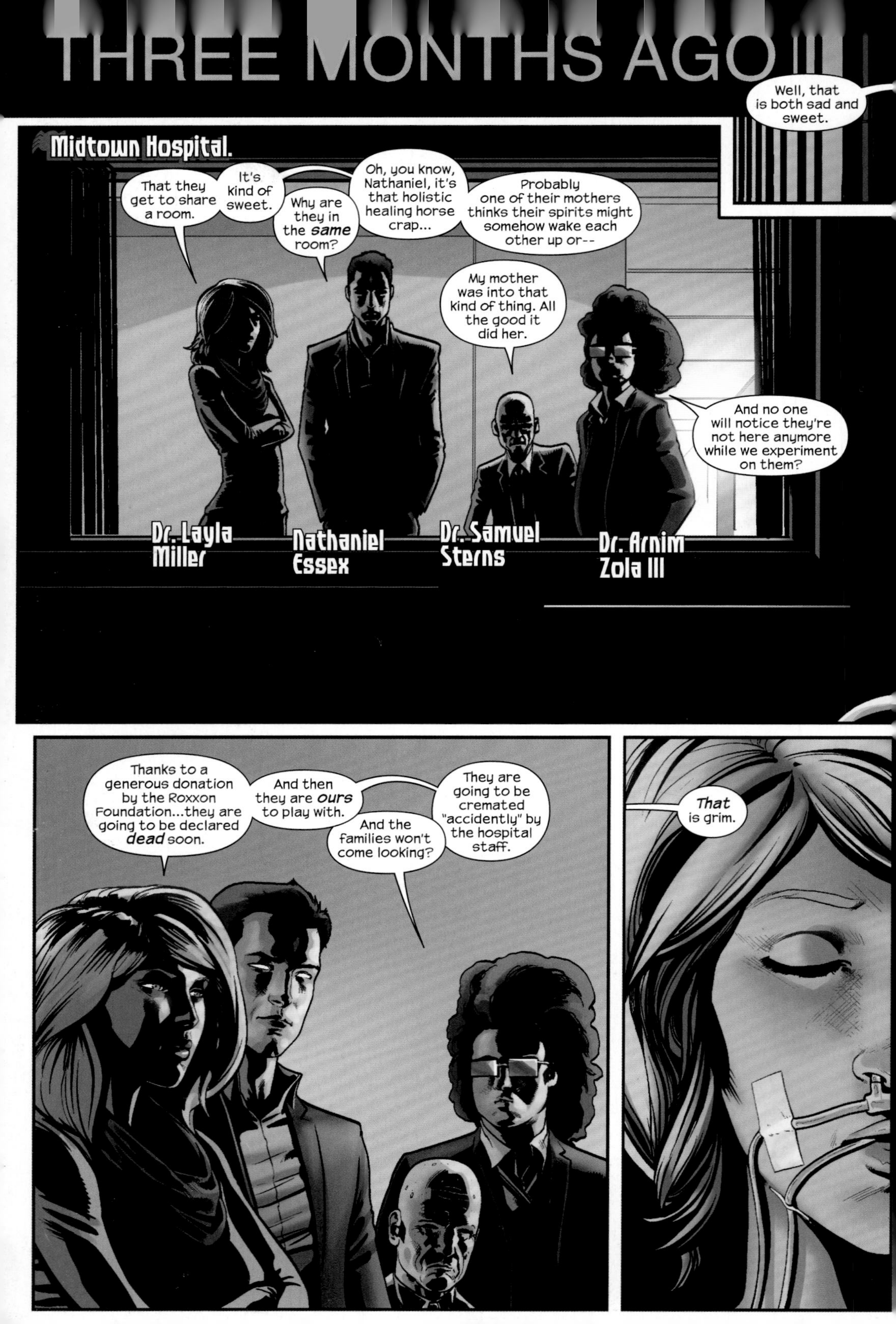
THREE MONTHS AGO III
Well, that is both sad and sweet.
Midtown Hospital.
That they get to share a room.
It's kind of sweet.
Why are they in the *same* room?
Oh, you know, Nathaniel, it's that holistic healing horse crap...
Probably one of their mothers thinks their spirits might somehow wake each other up or--
My mother was into that kind of thing. All the good it did her.
And no one will notice they're not here anymore while we experiment on them?
Dr. Layla Miller
Nathaniel Essex
Dr. Samuel Sterns
Dr. Arnim Zola III
Thanks to a generous donation by the Roxxon Foundation...they are going to be declared *dead* soon.
And then they are *ours* to play with.
And the families won't come looking?
They are going to be cremated "accidently" by the hospital staff.
That is grim.

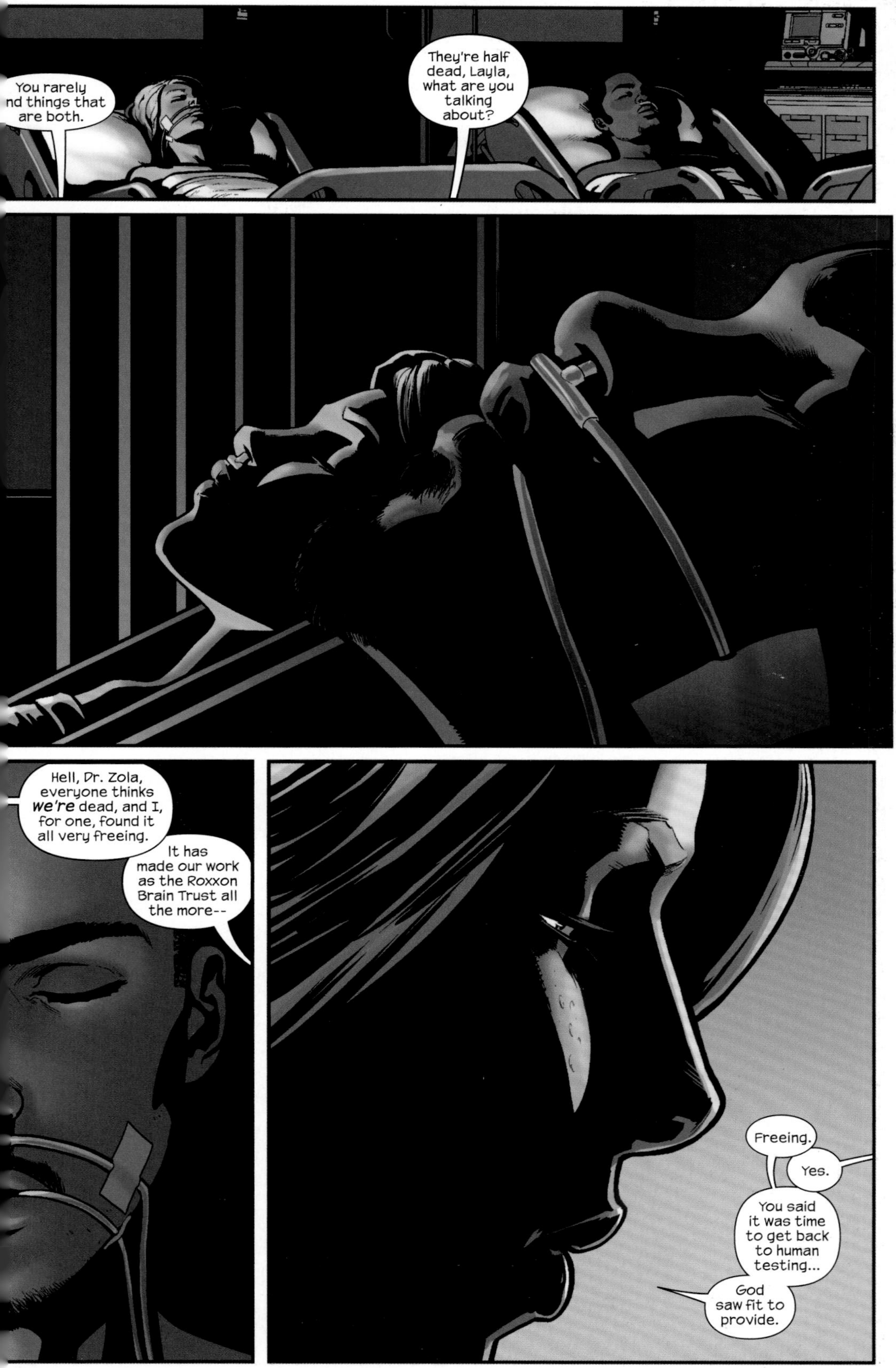
You rarely
nd things that are both.
They're half dead, Layla, what are you talking about?
Hell, Dr. Zola, everyone thinks *we're* dead, and I, for one, found it all very freeing.
It has made our work as the Roxxon Brain Trust all the more--
Freeing.
Yes.
You said it was time to get back to human testing...
God saw fit to provide.

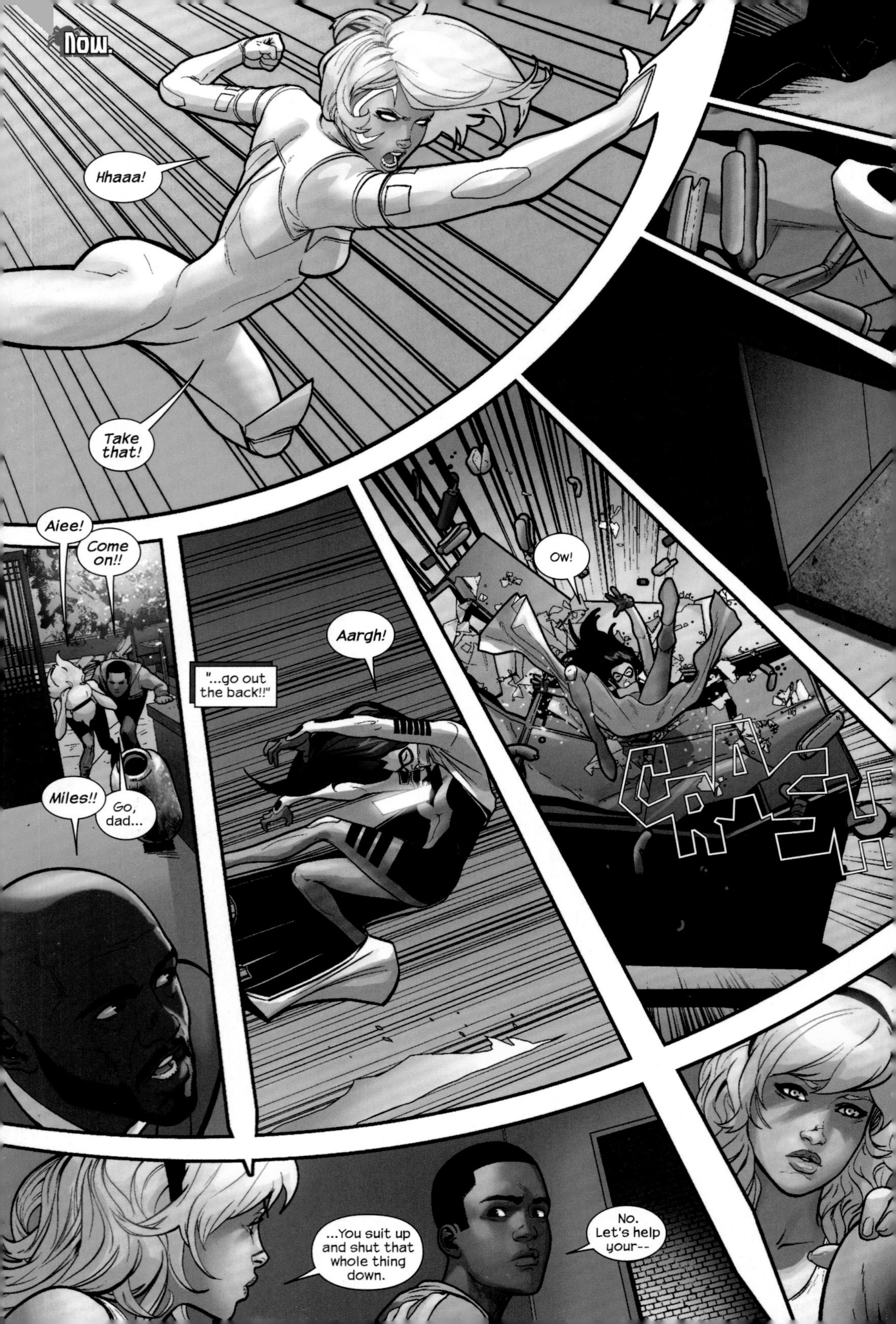
Now.
Hhaaa!
Take that!
Ow!
Aiee!
Come on!!
Aargh!
"...go out the back!!"
Miles!!
Go, dad...
...You suit up and shut that whole thing down.
No. Let's help your--

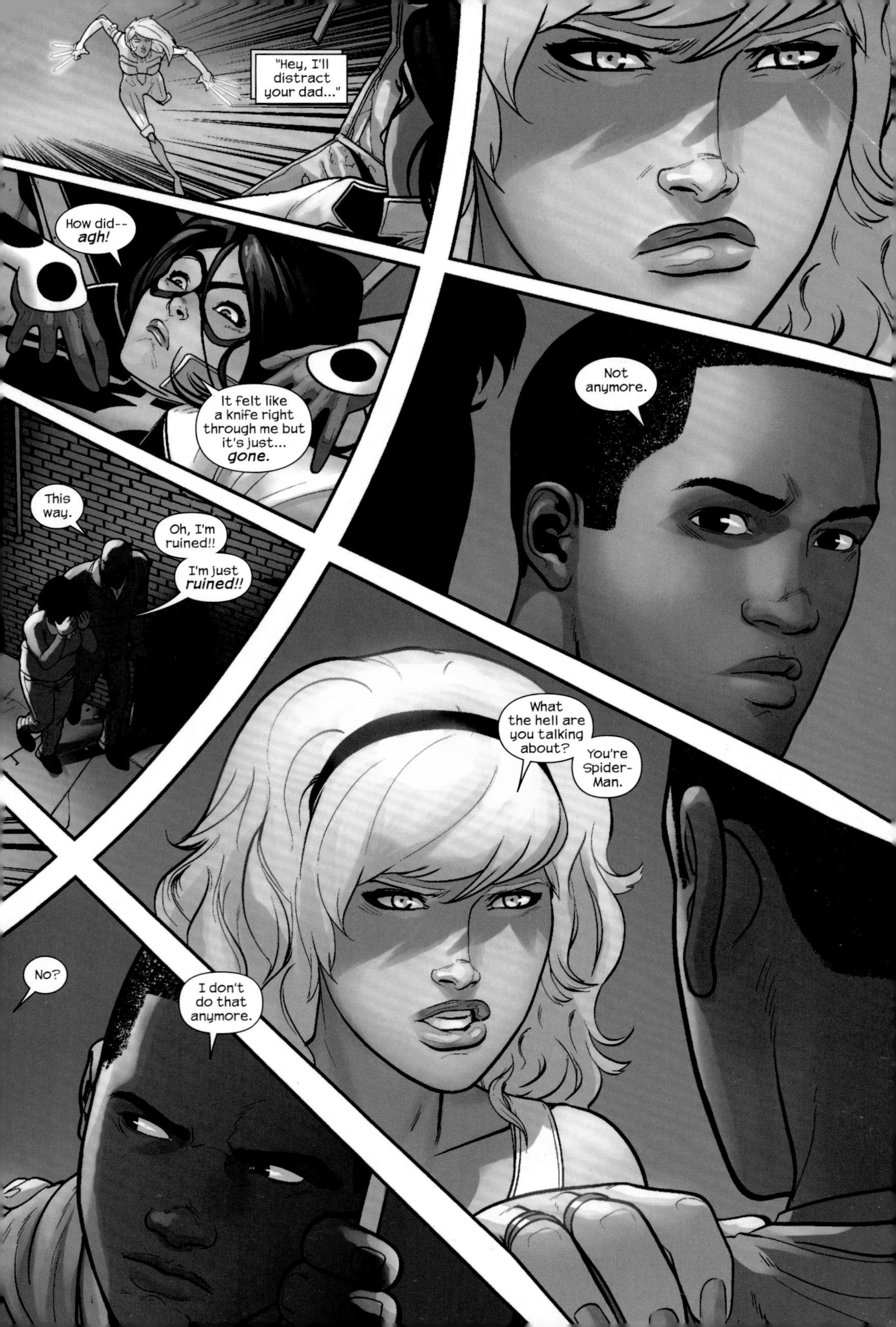
"Hey, I'll distract your dad..."
How did-- agh!
It felt like a knife right through me but it's just... gone.
Not anymore.
This way.
Oh, I'm ruined!!
I'm just ruined!!
What the hell are you talking about?
You're Spider-Man.
No?
I don't do that anymore.

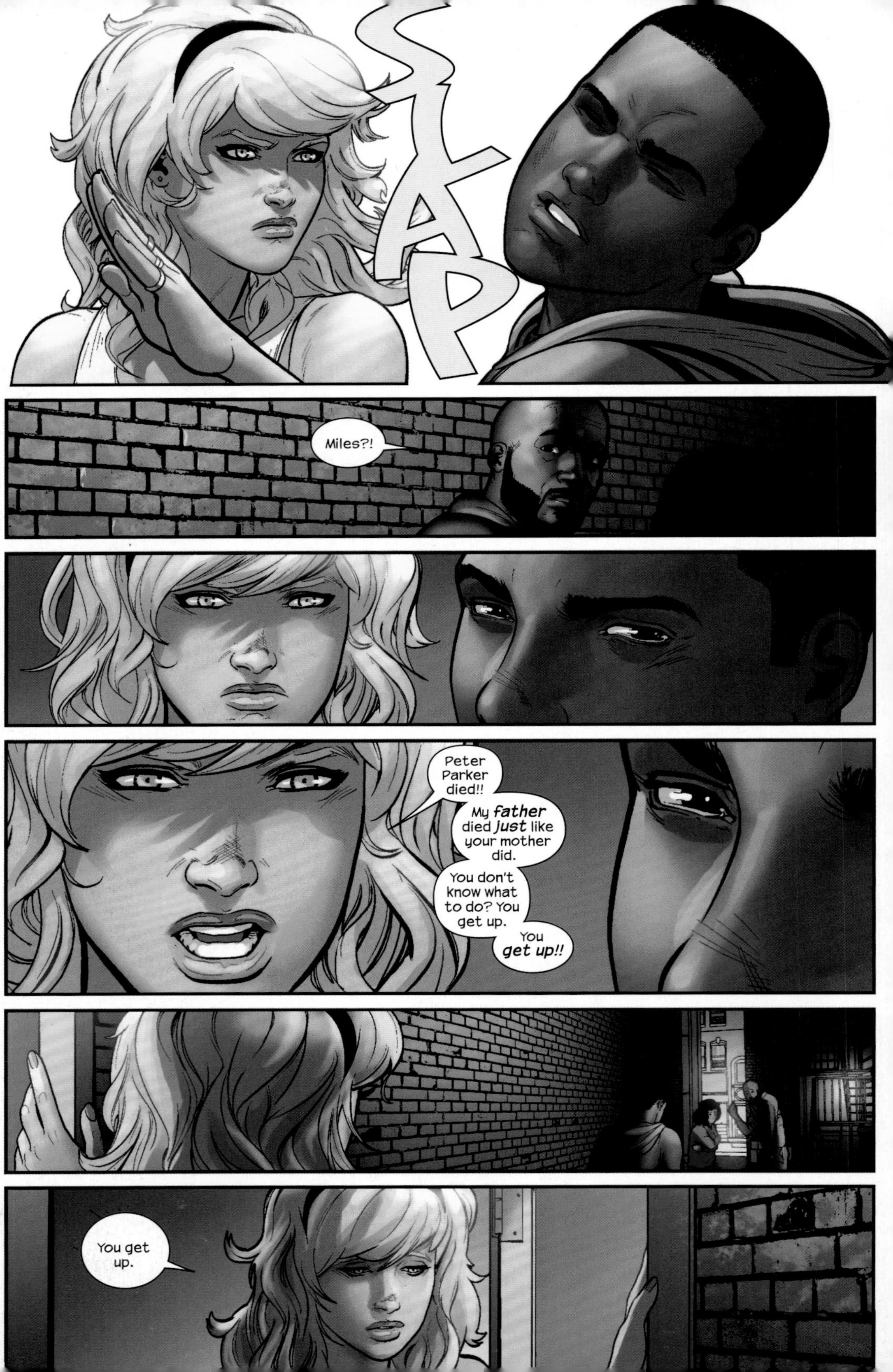
SLAP
Miles?!
Peter Parker died!!
My *father* died *just* like your mother did.
You don't know what to do? You get up.
You *get up!!*
You get up.

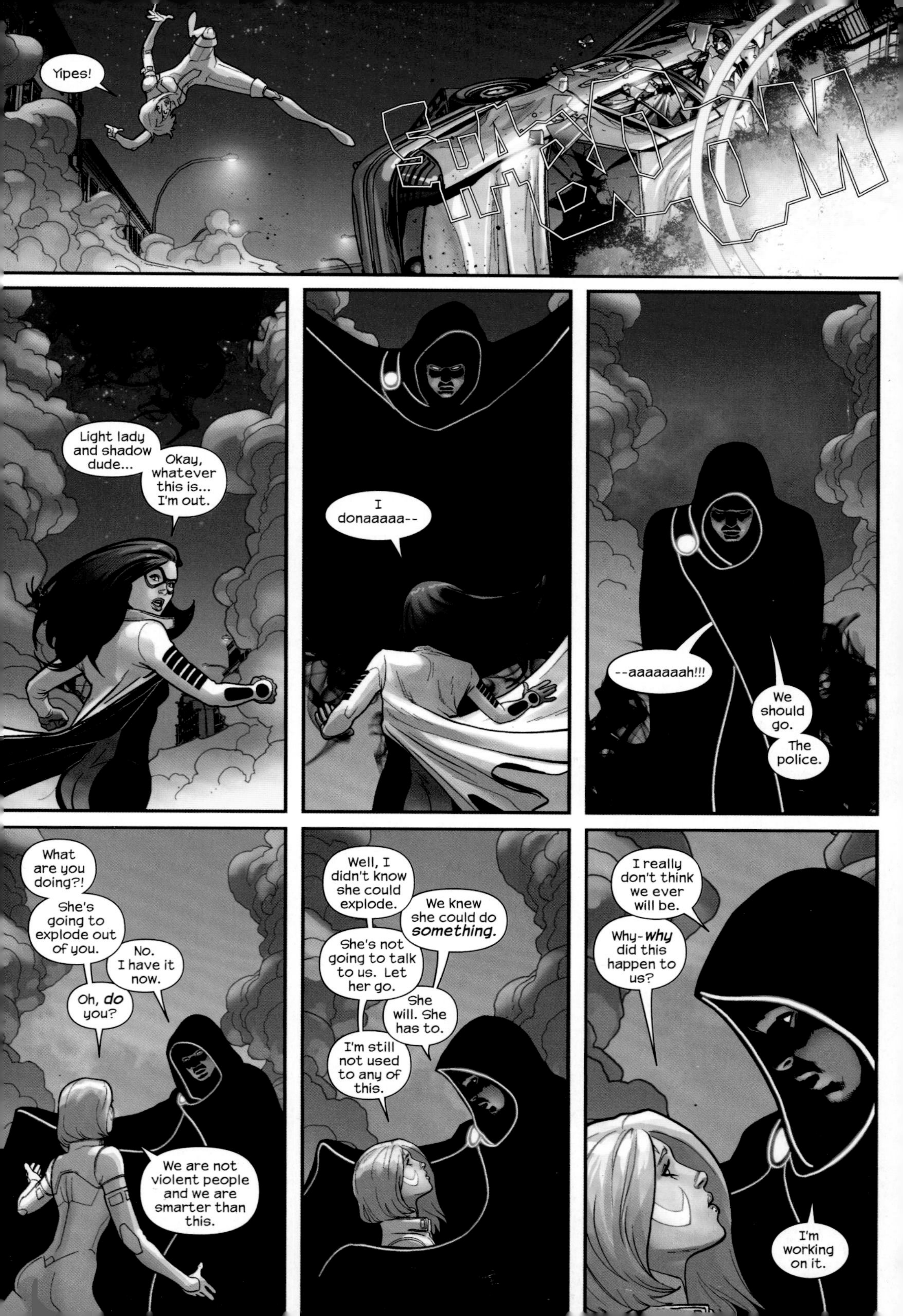
Yipes!
SHA-KOOM
Light lady and shadow dude...
Okay, whatever this is... I'm out.
I donaaaaa--
--aaaaaaah!!!
We should go.
The police.
What are you doing?!
She's going to explode out of you.
No. I have it now.
Oh, *do* you?
We are not violent people and we are smarter than this.
Well, I didn't know she could explode.
We knew she could do *something.*
She's not going to talk to us. Let her go.
She will. She has to.
I'm still not used to any of this.
I really don't think we ever will be.
Why-*why* did this happen to us?
I'm working on it.

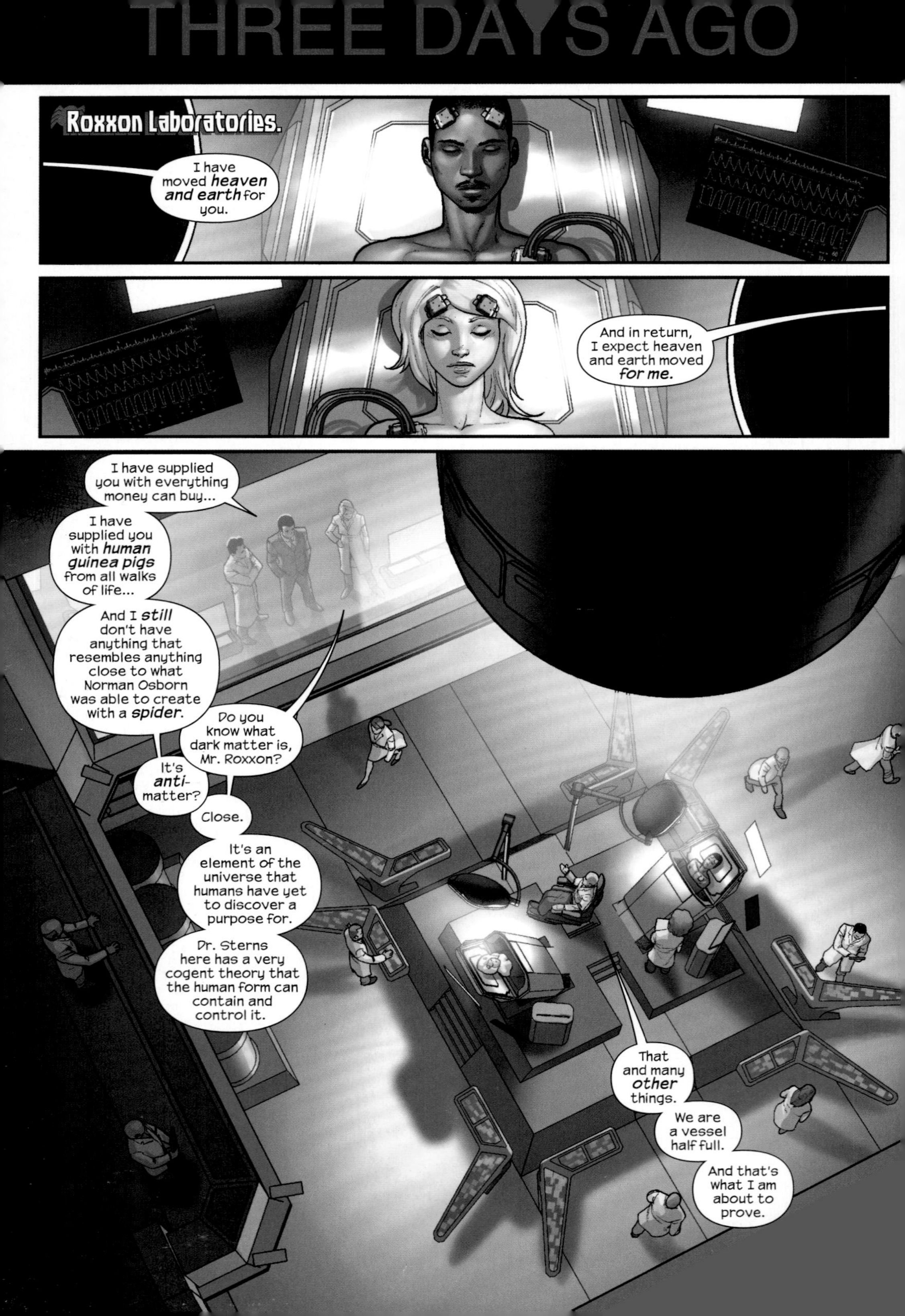
THREE DAYS AGO
Roxxon Laboratories.
I have moved heaven and earth for you.
And in return, I expect heaven and earth moved for me.
I have supplied you with everything money can buy...
I have supplied you with human guinea pigs from all walks of life...
And I still don't have anything that resembles anything close to what Norman Osborn was able to create with a spider.
Do you know what dark matter is, Mr. Roxxon?
It's anti-matter?
Close.
It's an element of the universe that humans have yet to discover a purpose for.
Dr. Sterns here has a very cogent theory that the human form can contain and control it.
That and many other things.
We are a vessel half full.
And that's what I am about to prove.

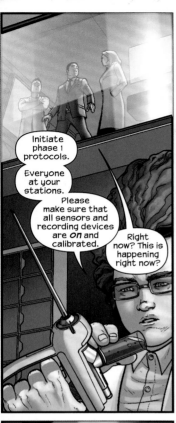

Initiate phase 1 protocols.

Everyone at your stations.

Please make sure that all sensors and recording devices are *on* and calibrated.

Right now? This is happening right now?

That's what we called you in for, boss.

Really? *Right* now?

You have moved heaven and earth for us... it's the least we can do.

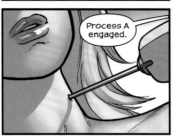

Process A engaged.

What are you injecting into the--?

Is--is-- is *that* dark matter?

It is a catalyst compound.

Vital signs are stable, Zola.

I think we are a go for Process B.

We already *have* dark matter inside of us.

Everything does. All things do.

It's the thing in between the things that make us *us*.

So is the *theory*...

You see...and I mean no offense, Mr. Roxxon, but the problem with your experiments up until now is that you keep trying to duplicate what Norman *Osborn* did.

What Norman Osborn created with his fractured Oz formula...

What the Parkers created with the symbiotes years ago...

Why would you try to duplicate failure?

Spider-Man was Osborn's penicillin, his accident...

But what it did show us, inarguably, was that there are energies inside all of us.

Untapped potential.

Things we can't even perceive yet.

Um, I think we have a--

Uh-oh.

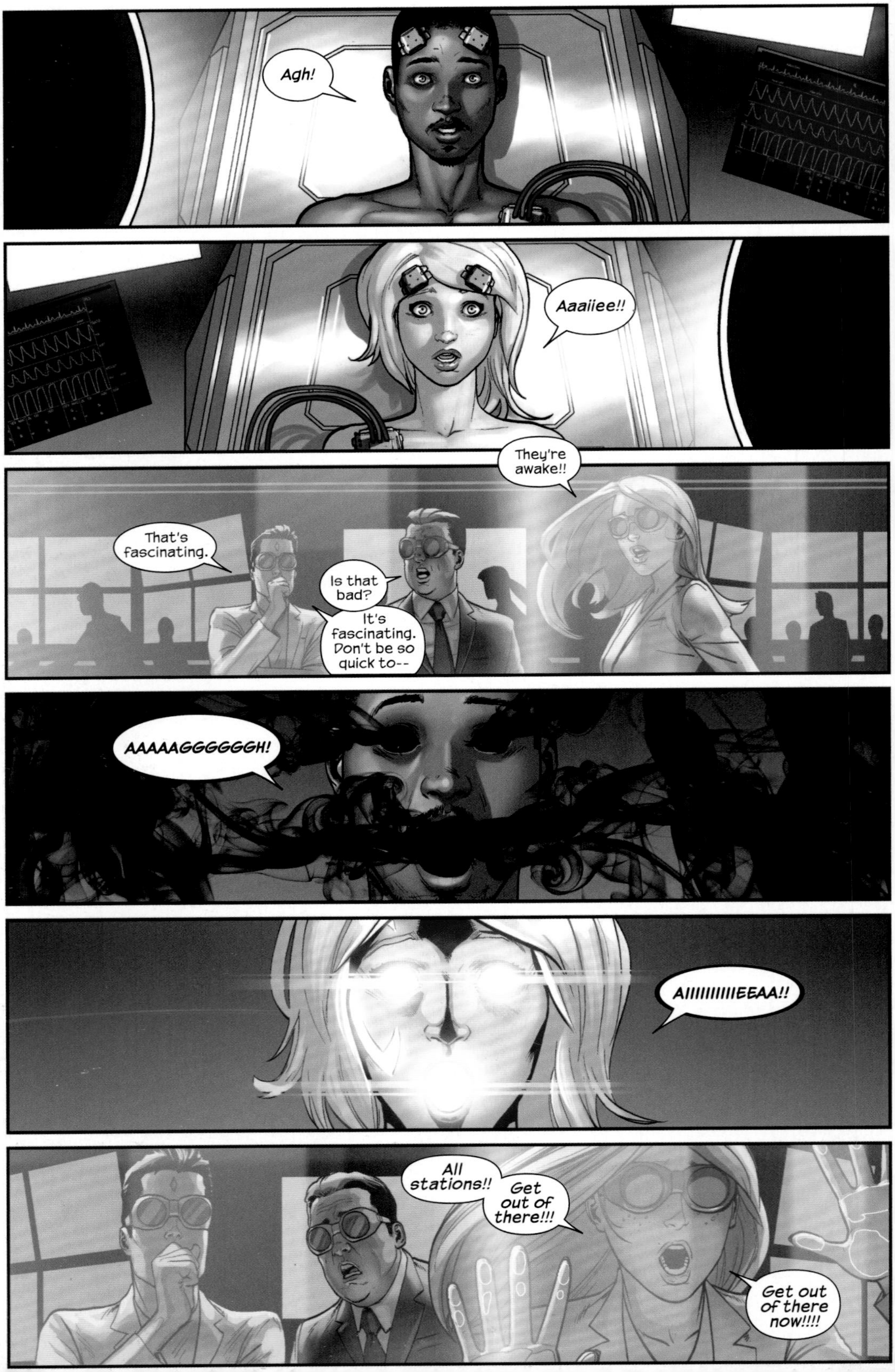
Agh!
Aaaiiee!!
They're awake!!
That's fascinating.
Is that bad?
It's fascinating. Don't be so quick to--
AAAAAGGGGGGH!
AIIIIIIIIIIEEAA!!
All stations!!
Get out of there!!!
Get out of there now!!!!

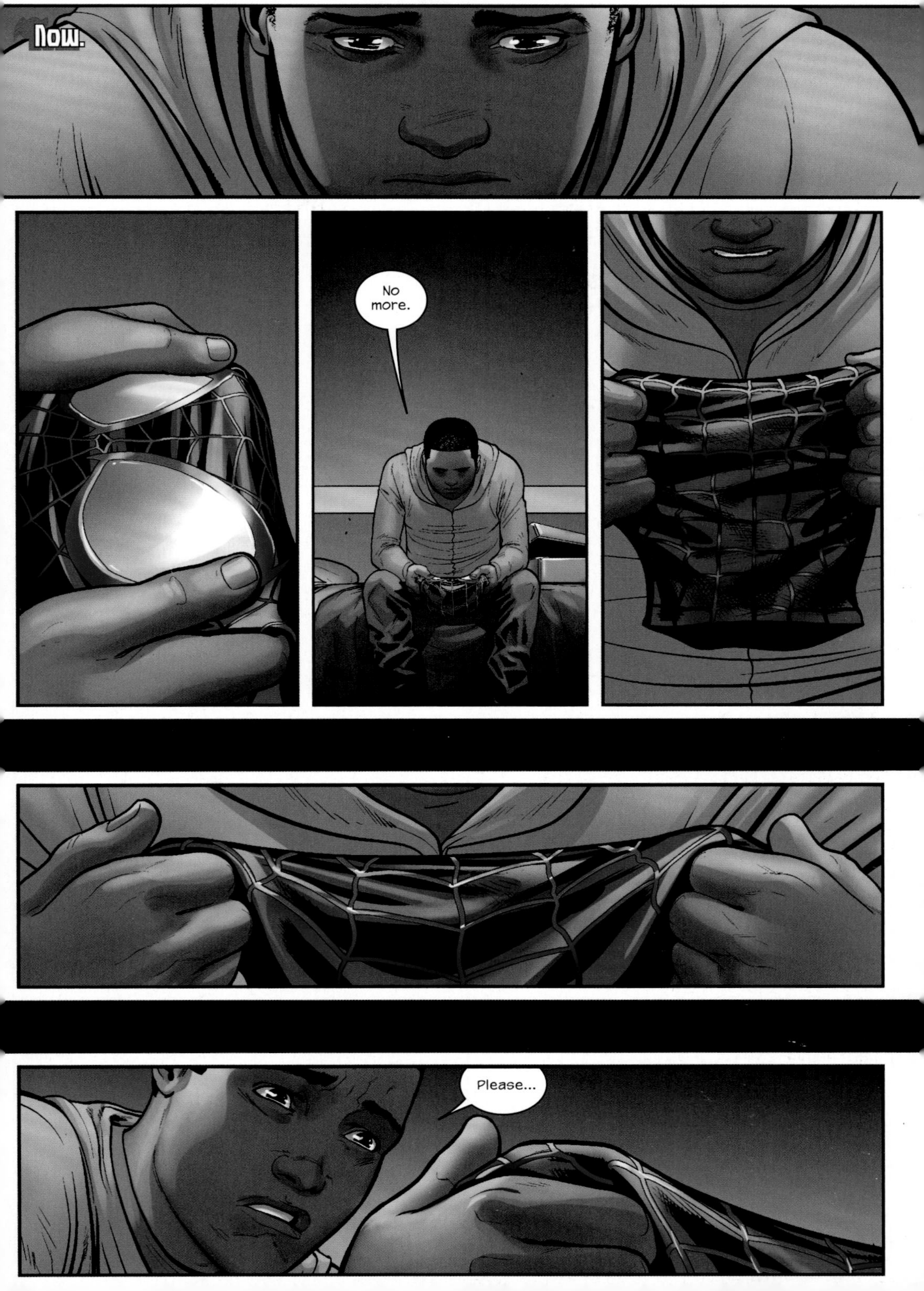
Now.
No more.
Please...

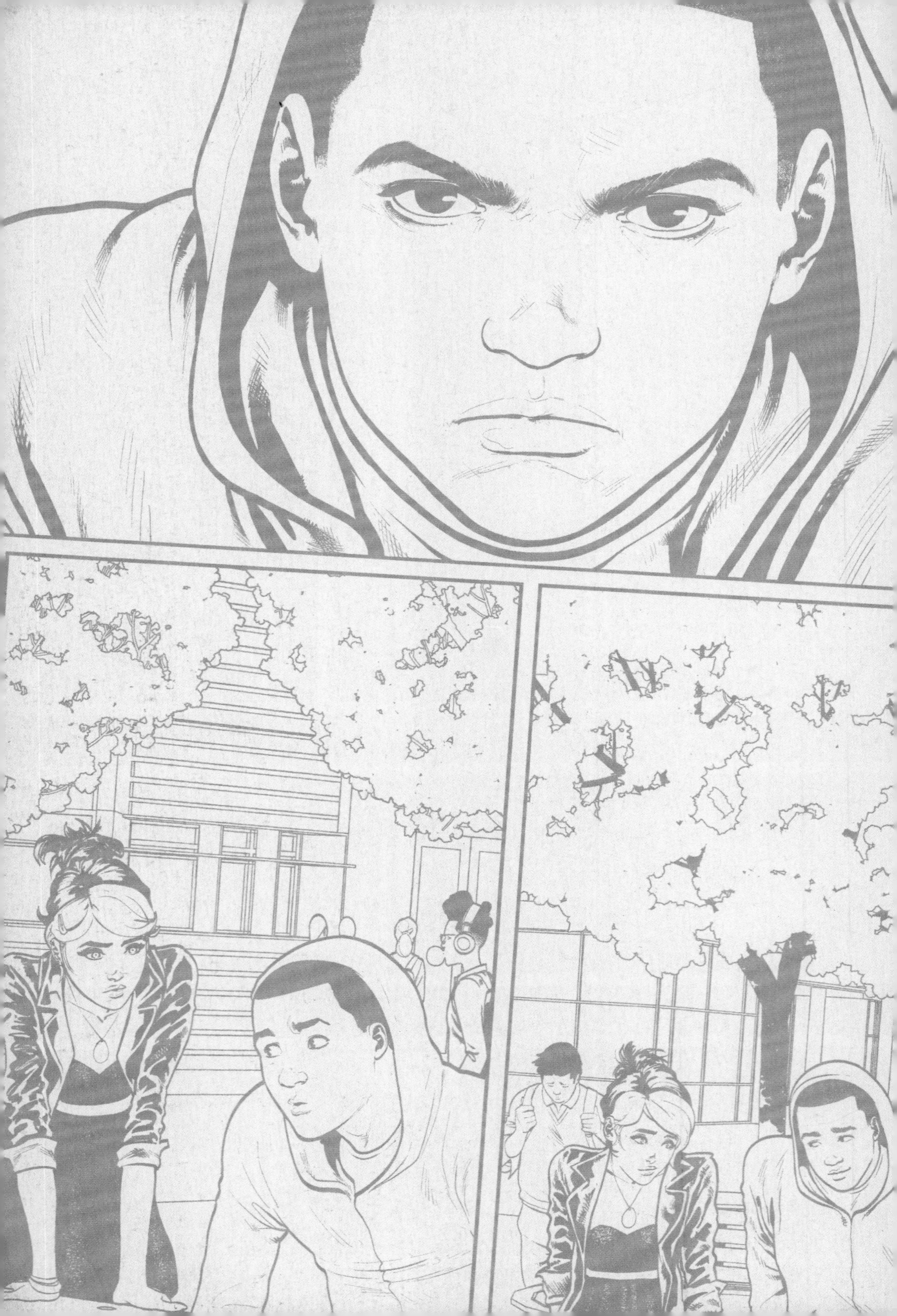

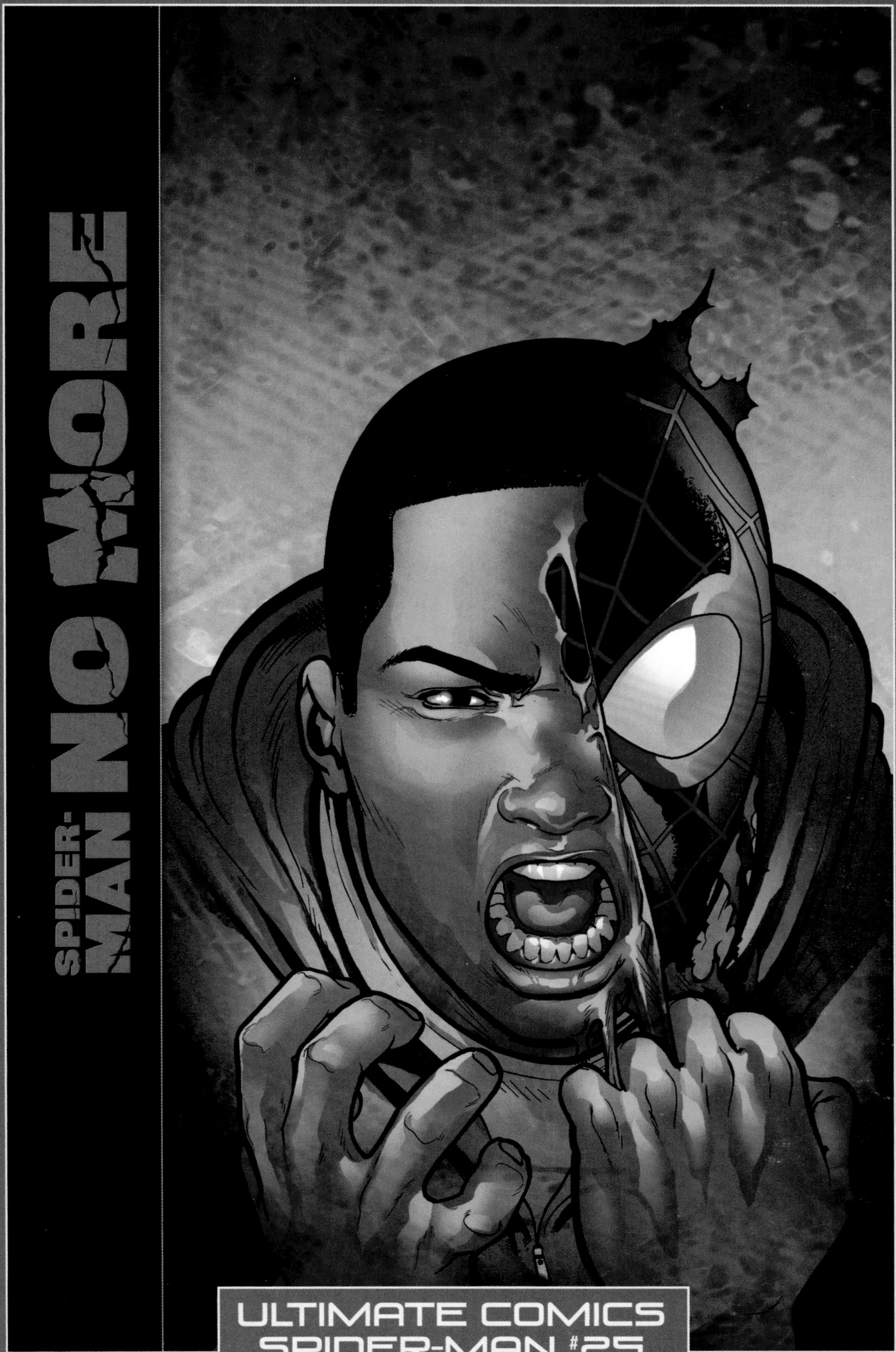
SPIDER-MAN NO MORE
ULTIMATE COMICS
SPIDER-MAN #25

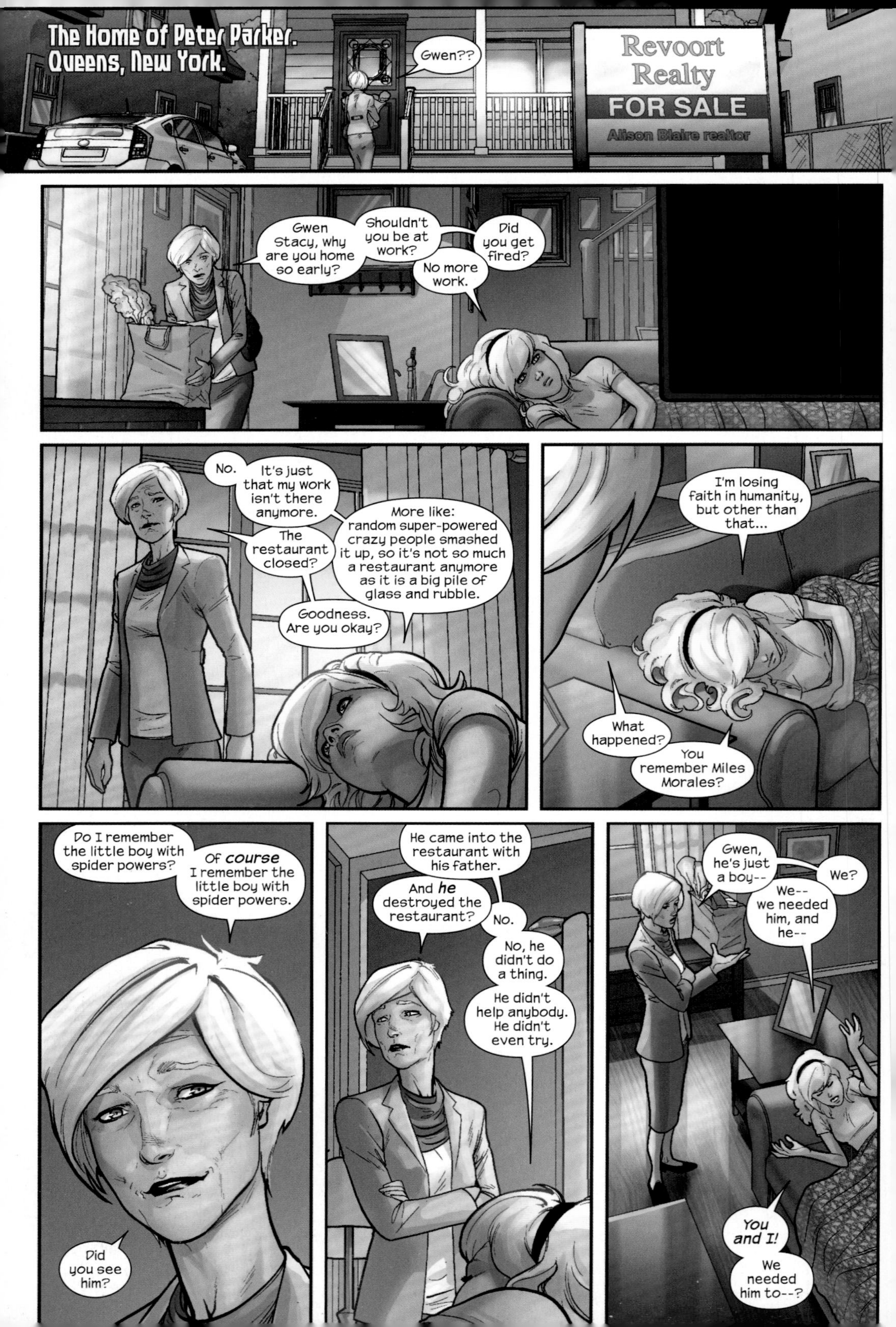

The Home of Peter Parker. Queens, New York.
Gwen??
Revoort Realty
FOR SALE
Alison Blaire realtor
Gwen Stacy, why are you home so early?
Shouldn't you be at work?
Did you get fired?
No more work.
No. It's just that my work isn't there anymore.
The restaurant closed?
More like: random super-powered crazy people smashed it up, so it's not so much a restaurant anymore as it is a big pile of glass and rubble.
Goodness. Are you okay?
I'm losing faith in humanity, but other than that...
What happened?
You remember Miles Morales?
Do I remember the little boy with spider powers?
Of *course* I remember the little boy with spider powers.
Did you see him?
He came into the restaurant with his father.
And *he* destroyed the restaurant?
No.
No, he didn't do a thing.
He didn't help anybody. He didn't even try.
Gwen, he's just a boy--
We?
We-- we needed him, and he--
You and I!
We needed him to--?

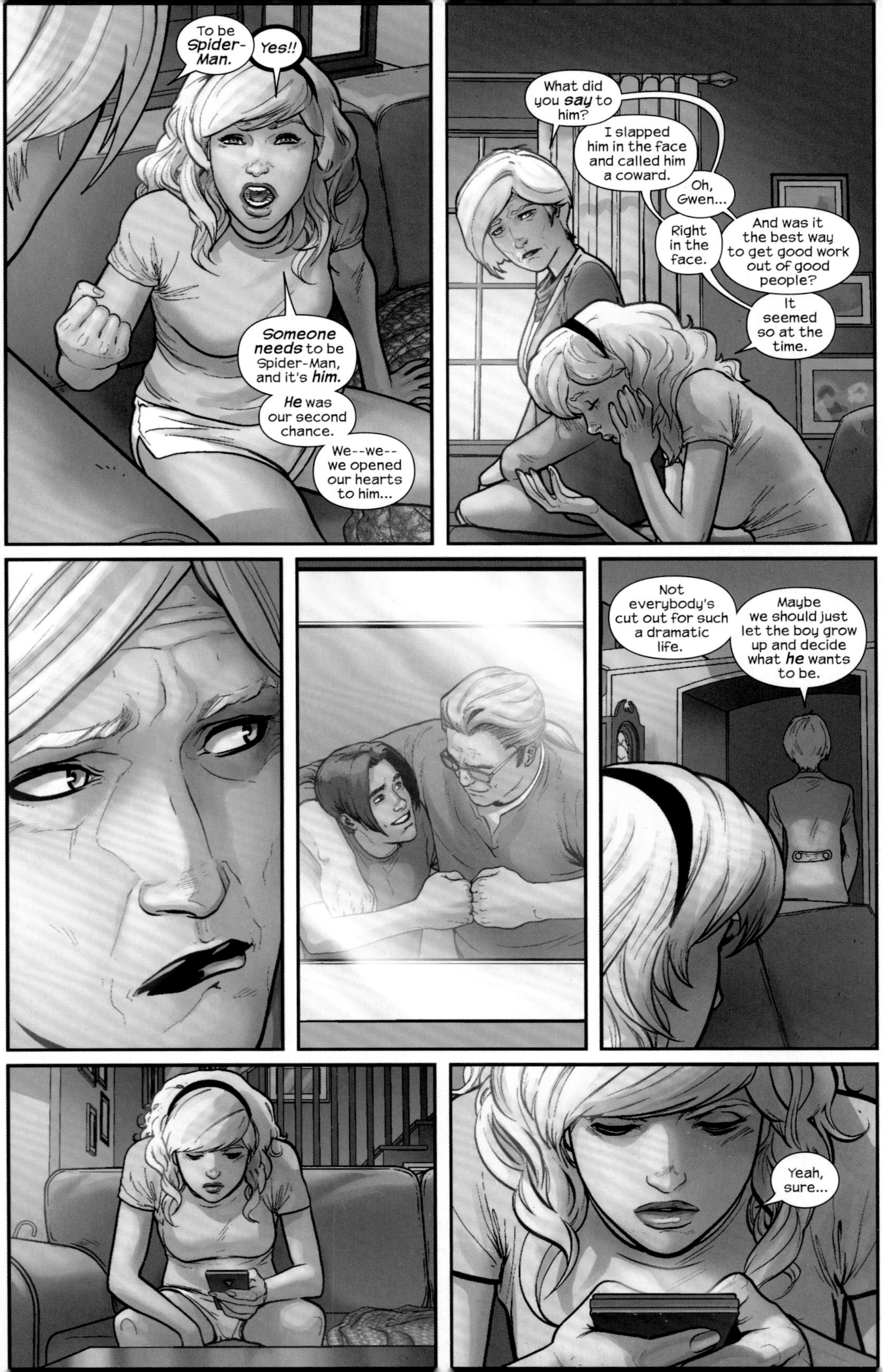
To be Spider-Man.
Yes!!
Someone needs to be Spider-Man, and it's him.
He was our second chance.
We--we--we opened our hearts to him...
What did you say to him?
I slapped him in the face and called him a coward.
Oh, Gwen...
Right in the face.
And was it the best way to get good work out of good people?
It seemed so at the time.
Not everybody's cut out for such a dramatic life.
Maybe we should just let the boy grow up and decide what he wants to be.
Yeah, sure...

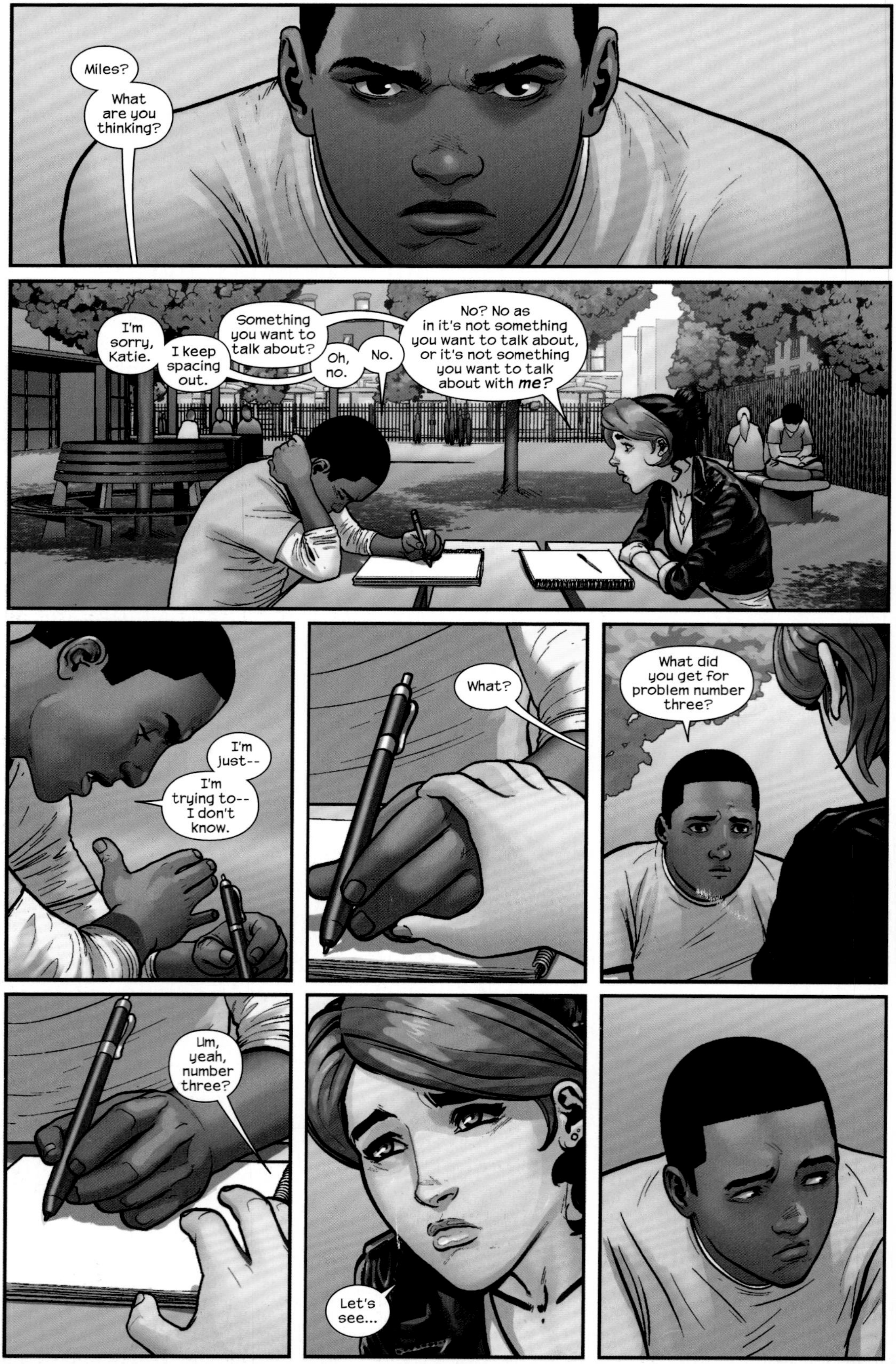
Miles?
What are you thinking?
I'm sorry, Katie.
I keep spacing out.
Something you want to talk about?
Oh, no.
No.
No? No as in it's not something you want to talk about, or it's not something you want to talk about with *me*?
I'm just--
I'm trying to-- I don't know.
What?
What did you get for problem number three?
Um, yeah, number three?
Let's see...

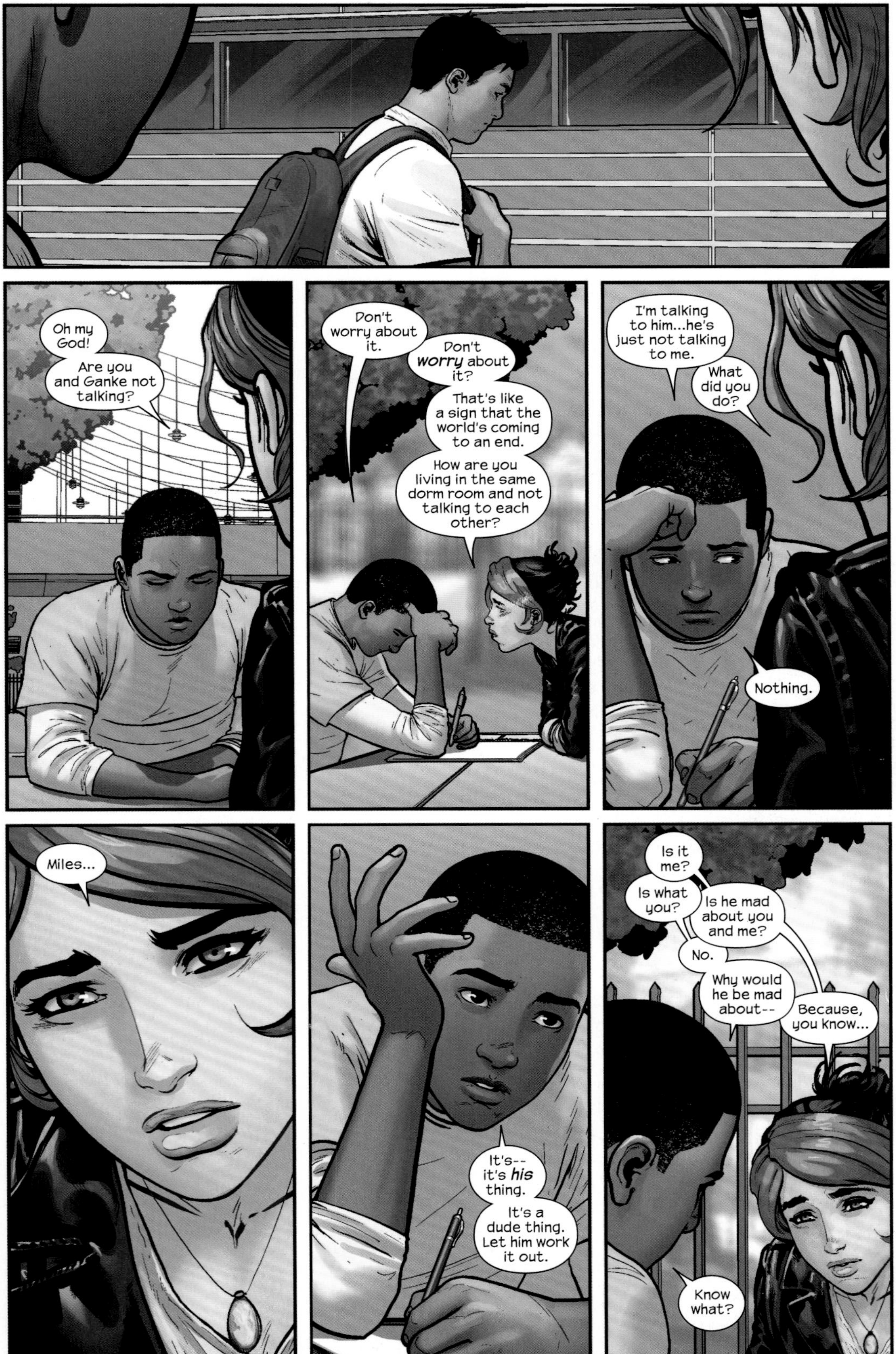

Oh my God!
Are you and Ganke not talking?
Don't worry about it.
Don't *worry* about it?
That's like a sign that the world's coming to an end.
How are you living in the same dorm room and not talking to each other?
I'm talking to him...he's just not talking to me.
What did you do?
Nothing.
Miles...
It's-- it's *his* thing.
It's a dude thing. Let him work it out.
Is it me?
Is what you?
Is he mad about you and me?
No.
Why would he be mad about--
Because, you know...
Know what?

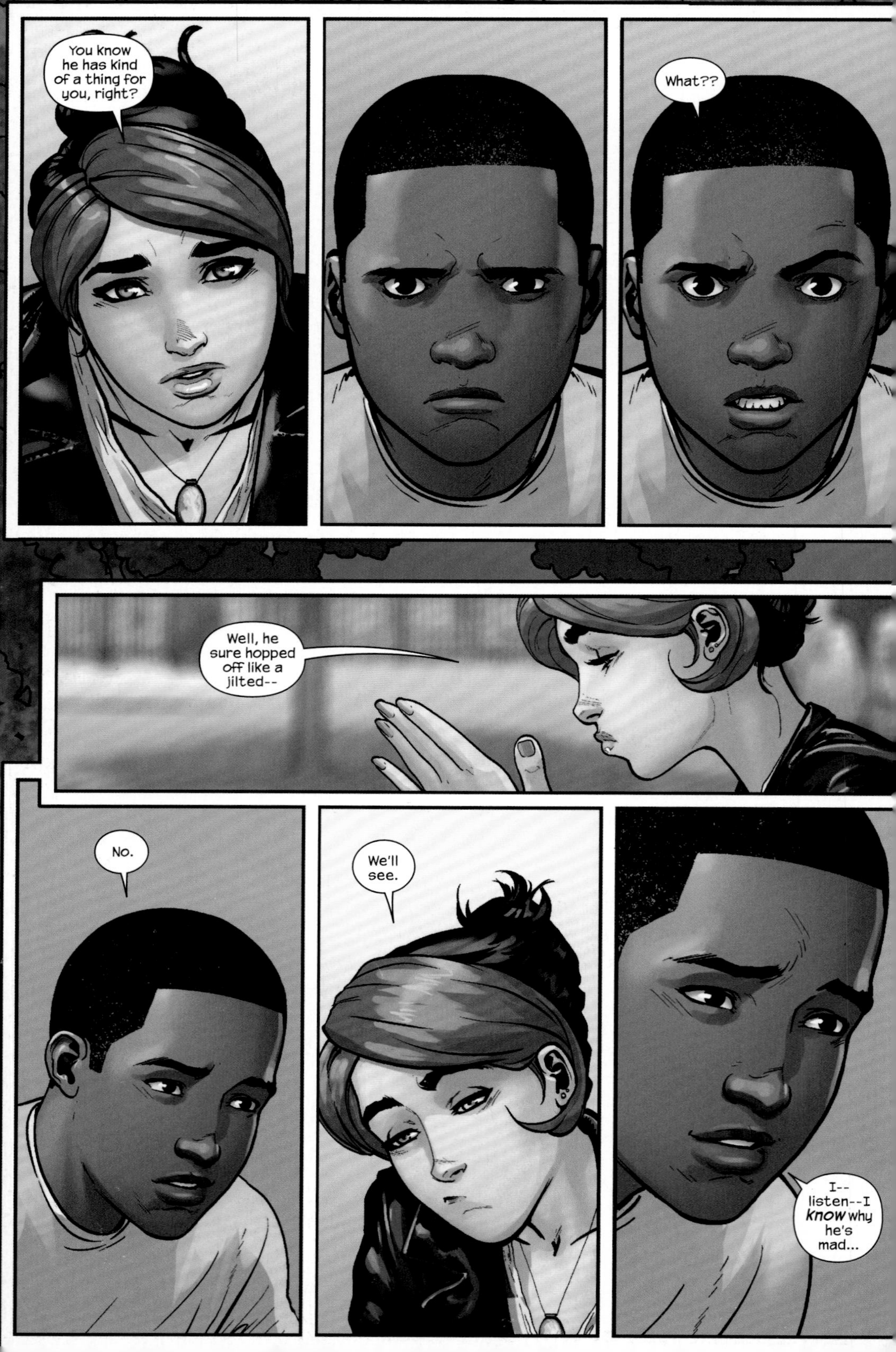
You know he has kind of a thing for you, right?
What??
Well, he sure hopped off like a jilted--
No.
We'll see.
I-- listen--I *KNOW* why he's mad...

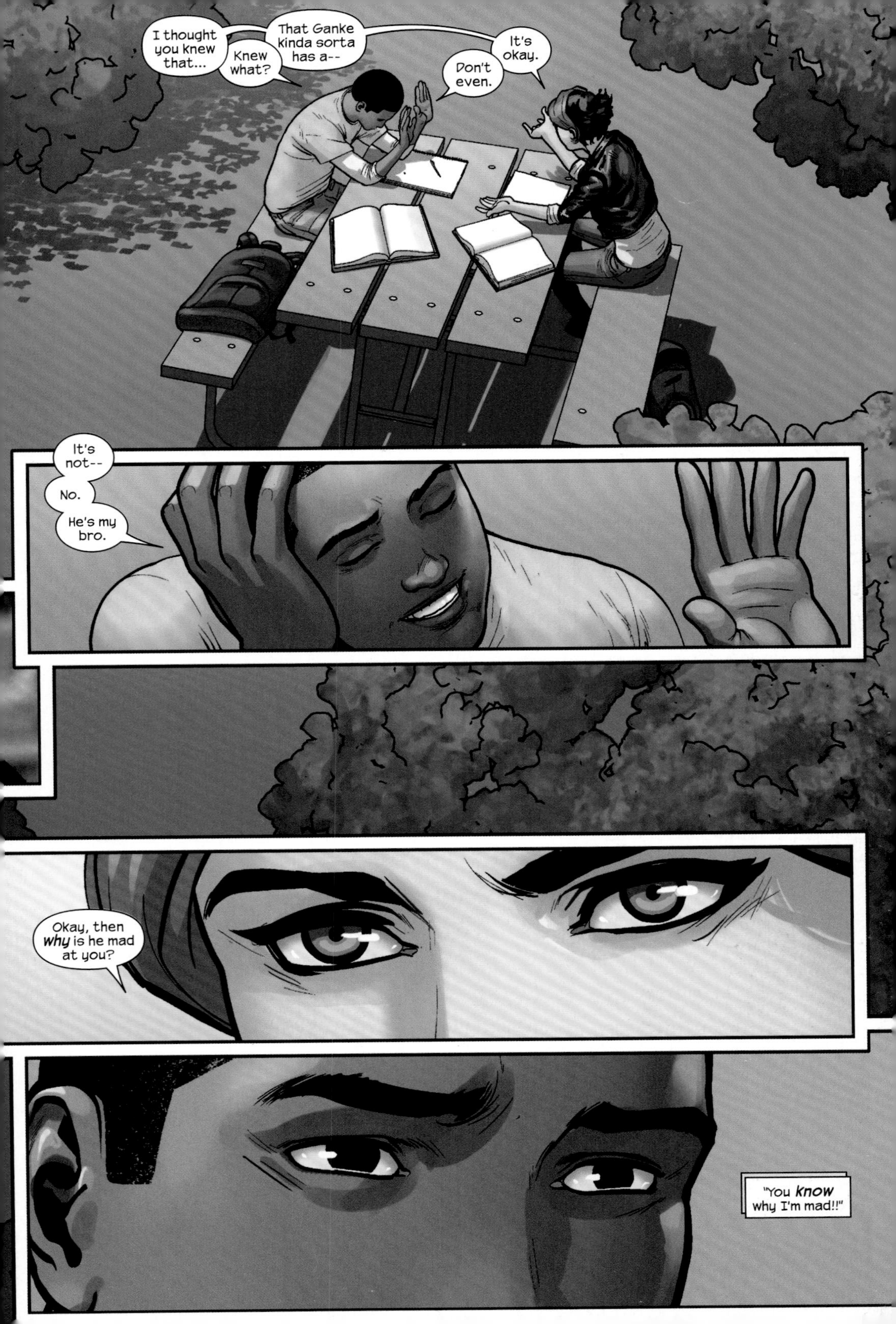

I thought you knew that...
Knew what?
That Ganke kinda sorta has a--
Don't even.
It's okay.
It's not--
No.
He's my bro.
Okay, then *why* is he mad at you?
"You *know* why I'm mad!!"

Because you're being selfish and--and a coward, and I've *had it!!*

Hey!

Miles, I mean it!

What?

I found out what happened at the Chinese restaurant.

You had a perfect opportunity to get in there and *do the right thing...*and you *ran away??*

Who told you that??

Gwen Stacy *texted* me.

Yeah...

You ran away.

To *help* my *father!*

The way she tells it, your father was already safe.

You *really* don't understand what's going *on* here?

You really don't get that I *lost my mother!!*

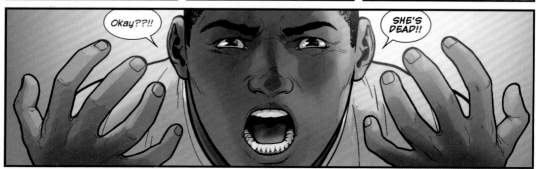

Okay??!!

SHE'S DEAD!!

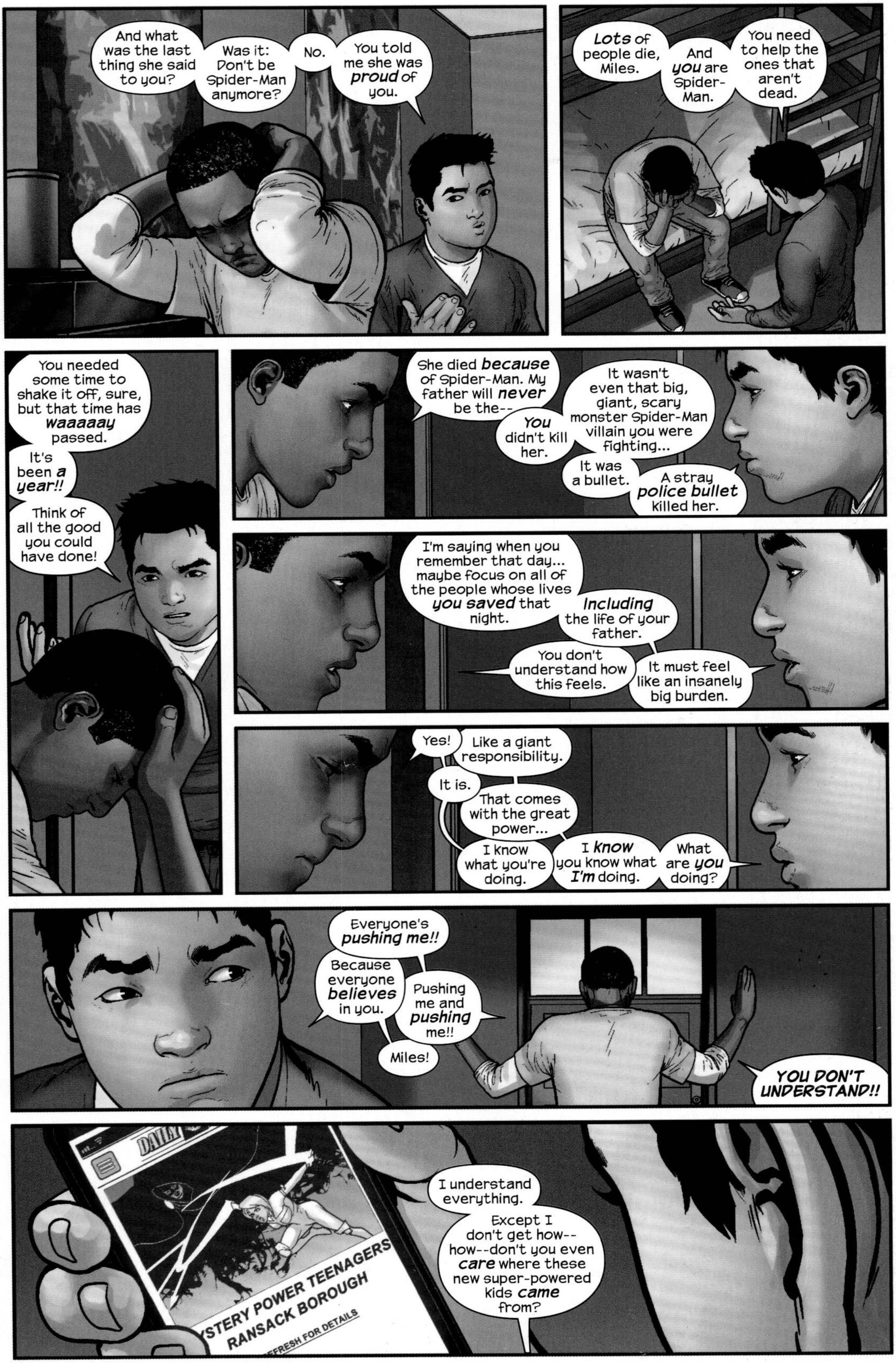

And what was the last thing she said to you?
Was it: Don't be Spider-Man anymore?
No.
You told me she was *proud* of you.
Lots of people die, Miles.
And *you* are Spider-Man.
You need to help the ones that aren't dead.
You needed some time to shake it off, sure, but that time has *waaaaay* passed.
It's been *a year!!*
Think of all the good you could have done!
She died *because* of Spider-Man. My father will *never* be the--
You didn't kill her.
It wasn't even that big, giant, scary monster Spider-Man villain you were fighting...
It was a bullet.
A stray *police bullet* killed her.
I'm saying when you remember that day... maybe focus on all of the people whose lives *you saved* that night.
Including the life of your father.
You don't understand how this feels.
It must feel like an insanely big burden.
Yes!
Like a giant responsibility.
It is.
That comes with the great power...
I know what you're doing.
I *know* you know what *I'm* doing.
What are *you* doing?
Everyone's *pushing me!!*
Because everyone *believes* in you.
Pushing me and *pushing* me!!
Miles!
YOU DON'T UNDERSTAND!!
DAILY
YSTERY POWER TEENAGERS
RANSACK BOROUGH
REFRESH FOR DETAILS
I understand everything.
Except I don't get how--how--don't you even *care* where these new super-powered kids *came* from?

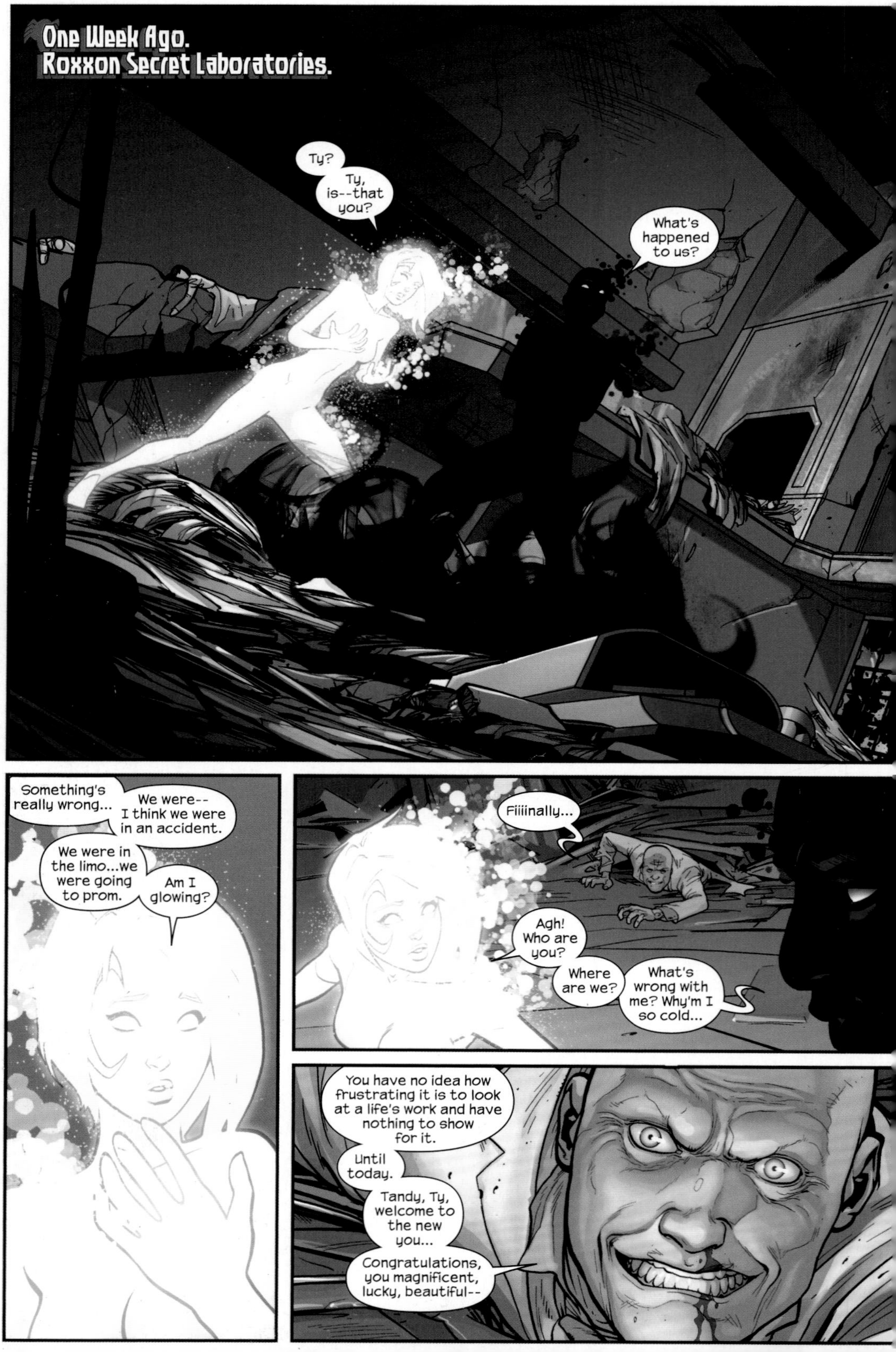
One Week Ago.
Roxxon Secret Laboratories.
Ty?
Ty, is--that you?
What's happened to us?
Something's really wrong...
We were-- I think we were in an accident.
We were in the limo...we were going to prom.
Am I glowing?
Fiiiinally...
Agh! Who are you?
Where are we?
What's wrong with me? Why'm I so cold...
You have no idea how frustrating it is to look at a life's work and have nothing to show for it.
Until today.
Tandy, Ty, welcome to the new you...
Congratulations, you magnificent, lucky, beautiful--

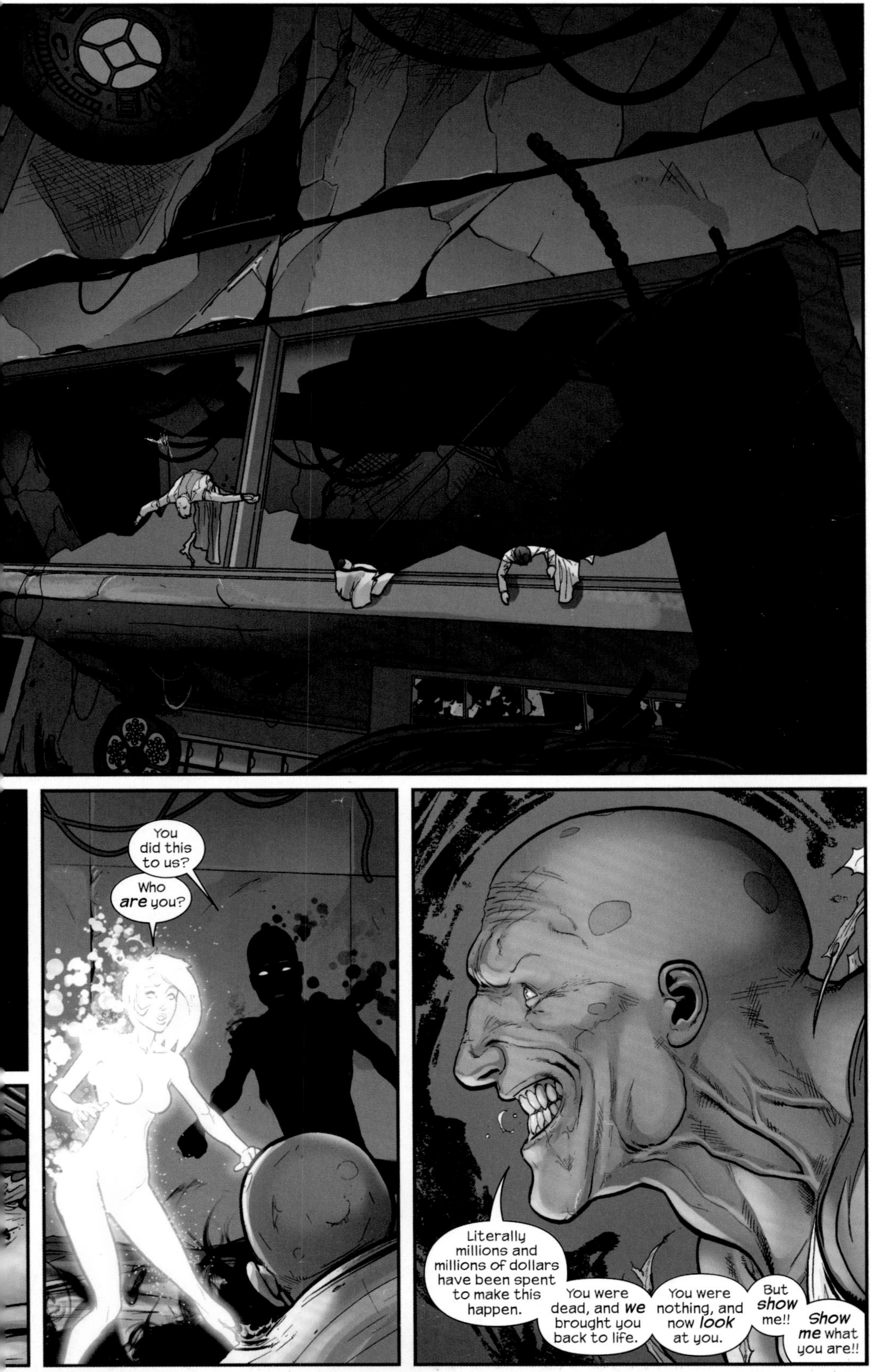

You did this to us?
Who *are* you?
Literally millions and millions of dollars have been spent to make this happen.
You were dead, and *we* brought you back to life.
You were nothing, and now *look* at you.
But *show* me!!
Show me what you are!!

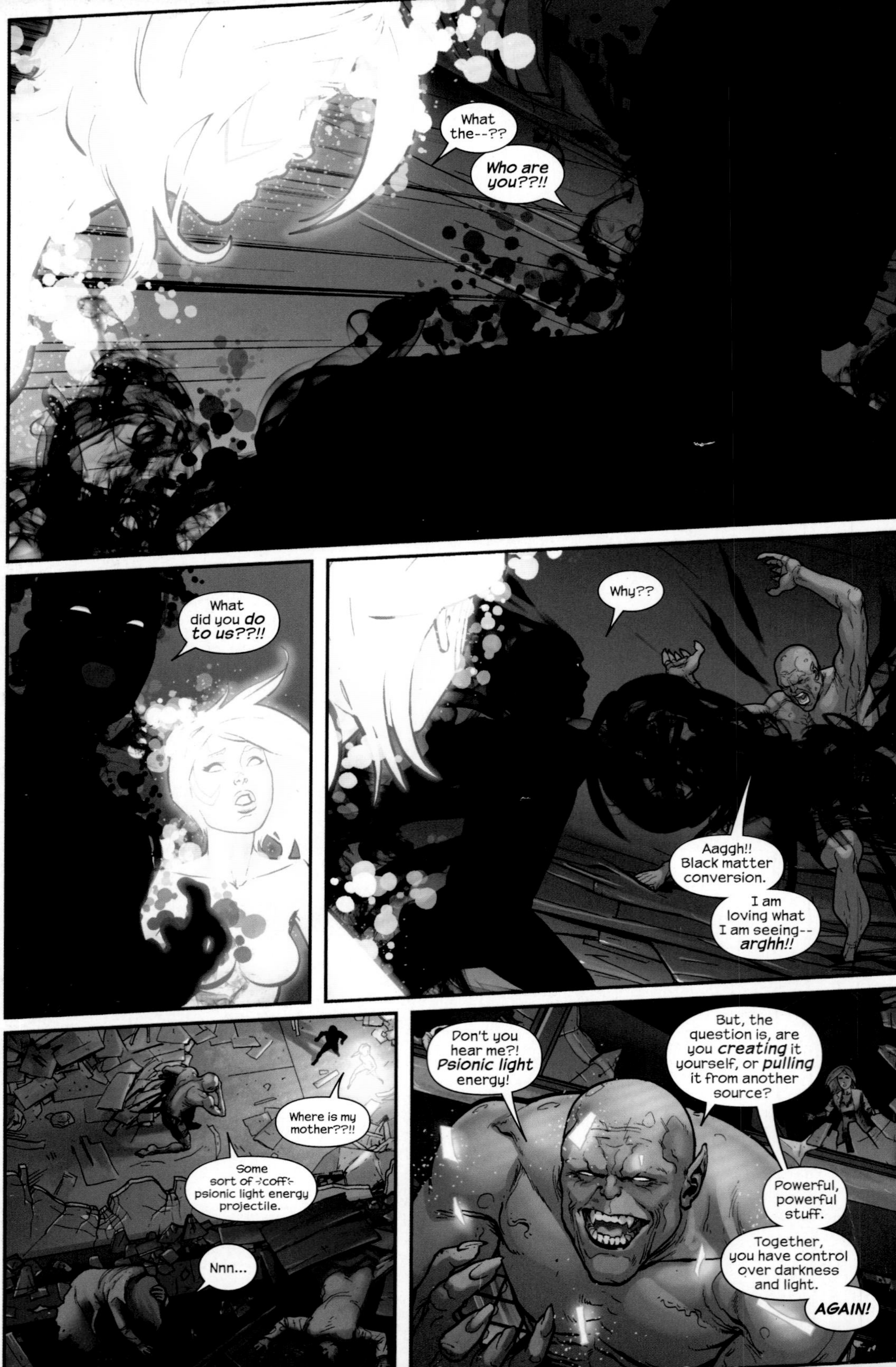

What the--??
Who are you??!!
What did you do to us??!!
Why??
Aaggh!! Black matter conversion.
I am loving what I am seeing-- arghh!!
Where is my mother??!!
Some sort of -coff- psionic light energy projectile.
Nnn...
Don't you hear me?! Psionic light energy!
But, the question is, are you creating it yourself, or pulling it from another source?
Powerful, powerful stuff.
Together, you have control over darkness and light.
AGAIN!

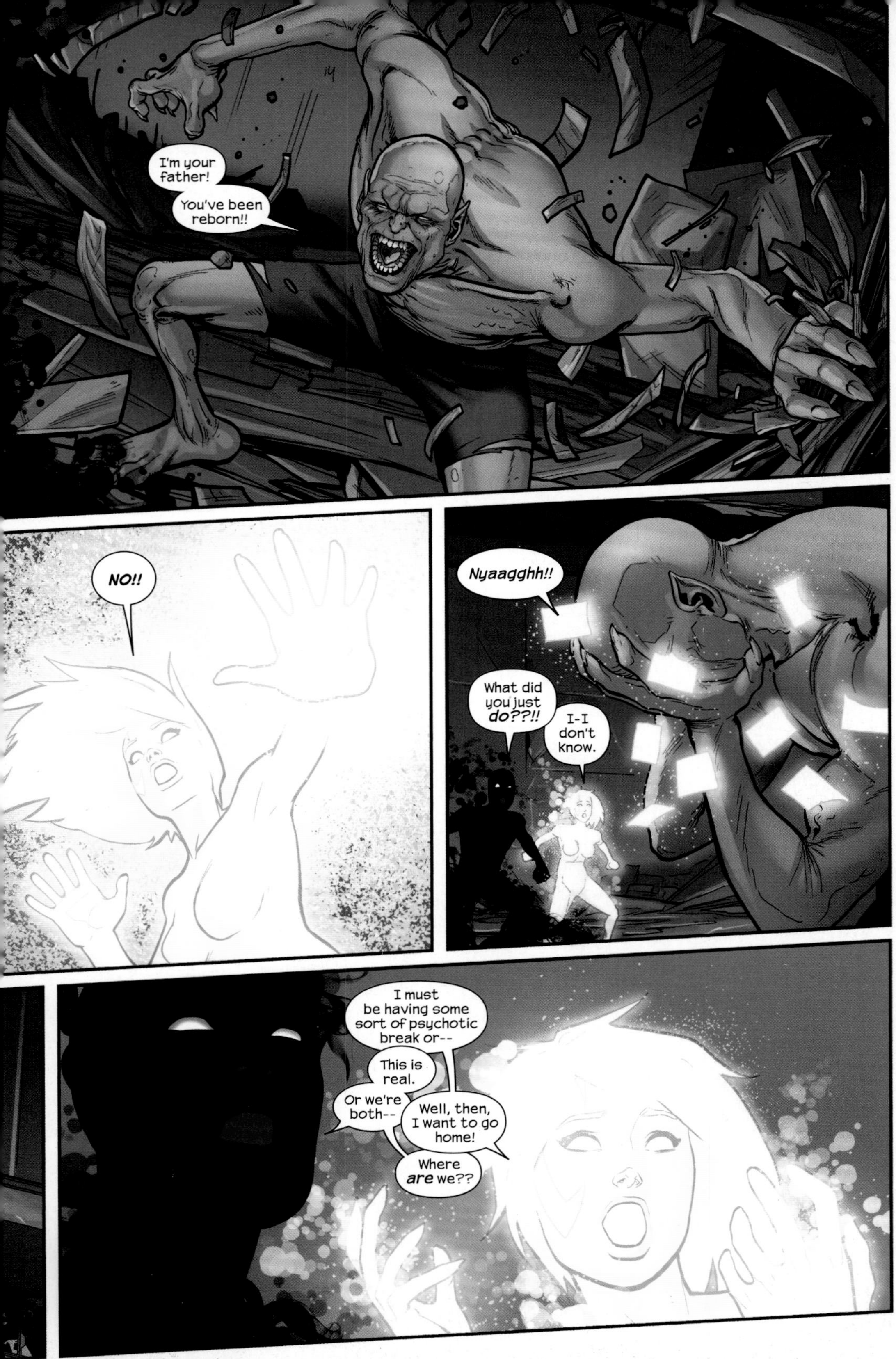
I'm your father!
You've been reborn!!
NO!!
Nyaagghh!!
What did you just do??!!
I-I don't know.
I must be having some sort of psychotic break or--
This is real.
Or we're both--
Well, then, I want to go home!
Where are we??

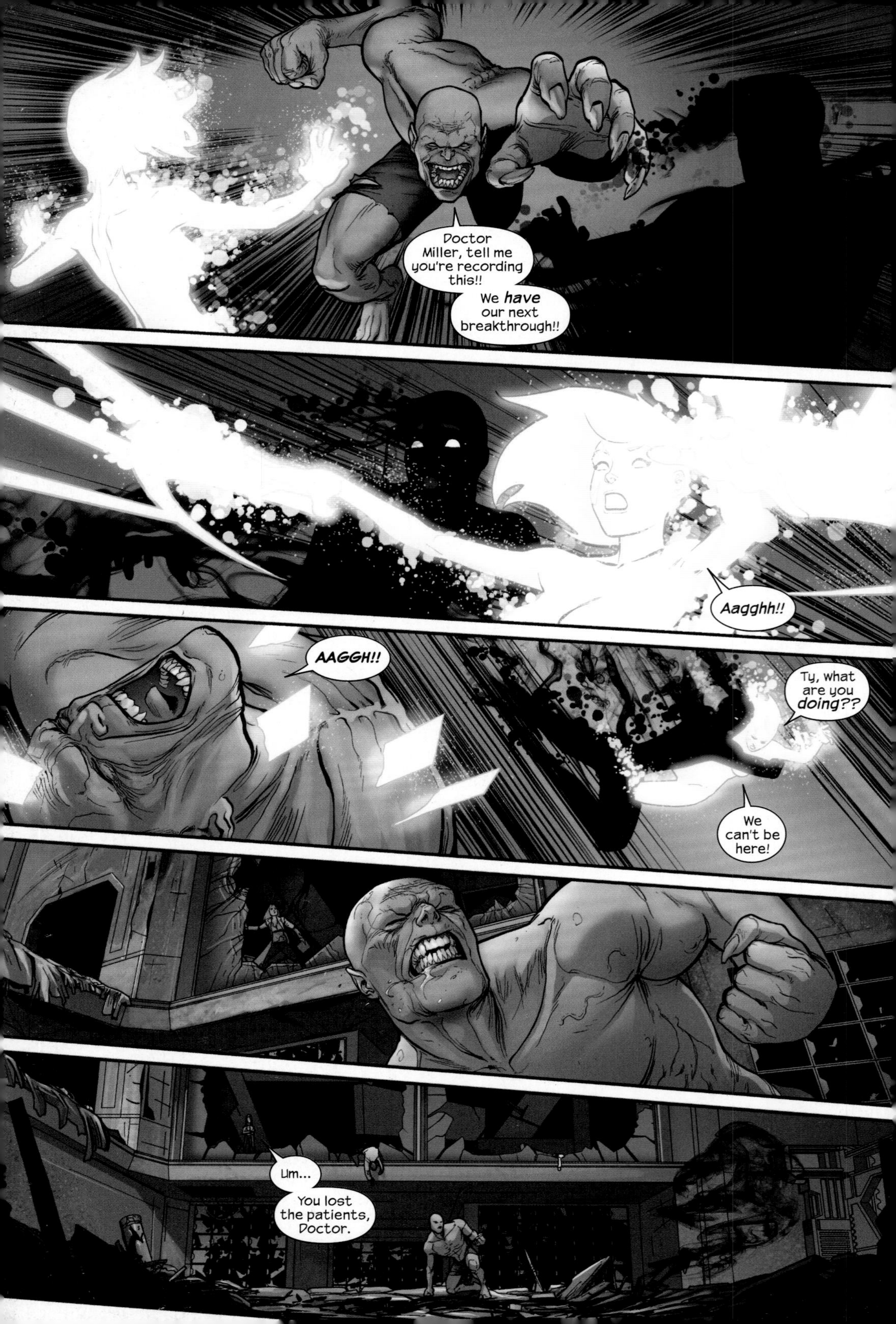
Doctor Miller, tell me you're recording this!!
We *have* our next breakthrough!!
Aagghh!!
AAGGH!!
Ty, what are you *doing*??
We can't be here!
Um...
You lost the patients, Doctor.

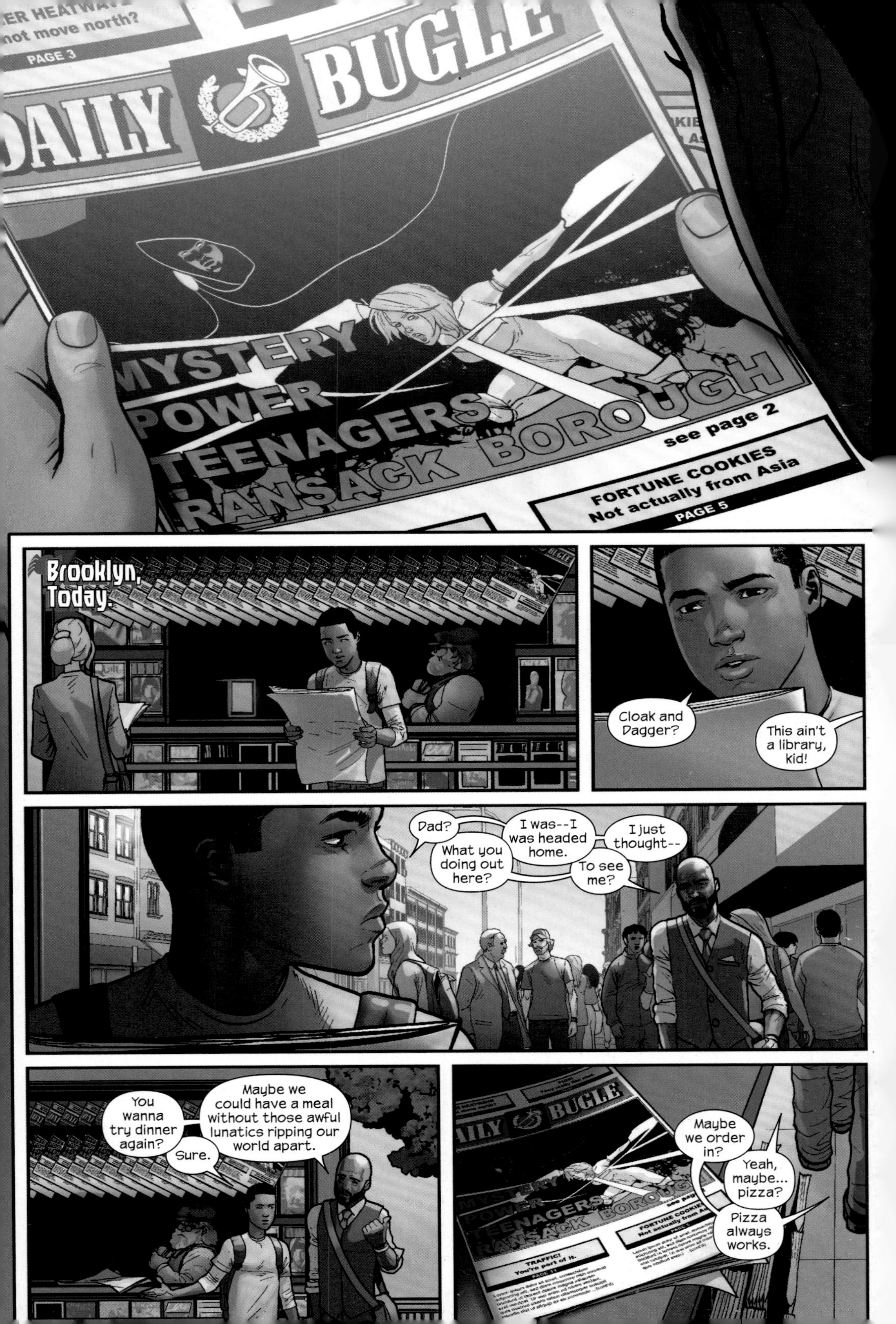

ER HEATWA
not move north?
PAGE 3
DAILY BUGLE
MYSTERY POWER TEENAGERS RANSACK BOROUGH
see page 2
FORTUNE COOKIES
Not actually from Asia
PAGE 5
Brooklyn, Today.
Cloak and Dagger?
This ain't a library, kid!
Dad?
What you doing out here?
I was--I was headed home.
I just thought--
To see me?
You wanna try dinner again?
Sure.
Maybe we could have a meal without those awful lunatics ripping our world apart.
Maybe we order in?
Yeah, maybe... pizza?
Pizza always works.
TRAFFIC!
You're part of it.

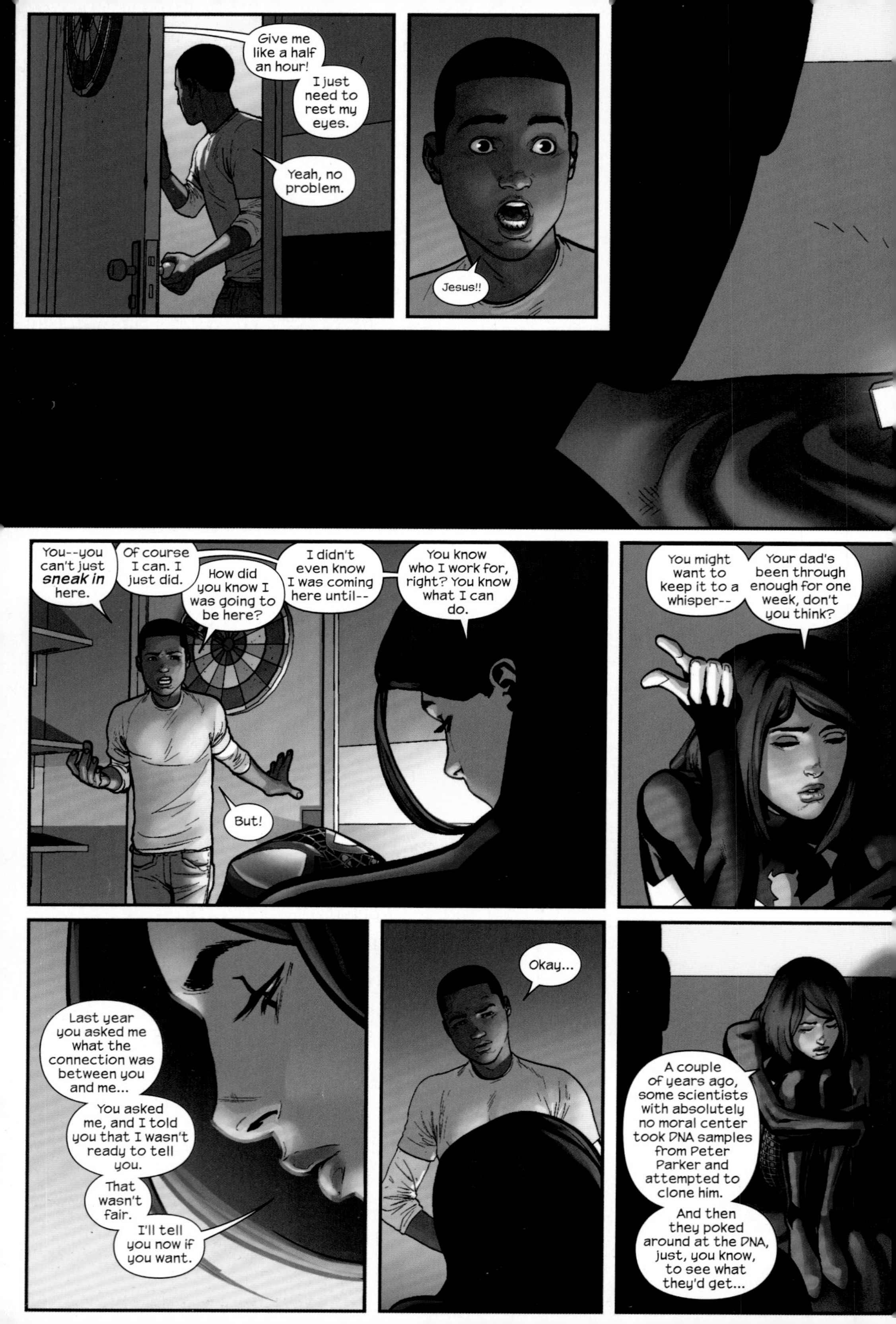
Give me like a half an hour!
I just need to rest my eyes.
Yeah, no problem.
Jesus!!
You--you can't just **sneak in** here.
Of course I can. I just did.
How did you know I was going to be here?
I didn't even know I was coming here until--
You know who I work for, right? You know what I can do.
But!
You might want to keep it to a whisper--
Your dad's been through enough for one week, don't you think?
Last year you asked me what the connection was between you and me...
You asked me, and I told you that I wasn't ready to tell you.
That wasn't fair.
I'll tell you now if you want.
Okay...
A couple of years ago, some scientists with absolutely no moral center took DNA samples from Peter Parker and attempted to clone him.
And then they poked around at the DNA, just, you know, to see what they'd get...

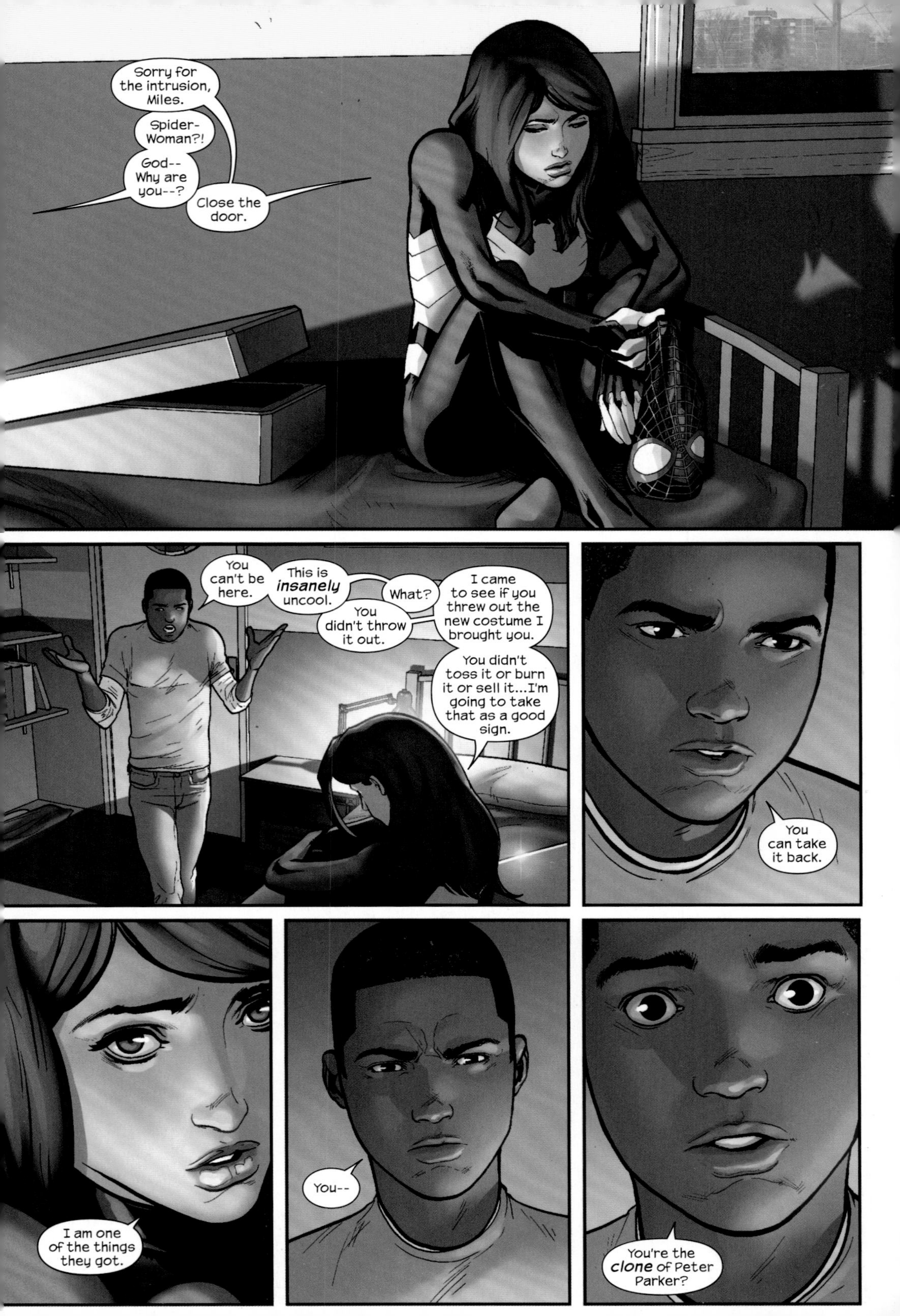
Sorry for the intrusion, Miles.
Spider-Woman?!
God-- Why are you--?
Close the door.
You can't be here.
This is *insanely* uncool.
What?
You didn't throw it out.
I came to see if you threw out the new costume I brought you.
You didn't toss it or burn it or sell it...I'm going to take that as a good sign.
You can take it back.
I am one of the things they got.
You--
You're the *clone* of Peter Parker?

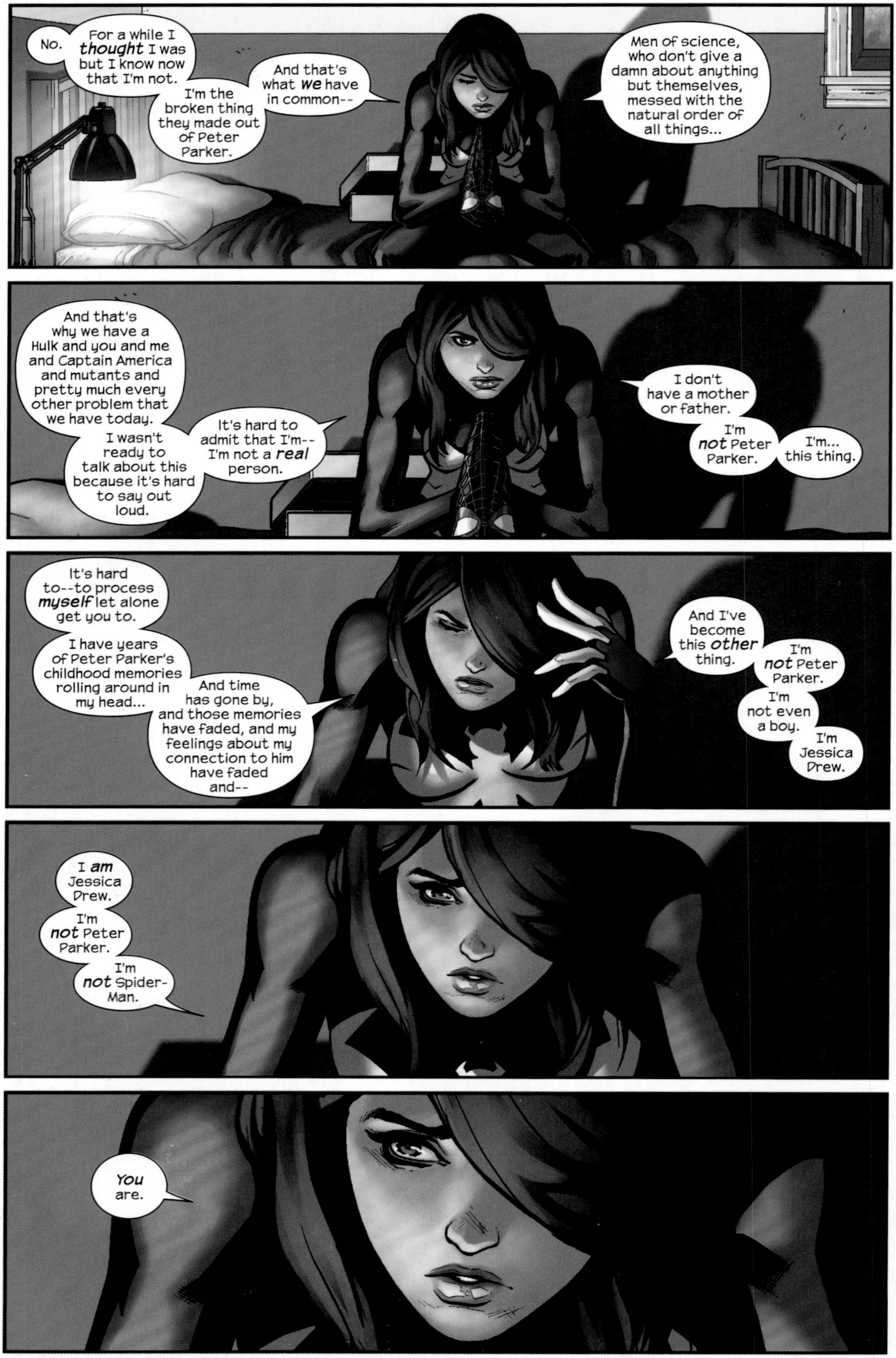
No.
For a while I *thought* I was but I know now that I'm not.
I'm the broken thing they made out of Peter Parker.
And that's what *we* have in common--
Men of science, who don't give a damn about anything but themselves, messed with the natural order of all things...
And that's why we have a Hulk and you and me and Captain America and mutants and pretty much every other problem that we have today.
I wasn't ready to talk about this because it's hard to say out loud.
It's hard to admit that I'm-- I'm not a *real* person.
I don't have a mother or father.
I'm *not* Peter Parker.
I'm... this thing.
It's hard to--to process *myself* let alone get you to.
I have years of Peter Parker's childhood memories rolling around in my head...
And time has gone by, and those memories have faded, and my feelings about my connection to him have faded and--
And I've become this *other* thing.
I'm *not* Peter Parker.
I'm not even a boy.
I'm Jessica Drew.
I *am* Jessica Drew.
I'm *not* Peter Parker.
I'm *not* Spider-Man.
You are.

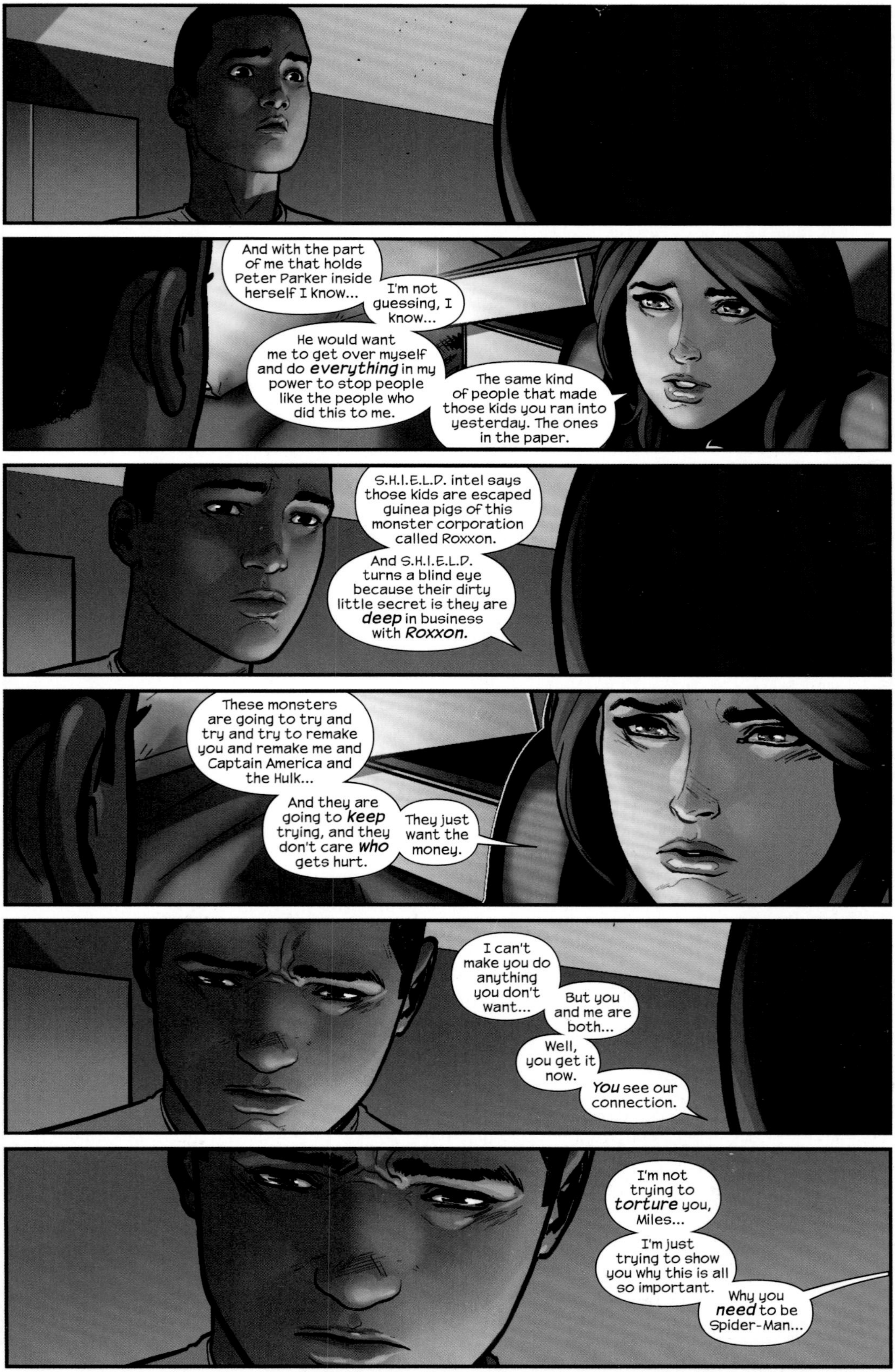

And with the part of me that holds Peter Parker inside herself I know...
I'm not guessing, I know...
He would want me to get over myself and do *everything* in my power to stop people like the people who did this to me.
The same kind of people that made those kids you ran into yesterday. The ones in the paper.
S.H.I.E.L.D. intel says those kids are escaped guinea pigs of this monster corporation called Roxxon.
And S.H.I.E.L.D. turns a blind eye because their dirty little secret is they are *deep* in business with *Roxxon.*
These monsters are going to try and try and try to remake you and remake me and Captain America and the Hulk...
And they are going to *keep* trying, and they don't care *who* gets hurt.
They just want the money.
I can't make you do anything you don't want...
But you and me are both...
Well, you get it now.
You see our connection.
I'm not trying to *torture* you, Miles...
I'm just trying to show you why this is all so important.
Why you *need* to be Spider-Man...

A doctor!! *I need a doctor!!*
Look at you.
Look what you can do.
Why there needs to be a Spider-Man.
had to go back to school. Forgot about a test. Call you tomorrow.

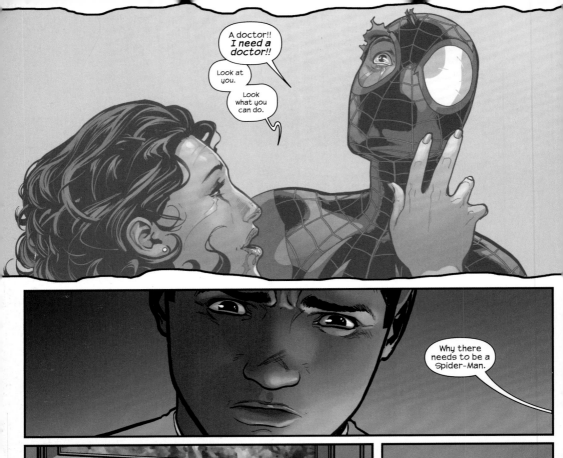

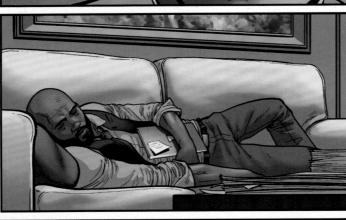

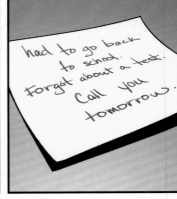

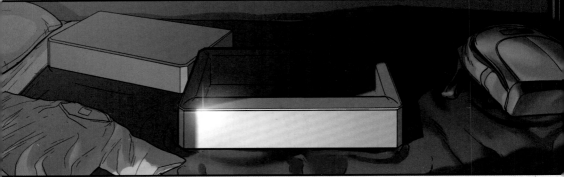

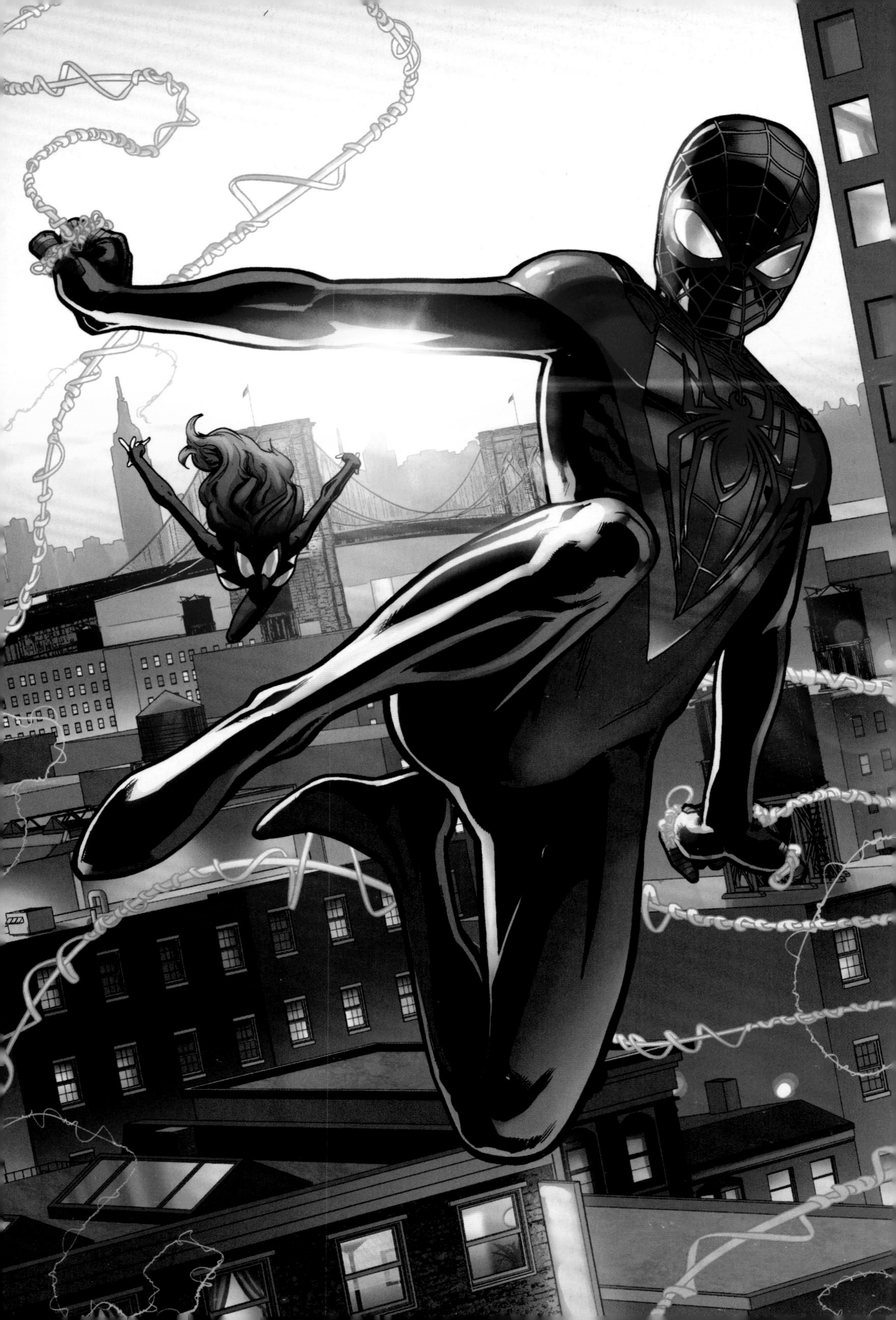

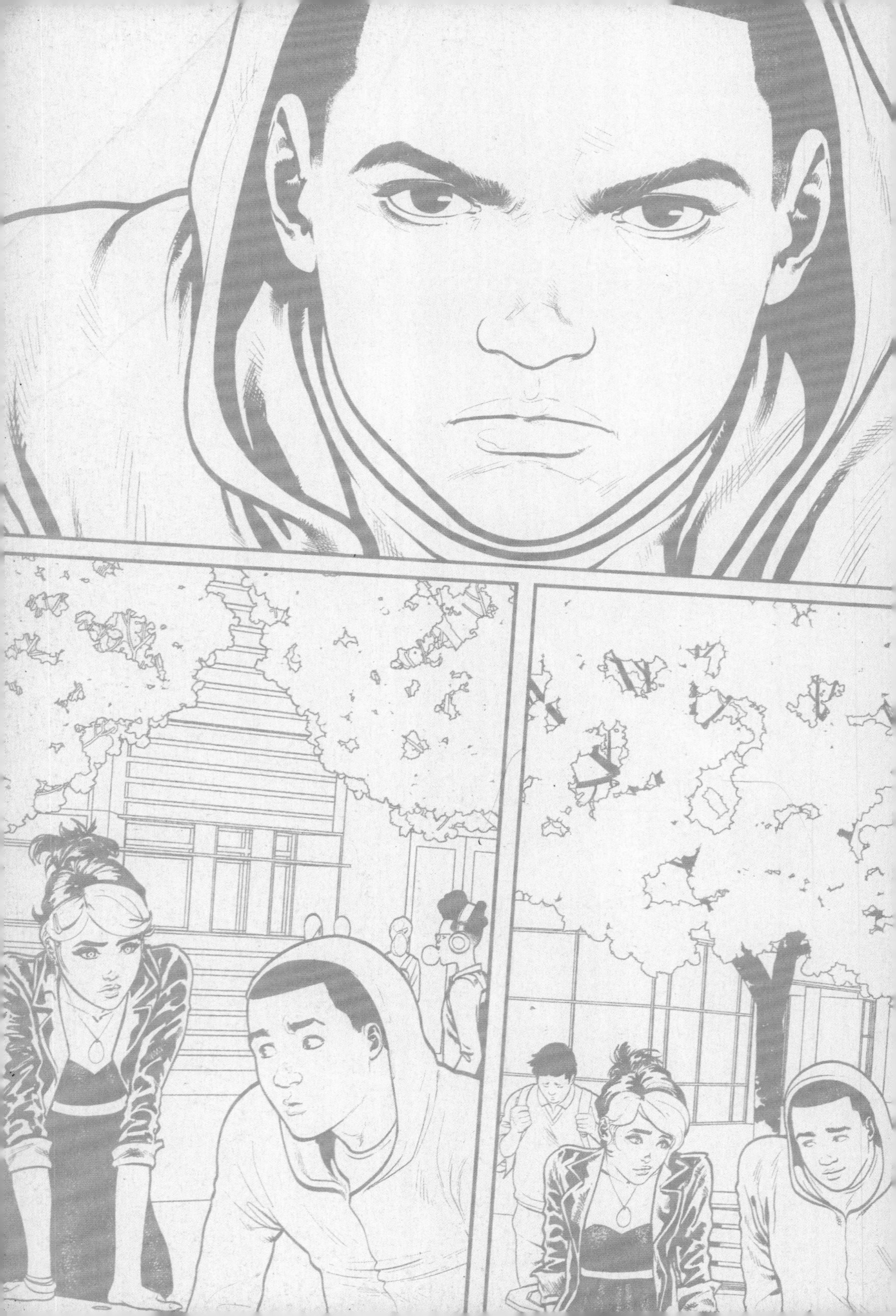

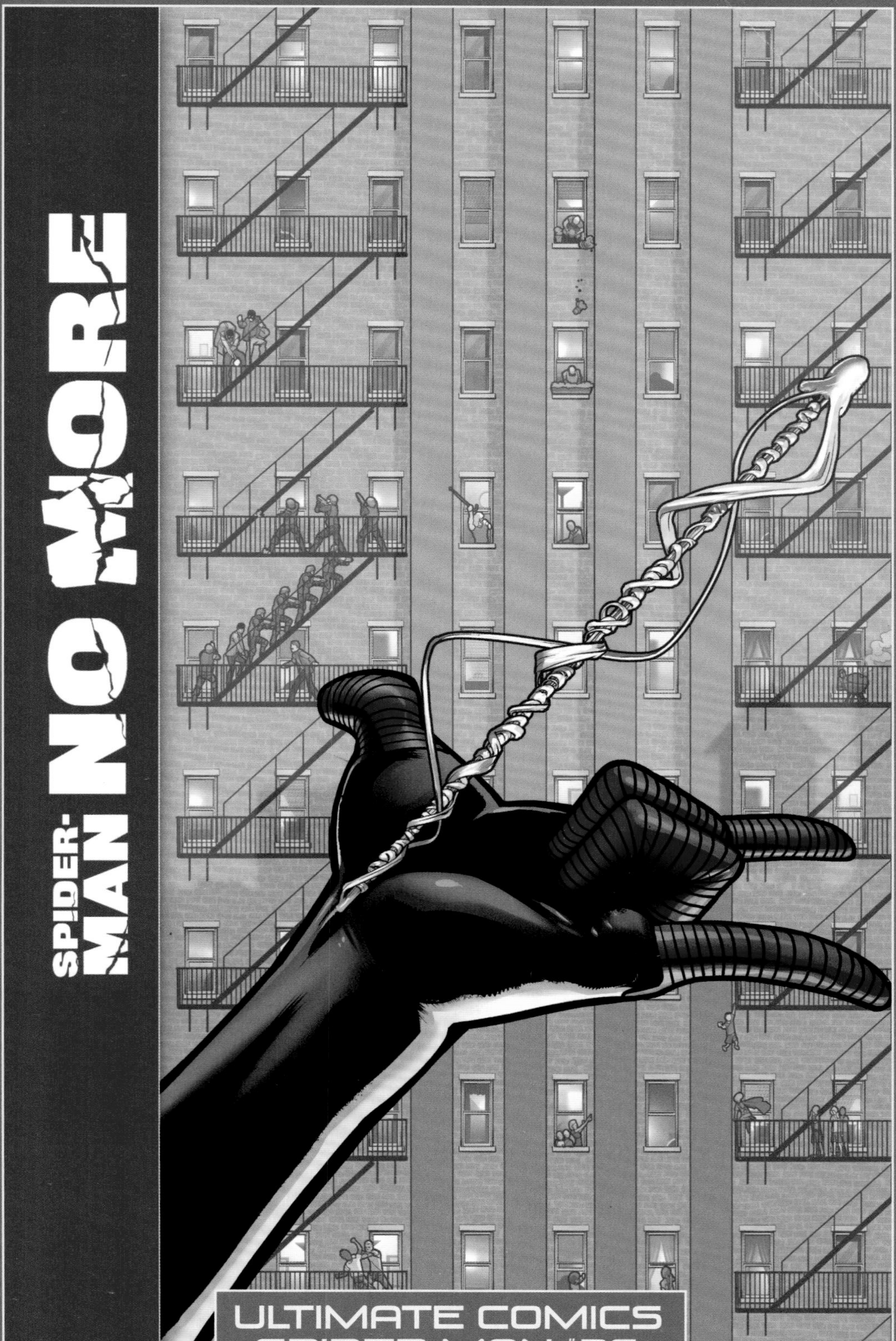
SPIDER-MAN NO MORE
ULTIMATE COMICS SPIDER-MAN #26

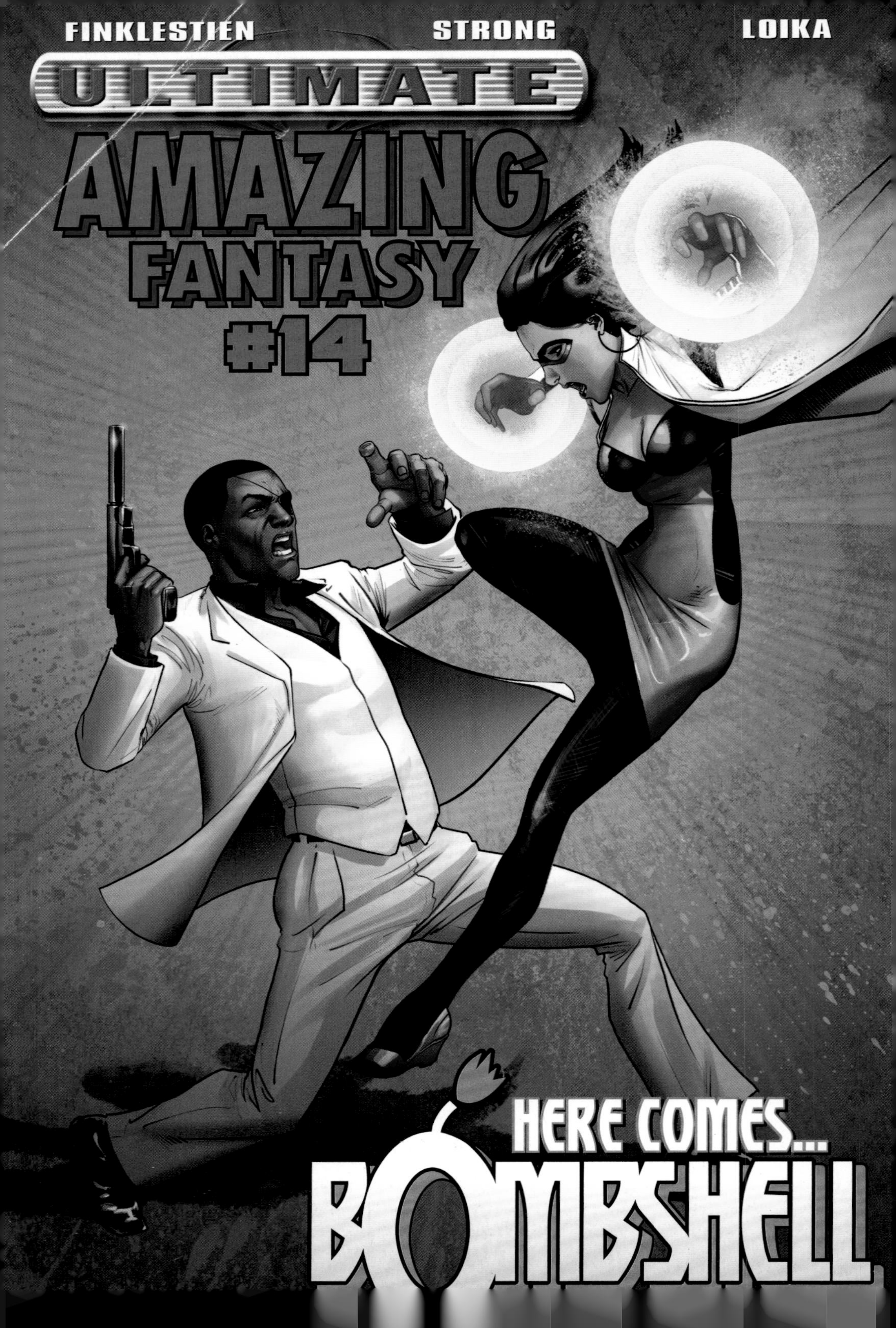
FINKLESTIEN
STRONG
LOIKA
ULTIMATE
AMAZING
FANTASY
#14
HERE COMES...
BOMBSHELL

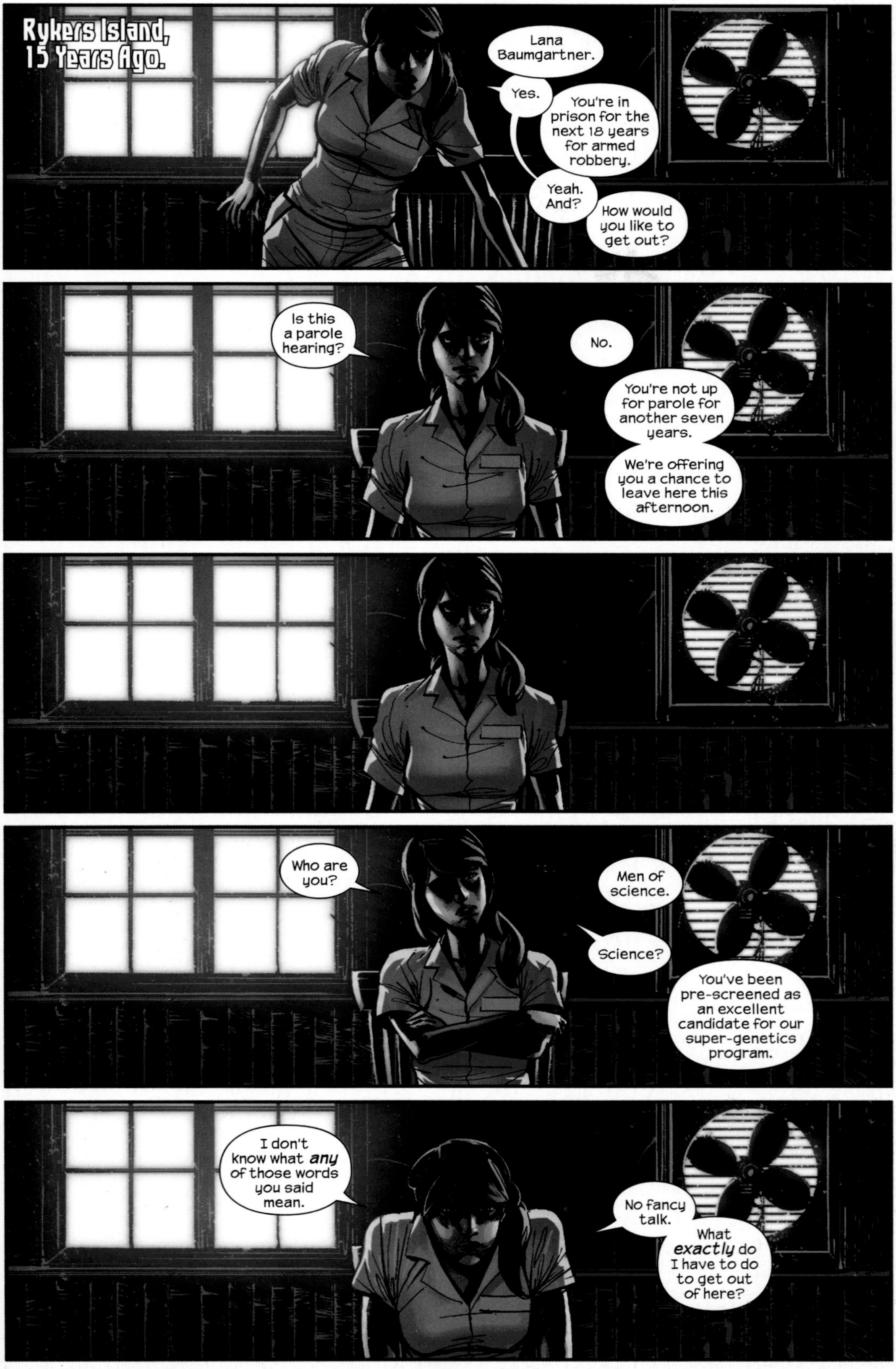
Rykers Island, 15 Years Ago.
Lana Baumgartner.
Yes.
You're in prison for the next 18 years for armed robbery.
Yeah. And?
How would you like to get out?
Is this a parole hearing?
No.
You're not up for parole for another seven years.
We're offering you a chance to leave here this afternoon.
Who are you?
Men of science.
Science?
You've been pre-screened as an excellent candidate for our super-genetics program.
I don't know what *any* of those words you said mean.
No fancy talk.
What *exactly* do I have to do to get out of here?

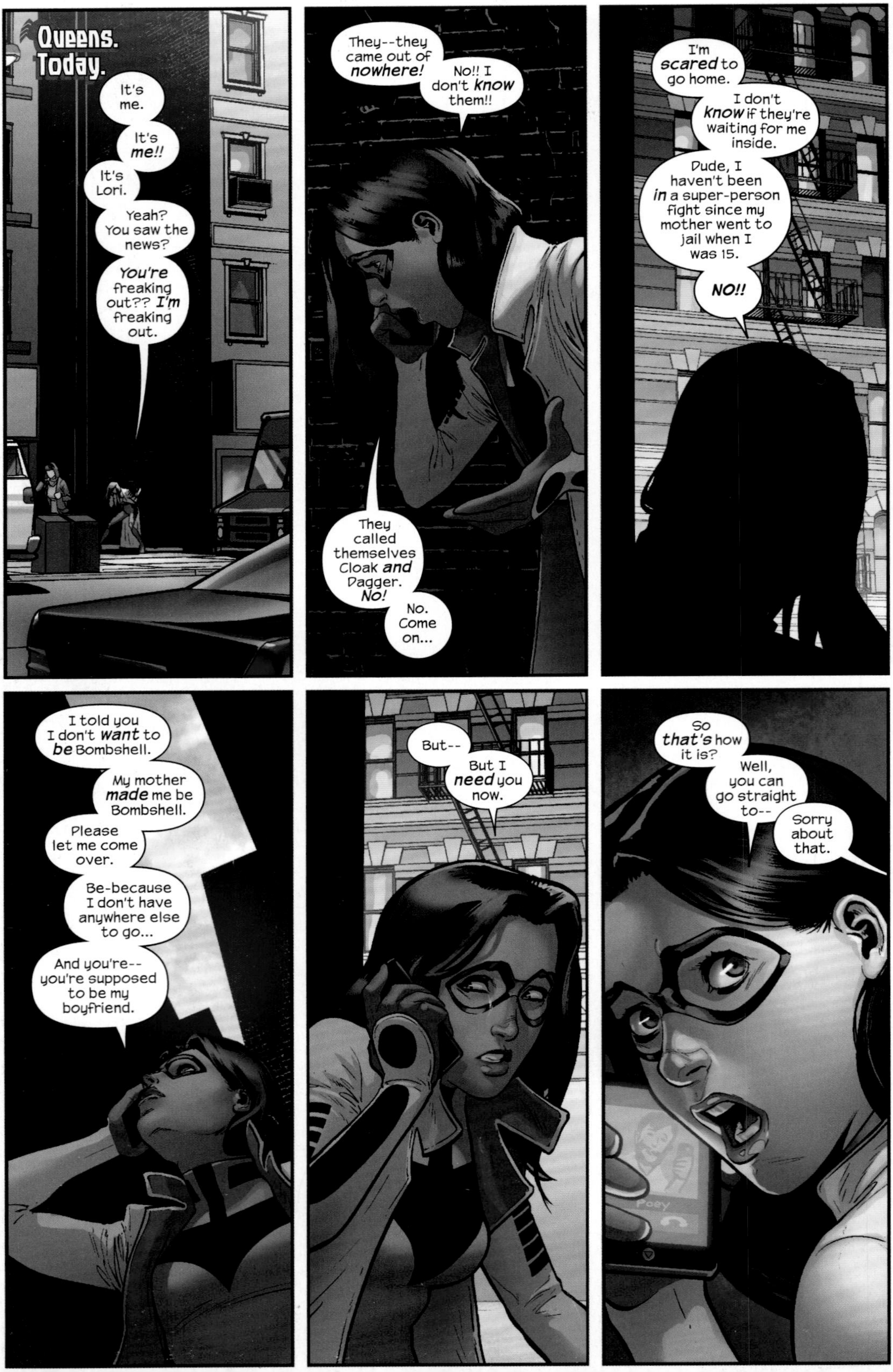
Queens. Today.
It's me.
It's me!!
It's Lori.
Yeah? You saw the news?
You're freaking out?? I'm freaking out.
They--they came out of nowhere!
No!! I don't know them!!
They called themselves Cloak and Dagger. No!
No. Come on...
I'm scared to go home.
I don't know if they're waiting for me inside.
Dude, I haven't been in a super-person fight since my mother went to jail when I was 15.
NO!!
I told you I don't want to be Bombshell.
My mother made me be Bombshell.
Please let me come over.
Be-because I don't have anywhere else to go...
And you're-- you're supposed to be my boyfriend.
But--
But I need you now.
So that's how it is?
Well, you can go straight to--
Sorry about that.
Poey

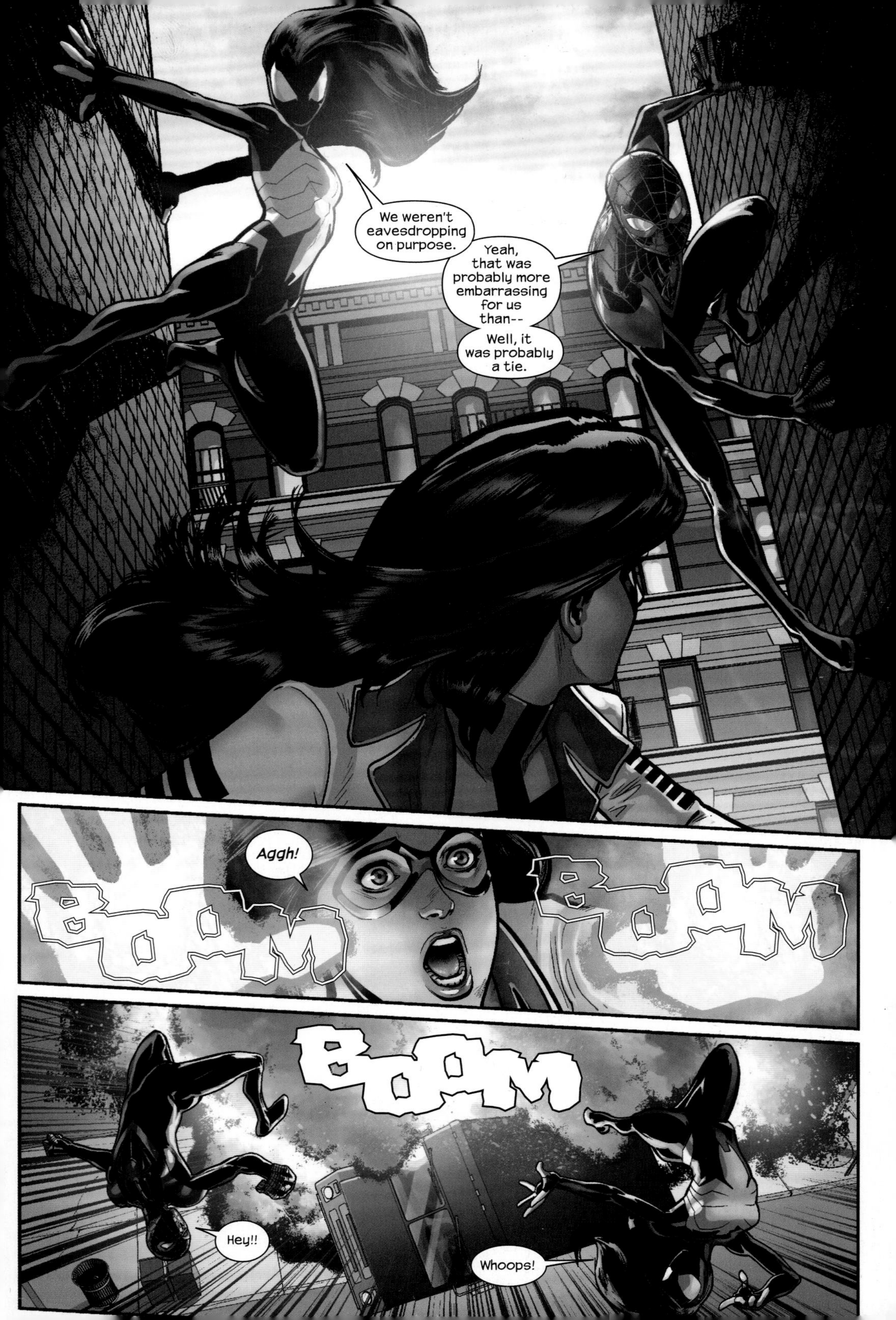
We weren't eavesdropping on purpose.
Yeah, that was probably more embarrassing for us than--
Well, it was probably a tie.
Aggh!
BOOM
BOOM
BOOM
Hey!!
Whoops!

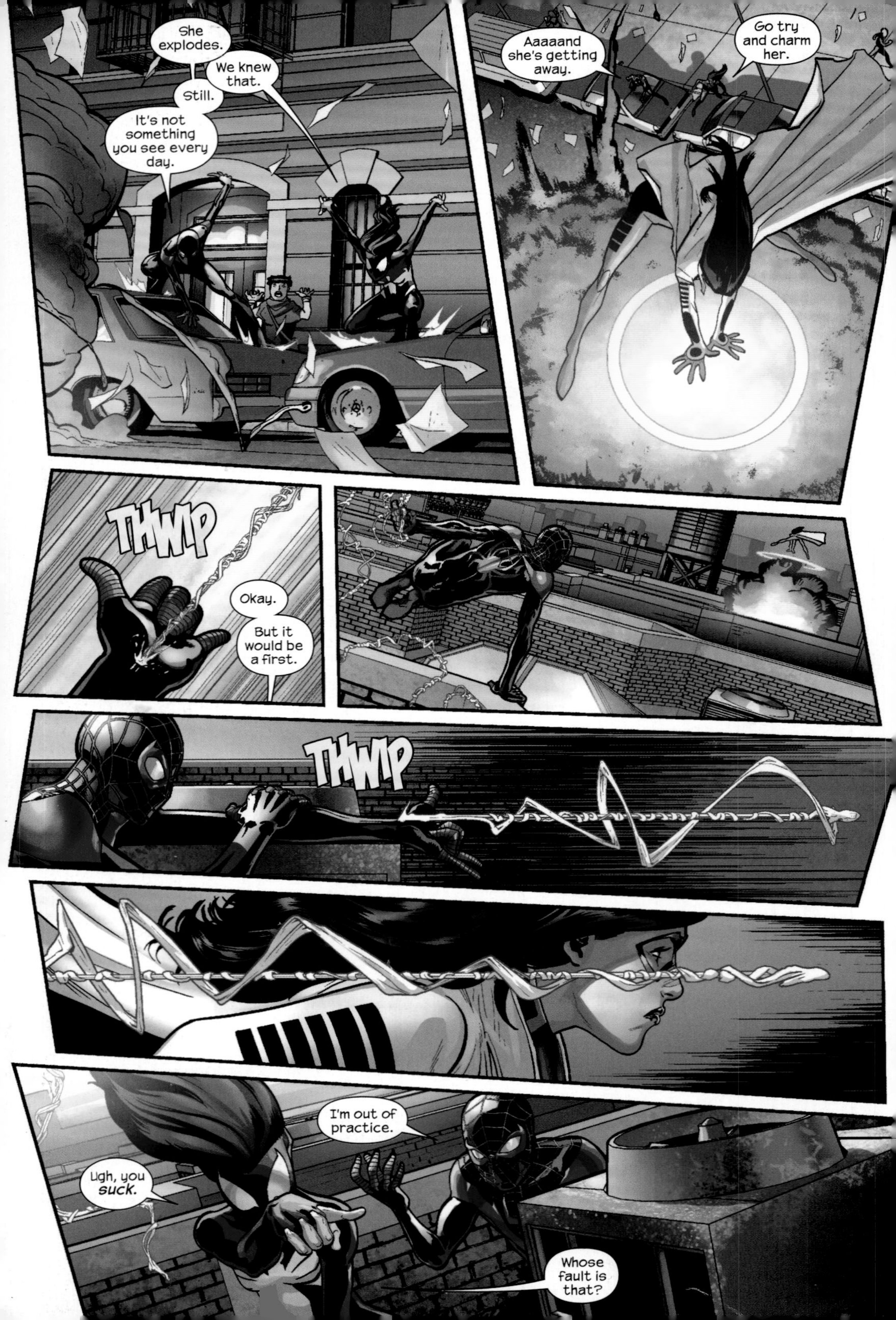
She explodes.
We knew that.
Still.
It's not something you see every day.
Aaaaand she's getting away.
Go try and charm her.
THWIP
Okay.
But it would be a first.
THWIP
I'm out of practice.
Ugh, you *suck.*
Whose fault is that?

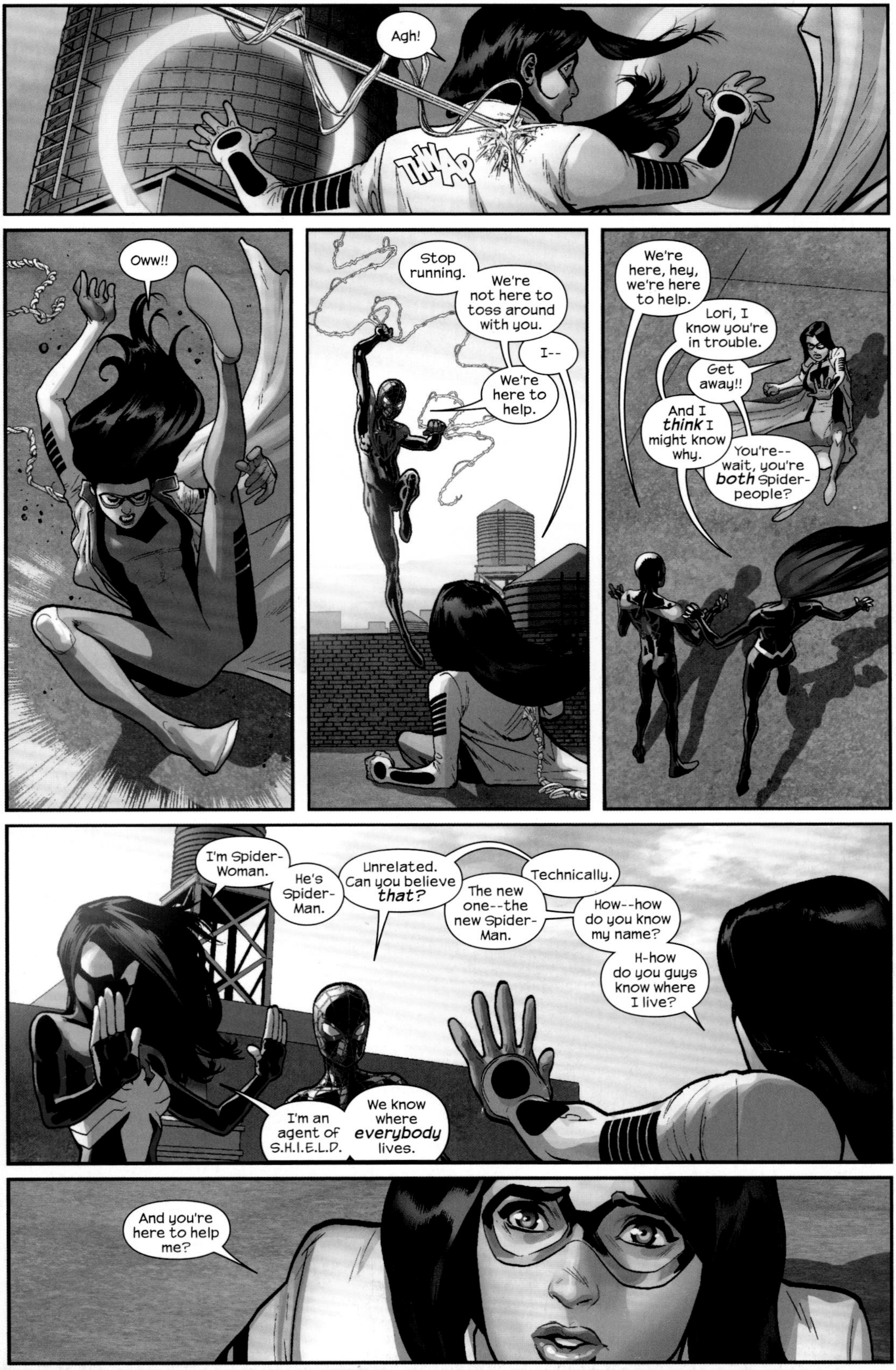

Agh!
THWAP
Oww!!
Stop running.
We're not here to toss around with you.
I--
We're here to help.
We're here, hey, we're here to help.
Lori, I know you're in trouble.
Get away!!
And I *think* I might know why.
You're--wait, you're *both* Spider-people?
I'm Spider-Woman.
He's Spider-Man.
Unrelated. Can you believe *that?*
Technically.
The new one--the new Spider-Man.
How--how do you know my name?
H-how do you guys know where I live?
I'm an agent of S.H.I.E.L.D.
We know where *everybody* lives.
And you're here to help me?

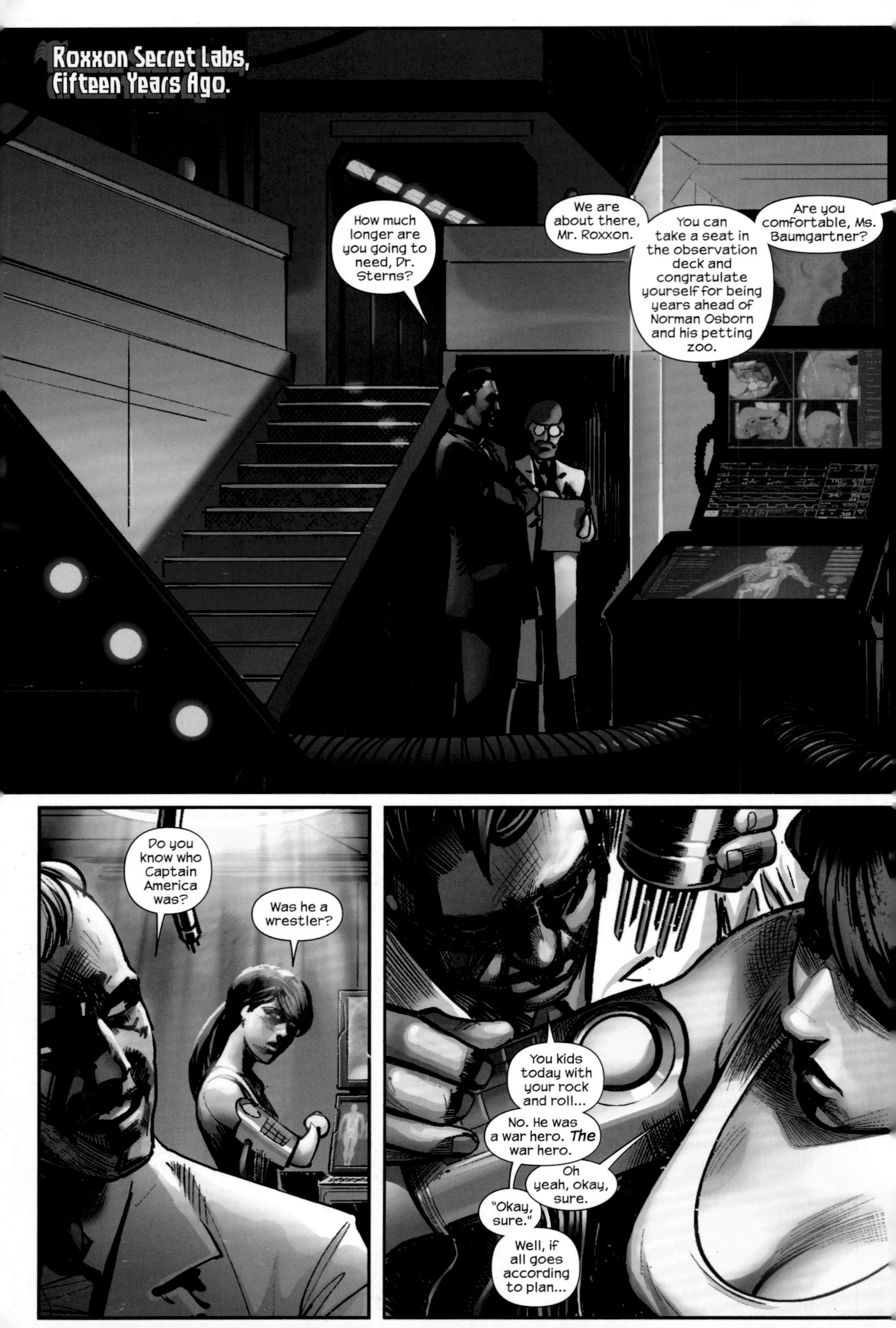
Roxxon Secret Labs, Fifteen Years Ago.
How much longer are you going to need, Dr. Sterns?
We are about there, Mr. Roxxon.
You can take a seat in the observation deck and congratulate yourself for being years ahead of Norman Osborn and his petting zoo.
Are you comfortable, Ms. Baumgartner?
Do you know who Captain America was?
Was he a wrestler?
You kids today with your rock and roll...
No. He was a war hero. *The* war hero.
Oh yeah, okay, sure.
"Okay, sure."
Well, if all goes according to plan...

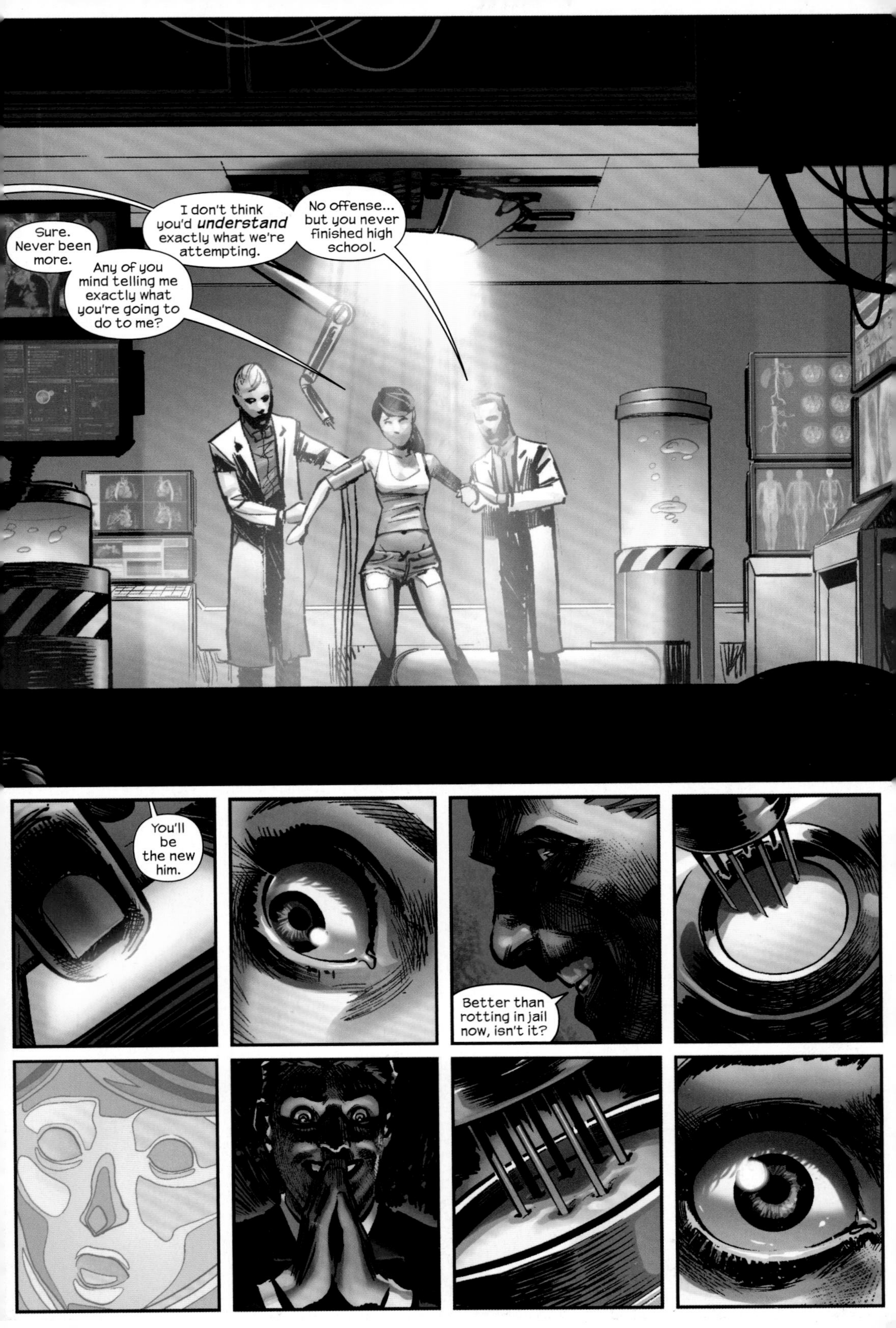
Sure. Never been more.
Any of you mind telling me exactly what you're going to do to me?
I don't think you'd *understand* exactly what we're attempting.
No offense... but you never finished high school.
You'll be the new him.
Better than rotting in jail now, isn't it?

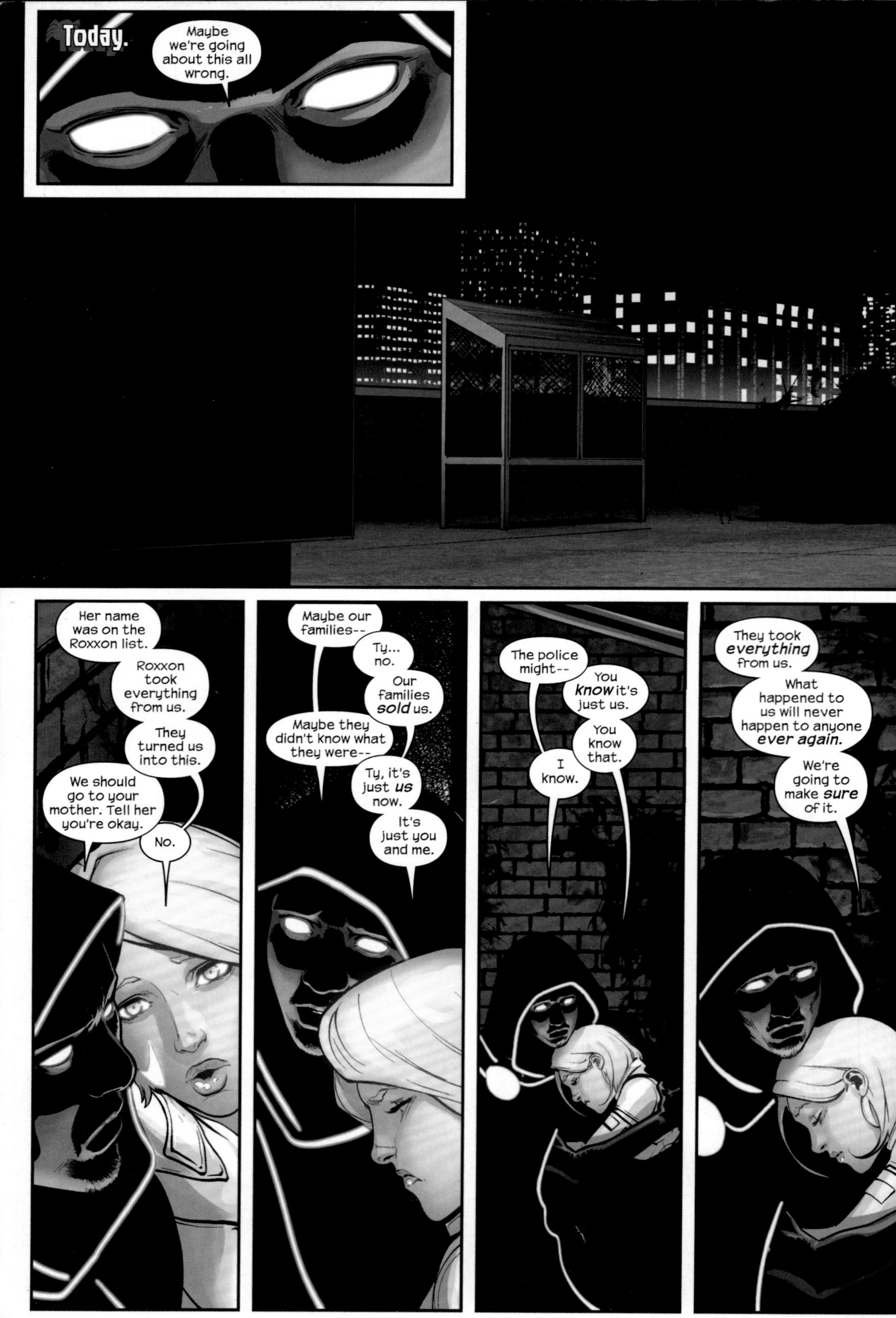
Today.
Maybe we're going about this all wrong.
Her name was on the Roxxon list.
Roxxon took everything from us.
They turned us into this.
We should go to your mother. Tell her you're okay.
No.
Maybe our families--
Ty... no.
Our families sold us.
Maybe they didn't know what they were--
Ty, it's just us now.
It's just you and me.
The police might--
You know it's just us.
You know that.
I know.
They took everything from us.
What happened to us will never happen to anyone ever again.
We're going to make sure of it.

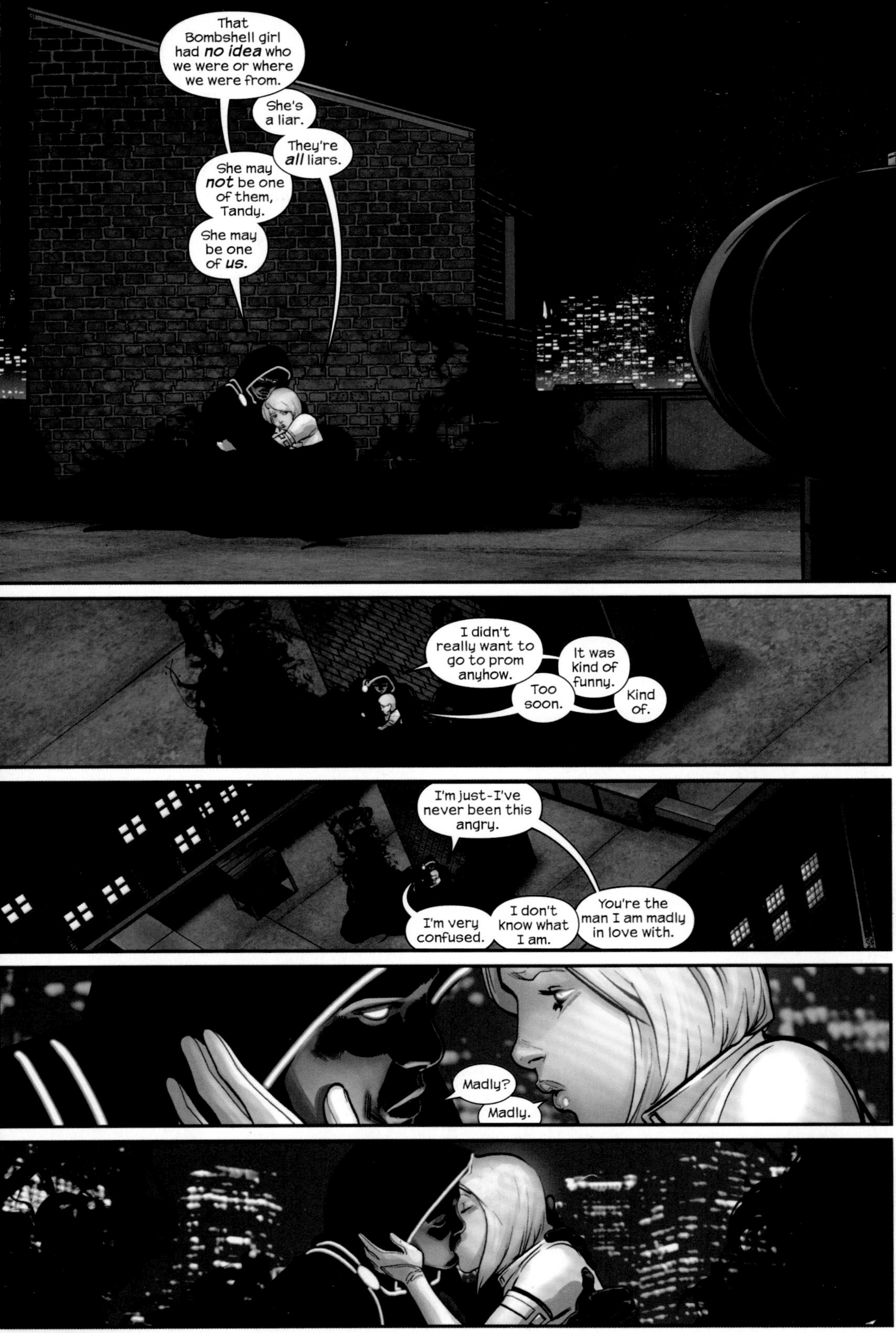
That Bombshell girl had *no idea* who we were or where we were from.
She's a liar.
They're *all* liars.
She may *not* be one of them, Tandy.
She may be one of *us.*
I didn't really want to go to prom anyhow.
It was kind of funny.
Too soon.
Kind of.
I'm just-I've never been this angry.
I'm very confused.
I don't know what I am.
You're the man I am madly in love with.
Madly?
Madly.

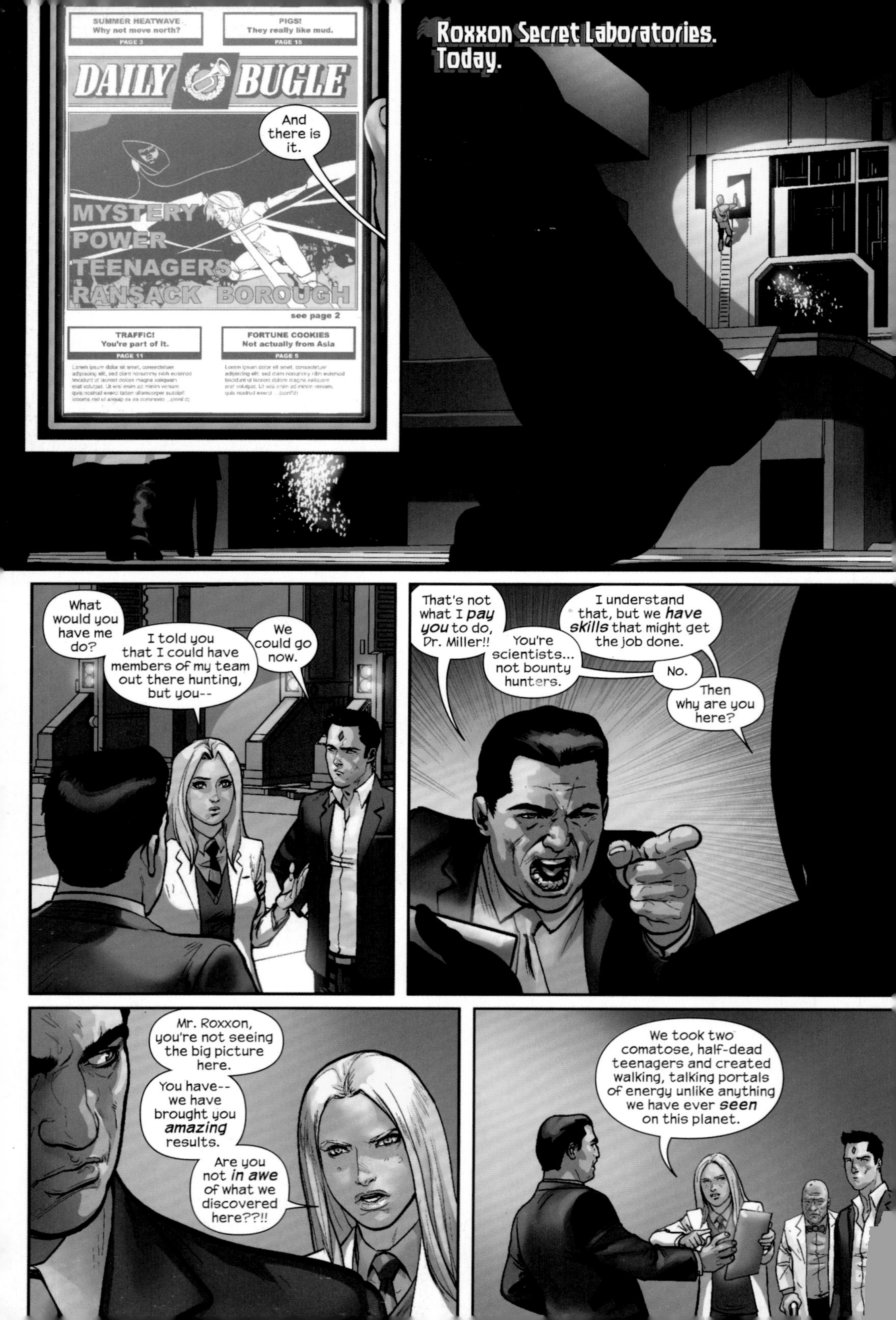

Roxxon Secret Laboratories. Today.
SUMMER HEATWAVE Why not move north?
PAGE 3
PIGS! They really like mud.
PAGE 15
DAILY BUGLE
MYSTERY POWER TEENAGERS RANSACK BOROUGH
see page 2
TRAFFIC! You're part of it.
PAGE 11
FORTUNE COOKIES Not actually from Asia
PAGE 5
And there is it.
What would you have me do?
I told you that I could have members of my team out there hunting, but you--
We could go now.
That's not what I *pay you* to do, Dr. Miller!!
I understand that, but we *have skills* that might get the job done.
You're scientists... not bounty hunters.
No.
Then why are you here?
Mr. Roxxon, you're not seeing the big picture here.
You have-- we have brought you *amazing* results.
Are you not *in awe* of what we discovered here??!!
We took two comatose, half-dead teenagers and created walking, talking portals of energy unlike anything we have ever *seen* on this planet.

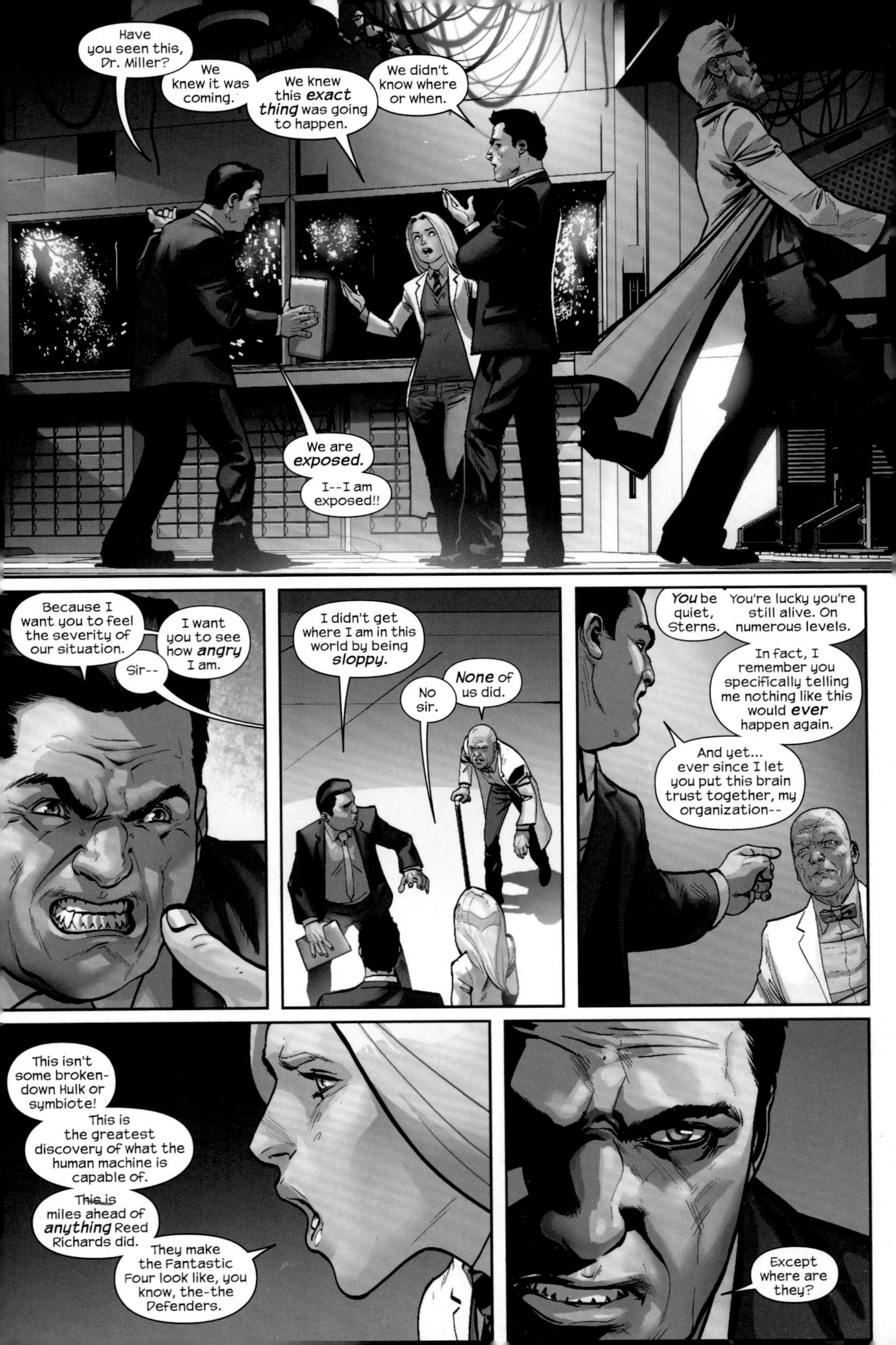

Have you seen this, Dr. Miller?
We knew it was coming.
We knew this *exact thing* was going to happen.
We didn't know where or when.
We are *exposed.*
I--I am exposed!!
Because I want you to feel the severity of our situation.
I want you to see how *angry* I am.
Sir--
I didn't get where I am in this world by being *sloppy.*
No sir.
None of us did.
You be quiet, Sterns.
You're lucky you're still alive. On numerous levels.
In fact, I remember you specifically telling me nothing like this would *ever* happen again.
And yet... ever since I let you put this brain trust together, my organization--
This isn't some broken-down Hulk or symbiote!
This is the greatest discovery of what the human machine is capable of.
This is miles ahead of *anything* Reed Richards did.
They make the Fantastic Four look like, you know, the-the Defenders.
Except where are they?

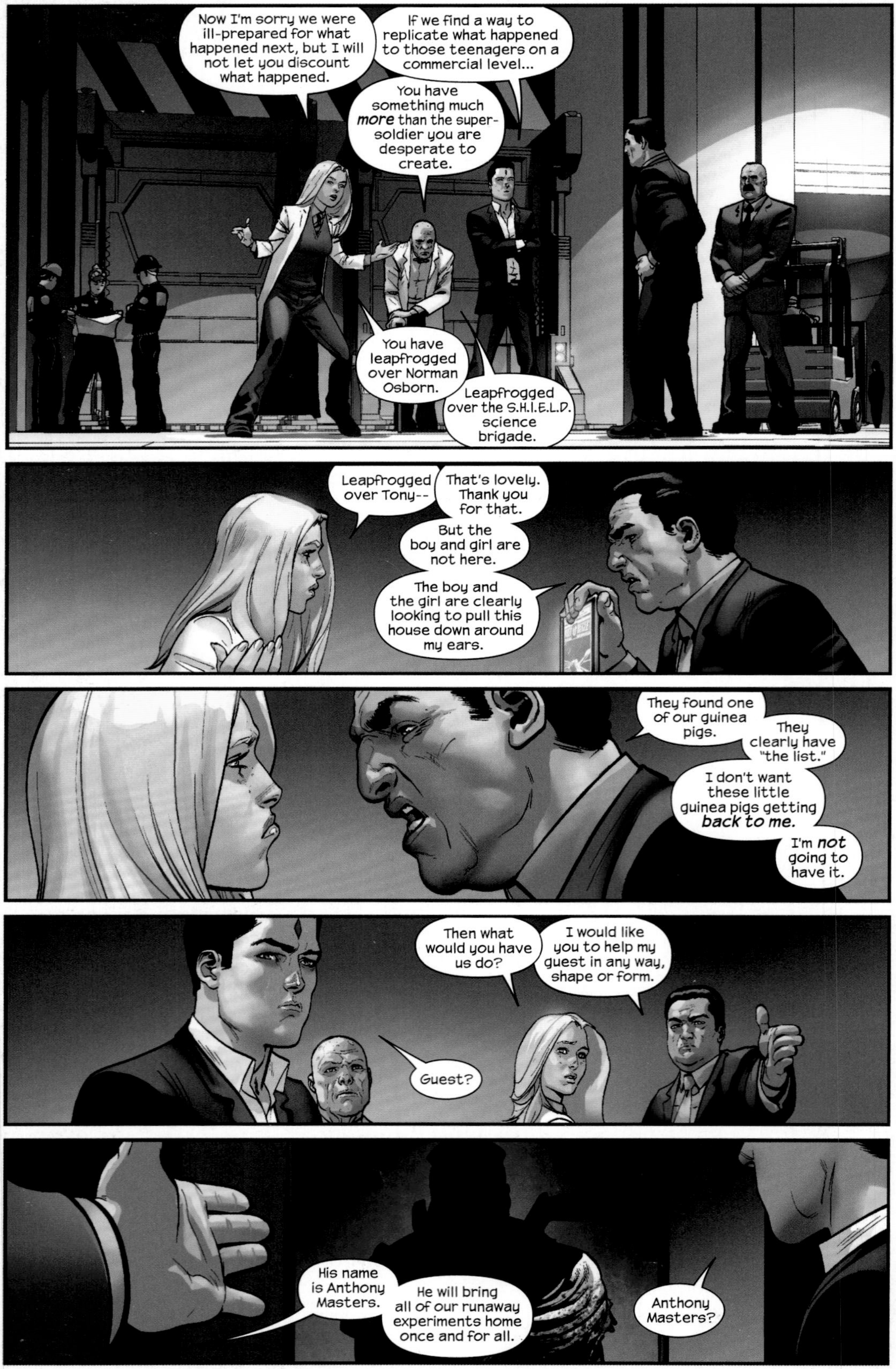

Now I'm sorry we were ill-prepared for what happened next, but I will not let you discount what happened.
If we find a way to replicate what happened to those teenagers on a commercial level...
You have something much *more* than the super-soldier you are desperate to create.
You have leapfrogged over Norman Osborn.
Leapfrogged over the S.H.I.E.L.D. science brigade.
Leapfrogged over Tony--
That's lovely. Thank you for that.
But the boy and girl are not here.
The boy and the girl are clearly looking to pull this house down around my ears.
They found one of our guinea pigs.
They clearly have "the list."
I don't want these little guinea pigs getting *back to me.*
I'm ***not*** going to have it.
Then what would you have us do?
I would like you to help my guest in any way, shape or form.
Guest?
His name is Anthony Masters.
He will bring all of our runaway experiments home once and for all.
Anthony Masters?

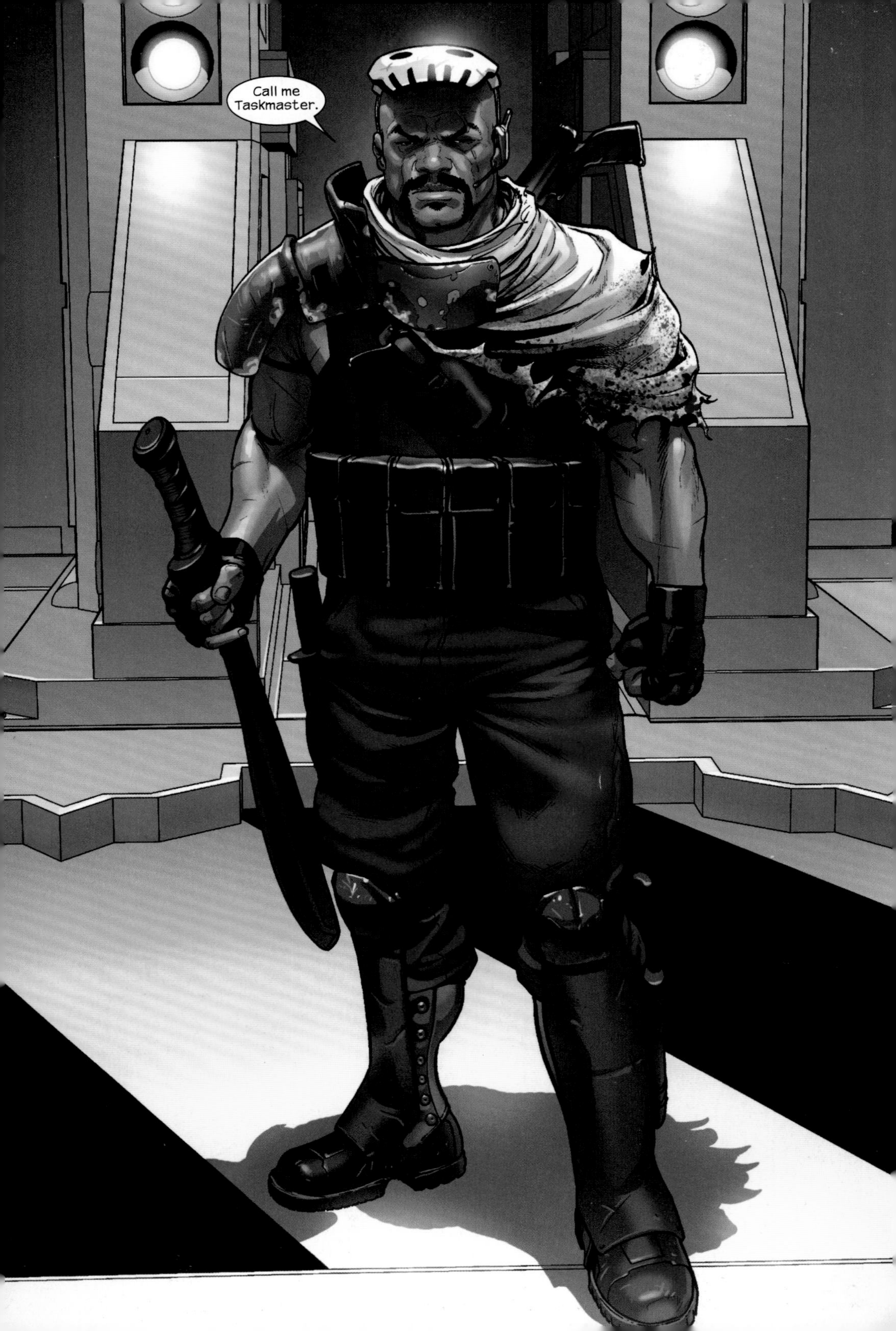
Call me Taskmaster.

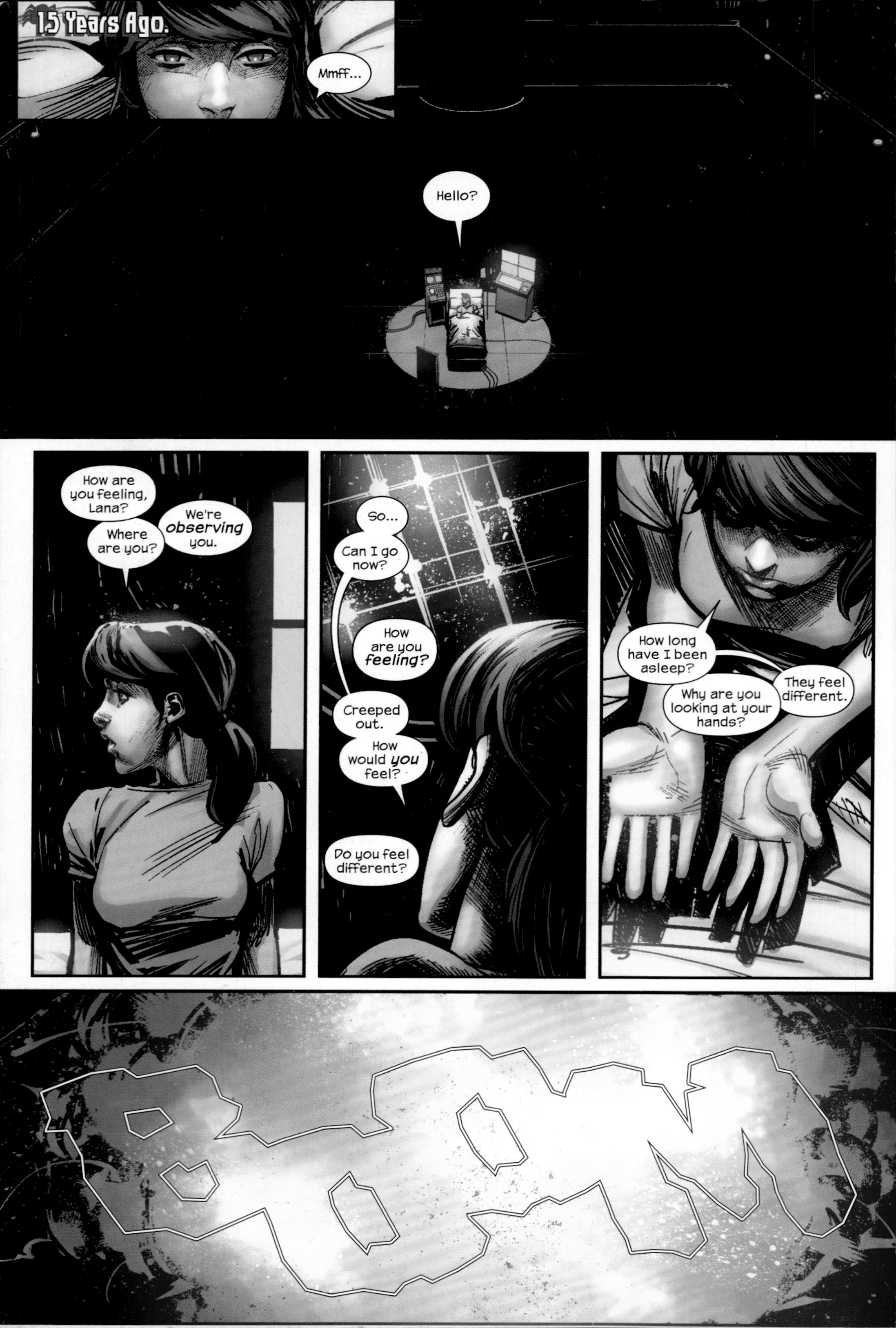
15 Years Ago.
Mmff...
Hello?
How are you feeling, Lana?
Where are you?
We're *observing* you.
So...
Can I go now?
How are you *feeling?*
Creeped out.
How would *you* feel?
Do you feel different?
How long have I been asleep?
Why are you looking at your hands?
They feel different.
BOOM

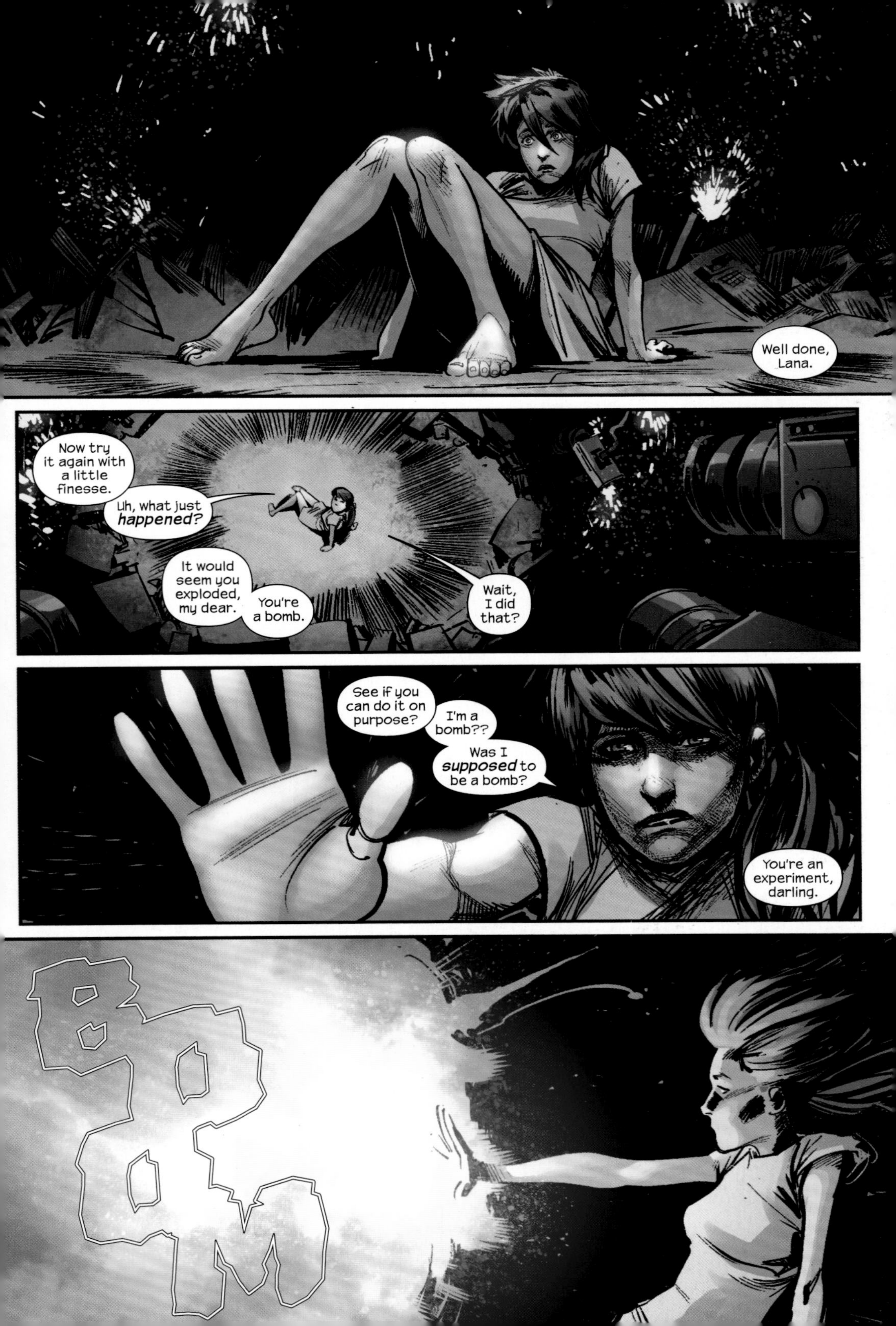

Well done, Lana.
Now try it again with a little finesse.
Uh, what just *happened?*
It would seem you exploded, my dear.
You're a bomb.
Wait, I did that?
See if you can do it on purpose?
I'm a bomb??
Was I *supposed* to be a bomb?
You're an experiment, darling.
BOOM

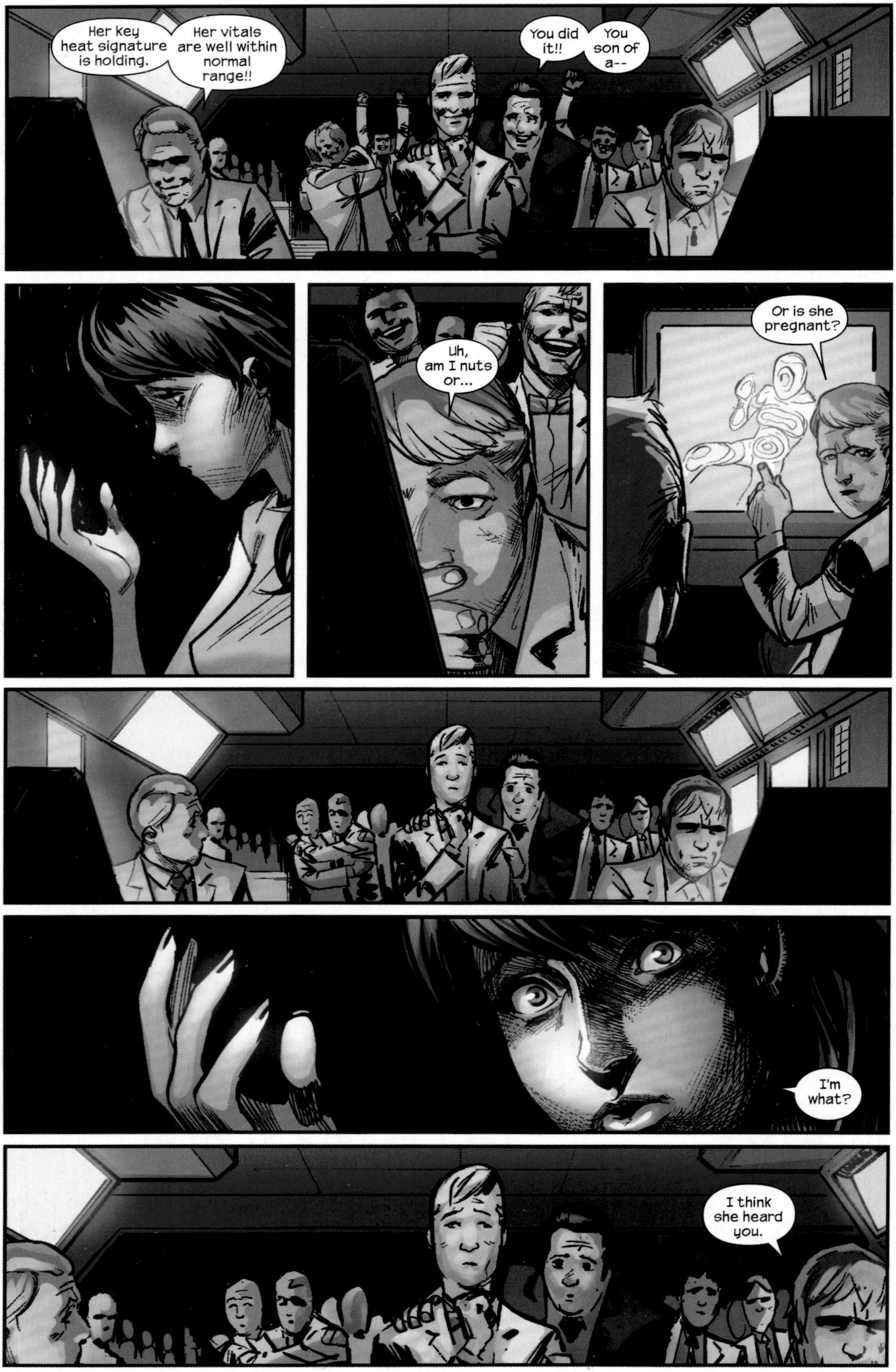
Her key heat signature is holding.
Her vitals are well within normal range!!
You did it!!
You son of a--
Uh, am I nuts or...
Or is she pregnant?
I'm what?
I think she heard you.

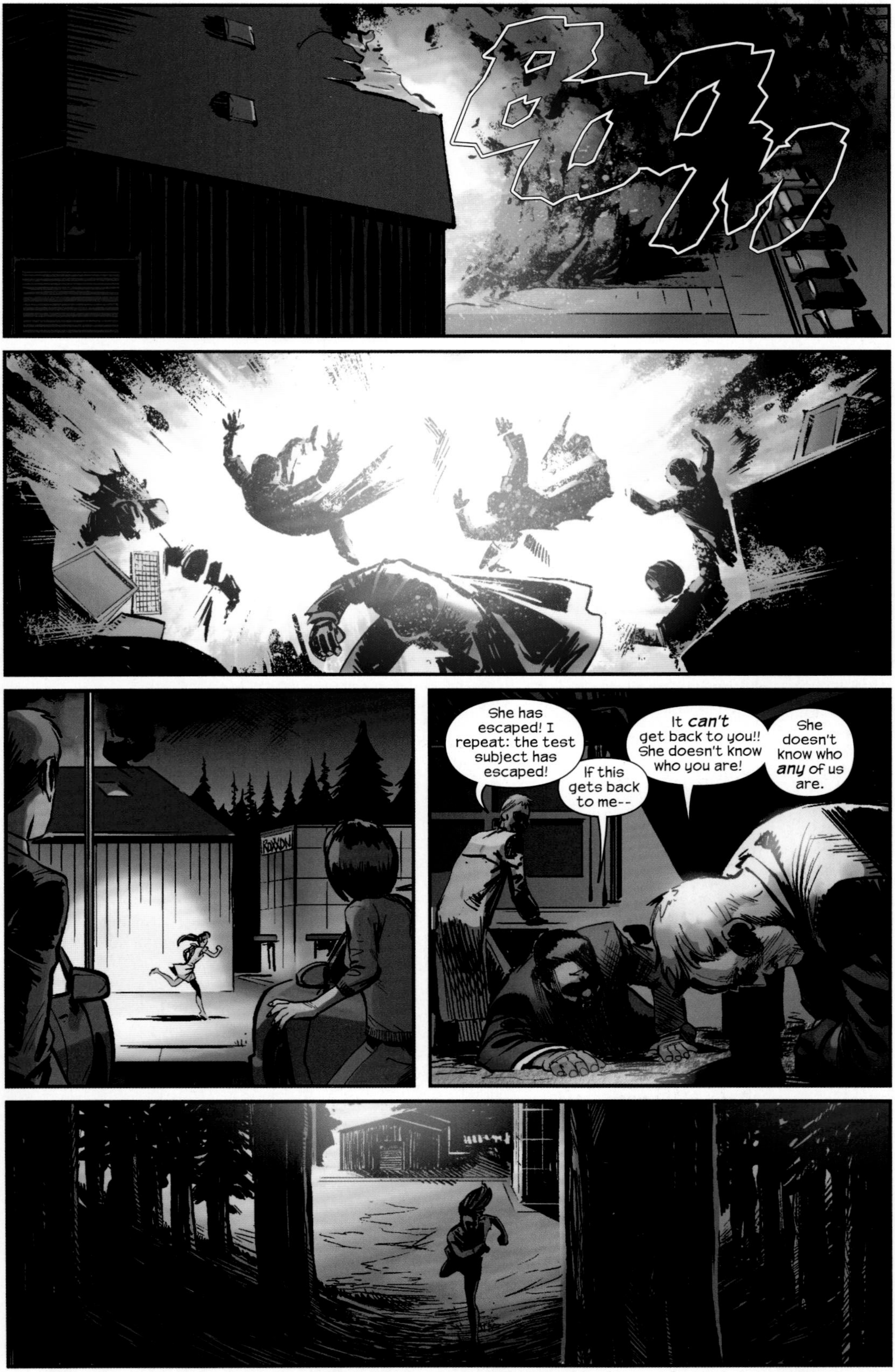
She has escaped! I repeat: the test subject has escaped!
If this gets back to me--
It *can't* get back to you!! She doesn't know who you are!
She doesn't know who *any* of us are.

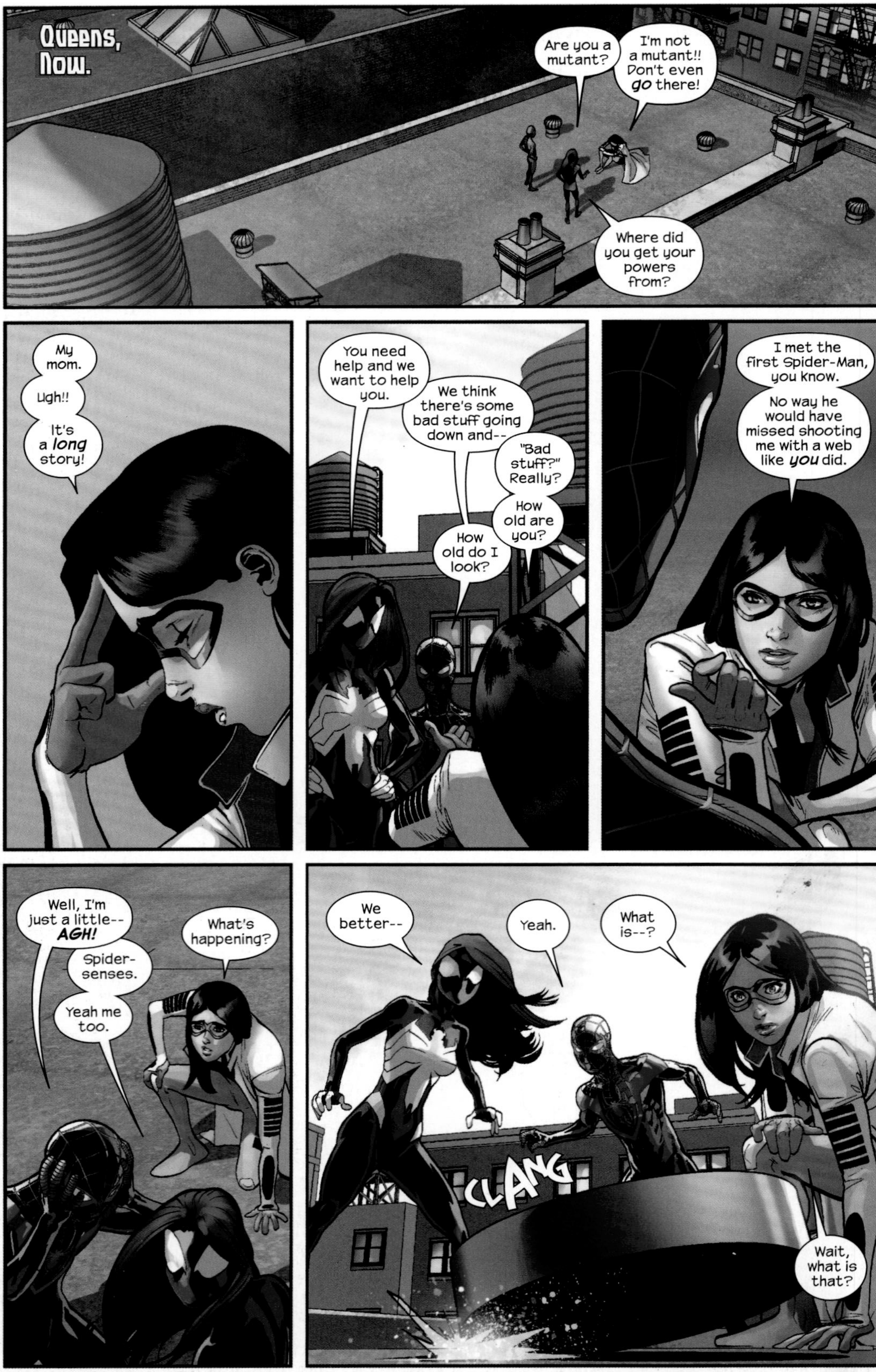
Queens, Now.
Are you a mutant?
I'm not a mutant!! Don't even go there!
Where did you get your powers from?
My mom.
Ugh!!
It's a long story!
You need help and we want to help you.
We think there's some bad stuff going down and--
"Bad stuff?" Really?
How old are you?
How old do I look?
I met the first Spider-Man, you know.
No way he would have missed shooting me with a web like you did.
Well, I'm just a little-- AGH!
What's happening?
Spider-senses.
Yeah me too.
We better--
Yeah.
What is--?
CLANG
Wait, what is that?

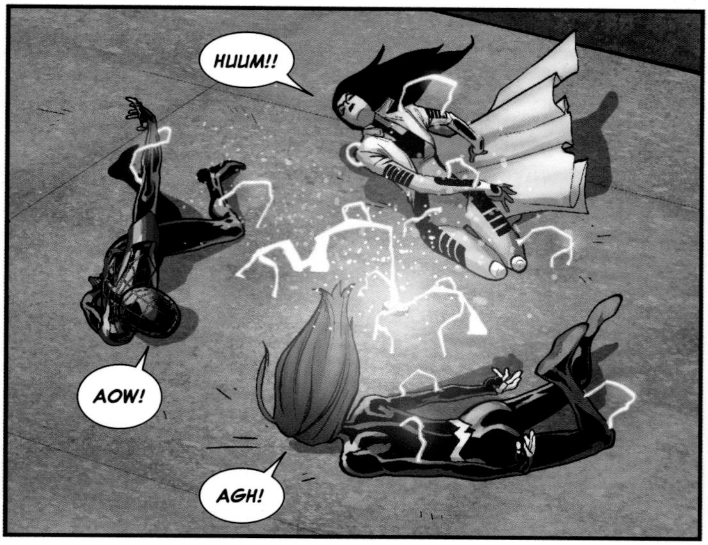
HUUM!!
AOW!
AGH!
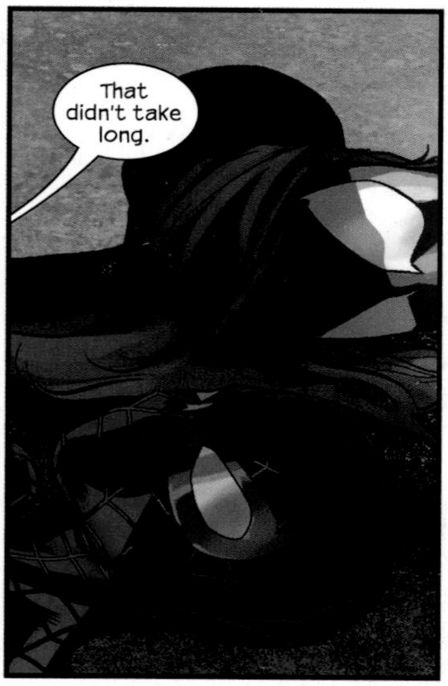
That didn't take long.
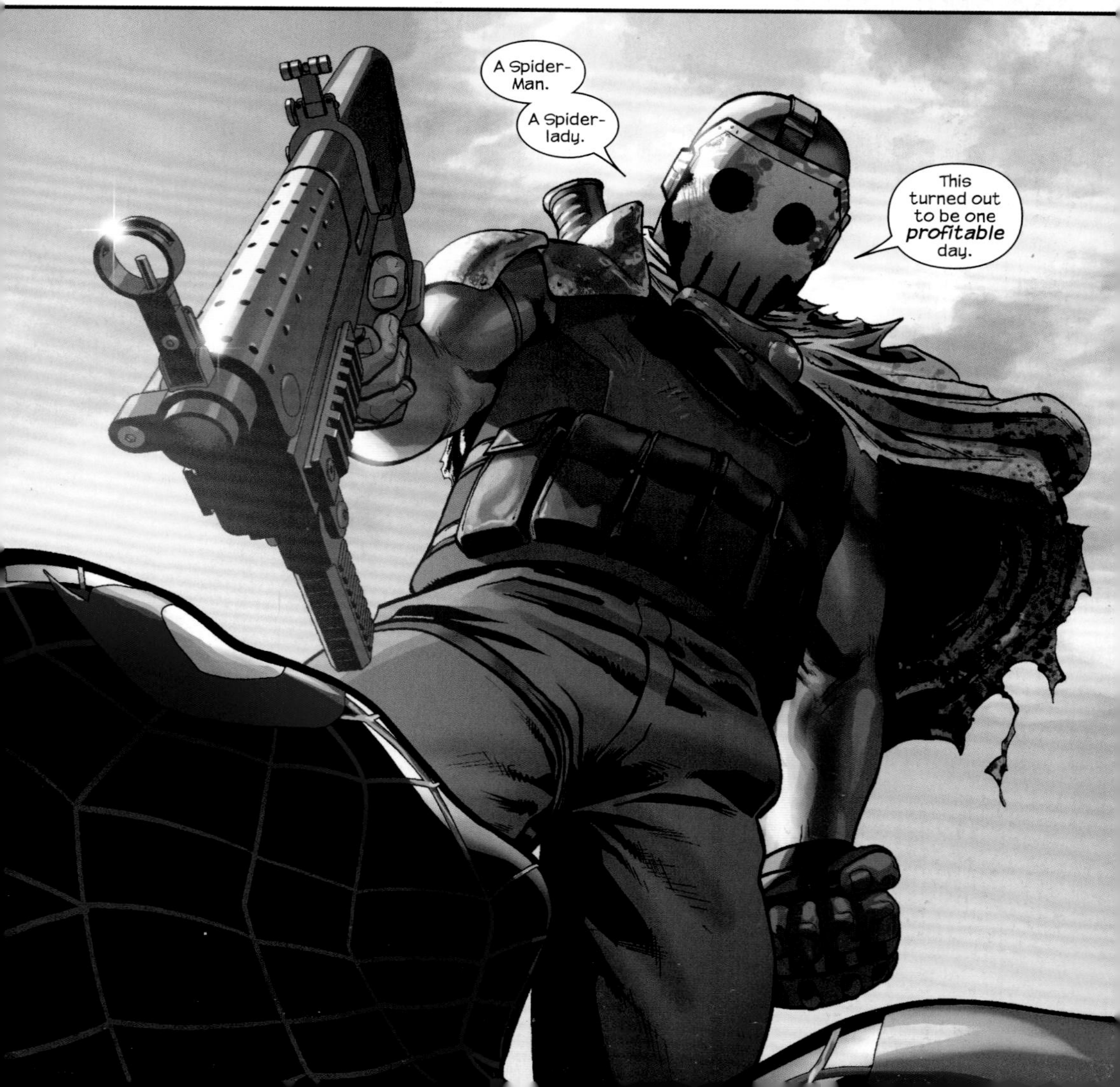
A Spider-Man.
A Spider-lady.
This turned out to be one *profitable* day.

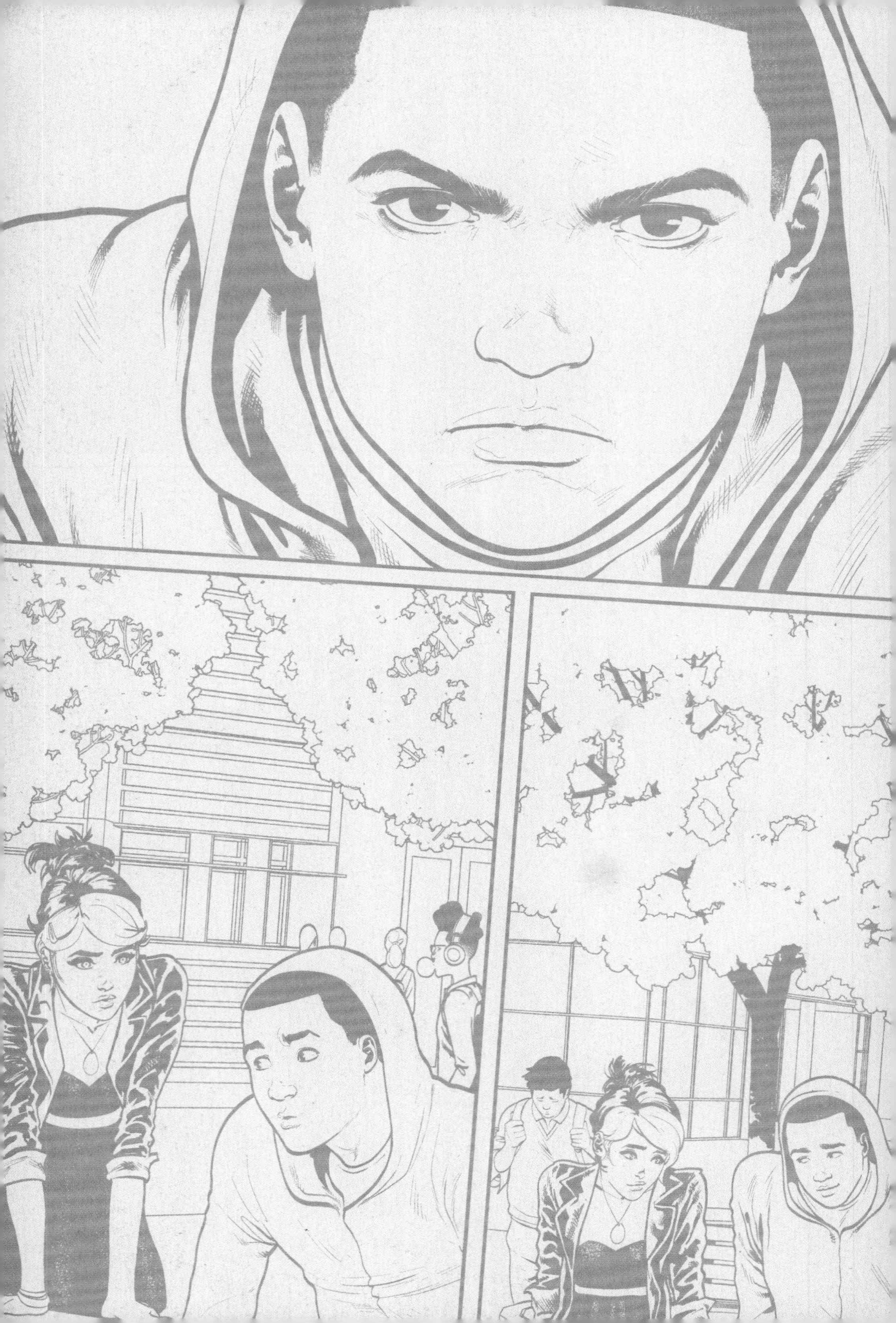

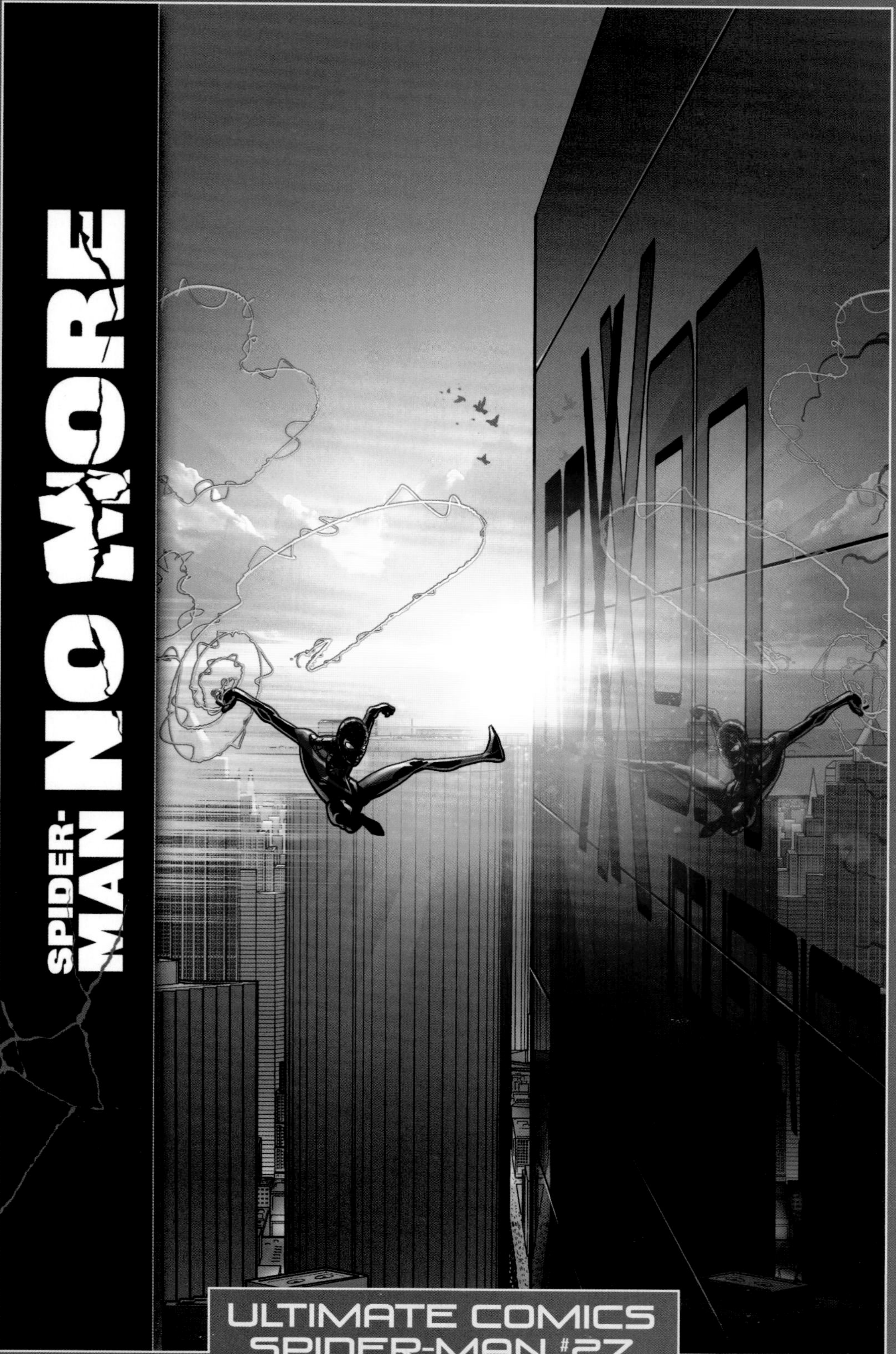
SPIDER-MAN NO MORE
ULTIMATE COMICS
SPIDER-MAN #27

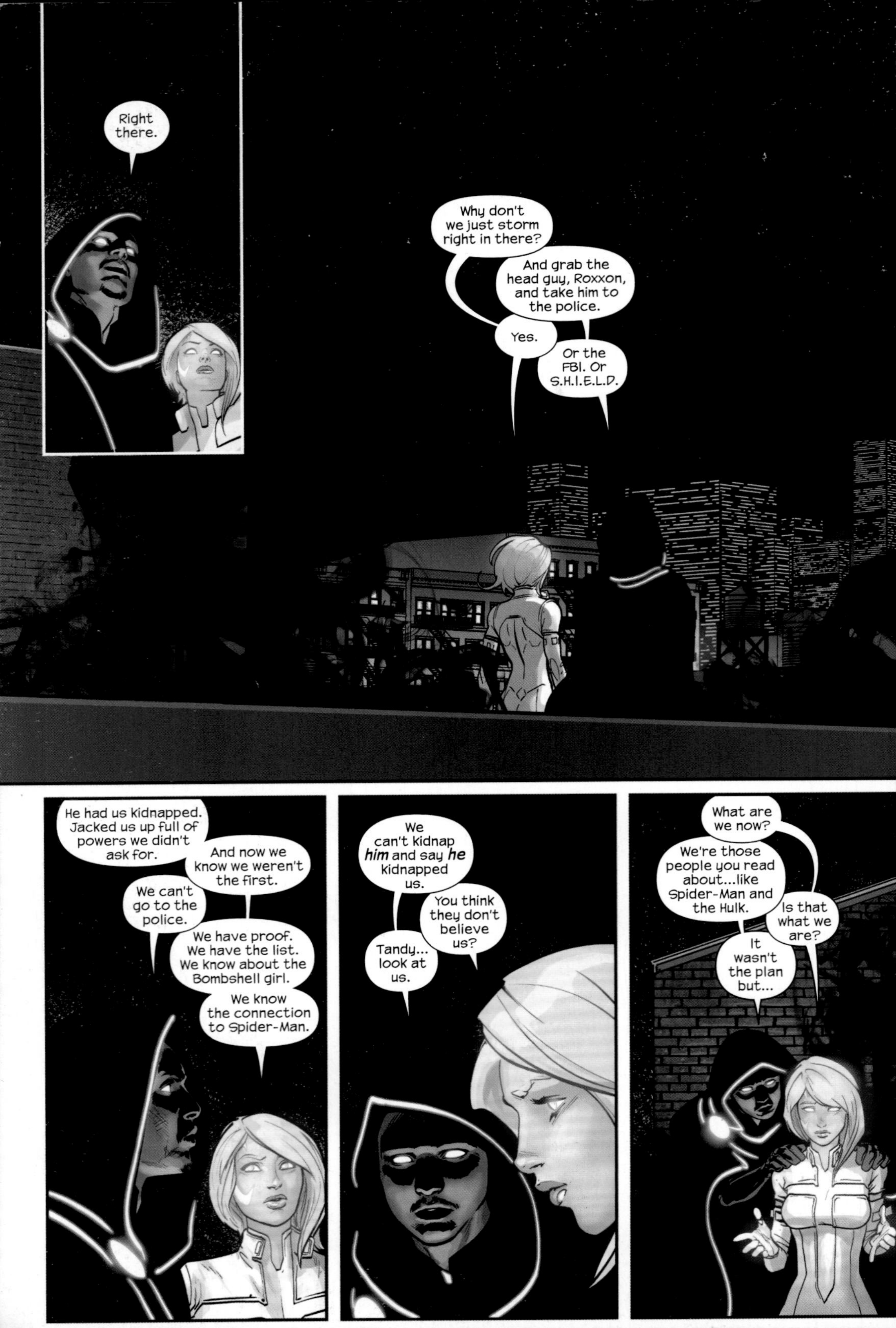
Right there.
Why don't we just storm right in there?
And grab the head guy, Roxxon, and take him to the police.
Yes.
Or the FBI. Or S.H.I.E.L.D.
He had us kidnapped. Jacked us up full of powers we didn't ask for.
And now we know we weren't the first.
We can't go to the police.
We have proof. We have the list. We know about the Bombshell girl.
We know the connection to Spider-Man.
We can't kidnap *him* and say *he* kidnapped us.
You think they don't believe us?
Tandy... look at us.
What are we now?
We're those people you read about...like Spider-Man and the Hulk.
Is that what we are?
It wasn't the plan but...

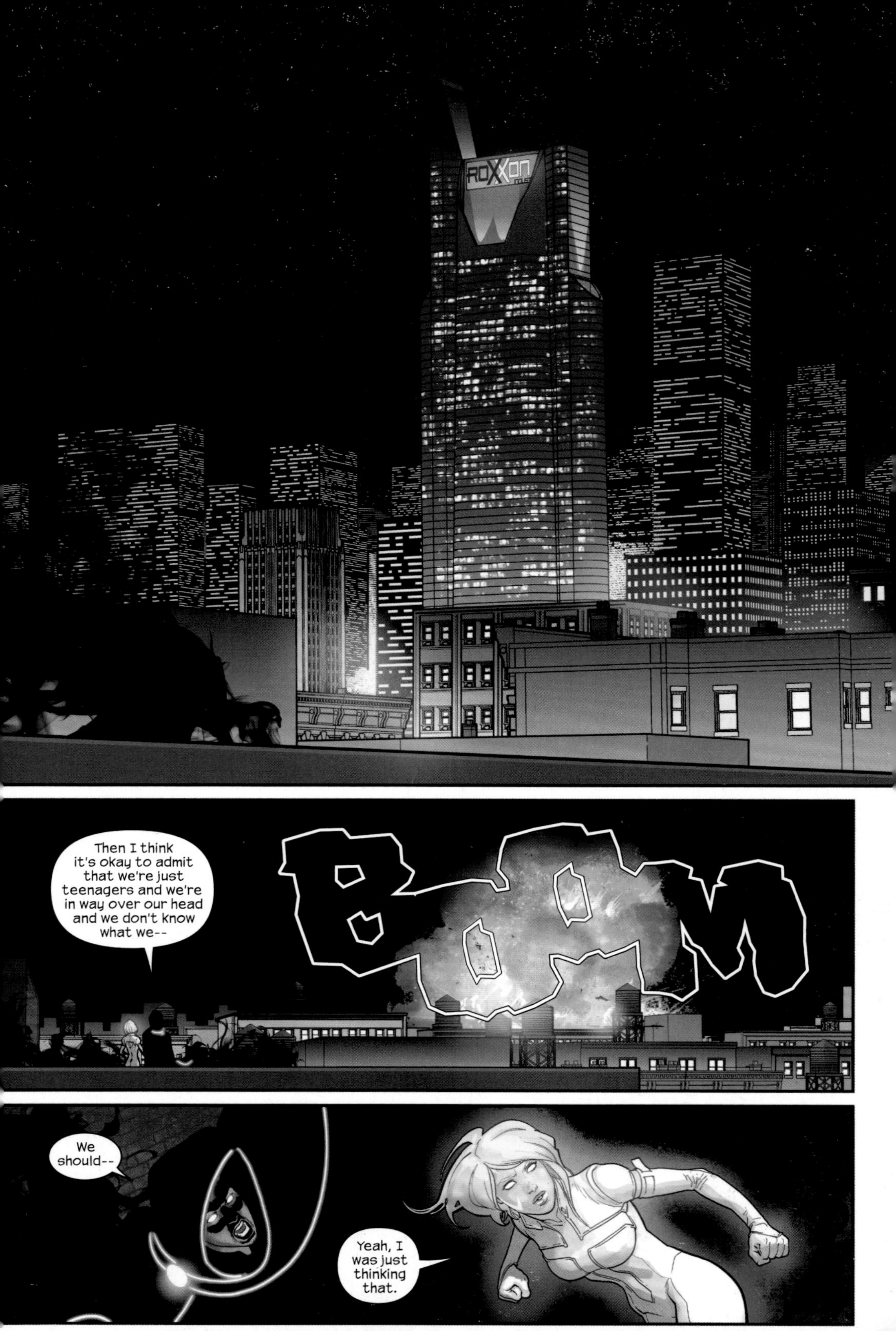

Then I think it's okay to admit that we're just teenagers and we're in way over our head and we don't know what we--
BOOM
We should--
Yeah, I was just thinking that.

up being Spider-Man?

Oh yeah, stuff like this.

I don't know who this guy is or *how* he found us or *what* he wants or how he has us all *paralyzed.*

(Which feels very freaky weird, by the way.)

Agh!

Aow!

HUUM!

I can't even move my mouth to ask--wait!!

What is he doing?

The *new* Spider-Man.

I bet I could turn this intel into a retirement.

Oh no.

He's going for my mask.

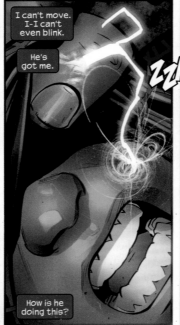

I can't move. I-I can't even blink.

He's got me.

ZZAAATTT

How is he doing this?

Ah!

What *the hell,* kid?!

You booby-trapped or--

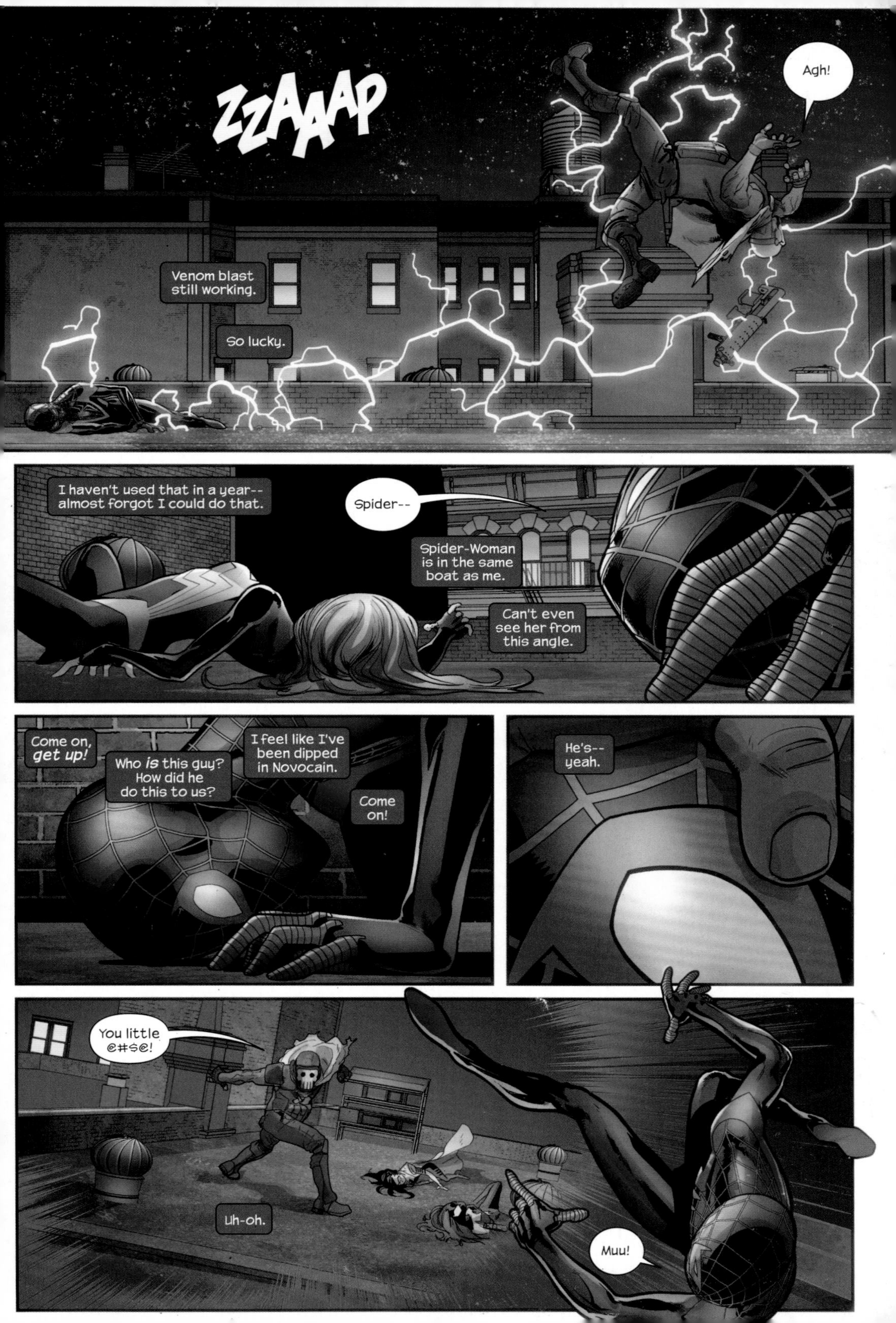
ZZAAAAP
Agh!
Venom blast still working.
So lucky.
I haven't used that in a year--almost forgot I could do that.
Spider--
Spider-Woman is in the same boat as me.
Can't even see her from this angle.
Come on, *get up!*
Who *is* this guy? How did he do this to us?
I feel like I've been dipped in Novocain.
Come on!
He's--yeah.
You little @#$@!
Uh-oh.
Muu!

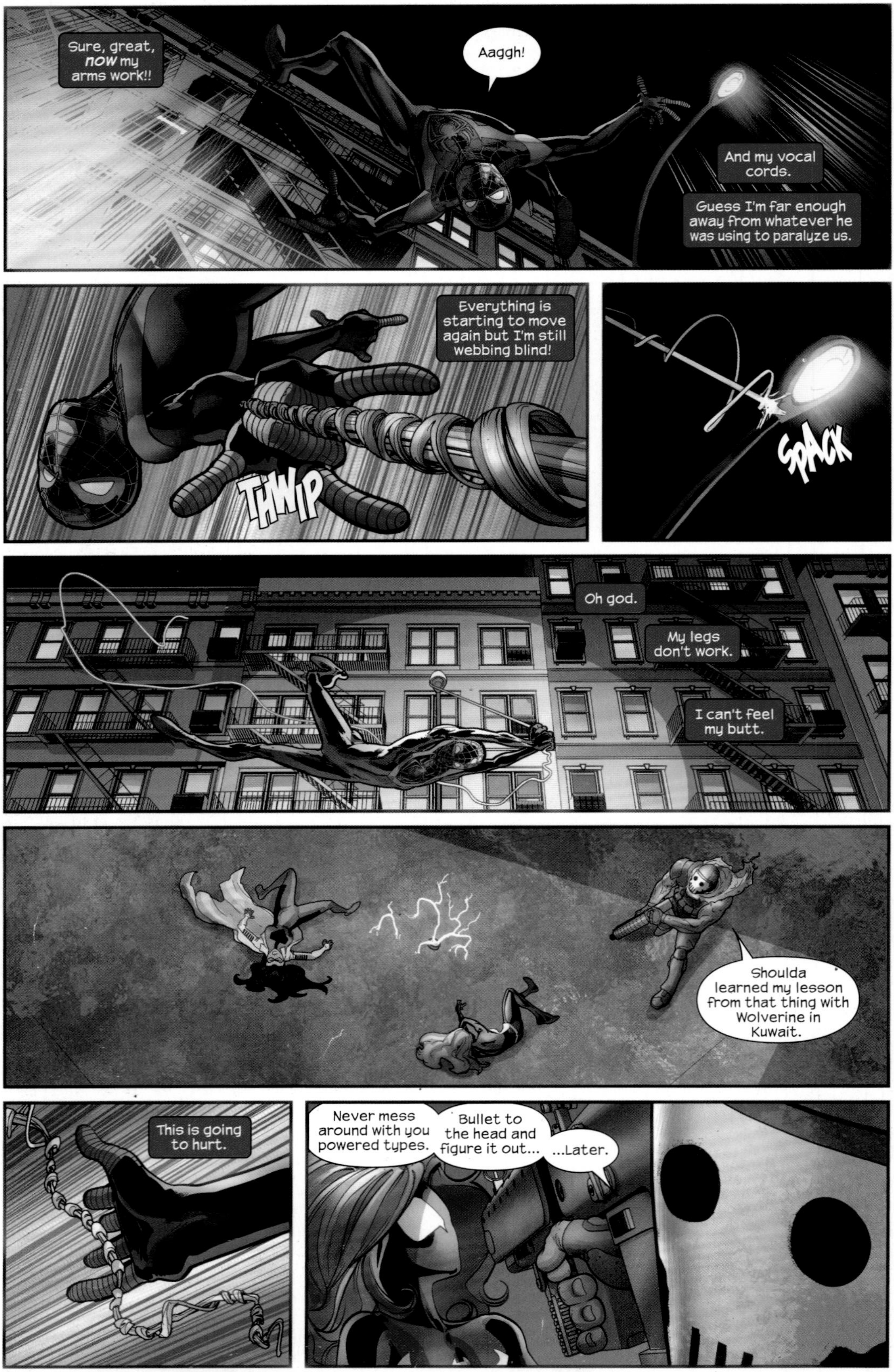
Sure, great, NOW my arms work!!
Aaggh!
And my vocal cords.
Guess I'm far enough away from whatever he was using to paralyze us.
Everything is starting to move again but I'm still webbing blind!
THWIP
SPACK
Oh god.
My legs don't work.
I can't feel my butt.
Shoulda learned my lesson from that thing with Wolverine in Kuwait.
This is going to hurt.
Never mess around with you powered types.
Bullet to the head and figure it out...
...Later.

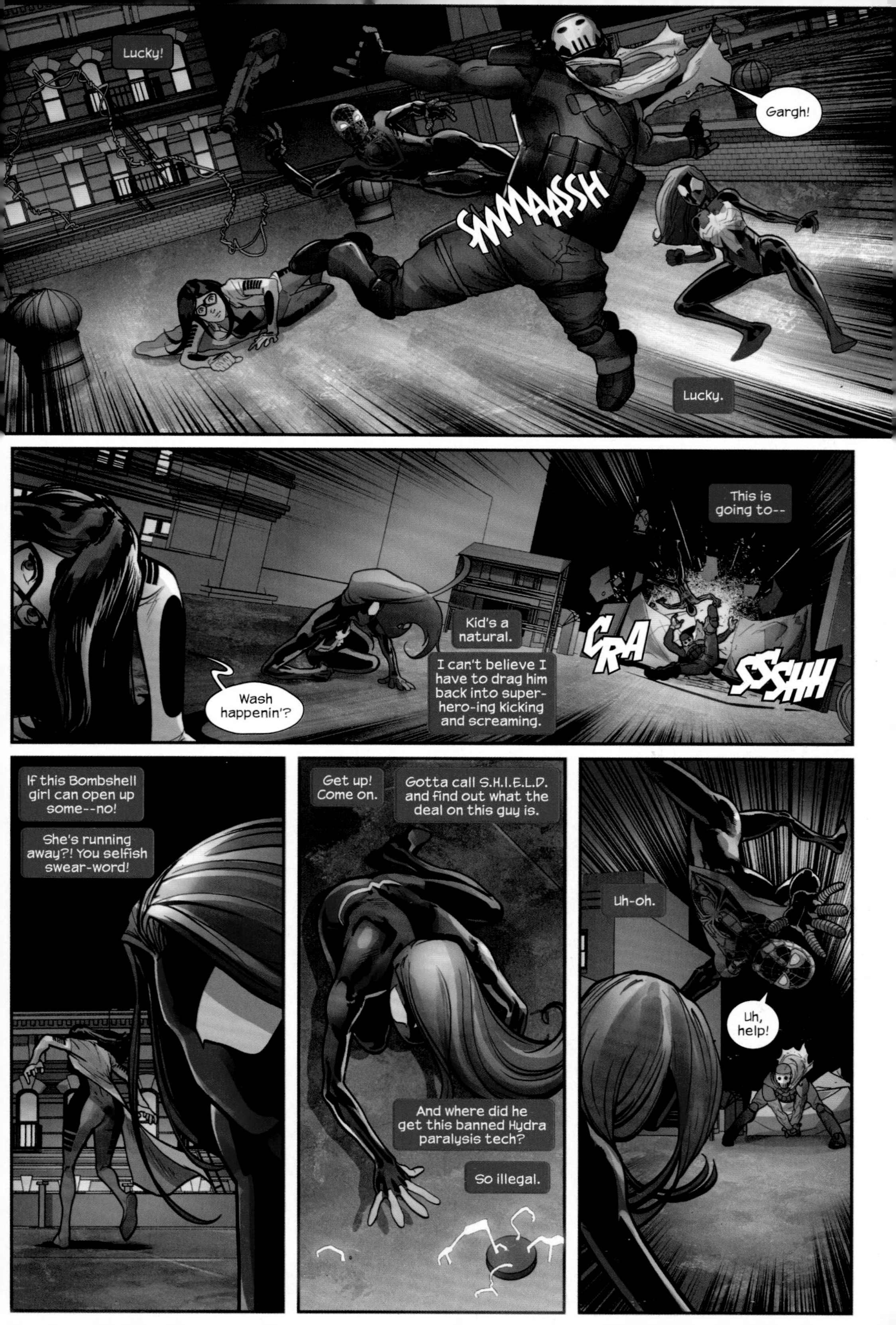

Lucky!
Gargh!
SMMAASSH
Lucky.
This is going to--
Kid's a natural.
I can't believe I have to drag him back into super-hero-ing kicking and screaming.
Wash happenin'?
CRA
SSSHH
If this Bombshell girl can open up some--no!
She's running away?! You selfish swear-word!
Get up! Come on.
Gotta call S.H.I.E.L.D. and find out what the deal on this guy is.
And where did he get this banned Hydra paralysis tech?
So illegal.
Uh-oh.
Uh, help!

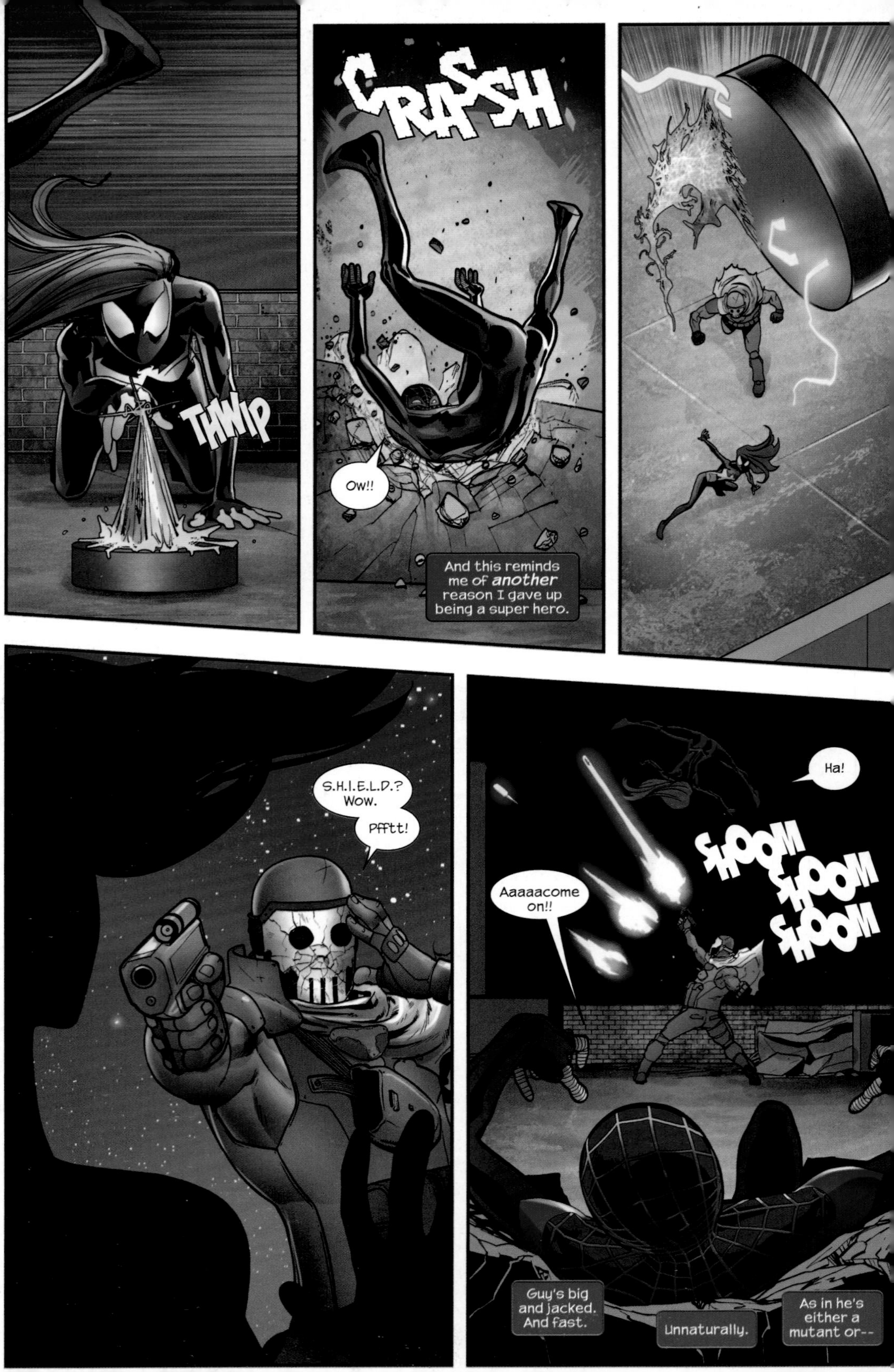
THWIP
CRASH
Ow!!
And this reminds me of *another* reason I gave up being a super hero.
S.H.I.E.L.D.? Wow.
Pffft!
Ha!
SHOOM SHOOM SHOOM
Aaaaacome on!!
Guy's big and jacked. And fast.
Unnaturally.
As in he's either a mutant or--

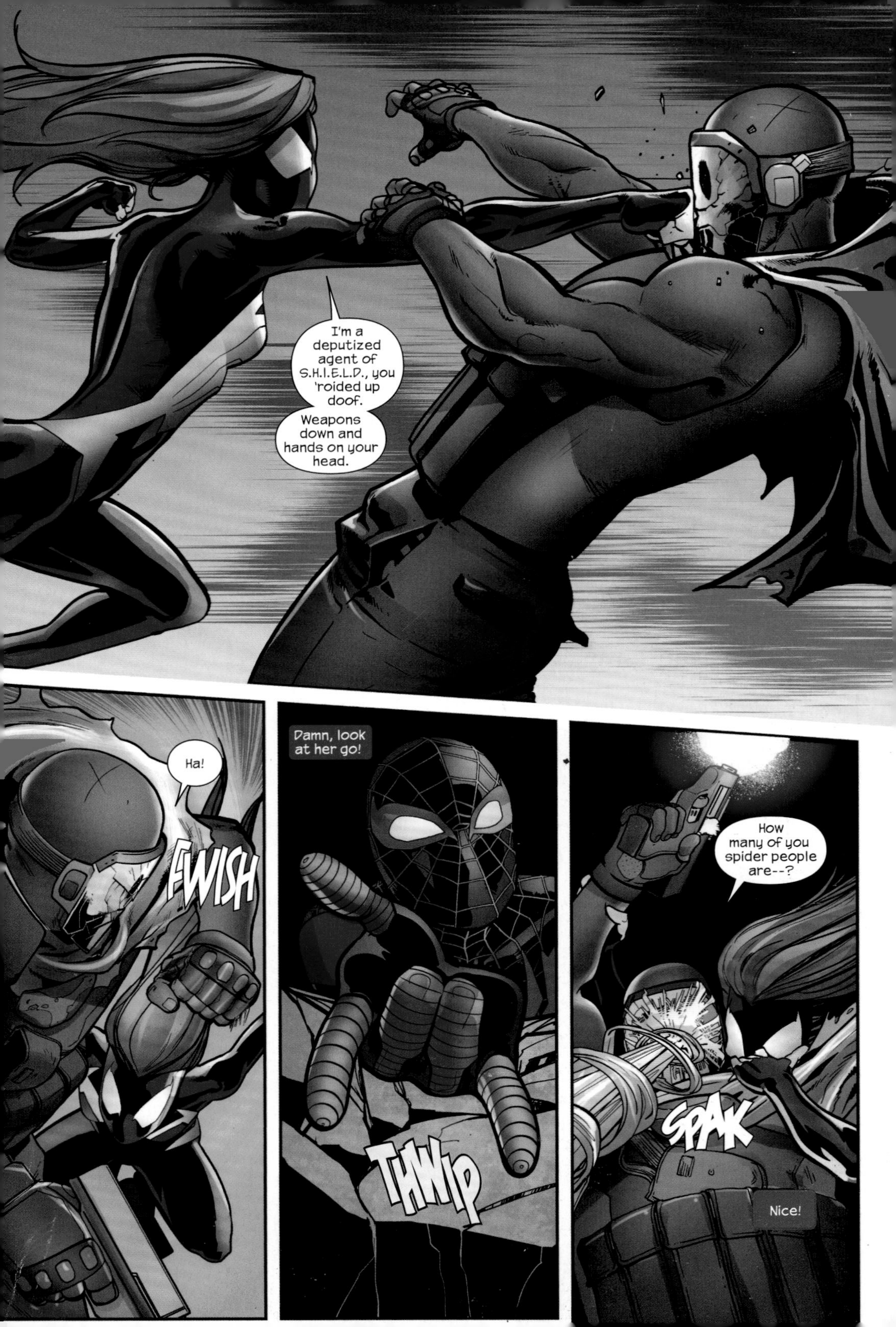
I'm a deputized agent of S.H.I.E.L.D., you 'roided up doof.
Weapons down and hands on your head.
Ha!
FWISH
Damn, look at her go!
THWIP
How many of you spider people are--?
SPAK
Nice!

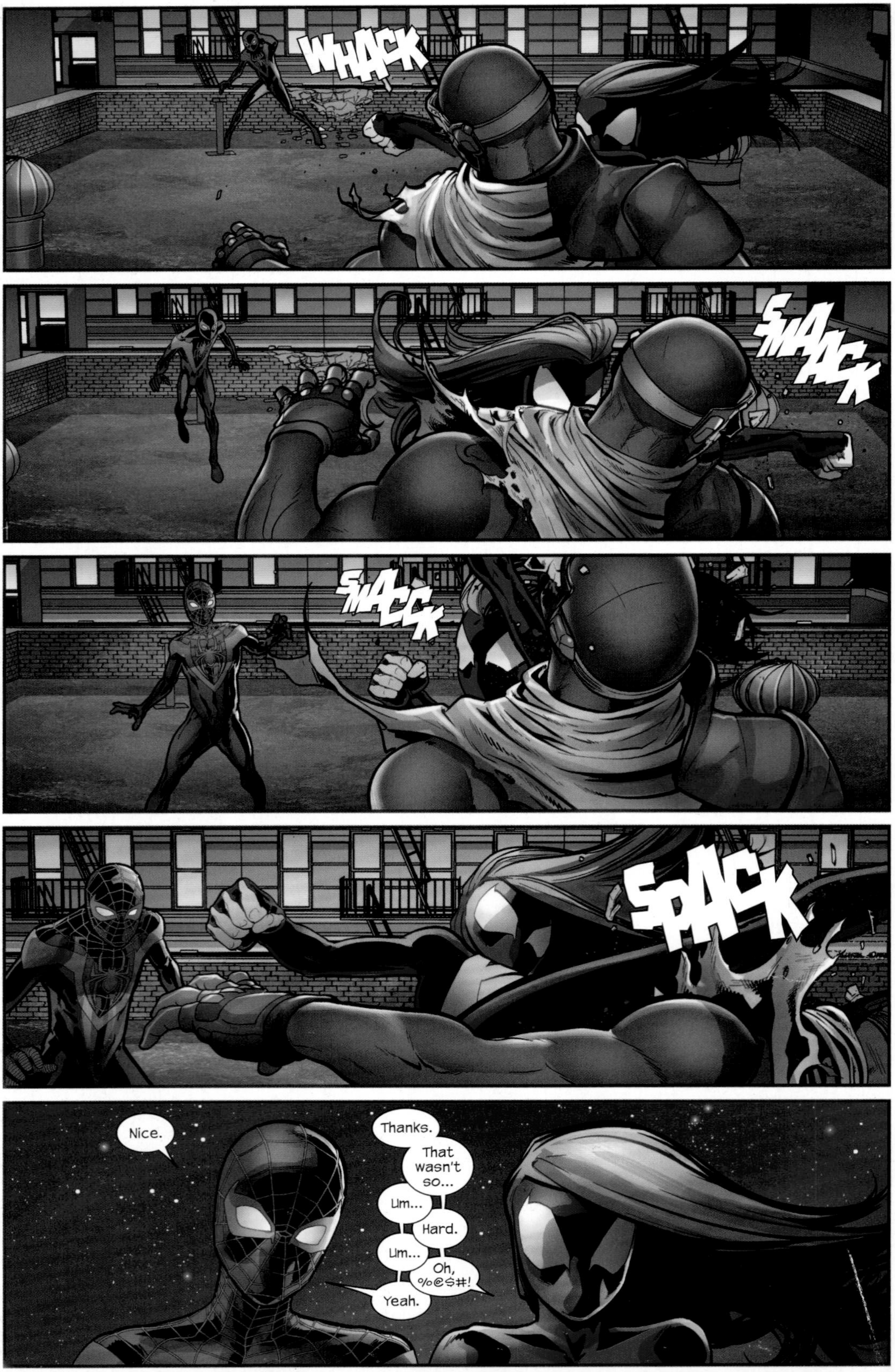
WHACK
SMACK
SMACK
SPACK
Nice.
Thanks.
That wasn't so...
Um...
Hard.
Um...
Oh, %@$#!
Yeah.

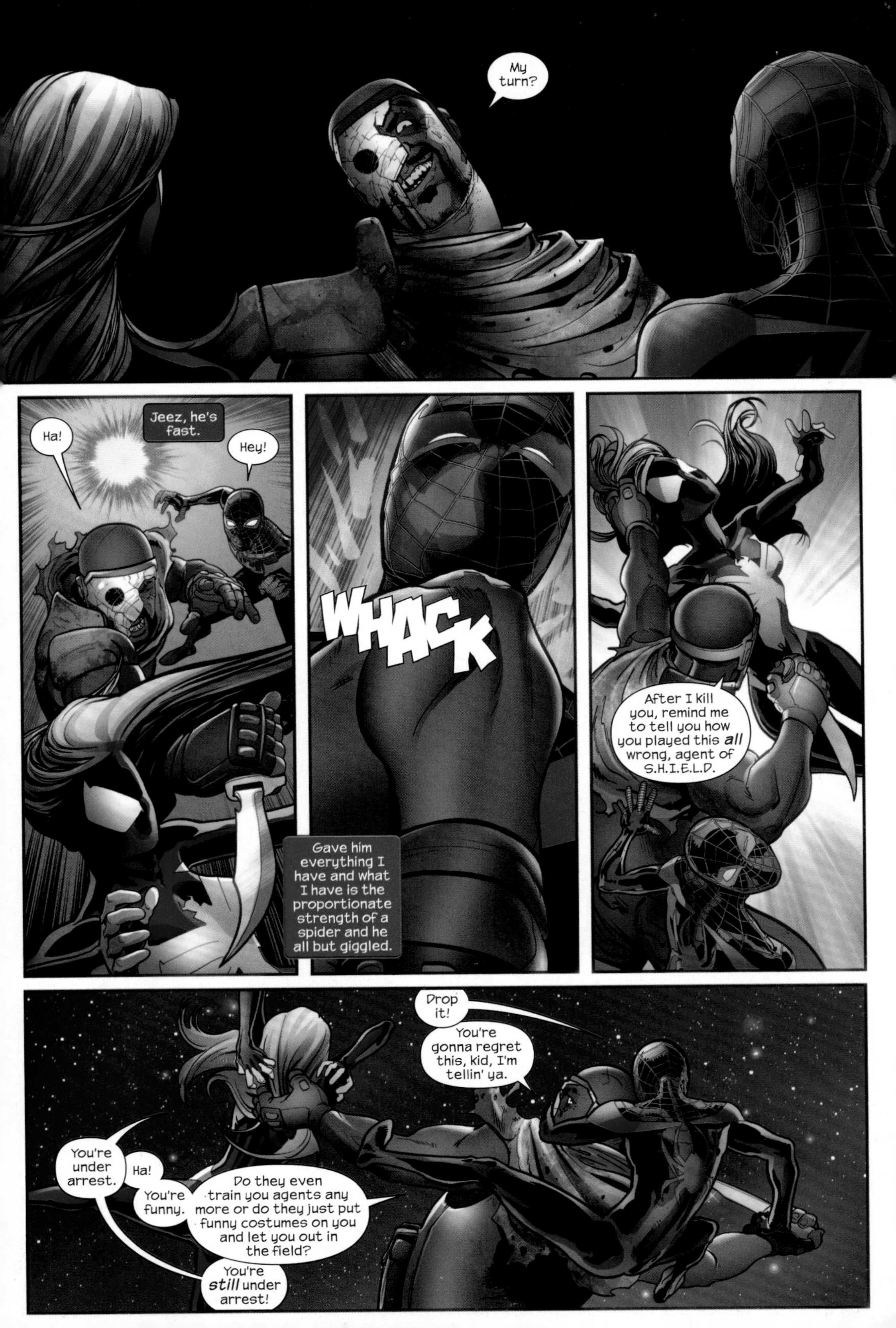
My turn?
Ha!
Jeez, he's fast.
Hey!
WHACK
Gave him everything I have and what I have is the proportionate strength of a spider and he all but giggled.
After I kill you, remind me to tell you how you played this all wrong, agent of S.H.I.E.L.D.
Drop it!
You're gonna regret this, kid, I'm tellin' ya.
You're under arrest.
Ha!
You're funny.
Do they even train you agents any more or do they just put funny costumes on you and let you out in the field?
You're still under arrest!

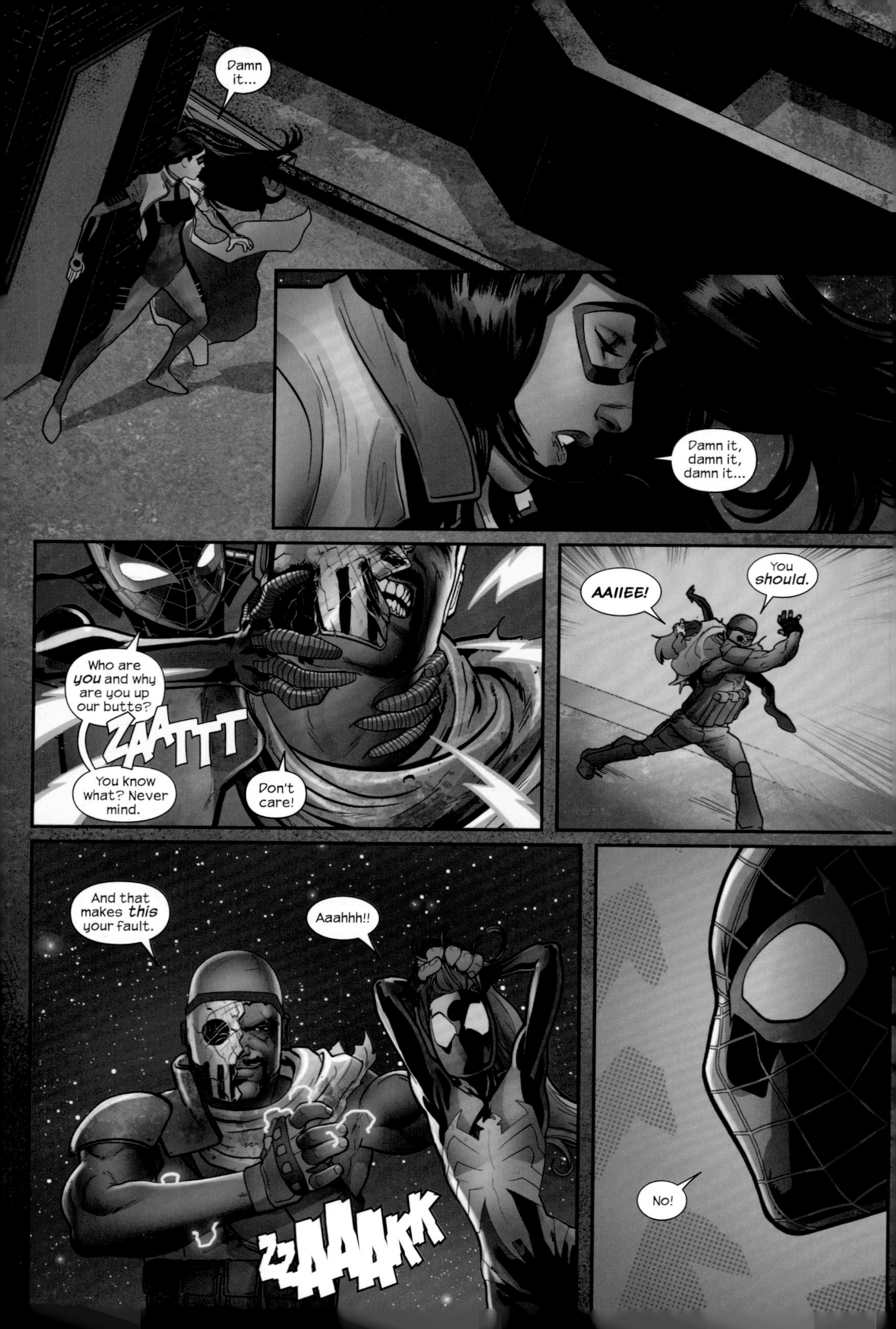

Damn it...
Damn it, damn it, damn it...
Who are *you* and why are you up our butts?
ZAATTT
You know what? Never mind.
Don't care!
AAIIEE!
You *should.*
And that makes *this* your fault.
Aaahhh!!
ZZAAAKK
No!

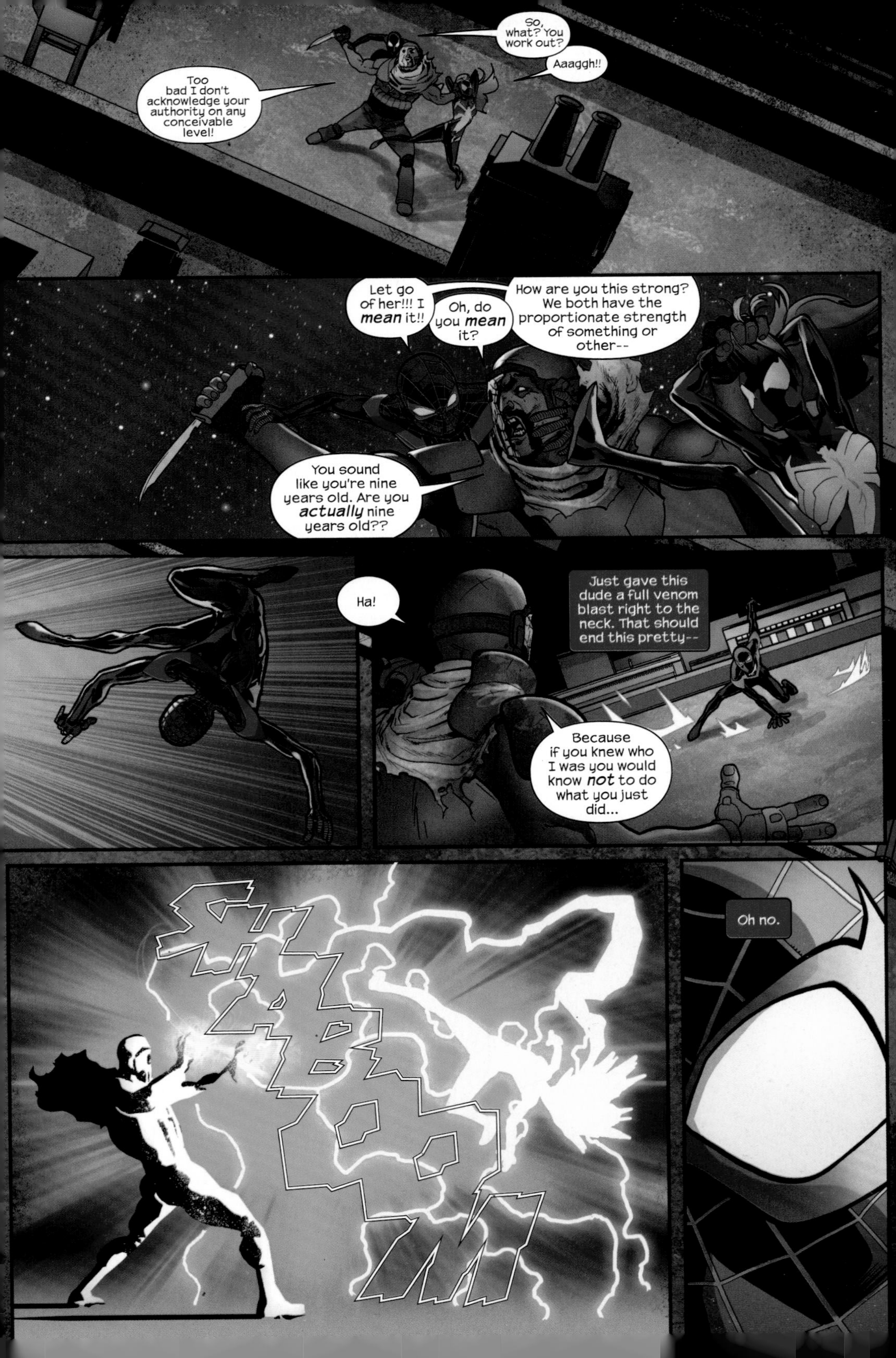

Too bad I don't acknowledge your authority on any conceivable level!
So, what? You work out?
Aaaggh!!
Let go of her!!! I *mean* it!!
Oh, do you *mean* it?
How are you this strong? We both have the proportionate strength of something or other--
You sound like you're nine years old. Are you *actually* nine years old??
Ha!
Just gave this dude a full venom blast right to the neck. That should end this pretty--
Because if you knew who I was you would know *not* to do what you just did...
Oh no.

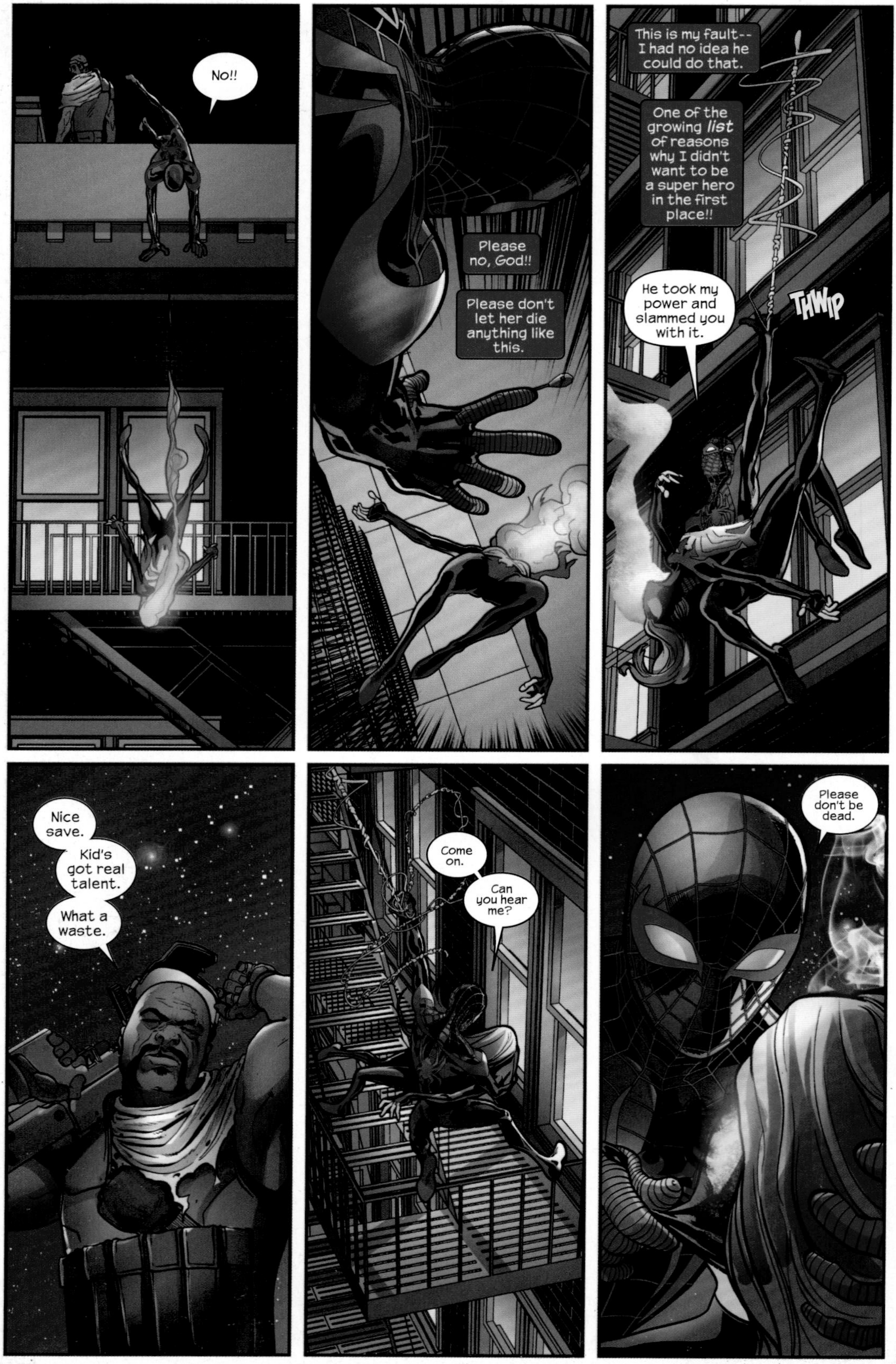
No!!
Please no, God!!
Please don't let her die anything like this.
This is my fault-- I had no idea he could do that.
One of the growing *list* of reasons why I didn't want to be a super hero in the first place!!
He took my power and slammed you with it.
THWIP
Nice save.
Kid's got real talent.
What a waste.
Come on.
Can you hear me?
Please don't be dead.

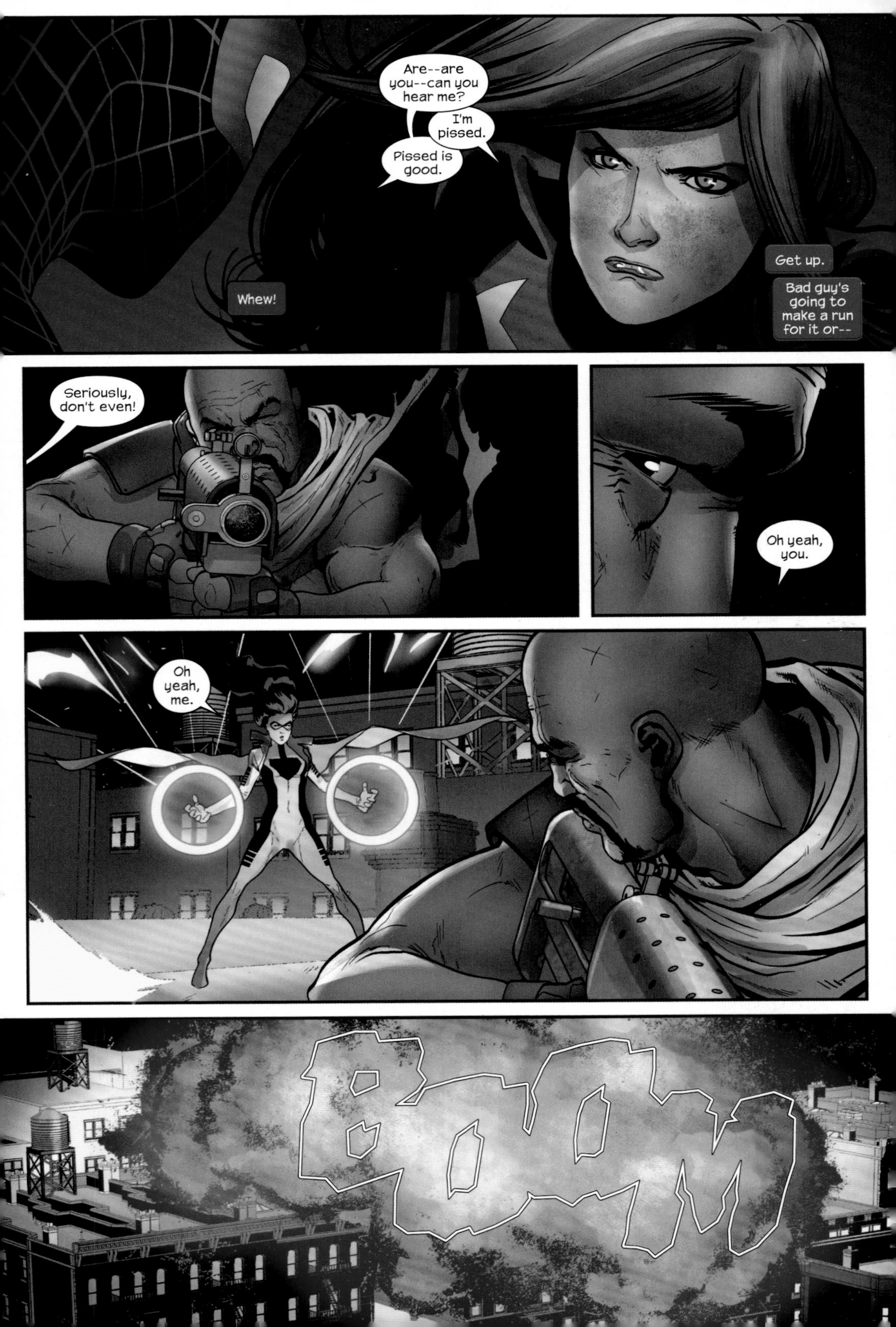
Are--are you--can you hear me?
I'm pissed.
Pissed is good.
Whew!
Get up.
Bad guy's going to make a run for it or--
Seriously, don't even!
Oh yeah, you.
Oh yeah, me.
BOOM

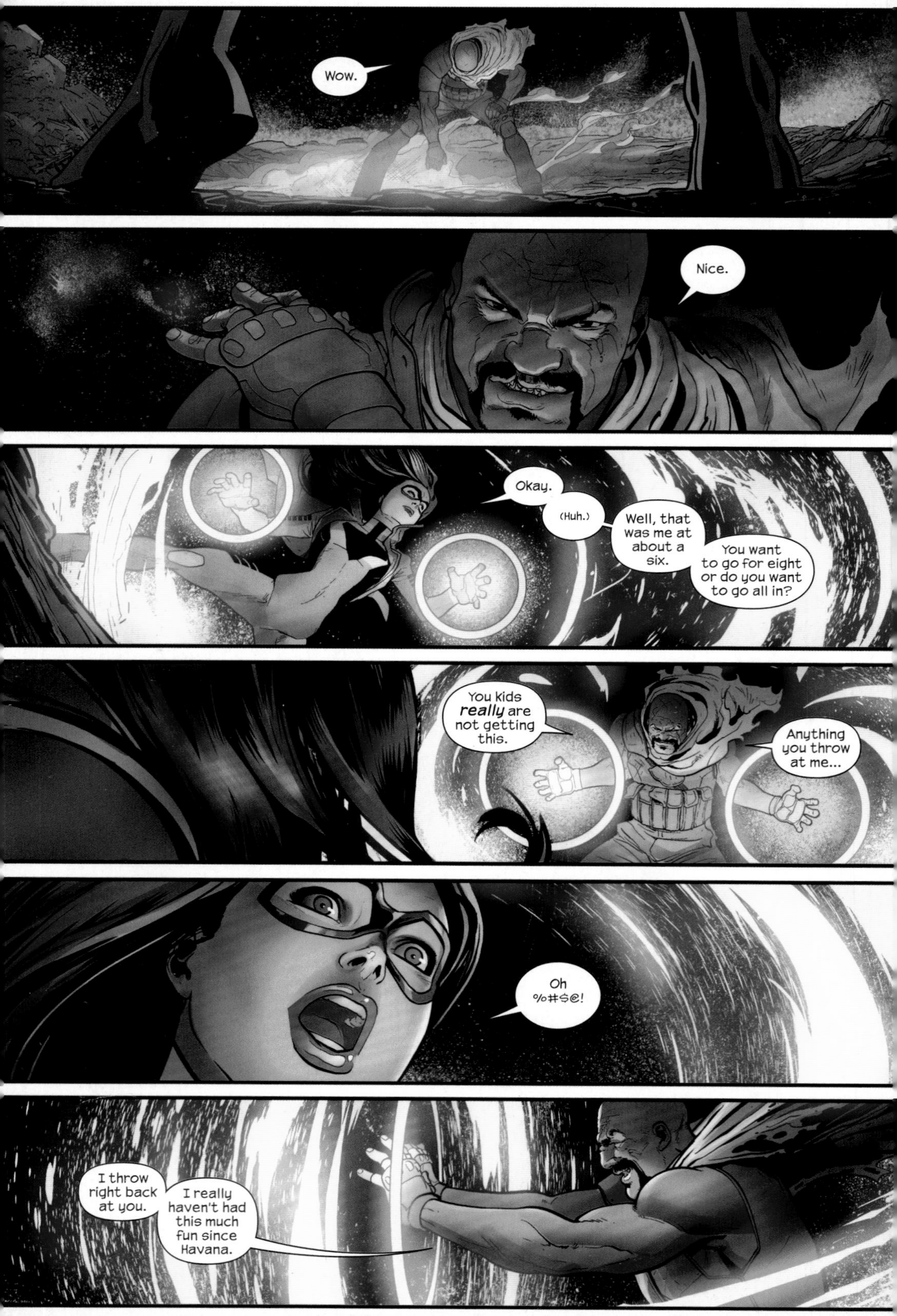
Wow.
Nice.
Okay.
(Huh.)
Well, that was me at about a six.
You want to go for eight or do you want to go all in?
You kids *really* are not getting this.
Anything you throw at me...
Oh %#$@!
I throw right back at you.
I really haven't had this much fun since Havana.

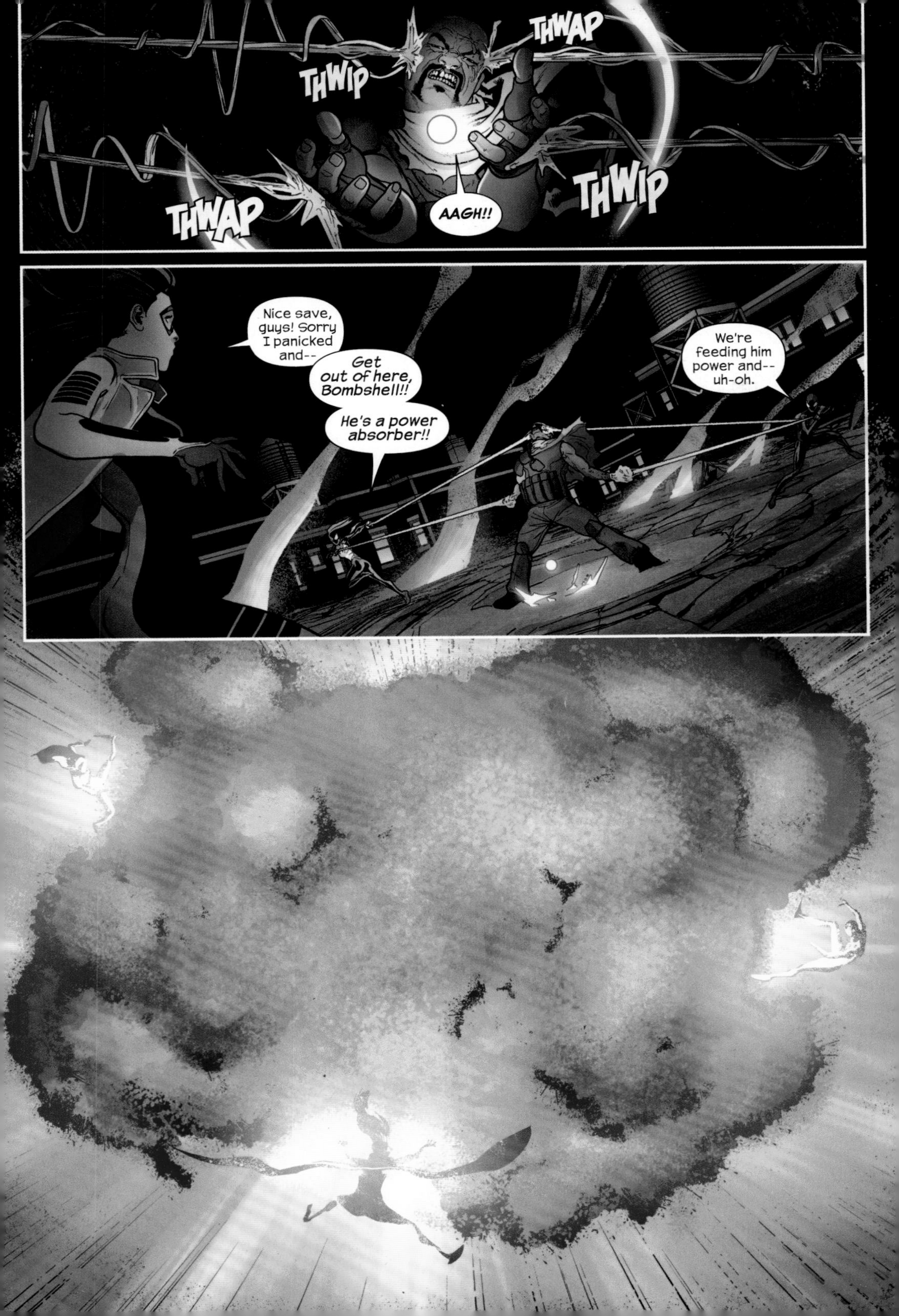
THWIP
THWAP
THWAP
THWIP
AAGH!!
Nice save, guys! Sorry I panicked and--
Get out of here, Bombshell!!
He's a power absorber!!
We're feeding him power and-- uh-oh.

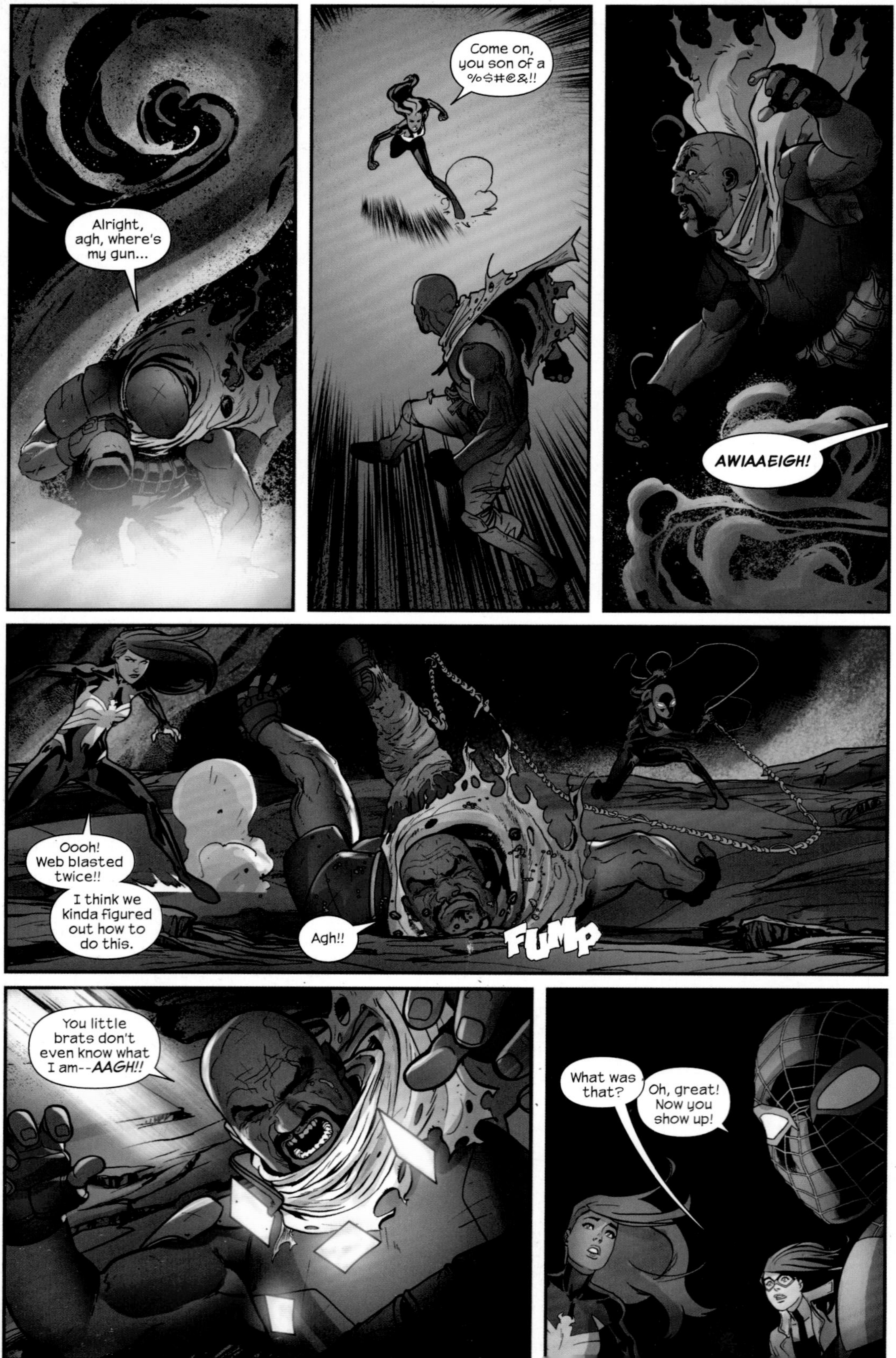

Alright, agh, where's my gun...
Come on, you son of a %$#@&!!
AWIAAEIGH!
Oooh! Web blasted twice!!
I think we kinda figured out how to do this.
Agh!!
FUMP
You little brats don't even know what I am--AAGH!!
What was that?
Oh, great! Now you show up!

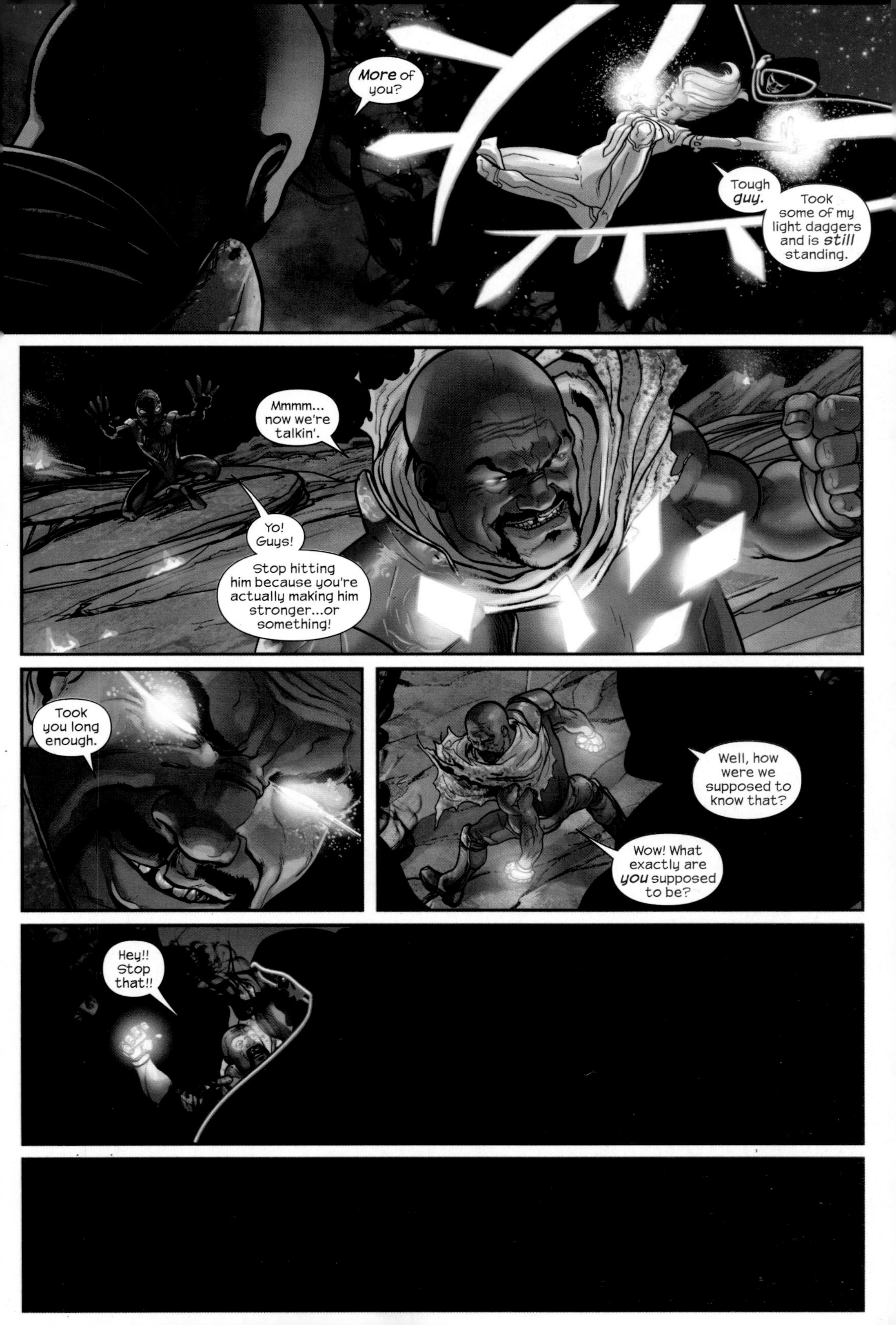
More of you?
Tough guy.
Took some of my light daggers and is still standing.
Mmmm... now we're talkin'.
Yo! Guys!
Stop hitting him because you're actually making him stronger...or something!
Took you long enough.
Well, how were we supposed to know that?
Wow! What exactly are you supposed to be?
Hey!! Stop that!!

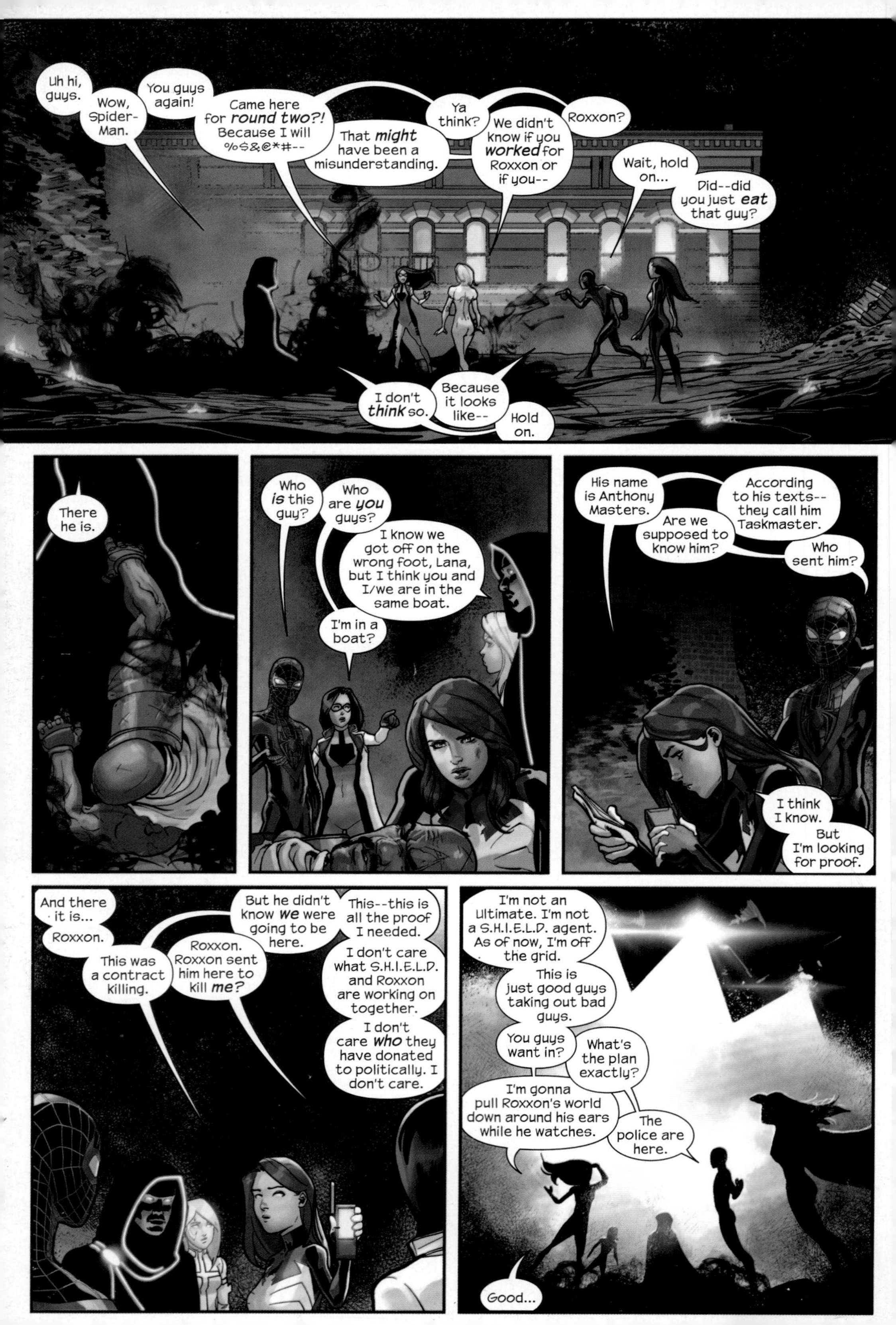

Uh hi, guys.
Wow, Spider-Man.
You guys again!
Came here for round two?! Because I will %$&@*#--
That might have been a misunderstanding.
Ya think?
We didn't know if you worked for Roxxon or if you--
Roxxon?
Wait, hold on...
Did--did you just eat that guy?
I don't think so.
Because it looks like--
Hold on.
There he is.
Who is this guy?
Who are you guys?
I know we got off on the wrong foot, Lana, but I think you and I/we are in the same boat.
I'm in a boat?
His name is Anthony Masters.
According to his texts-- they call him Taskmaster.
Are we supposed to know him?
Who sent him?
I think I know.
But I'm looking for proof.
And there it is...
Roxxon.
This was a contract killing.
Roxxon. Roxxon sent him here to kill me?
But he didn't know we were going to be here.
This--this is all the proof I needed.
I don't care what S.H.I.E.L.D. and Roxxon are working on together.
I don't care who they have donated to politically. I don't care.
I'm not an Ultimate. I'm not a S.H.I.E.L.D. agent. As of now, I'm off the grid.
This is just good guys taking out bad guys.
You guys want in?
What's the plan exactly?
I'm gonna pull Roxxon's world down around his ears while he watches.
The police are here.
Good...

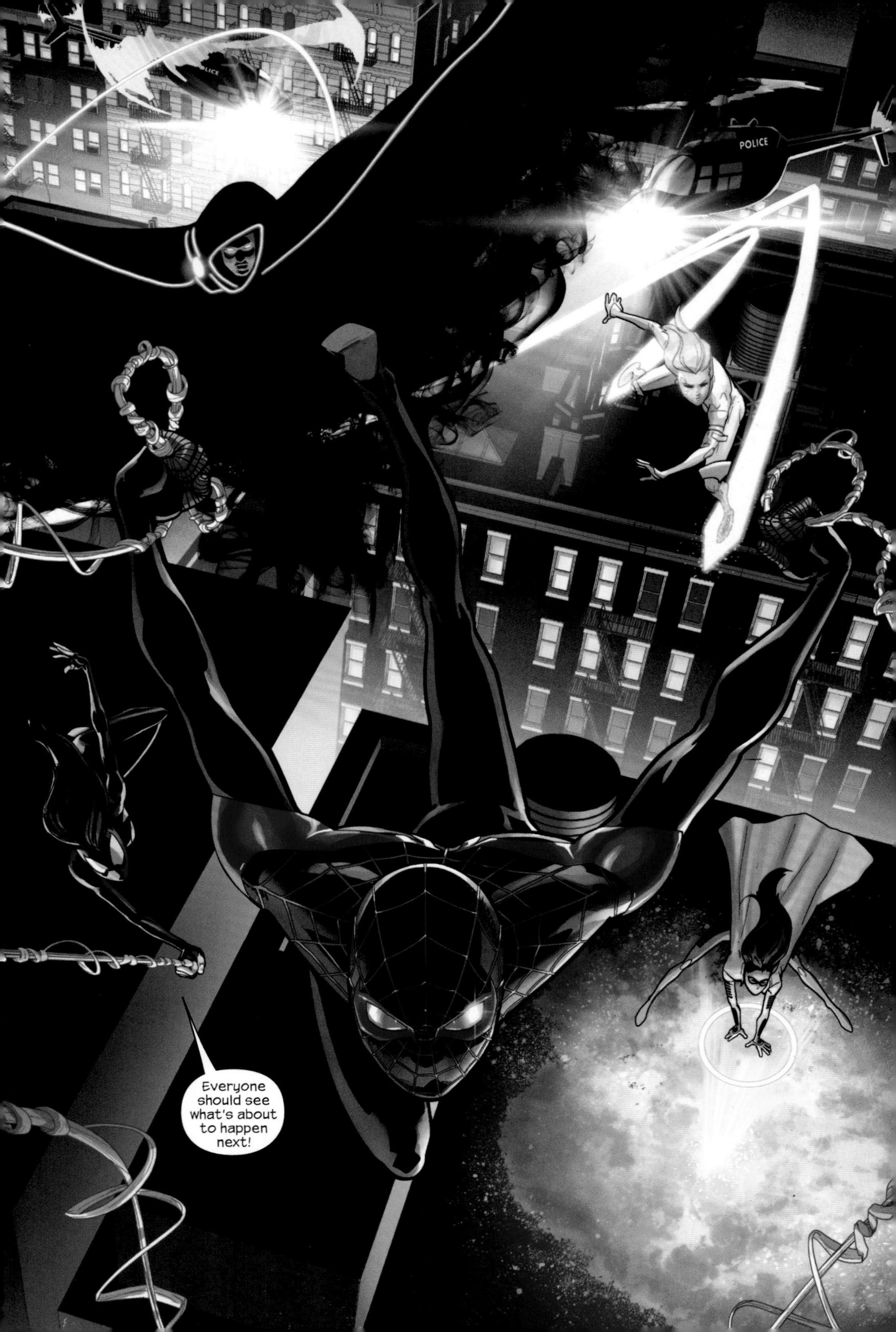
POLICE
POLICE
Everyone should see what's about to happen next!

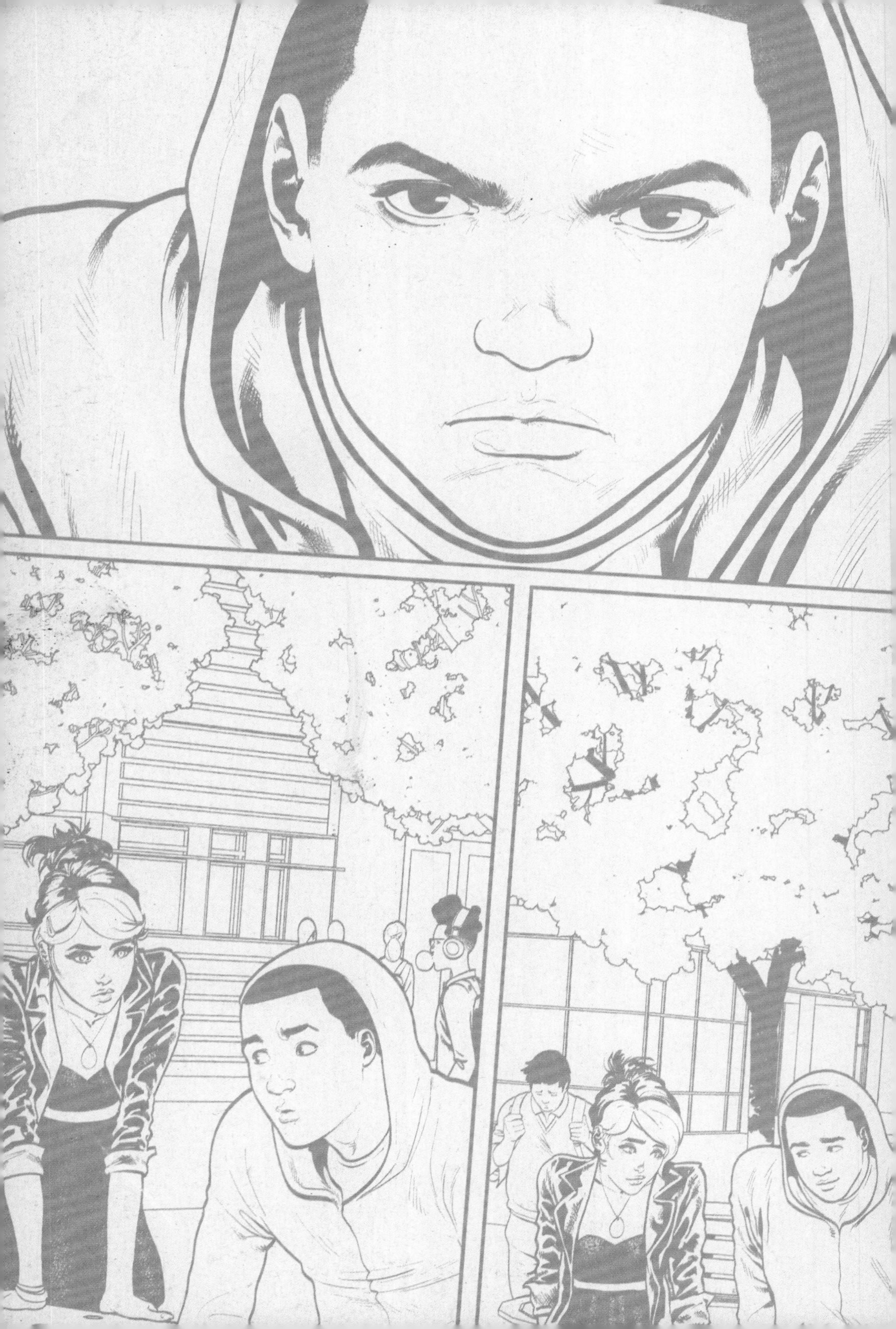

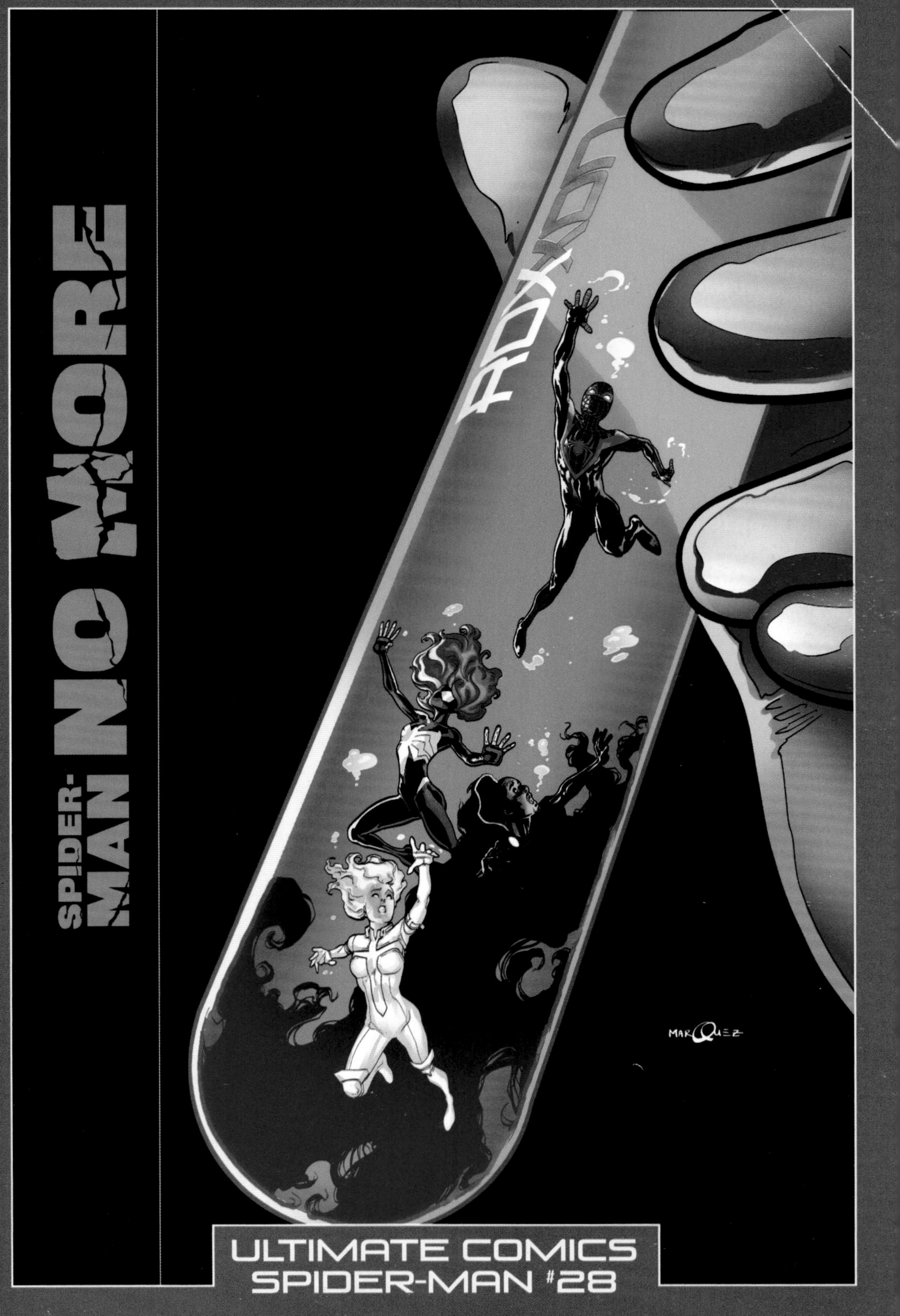
SPIDER-MAN NO MORE
MARQUEZ
ULTIMATE COMICS
SPIDER-MAN #28

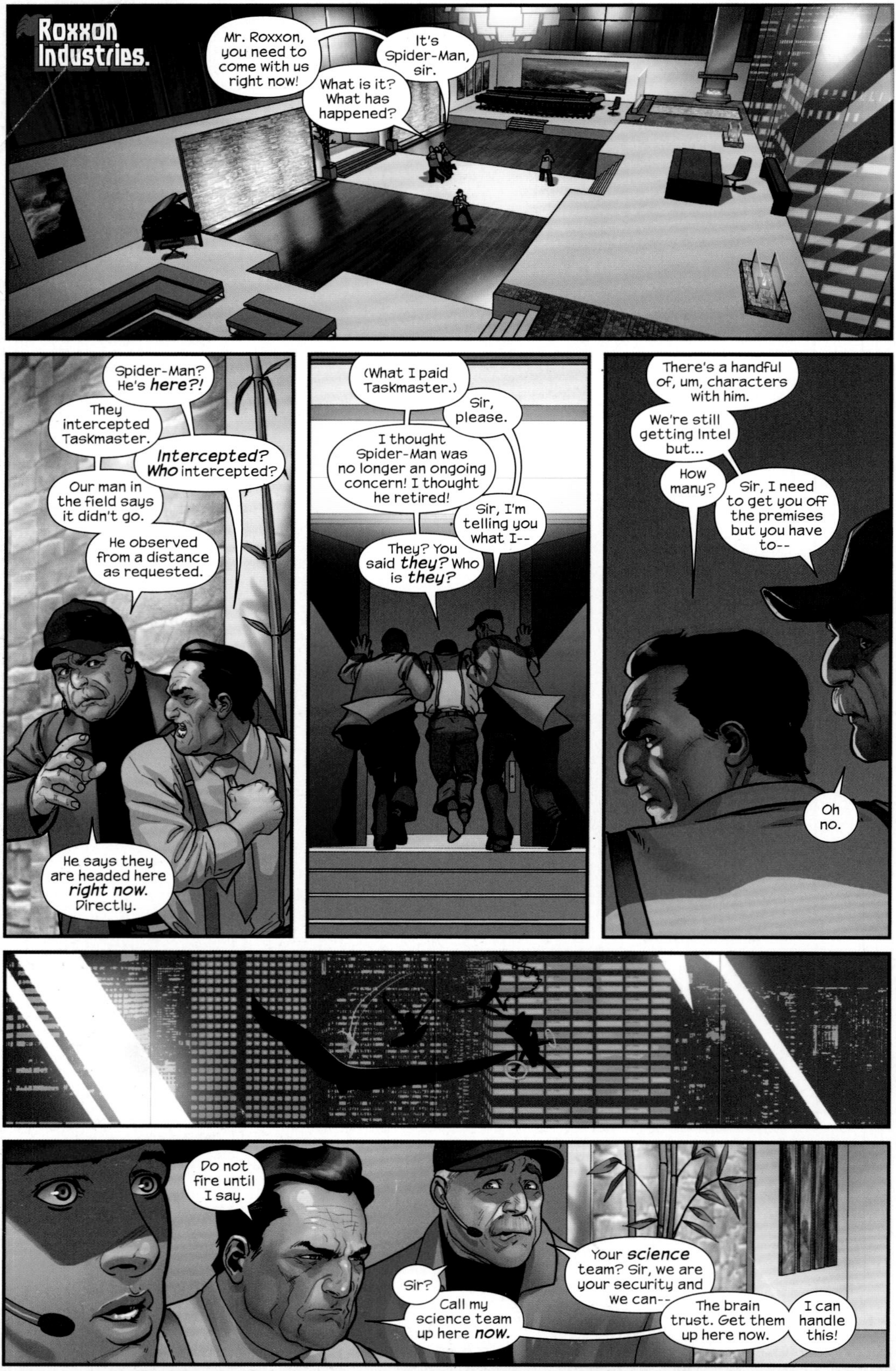
Roxxon Industries.
Mr. Roxxon, you need to come with us right now!
It's Spider-Man, sir.
What is it? What has happened?
Spider-Man? He's here?!
They intercepted Taskmaster.
Intercepted? Who intercepted?
Our man in the field says it didn't go.
He observed from a distance as requested.
He says they are headed here right now. Directly.
(What I paid Taskmaster.)
Sir, please.
I thought Spider-Man was no longer an ongoing concern! I thought he retired!
Sir, I'm telling you what I--
They? You said they? Who is they?
There's a handful of, um, characters with him.
We're still getting Intel but...
How many?
Sir, I need to get you off the premises but you have to--
Oh no.
Do not fire until I say.
Sir?
Call my science team up here now.
Your science team? Sir, we are your security and we can--
The brain trust. Get them up here now.
I can handle this!

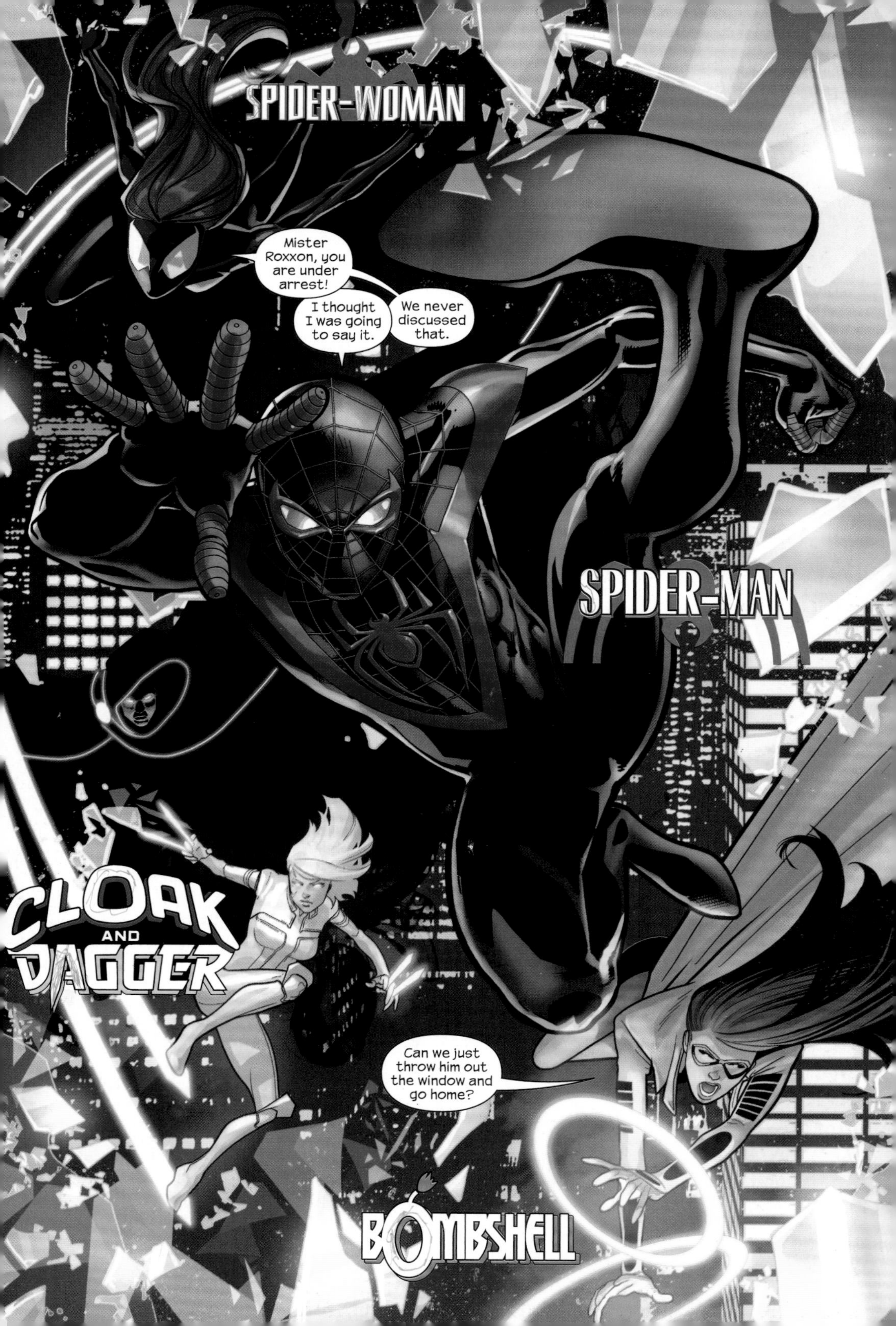
SPIDER-WOMAN
Mister Roxxon, you are under arrest!
I thought I was going to say it.
We never discussed that.
SPIDER-MAN
CLOAK AND DAGGER
Can we just throw him out the window and go home?
BOMBSHELL

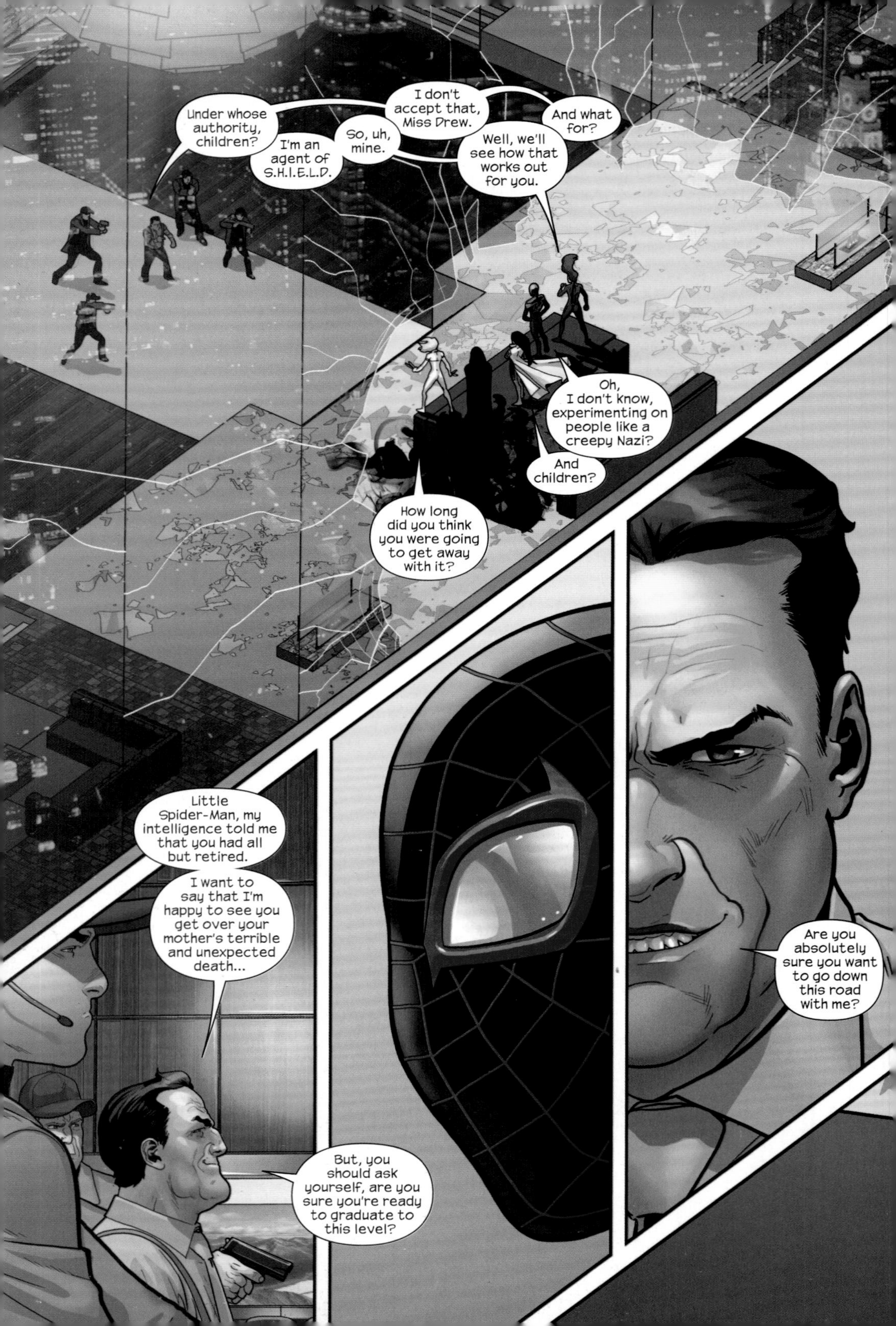
Under whose authority, children?
I'm an agent of S.H.I.E.L.D.
So, uh, mine.
I don't accept that, Miss Drew.
Well, we'll see how that works out for you.
And what for?
Oh, I don't know, experimenting on people like a creepy Nazi?
And children?
How long did you think you were going to get away with it?
Little Spider-Man, my intelligence told me that you had all but retired.
I want to say that I'm happy to see you get over your mother's terrible and unexpected death...
But, you should ask yourself, are you sure you're ready to graduate to this level?
Are you absolutely sure you want to go down this road with me?

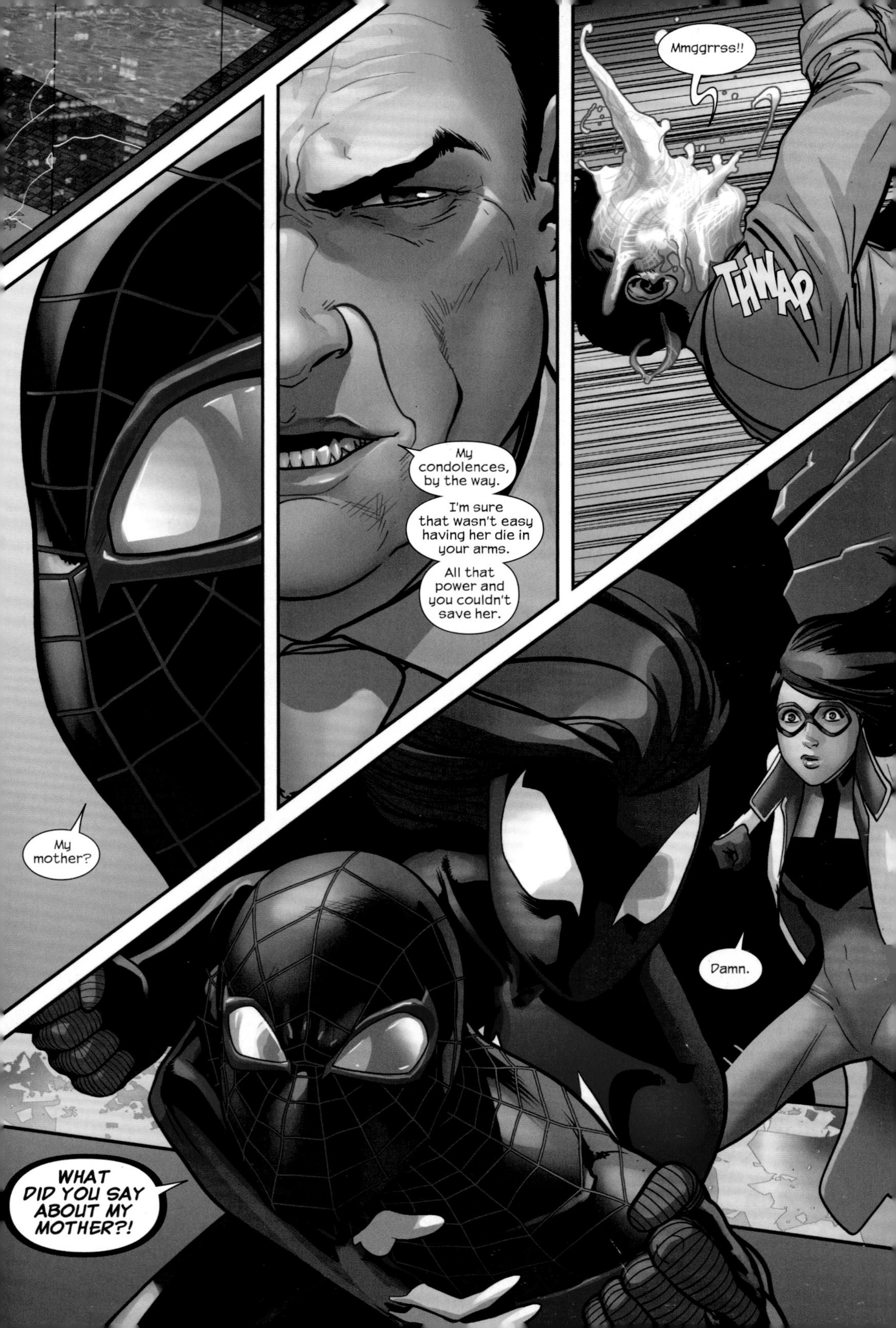
Mmggrrss!!
THWAP
My condolences, by the way.
I'm sure that wasn't easy having her die in your arms.
All that power and you couldn't save her.
My mother?
Damn.
WHAT DID YOU SAY ABOUT MY MOTHER?!

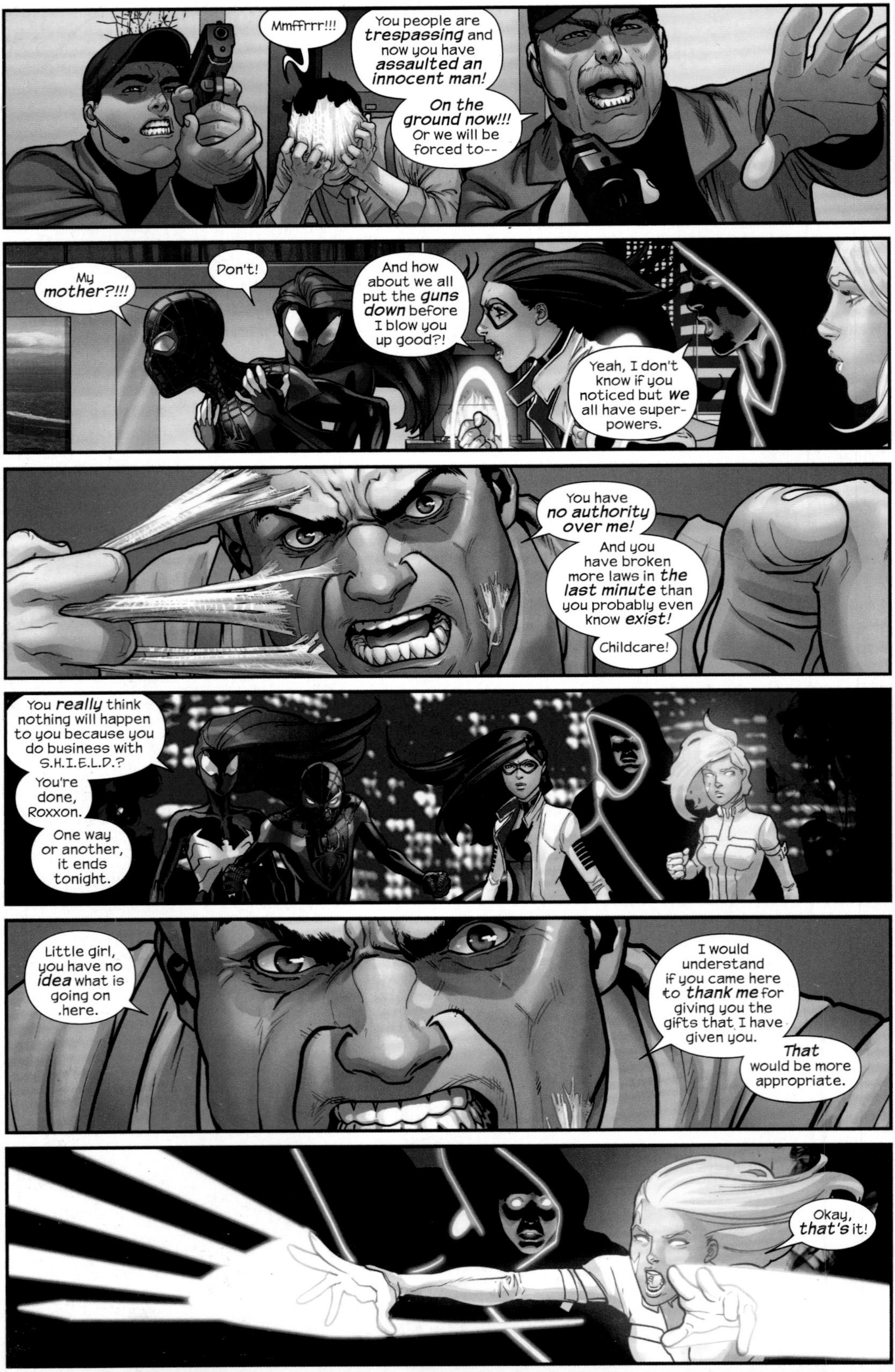
Mmffrrr!!!
You people are *trespassing* and now you have *assaulted an innocent man!*
On the ground now!!! Or we will be forced to--
My *mother?!!!*
Don't!
And how about we all put the *guns down* before I blow you up good?!
Yeah, I don't know if you noticed but *we* all have super-powers.
You have *no authority over me!*
And you have broken more laws in *the last minute* than you probably even know *exist!*
Childcare!
You *really* think nothing will happen to you because you do business with S.H.I.E.L.D.?
You're done, Roxxon.
One way or another, it ends tonight.
Little girl, you have no *idea* what is going on .here.
I would understand if you came here to *thank me* for giving you the gifts that I have given you.
That would be more appropriate.
Okay, *that's* it!

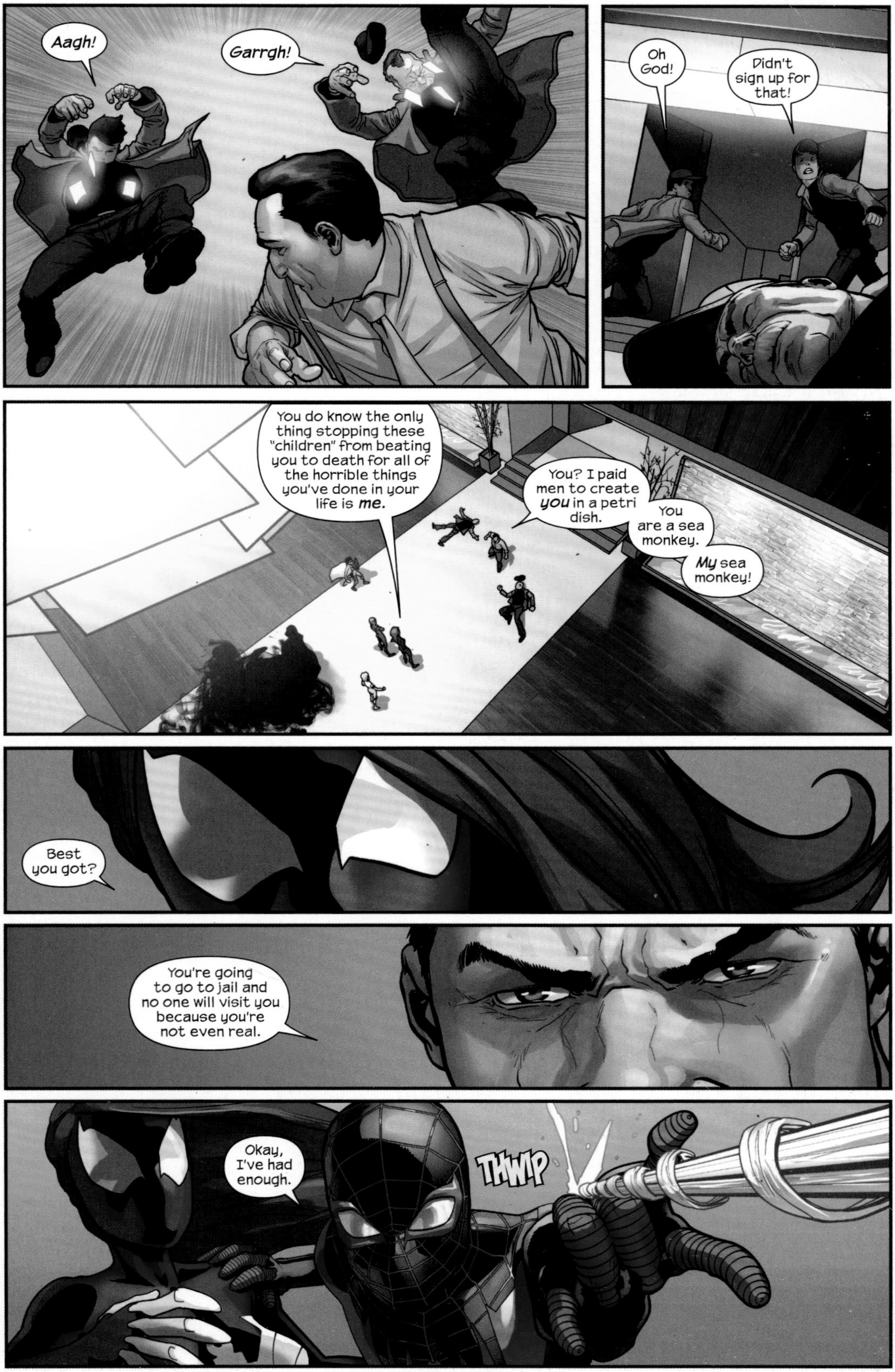
Aagh!
Garrgh!
Oh God!
Didn't sign up for that!
You do know the only thing stopping these "children" from beating you to death for all of the horrible things you've done in your life is *me.*
You? I paid men to create *you* in a petri dish.
You are a sea monkey.
My sea monkey!
Best you got?
You're going to go to jail and no one will visit you because you're not even real.
Okay, I've had enough.
THWIP

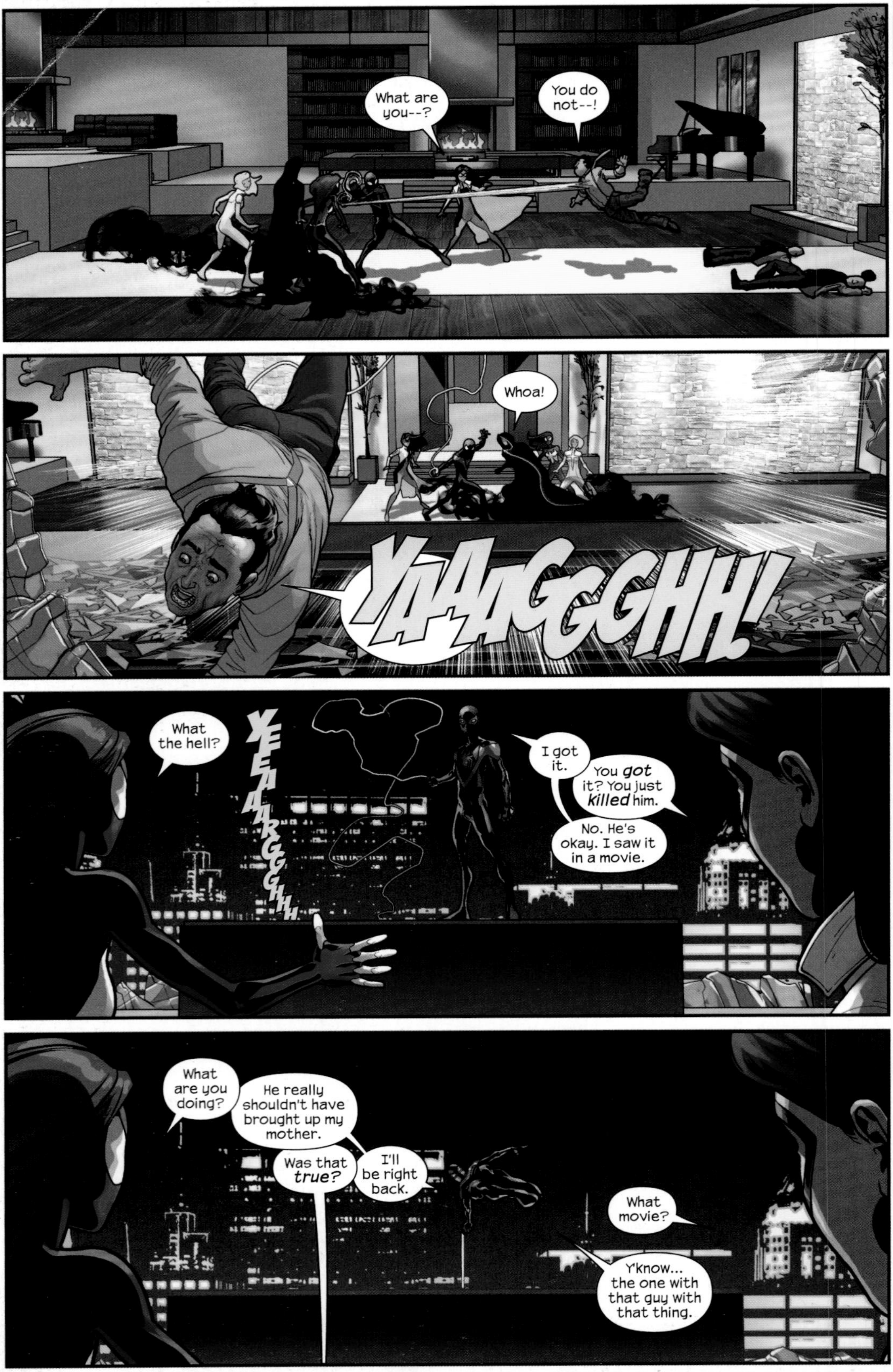
What are you--?
You do not--!
Whoa!
YAAAGGGHH!
What the hell?
YEAAARGGGHHH
I got it.
You *got* it? You just *killed* him.
No. He's okay. I saw it in a movie.
What are you doing?
He really shouldn't have brought up my mother.
Was that *true*?
I'll be right back.
What movie?
Y'know... the one with that guy with that thing.

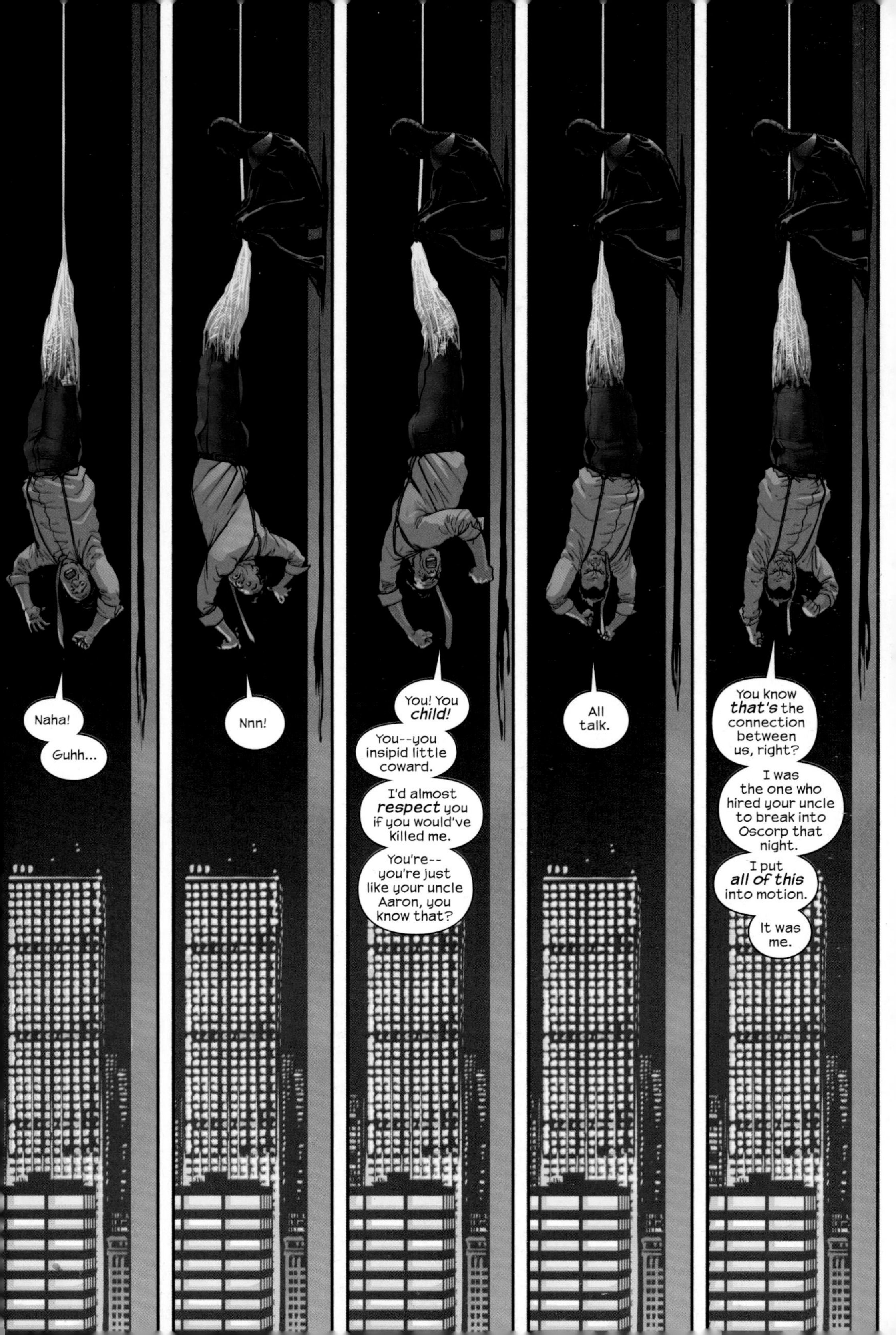
Naha!
Guhh...
Nnn!
You! You child!
You--you insipid little coward.
I'd almost respect you if you would've killed me.
You're--you're just like your uncle Aaron, you know that?
All talk.
You know that's the connection between us, right?
I was the one who hired your uncle to break into Oscorp that night.
I put all of this into motion.
It was me.

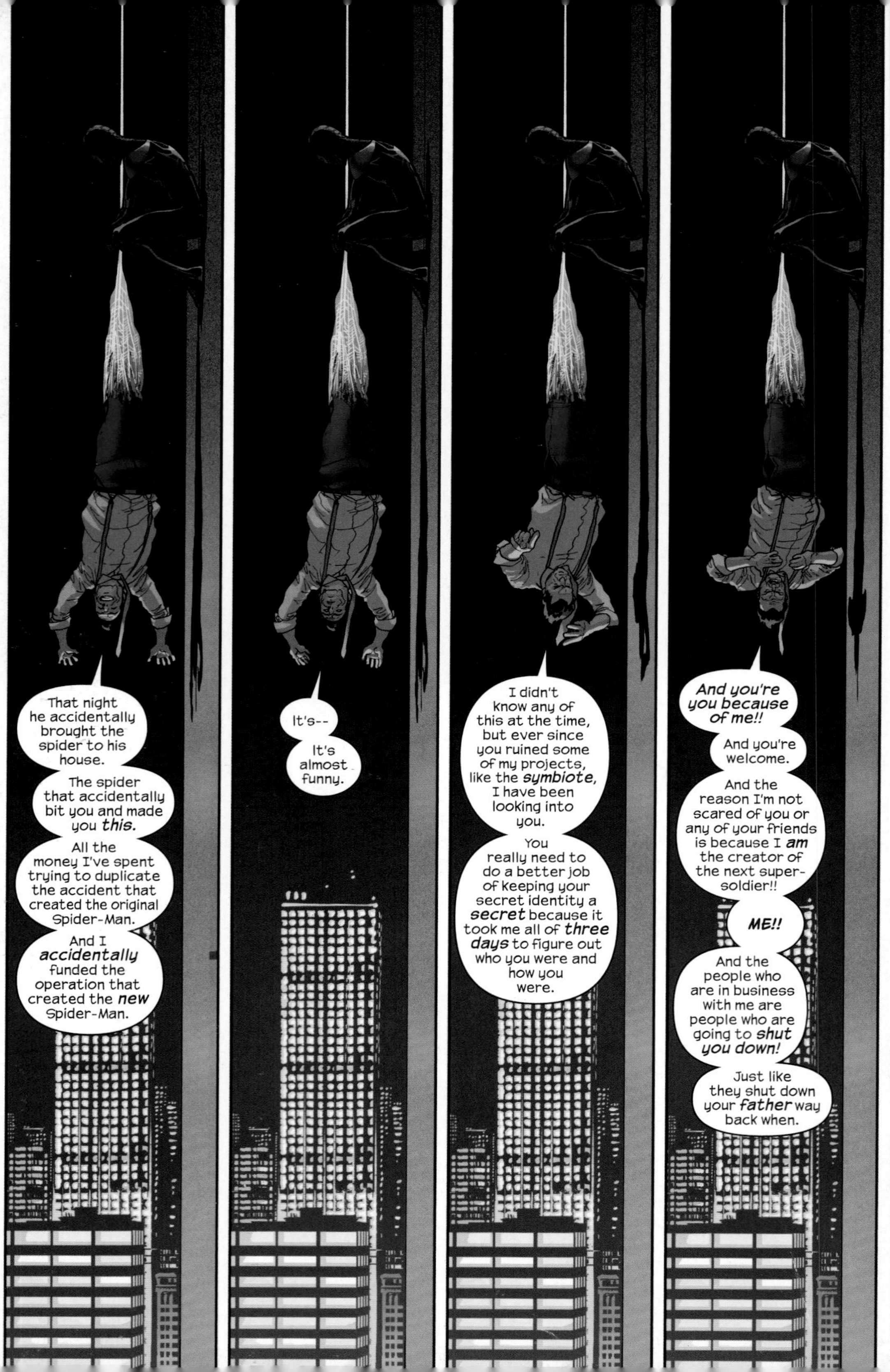

That night he accidentally brought the spider to his house.
The spider that accidentally bit you and made you *this.*
All the money I've spent trying to duplicate the accident that created the original Spider-Man.
And I *accidentally* funded the operation that created the *new* Spider-Man.
It's--
It's almost funny.
I didn't know any of this at the time, but ever since you ruined some of my projects, like the *symbiote*, I have been looking into you.
You really need to do a better job of keeping your secret identity a *secret* because it took me all of *three days* to figure out who you were and how you were.
And you're you because of me!!
And you're welcome.
And the reason I'm not scared of you or any of your friends is because I *am* the creator of the next super-soldier!!
ME!!
And the people who are in business with me are people who are going to *shut you down!*
Just like they shut down your *father* way back when.

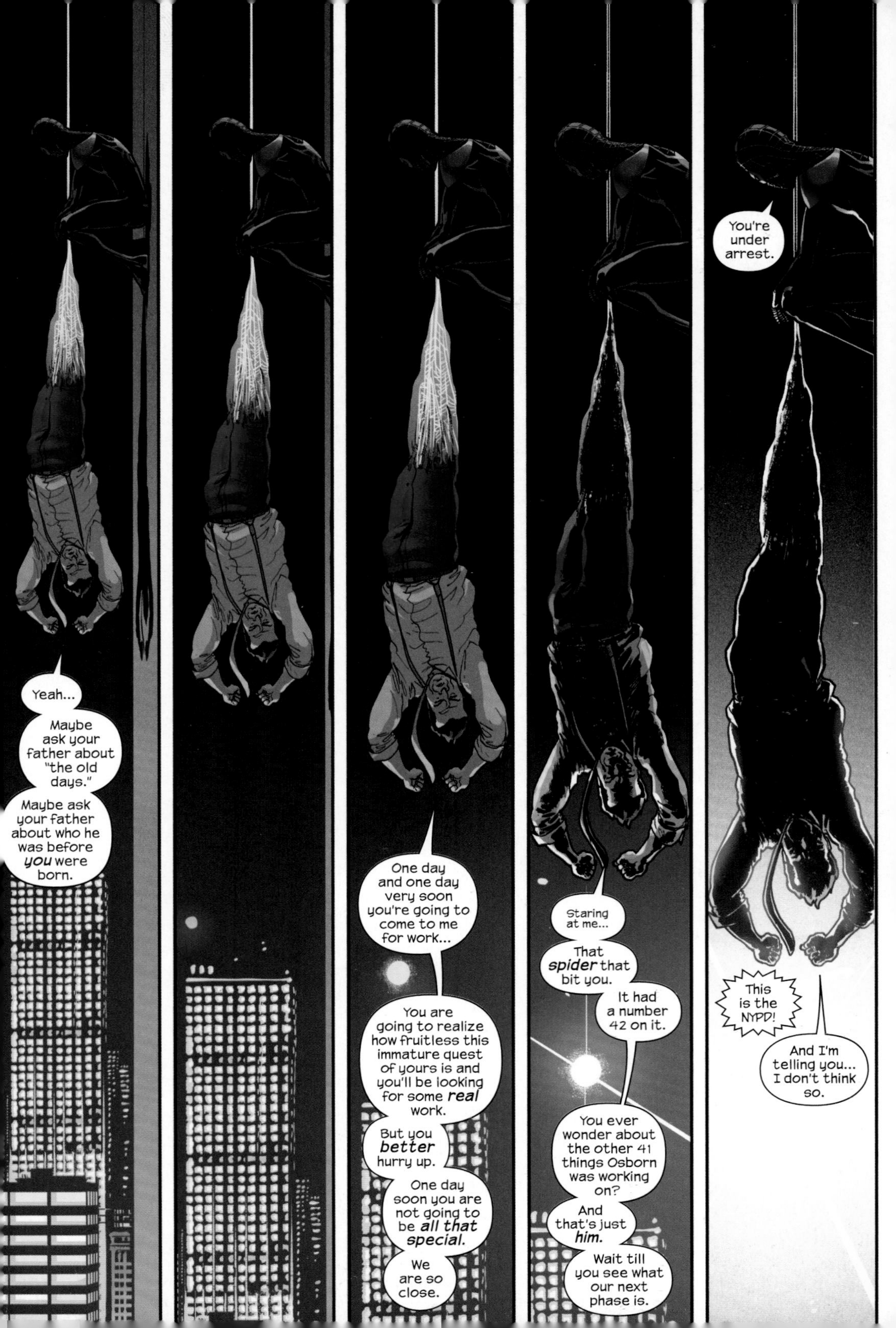
Yeah...
Maybe ask your father about "the old days."
Maybe ask your father about who he was before *you* were born.
One day and one day very soon you're going to come to me for work...
You are going to realize how fruitless this immature quest of yours is and you'll be looking for some *real* work.
But you *better* hurry up.
One day soon you are not going to be *all that special*.
We are so close.
Staring at me...
That *spider* that bit you.
It had a number 42 on it.
You ever wonder about the other 41 things Osborn was working on?
And that's just *him*.
Wait till you see what our next phase is.
You're under arrest.
This is the NYPD!
And I'm telling you... I don't think so.

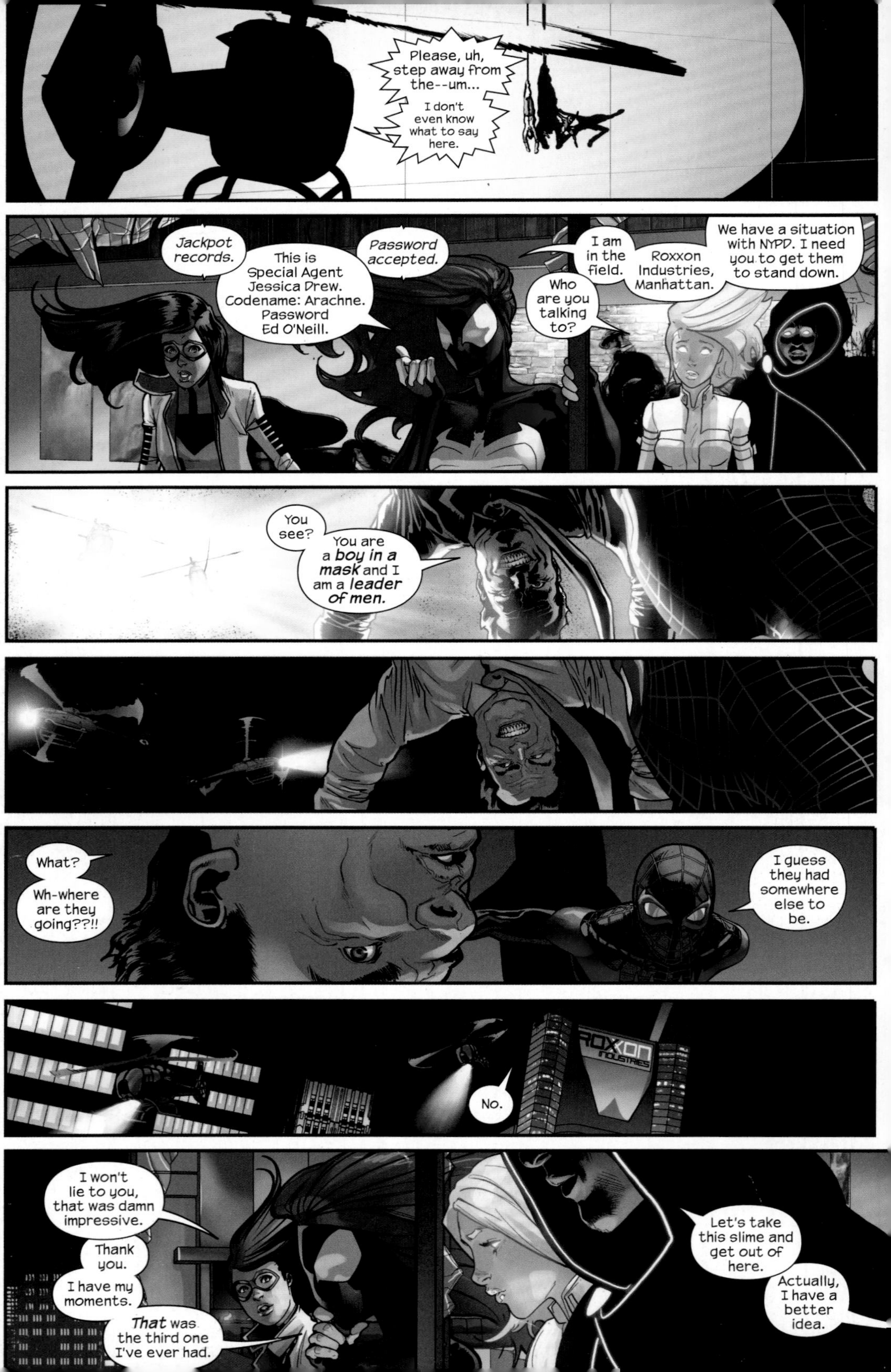
Please, uh, step away from the--um...
I don't even know what to say here.
Jackpot records.
This is Special Agent Jessica Drew. Codename: Arachne. Password Ed O'Neill.
Password accepted.
I am in the field.
Who are you talking to?
Roxxon Industries, Manhattan.
We have a situation with NYPD. I need you to get them to stand down.
You see?
You are a ***boy in a mask*** and I am a ***leader of men.***
What?
Wh-where are they going??!!
I guess they had somewhere else to be.
ROXXON INDUSTRIES
No.
I won't lie to you, that was damn impressive.
Thank you.
I have my moments.
That was the third one I've ever had.
Let's take this slime and get out of here.
Actually, I have a better idea.

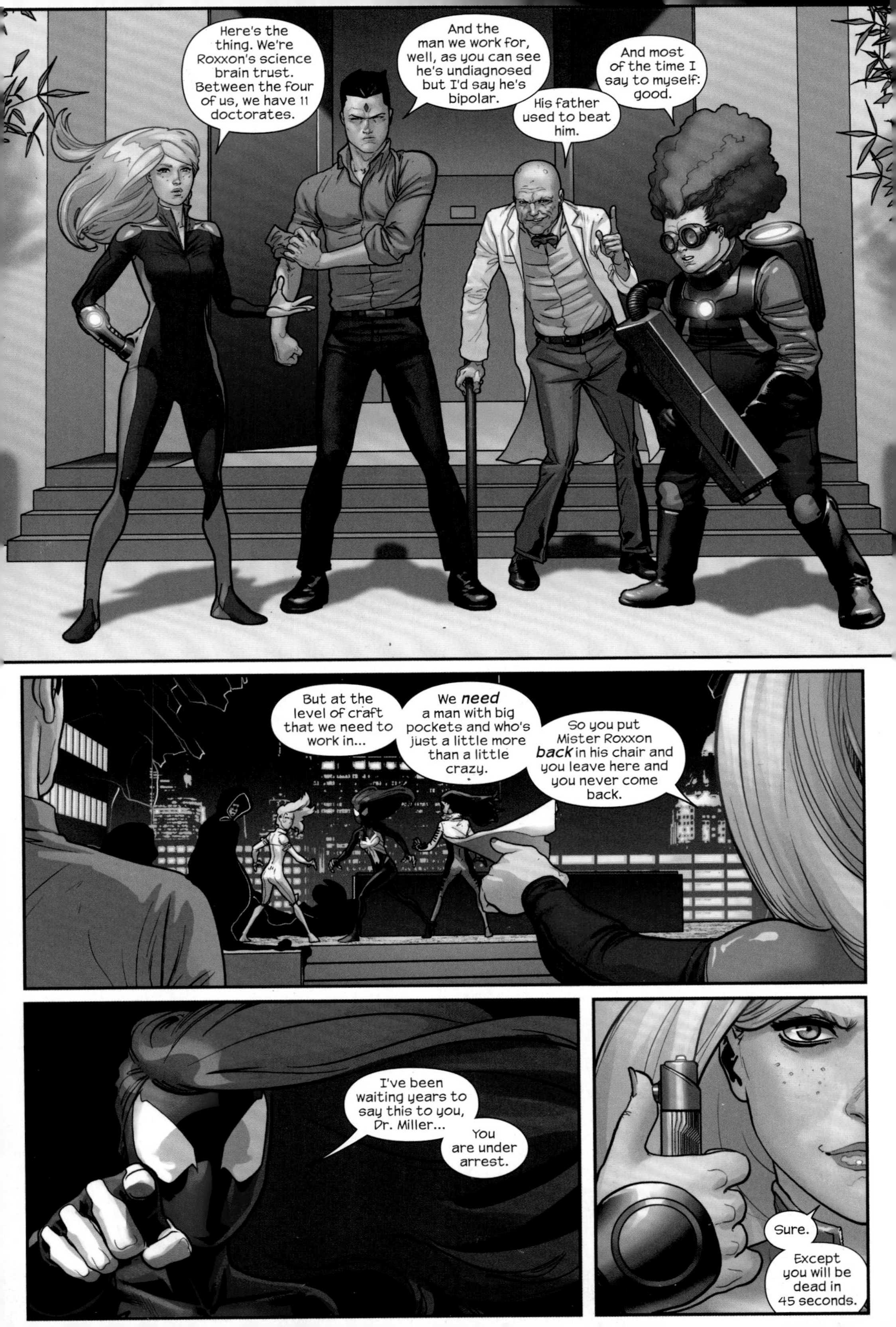
Here's the thing. We're Roxxon's science brain trust. Between the four of us, we have 11 doctorates.
And the man we work for, well, as you can see he's undiagnosed but I'd say he's bipolar.
His father used to beat him.
And most of the time I say to myself: good.
But at the level of craft that we need to work in...
We *need* a man with big pockets and who's just a little more than a little crazy.
So you put Mister Roxxon *back* in his chair and you leave here and you never come back.
I've been waiting years to say this to you, Dr. Miller...
You are under arrest.
Sure.
Except you will be dead in 45 seconds.

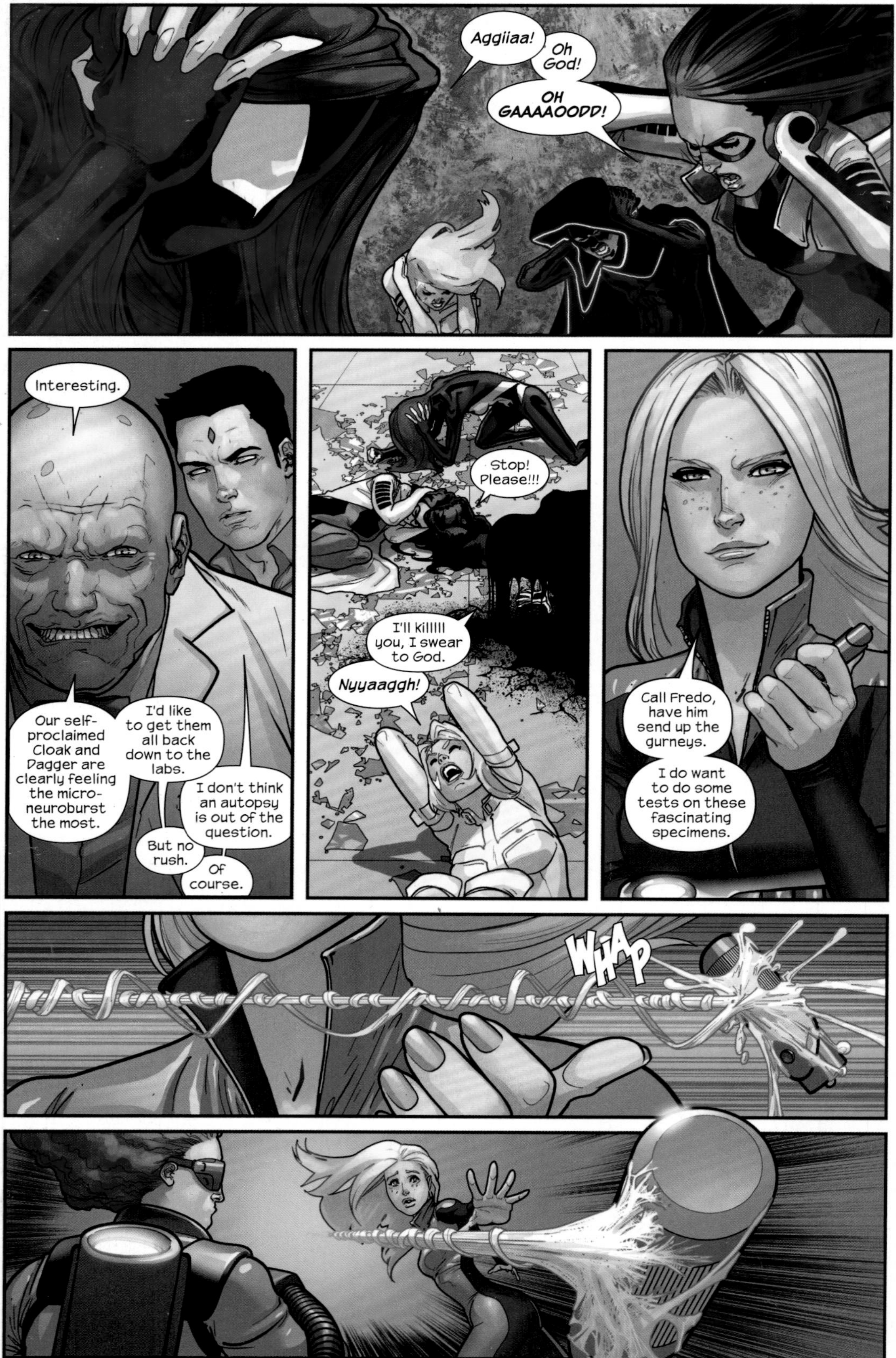

Aggiiaa!
Oh God!
OH GAAAAOODD!
Interesting.
Our self-proclaimed Cloak and Dagger are clearly feeling the micro-neuroburst the most.
I'd like to get them all back down to the labs.
But no rush.
I don't think an autopsy is out of the question.
Of course.
Stop! Please!!!
I'll kilIIII you, I swear to God.
Nyyaaggh!
Call Fredo, have him send up the gurneys.
I do want to do some tests on these fascinating specimens.
WHAP

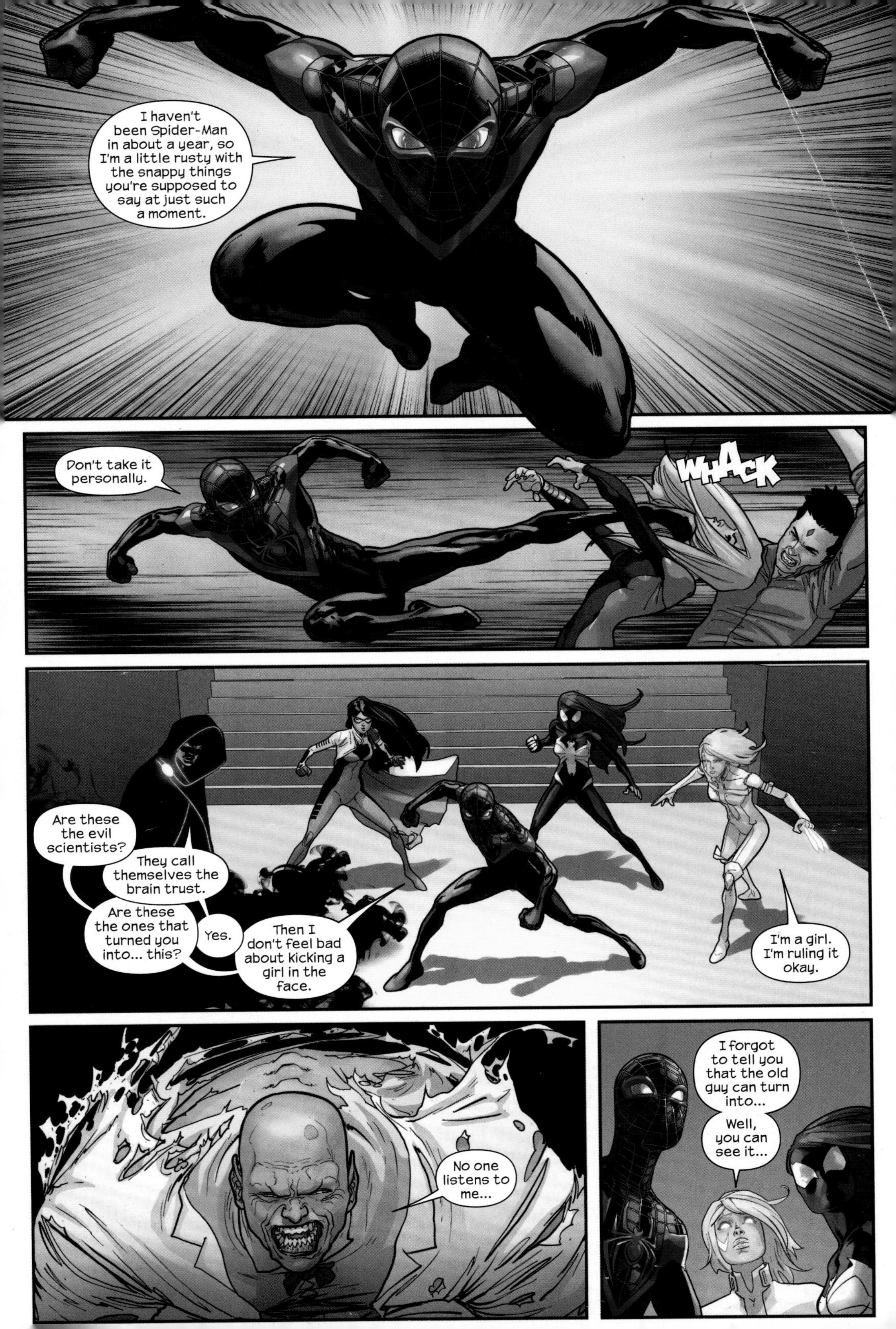
I haven't been Spider-Man in about a year, so I'm a little rusty with the snappy things you're supposed to say at just such a moment.
Don't take it personally.
WHACK
Are these the evil scientists?
They call themselves the brain trust.
Are these the ones that turned you into... this?
Yes.
Then I don't feel bad about kicking a girl in the face.
I'm a girl. I'm ruling it okay.
No one listens to me...
I forgot to tell you that the old guy can turn into...
Well, you can see it...

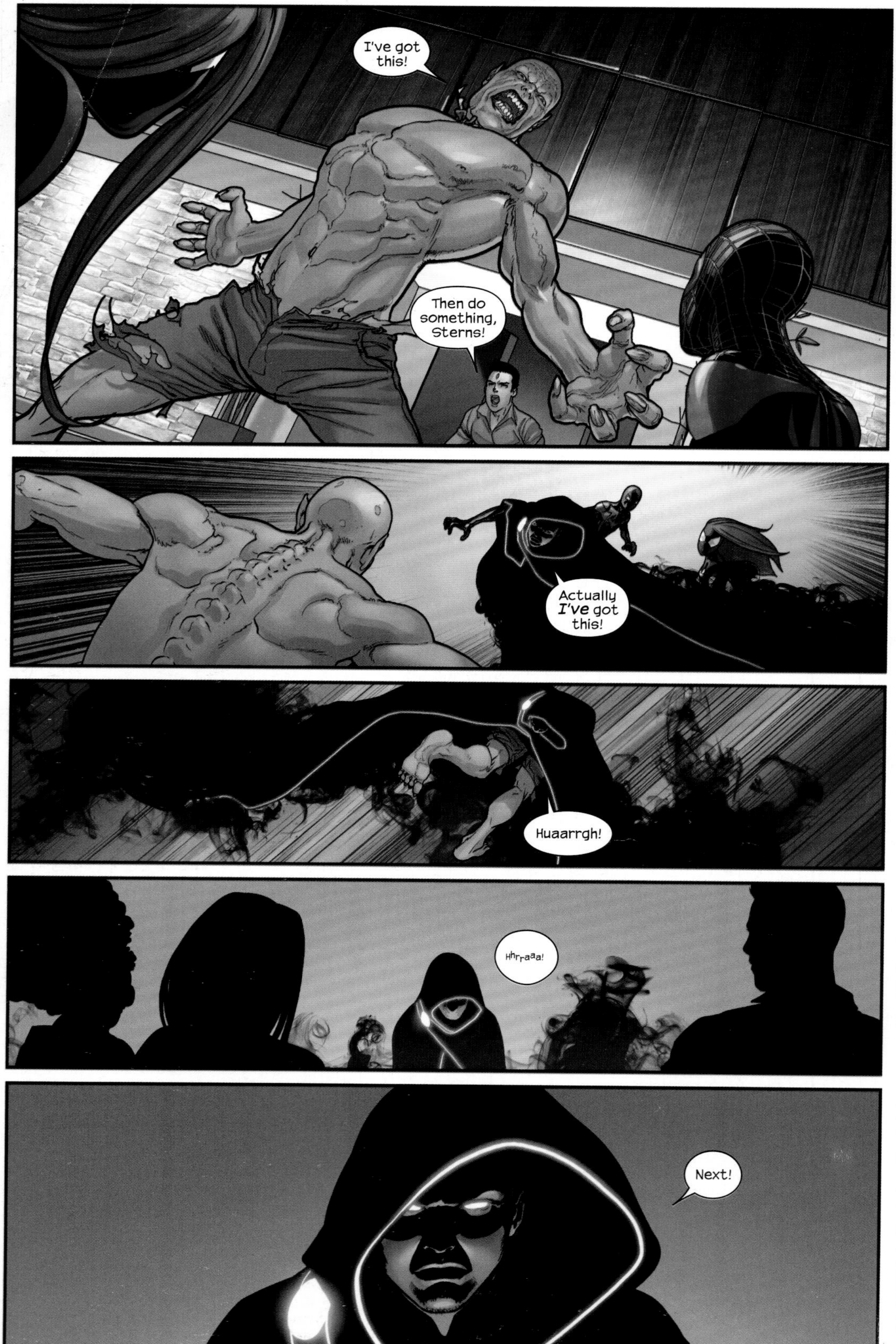

I've got this!
Then do something, Sterns!
Actually *I've* got this!
Huaarrgh!
Hhrraaa!
Next!

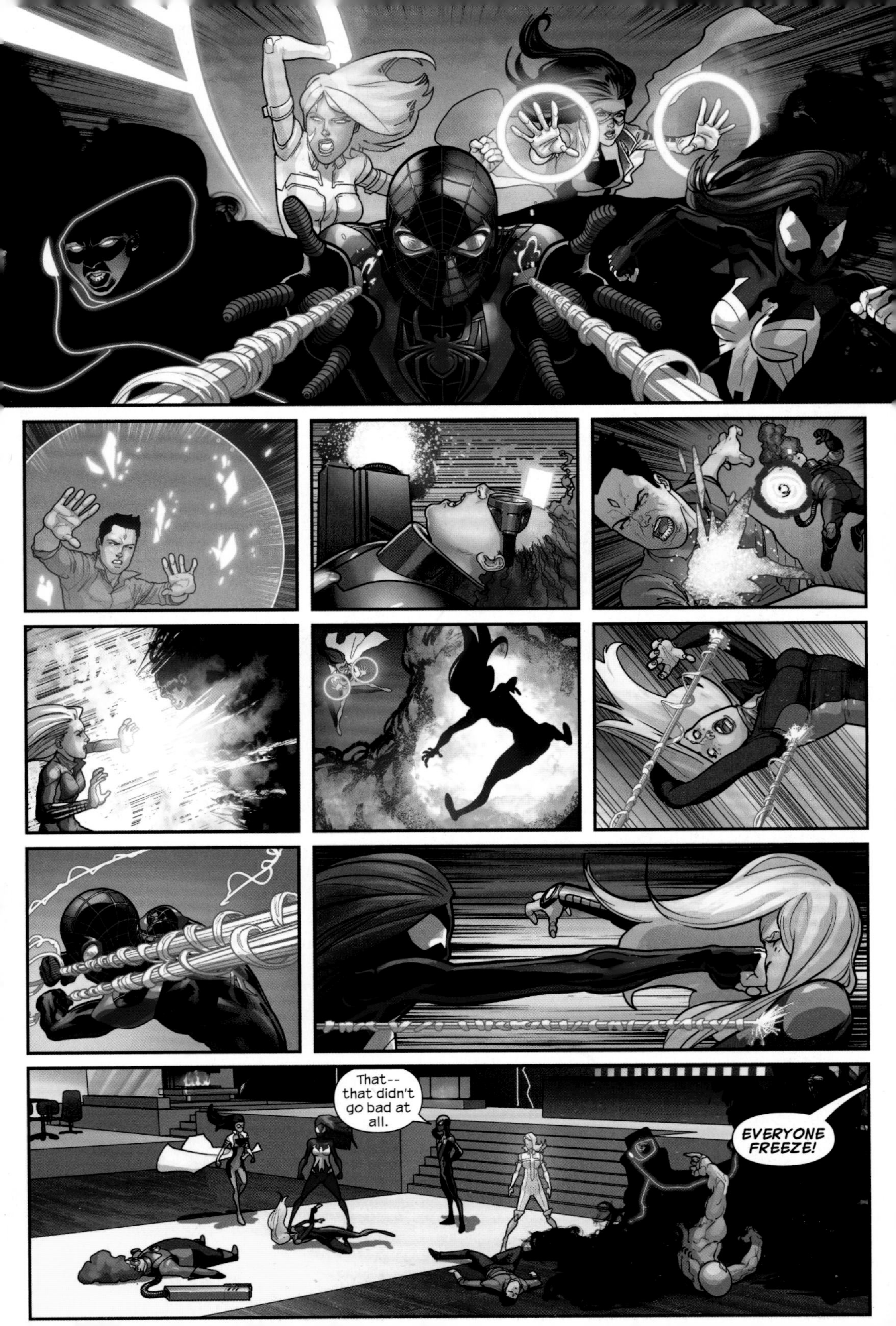
That--
that didn't
go bad at
all.
EVERYONE
FREEZE!

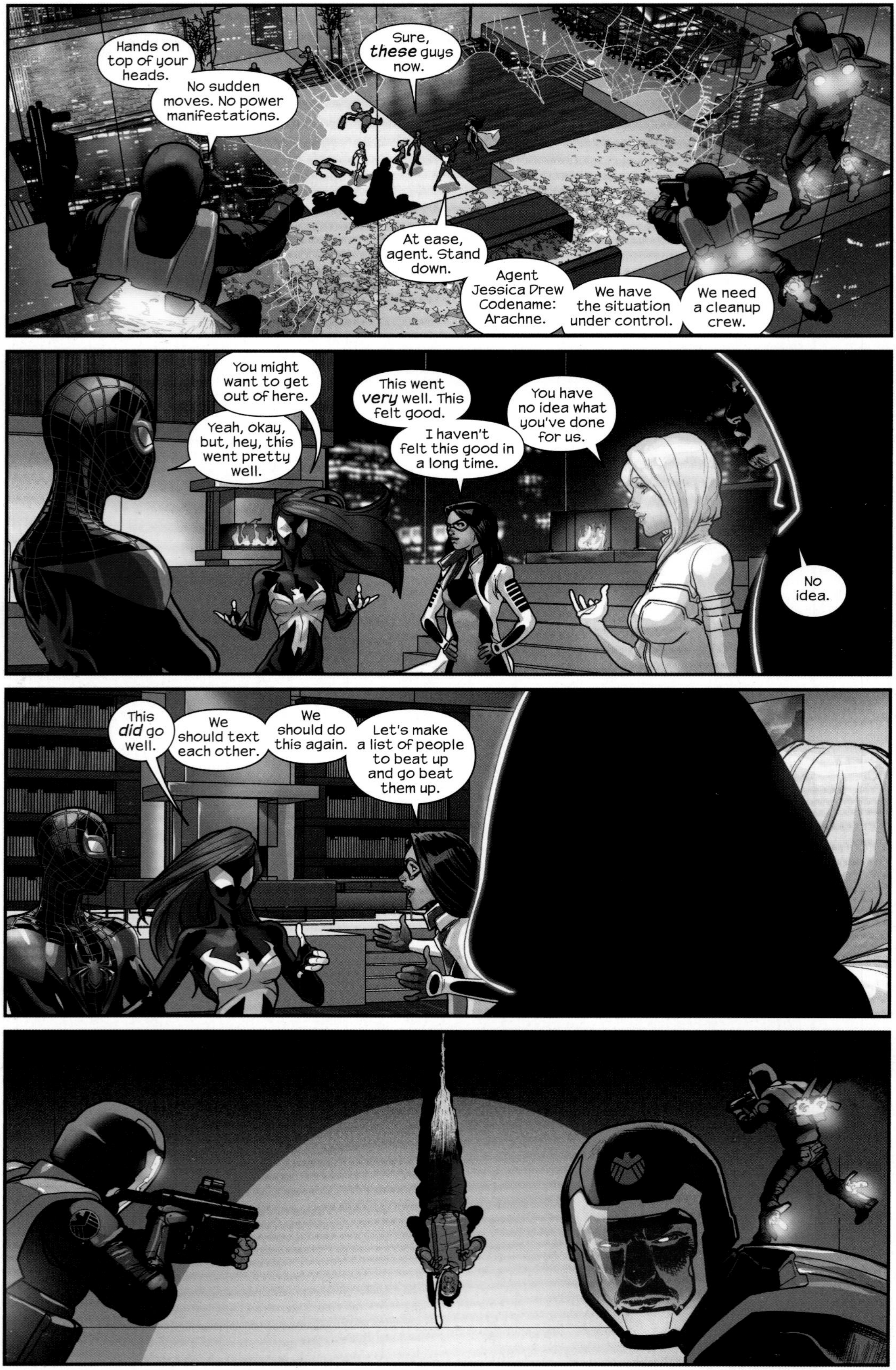
Hands on top of your heads.
No sudden moves. No power manifestations.
Sure, *these* guys now.
At ease, agent. Stand down.
Agent Jessica Drew Codename: Arachne.
We have the situation under control.
We need a cleanup crew.
You might want to get out of here.
Yeah, okay, but, hey, this went pretty well.
This went *very* well. This felt good.
I haven't felt this good in a long time.
You have no idea what you've done for us.
No idea.
This *did* go well.
We should text each other.
We should do this again.
Let's make a list of people to beat up and go beat them up.

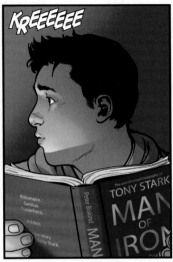

KREEEEEE

The unauthorized biography of

TONY STARK

Peter Biskind

MAN OF IRON

Billionaire.
Genius.
Superhero.
Addict.

The story of Tony Stark.

Dude.

Sshh!

Dude, are--are you--

Ganke, whisper.

Are you-- are you *back*? Are you, you know, *him* again?

Just listen...

I'm sorry I was being like that and I'm sorry I was making you mad.

You were right.

Thank you for hanging in there with me.

Just, you know, thank you.

For everything.

Aw...

Dude.

Just tell me you're back for real.

Tell me this is for real.

I'm telling you...you're right, Ganke.

You were totally right.

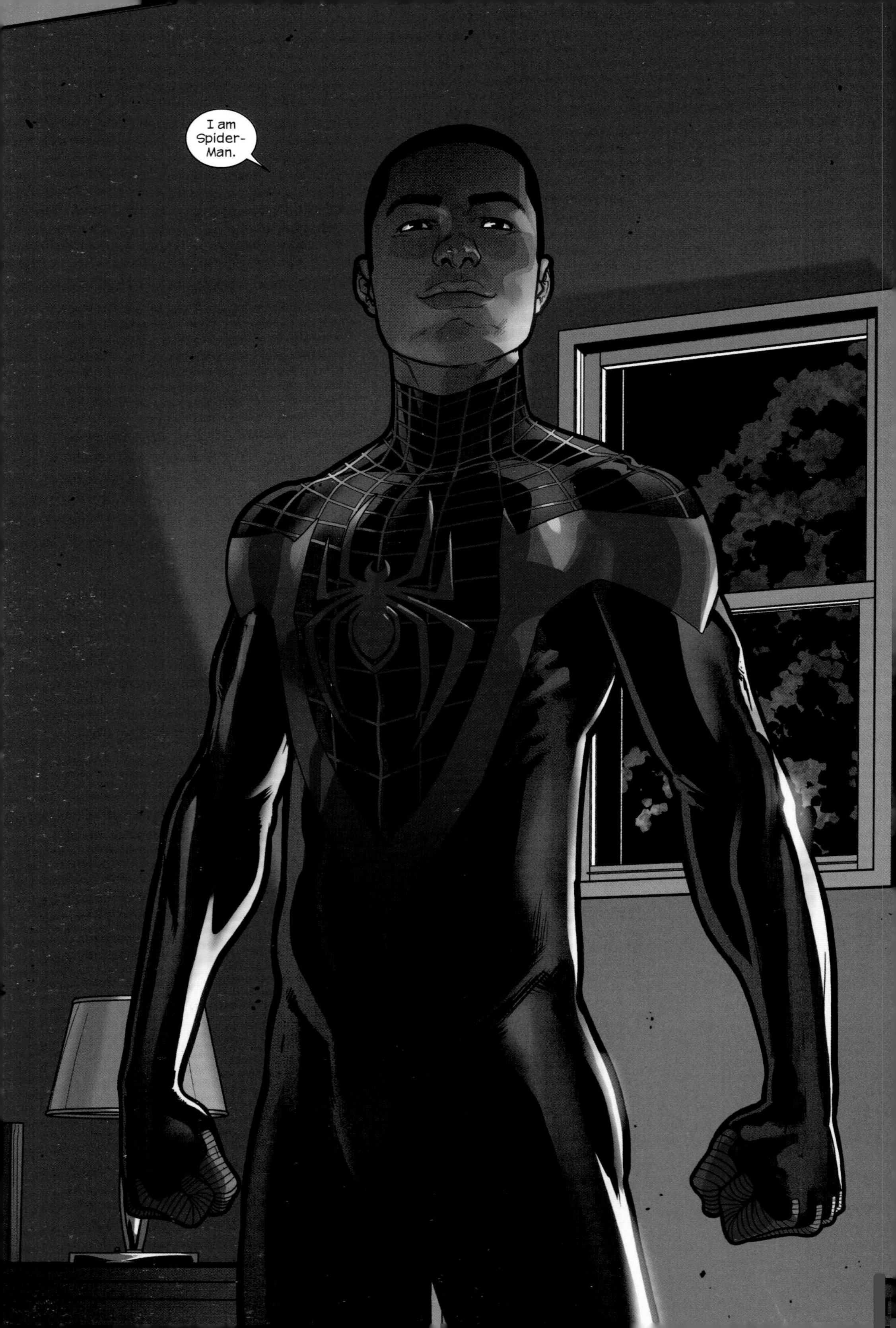
I am Spider-Man.

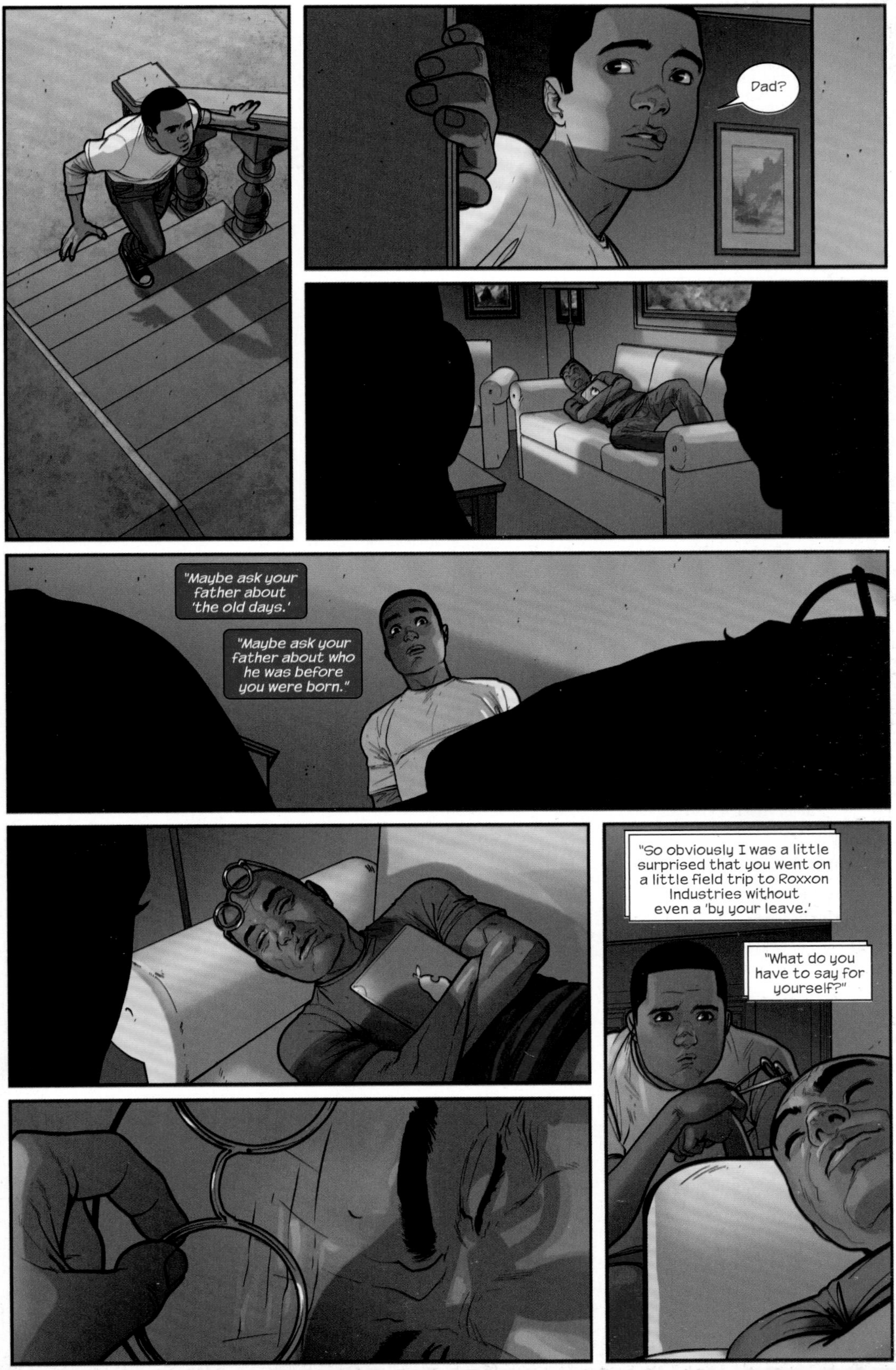
Dad?
"Maybe ask your father about 'the old days.'
"Maybe ask your father about who he was before you were born."
"So obviously I was a little surprised that you went on a little field trip to Roxxon Industries without even a 'by your leave.'
"What do you have to say for yourself?"

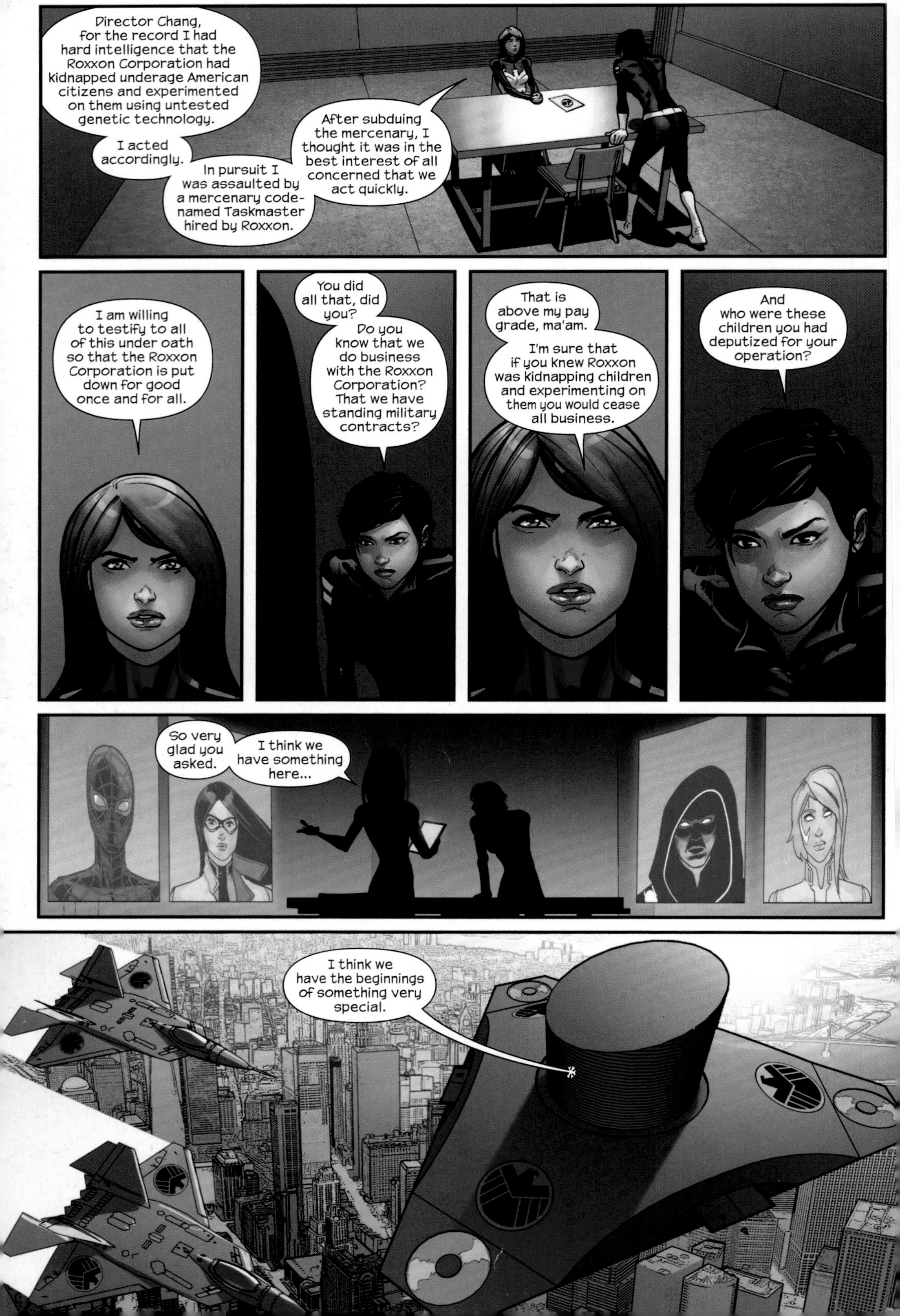
Director Chang, for the record I had hard intelligence that the Roxxon Corporation had kidnapped underage American citizens and experimented on them using untested genetic technology.
I acted accordingly.
In pursuit I was assaulted by a mercenary code-named Taskmaster hired by Roxxon.
After subduing the mercenary, I thought it was in the best interest of all concerned that we act quickly.
I am willing to testify to all of this under oath so that the Roxxon Corporation is put down for good once and for all.
You did all that, did you?
Do you know that we do business with the Roxxon Corporation? That we have standing military contracts?
That is above my pay grade, ma'am.
I'm sure that if you knew Roxxon was kidnapping children and experimenting on them you would cease all business.
And who were these children you had deputized for your operation?
So very glad you asked.
I think we have something here...
I think we have the beginnings of something very special.

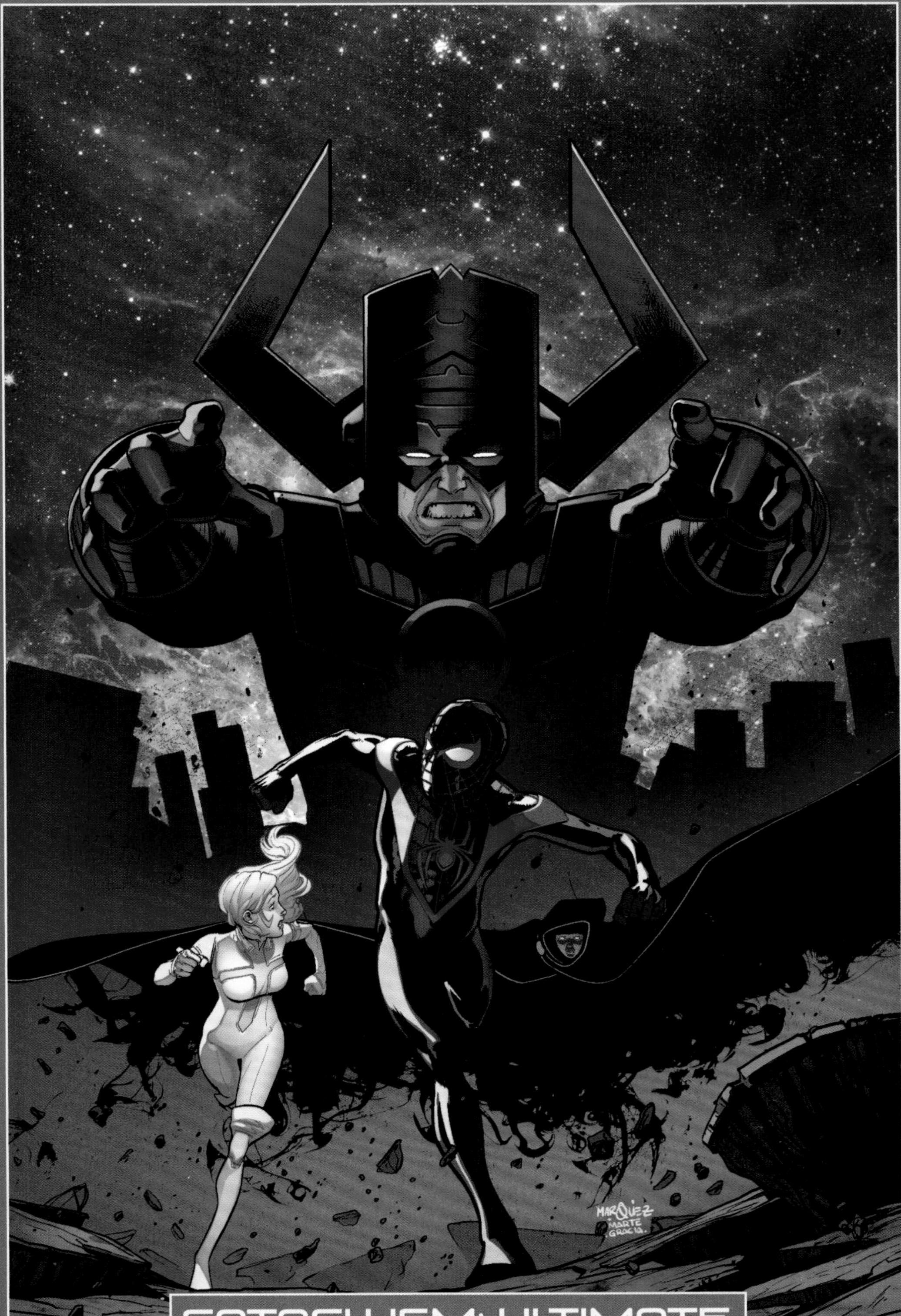
MARQUEZ
MARTE GRACIA.

CATACLYSM: ULTIMATE SPIDER-MAN #1

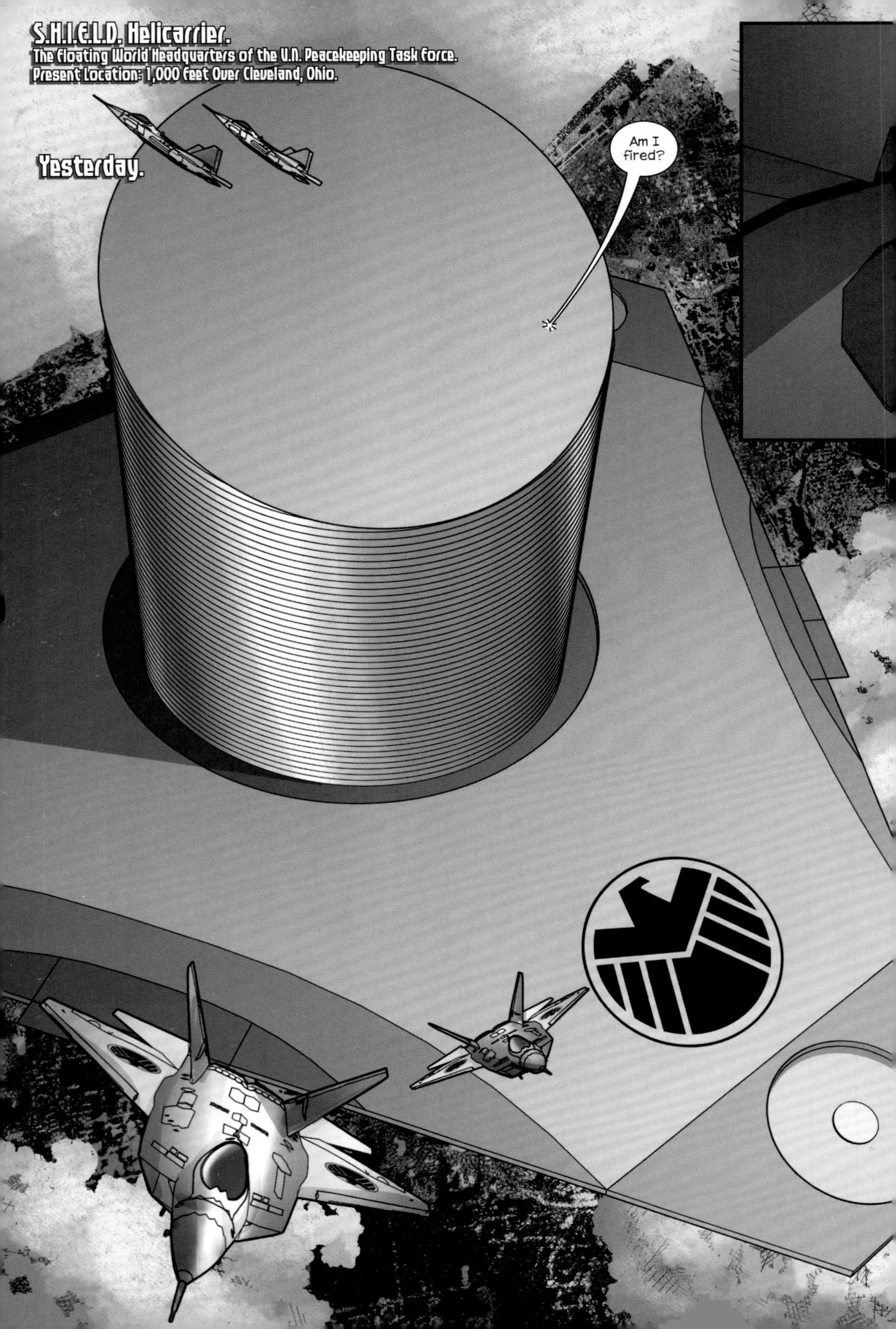
S.H.I.E.L.D. Helicarrier.
The Floating World Headquarters of the U.N. Peacekeeping Task Force.
Present Location: 1,000 Feet Over Cleveland, Ohio.
Yesterday.
Am I fired?

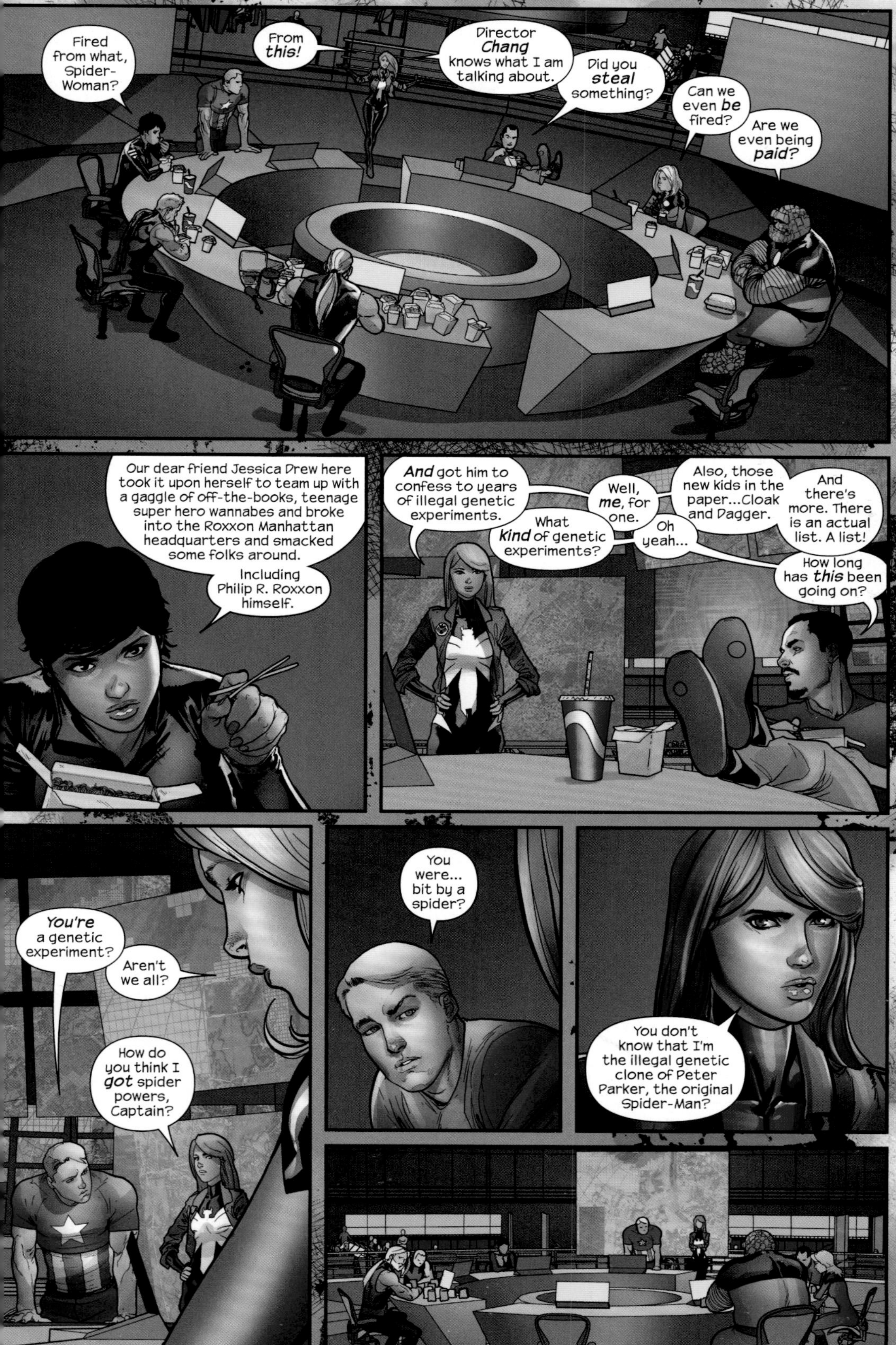

Fired from what, Spider-Woman?
From this!
Director Chang knows what I am talking about.
Did you steal something?
Can we even be fired?
Are we even being paid?
Our dear friend Jessica Drew here took it upon herself to team up with a gaggle of off-the-books, teenage super hero wannabes and broke into the Roxxon Manhattan headquarters and smacked some folks around.
Including Philip R. Roxxon himself.
And got him to confess to years of illegal genetic experiments.
Well, me, for one.
Also, those new kids in the paper...Cloak and Dagger.
And there's more. There is an actual list. A list!
What kind of genetic experiments?
Oh yeah...
How long has this been going on?
You're a genetic experiment?
Aren't we all?
How do you think I got spider powers, Captain?
You were... bit by a spider?
You don't know that I'm the illegal genetic clone of Peter Parker, the original Spider-Man?

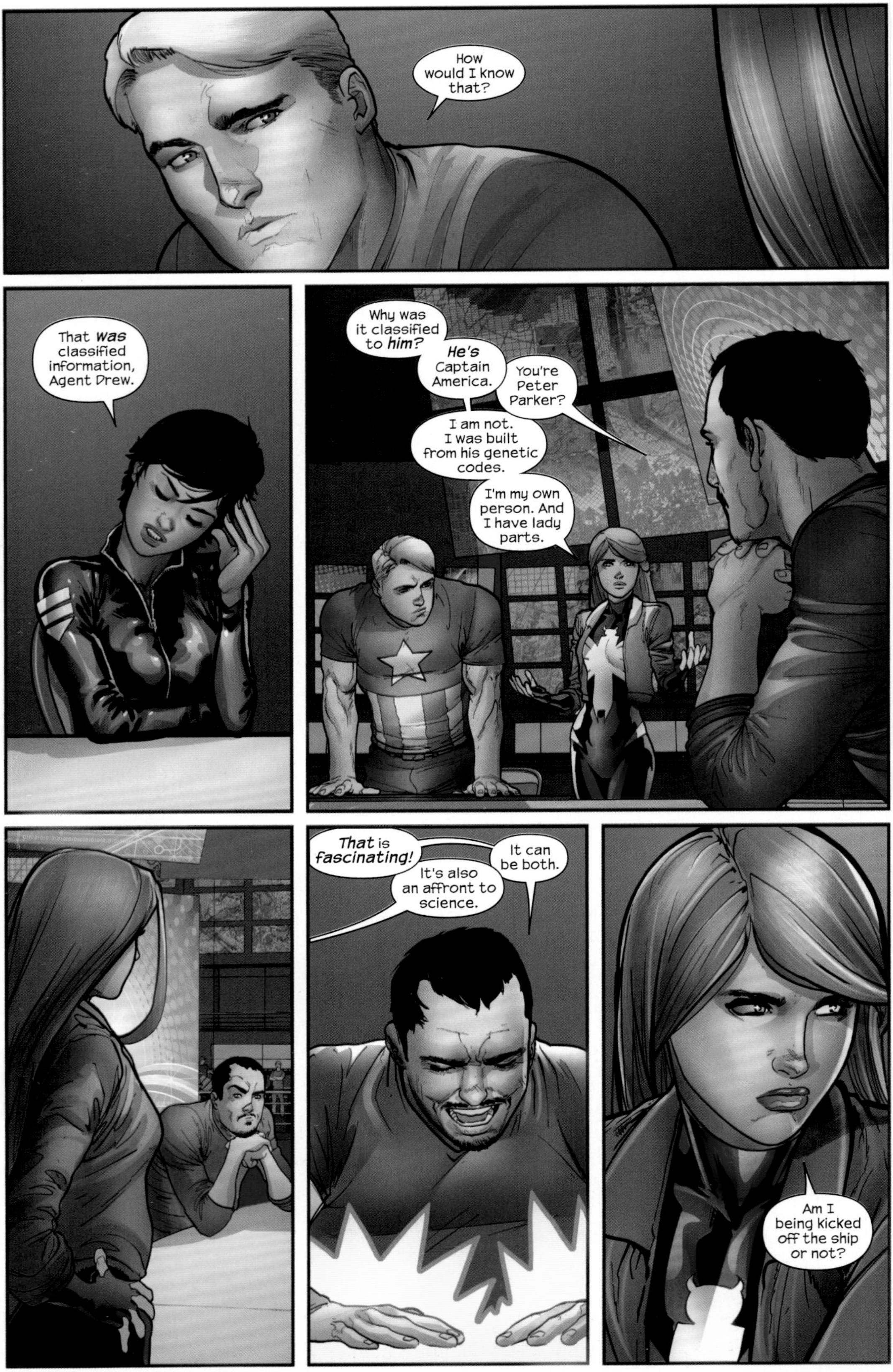
How would I know that?
That *was* classified information, Agent Drew.
Why was it classified to *him*?
He's Captain America.
You're Peter Parker?
I am not. I was built from his genetic codes.
I'm my own person. And I have lady parts.
That is *fascinating!*
It's also an affront to science.
It can be both.
Am I being kicked off the ship or not?

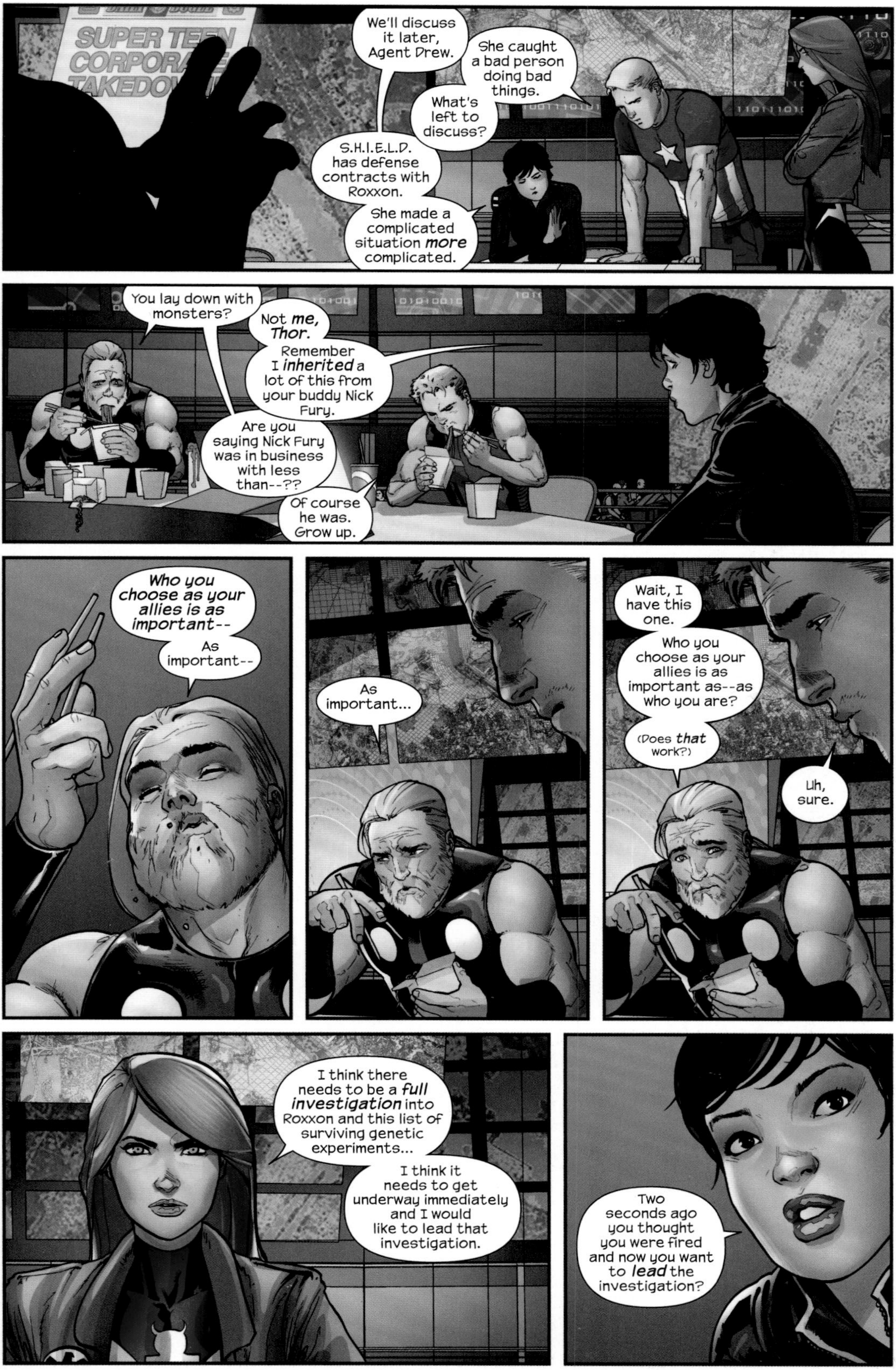
SUPER TEEN CORPORATE TAKEDOW
We'll discuss it later, Agent Drew.
She caught a bad person doing bad things.
What's left to discuss?
S.H.I.E.L.D. has defense contracts with Roxxon.
She made a complicated situation *more* complicated.
You lay down with monsters?
Not *me, Thor.*
Remember I *inherited* a lot of this from your buddy Nick Fury.
Are you saying Nick Fury was in business with less than--??
Of course he was. Grow up.
Who you choose as your allies is as important--
As important--
As important...
Wait, I have this one.
Who you choose as your allies is as important as--as who you are?
(Does *that* work?)
Uh, sure.
I think there needs to be a *full investigation* into Roxxon and this list of surviving genetic experiments...
I think it needs to get underway immediately and I would like to lead that investigation.
Two seconds ago you thought you were fired and now you want to *lead* the investigation?

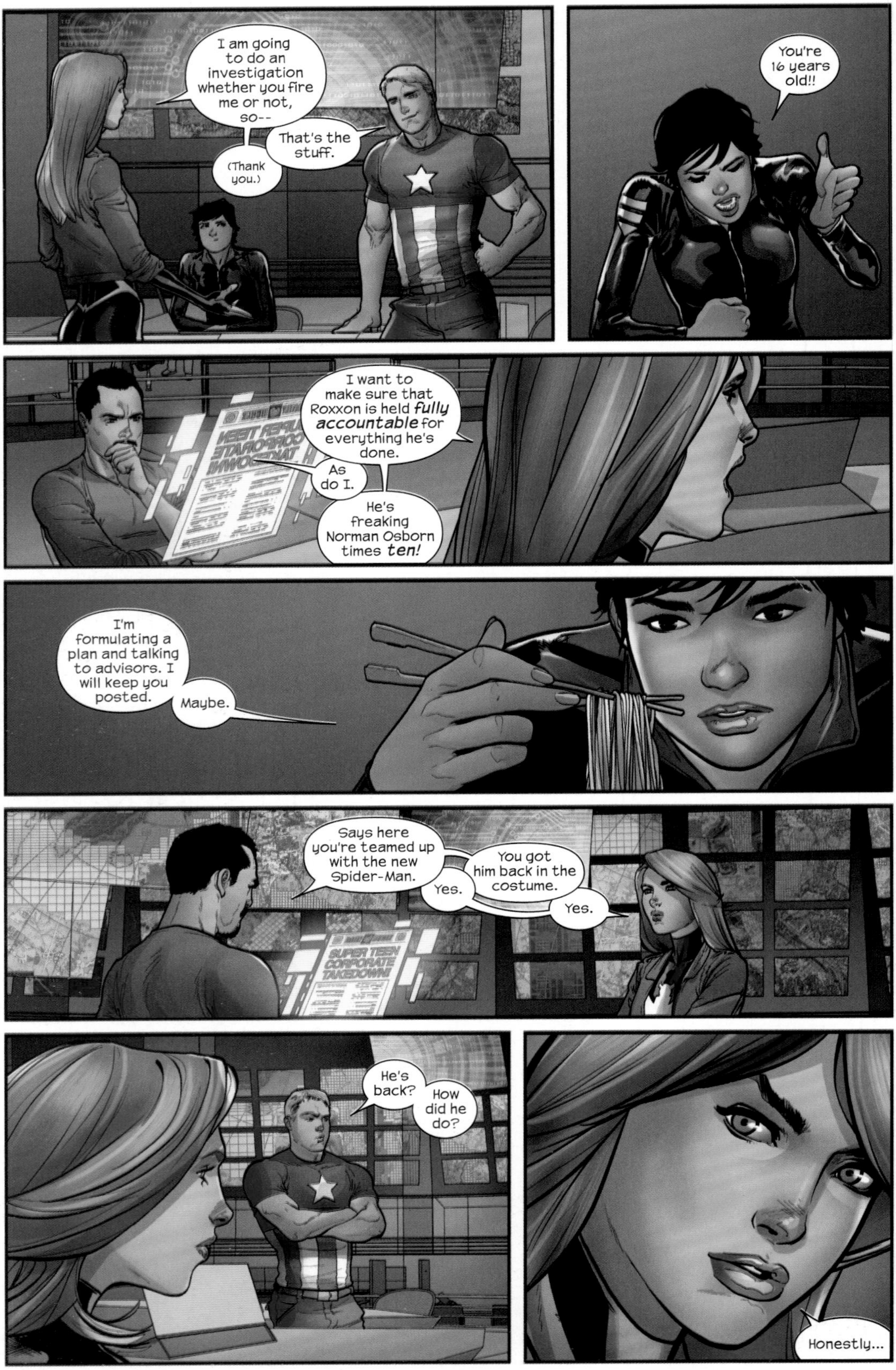
I am going to do an investigation whether you fire me or not, so--
(Thank you.)
That's the stuff.
You're 16 years old!!
I want to make sure that Roxxon is held *fully accountable* for everything he's done.
As do I.
He's freaking Norman Osborn times *ten!*
SUPER TEEN CORPORATE TAKEDOWN!
I'm formulating a plan and talking to advisors. I will keep you posted.
Maybe.
Says here you're teamed up with the new Spider-Man.
Yes.
You got him back in the costume.
Yes.
SUPER TEEN CORPORATE TAKEDOWN!
He's back?
How did he do?
Honestly...

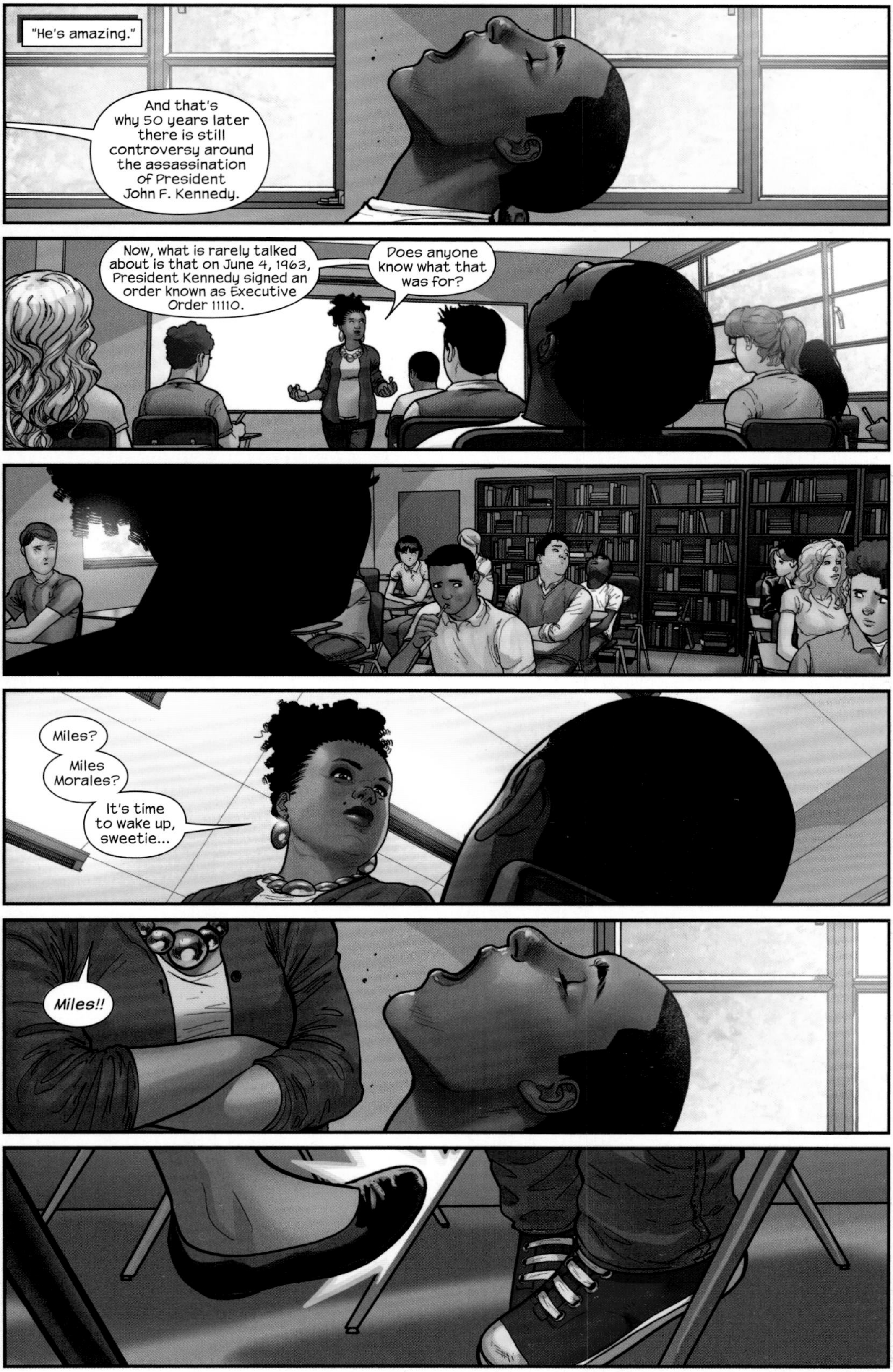
"He's amazing."
And that's why 50 years later there is still controversy around the assassination of President John F. Kennedy.
Now, what is rarely talked about is that on June 4, 1963, President Kennedy signed an order known as Executive Order 11110.
Does anyone know what that was for?
Miles?
Miles Morales?
It's time to wake up, sweetie...
Miles!!

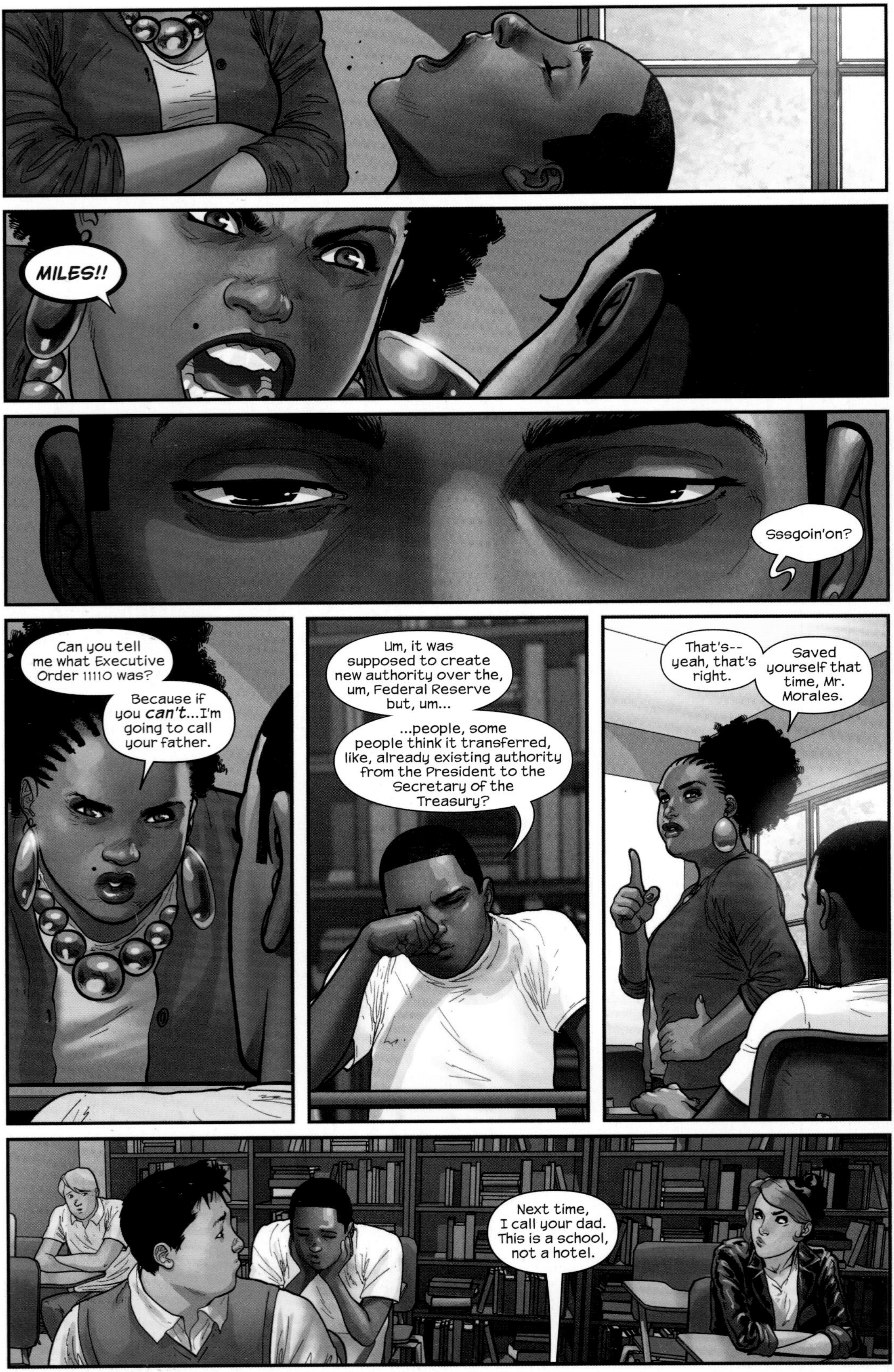
MILES!!
Sssgoin'on?
Can you tell me what Executive Order 11110 was?
Because if you *can't*...I'm going to call your father.
Um, it was supposed to create new authority over the, um, Federal Reserve but, um...
...people, some people think it transferred, like, already existing authority from the President to the Secretary of the Treasury?
That's-- yeah, that's right.
Saved yourself that time, Mr. Morales.
Next time, I call your dad. This is a school, not a hotel.

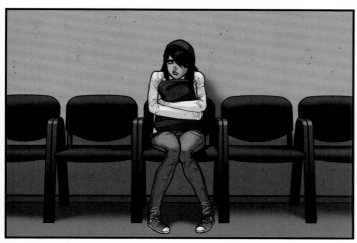

Lana Baumgartner?

Yeah.

I assume this was you?

Yes.

I was *one* of them.

You know that means you broke your juvenile detention parole.

That means I have to call the police *and* S.H.I.E.L.D. and tell them Bombshell broke her parole agreement.

SUPER TEEN CORPORATE TAKEDOWN!

S.H.I.E.L.D. and the police were there.

Spider-Woman is an *agent* of S.H.I.E.L.D.

She--we were following *her.*

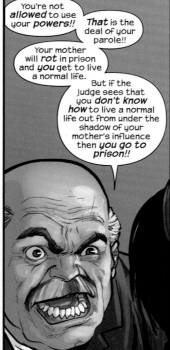

You're not *allowed* to use your *powers!!*

That is the deal of your parole!!

Your mother will *rot* in prison and *you* get to live a normal life.

But if the judge sees that you *don't know how* to live a normal life out from under the shadow of your mother's influence then *you go to prison!!*

I think maybe I--

I think I'm supposed to be a super hero.

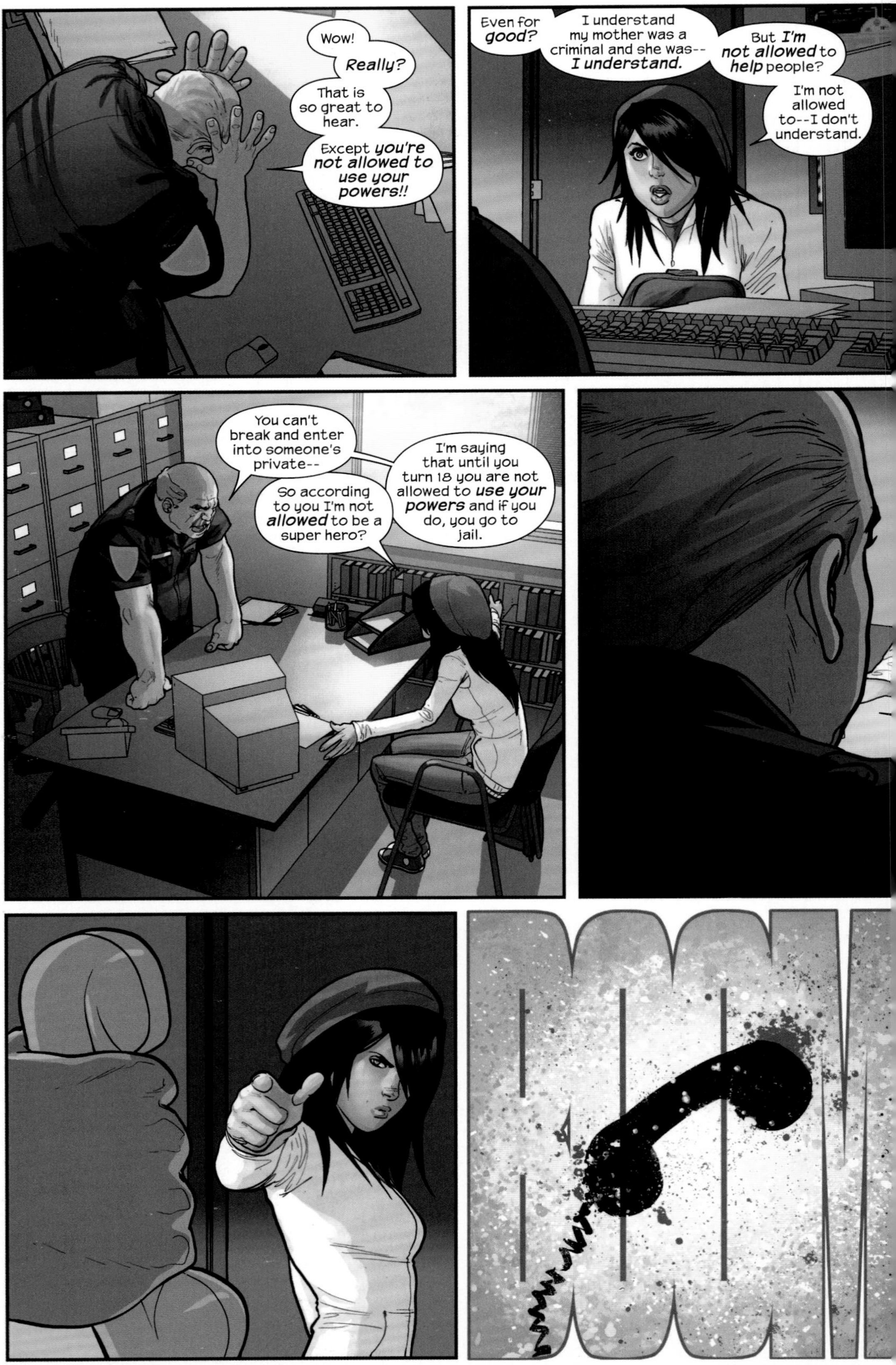

Wow!
Really?
That is so great to hear.
Except you're not allowed to use your powers!!
Even for good?
I understand my mother was a criminal and she was-- I understand.
But I'm not allowed to help people?
I'm not allowed to--I don't understand.
You can't break and enter into someone's private--
I'm saying that until you turn 18 you are not allowed to use your powers and if you do, you go to jail.
So according to you I'm not allowed to be a super hero?

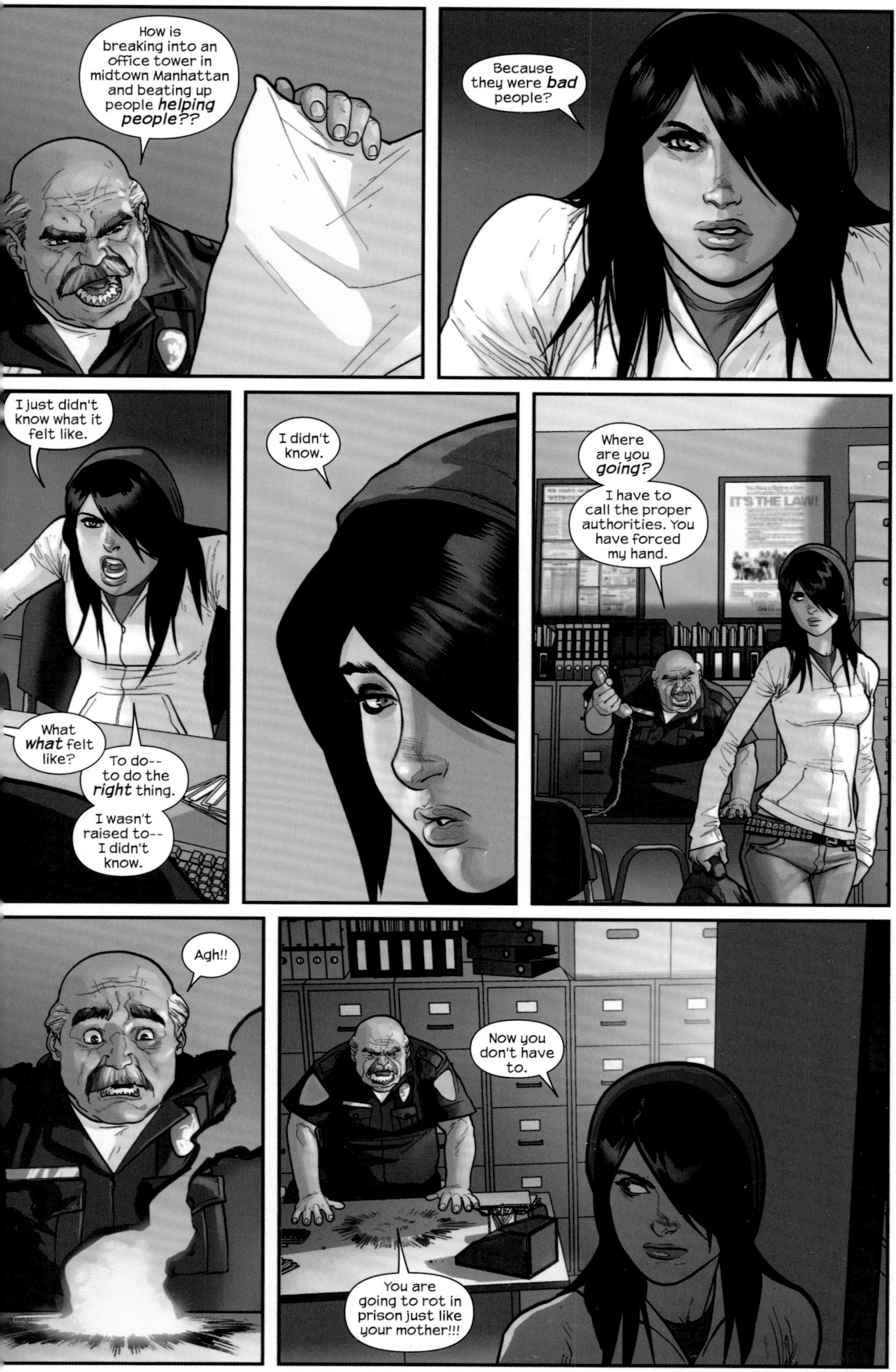
How is breaking into an office tower in midtown Manhattan and beating up people *helping people*??
Because they were *bad* people?
I just didn't know what it felt like.
What *what* felt like?
To do-- to do the *right* thing.
I wasn't raised to-- I didn't know.
I didn't know.
Where are you *going?*
I have to call the proper authorities. You have forced my hand.
IT'S THE LAW!
Agh!!
Now you don't have to.
You are going to rot in prison just like your mother!!!

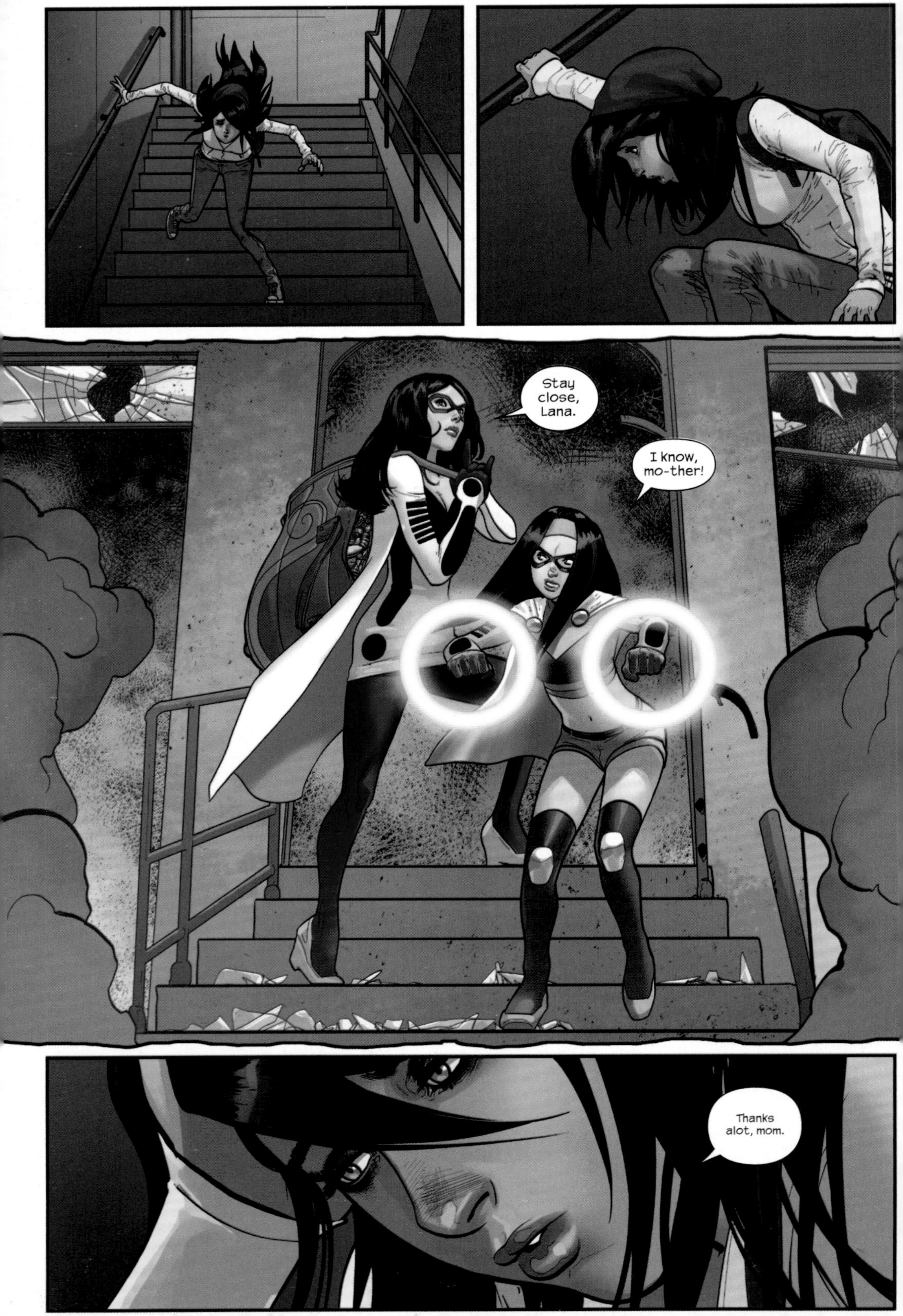
Stay close, Lana.
I know, mo-ther!
Thanks alot, mom.

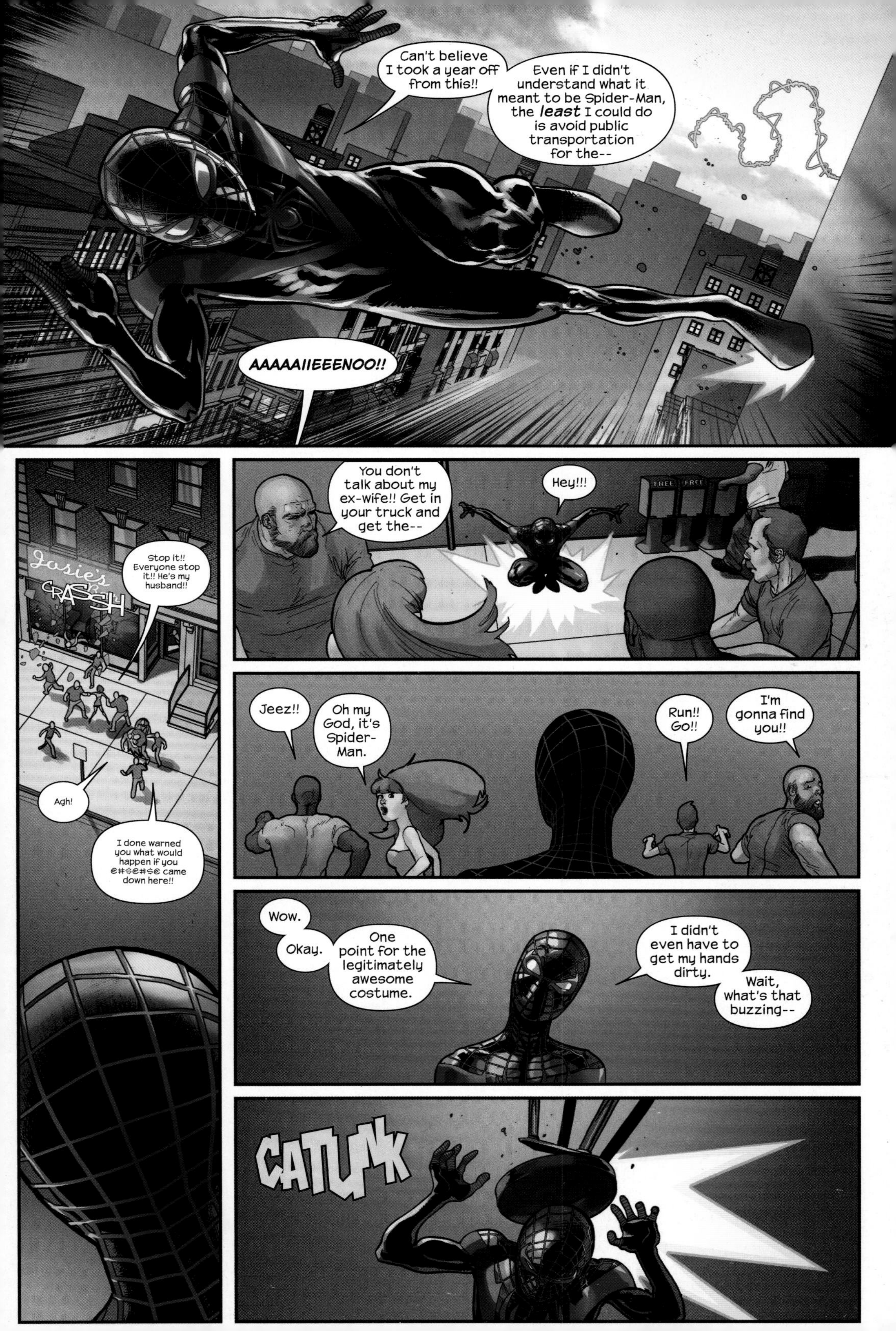
Can't believe I took a year off from this!!
Even if I didn't understand what it meant to be Spider-Man, the *least* I could do is avoid public transportation for the--
AAAAAIIEEENOO!!
Josie's
CRASSSH
Stop it!! Everyone stop it!! He's my husband!!
Agh!
I done warned you what would happen if you @#$@#$@ came down here!!
You don't talk about my ex-wife!! Get in your truck and get the--
Hey!!!
FREE
FREE
Jeez!!
Oh my God, it's Spider-Man.
Run!! Go!!
I'm gonna find you!!
Wow.
Okay.
One point for the legitimately awesome costume.
I didn't even have to get my hands dirty.
Wait, what's that buzzing--
CATUNK

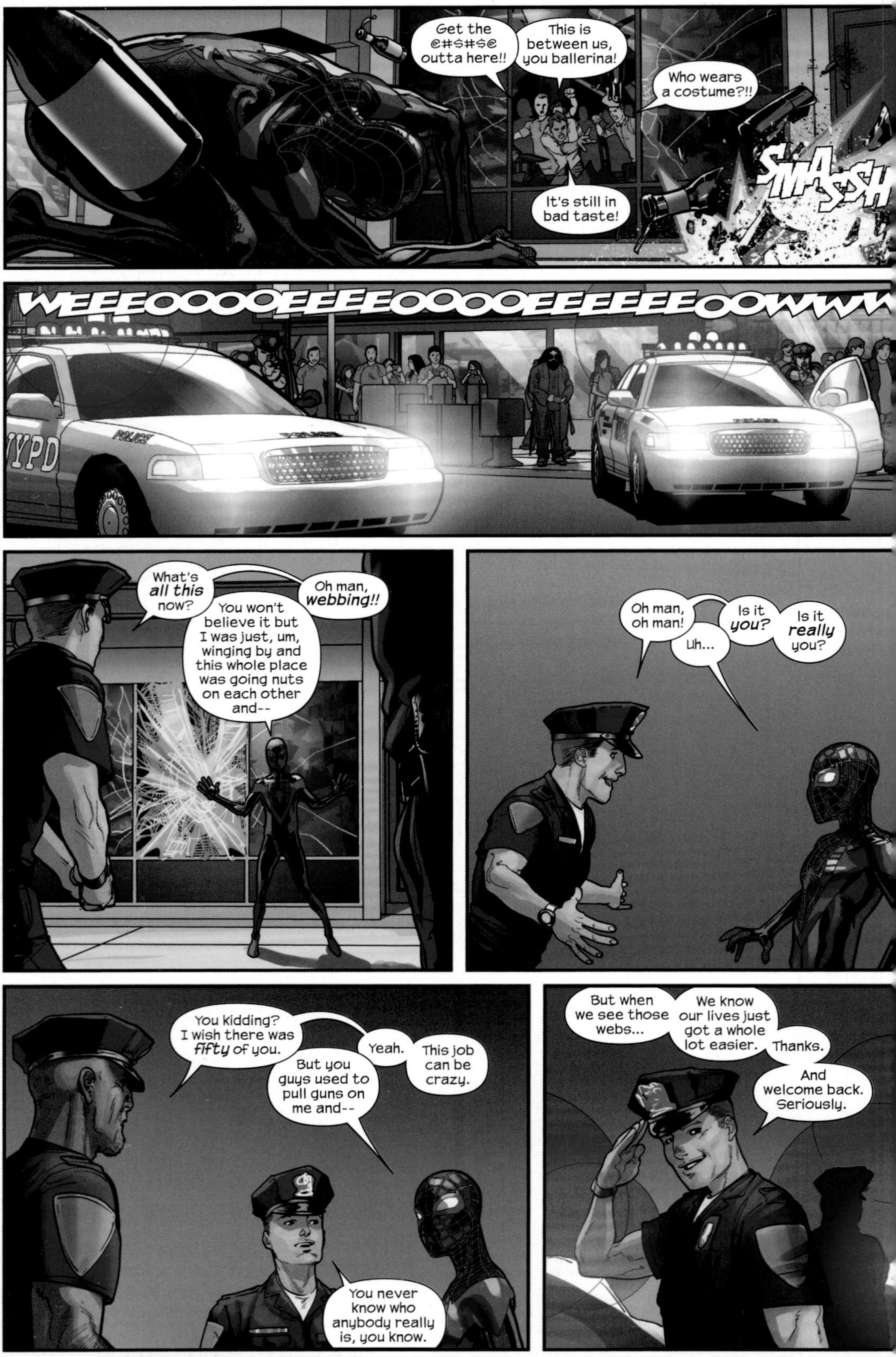

Get the @#$#$@ outta here!!
This is between us, you ballerina!
Who wears a costume?!!
It's still in bad taste!
SMASH
WEEEOOOOEEEEOOOOEEEEEEOOWWW
What's *all this* now?
Oh man, *webbing!!*
You won't believe it but I was just, um, winging by and this whole place was going nuts on each other and--
Oh man, oh man!
Uh...
Is it *you?*
Is it *really* you?
You kidding? I wish there was *fifty* of you.
Yeah.
This job can be crazy.
But you guys used to pull guns on me and--
You never know who anybody really is, you know.
But when we see those webs...
We know our lives just got a whole lot easier.
Thanks.
And welcome back. Seriously.

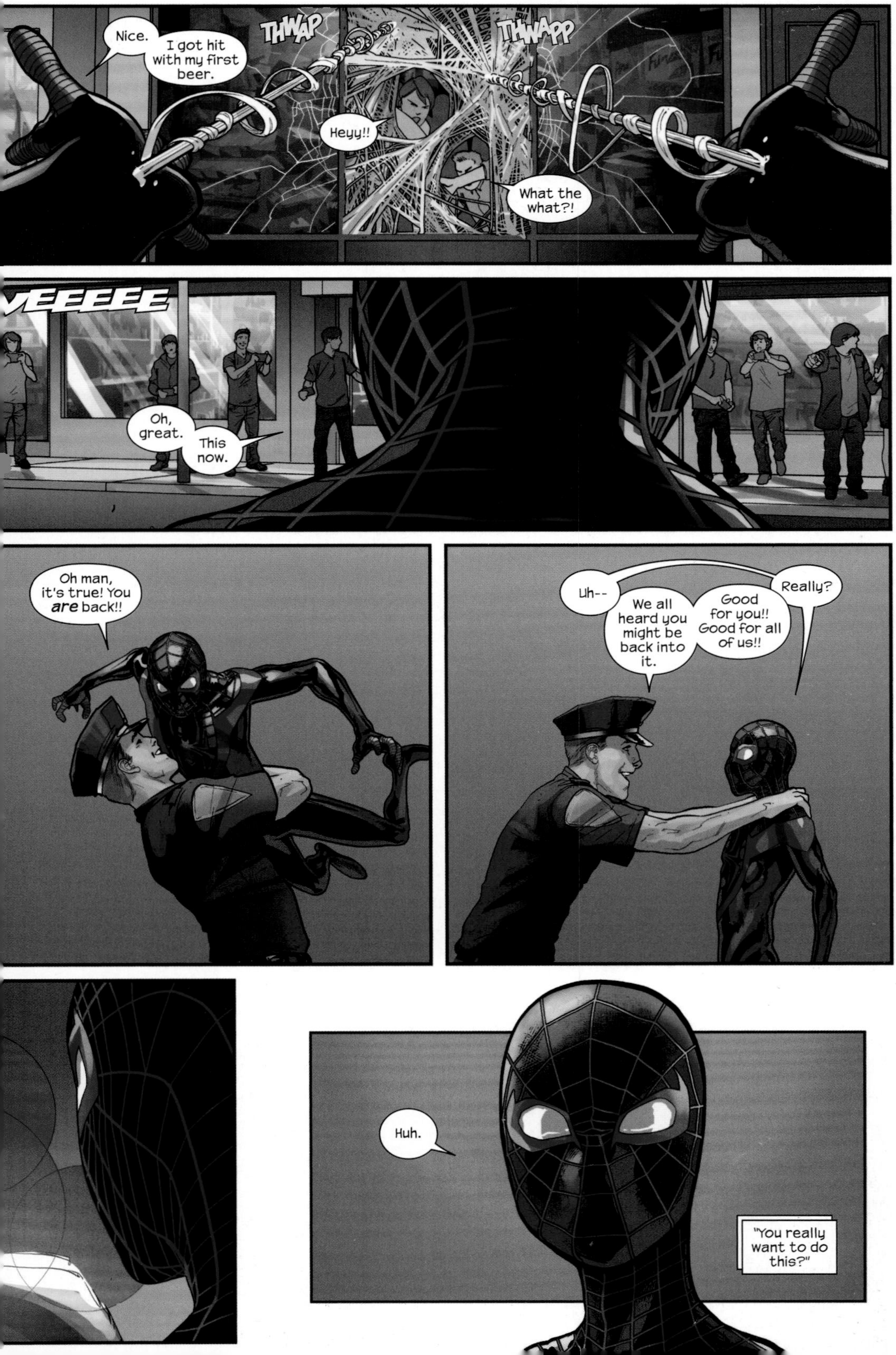
Nice.
I got hit with my first beer.
THWAP
THWAPP
Heyy!!
What the what?!
VEEEEEE
Oh, great.
This now.
Oh man, it's true! You *are* back!!
Uh--
We all heard you might be back into it.
Good for you!! Good for all of us!!
Really?
Huh.
"You really want to do this?"

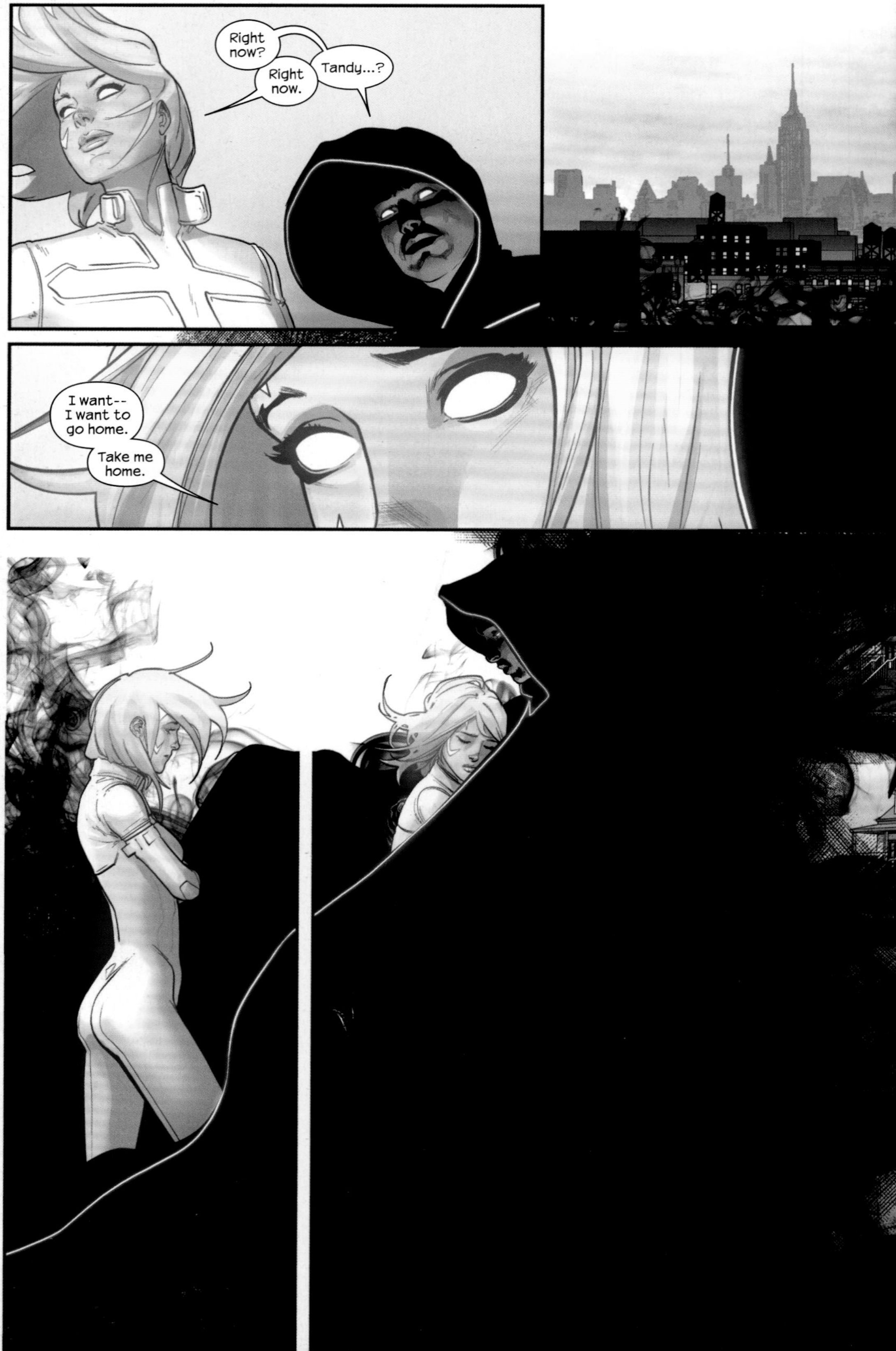
Right now?
Tandy...?
Right now.
I want-- I want to go home.
Take me home.

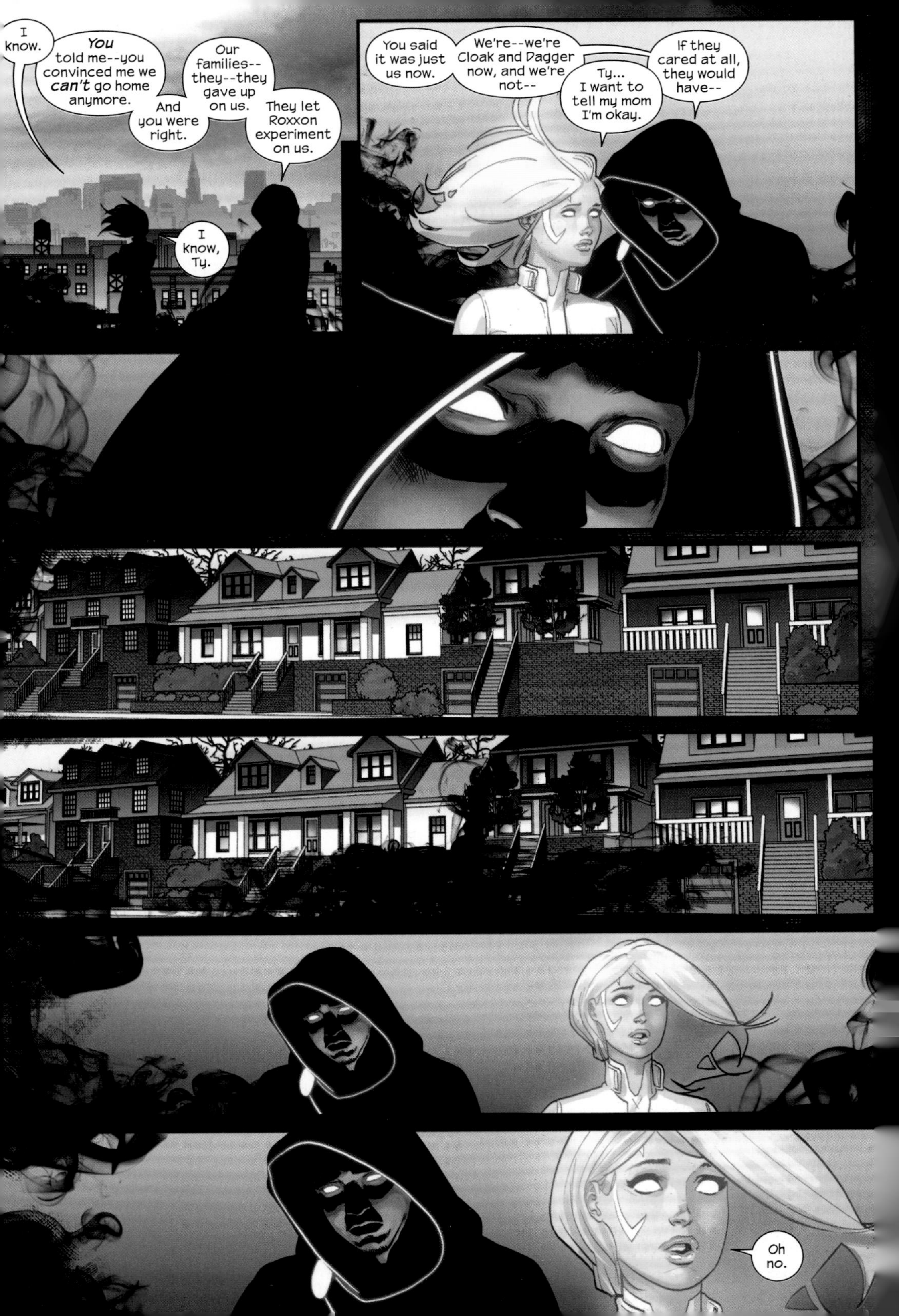
I know.
You told me--you convinced me we can't go home anymore.
And you were right.
Our families--they--they gave up on us.
They let Roxxon experiment on us.
I know, Ty.
You said it was just us now.
We're--we're Cloak and Dagger now, and we're not--
If they cared at all, they would have--
Ty... I want to tell my mom I'm okay.
Oh no.

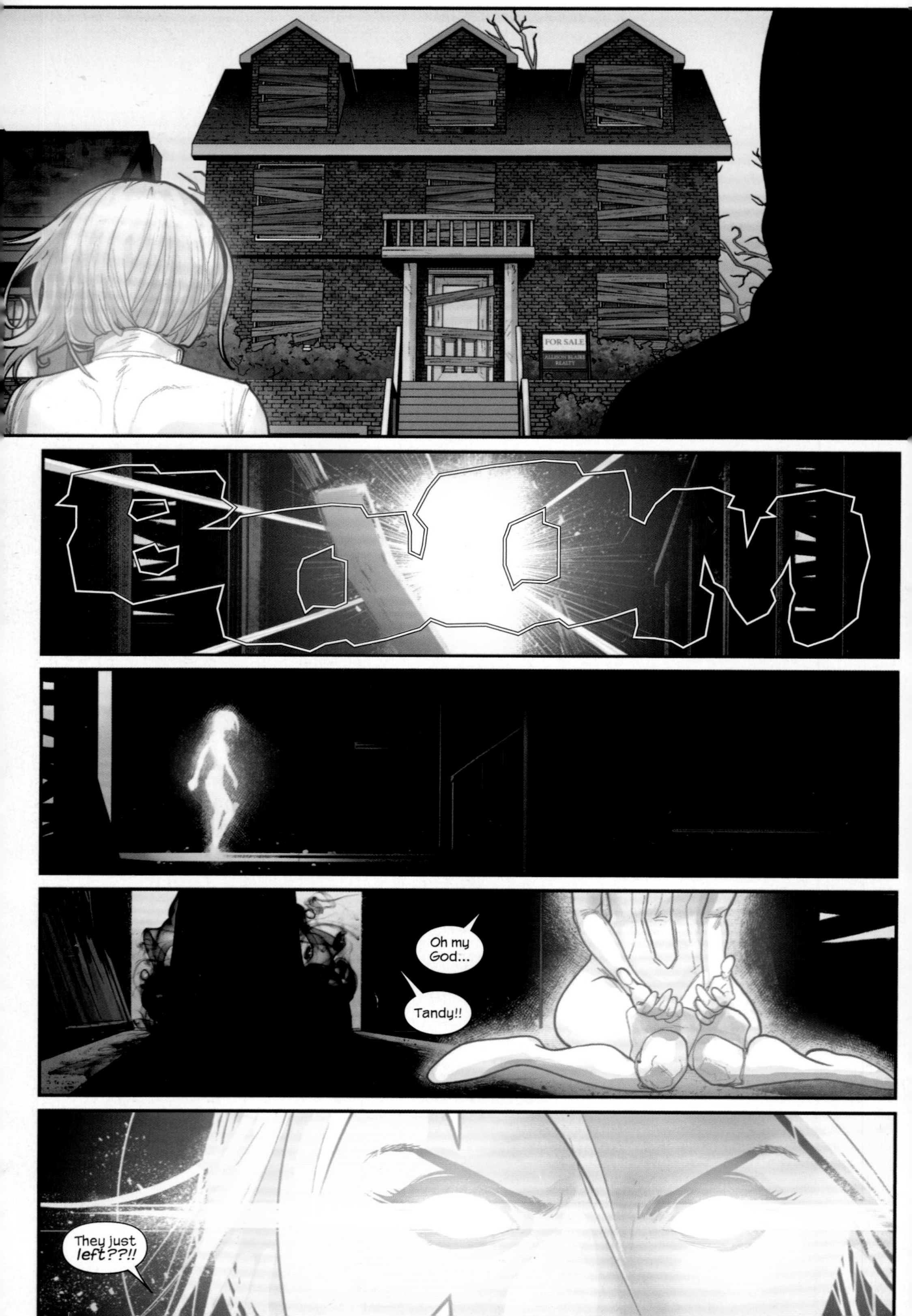
FOR SALE
ALLISON BLAIRE REALTY
BOOM
Oh my God...
Tandy!!
They just left??!!

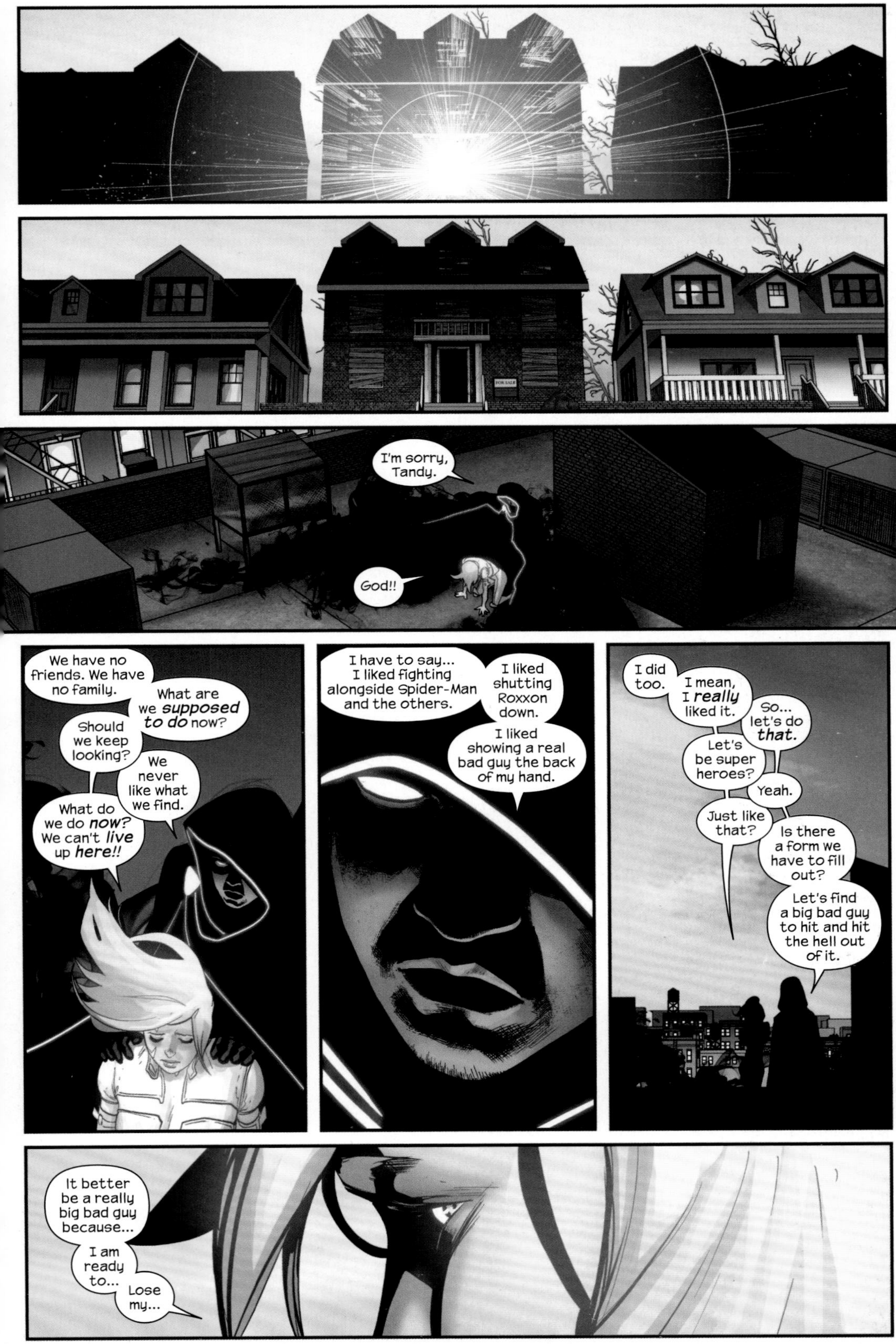

I'm sorry, Tandy.
God!!
We have no friends. We have no family.
What are we *supposed to do* now?
Should we keep looking?
We never like what we find.
What do we do *now?* We can't *live* up *here!!*
I have to say... I liked fighting alongside Spider-Man and the others.
I liked shutting Roxxon down.
I liked showing a real bad guy the back of my hand.
I did too.
I mean, I *really* liked it.
So... let's do *that.*
Let's be super heroes?
Yeah.
Just like that?
Is there a form we have to fill out?
Let's find a big bad guy to hit and hit the hell out of it.
It better be a really big bad guy because...
I am ready to...
Lose my...

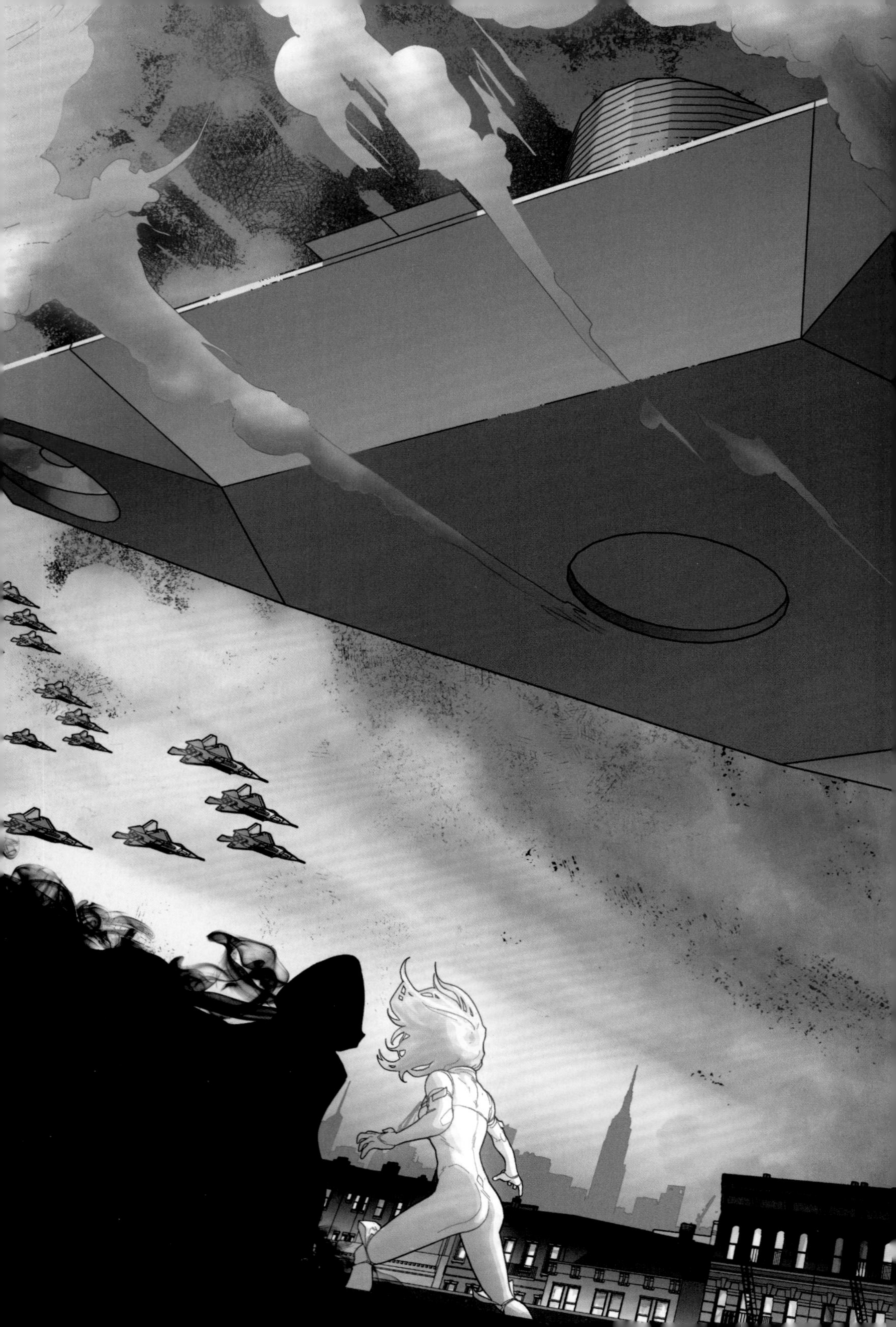

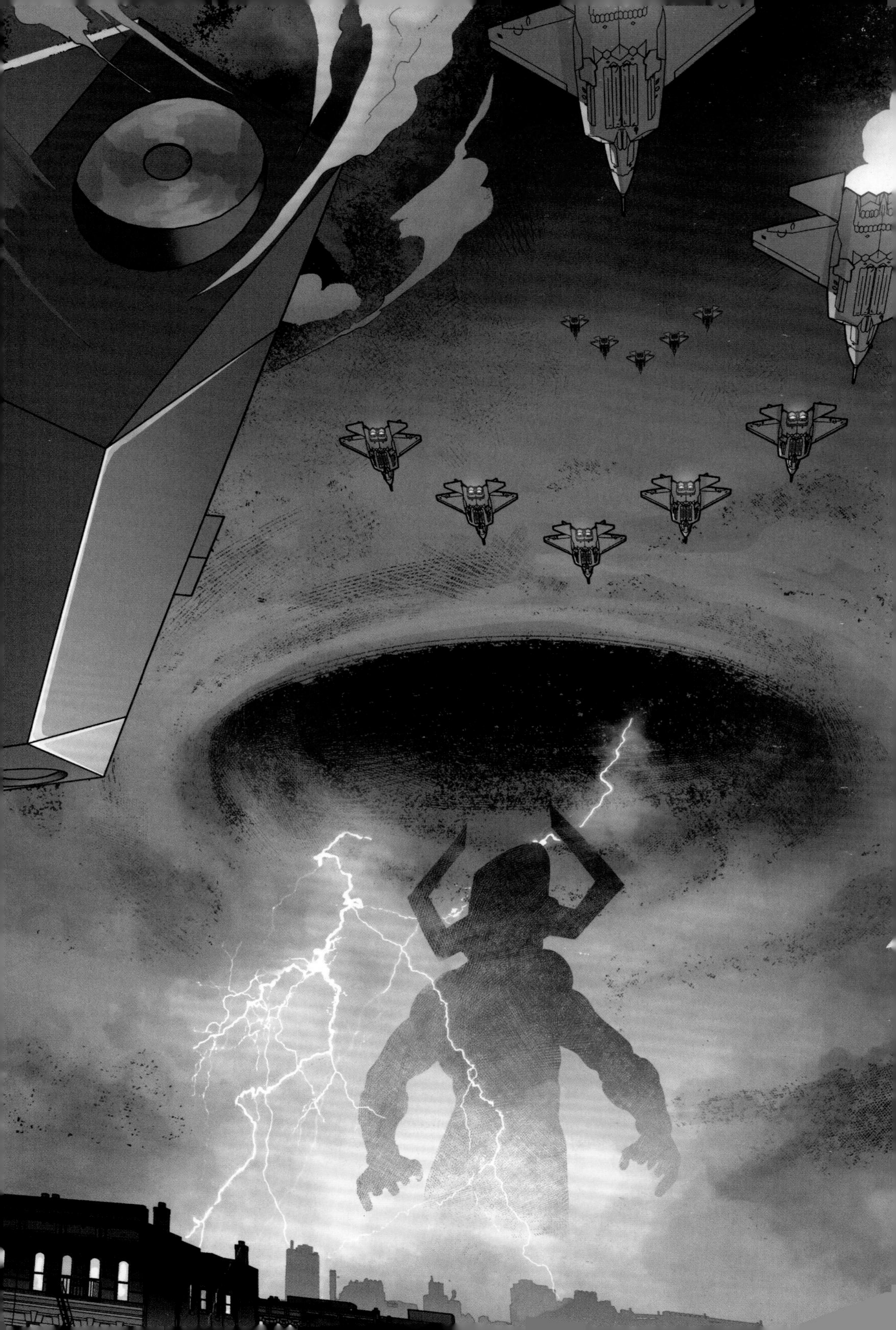

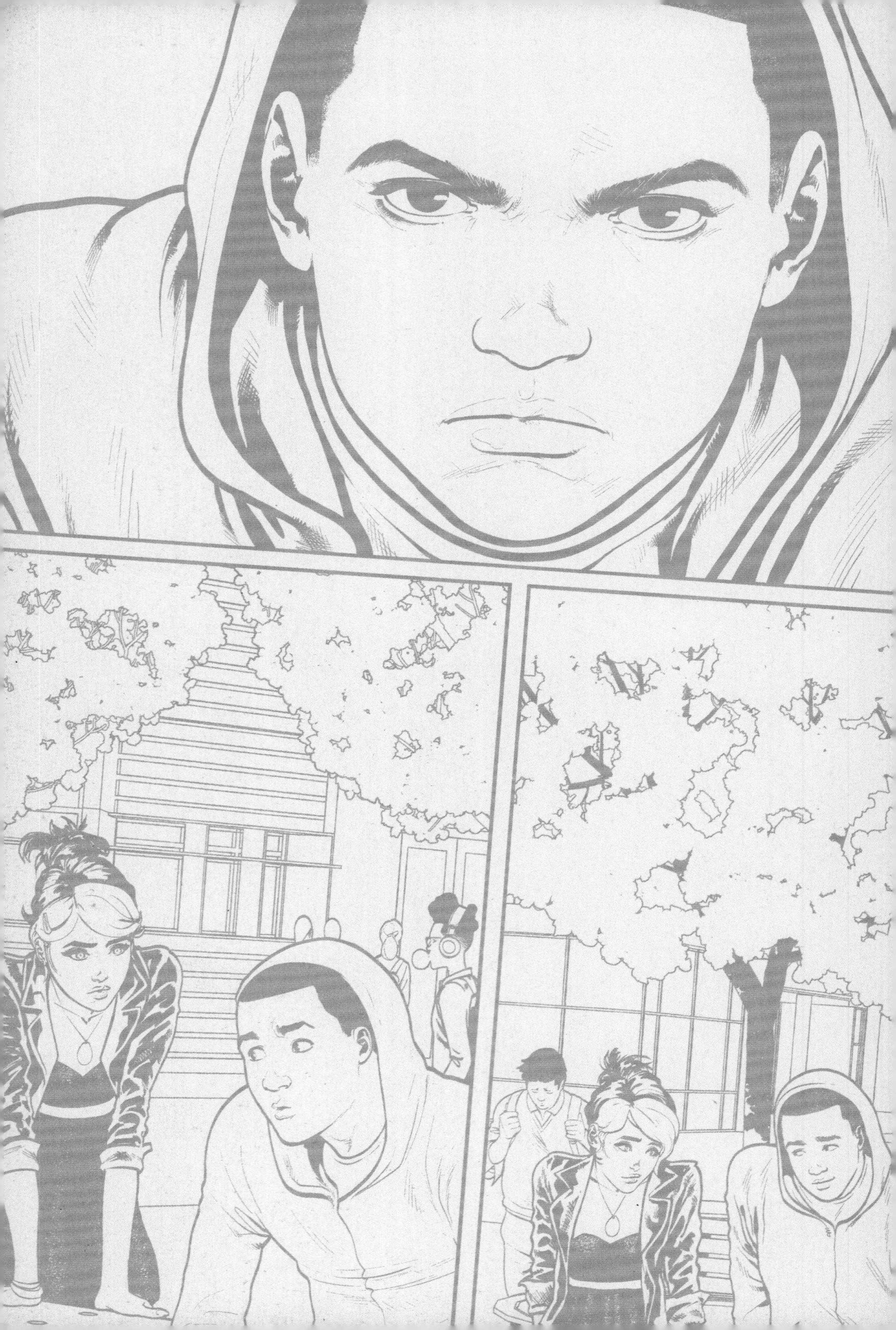

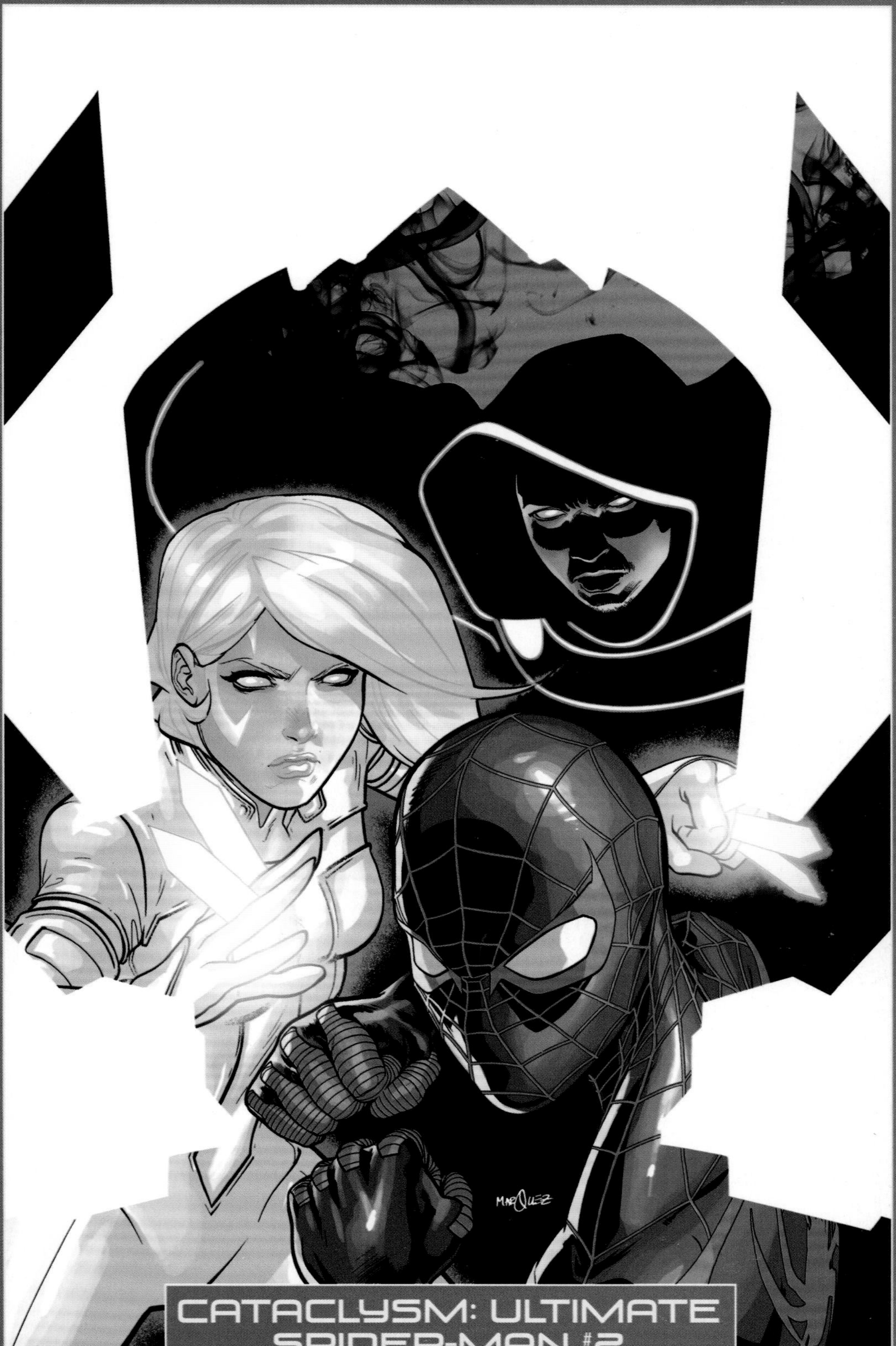
MARQUEZ
CATACLYSM: ULTIMATE
SPIDER-MAN #2

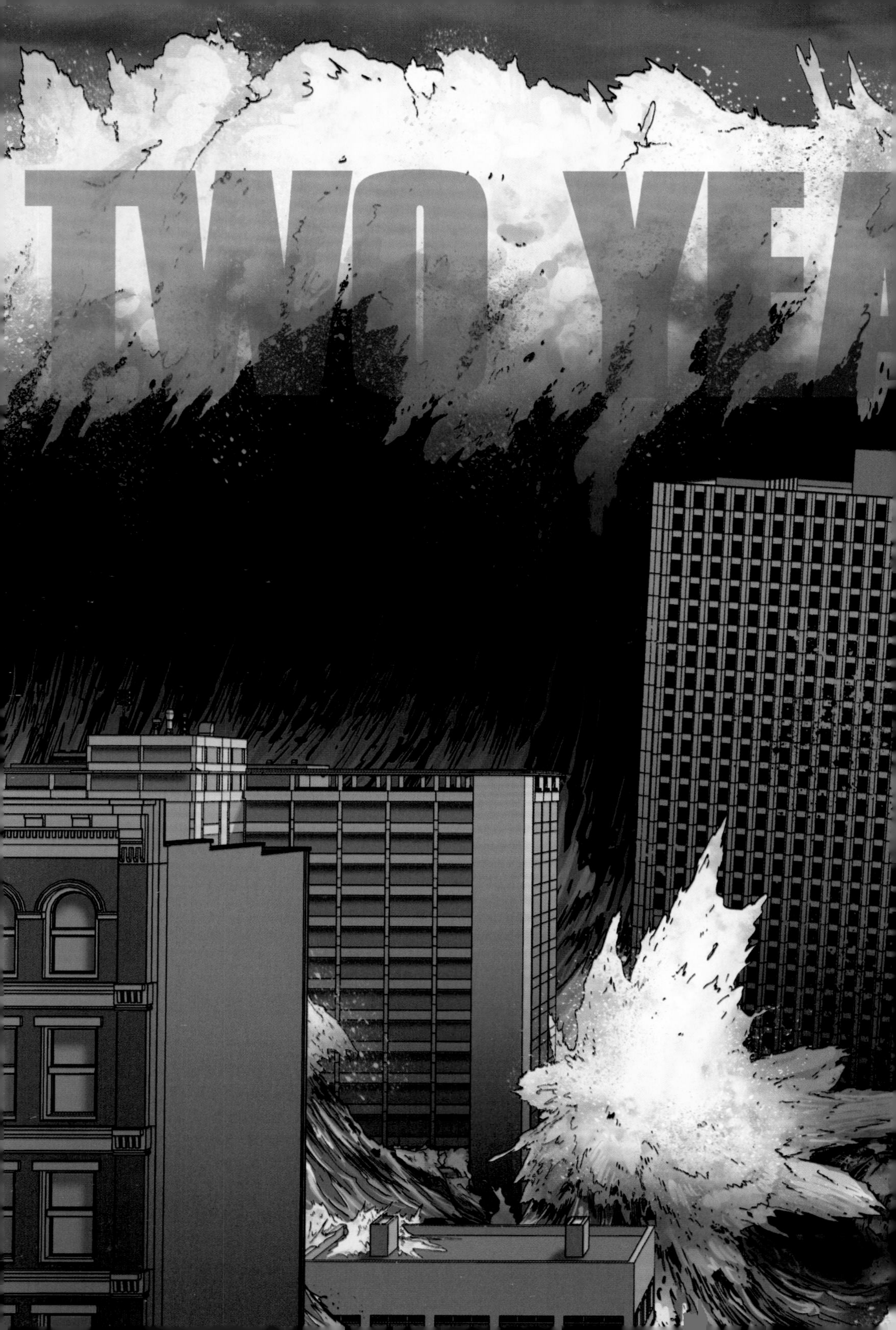
TWO YEA

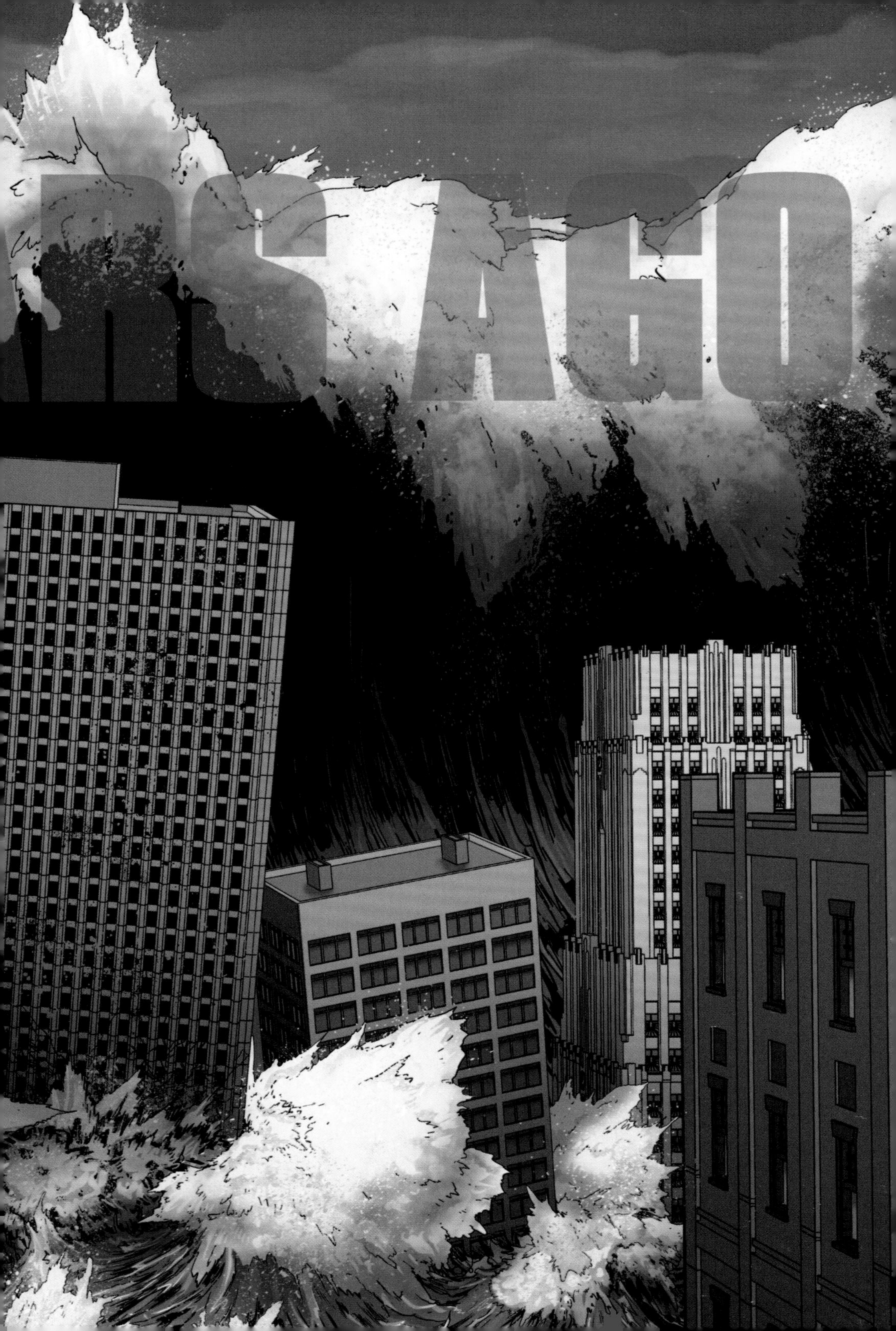
RS AGO

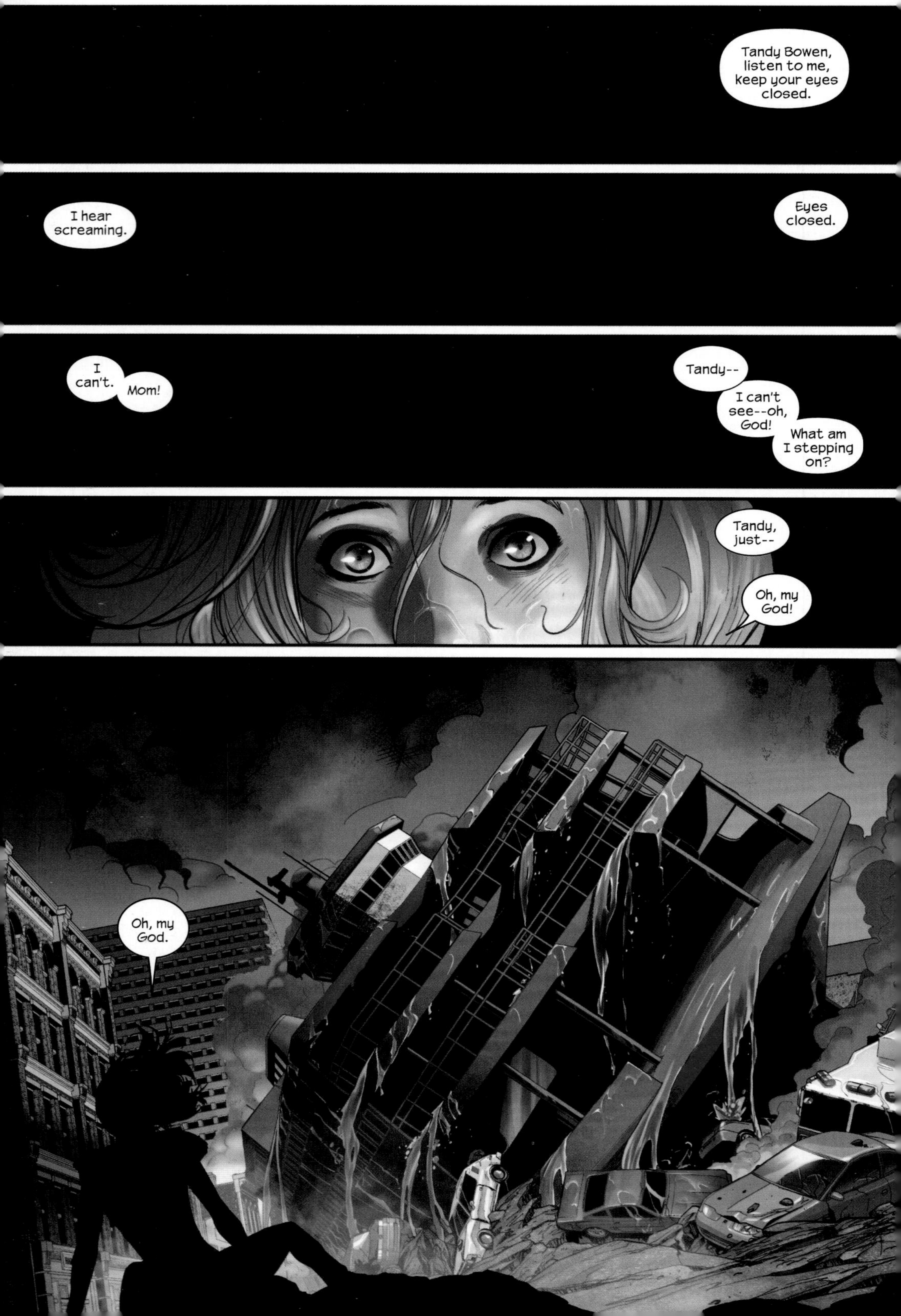
Tandy Bowen, listen to me, keep your eyes closed.
I hear screaming.
Eyes closed.
I can't.
Mom!
Tandy--
I can't see--oh, God!
What am I stepping on?
Tandy, just--
Oh, my God!
Oh, my God.

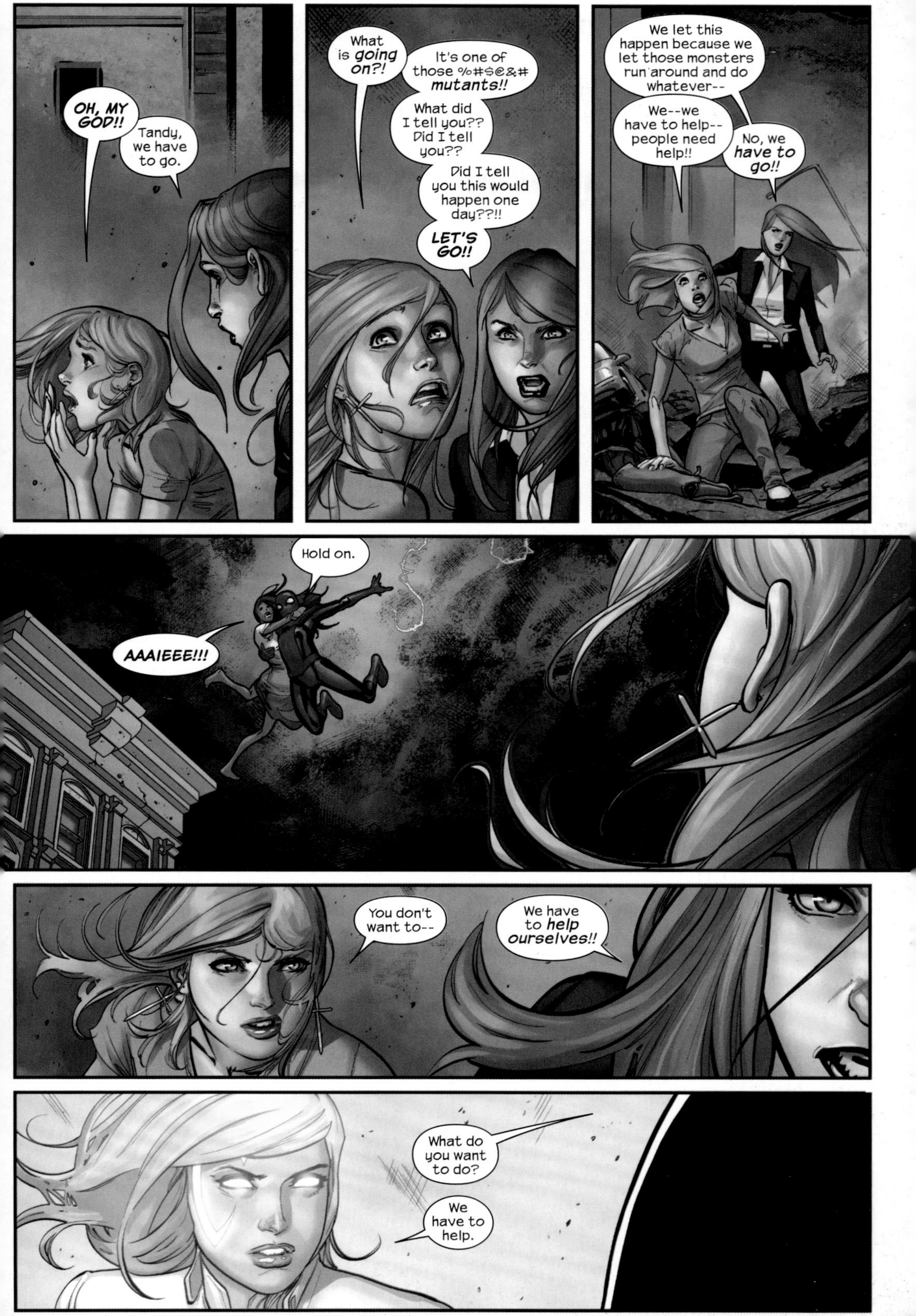

OH, MY GOD!!
Tandy, we have to go.
What is *going on?!*
It's one of those %#$@&# *mutants!!*
What did I tell you?? Did I tell you??
Did I tell you this would happen one day??!!
LET'S GO!!
We let this happen because we let those monsters run around and do whatever--
We--we have to help--people need help!!
No, we *have to go!!*
Hold on.
AAAIEEE!!!
You don't want to--
We have to *help ourselves!!*
What do you want to do?
We have to help.

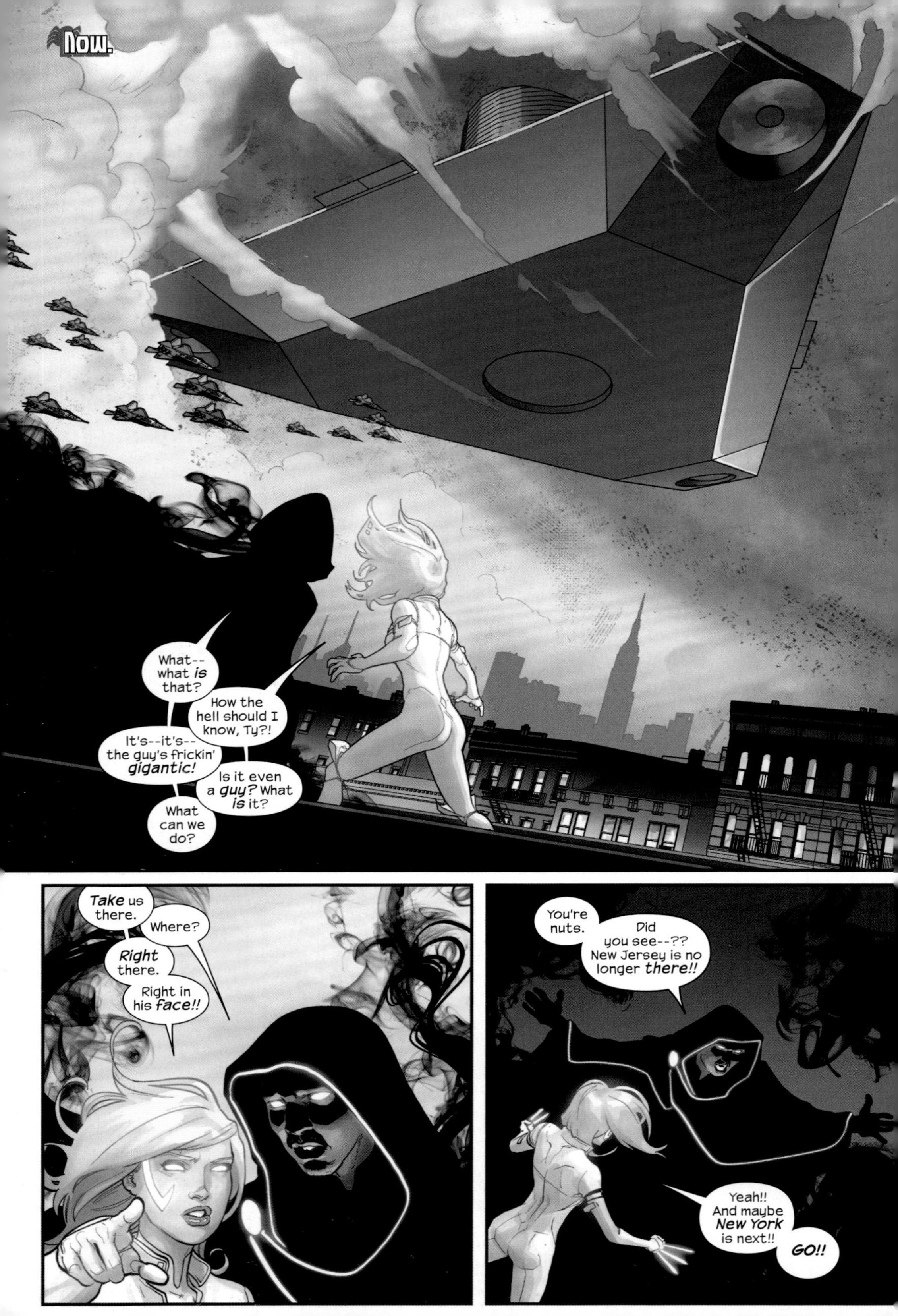
Now.
What-- what *is* that?
How the hell should I know, Ty?!
It's--it's-- the guy's frickin' *gigantic!*
Is it even a *guy?* What *is* it?
What can we do?
Take us there.
Where?
Right there.
Right in his *face!!*
You're nuts.
Did you see--?? New Jersey is no longer *there!!*
Yeah!! And maybe *New York* is next!!
GO!!

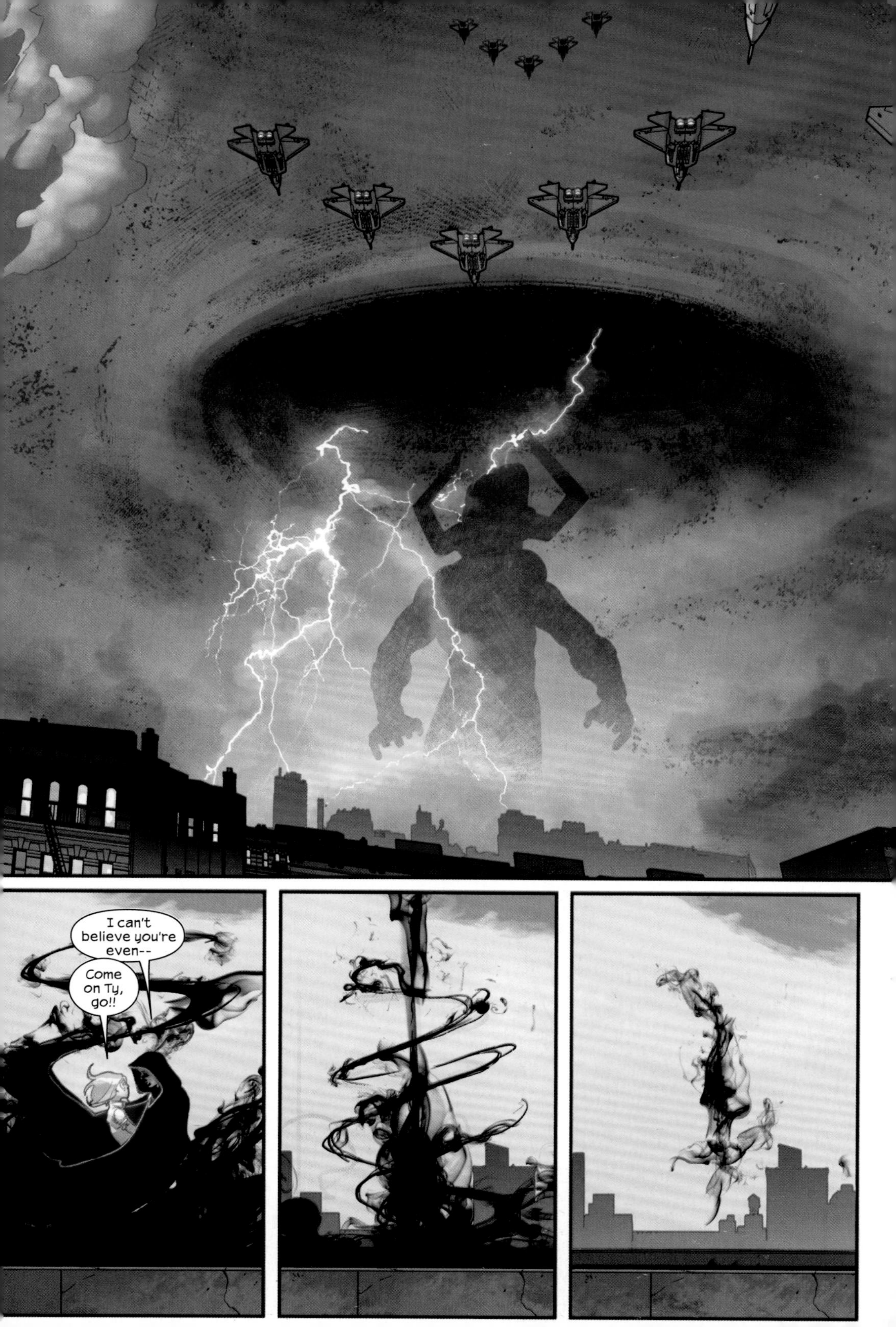

I can't believe you're even--
Come on Ty, go!!

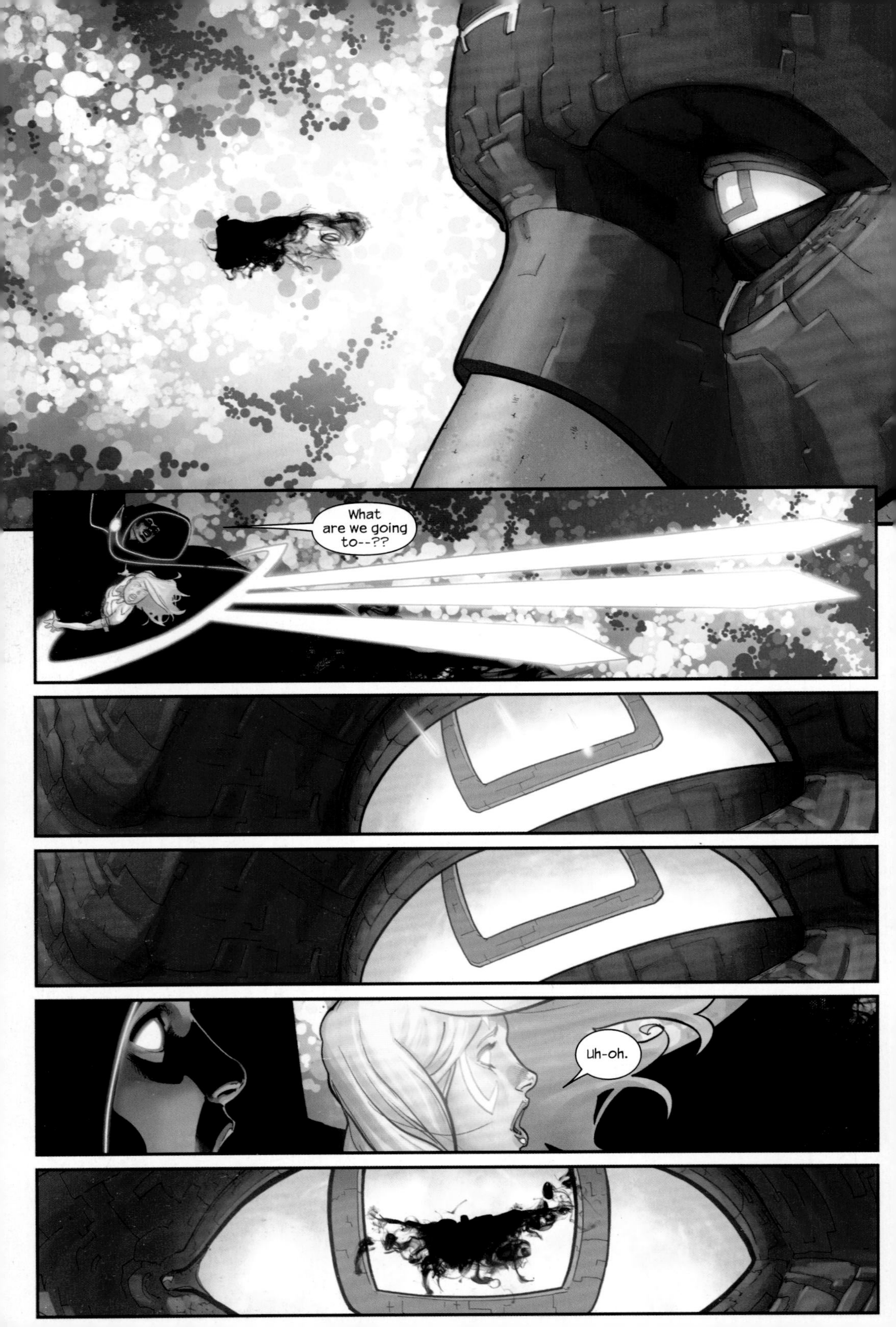
What are we going to--??
Uh-oh.

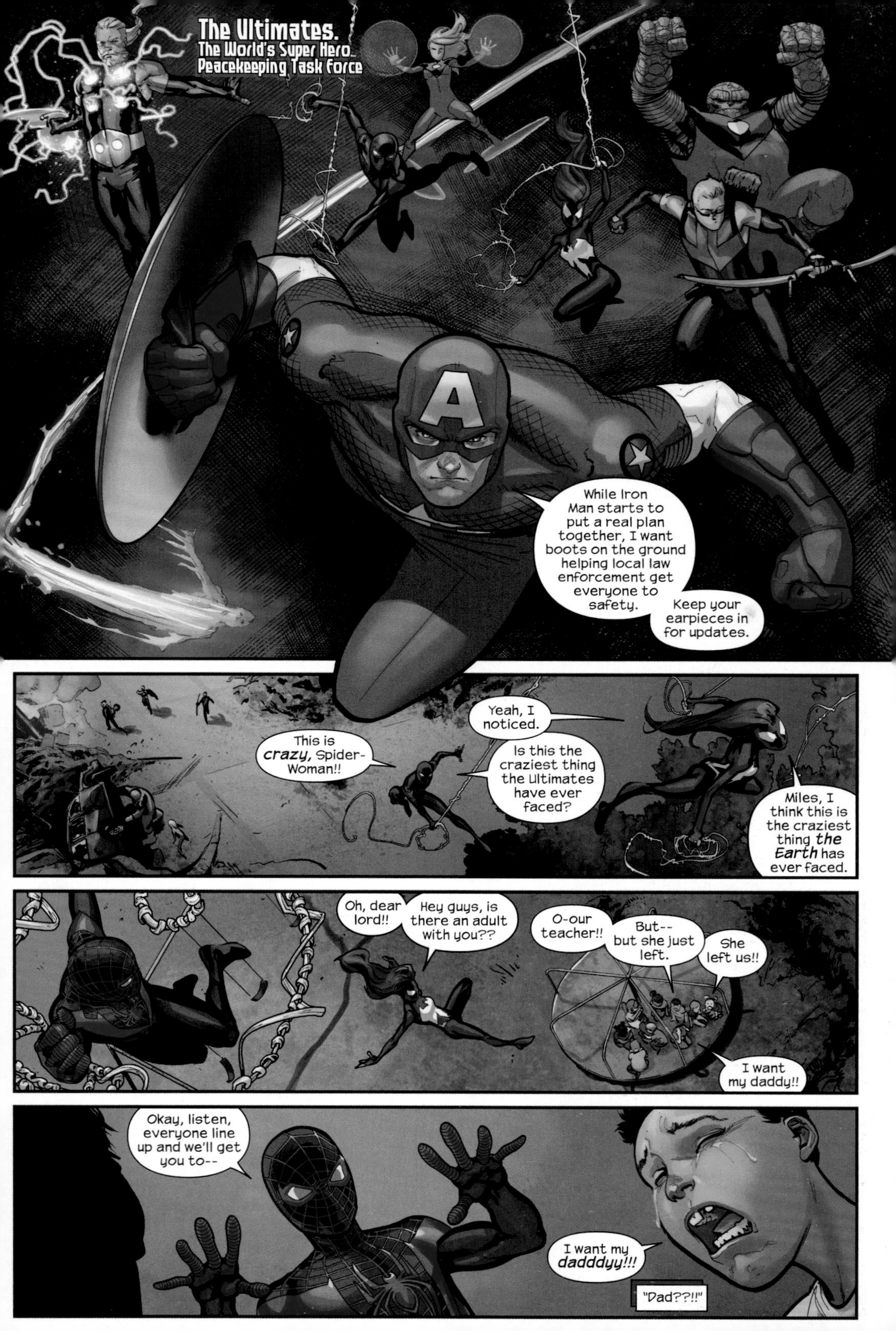

The Ultimates.
The World's Super Hero Peacekeeping Task Force
While Iron Man starts to put a real plan together, I want boots on the ground helping local law enforcement get everyone to safety.
Keep your earpieces in for updates.
This is crazy, Spider-Woman!!
Yeah, I noticed.
Is this the craziest thing the Ultimates have ever faced?
Miles, I think this is the craziest thing the Earth has ever faced.
Oh, dear lord!!
Hey guys, is there an adult with you??
O-our teacher!!
But-- but she just left.
She left us!!
I want my daddy!!
Okay, listen, everyone line up and we'll get you to--
I want my dadddyy!!!
"Dad??!!"

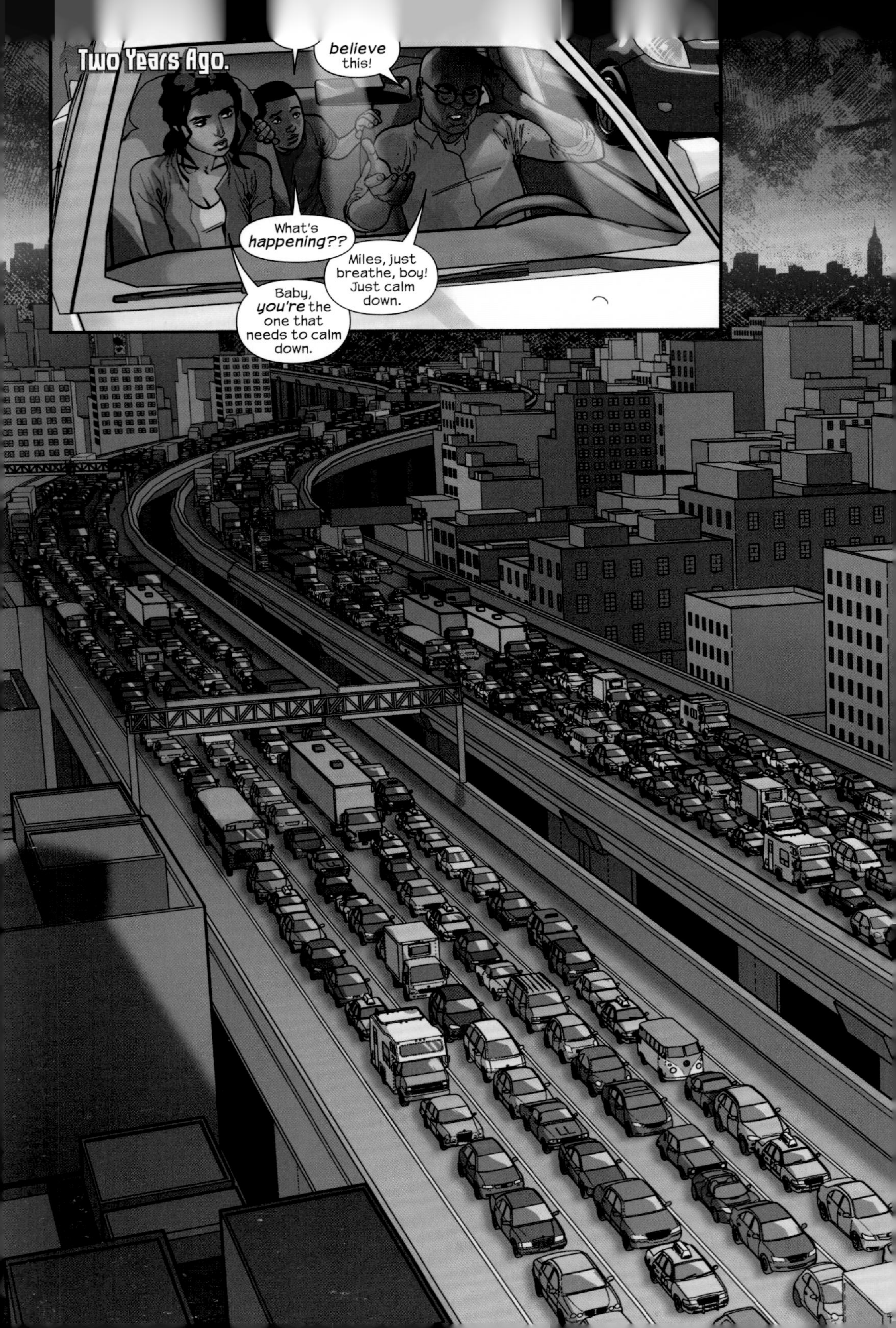

Two Years Ago.
believe this!
What's happening??
Miles, just breathe, boy! Just calm down.
Baby, you're the one that needs to calm down.

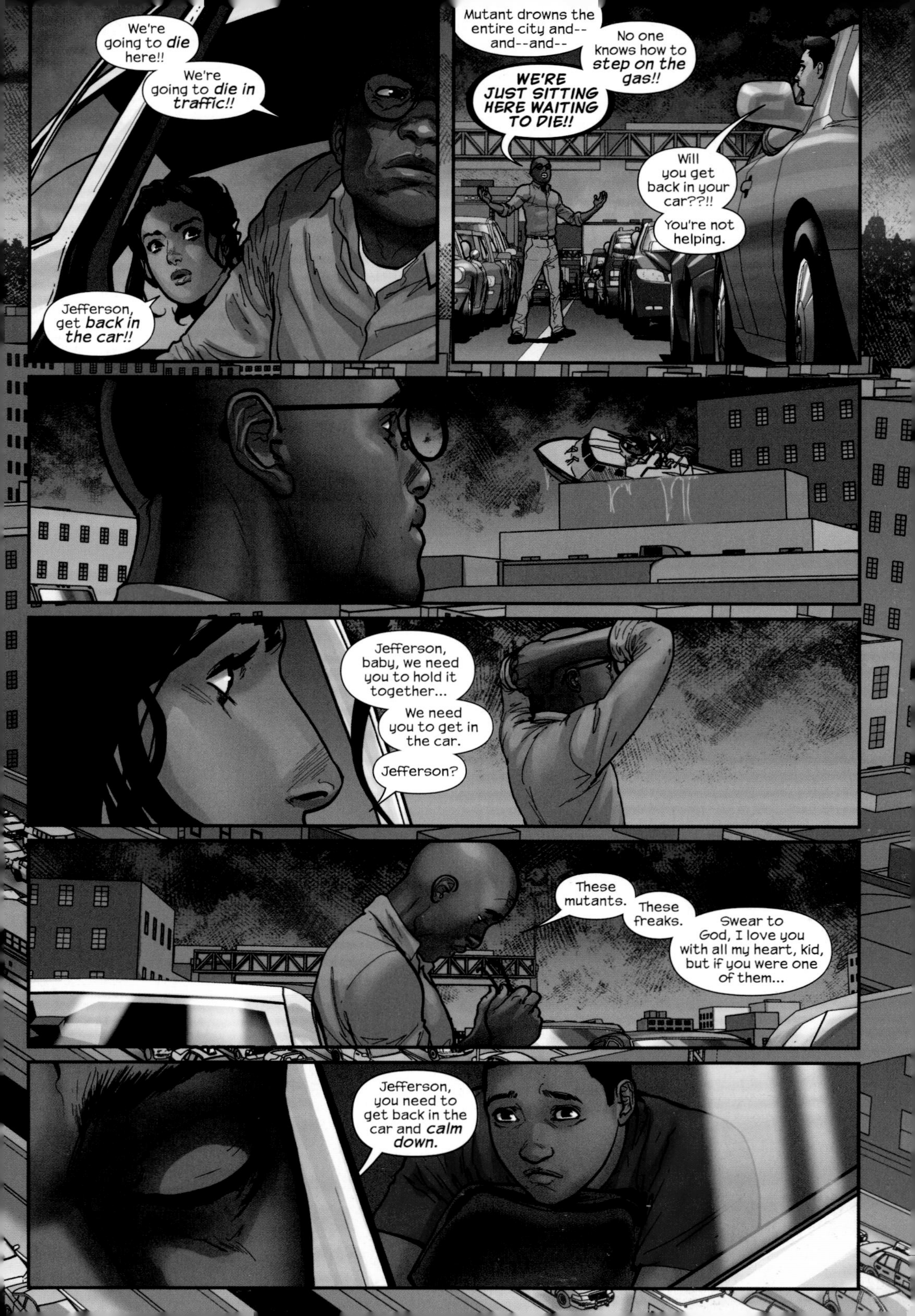

We're going to *die* here!!
We're going to *die in traffic!!*
Jefferson, get *back in the car!!*
Mutant drowns the entire city and-- and--and--
No one knows how to *step on the gas!!*
WE'RE JUST SITTING HERE WAITING TO DIE!!
Will you get back in your car??!!
You're not helping.
Jefferson, baby, we need you to hold it together...
We need you to get in the car.
Jefferson?
These mutants.
These freaks.
Swear to God, I love you with all my heart, kid, but if you were one of them...
Jefferson, you need to get back in the car and *calm down.*

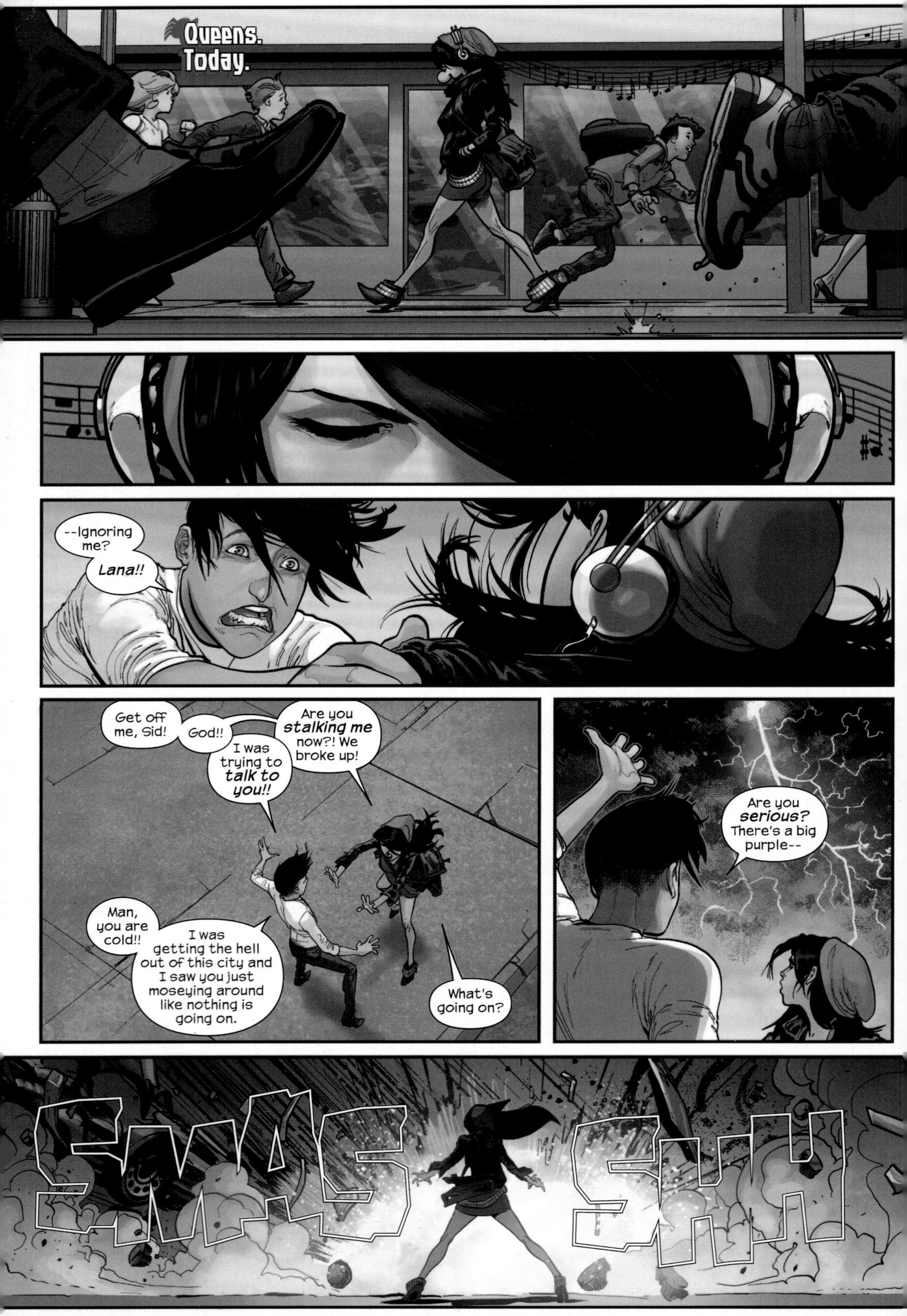
Queens. Today.
--Ignoring me?
Lana!!
Get off me, Sid!
God!!
Are you stalking me now?! We broke up!
I was trying to talk to you!!
Man, you are cold!!
I was getting the hell out of this city and I saw you just moseying around like nothing is going on.
What's going on?
Are you serious? There's a big purple--
SMASH

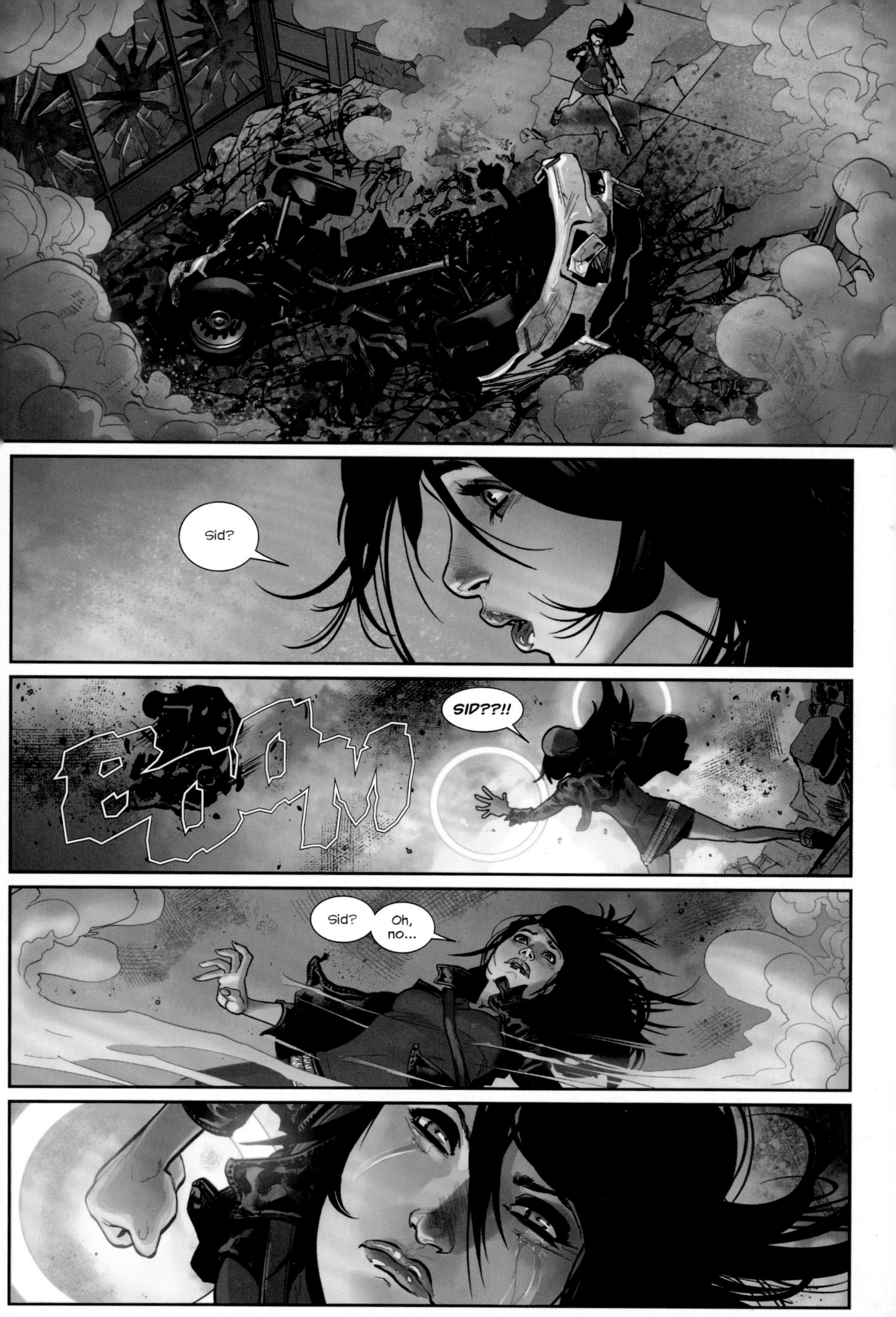
Sid?
BOOM
SID??!!
Sid?
Oh, no...

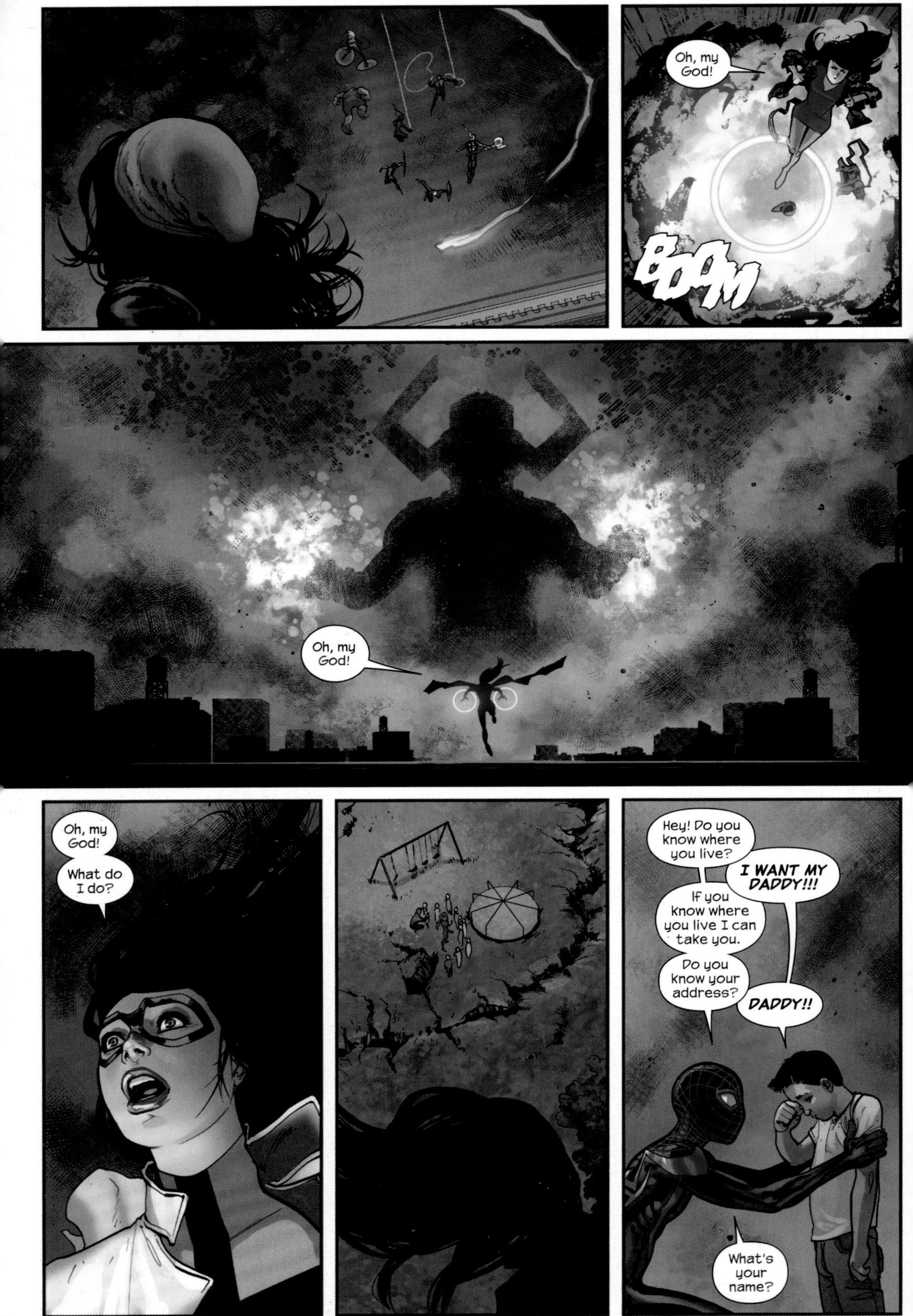
Oh, my God!
BOOM
Oh, my God!
Oh, my God!
What do I do?
Hey! Do you know where you live?
I WANT MY DADDY!!!
If you know where you live I can take you.
Do you know your address?
DADDY!!
What's your name?

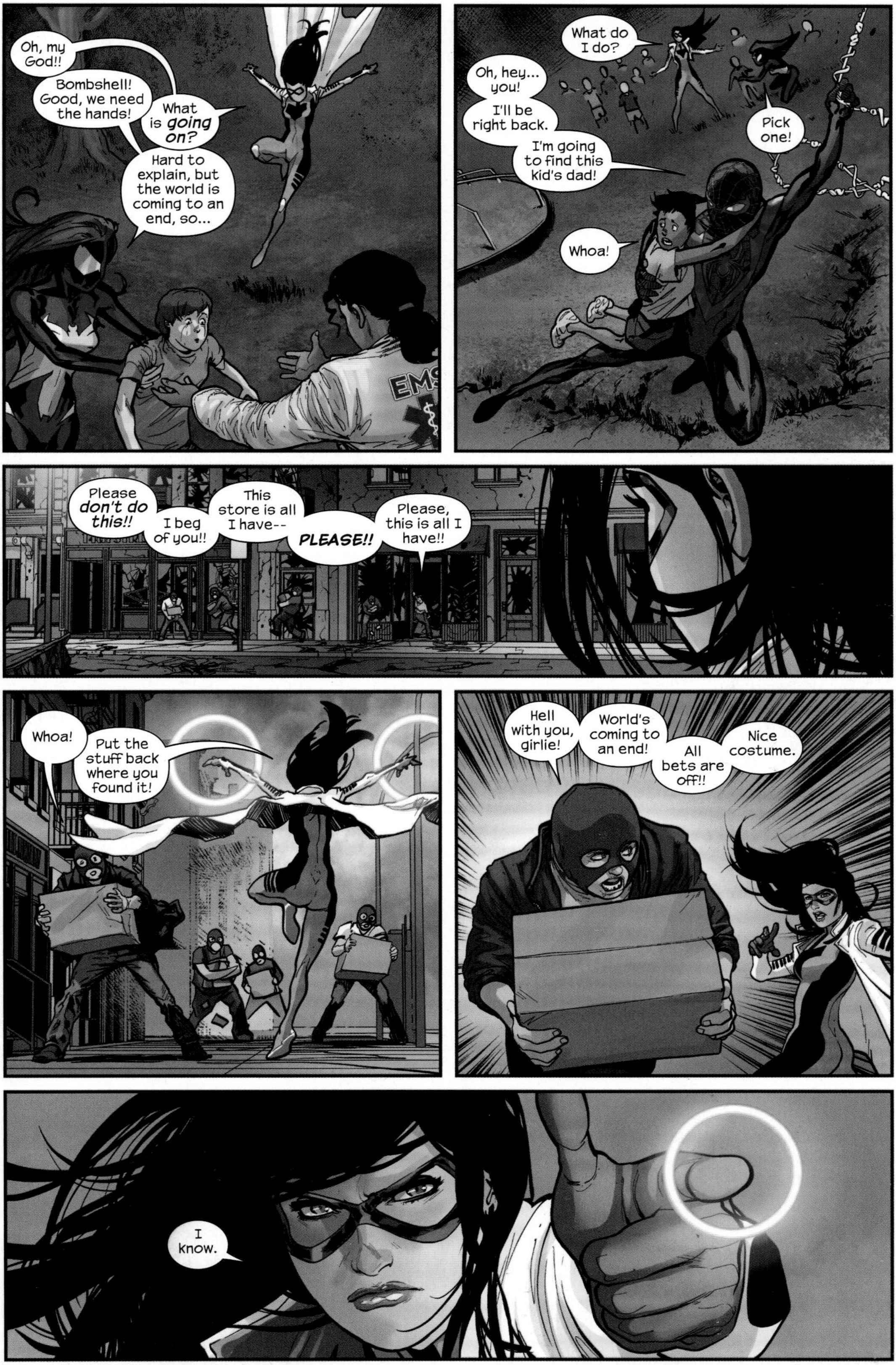

Oh, my God!!
Bombshell! Good, we need the hands!
What is *going on?*
Hard to explain, but the world is coming to an end, so...
EMS
What do I do?
Oh, hey... you!
I'll be right back.
I'm going to find this kid's dad!
Pick one!
Whoa!
Please *don't do this!!*
I beg of you!!
This store is all I have--
PLEASE!!
Please, this is all I have!!
Whoa!
Put the stuff back where you found it!
Hell with you, girlie!
World's coming to an end!
All bets are off!!
Nice costume.
I know.

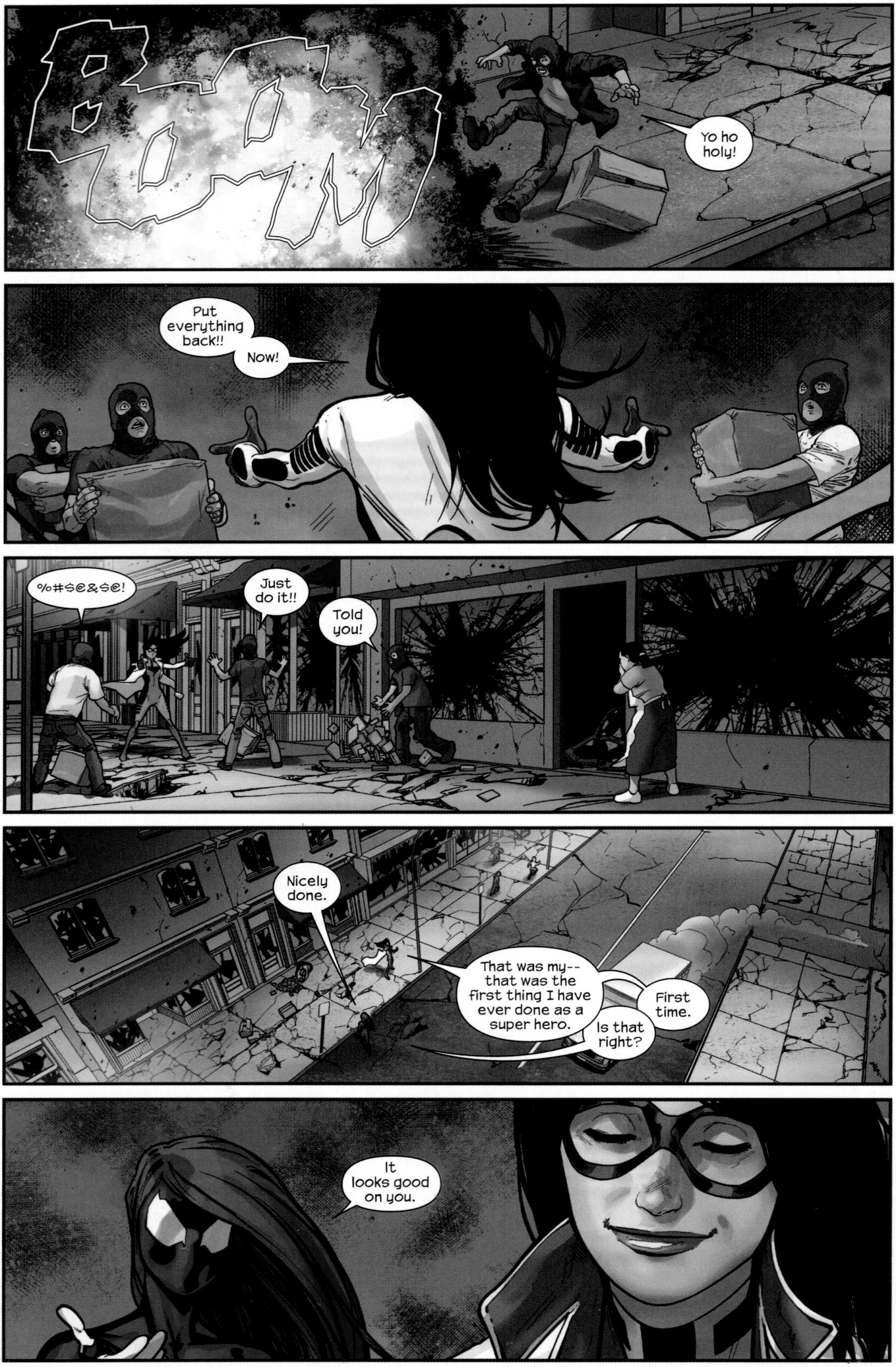
BOOM
Yo ho holy!
Put everything back!!
Now!
%#$@&$@!
Just do it!!
Told you!
Nicely done.
That was my-- that was the first thing I have ever done as a super hero.
First time.
Is that right?
It looks good on you.

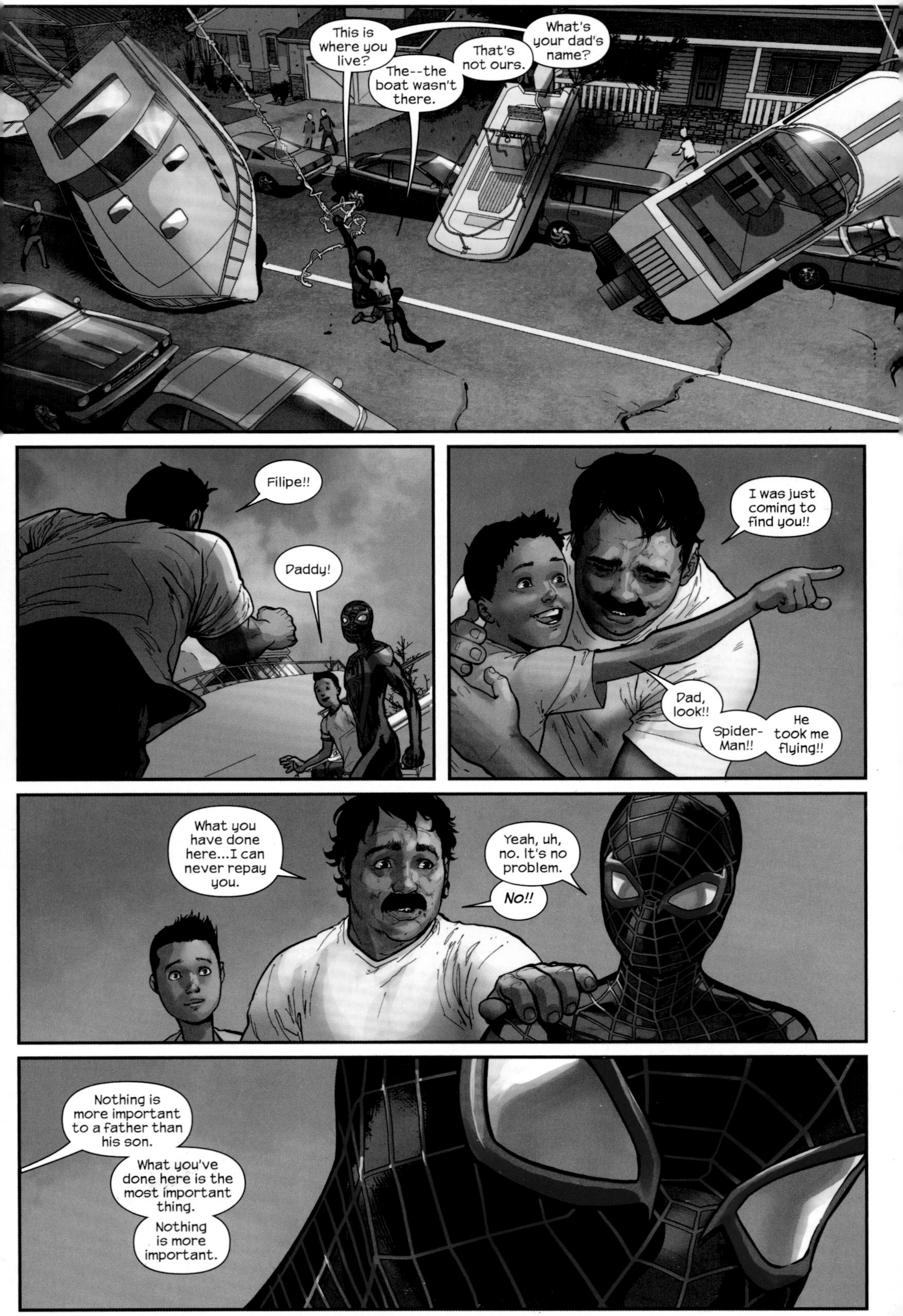
This is where you live?
What's your dad's name?
That's not ours.
The--the boat wasn't there.
Filipe!!
Daddy!
I was just coming to find you!!
Dad, look!!
Spider-Man!!
He took me flying!!
What you have done here...I can never repay you.
Yeah, uh, no. It's no problem.
NO!!
Nothing is more important to a father than his son.
What you've done here is the most important thing.
Nothing is more important.

Ty!!
Ty!!!
TY!!!
Agh!!
Oh, my God!!
What is that?!
What is it doing?
We have to get these people out of here...

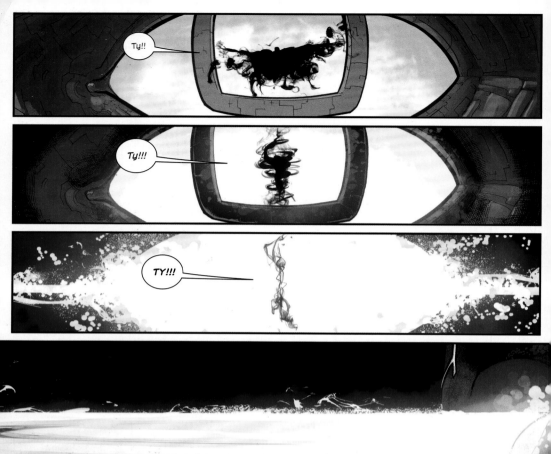

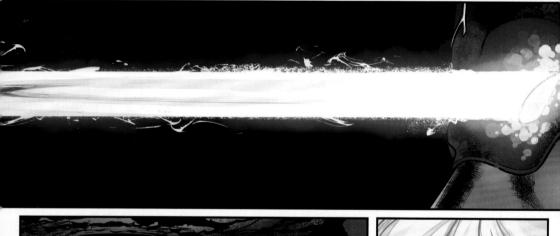

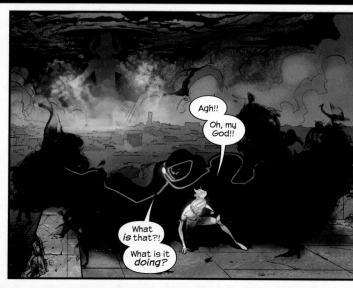

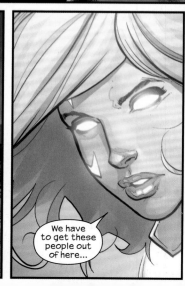

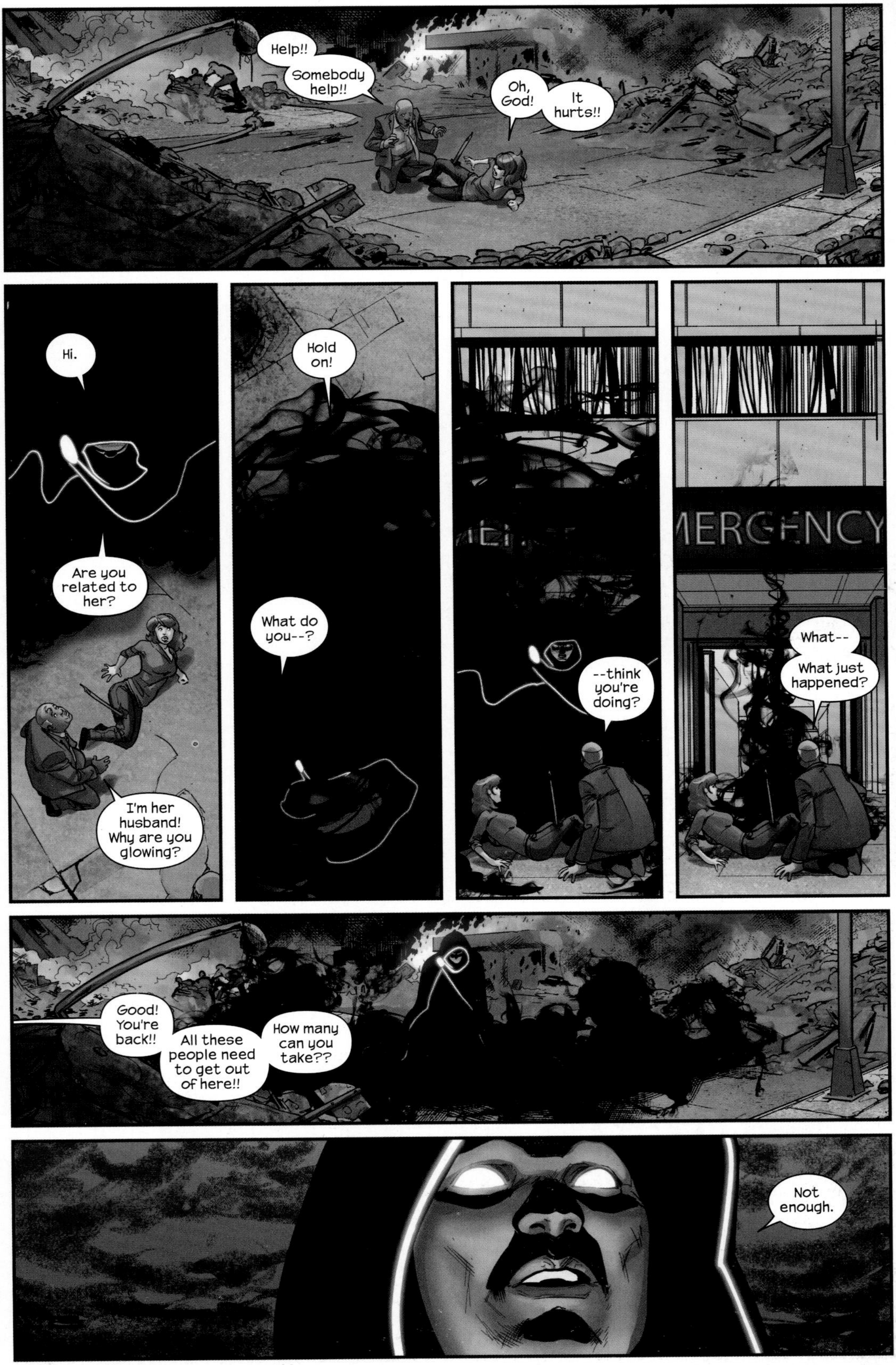
Help!!
Somebody help!!
Oh, God!
It hurts!!
Hi.
Are you related to her?
I'm her husband! Why are you glowing?
Hold on!
What do you--?
--think you're doing?
MERGENCY
What--
What just happened?
Good! You're back!!
All these people need to get out of here!!
How many can you take??
Not enough.

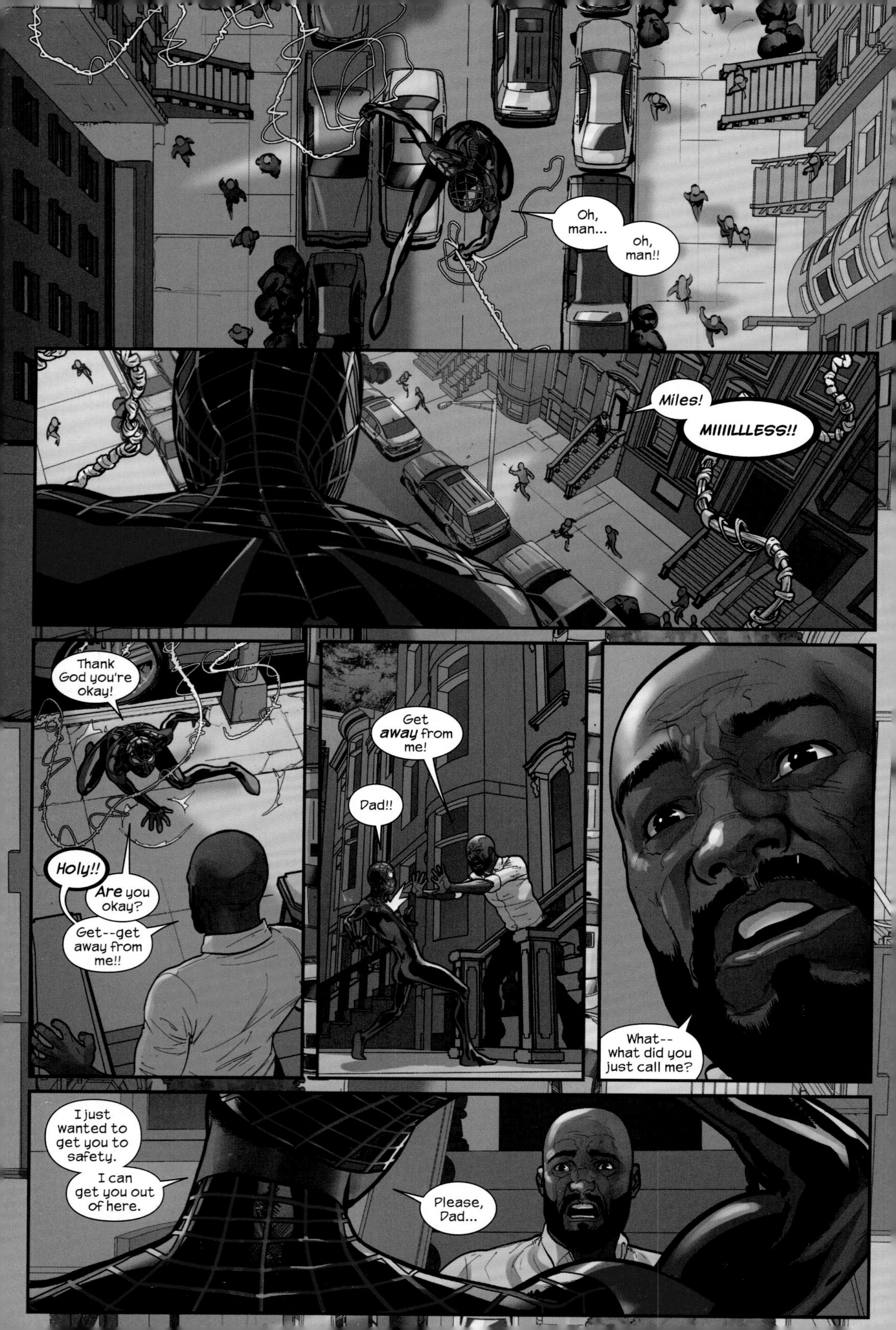
Oh, man...
oh, man!!
Miles!
MIIIILLLESS!!
Thank God you're okay!
Holy!!
Are you okay?
Get--get away from me!!
Get away from me!
Dad!!
What-- what did you just call me?
I just wanted to get you to safety.
I can get you out of here.
Please, Dad...

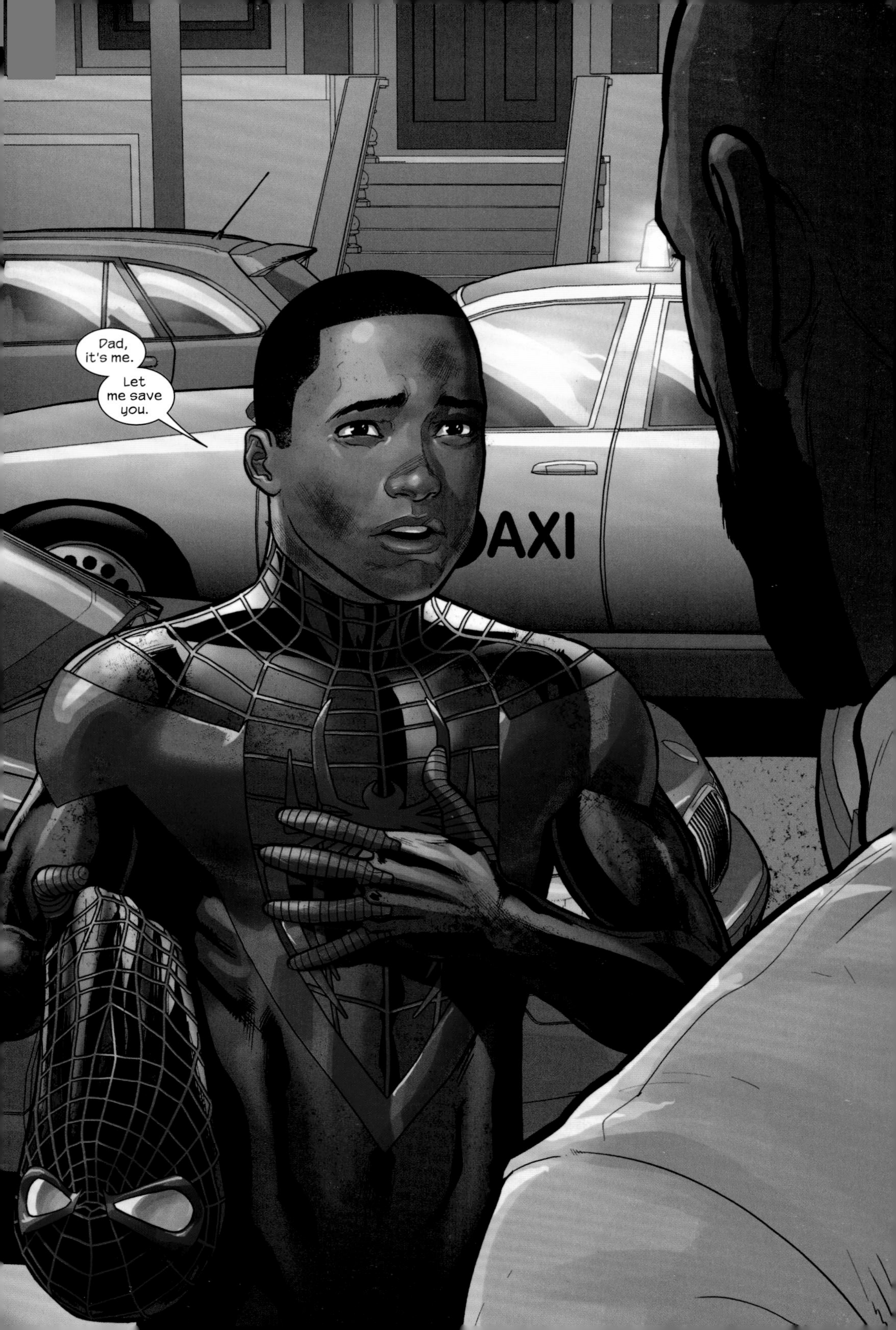
Dad, it's me.
Let me save you.
AXI

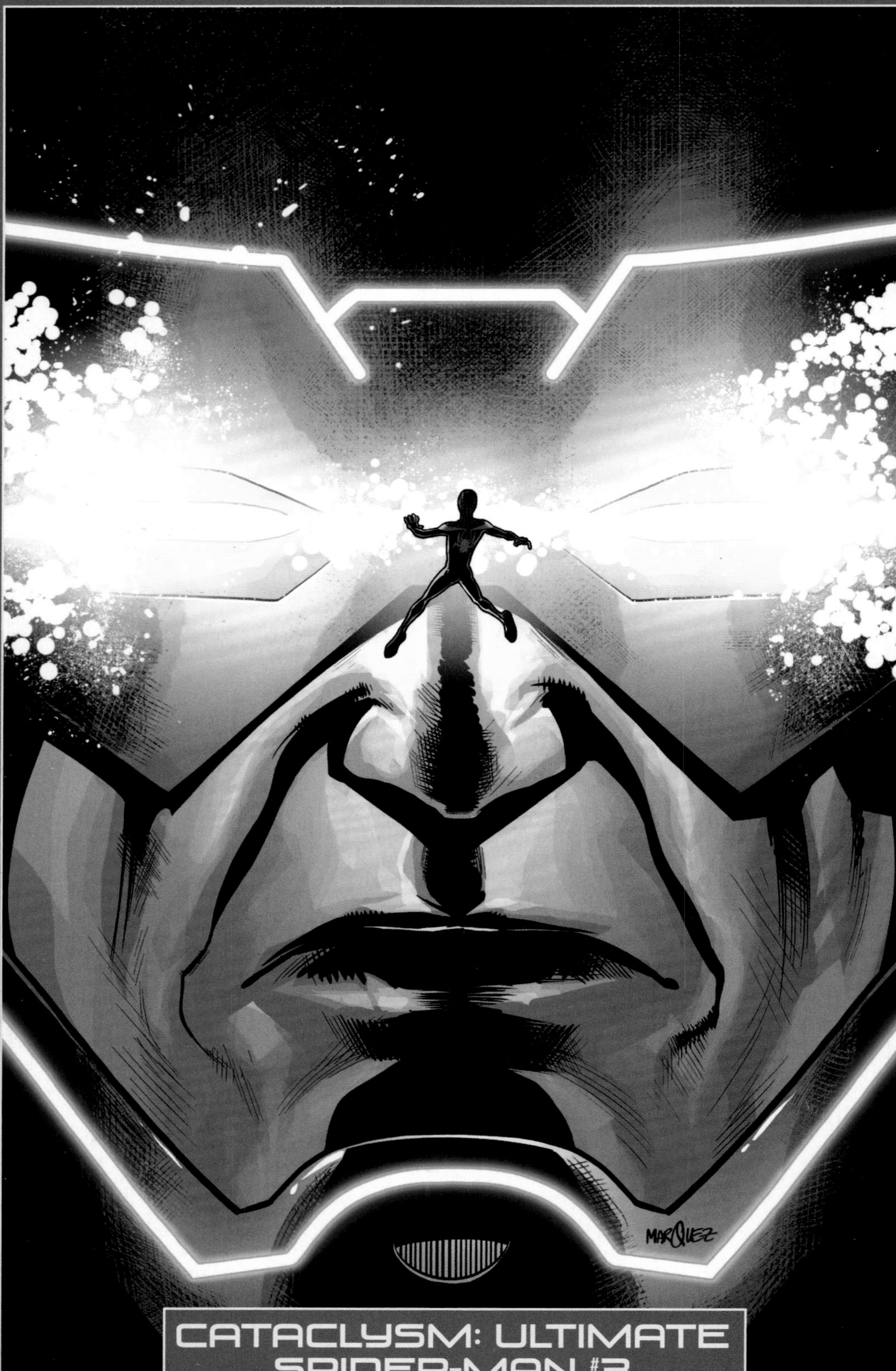
MARQUEZ
CATACLYSM: ULTIMATE SPIDER-MAN #3

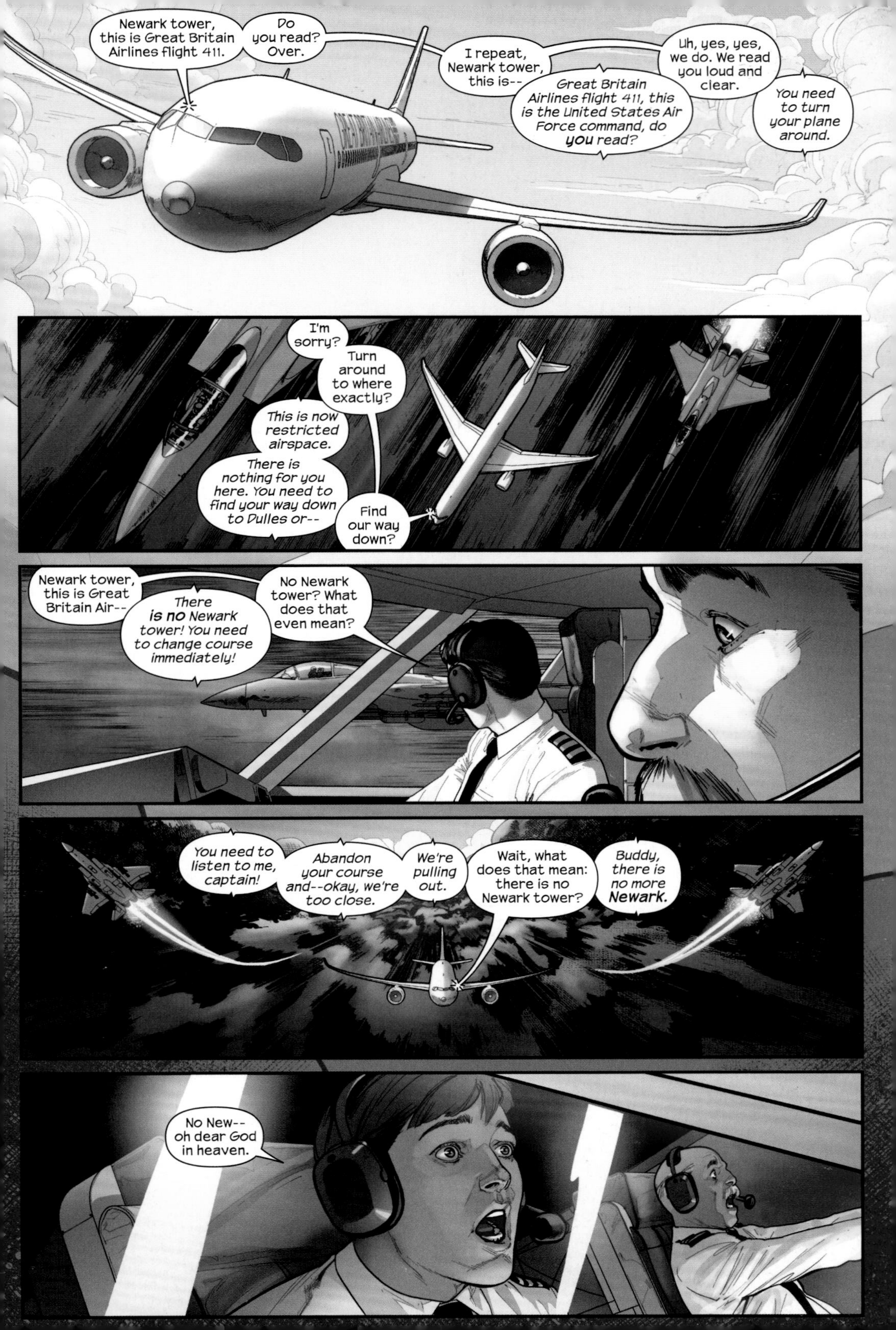
Newark tower, this is Great Britain Airlines flight 411.
Do you read? Over.
I repeat, Newark tower, this is--
Great Britain Airlines flight 411, this is the United States Air Force command, do you read?
Uh, yes, yes, we do. We read you loud and clear.
You need to turn your plane around.
I'm sorry?
Turn around to where exactly?
This is now restricted airspace.
There is nothing for you here. You need to find your way down to Dulles or--
Find our way down?
Newark tower, this is Great Britain Air--
There is no Newark tower! You need to change course immediately!
No Newark tower? What does that even mean?
You need to listen to me, captain!
Abandon your course and--okay, we're too close.
We're pulling out.
Wait, what does that mean: there is no Newark tower?
Buddy, there is no more Newark.
No New--oh dear God in heaven.

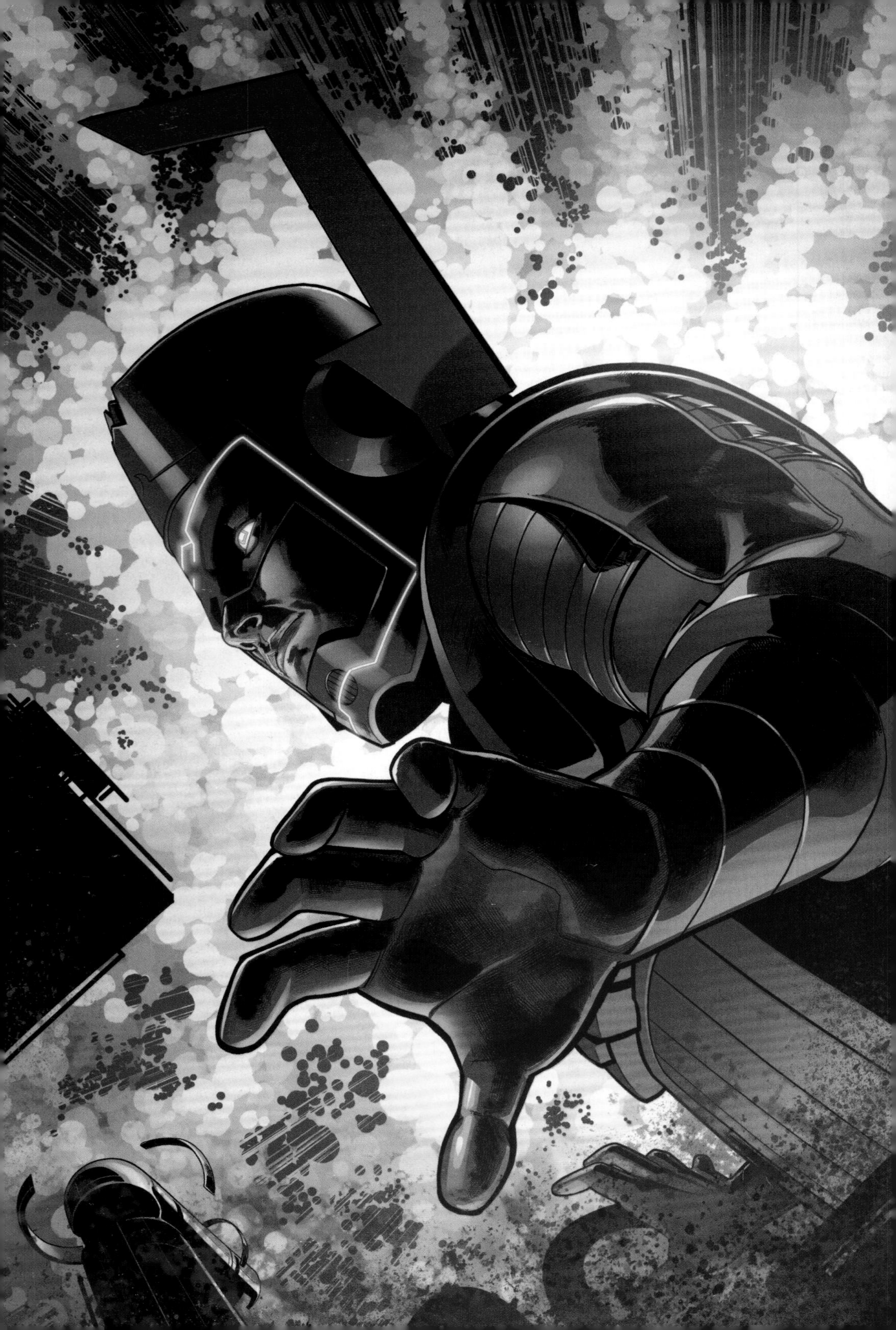

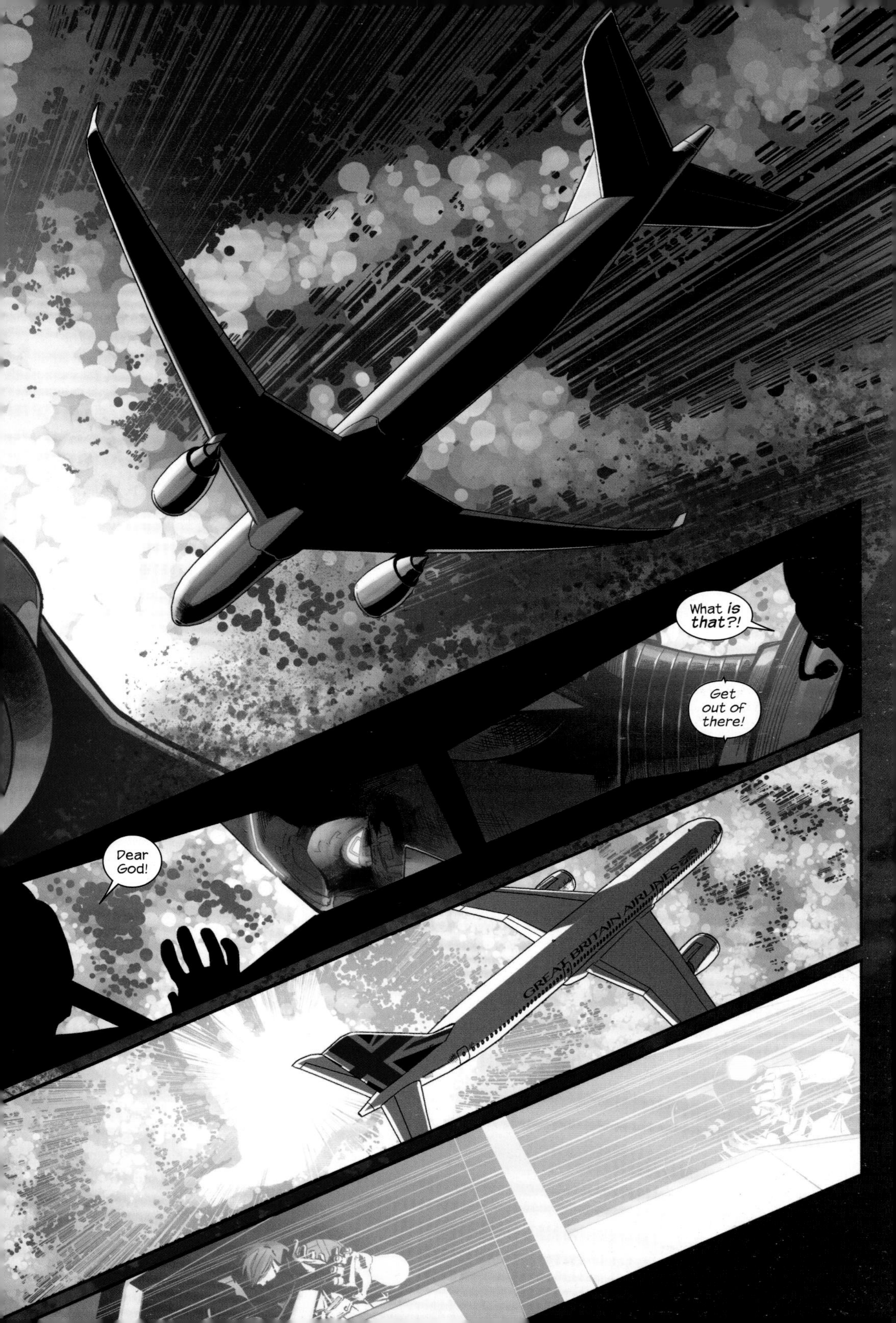
What is that?!
Get out of there!
Dear God!
GREAT BRITAIN AIRLINES

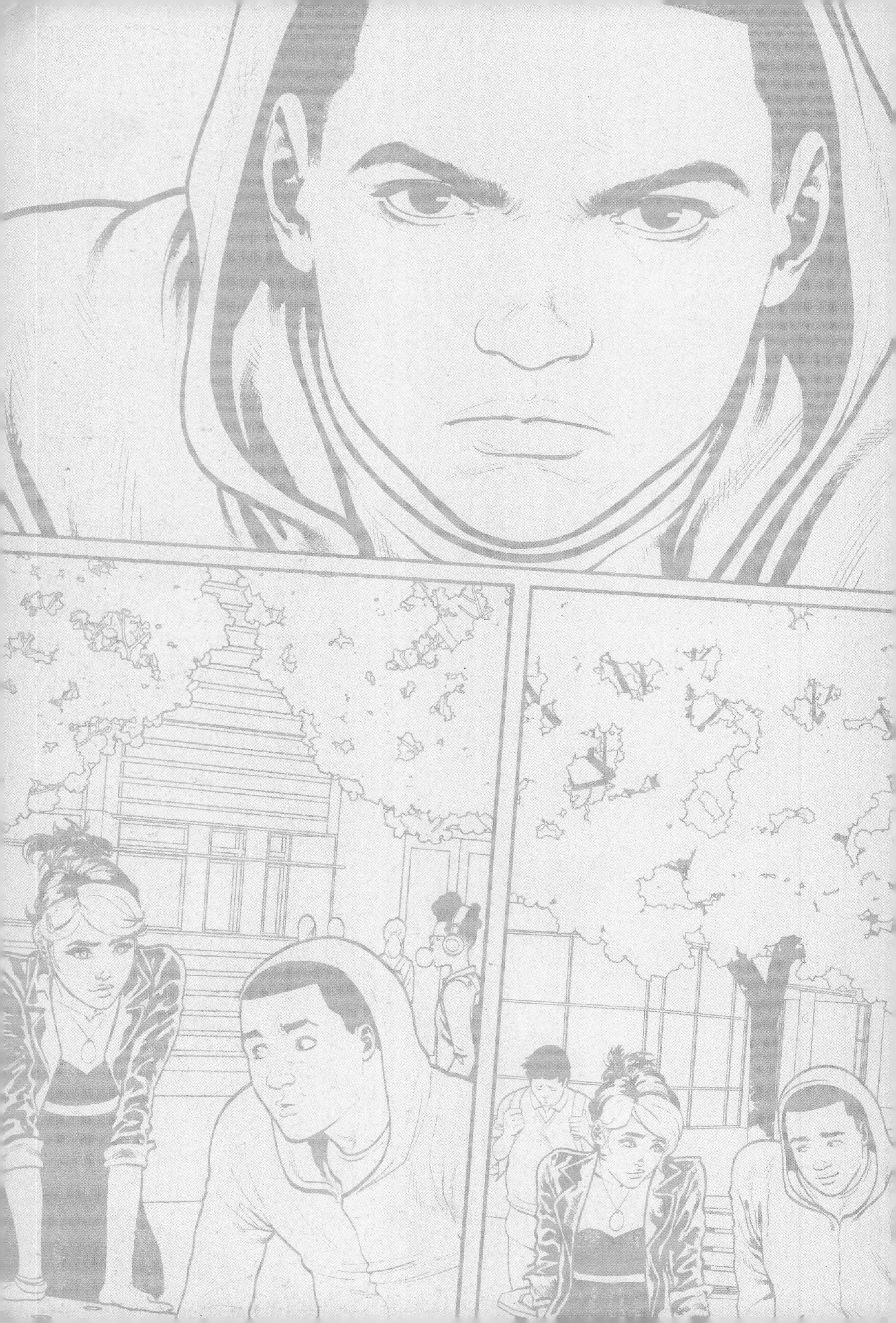

Brooklyn, New York.

Dad, *it's me.*

Please let me take you out of here! Let me save you.

M-Miles?

And we can talk about this, literally, *any* other time.

I'm going to take you out of this city and then I'm going to--

No!

Dad! *Please!*

DAD! This is bigger than whatever you think is wrong with super heroes and all that.

The world is *literally* going crazy.

New Jersey is gone! It's *all* gone! And New York *might be next!*

I've seen it! I've seen it with my own eyes!

I came back here to get you. We're all that we have. I *need* to get you somewhere safe.

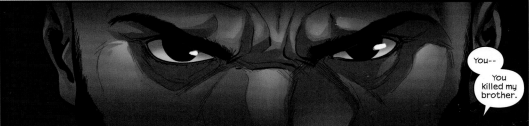

You-- You killed my brother.

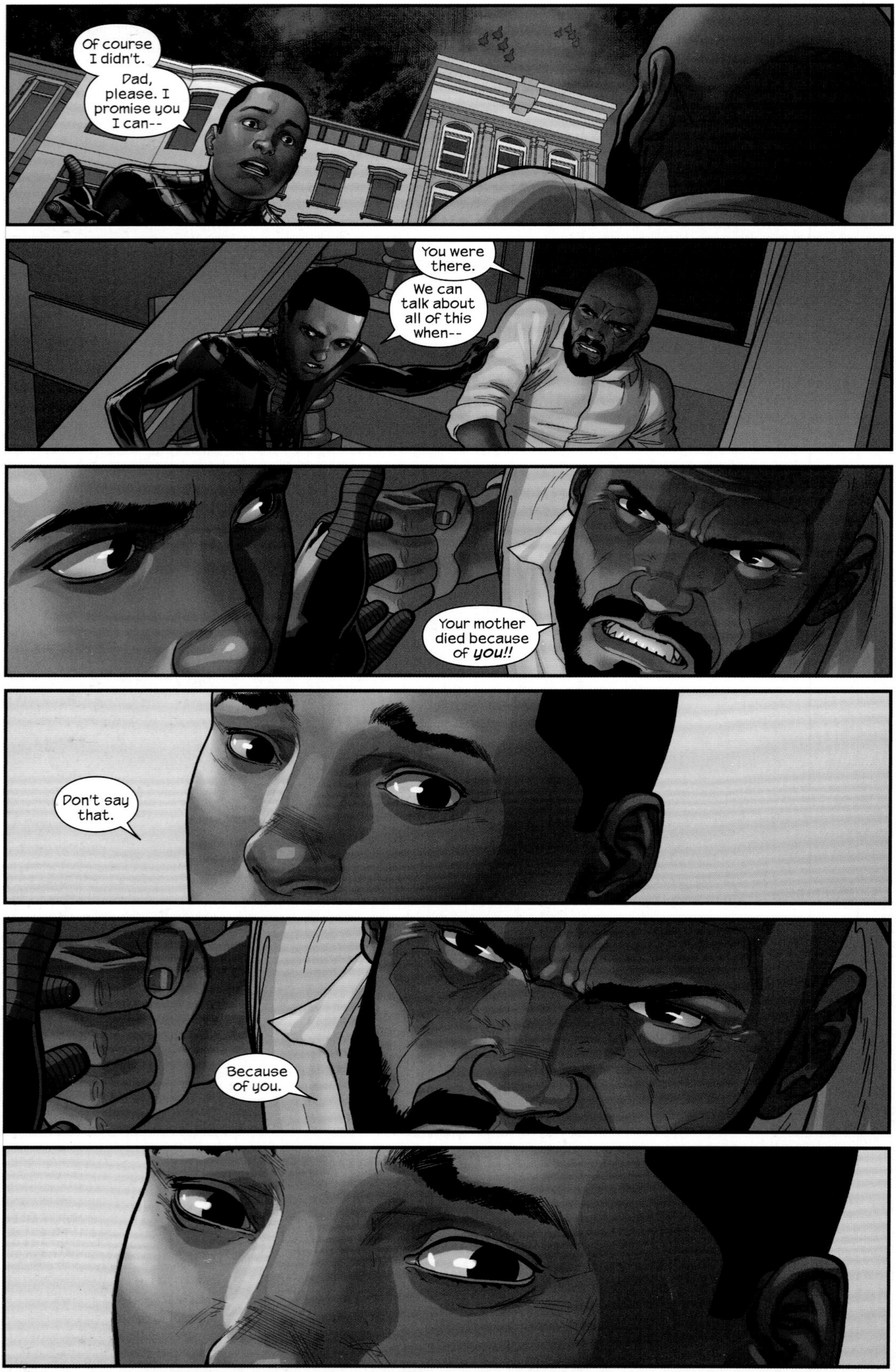
Of course I didn't.
Dad, please. I promise you I can--
You were there.
We can talk about all of this when--
Your mother died because of *you!!*
Don't say that.
Because of you.

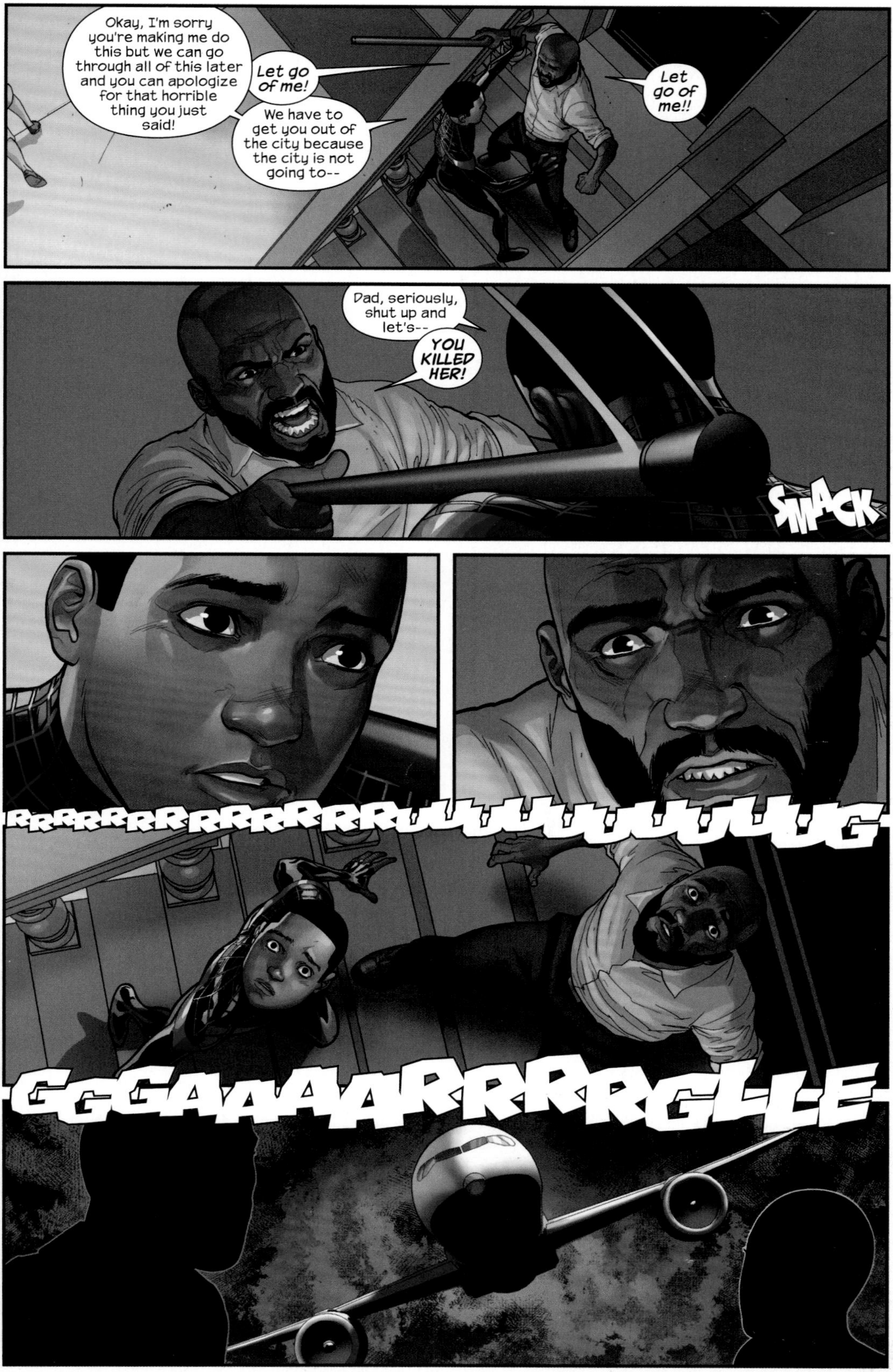
Okay, I'm sorry you're making me do this but we can go through all of this later and you can apologize for that horrible thing you just said!
Let go of me!
We have to get you out of the city because the city is not going to--
Let go of me!!
Dad, seriously, shut up and let's--
YOU KILLED HER!
SMACK
RRRRRRRRRRRRRUUUUUUUUUG
GGGAAAAARRRRRGLLE

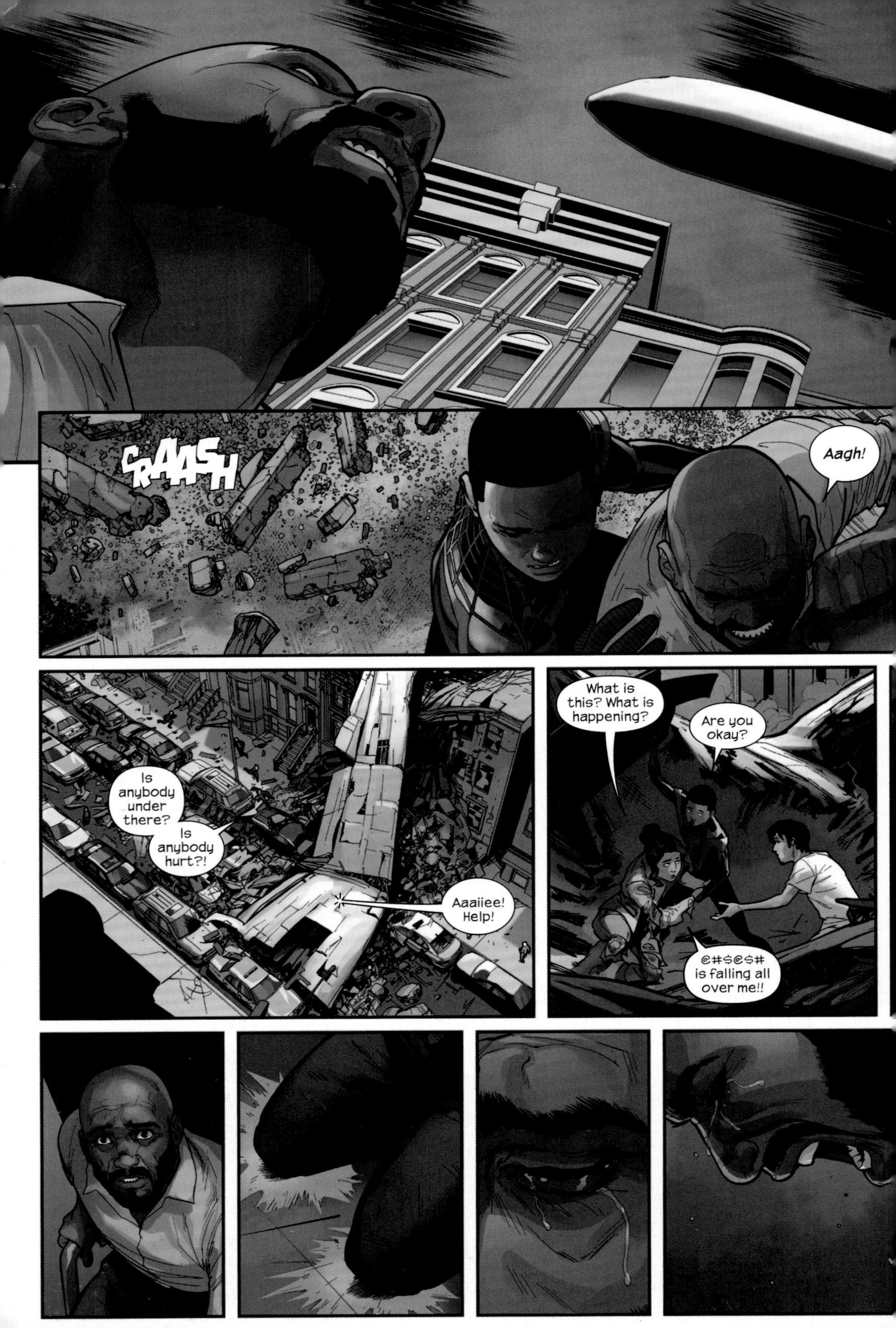
CRAASH
Aagh!
Is anybody under there?
Is anybody hurt?!
Aaaiiee! Help!
What is this? What is happening?
Are you okay?
@#$@$# is falling all over me!!

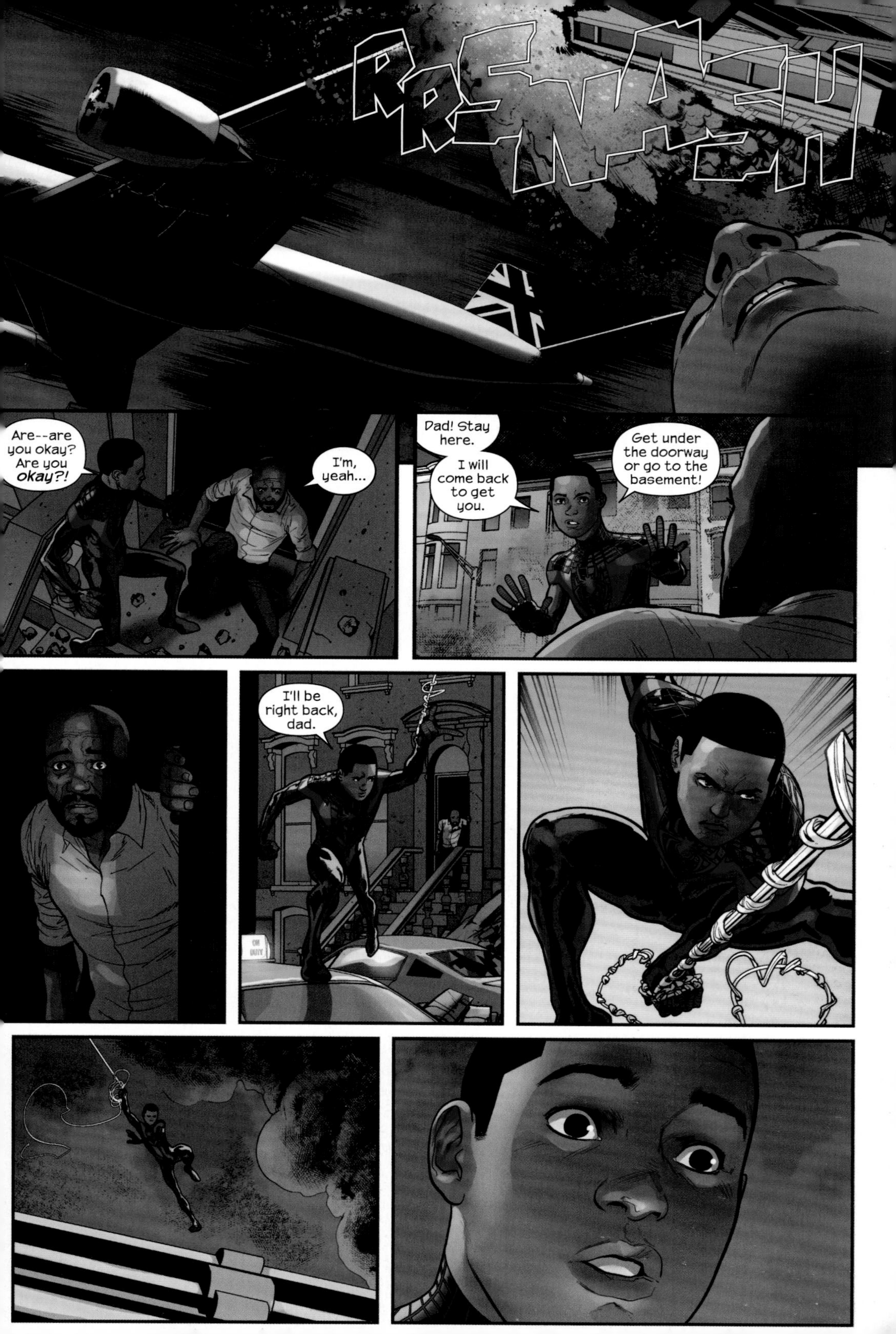

Are--are you okay? Are you *okay?!*
I'm, yeah...
Dad! Stay here.
I will come back to get you.
Get under the doorway or go to the basement!
I'll be right back, dad.

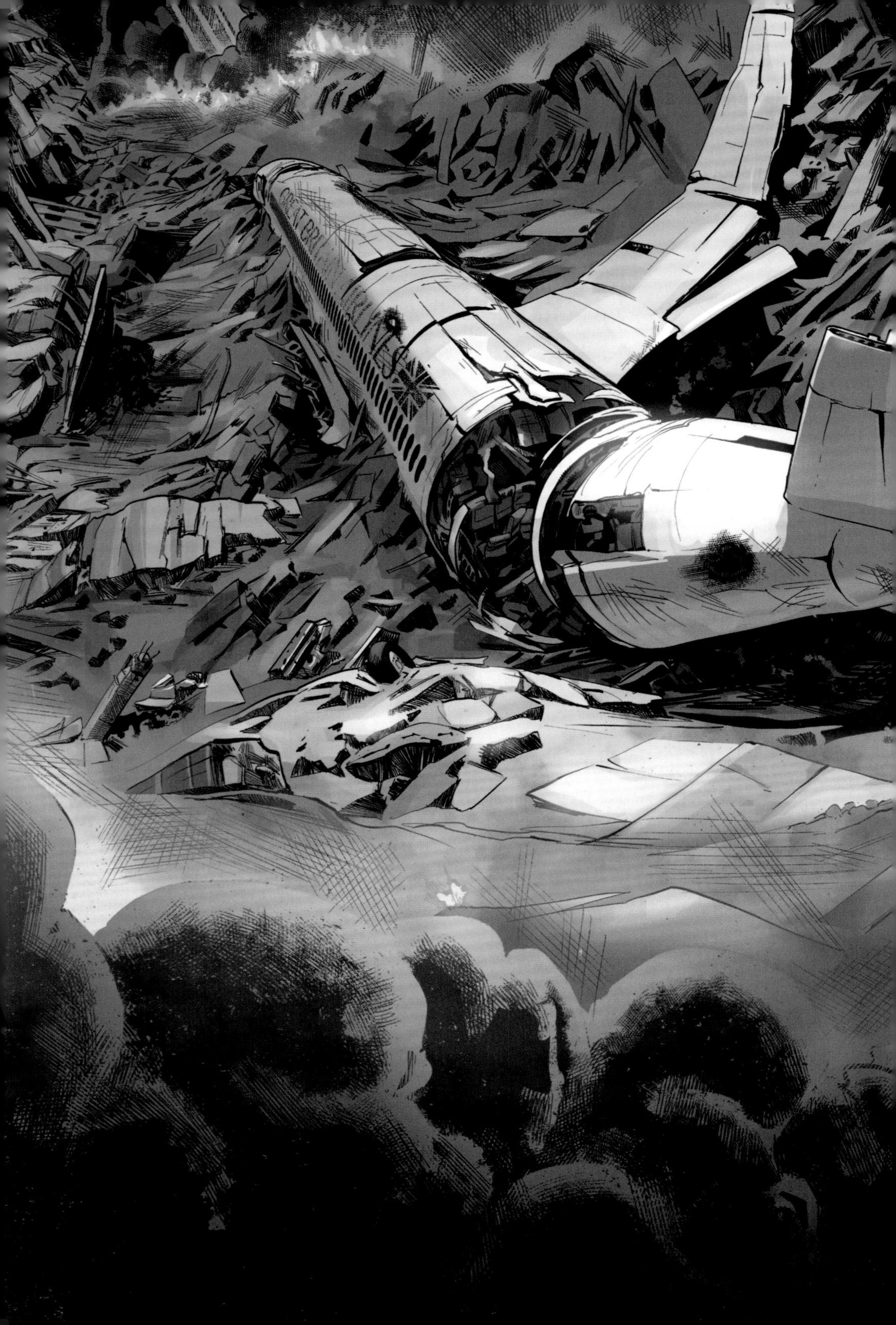

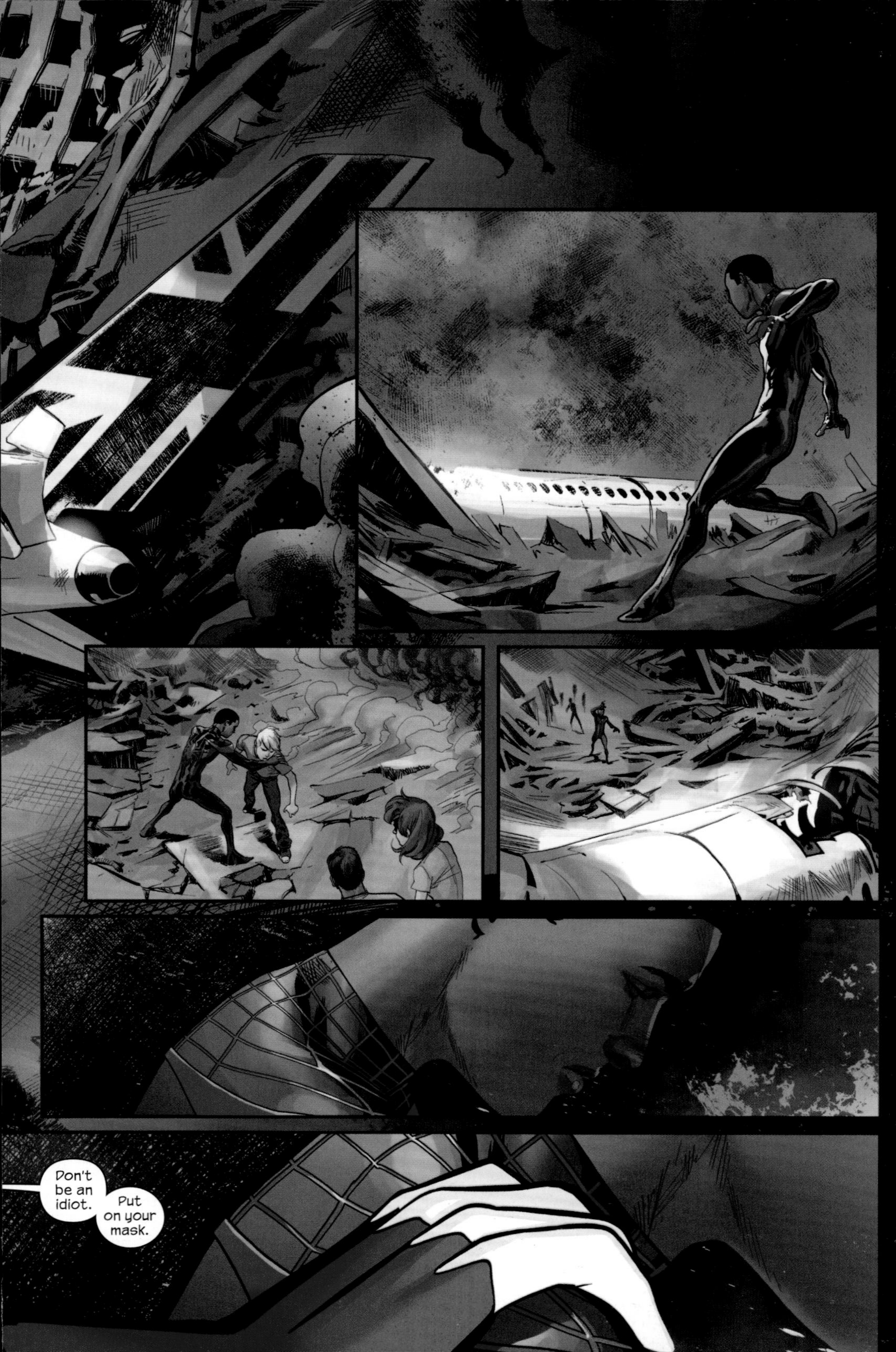
Don't be an idiot.
Put on your mask.

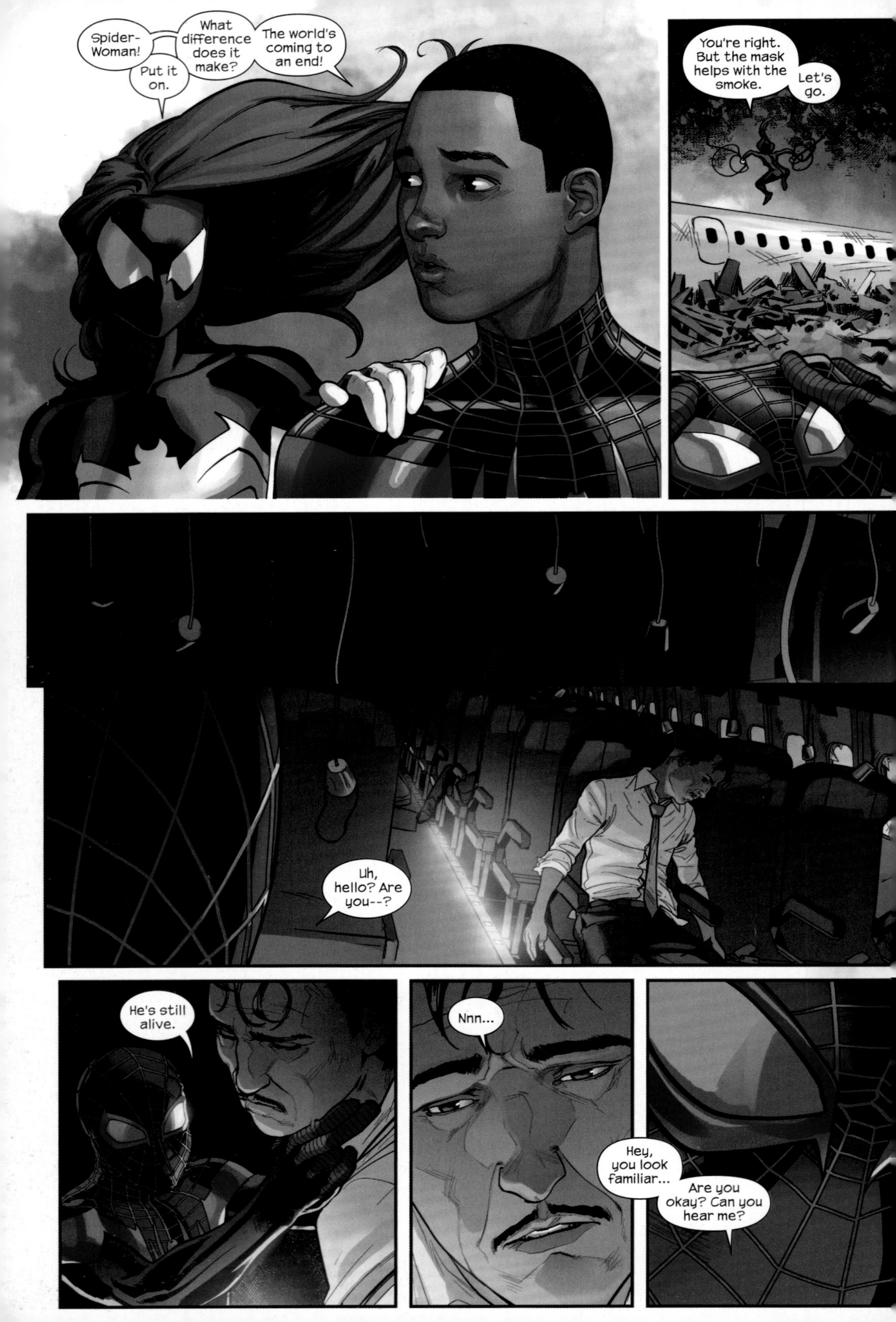
Spider-Woman!
Put it on.
What difference does it make?
The world's coming to an end!
You're right. But the mask helps with the smoke.
Let's go.
Uh, hello? Are you--?
He's still alive.
Nnn...
Hey, you look familiar...
Are you okay? Can you hear me?

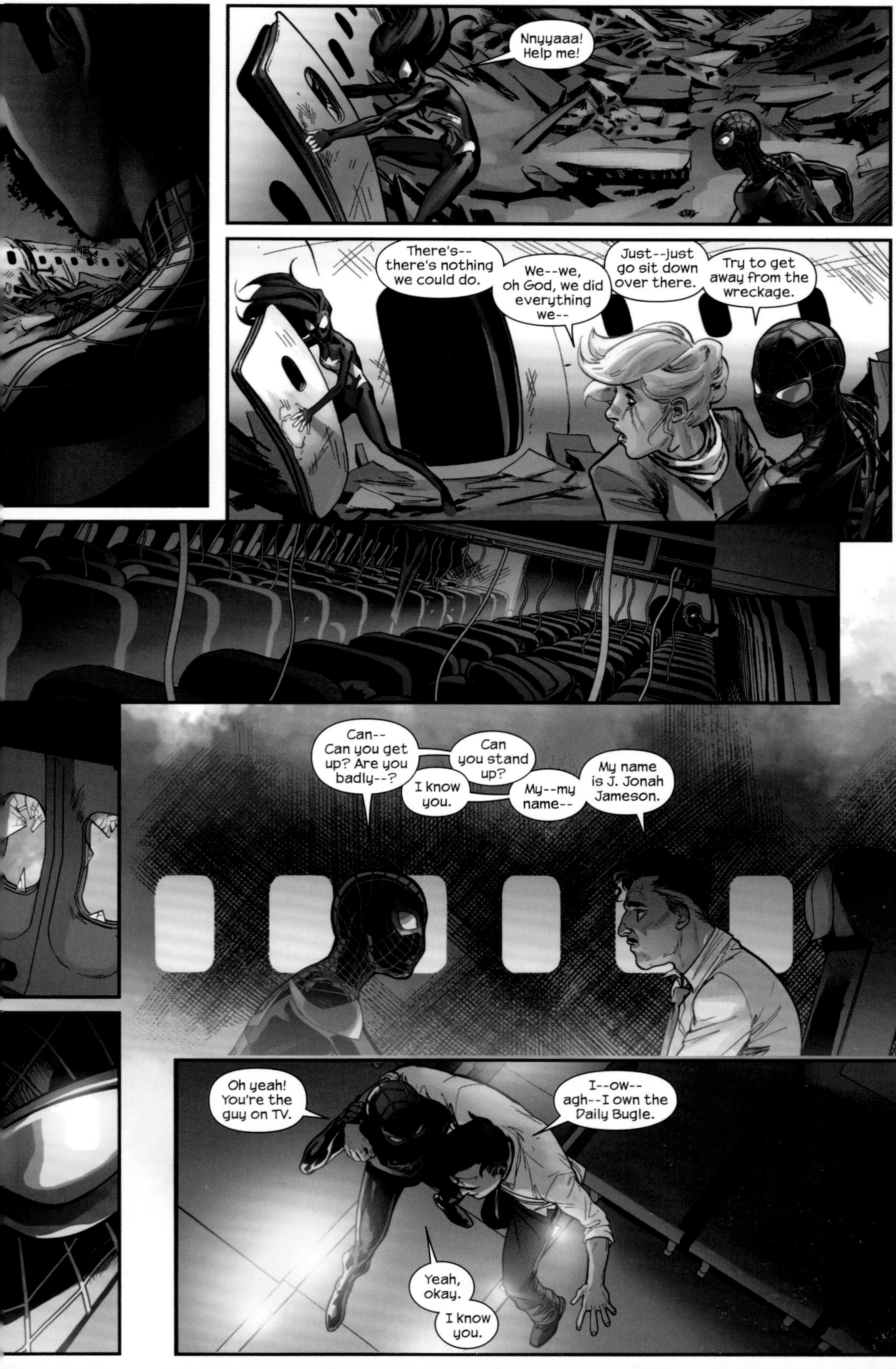
Nnyyaaa! Help me!
There's-- there's nothing we could do.
We--we, oh God, we did everything we--
Just--just go sit down over there.
Try to get away from the wreckage.
Can-- Can you get up? Are you badly--?
Can you stand up?
I know you.
My--my name--
My name is J. Jonah Jameson.
Oh yeah! You're the guy on TV.
I--ow-- agh--I own the Daily Bugle.
Yeah, okay.
I know you.

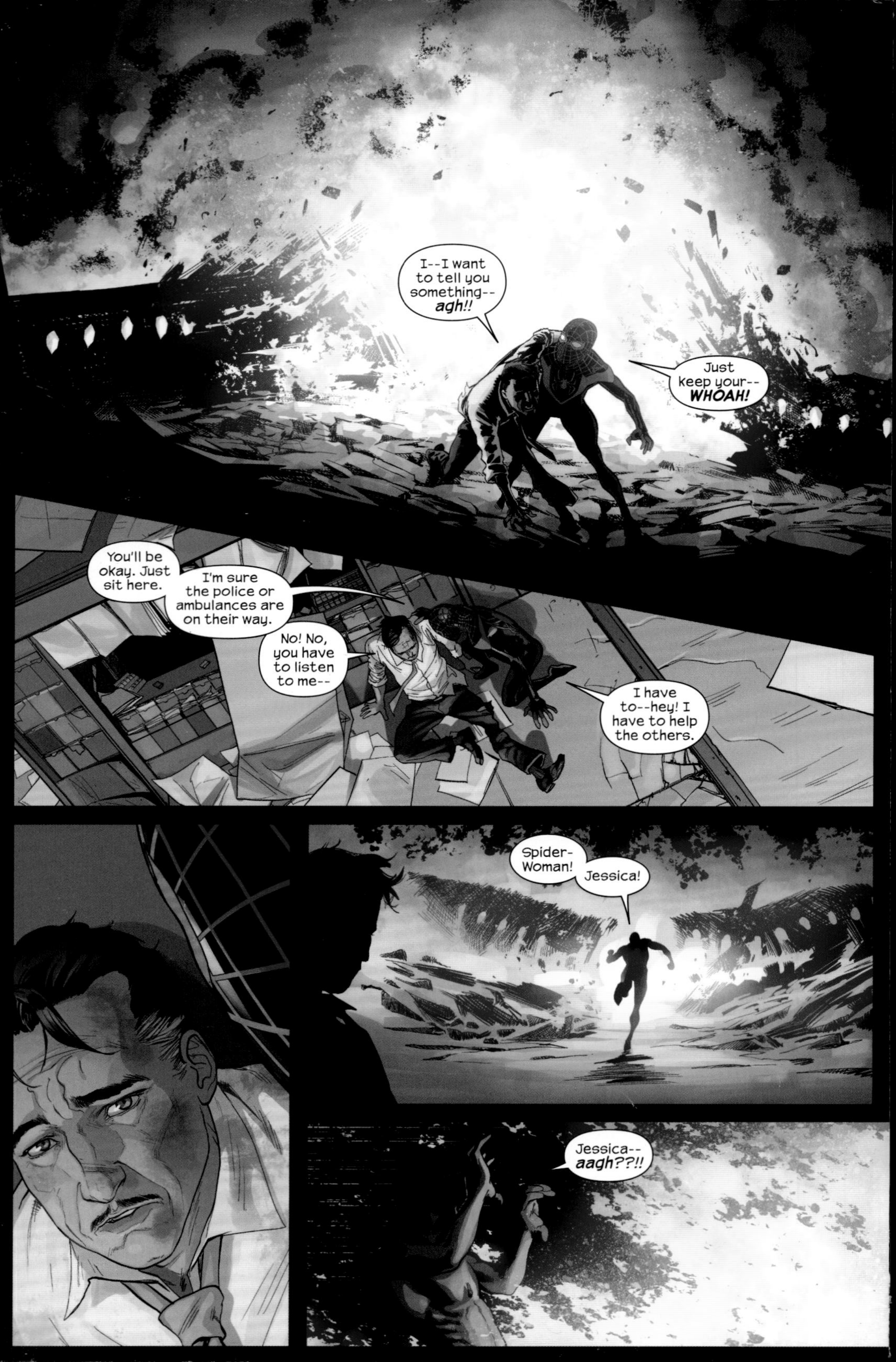
I--I want to tell you something-- *agh!!*
Just keep your-- ***WHOAH!***
You'll be okay. Just sit here.
I'm sure the police or ambulances are on their way.
No! No, you have to listen to me--
I have to--hey! I have to help the others.
Spider-Woman!
Jessica!
Jessica-- ***aagh??!!***

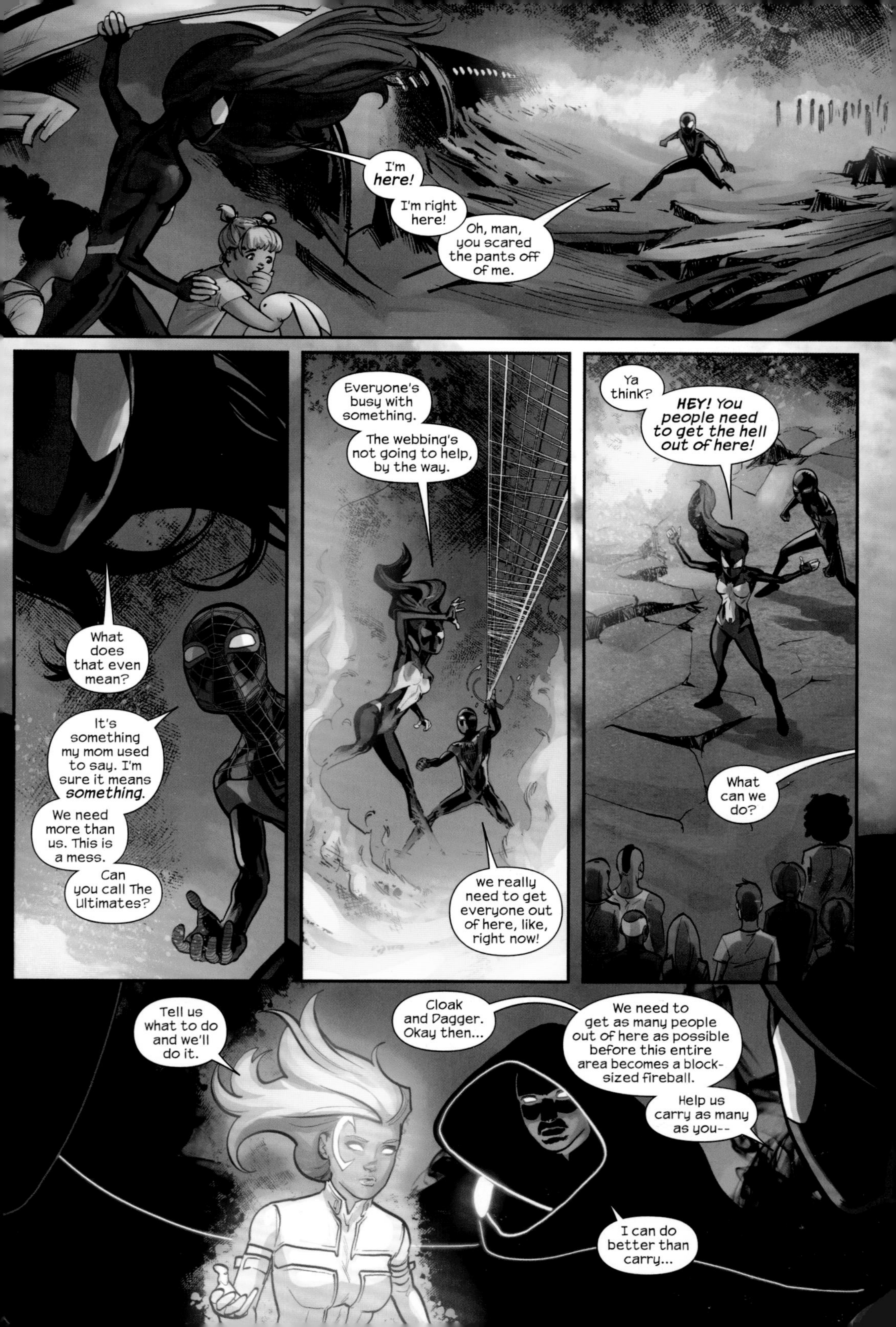
I'm *here!*
I'm right here!
Oh, man, you scared the pants off of me.
What does that even mean?
It's something my mom used to say. I'm sure it means *something*.
We need more than us. This is a mess.
Can you call The Ultimates?
Everyone's busy with something.
The webbing's not going to help, by the way.
We really need to get everyone out of here, like, right now!
Ya think?
HEY! You people need to get the hell out of here!
What can we do?
Tell us what to do and we'll do it.
Cloak and Dagger. Okay then...
We need to get as many people out of here as possible before this entire area becomes a block-sized fireball.
Help us carry as many as you--
I can do better than carry...

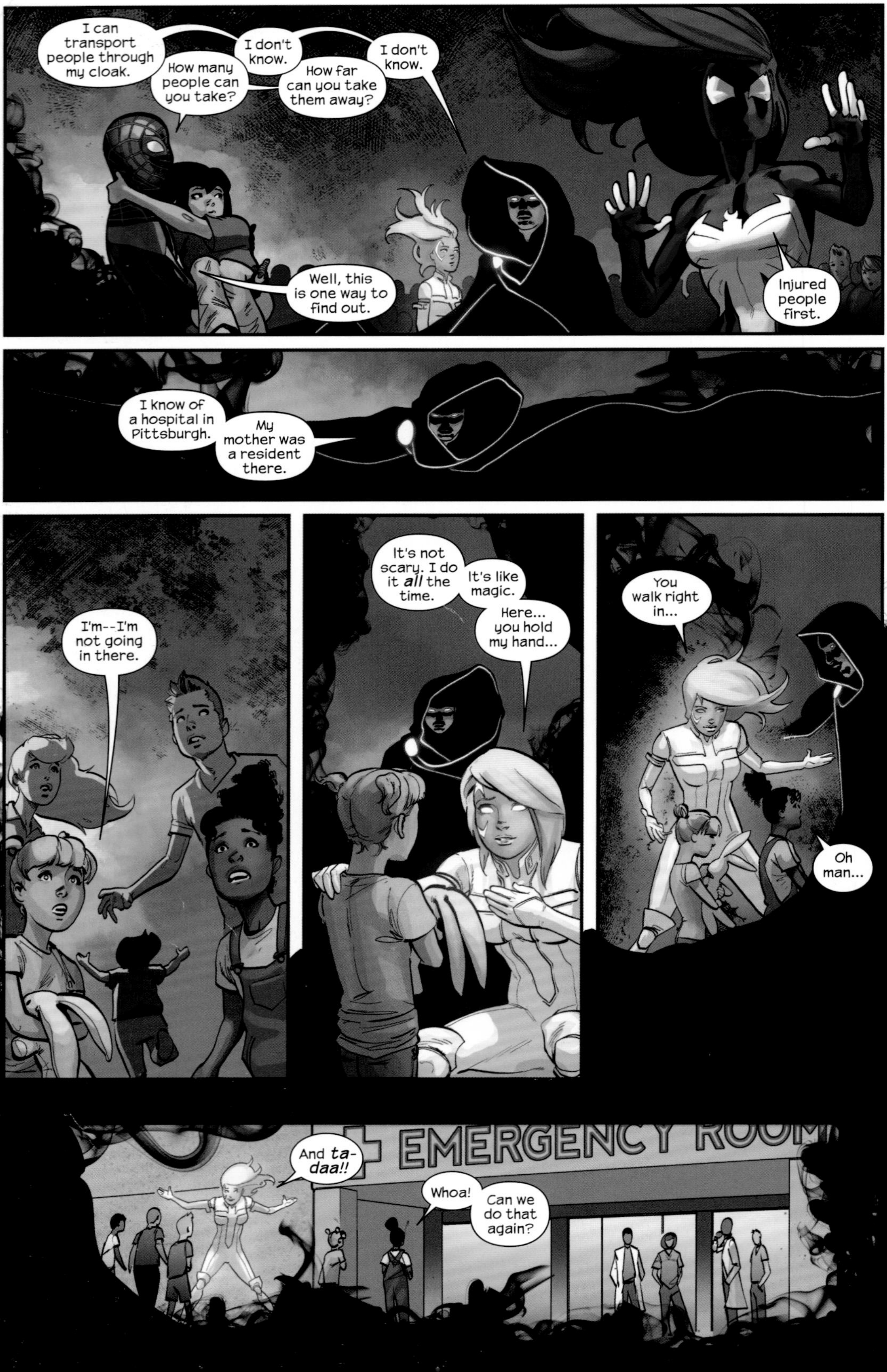
I can transport people through my cloak.
How many people can you take?
I don't know.
How far can you take them away?
I don't know.
Well, this is one way to find out.
Injured people first.
I know of a hospital in Pittsburgh.
My mother was a resident there.
I'm--I'm not going in there.
It's not scary. I do it *all* the time.
It's like magic.
Here... you hold my hand...
You walk right in...
Oh man...
EMERGENCY ROOM
And *ta-daa!!*
Whoa!
Can we do that again?

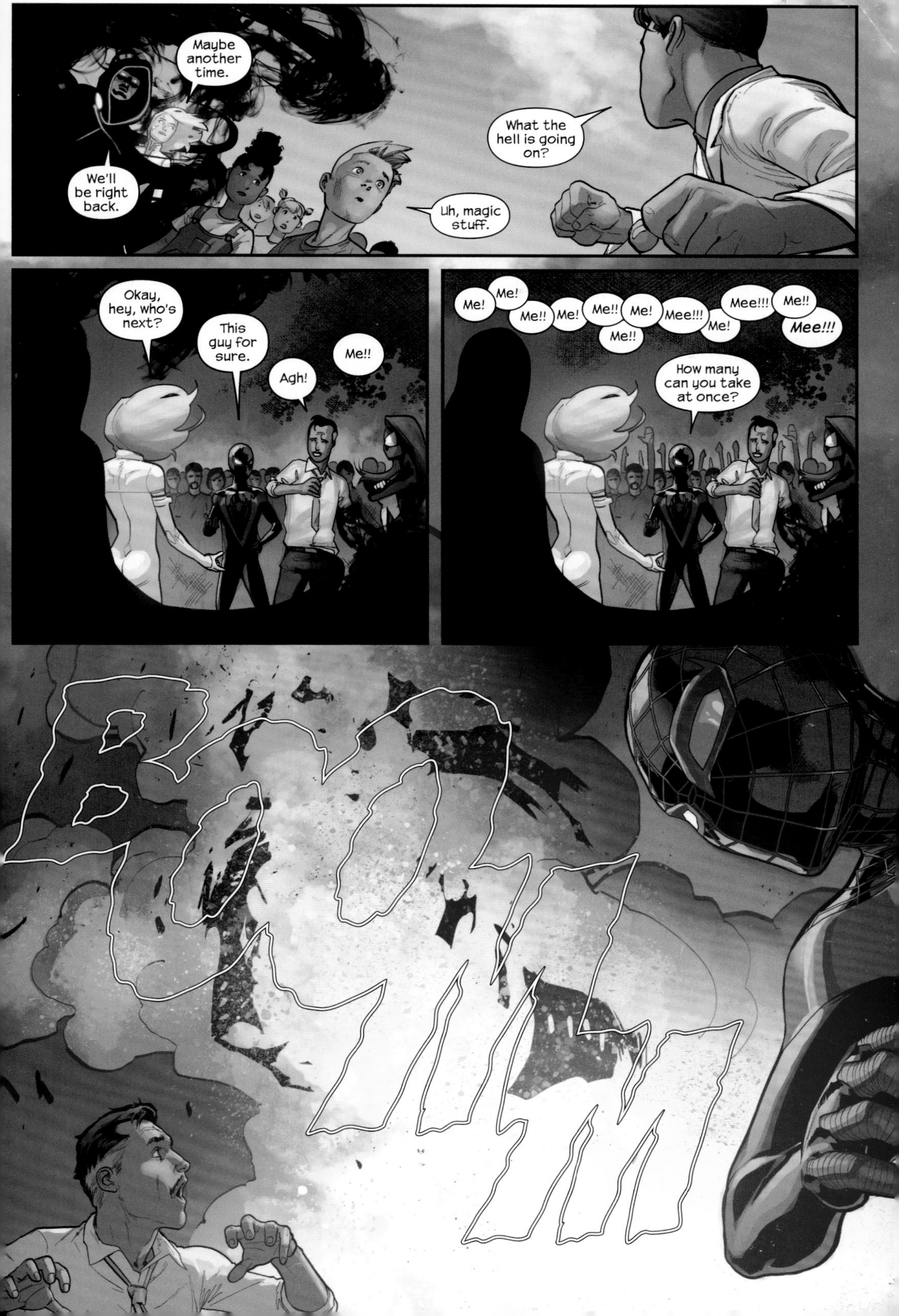
Maybe another time.
We'll be right back.
What the hell is going on?
Uh, magic stuff.
Okay, hey, who's next?
This guy for sure.
Agh!
Me!!
Me!
Me!
Me!!
Me!
Me!!
Me!!
Me!
Mee!!!
Me!
Mee!!!
Me!!
Mee!!!
How many can you take at once?

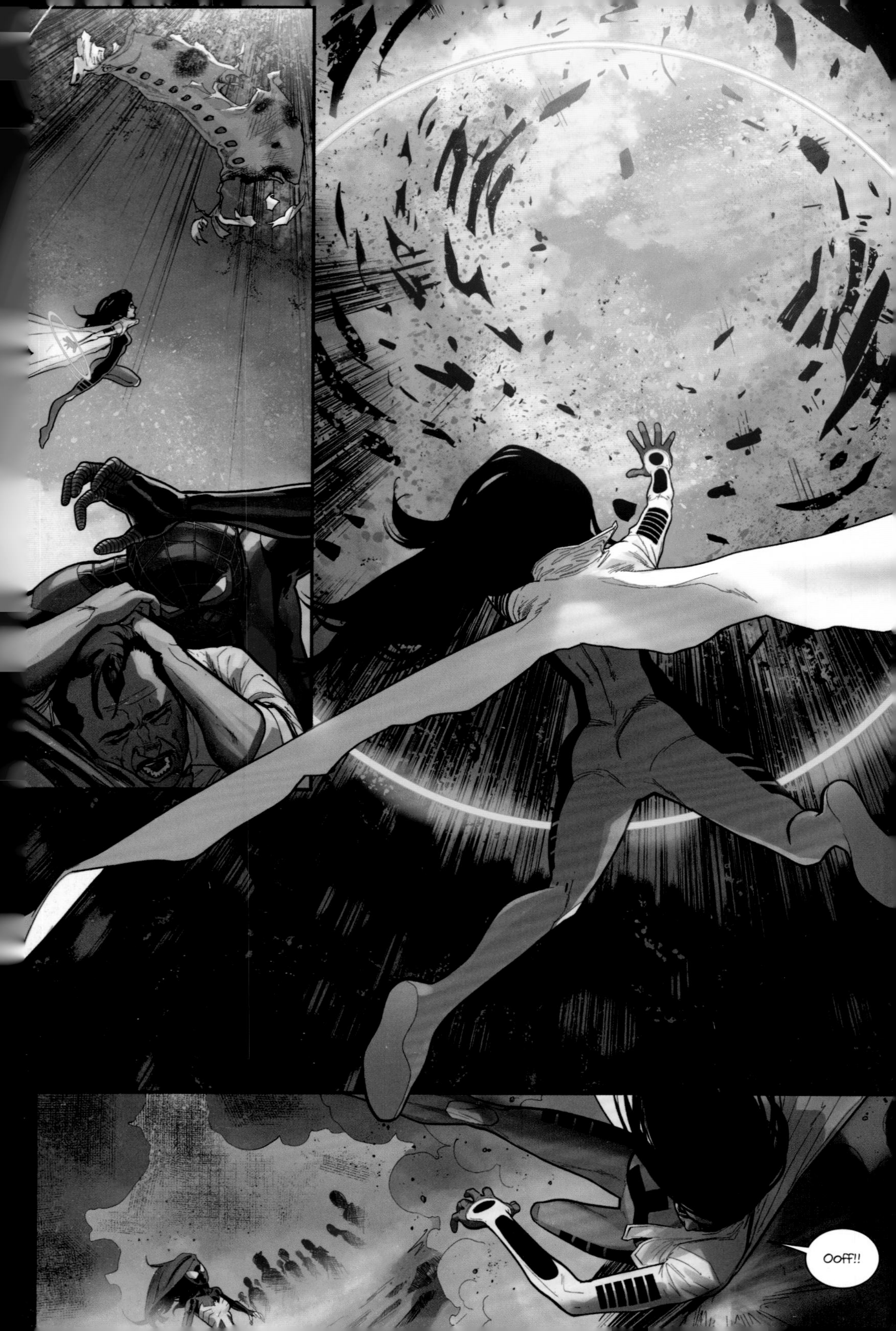
Ooff!!

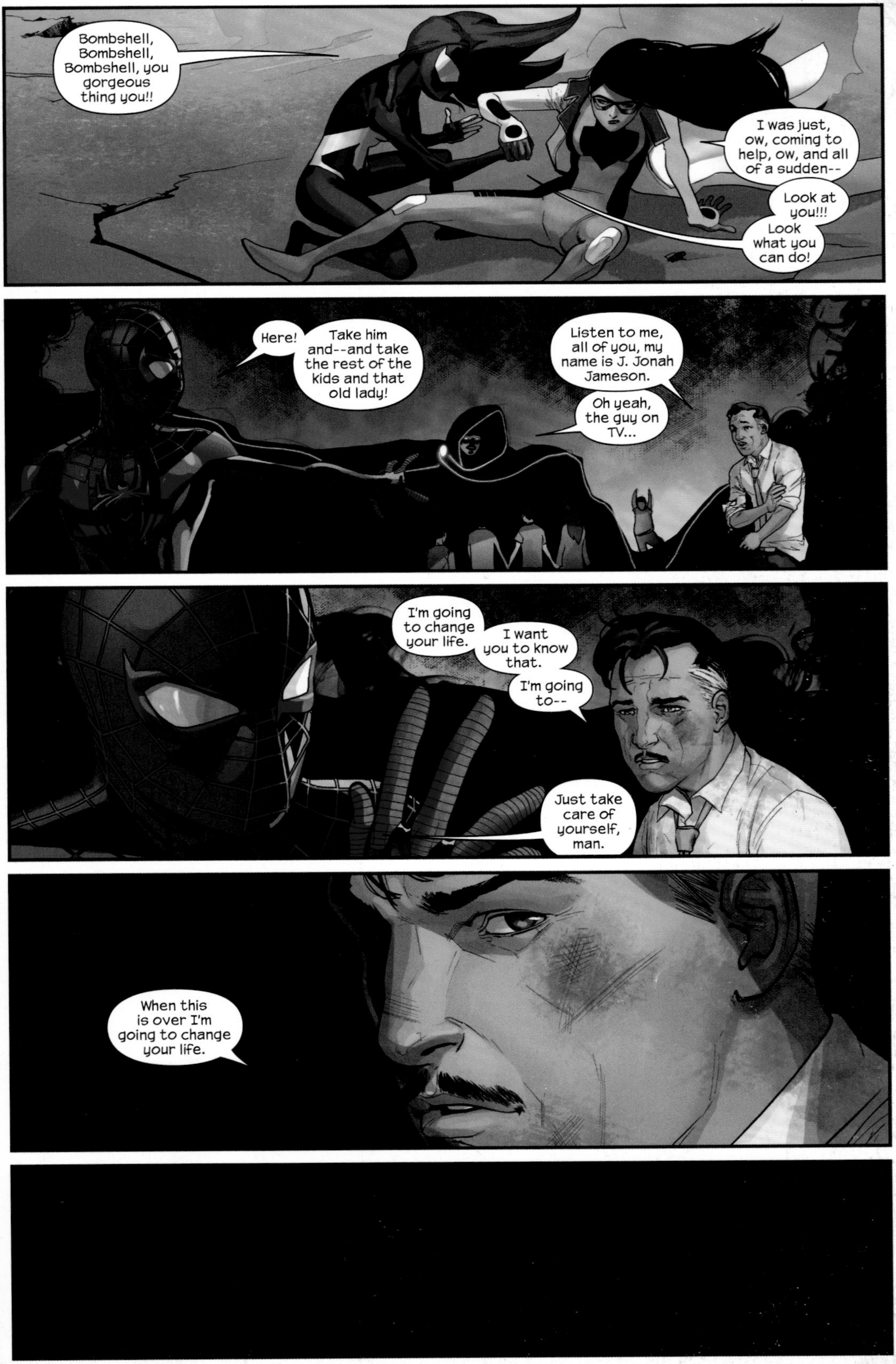
Bombshell, Bombshell, Bombshell, you gorgeous thing you!!
I was just, ow, coming to help, ow, and all of a sudden--
Look at you!!!
Look what you can do!
Here!
Take him and--and take the rest of the kids and that old lady!
Listen to me, all of you, my name is J. Jonah Jameson.
Oh yeah, the guy on TV...
I'm going to change your life.
I want you to know that.
I'm going to--
Just take care of yourself, man.
When this is over I'm going to change your life.

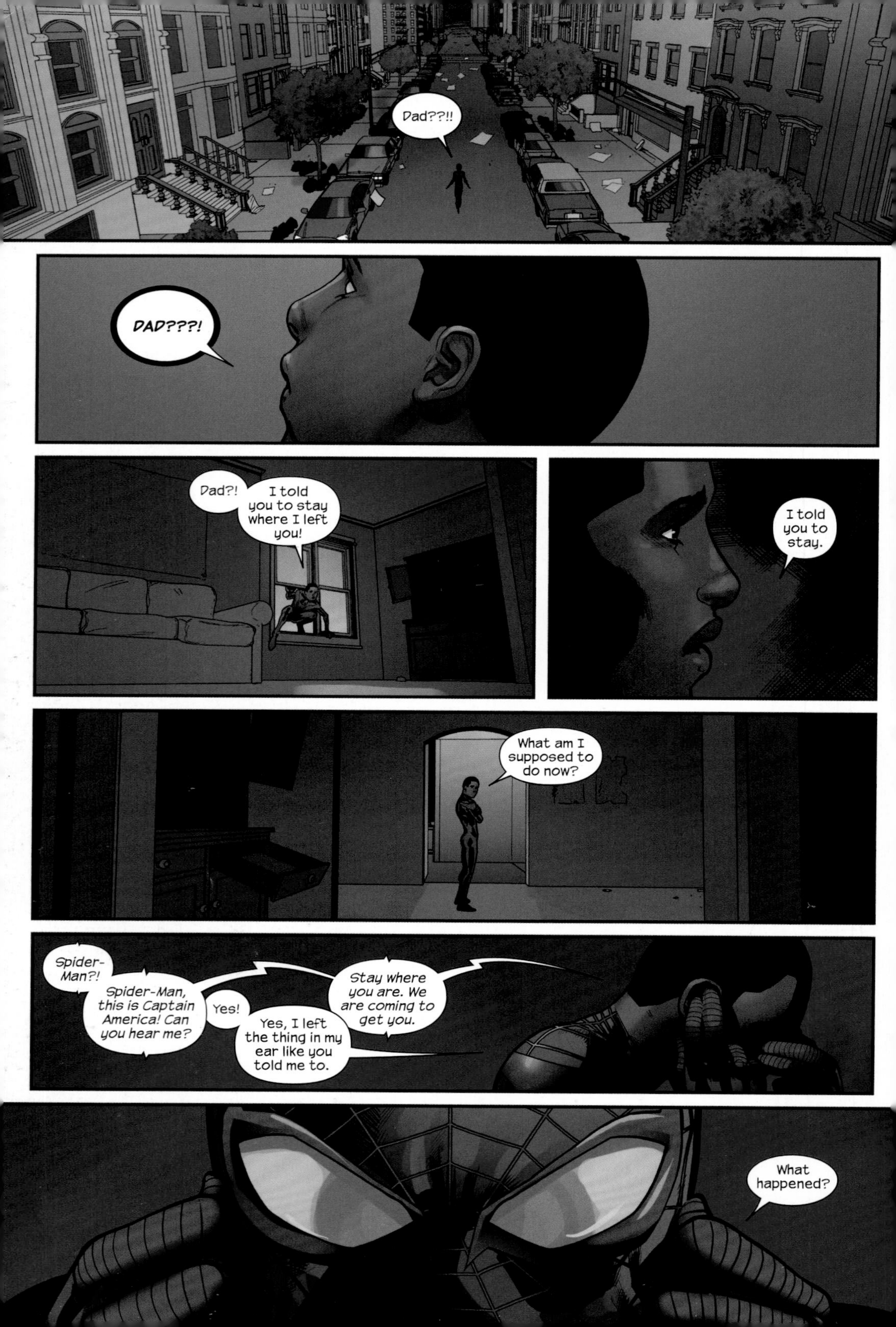
Dad??!!
DAD???!
Dad?!
I told you to stay where I left you!
I told you to stay.
What am I supposed to do now?
Spider-Man?!
Spider-Man, this is Captain America! Can you hear me?
Yes!
Yes, I left the thing in my ear like you told me to.
Stay where you are. We are coming to get you.
What happened?

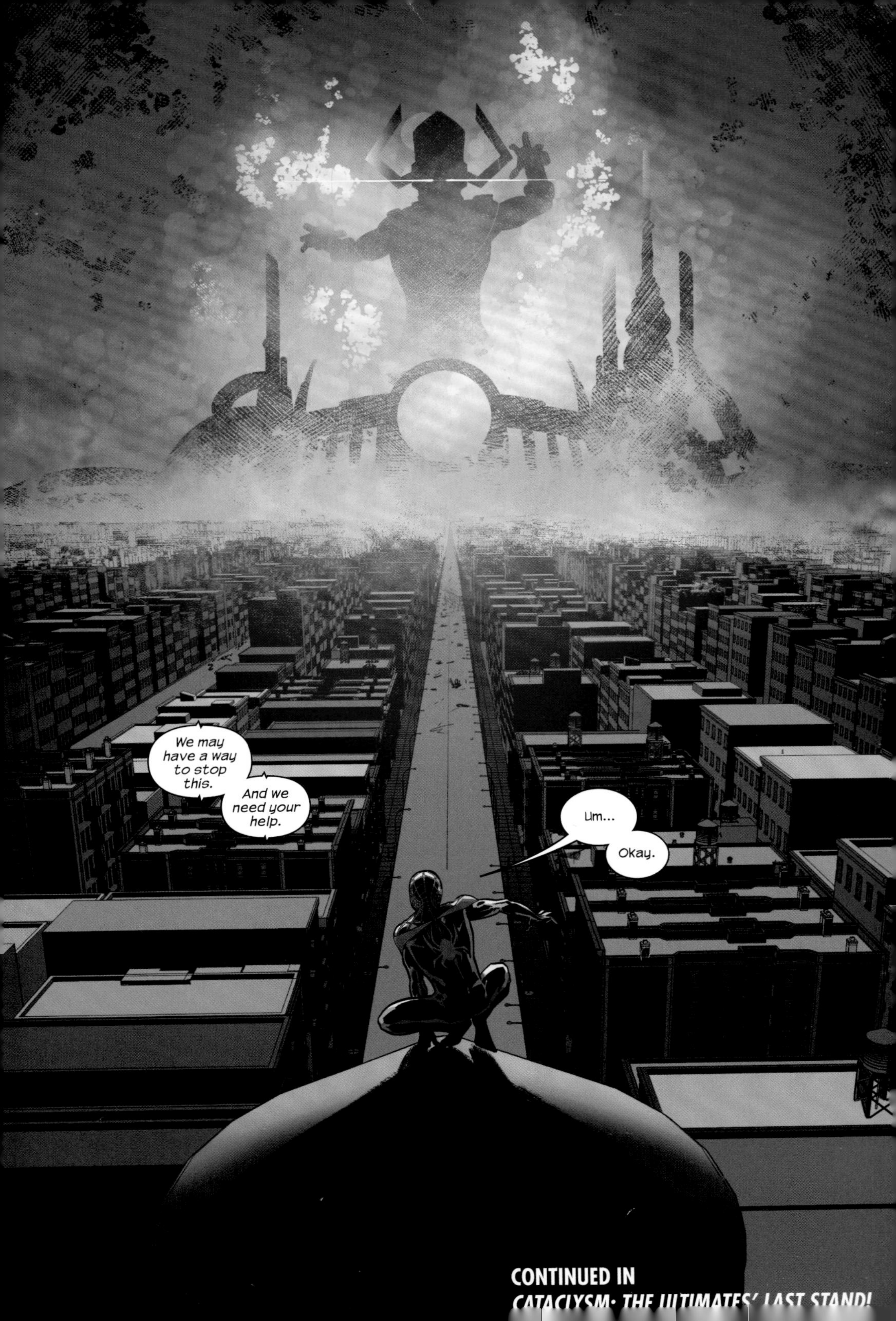
We may have a way to stop this.
And we need your help.
Um...
Okay.
CONTINUED IN
CATACLYSM: THE ULTIMATES' LAST STAND!

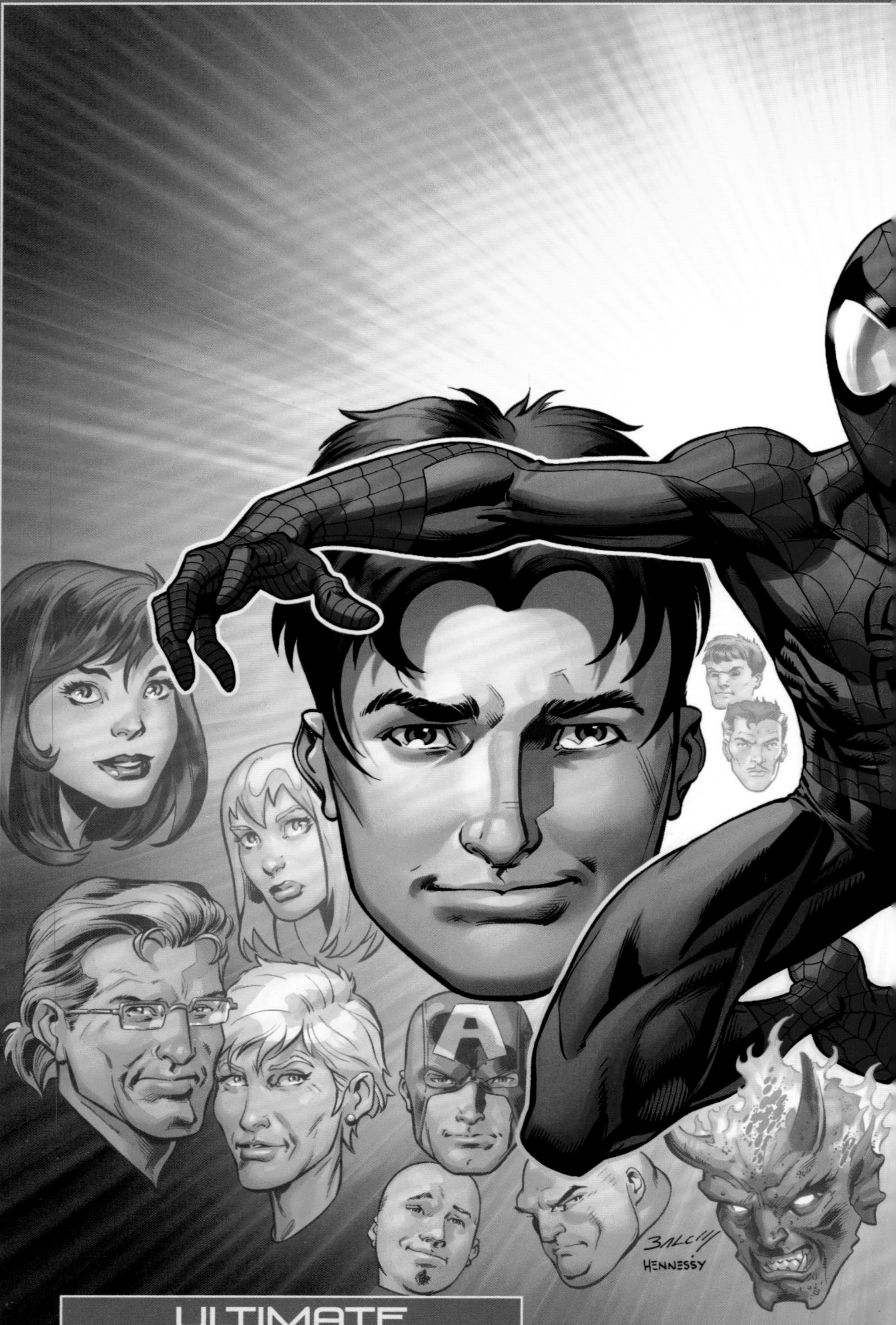
HENNESSY

ULTIMATE
SPIDER-MAN #200

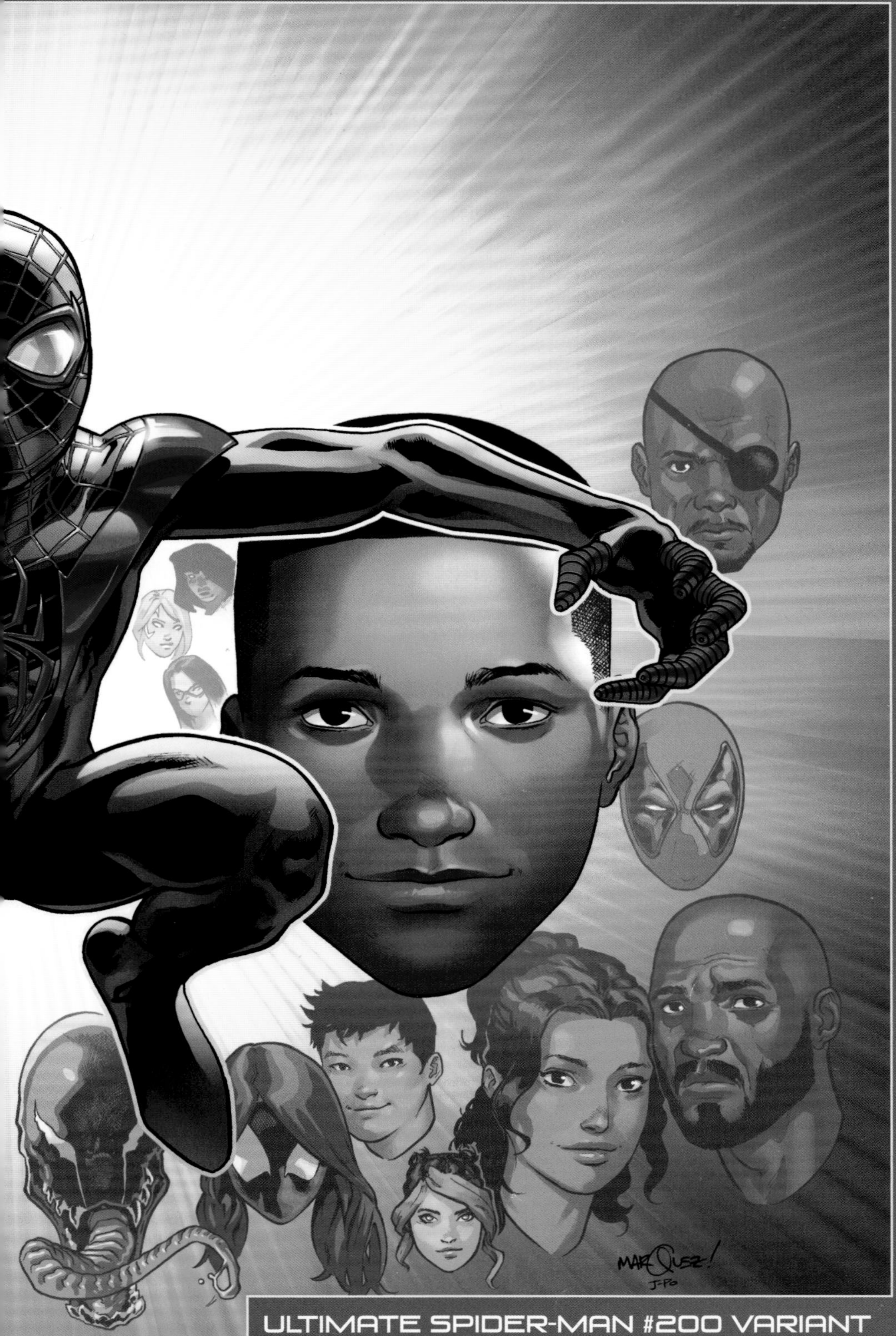

ULTIMATE SPIDER-MAN #200 VARIANT
BY DAVID MARQUEZ & JUSTIN PONSOR

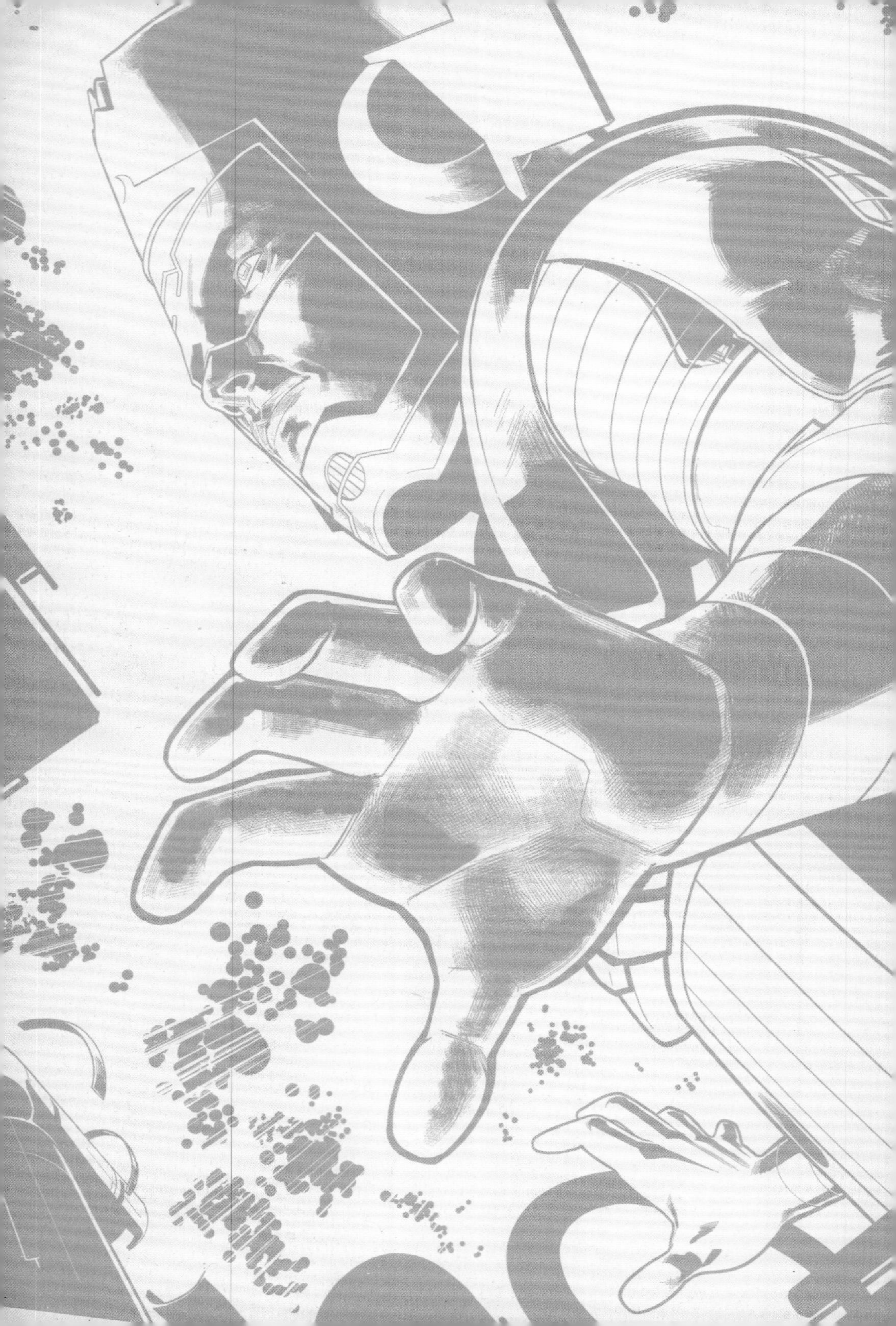

PREVIOUSLY IN *CATACLYSM*

**Galactus destroyed most of New Jersey before
all the super heroes could team up and fight him.
Galactus was defeated, but not without great loss
and sacrifice.**

**Miles has not seen his father since revealing his
secret identity to him.**

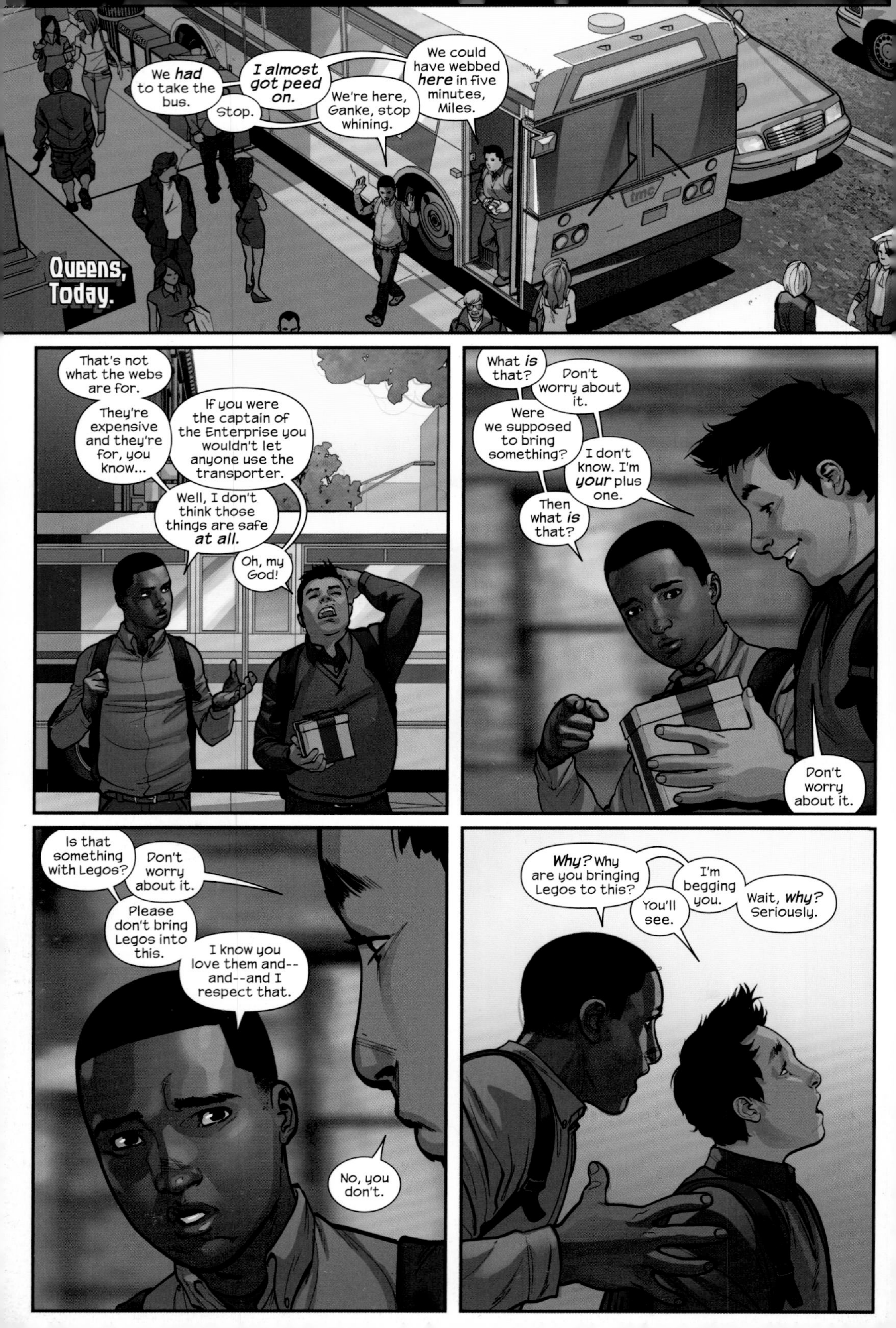
Queens, Today.
We had to take the bus.
I almost got peed on.
Stop.
We could have webbed here in five minutes, Miles.
We're here, Ganke, stop whining.
That's not what the webs are for.
They're expensive and they're for, you know...
If you were the captain of the Enterprise you wouldn't let anyone use the transporter.
Well, I don't think those things are safe at all.
Oh, my God!
What is that?
Don't worry about it.
Were we supposed to bring something?
I don't know. I'm your plus one.
Then what is that?
Don't worry about it.
Is that something with Legos?
Don't worry about it.
Please don't bring Legos into this.
I know you love them and--and--and I respect that.
No, you don't.
Why? Why are you bringing Legos to this?
I'm begging you.
You'll see.
Wait, why? Seriously.

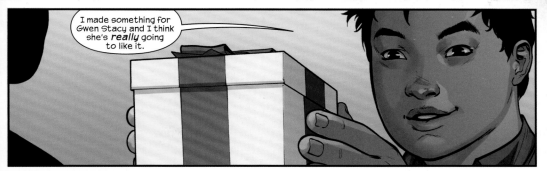

I made something for Gwen Stacy and I think she's *really* going to like it.

Oh, dear God. No!

Please don't do this.

It's done.

This will not go well.

It will.

Ganke, please. She's--she's older than you.

Oh, I know.

She will not appreciate your little X-Wing fighter or whatever it is you--

She will.

I made it for *her*.

She won't.

She will.

You spend too much time alone with those things.

You--you don't know-- girls don't--

Hey, it's done.

The Home of Peter Parker.

The Home of Peter Parker

FOR SALE

Alison Blaire realtor

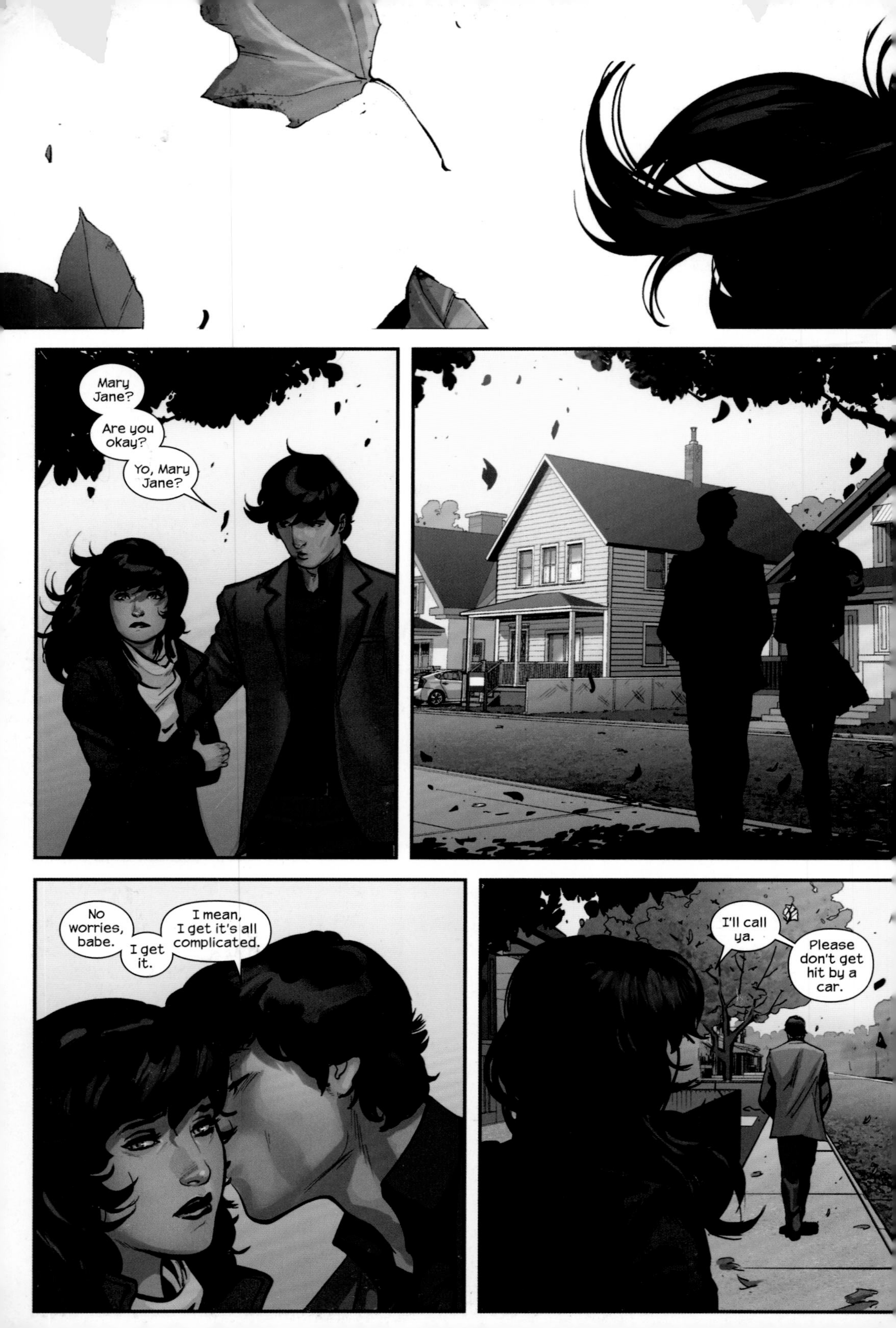
Mary Jane?
Are you okay?
Yo, Mary Jane?
No worries, babe.
I get it.
I mean, I get it's all complicated.
I'll call ya.
Please don't get hit by a car.

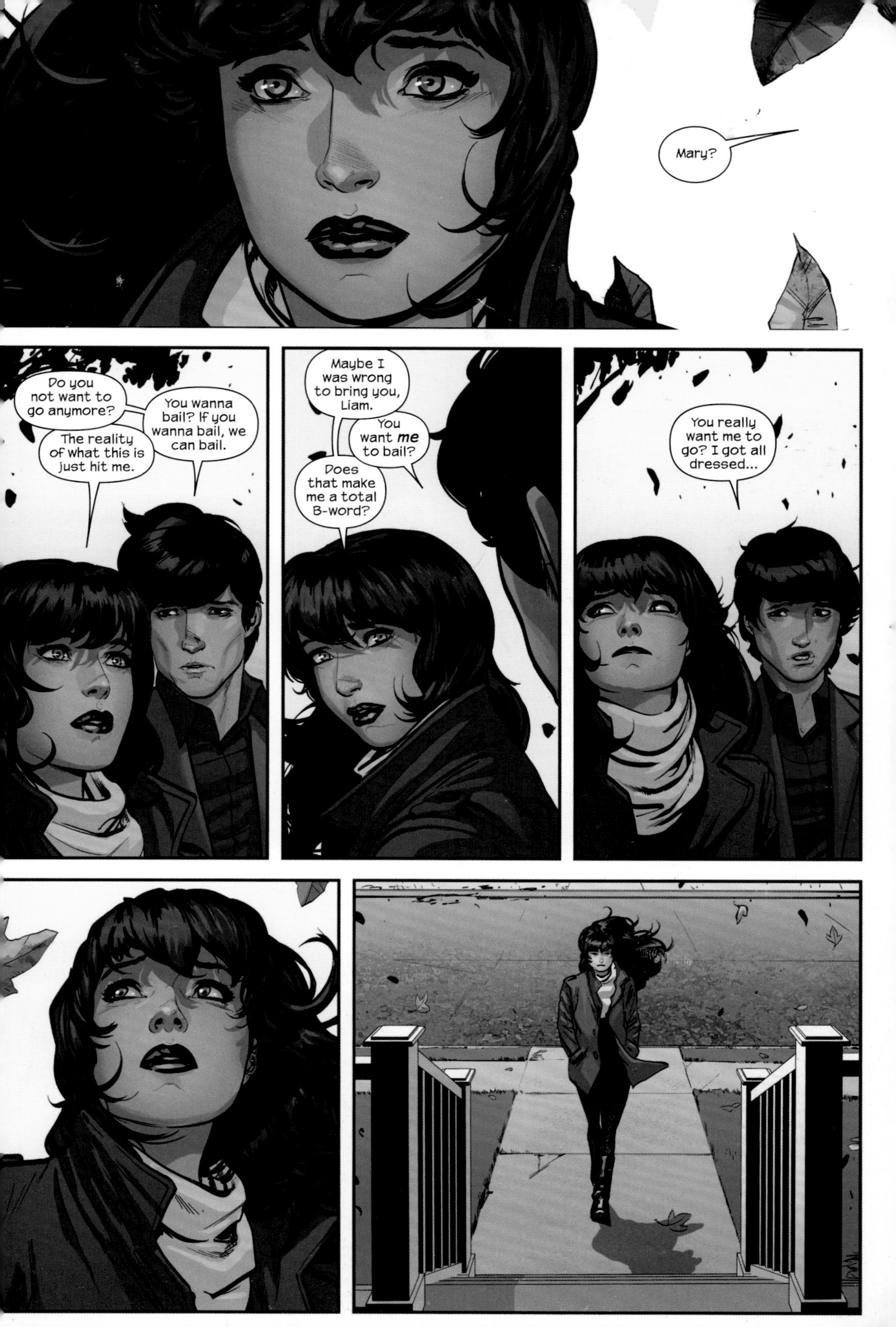

Mary?
Do you not want to go anymore?
You wanna bail? If you wanna bail, we can bail.
The reality of what this is just hit me.
Maybe I was wrong to bring you, Liam.
You want *me* to bail?
Does that make me a total B-word?
You really want me to go? I got all dressed...

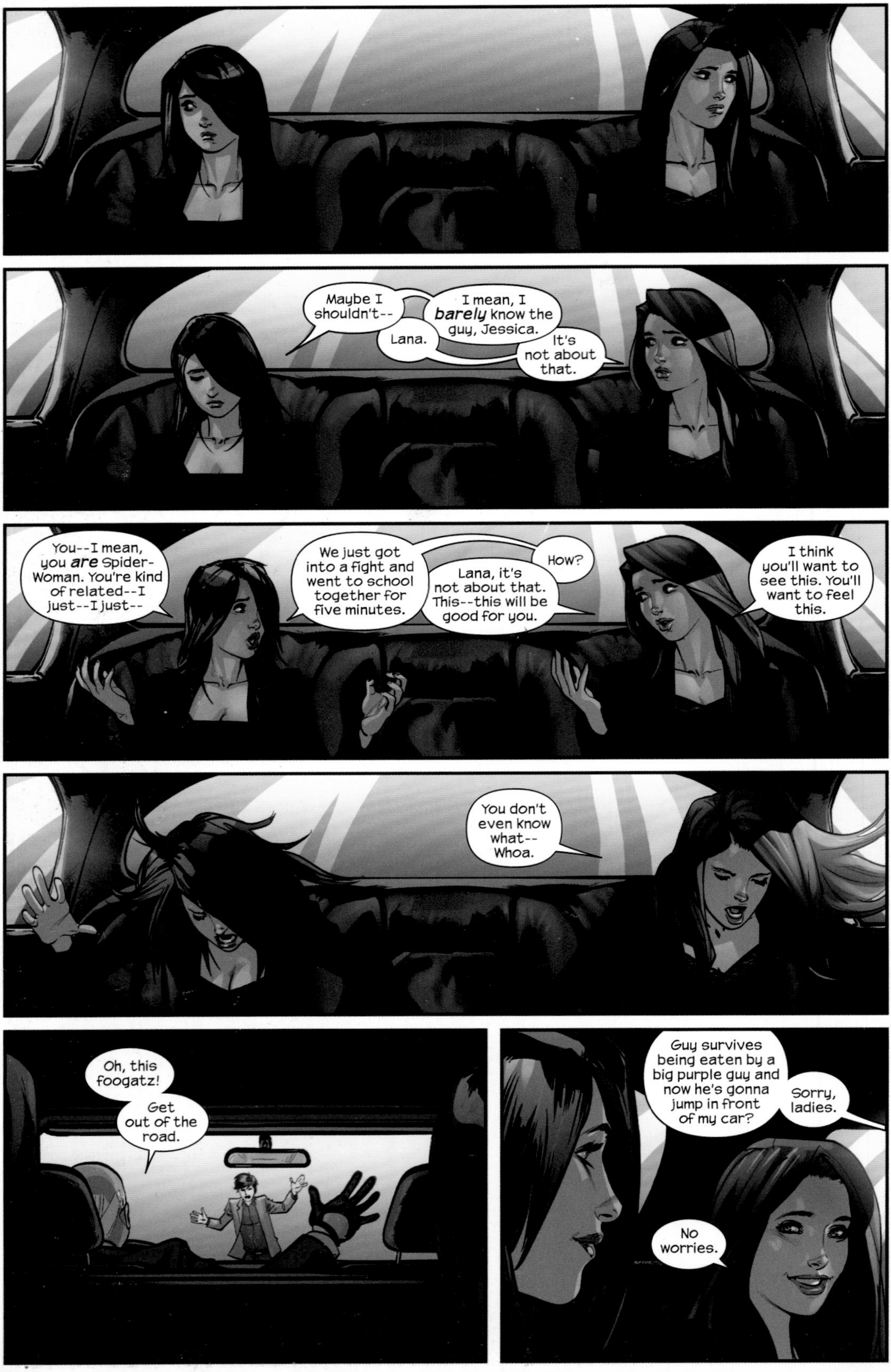

Maybe I shouldn't--
I mean, I *barely* know the guy, Jessica.
Lana.
It's not about that.
You--I mean, you *are* Spider-Woman. You're kind of related--I just--I just--
We just got into a fight and went to school together for five minutes.
How?
Lana, it's not about that. This--this will be good for you.
I think you'll want to see this. You'll want to feel this.
You don't even know what--
Whoa.
Oh, this foogatz!
Get out of the road.
Guy survives being eaten by a big purple guy and now he's gonna jump in front of my car?
Sorry, ladies.
No worries.

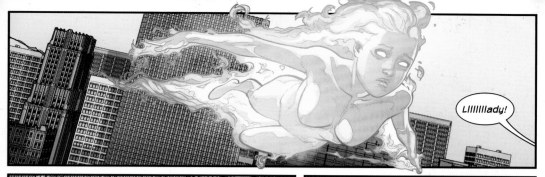

LIIIIIIlady!

Bobby! You scared me!

Are we headed to the same place, Miss Allen?

I don't want to.

You don't *want* to?

I *really* don't want to. I *hate* things like this.

There's going to be *food.*

Do you ever worry about how emotionally disconnected you are to the rest of the--

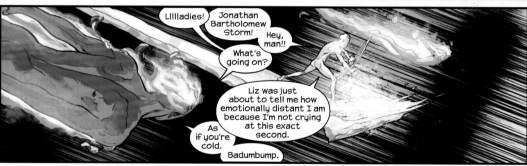

LIIIIladies!

Jonathan Bartholomew Storm!

What's going on?

Hey, man!!

Liz was just about to tell me how emotionally distant I am because I'm not crying at this exact second.

As if you're cold.

Badumbump.

Is your middle name Bartholomew?

No. He's an idiot.

Ugh, there's too much fire on either side of me and I'm gonna--

I'm okay!

From:
silverhippy@jeemail.com
Subject:
a celebration of Peter Parker

To commemorate the second anniversary of our dear Peter's untimely passing we are having a small get-together at the house. This is a celebration of his life, not a mourning of his passing.

There will be food, drink and friends. I truly believe Peter would want us to do this and would want you there. I hope to see you there.

Please RSVP.
May Parker

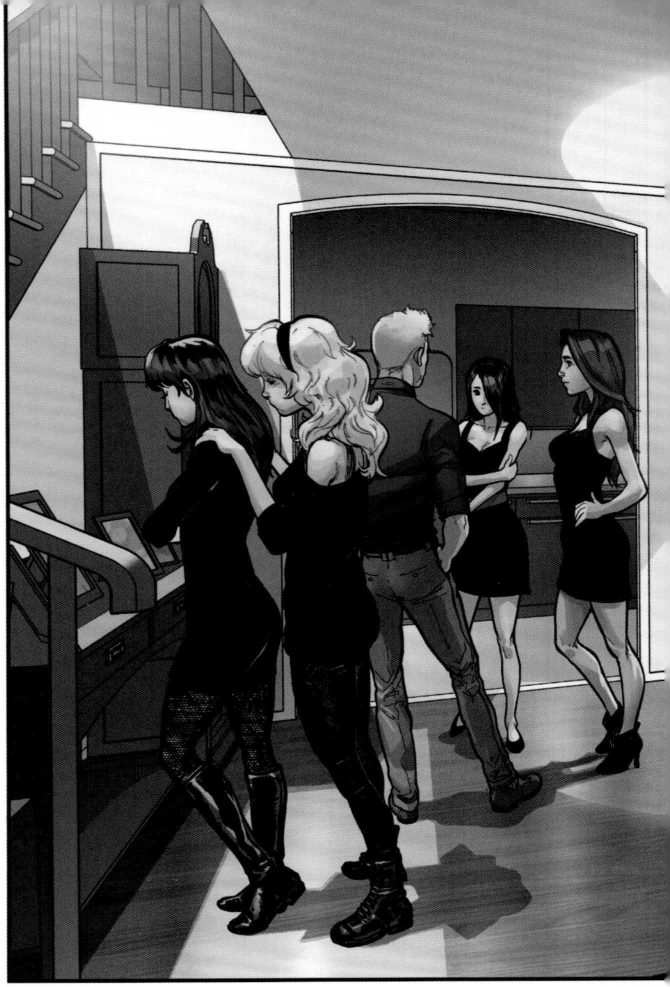

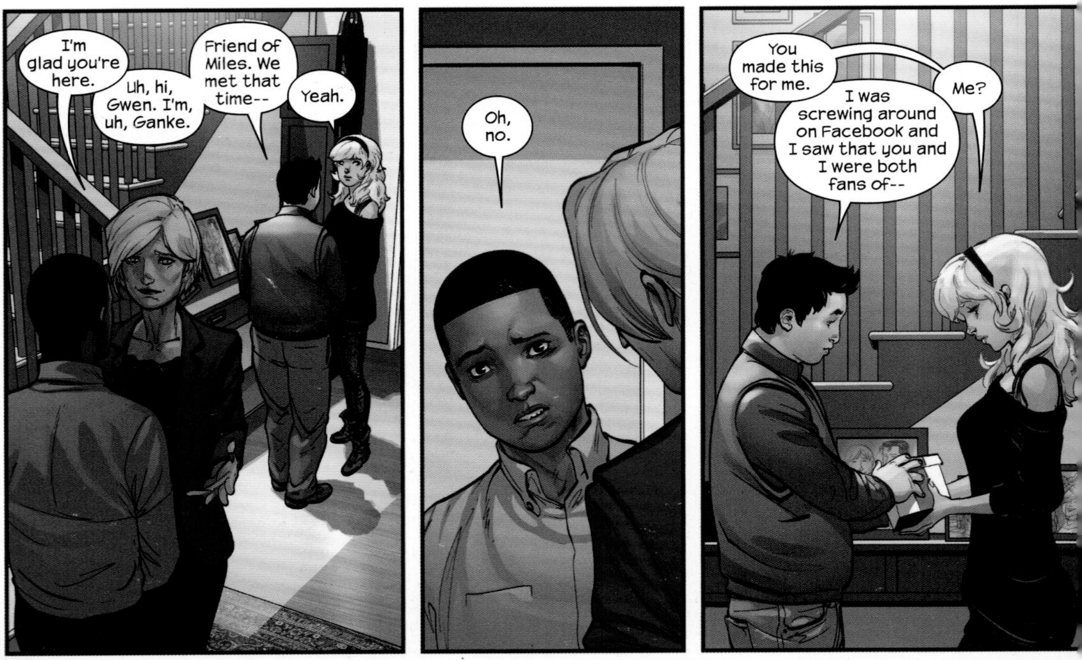
I'm glad you're here.
Uh, hi, Gwen. I'm, uh, Ganke.
Friend of Miles. We met that time--
Yeah.
Oh, no.
You made this for me.
Me?
I was screwing around on Facebook and I saw that you and I were both fans of--

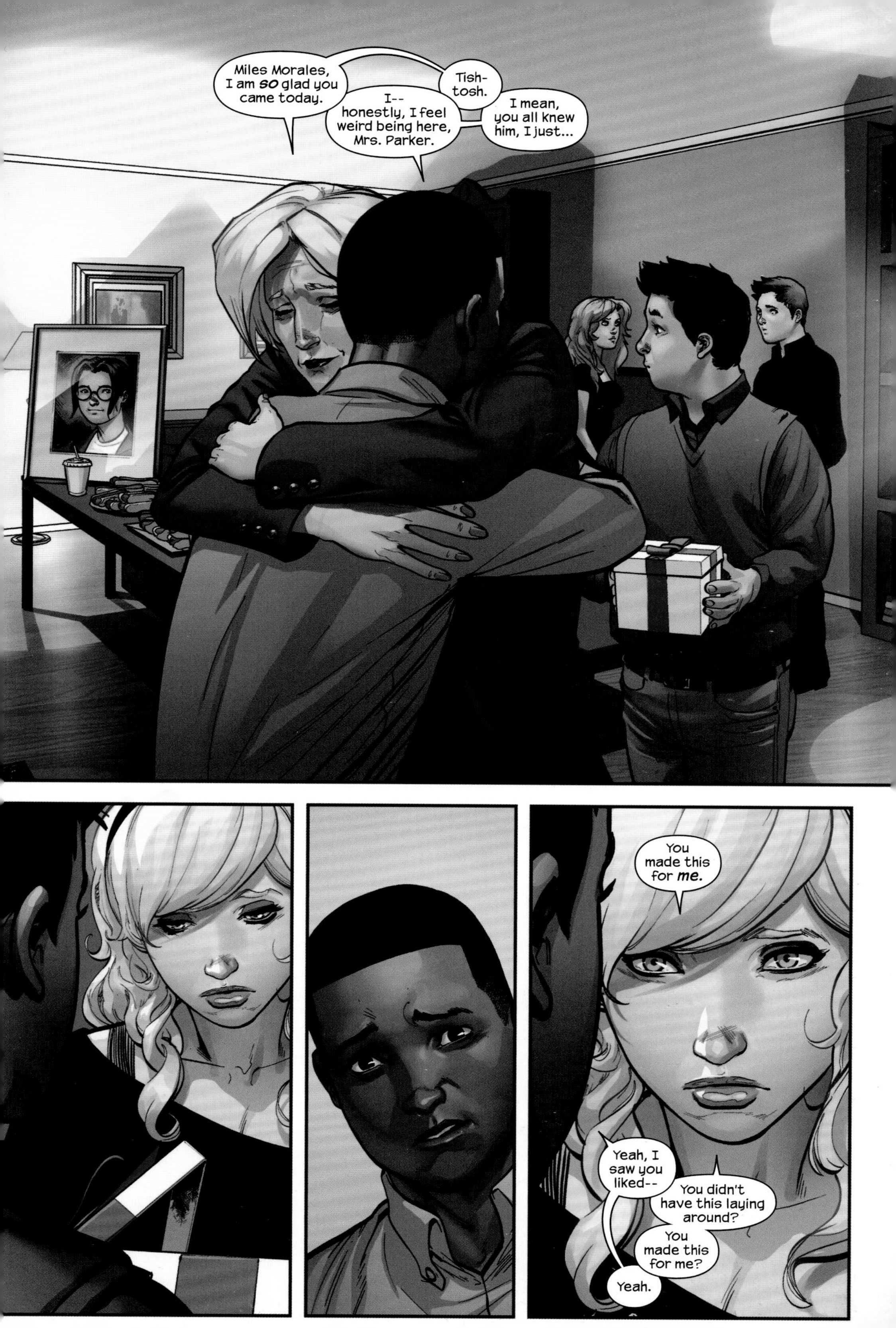
Miles Morales, I am *SO* glad you came today.
I-- honestly, I feel weird being here, Mrs. Parker.
Tish-tosh.
I mean, you all knew him, I just...
You made this for *me.*
Yeah, I saw you liked--
You didn't have this laying around?
You made this for me?
Yeah.

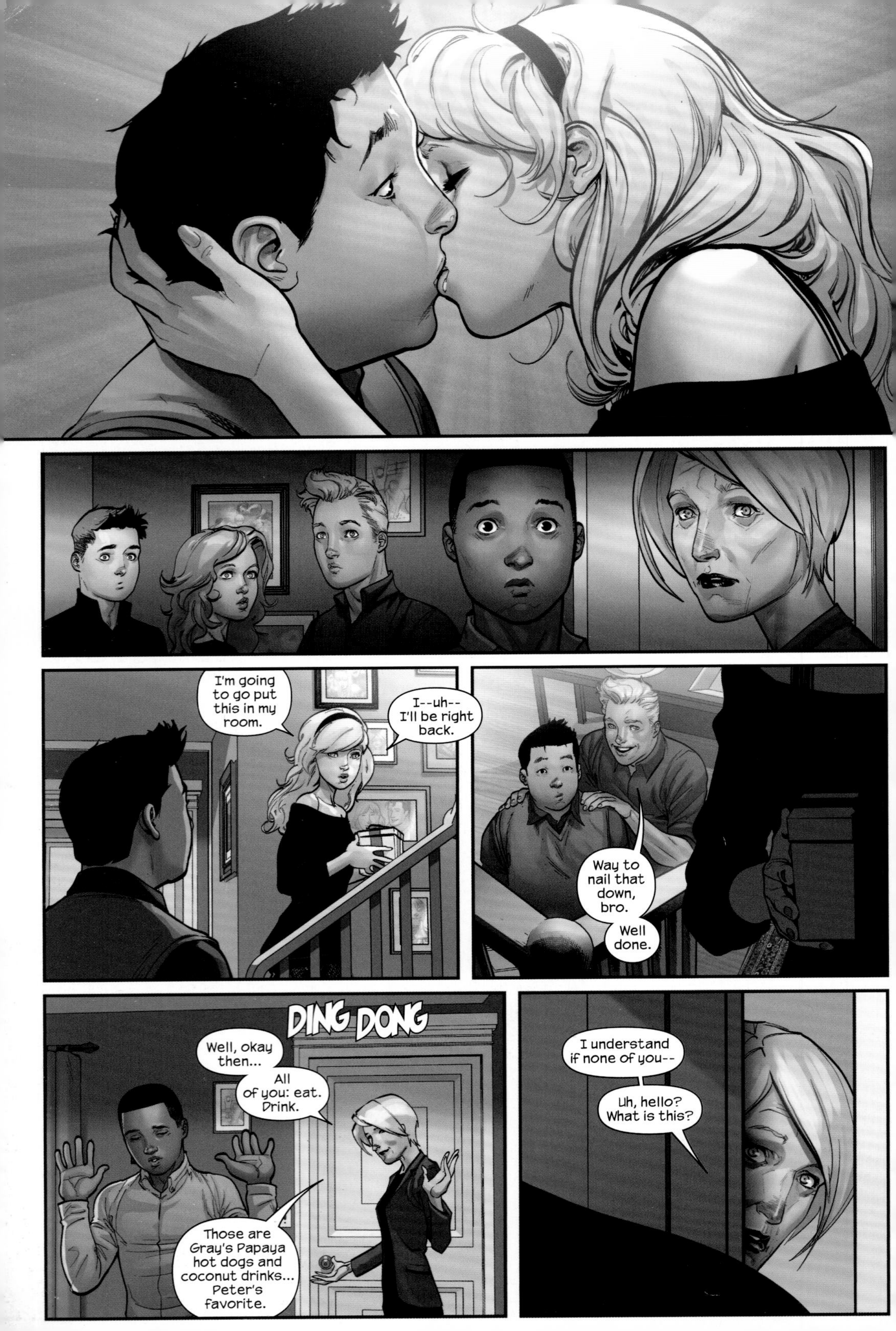
I'm going to go put this in my room.
I--uh-- I'll be right back.
Way to nail that down, bro.
Well done.
DING DONG
Well, okay then...
All of you: eat. Drink.
Those are Gray's Papaya hot dogs and coconut drinks... Peter's favorite.
I understand if none of you--
Uh, hello? What is this?

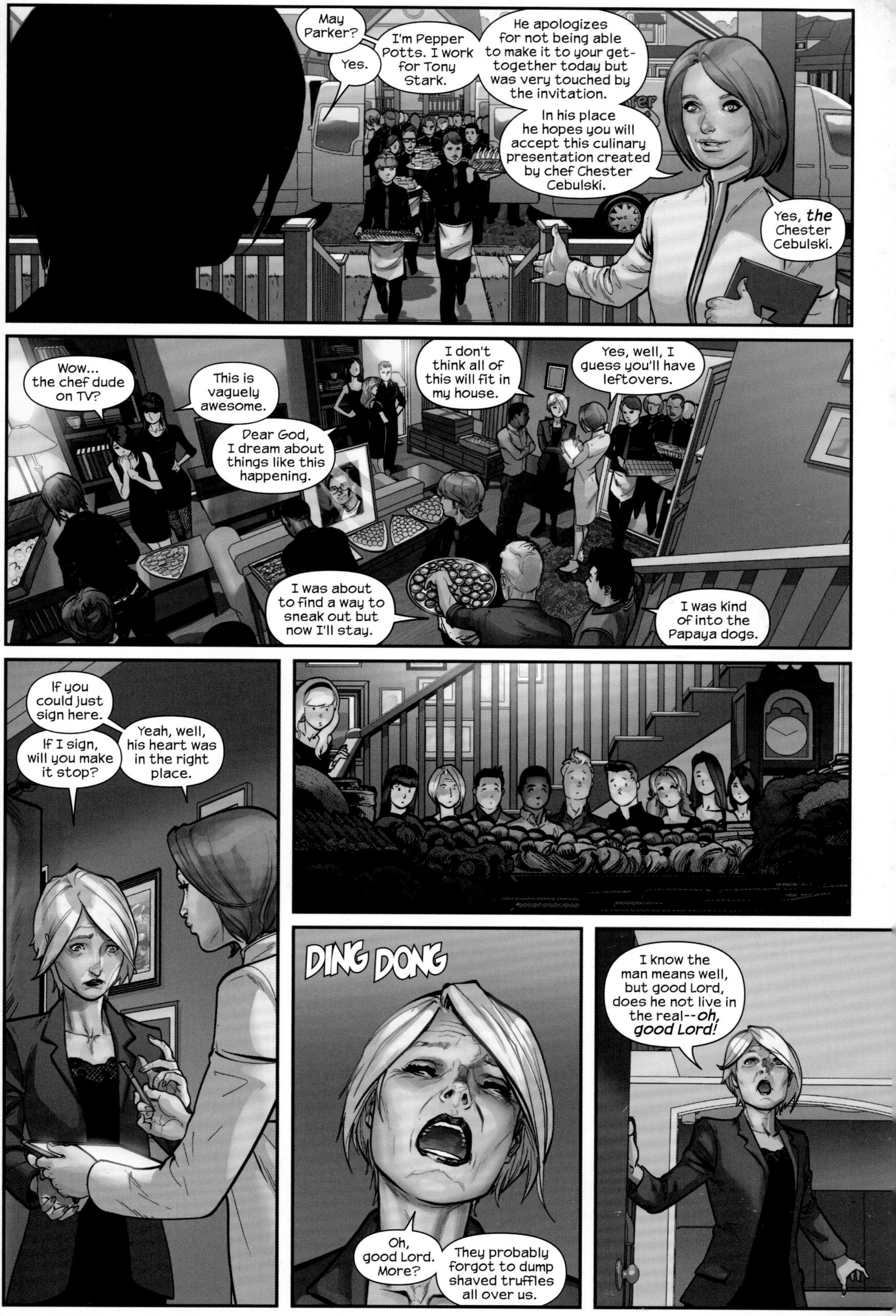
May Parker?
Yes.
I'm Pepper Potts. I work for Tony Stark.
He apologizes for not being able to make it to your get-together today but was very touched by the invitation.
In his place he hopes you will accept this culinary presentation created by chef Chester Cebulski.
Yes, *the* Chester Cebulski.
Wow... the chef dude on TV?
This is vaguely awesome.
Dear God, I dream about things like this happening.
I don't think all of this will fit in my house.
Yes, well, I guess you'll have leftovers.
I was about to find a way to sneak out but now I'll stay.
I was kind of into the Papaya dogs.
If you could just sign here.
If I sign, will you make it stop?
Yeah, well, his heart was in the right place.
DING DONG
Oh, good Lord. More?
They probably forgot to dump shaved truffles all over us.
I know the man means well, but good Lord, does he not live in the real--*oh, good Lord!*

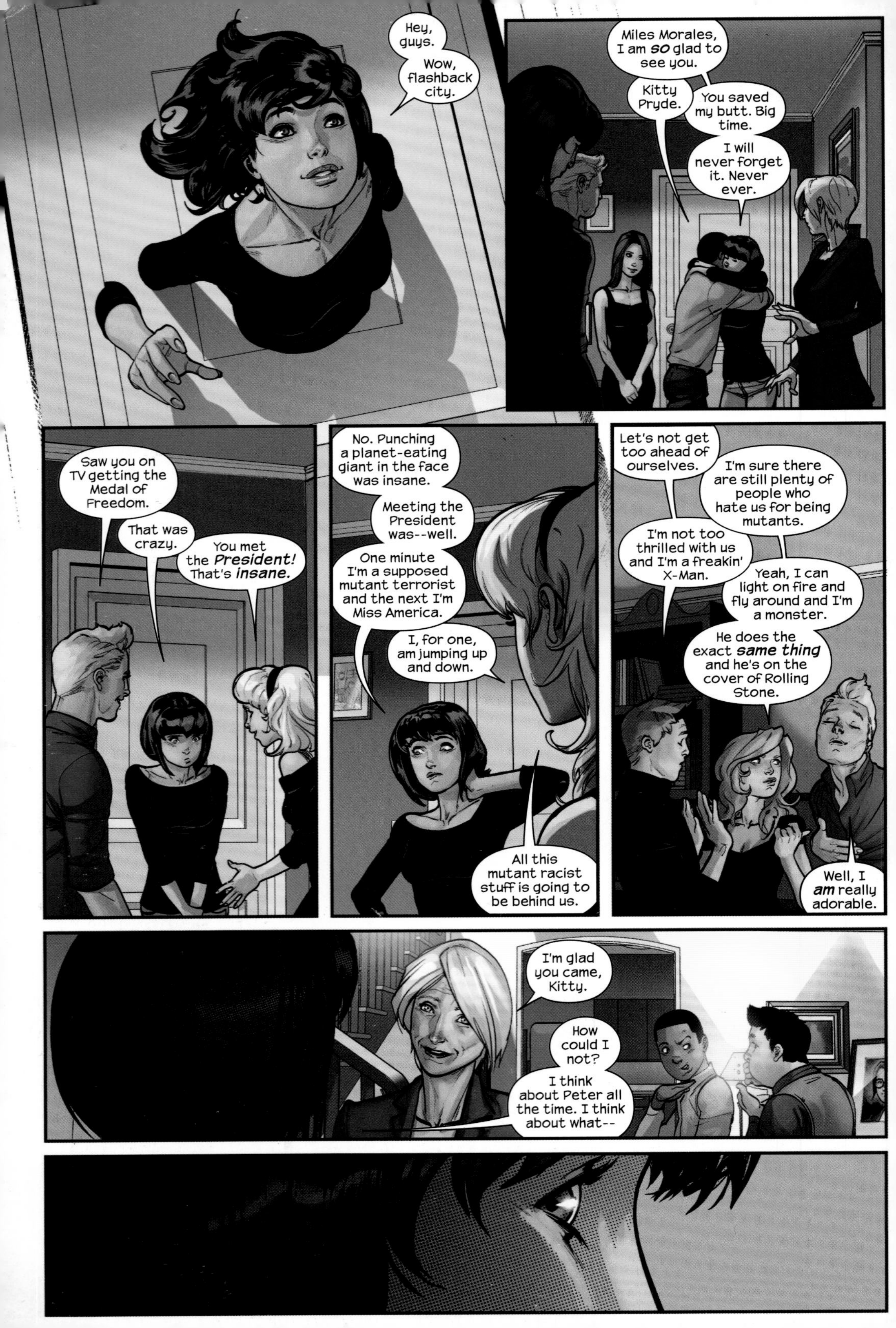
Hey, guys.
Wow, flashback city.
Miles Morales, I am SO glad to see you.
Kitty Pryde.
You saved my butt. Big time.
I will never forget it. Never ever.
Saw you on TV getting the Medal of Freedom.
That was crazy.
You met the President! That's insane.
No. Punching a planet-eating giant in the face was insane.
Meeting the President was--well.
One minute I'm a supposed mutant terrorist and the next I'm Miss America.
I, for one, am jumping up and down.
All this mutant racist stuff is going to be behind us.
Let's not get too ahead of ourselves.
I'm sure there are still plenty of people who hate us for being mutants.
I'm not too thrilled with us and I'm a freakin' X-Man.
Yeah, I can light on fire and fly around and I'm a monster.
He does the exact same thing and he's on the cover of Rolling Stone.
Well, I am really adorable.
I'm glad you came, Kitty.
How could I not?
I think about Peter all the time. I think about what--

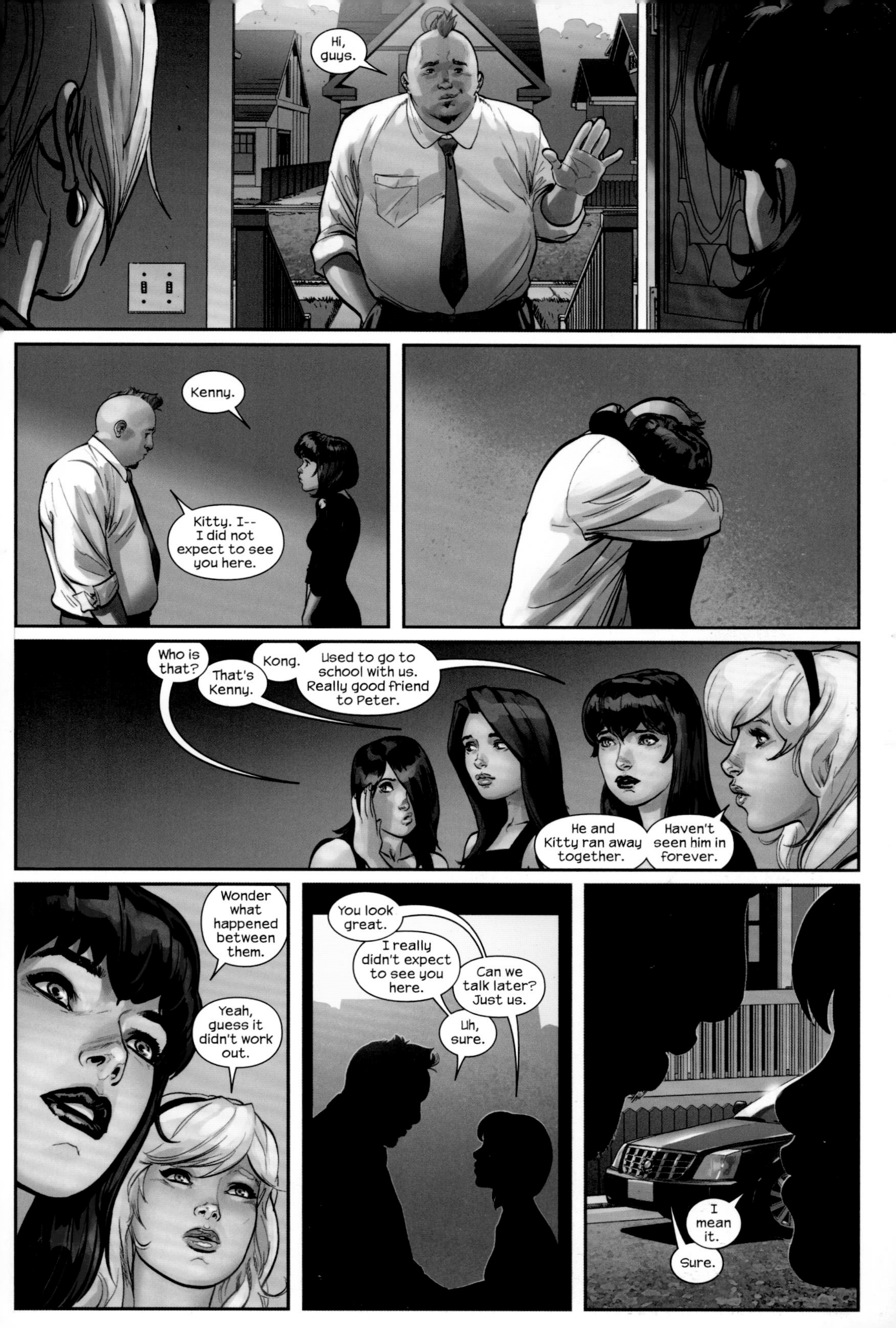
Hi, guys.
Kenny.
Kitty. I-- I did not expect to see you here.
Who is that?
That's Kenny.
Kong.
Used to go to school with us. Really good friend to Peter.
He and Kitty ran away together.
Haven't seen him in forever.
Wonder what happened between them.
Yeah, guess it didn't work out.
You look great.
I really didn't expect to see you here.
Can we talk later? Just us.
Uh, sure.
I mean it.
Sure.

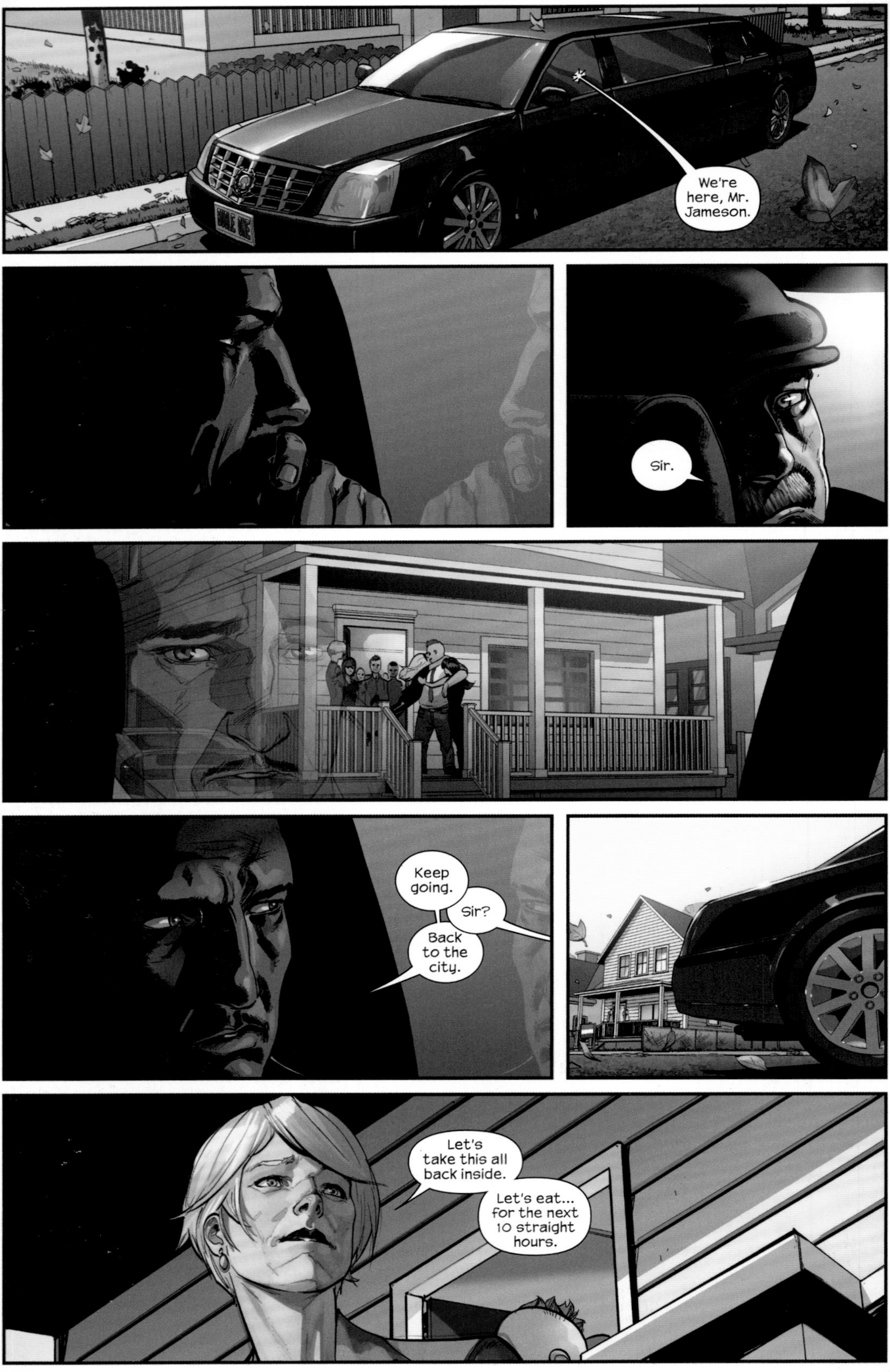
We're here, Mr. Jameson.
Sir.
Keep going.
Sir?
Back to the city.
Let's take this all back inside.
Let's eat... for the next 10 straight hours.

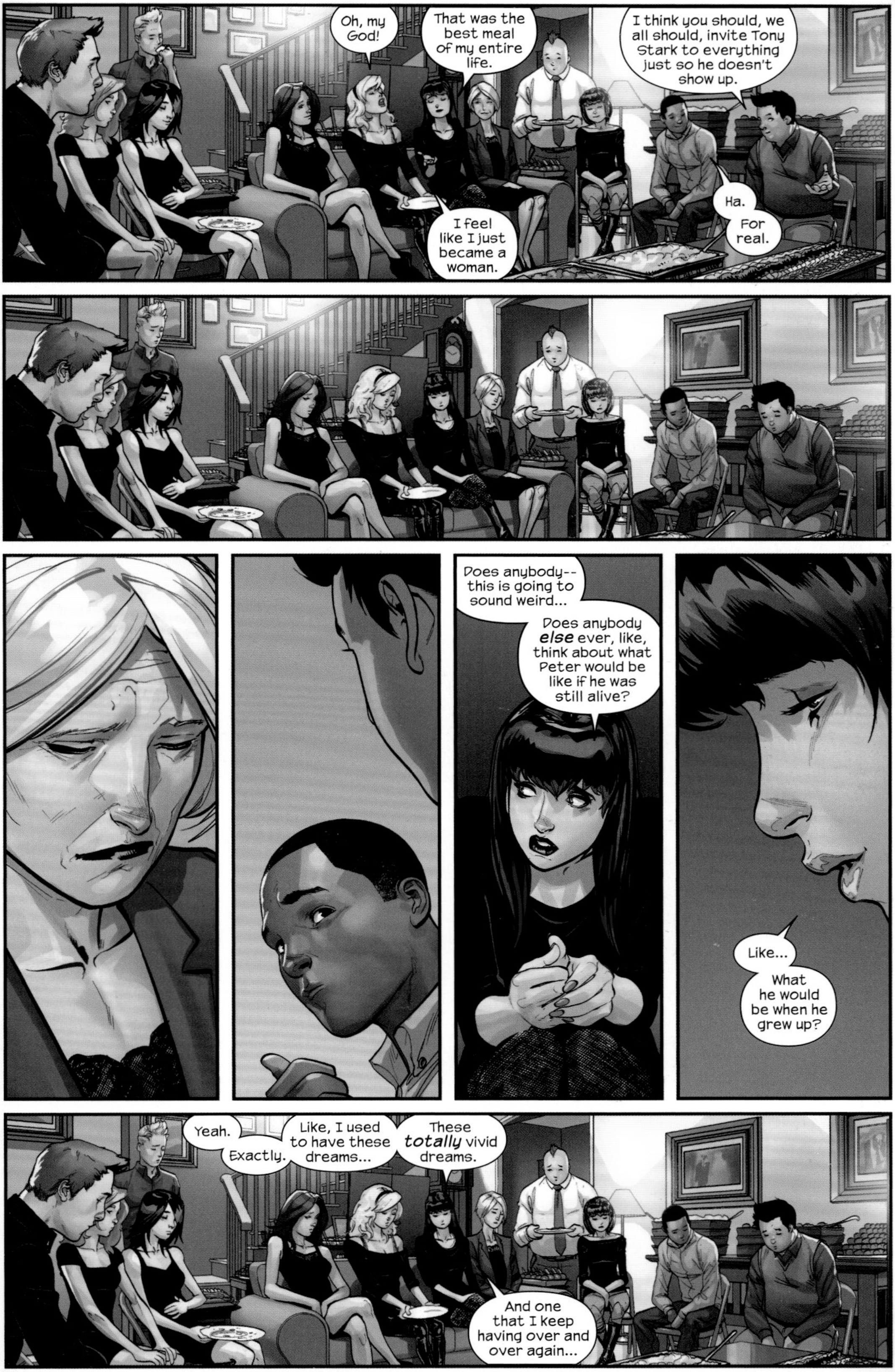
Oh, my God!
That was the best meal of my entire life.
I feel like I just became a woman.
I think you should, we all should, invite Tony Stark to everything just so he doesn't show up.
Ha.
For real.
Does anybody-- this is going to sound weird...
Does anybody *else* ever, like, think about what Peter would be like if he was still alive?
Like...
What he would be when he grew up?
Yeah.
Exactly.
Like, I used to have these dreams...
These *totally* vivid dreams.
And one that I keep having over and over again...

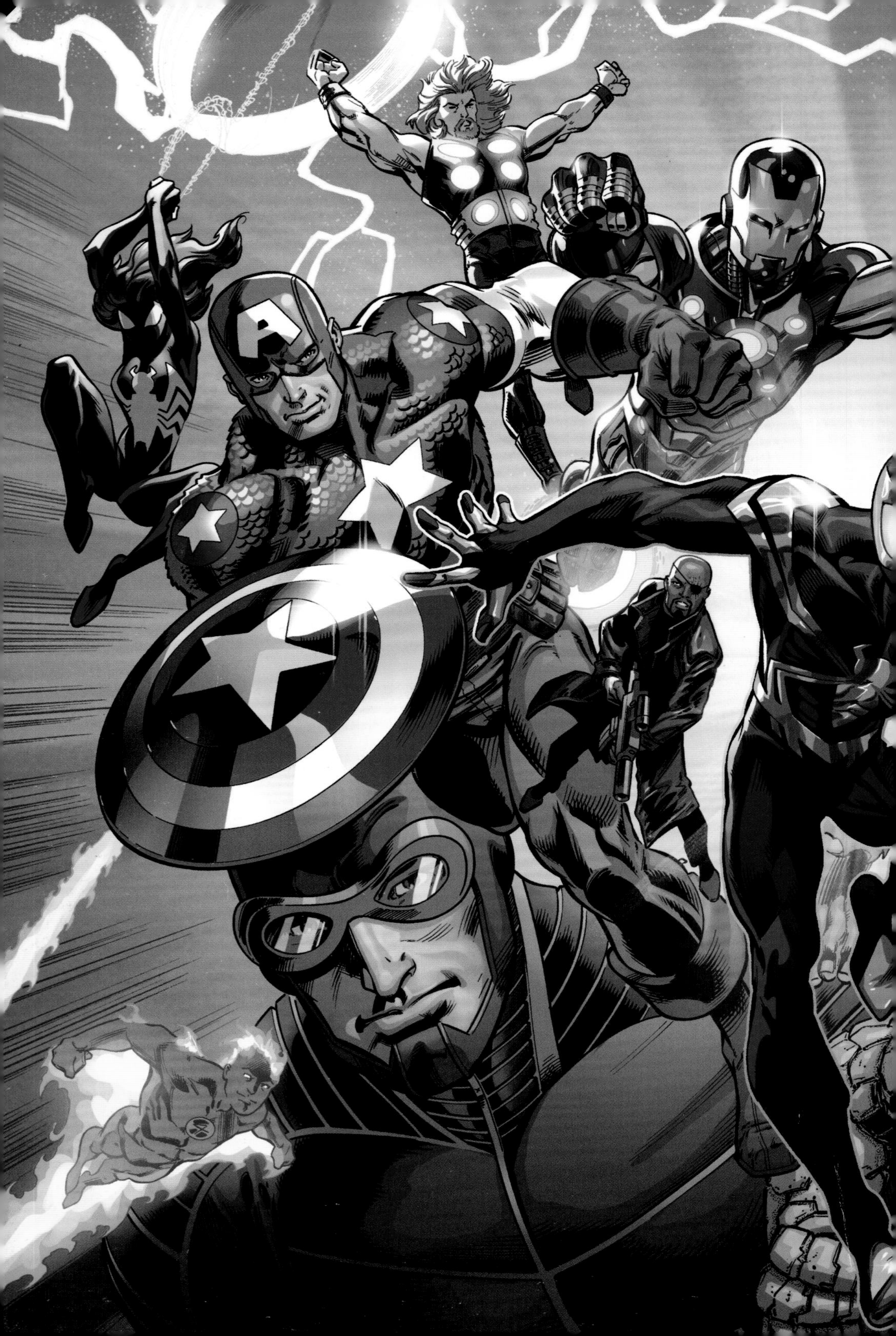

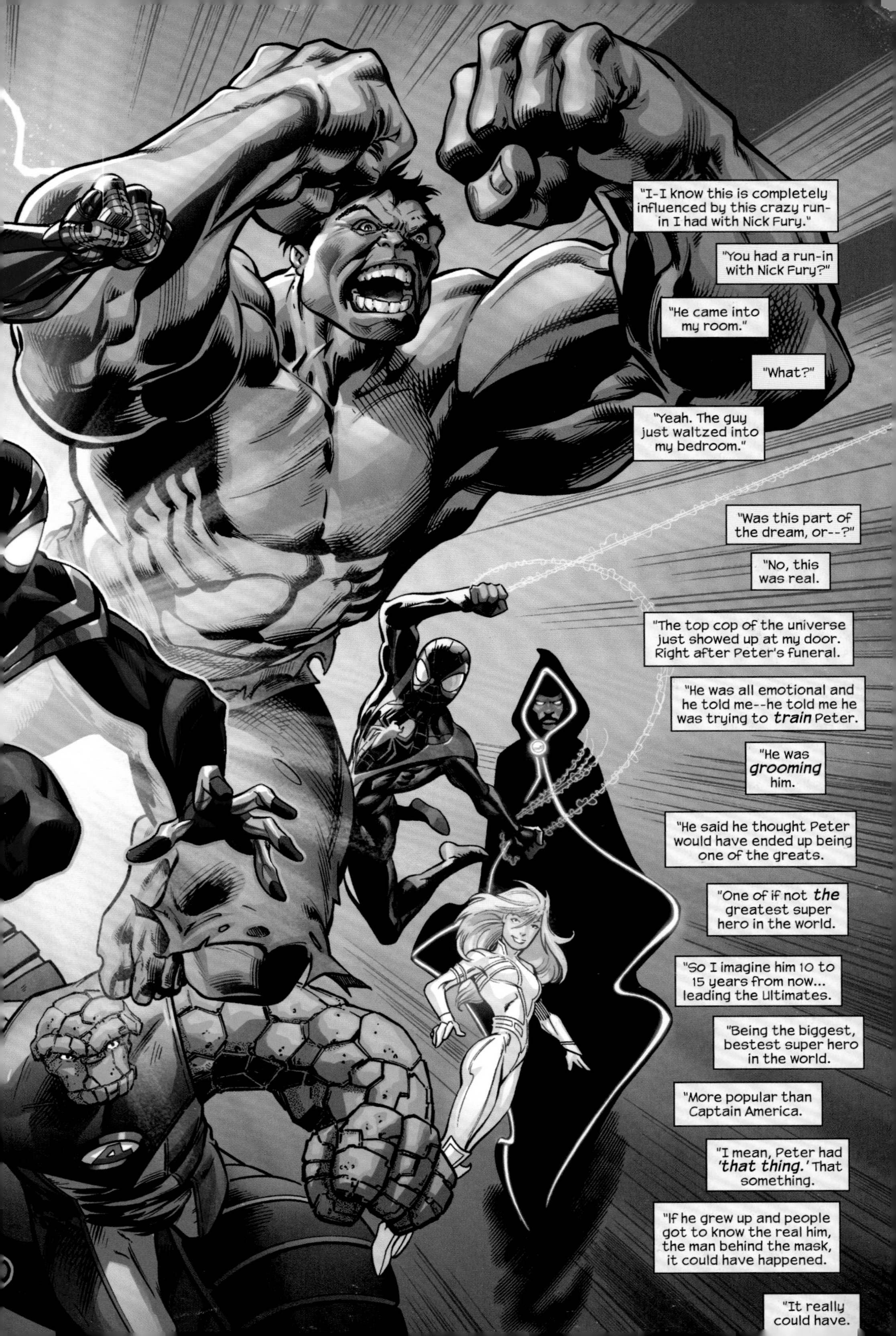
"I-I know this is completely influenced by this crazy run-in I had with Nick Fury."
"You had a run-in with Nick Fury?"
"He came into my room."
"What?"
"Yeah. The guy just waltzed into my bedroom."
"Was this part of the dream, or--?"
"No, this was real.
"The top cop of the universe just showed up at my door. Right after Peter's funeral.
"He was all emotional and he told me--he told me he was trying to *train* Peter.
"He was *grooming* him.
"He said he thought Peter would have ended up being one of the greats.
"One of if not *the* greatest super hero in the world.
"So I imagine him 10 to 15 years from now... leading the Ultimates.
"Being the biggest, bestest super hero in the world.
"More popular than Captain America.
"I mean, Peter had *'that thing.'* That something.
"If he grew up and people got to know the real him, the man behind the mask, it could have happened.
"It really could have.

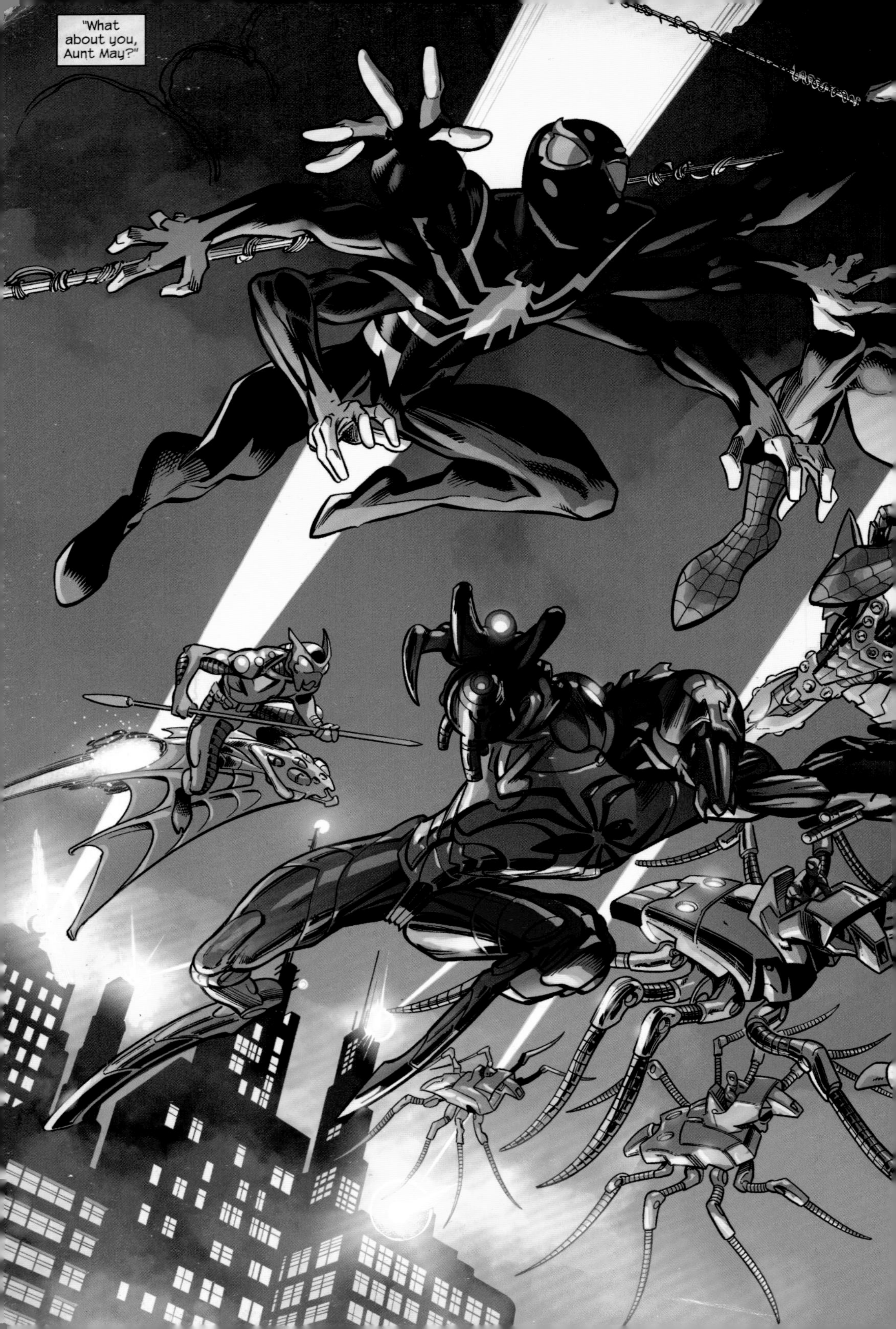
"What about you, Aunt May?"

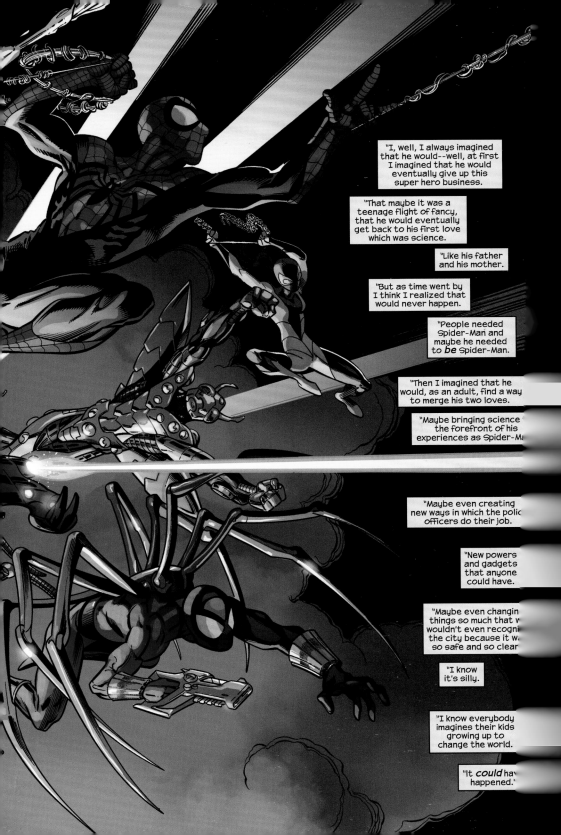

"I, well, I always imagined that he would--well, at first I imagined that he would eventually give up this super hero business.

"That maybe it was a teenage flight of fancy, that he would eventually get back to his first love which was science.

"Like his father and his mother.

"But as time went by I think I realized that would never happen.

"People needed Spider-Man and maybe he needed to *be* Spider-Man.

"Then I imagined that he would, as an adult, find a way to merge his two loves.

"Maybe bringing science the forefront of his experiences as Spider-Ma

"Maybe even creating new ways in which the polic officers do their job.

"New powers and gadgets that anyone could have.

"Maybe even changin things so much that v wouldn't even recogni the city because it wa so safe and so clear

"I know it's silly.

"I know everybody imagines their kids growing up to change the world.

"It *could* hav happened.'

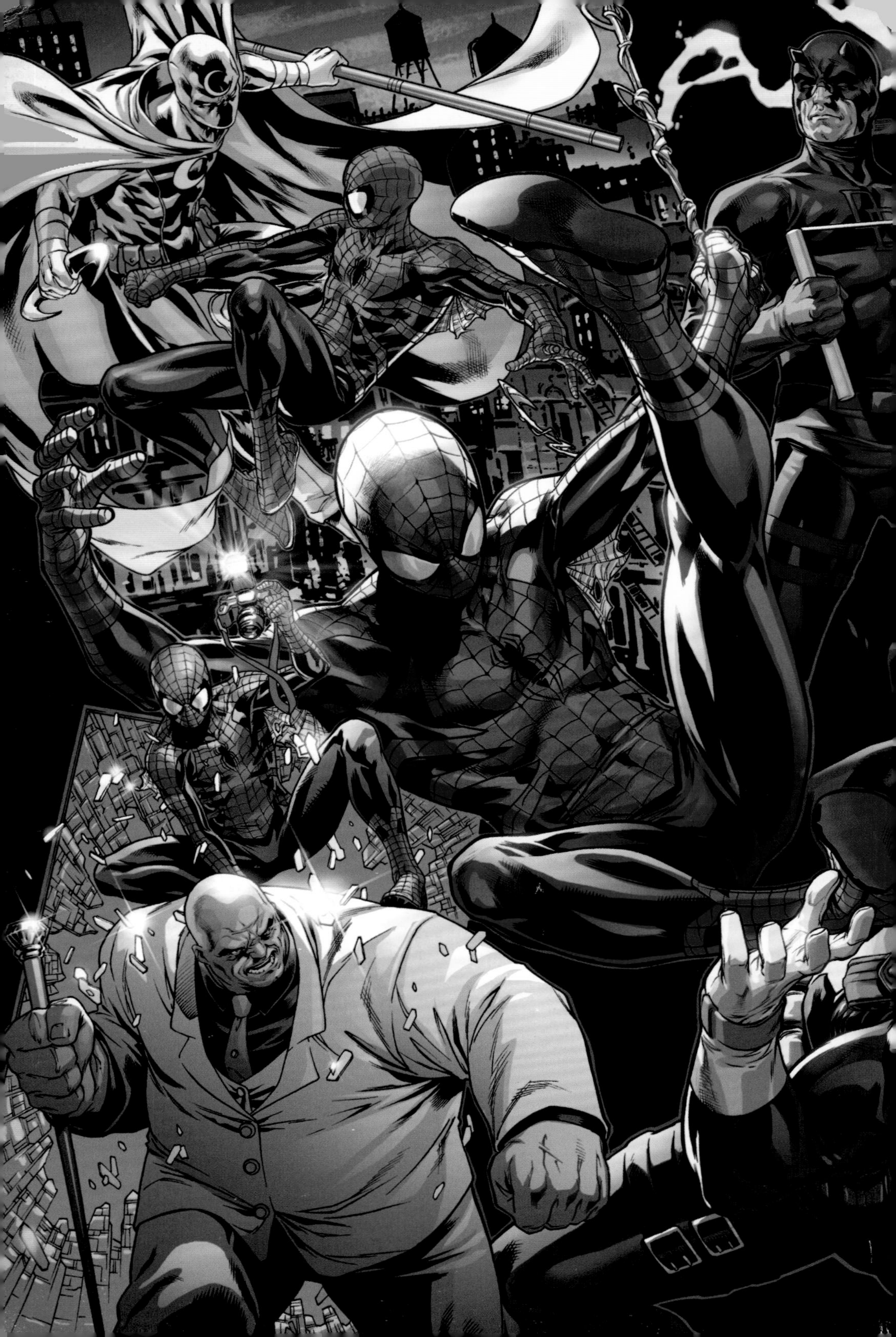

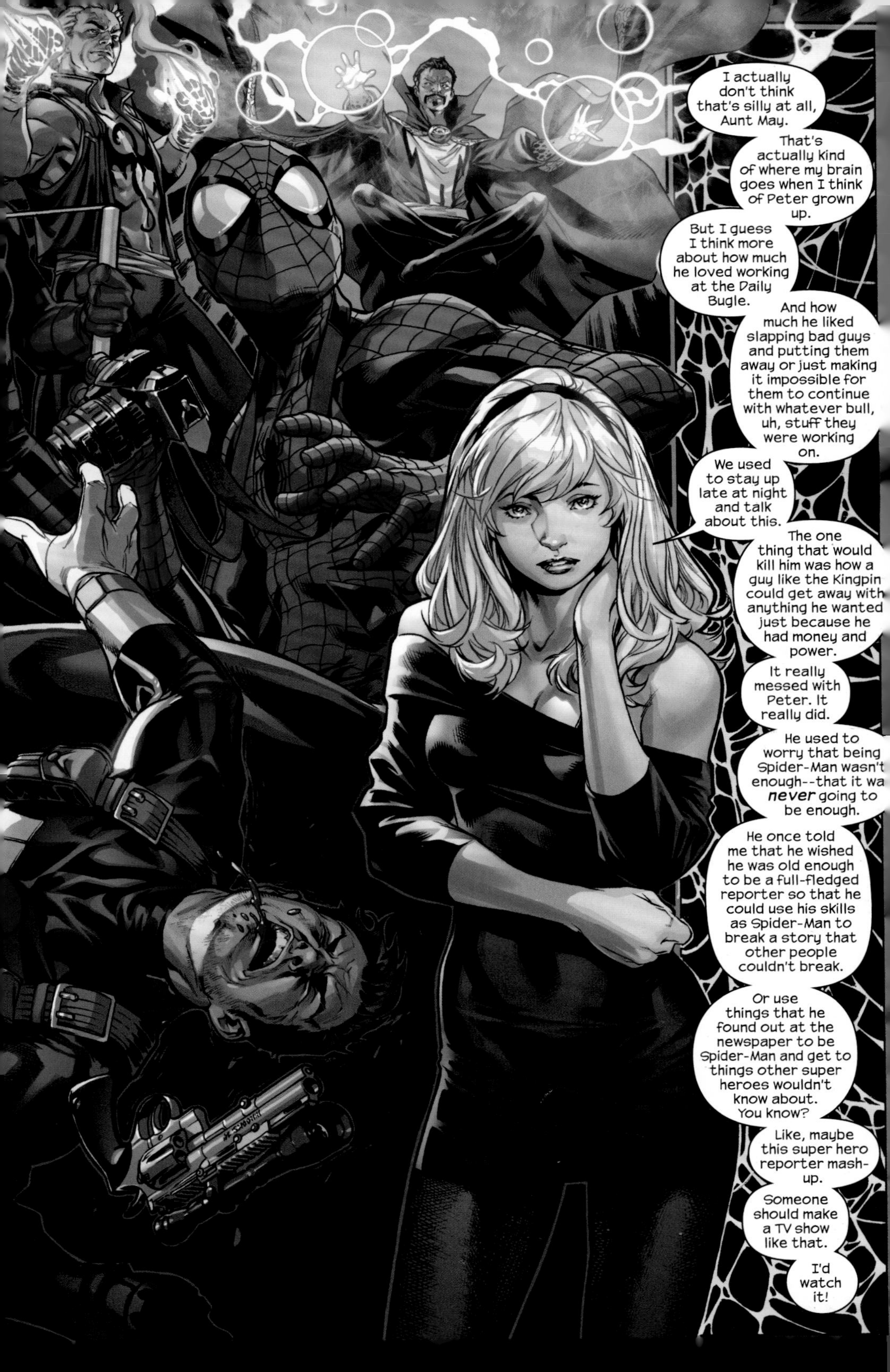
I actually don't think that's silly at all, Aunt May.
That's actually kind of where my brain goes when I think of Peter grown up.
But I guess I think more about how much he loved working at the Daily Bugle.
And how much he liked slapping bad guys and putting them away or just making it impossible for them to continue with whatever bull, uh, stuff they were working on.
We used to stay up late at night and talk about this.
The one thing that would kill him was how a guy like the Kingpin could get away with anything he wanted just because he had money and power.
It really messed with Peter. It really did.
He used to worry that being Spider-Man wasn't enough--that it wa *never* going to be enough.
He once told me that he wished he was old enough to be a full-fledged reporter so that he could use his skills as Spider-Man to break a story that other people couldn't break.
Or use things that he found out at the newspaper to be Spider-Man and get to things other super heroes wouldn't know about. You know?
Like, maybe this super hero reporter mash-up.
Someone should make a TV show like that.
I'd watch it!

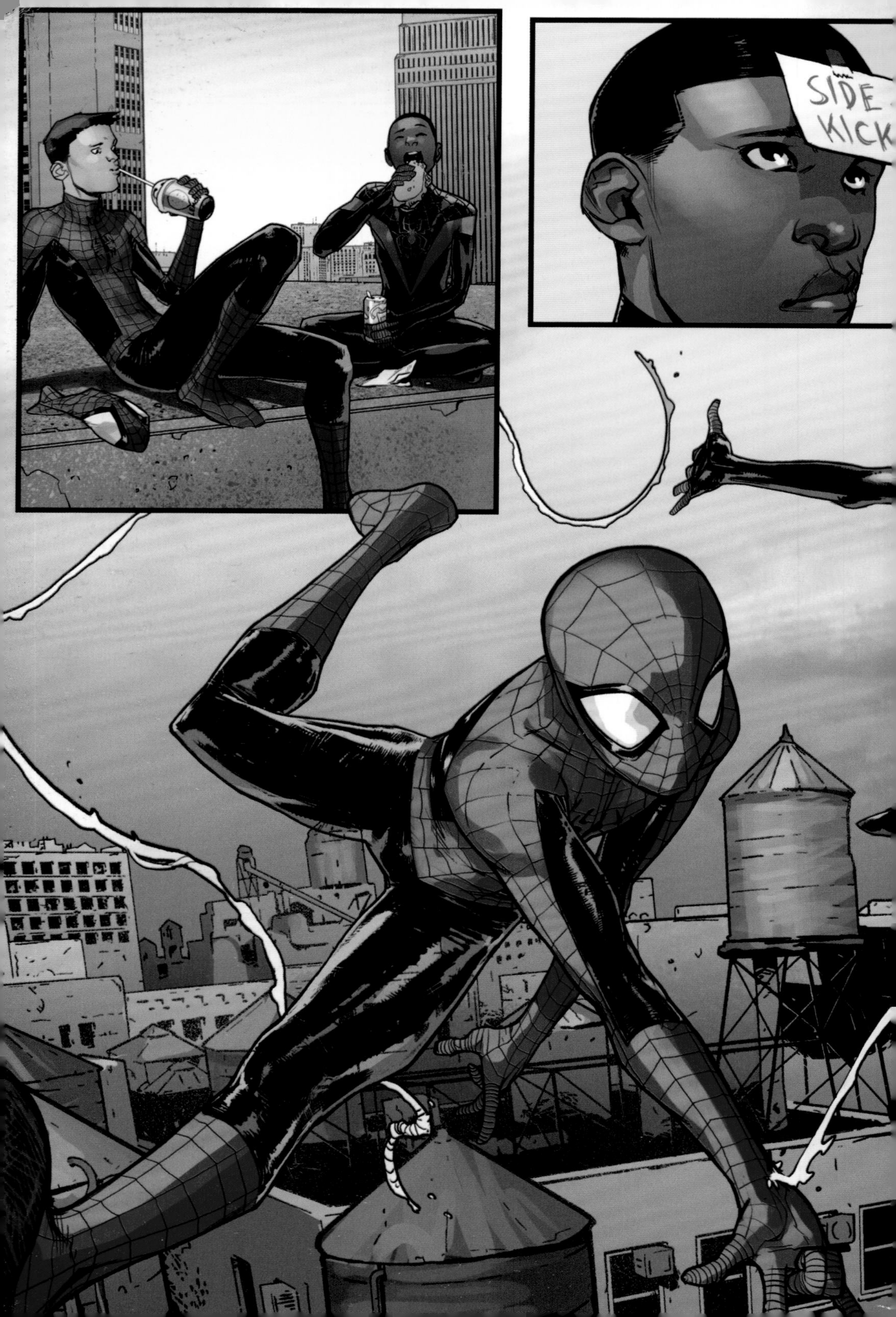
SIDE KICK

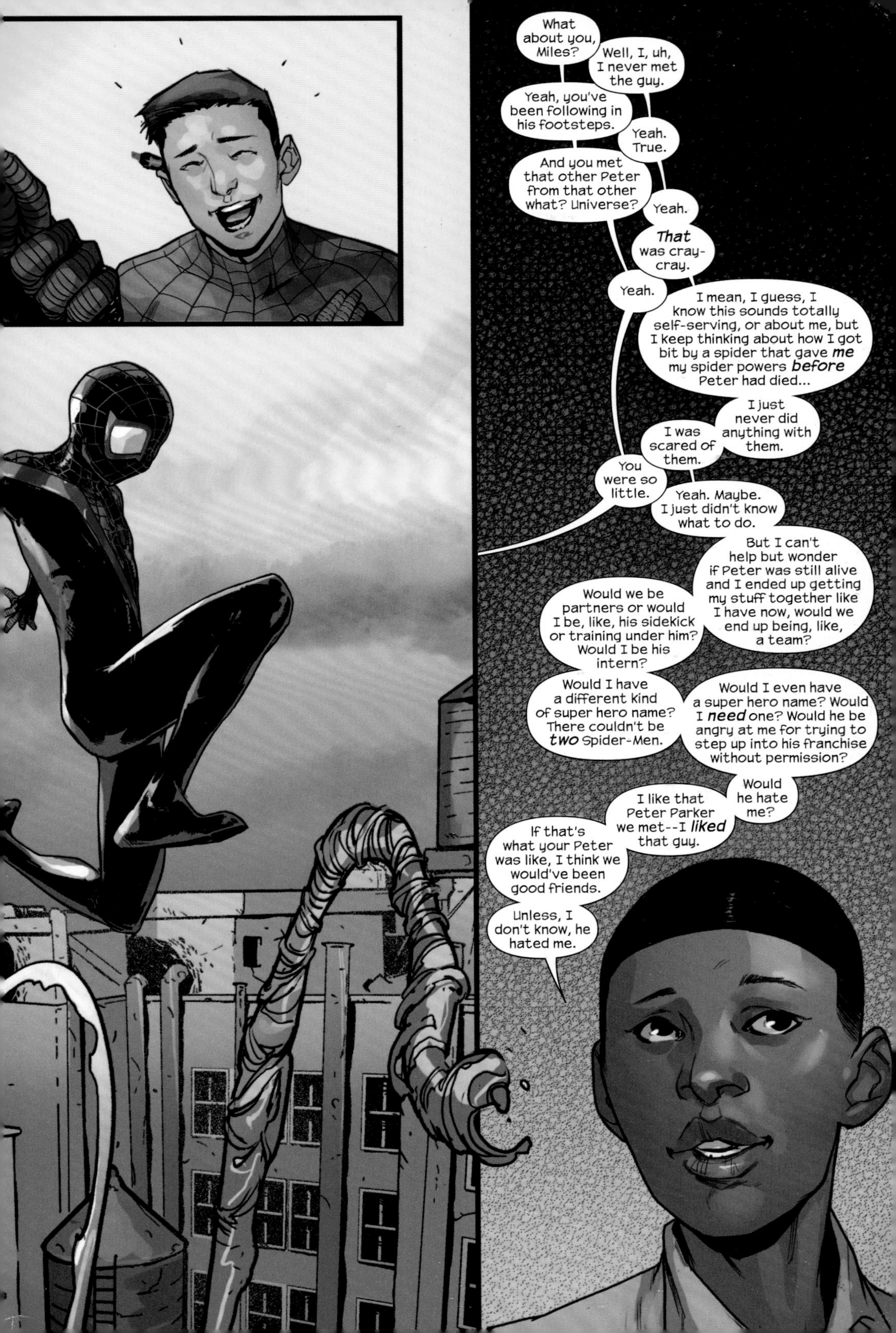

What about you, Miles?
Well, I, uh, I never met the guy.
Yeah, you've been following in his footsteps.
Yeah. True.
And you met that other Peter from that other what? Universe?
Yeah.
That was cray-cray.
Yeah.
I mean, I guess, I know this sounds totally self-serving, or about me, but I keep thinking about how I got bit by a spider that gave *me* my spider powers *before* Peter had died...
I just never did anything with them.
I was scared of them.
You were so little.
Yeah. Maybe. I just didn't know what to do.
But I can't help but wonder if Peter was still alive and I ended up getting my stuff together like I have now, would we end up being, like, a team?
Would we be partners or would I be, like, his sidekick or training under him? Would I be his intern?
Would I have a different kind of super hero name? There couldn't be *two* Spider-Men.
Would I even have a super hero name? Would I *need* one? Would he be angry at me for trying to step up into his franchise without permission?
Would he hate me?
I like that Peter Parker we met--I *liked* that guy.
If that's what your Peter was like, I think we would've been good friends.
Unless, I don't know, he hated me.

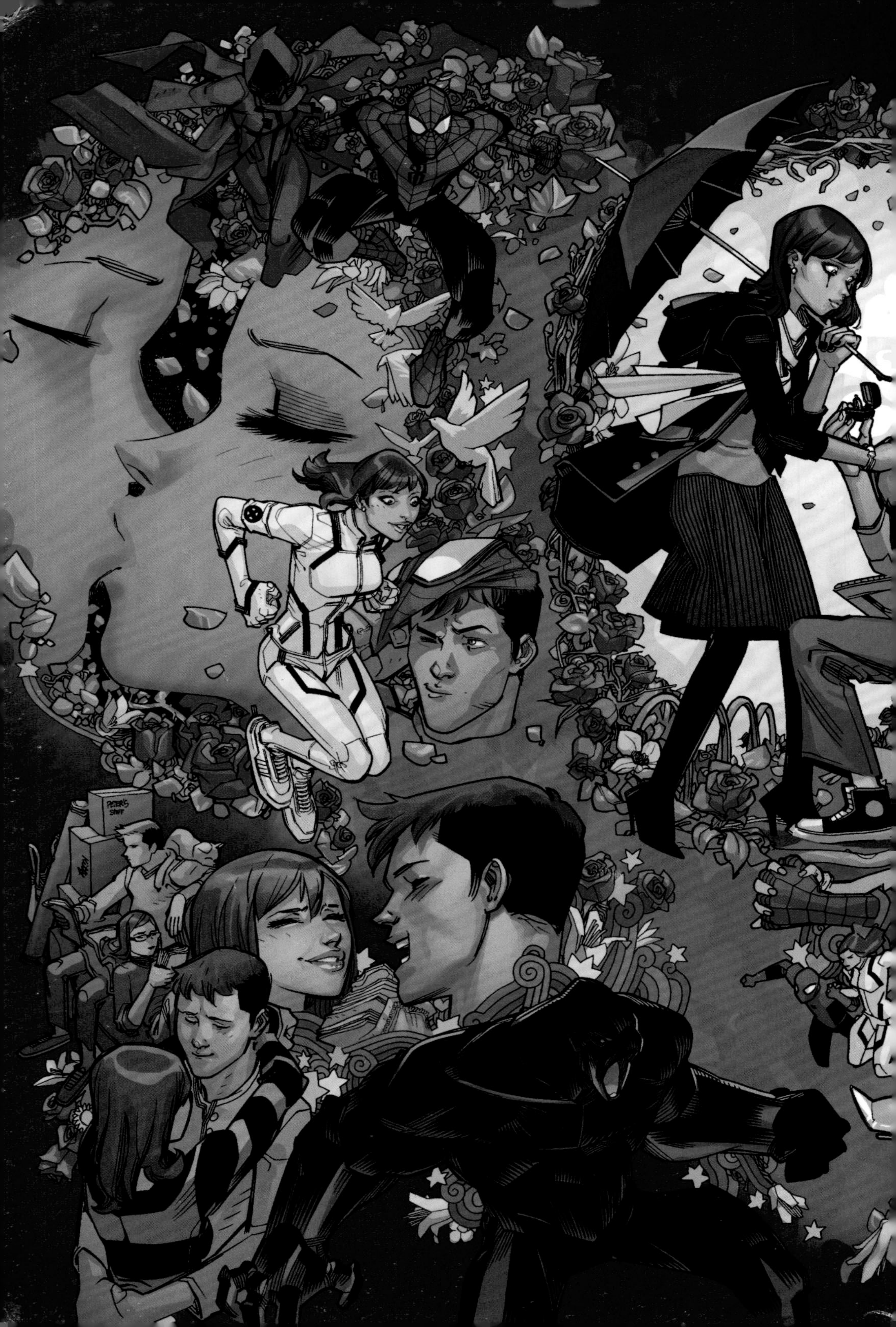
PETER'S STUFF

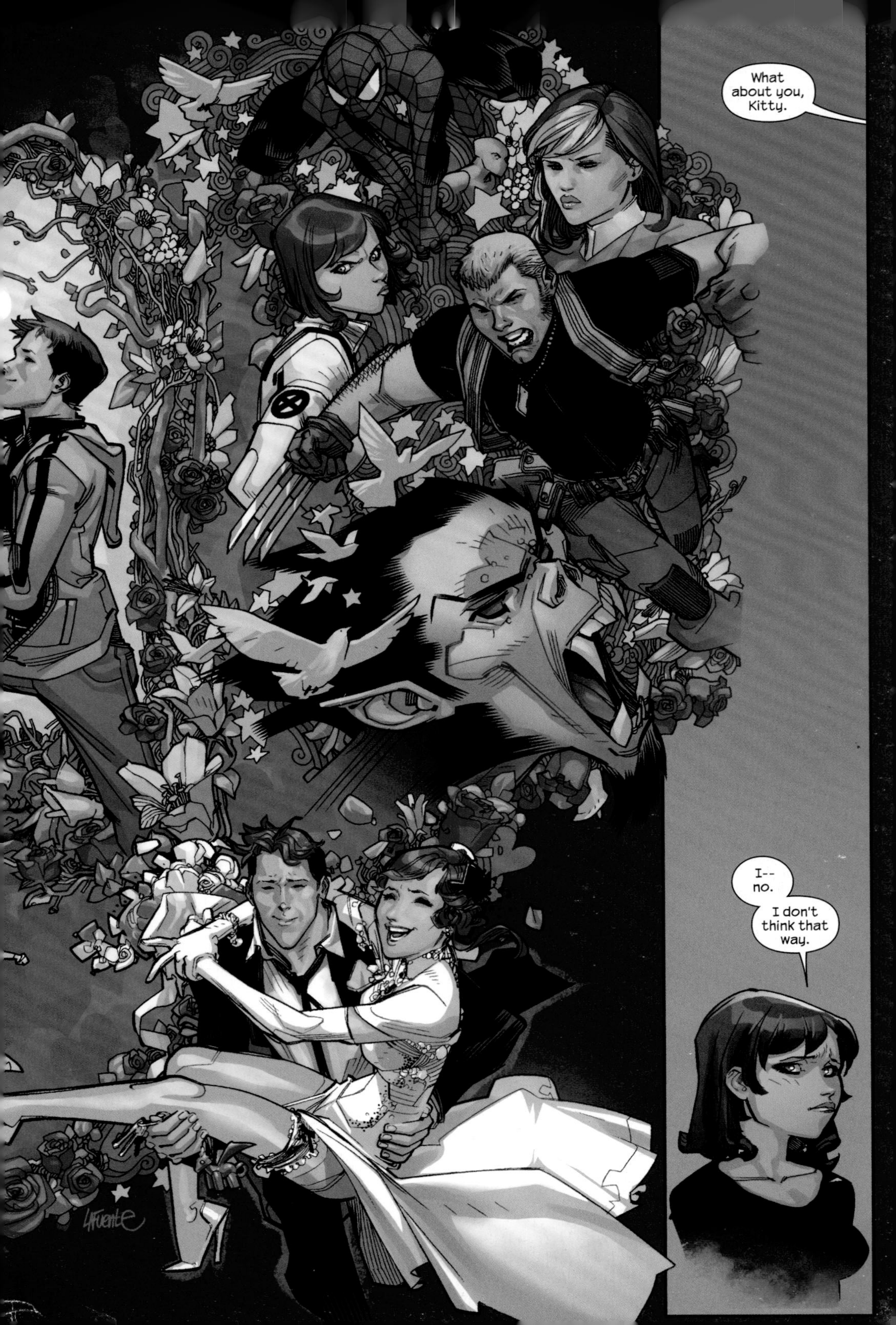
What about you, Kitty.
I-- no.
I don't think that way.
LaFuente

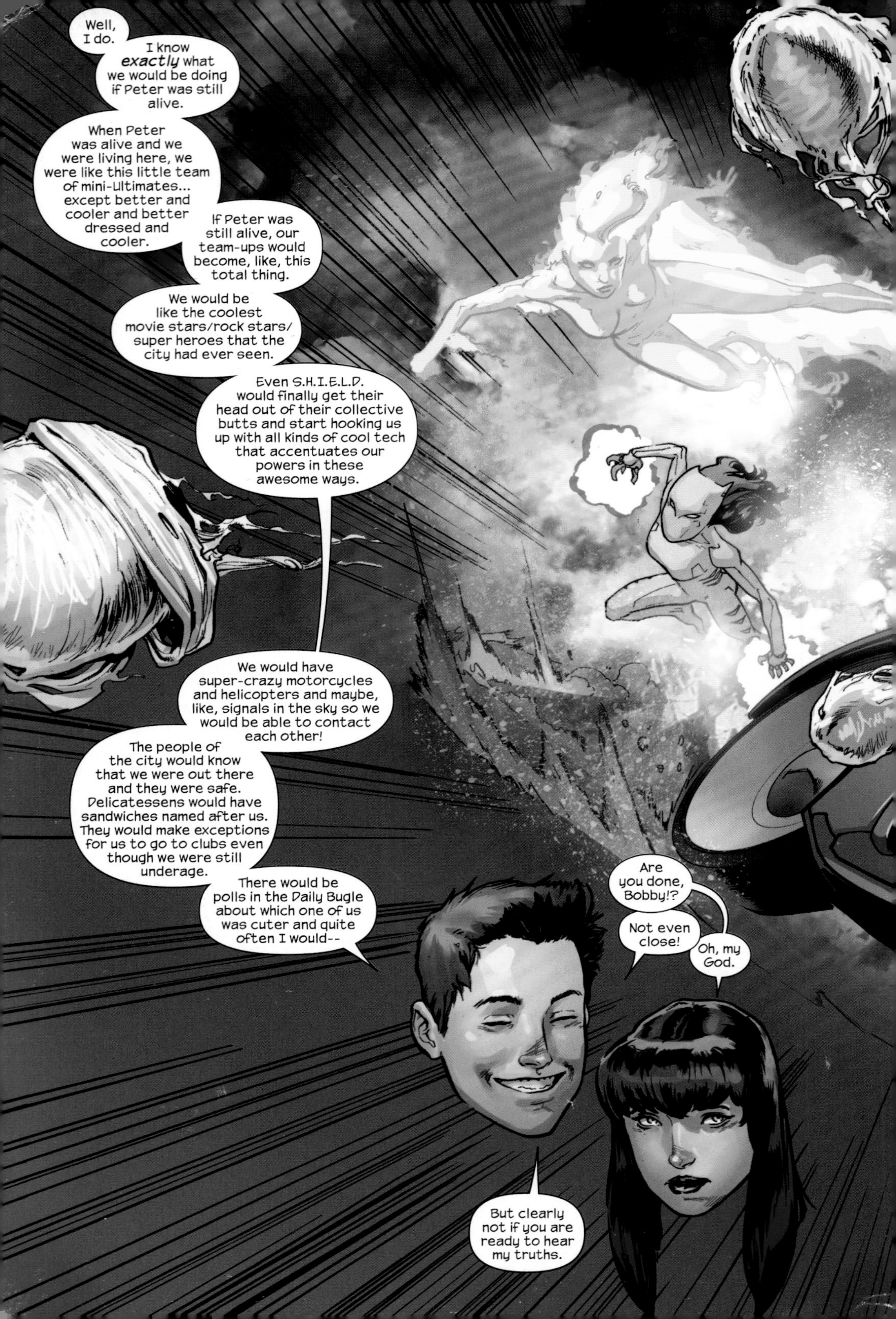
Well, I do.
I know *exactly* what we would be doing if Peter was still alive.
When Peter was alive and we were living here, we were like this little team of mini-Ultimates... except better and cooler and better dressed and cooler.
If Peter was still alive, our team-ups would become, like, this total thing.
We would be like the coolest movie stars/rock stars/ super heroes that the city had ever seen.
Even S.H.I.E.L.D. would finally get their head out of their collective butts and start hooking us up with all kinds of cool tech that accentuates our powers in these awesome ways.
We would have super-crazy motorcycles and helicopters and maybe, like, signals in the sky so we would be able to contact each other!
The people of the city would know that we were out there and they were safe. Delicatessens would have sandwiches named after us. They would make exceptions for us to go to clubs even though we were still underage.
There would be polls in the Daily Bugle about which one of us was cuter and quite often I would--
Are you done, Bobby!?
Not even close!
Oh, my God.
But clearly not if you are ready to hear my truths.

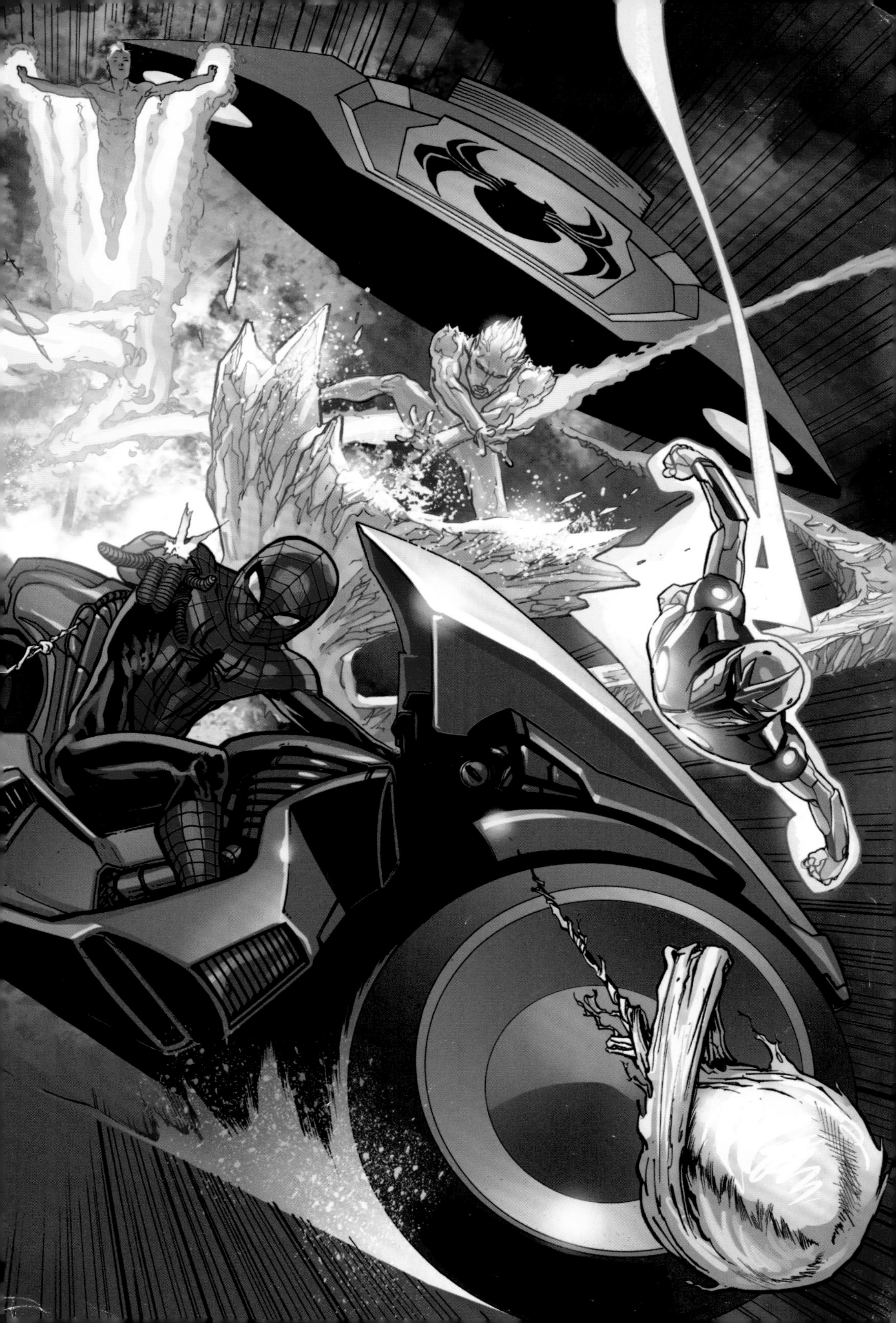

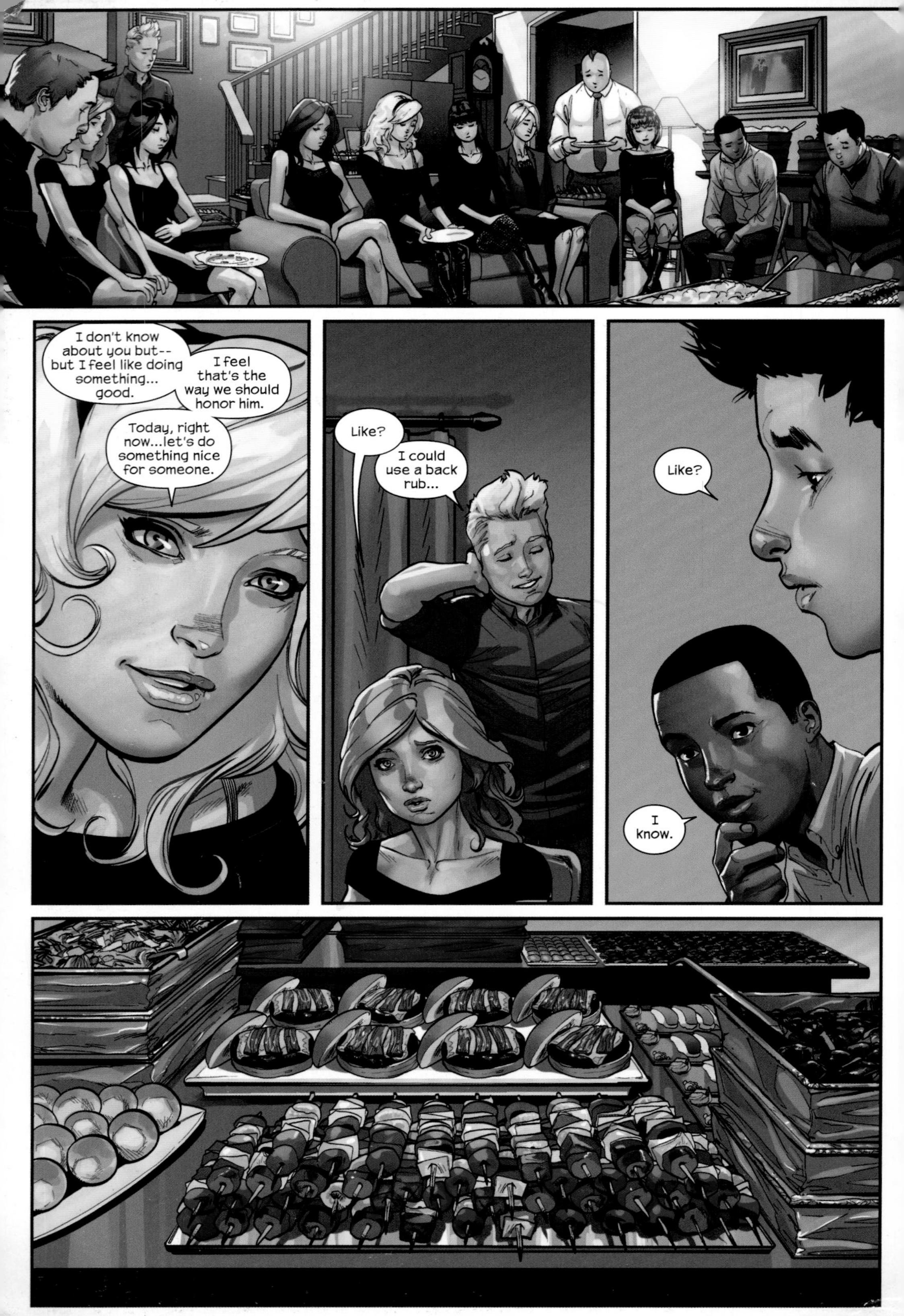
I don't know about you but-- but I feel like doing something... good.
I feel that's the way we should honor him.
Today, right now...let's do something nice for someone.
Like?
I could use a back rub...
Like?
I know.

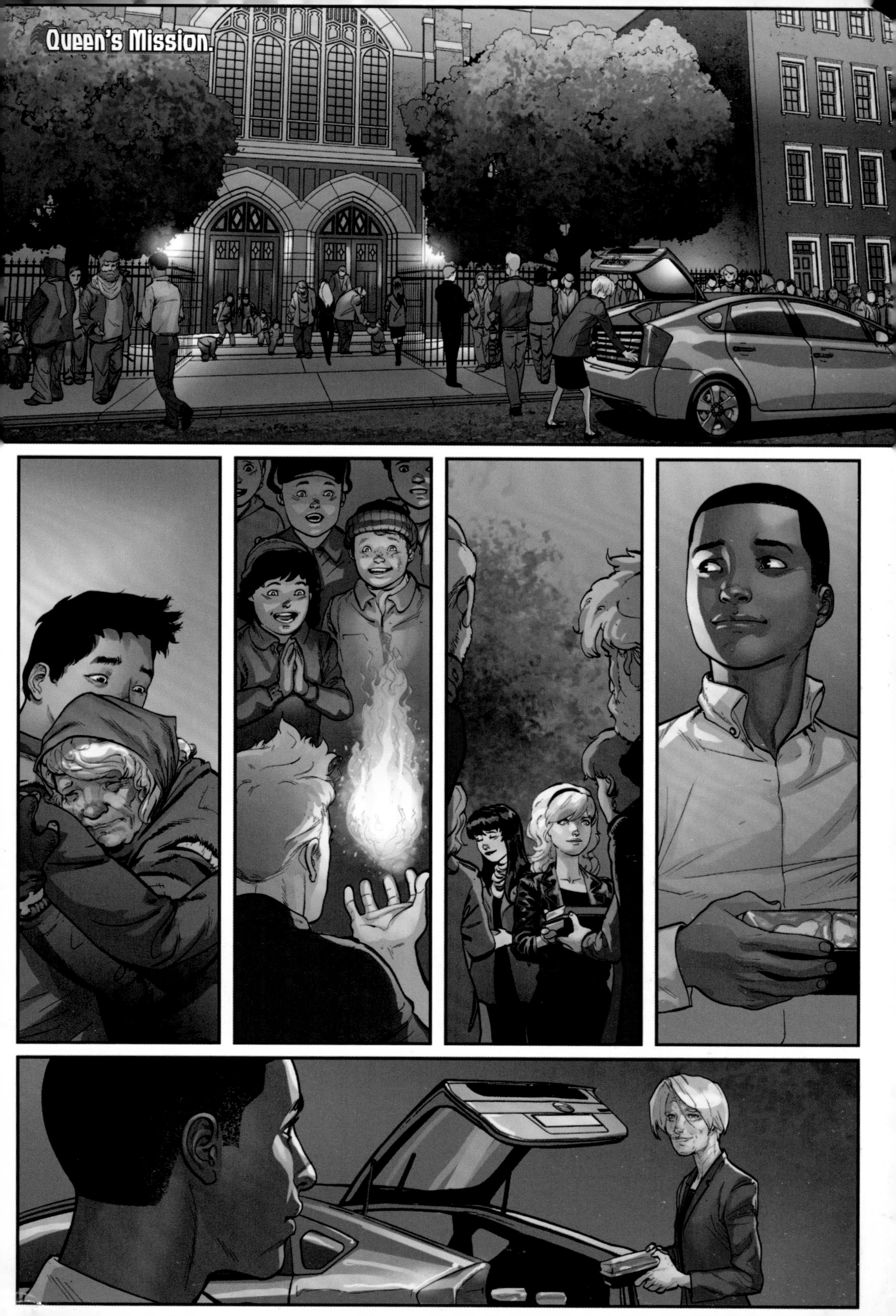
Queen's Mission.

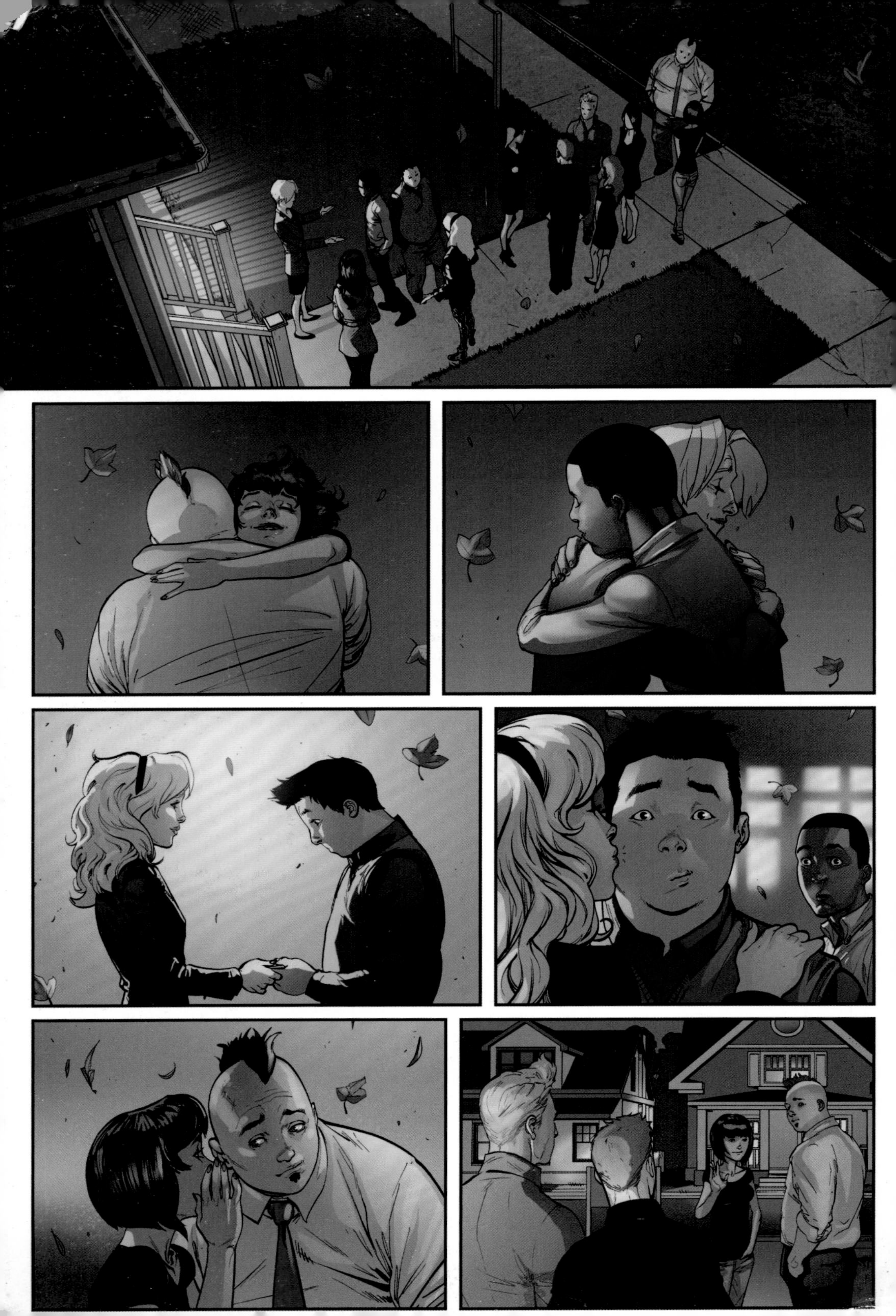

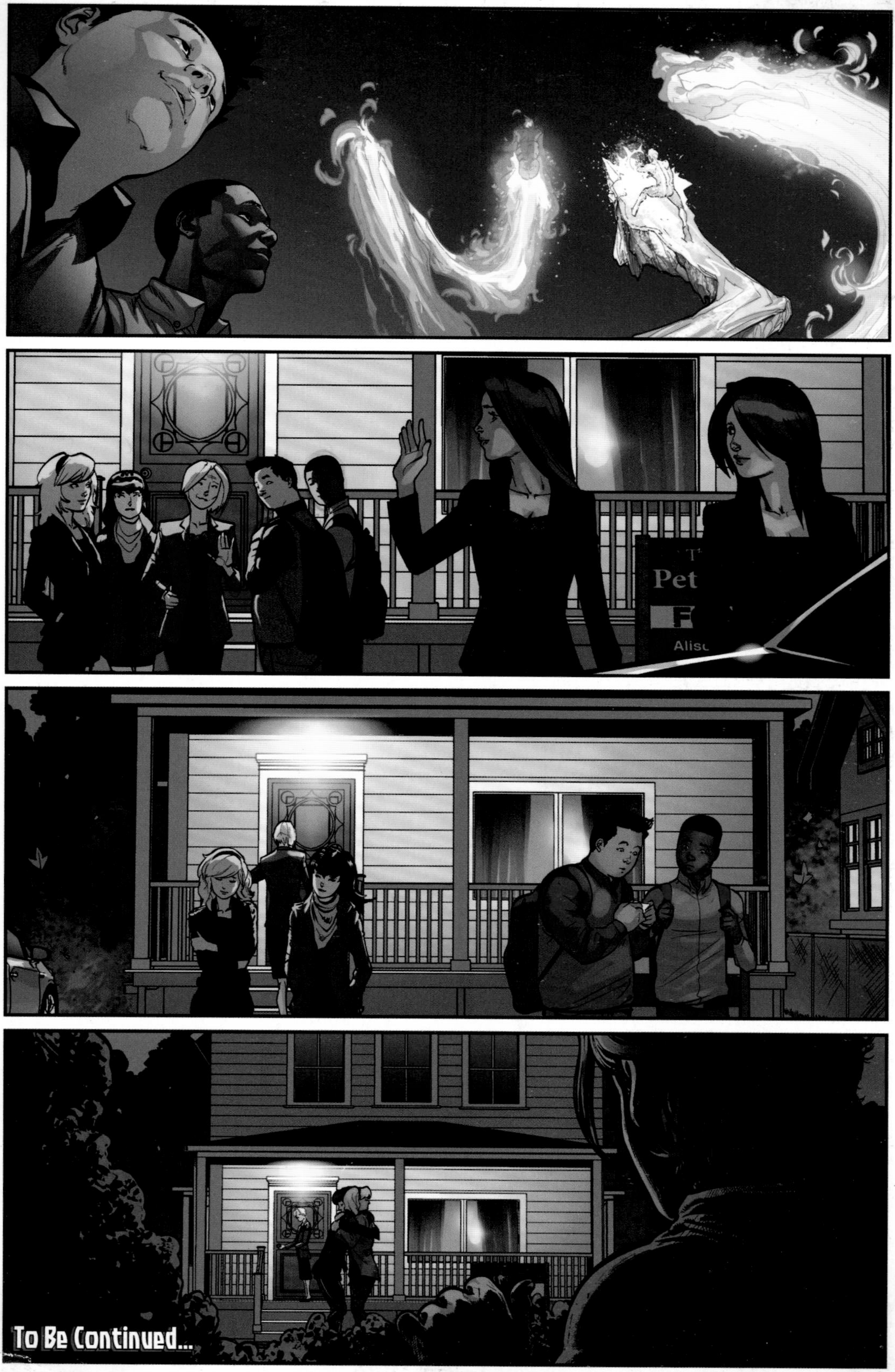
To Be Continued...

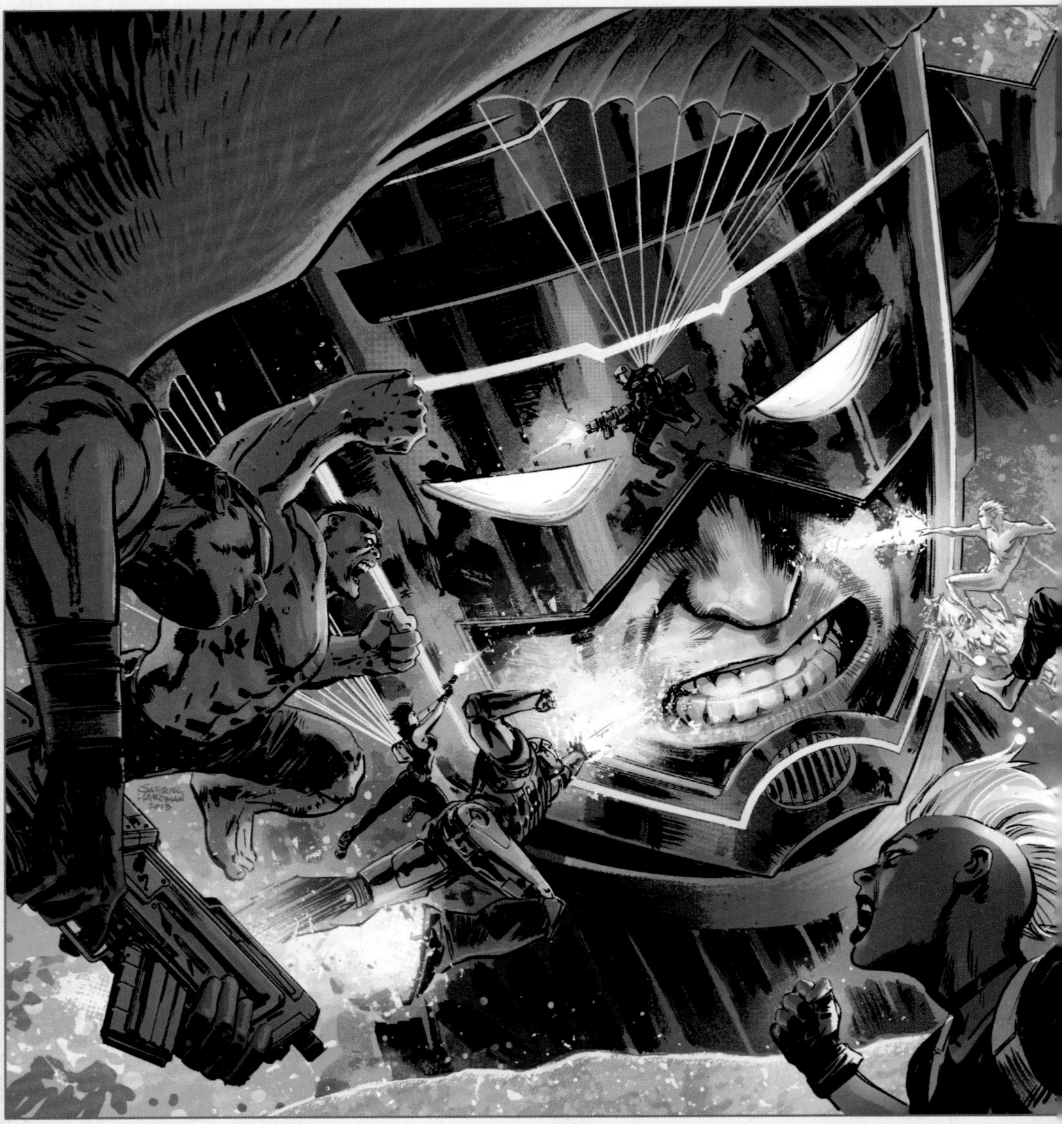
GABRIEL HARDMAN 2013

CATACLYSM: ULTIMATES #1, CATACLYSM: ULIMATE X-MEN #1 & CATACLYSM: ULTIMATE SPIDER-MAN #1 COMBINED VARIANTS

BY GABRIEL HARDMAN & ELIZABETH DISMANG BREITWEISER

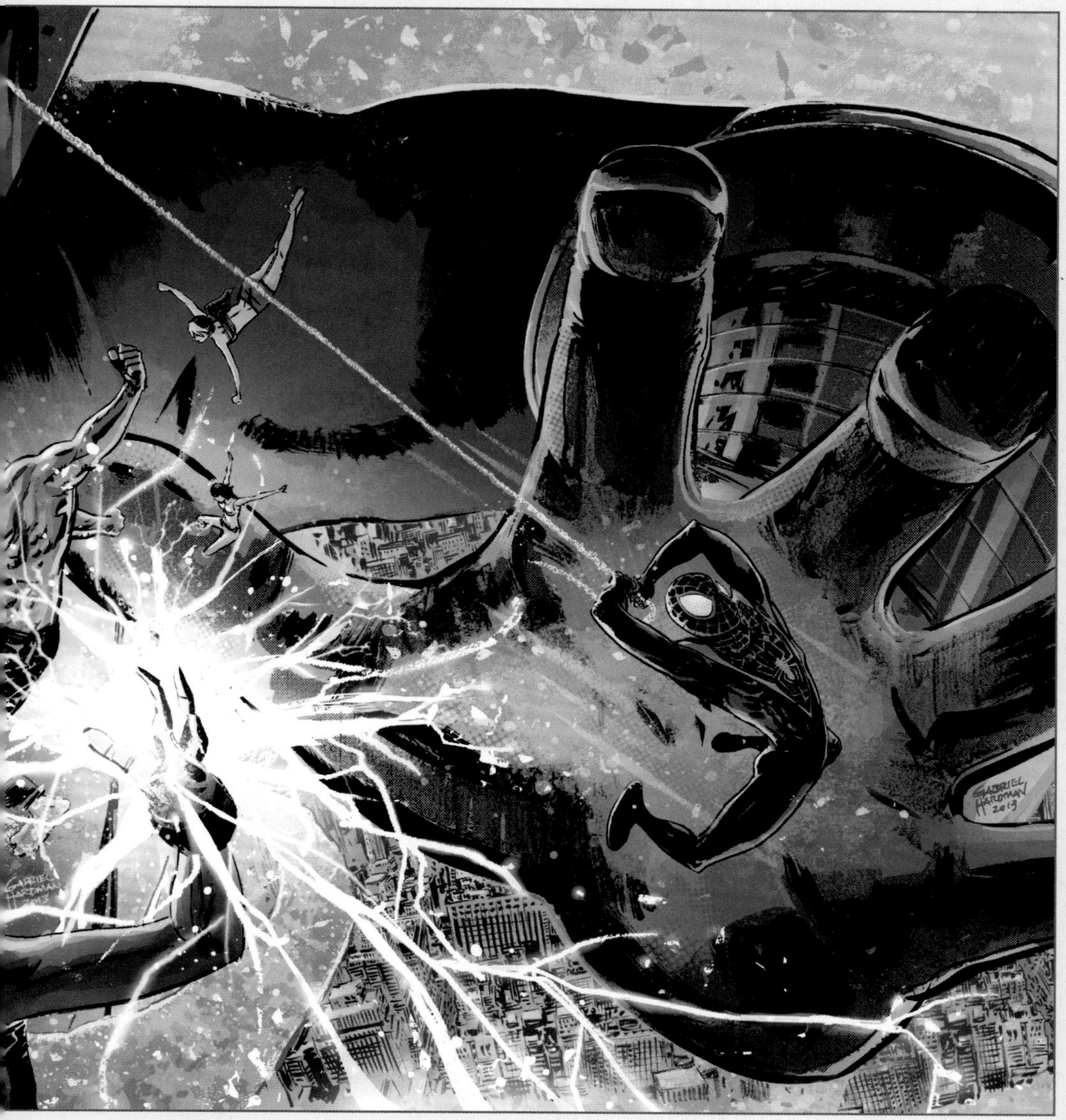
GABRIEL HARDMAN 2013

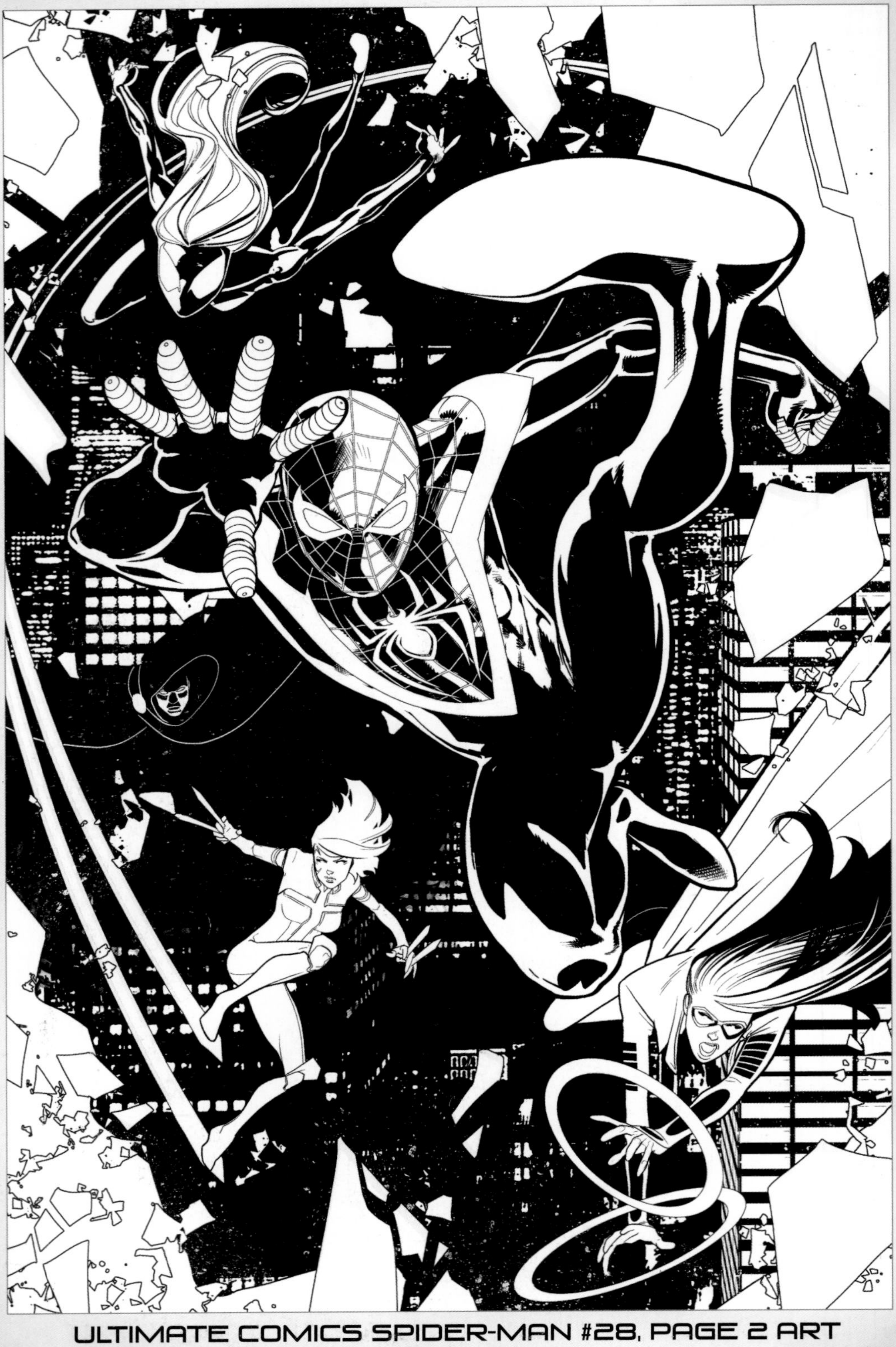

ULTIMATE COMICS SPIDER-MAN #28, PAGE 2 ART

BY DAVID MARQUEZ